Act of Contrition

A Trent Carter Novel

by

Richard Trice

Dear Merrill:
Dana, your book buddy since 1988, wants you to have a copy of my first novel. She tells me that she is certain you will like it very much!
Richard Trice

Inquiries should be addressed to the author at:
TriceTunes
PO Box 727
Raton, New Mexico 87740
Or
Email: tricetunes@gmail.com

ISBN 10: 1985319330
ISBN 13: 9781985319332

ASIN: B07CMTJ8FB

DEDICATION

For my father, my sister, my brother, and all those others who have gone on before me and contributed their own wonderfully frayed threads and beautifully stained patterns to the fabric of my life.

CONTENTS

ACKNOWLEDGMENTS

Although I have been writing for most of my life, those endeavors have consisted primarily of short stories, articles, teachings, business policies and manuals, love songs, ballads, and the occasional foray into dreadful poetry. This current labor of love, however, marks my first completed novel and has taken over four years to come to fruition. At turns frustrating and fulfilling, the task would have proven downright impossible had it not been for the dedicated assistance and encouragement of the following people, to whom I give my undying thanks:

First of all, I would be remiss to not go all the way back to Mrs. Gwen Marshall, my high school English teacher in Jal, New Mexico, who not only birthed within me the hunger to write, but, to my shock, convinced me I also had the raw ability to do so;

To my friends and colleagues at the Accidental Writers Guild in Raton, New Mexico, for their welcome and honest perusal and feedback regarding the first few chapters when the notion of writing this novel was still germinating in my mind, and whose initial encouragements kept me moving forward at a time when I was ready to abandon the entire idea;

To my faithful friends who strongly supported and encouraged my completion of *Act of Contrition* on an ongoing basis, most notably Judy Moore, Lucille Vigil Arvizo, Paula Graham Glover, Dana Lee McLaughlin Tasharshki, Susan Benham, Dr. Larry Stolarczyk, and Lynn Bernard for their steady feedback and cheerleading;

To my wonderful relatives, including my precious mother, Betty Owens Trice, my three amazing children Nathan, Lauren, and Jillian, and my brother-in-law Quentin Wills, all of whom took their valuable time to read the entire manuscript, all of whom claim to have actually liked it, and all of whom remain my most dedicated champions;

A huge thanks to my amazing editor and professor of English extraordinaire, Dr. Pamela R. Howell, whose keen and practiced eye and hand have made at least my most egregious abuses of the language go bye-bye, as well as surgically improved and tightened up innumerable phrases, dialogue, paragraphs, characterization, and just plain dumb grammatical errors (water guns at fifteen paces, Pam! And let's do this again real soon.);

And last, but by no stretch of the imagination, least, to my wonderful wife Linda, who not only patiently gave me up to countless hours, evenings, weekends, holidays, weeks, months, and years as I obsessed with this project, but also diligently proofread every single jot and tittle that rolled off the printer during all the seemingly interminable rewrites, making invaluable suggestions as to character delineation and continuity problems.

If I have missed thanking anyone else in particular, I humbly apologize.

May God richly bless and keep each and every one of you.

Richard C. Trice
Raton, New Mexico
April, 2018

PROLOGUE
A TIME TO KILL

Love, like war, is a military campaign, a surprise invasion of the most ill-protected part of a person's being – the heart.

Love, like war, attacks and takes no prisoners. It ultimately demands unconditional surrender, to which the vanquished must capitulate or be totally annihilated.

Love, like war, is not for the unprepared, or the weak of mind, will, or stamina. And perish the thought that someone will come out of it whole and unscathed, or in total possession of their reasoning or sense of well-being.

For when it's all over, love – like war – will have produced many wounds in a person that cannot easily be healed, or even seen by the naked eye, a sort of post-traumatic stress disorder that is every bit as debilitating as physical injury, if not properly dealt with. And everything someone once held dear in their very soul will now feel like it has been plundered and violently ripped from them, invasively handled by unfamiliar, rapacious fingers, and then tossed back, unrecognizable, into their bleeding and bandaged hands to try and put back into some semblance of what love once meant to them.

For with love, like with war, a person will be quite blessed, indeed, if they eventually discover, in the end, just what purpose any of these scars served at all.

And that is what will always take the greatest amount of faith.

#

Mirielle didn't know where she was. She exhaled slowly. Her eyes were held tightly shut. She tried to inhale, only to breathe dirt into her nostrils and throat, which caused her to choke and cough, in turn, sending a spasm of excruciating pain tearing down her right side. She tasted blood in her mouth and then spat out a muddy mixture of dirt and blood. She opened her eyes, but at first everything was too bright and she couldn't focus. Gradually, she began to identify tufts of grass and small rocks right in front of her; the blades of grass tickled her nose and poked into her ear. She finally realized she was lying face down on the ground with her right arm painfully folded beneath her. She moved her other arm and hand to try and push herself up until a thrill of terror went through her as she discovered she couldn't move; she was pinned by some great mass on her back. She pushed hard again, heard a deep groan, and froze. She smelled stale, sweaty clothes, and felt something damp and warm trickling over her back and side.

Mirielle was paralyzed in fear as a large, strong hand gently but firmly pressed her head back down to the dirt, and a familiar voice croaked softly into her ear.

"Shhh – shhhh," it whispered. "Be very, very still, *mi amore!*"

Mirielle's heart skipped a beat.

"Rogelio?" she called out and tried to raise her head against the pressure of the hand. "What is happening, Rogelio?" she asked, her panic rising again. She didn't understand why she was being pinned to the ground by her husband who lay heavily on top of her back.

"Let me up! Why are you holding me down?"

"You must be very quiet, Mirielle," he whispered soothingly at first – then more harshly: "They are coming!"

Rogelio's voice possessed an urgency that she had never heard before, even though he also sounded very weak, groaning in what seemed to be great pain.

Suddenly, she detected the sound of a truck engine growling in the distance and growing louder by the moment, coming toward them.

Then she remembered.

She recalled that Rogelio and she had walked the great distance from *México,* across the Rio Bravo into the United States, trying to get to relatives who lived in *Norte de Nuevo México.* For days they had traveled, ever northward – eluding the border authorities, but accepting help and rides whenever they thought it safe to do so.

But this last ride had been different – the men in their black pickup truck had appeared friendly at first, offering to allow them to ride in the back. Later, though, after turning off the main highway onto a long, desolate dirt road, they had revealed themselves to be something else entirely. The truck had at last stopped; the men got out with long guns in their hands, dropped the tailgate, then had pounded on it and yelled at Rogelio and Mirielle to run – *run for your lives!* – and they had laughed.

Rogelio and Mirielle began running and running, faster than she had ever run before, Rogelio shouting at her from behind, occasionally touching her shoulder with his strong hand, encouraging and pleading with her to go faster, faster. Even so, she had finally grown so winded and weak that she was weeping and begging her husband to stop and rest.

Then had come the gunshots – and her husband had shoved her, and she had fallen – and had remembered nothing more, until now.

She now stiffened again and grew as still as possible. Sounds and smells became unnaturally amplified for her: the truck engine drew nearer, now stopped; the doors opened and slammed; boots crunched on the ground; the rich smell of burning cigarette tobacco; the voices of the two men as they chuckled and laughed and now seemed to be only a few yards behind her where she could not see as she lay underneath her husband.

"Shhh – Mirielle! Please! Do not move a muscle," Rogelio whispered desperately into her ear. The footsteps approached closer, and then stopped, even nearer. One of the men hacked and spit. She heard the shuffle of their feet on the rocky soil, talking softly, and smelled their sweat. But suddenly, she heard a strange new noise – a soft, whirring sound. She could not understand their English very well, but she thought she had understood one of them to use the word *camera…cámara?* Mirielle was terrified, but somewhere within her terror she was curious enough to want to know what they were doing back there – taking photos?

She squirmed, but now another sound gripped her heart – the click of the bolt being racked on a rifle. Only at that sound, she realized with horror that the warmth she felt trickling down her side had to be blood, but whether her own blood or her husband's she couldn't immediately identify.

She shuddered. She knew that she was hurt, possibly even shot, for her side burned and throbbed – had she been shot? She didn't know what it was supposed to feel like, being shot, but for some reason she didn't think she had – perhaps it was merely a broken rib or two that tormented her –

which could only mean that it was Rogelio's blood she felt.

Dear God! He is bleeding to death on top of me! He had pushed her to the ground and dropped onto her to shield her with his own body.

Mirielle's mind screamed, now on the brink of uncontrolled insanity; she could take it no more and she squirmed again and took a sharp breath to finally give release to her terror. Perhaps they might still run and escape this horrible nightmare. But she again felt Rogelio's strong calloused hand slip around her face to cover her mouth and stifle any sound. His lips moved to within millimeters of her ear where he kissed her hair softly and spoke quietly again.

"Whatever happens now, *mi amore…*" Rogelio winced and gasped painfully, "you must stay so very still…as if you are really…dead!"

"Rogelio!" she cried, but her voice was muffled under the palm of his strong hand. Hot tears streamed down her cheeks, mixing with the dirt and leaving muddy streaks on her face.

"I love you for an eternity, *mi querida esposa*!" he whispered fiercely. "Remember forever, Mirielle… I…"

Rogelio's voice was cut brutally short by the deafening crack of a gunshot, only feet away. Mirielle gasped as he suddenly jerked violently against her and went still, blood and other matter spraying out across the ground just in front her, some of it striking her warmly on the back of her head and cheek as the echo of the shot bounced around the surrounding hills. A scream formed again involuntarily, deep in her throat, but when she heard footsteps approach again slowly, she sucked her breath in and held it, desperately squeezing her eyes shut and pressing her entire face into the earth – praying to God she would remain still and lifeless as Rogelio had warned her to. She heard the *snick-snick* sound of the rifle bolt again, and after an interminable and maddening delay, one of the men asked the other a question, which she didn't understand, then silence for what seemed an eternity. She continued to try and control her breathing. Suddenly, she heard a couple of quick steps right beside her; she was roughly jostled; she swooned, and almost passed out as rough hands rolled the weight of her dead husband off of her.

Mirielle's heart raced; she let her arms flop limply, desperately trying to also appear dead, but she felt certain the killers would still see the pulse throbbing in her neck. Absolute panic and indescribable pain flooded over her as she distinctly felt the muzzle of a rifle poke sharply into her injured side several times.

She pressed her eyes and lips shut, the pain pulsing unbearably, until blessed insanity wrapped its cool arms around her fevered mind, and everything finally – mercifully – went dark.

CHAPTER 1
DREAMS AND VISIONS

Trent Carter sits against a pine tree, sipping an ice-cold beer and gazing across a valley of gold and red and green. A carpet of aspen and oak and pine spreads like a king's ransom below and beyond as far as he can see. His eyes wander over to where his wife stands just a few yards away, silhouetted against the late afternoon sun: brown hair flecked with spun gold in the sunlight, slight breezes lifting her hair from her shoulders, waving it like a banner. Her light blue sundress provides a pleasant counterpoint to the palette of colors sparkling around her; she might have stepped out of a Monet painting. The tall grass and wildflowers break softly against her calves like waves, up to her knees, so that instead of walking, she appears to float and glide across the meadow as she moves along. Her camera obscures her face as she clicks away at varied subjects. She senses his gaze, turns, and catches him looking at her. She purses her lips with the beginnings of a smile, lifts the camera, aims it his way, and rapidly snaps off three or four shots. He is embarrassed, but grins and ducks his chin to his chest to avoid the camera's all-seeing eye.

When he looks again, she is coming toward him, skipping uphill like a little girl – and just like a little girl, she plops down, settles almost effortlessly beside him, grabs a handful of his hair, and pulls it playfully.

"You need a haircut," she murmurs, her voice low and silky.

He grabs her forearm – gently pulls her across his lap until they are face-to-face. Her finger drifts over to the widow's peak on his forehead – plays with a lock of his hair there, twisting it. "But don't you ever get rid of this," she purrs. He swims deeply into her blue-green eyes.

Moments – hours – days, they sit this way together, close, drinking in each other.

"Are you real?" she whispers.

He smiles. "I don't know. Are you?"

"Do you know how to make time stop?" she hums into his ear softly.

He shrugs. "Do you?"

"Those aren't answers – just more questions!" she pouts, elbowing him playfully. She looks shyly up into his eyes, and then continues, "And yes, I do."

She slips her hand around the back of his neck and pulls his head closer, until all he can possibly do is kiss her – for minutes, hours – days.

Time, indeed, stands still.

He then shivers as a sudden, ominous cold breeze raises goose bumps on his arms. She senses his disturbance and pulls away momentarily. He looks around – a sense of foreboding thumps in his chest.

"What's wrong?" she complains.

He shakes it off, bends back down, and kisses her quickly on her forehead.

"We need to go," he whispers as he glances around once more, uncomfortably. A mood has changed in the air.

They gather the remnants of their picnic and load everything back into the Jeep, jump in, crank the engine, and head up the narrow road that winds its way up the mountain. The road meanders back and forth, up and down, following switchbacks and curves, and crosses the tops of ridges that fall away several hundred feet into dark wooded areas below. He brakes near the curves, speeds back up on the straight-aways.

He glances over at her. Dappled light filters through the silvered leaves of aspen and plays across her face and hair. She smiles, not looking at him, but knows he is looking at her. She hums a vaguely familiar melody.

He starts to smile back.

At that moment, heaven comes to an end; hell begins.

From somewhere and everywhere, he hears a tremendous bang and feels the steering wheel jerk hard out of his hands. Time slows again, a dream within a dream – he is flying, a familiar occurrence in many of his dreams, but throughout this particular nightmare – for it is, certainly, now a nightmare – are woven vividly colored threads of panic, pain, and terror, punctuated periodically by horrific sounds of rending, screeching metal, of crashing tree limbs, and the piercing stabs of a woman's never ending scream.

Trent tells himself to wake up – but some other part of him refuses, seeking, instead, to get to the end of the dream as if on a mission; maybe this time he will find the answers that always elude him and in so doing, perhaps find ultimate healing for his torn, damaged mind, or at the very least, drift back into peaceful, restful sleep.

But peace never comes because this dream is not the stuff of tangled sleep but is born out of reality. Even within the nightmare, he suspects that these events have actually happened before, but knows he can never quite grasp the dream in its entirety. Important details are missing; he never understands why and he can never stop searching: the dream contains his only clues, and, reluctantly, he must always pursue what comes next.

A sudden excruciating pain explodes in his head – stabs through his entire body, followed by sudden stillness and haunting silence. The screams and the crashes subside, and he finds himself in that otherworldly Neverland that lies between sleep and wakefulness. He tries to speak, but only moans. He tries to move, but something presses down on him – something massive – until he is certain he will be crushed. He gasps for air; each breath only serves to produce indescribable pain to a degree that he has never before known, asleep or awake. When he tries to open his eyes, his sight blurs as the world swirls around him.

As he sinks into darkness, he strangely welcomes it, embraces it, loves it, and wills himself to slip even deeper into it, even as he is aware of a terrible nagging that nothing is at all right, nor will it likely ever be again.

His last foreboding sensation is of hearing faraway music – the thumping of some terrible, modern country song accompanied by the faint growl of a powerful truck engine – along with inexplicable, chilling laughter, all fading away into the unseen distance.

Suddenly, he is awake.

His first startling thought upon jarring wide awake in an ever-present cold sweat is the simple but unanswerable question – *Where is she? Vicky!*

Trent Carter is no longer dreaming.

The dream, however, remains with him always; he knows he has dreamt it before; he knows he will dream it again – asleep and awake, a gnawing, and growing obsession.

#

That afternoon, Trent Carter still contemplated his dreams. He lit a cheap cigar and clung to a brimming tumbler of Kentucky bourbon like his life depended on it. He settled back painfully into the old wooden rocker on the large redwood deck that clung, in turn, to the back of his rambling ranch style house, which itself clung midway up the side of Bartlett Mesa as if its life depended on it. The mesa rolled away northwards until it joined Raton Pass, which straddled the New Mexico-Colorado state line ten miles away.

The dreams were recurring, filled with incredible detail, and painted throughout with amazingly sensuous and distracting elements that took his breath away. Trent should have been able to dismiss them, like most dreams. But these were not only disturbing but clearly drawn from the clinical and cold realities of his own history – a past that stood out each night in stark relief against an even starker backdrop of a mind that possessed far too many gaps of reality, and a past that contained too many missing chunks of his memory to be ignored.

Therein lived the most frustration for Trent, for somewhere within the glittering mists of this so-called dream, he suspected laid the hard-sought answers about his missing past.

He took a long, slow sip of the whisky, feeling it burn down his throat, and rubbed the palm of his hand on the rough-hewn wooden armrest of the older rocker, just to make himself feel alive. The old chair had been built by his father at the same time he had built the old house itself, stick by stick, over fifty years ago. None of the rambling floor plan had been expertly fabricated, but it was still sturdy and functional like the old man himself had been for most of his life – until recently.

Trent had been raised in this house, and it had always drawn him back like a magnet throughout his adult life, no matter what that life brought, whether he had been away to college or the army or working with the New Mexico State Police in Santa Fe. His mother had died of a heart attack the year after he had returned from Desert Shield; shortly before her death, his father had been injured badly on the job with the railroad, become disabled, and was now in a rehab center in Clayton, about eighty miles to the east.

This was home, Trent had always felt safe here, Vicky had loved it, and that had been that. He had taken early retirement from the state police and they had moved back home to Raton, where he had reluctantly gone to work for the Colfax County Sheriff's Department.

Trent had been sitting now for a couple of hours, sipping whisky, and puffing his cigar. He used this daily ritual to try and give some semblance of structure and purpose to his afternoons. He looked south, out over the tired little town of Raton, which spread out in the valley below him. Since the 1800s, the town had flourished with mining, railroads, and ranching; but in recent decades, the mines had closed, the railways had dwindled, and the town now languished. *An appropriate metaphor for a burned out lawman*, Trent mused with an audible grunt as he rocked slowly, awaiting the waning light of day. He grabbed a bottle from the small table at his elbow and refilled his glass.

The air was growing crisp as the fall of the year crept up, just as the autumn of his 64 years of life crept up on him. Soon, the clouds on the horizon would explode into one of those spectacular panoramas of New Mexican color that moviemakers were enamored of these days.

His gaze took in the vista beyond – wide grassy pasturelands, interrupted here and there by abrupt intrusions of volcanic buttes and mesas that paraded away to the southeast across the New Mexican plains in ever-varying shades of purple. Somewhere out there over the horizon, he knew that the high desert terrain spilled away and onto the West Texas Panhandle.

Over to the southwest, dark rain clouds were piling up behind the town along the ridge of foothills that climbed away to the distant peaks of the Sangre de Cristo Mountains. The view from up here was timeless, rugged, and staggeringly beautiful, the light always shifting like a series of impressionistic paintings whose splashes of color and shadow could never be reproduced the same way.

Trent was not impressed with any of it.

Not anymore.

He continued to stare out blankly, squinting at the horizon toward something unseen, something ambiguous. He tried to coax that elusive something into view, but was unsuccessful.

Whatever it was, it refused to manifest itself in his memory, and chose, instead, to remain hidden in the torn parts of his mind. He raised his glass, took another sip of the amber liquid, and reflected on the dullness that beat mercilessly in his chest as if marking time in some relentless, inevitable countdown to eternity.

Trent's own long war of the heart and soul had left deep scars, just as his body bore the physical evidence of long years putting it all on the line – high school football, the military police in Germany, Iraq, and various wounds received during his twenty years in law enforcement.

Trent took another long sip as the memories, like specters, materialized before him.

The accident had left him in traction and in a coma for almost three months. Upon regaining consciousness, he had discovered he now also suffered loss of memory, loss of some minor cognitive abilities, and the loss of something even more unimaginable and unspeakable – his wife.

The truth continued to assault him: Vicky was gone, her death had been his fault, and the accident would haunt him forever.

After over a year of grueling physical therapy, which had finally enabled him to walk, first with the aid of a walker and later with a cane, he still awakened most days with his bed sheets soaked with sweat and to a fresh reality of everything his battles had cost him. He had refused to give himself any time to properly grieve, and, in fact, desperately wanted to take his mind elsewhere – anywhere – to stop dwelling on the memories, incomplete and damaged as they were. He couldn't wait to finally get back to a work routine, to start exercising his mind as well as his body. But his attempt to use work to drown his grief and massage his memories hadn't really worked, and he knew it.

Soon, Trent was only going through the motions, sometimes sitting in his office staring out the window or drifting off during meetings or phone calls. Often, he found himself in his pickup truck in the parking lot, staring off into space, having forgotten where he was headed to or exactly what he was supposed to be doing. The other deputies and staff noticed these lapses – seemed like everyone noticed it, including the sheriff.

The comforting smell of wood-smoke and pinesap wafted on the late afternoon breeze, just like the liquor wafted through his system and numbed his troubled mind. This daily routine to exorcise his demons of loss sometimes worked, but never lasted long.

"Dad, I'm going to town to get groceries," Sophie called through the sliding glass door screen, breaking in on his reverie. "Do you need me to pick up anything?"

Sophie Carter, Trent's 28-year-old daughter, was five-foot-two, slight build, with long sandy blond hair like her mother's, and every bit as beautiful. She had inherited her good looks from her mother, her stubborn streak from her father.

She had pretty much put her own life on hold to help nurse him back to some semblance of health. Sophie was well educated, independent, and smart, and upon earning her journalism degree from the University of New Mexico had taken a good position with *The Albuquerque Journal.* She had almost married after that, but her fiancée had been killed in Afghanistan. In barely a year she had also experienced the loss of her mother. After the accident, she had decided to come home to take care of her father for a while. With her background she had easily gotten on with the local newspaper as a staff reporter. Though taking a huge cut in pay, she told herself it was for her dad's sake and that he was the one who needed help. Trent, himself, though, suspected that the change had also been for Sophie's sake; she, too, needed the time to grieve and properly heal.

Trent was grateful and yet found himself emotionally stunted and unable to show her the proper gratitude. He felt he was only a burden on his daughter.

"Nope, can't think of a thing," he answered her and took another sip of whisky. He could feel Sophie's disapproving scowl on the back of his neck.

"Haven't you had enough for the day?"

Trent glanced over at the bottle on the table. It was almost empty. "Nope," he lied, "just barely cracked the bottle."

"I was referring to that one, plus this empty you tossed in the trash earlier!" He twisted around far enough to see her wag an empty bottle at him.

"That one was from yesterday," he smirked and then raised his glass as if to toast her and turned back to the view. He cringed as she slammed the sliding door shut and stamped away through the house. Shortly after, he heard the front door slam and her car start up. It spun gravel as it sped out of the circular drive.

"Way to go, Jerk," he muttered to himself.

Let's face it, Trent thought. It sometimes felt good to be miserable, and misery – as people were wont to say – often liked a little company.

To the extent that on one beautiful Friday afternoon, after being thoroughly chewed out by his exasperated boss, Sheriff Ben Ferguson, Trent had stood up, wished everyone a good weekend, tossed his service weapon and shield on the desk, and walked out of the office. That piece of theatre had been almost three weeks ago now; he had had more than enough and should have felt liberated.

He didn't.

He drained his glass, felt the harsh liquor burn as it went down, and grimaced with disgust with himself. This unending plague of mental and emotional instability, which tugged the hardest and most cruelly at this time of day was something he could seldom control anymore, without his drug of choice. He could feel the self-medication finally – gratefully – taking on a glow of ennui in both his mind and his face. Trent told himself he wasn't an alcoholic – at least, he didn't believe he was one –not yet. The thought caused a brief smile to play at the corner of his mouth as he reflected, *isn't that the first thing a real alcoholic denied to himself?*

He rose slowly and painfully from the rocker, grabbed his empty glass, and stumbled into the house to get a new bottle, which after much searching he eventually found in the bottom of the dining room china cabinet. The whisky gurgled and chuckled at him as it spilled into his tumbler with the wet promise of continued numbness. He drained half of it slowly and wiped his mouth on the back of his hand. His eyes roamed the room languidly and stopped as they lit on an old guitar resting undisturbed on its stand in the corner of the room.

Trent grunted, set the glass on the dining table, and shuffled over until he stood over the old Martin six-string guitar and stared down at the instrument as if he had never seen it before. He reached over and tentatively plucked the lower three strings with a forefinger.

It was the first time he had touched the instrument since the accident.

A familiar tune began to echo in the back of his mind and he suddenly recognized it as the one Vicky had been humming in the Jeep that day, the one she always sang in his dream – the one he had written just for her:

"I am Far and Away from the one that I love,
Far and Away from my home…"

"Damn song," he snorted, cutting the tune off in his head before it became a full-fledged earworm. *Why does that have to be one of the few memories I didn't lose?*

He retrieved his whisky before meandering back out to the deck, where he eased himself back into the rocker just as a huge yellow-orange tomcat suddenly jumped onto the deck from where it had been prowling below, startling Trent.

"Dammit, Jarhead!" he exclaimed, knocking over the bottle on the table with his elbow and sloshing his drink all over his shirt. The large cat sat down unconcernedly, stretched a hind leg in front of itself, and licked it. It then regally approached Trent, rubbed itself against his leg, purred loudly, as if giving permission for him to pay it some attention. The cat sported a major scar or two, including a nicked ear, testifying to its prowess in battle, and deigned now to allow Trent to reach over and scratch behind its ears for a few moments before turning without warning and grabbing Trent's wrist with its front paws, claws out and clinging, barely breaking the skin, as if to say, "*That's quite enough,*" before darting away.

Trent stared after the animal. Even the cat had no patience for him these days.

He slumped down into the rocker, reached over to rescue the remains of his whisky bottle, relit the stub of his cigar, and propped his boots up on the railing of the porch. He created a "gun sight" effect through the toes of his boots and squinted along his jeaned legs and straight downhill along the highway that ran to and from Texas. The distant truck rigs, family RVs, and ranch trucks crawled back and forth like ants out to where the road faded into vermillion desert landscape. From this elevation, the muted whir of their tires created a soothing white noise flange effect, causing Trent's mind to wander.

His eyelids drooped and his head lolled when suddenly the pocket of his denim shirt buzzed and vibrated insistently, like an angry, trapped hornet. He jerked awake, then retrieved and flipped open the cell phone in one practiced move. It was one of those older clamshell type phones, as he had refused to own one of the newer, so-called "smart" phones.

"Carter," he mouthed gruffly around the cigar in his mouth.

"Trent? That you?"

Trent and Molly Swindoll, the sheriff's department dispatcher, had known each other forever, or at least since they had dated a couple of times in high school decades ago. He might have fantasized back then about marrying her, but life had pushed them both along other pathways and on to other people. She was now widowed and semi-retired with six grandchildren, and Trent was – well, Trent was now worlds away from all that.

"Well, now, Molly, you're the one calling me," he muttered, trying to verbalize it so that she could envision the rolling of his eyes. "Who else do you expect to be answering this particular phone?"

Molly refused to rise to the bait. "Sounds like you've got a mouthful of mud," she continued, unperturbed, "and I am so very sorry to interrupt your busy day, but we've got a situation out at the Van Ryan place – I think you're going to have to deal with it personally. That is, unless you're too far along there in the washing and rinsing of your brain, which seems like you may be, from the sound of it!"

"Molly, may I remind you that I am no longer an employee of the Colfax County Sheriff's Department. Or hadn't you received that memo?"

"Oh, I got it. But I'm guessing someone forgot to give Miz Van Ryan the same information," she replied, exaggerating the "Ms."

Trent took the now dead cigar out of his mouth and rolled his eyes again, but this time for his own benefit. He held the phone away from his ear for a moment and pinched the bridge of his nose. He mumbled softly under his breath and then resignedly raised the phone again.

"What's she want now, or did she finally shoot somebody?" he asked.

"Who knows? She won't talk to anybody but you. I've tried." Molly continued to ramble on, non-stop now: "She's called in here five times already today, asking specifically for 'Deputy Carter,' in that tone of hers, you know. I tried to tell her you no longer work here. That's when she started in, going on and on about somebody better *'get off their ass and respond to the needs of the taxpayers in this county when they have a problem or there is going to be hell to pay this time,'* and threatening to come up here and pull me out into the street by my hair if I didn't give her your phone number, and then I – well, uh – I'm too much a lady to say what I told her. But anyway, let's just say I finally hung up on her!"

The silence on both ends of the line was palpable for a few seconds. "Trent? You listening to me?"

"Yeah, I'm listening. Is Ben around? What's he say about this?"

"Sheriff's down in Santa Fe, at that annual budget meeting. Won't be back till Monday—I wasn't about to bother him with any of this. But you better call her right away because she's just the kind of gal that'll be here kicking some butt!"

She paused.

"You want her number, Trent?" Molly paused once again, listening to Trent breathing hard. "Besides, I think she kinda likes you!" she added impishly.

Trent pulled his boots off of the deck rail and stood up cautiously, wincing as his back caught him. He cursed and leaned painfully against the railing, allowing his stiff joints to creak into place.

"No, I don't want her damn number," he growled, then sighed. "Look, Molly," he continued with almost an apologetic tone, "I'll just head on out there; but do me a couple of favors. Call and leave Ben a message about this, just so he doesn't come back here and put me into more of a shit storm than I am already about to step into." He groaned as he slowly straightened up, still leaning on the railing.

He added with a ceremonious tone, "Tell him I'm only doing this as a favor, you know, uh, as a concerned citizen."

"Right."

"And Molly, if Ms. Van Ryan calls back again, do not – DO NOT – under any circumstances, give her my number! And please try not to get her riled up any more than you already have." As he snapped the phone shut, he could just hear Molly begin to protest loudly before her voice disappeared.

Trent started to finish his drink, paused to study the half full tumbler of amber for a moment, then poured it out over the railing onto the ground below. He looked back out to the southeast where white jet contrails threaded and danced together as they spun away to the East and West. "Flyover country," he mumbled, visualizing all the people on those planes, looking down in his direction right now, wishing he were with them. *Everyone wants to go somewhere else, but when they get there nobody wants to stay*, he thought. Behind him and to the west over the foothills undulated the dark purples and grays of threatening rain clouds tumbling above the horizon.

Trent shook his head and turned back to the house. It would be late afternoon and probably raining once he got to the Van Ryan ranch. He opened the sliding door into the dining area just as Jarhead raced from under the deck table and scooted between his feet to beat him through the door, almost tripping him.

"Perfect timing once again, cat," he snapped. "But go ahead – it's gonna be a long night, so you might as well settle in for the duration."

He fed Jarhead, then limped to the bathroom, peeled off his shirt, leaned on the sink, and stared for two full minutes at his haggard reflection in the mirror, studiously trying to ignore the roadmap of scars across his body – the few small ones on his face and neck, and the larger ones on his arms and across his torso, including a round, purplish one on his right shoulder, the result of a bullet and a routine traffic stop gone bad. He ducked his head and splashed copious amounts of cold water on his face and head and then deliberately frowned again into the mirror at his dripping, puffy face. He looked ten years older than he really was, and felt twenty years older. He shook his head, finished undressing, turned the shower on as hot as he could stand it, and stood under the hot spray for a good ten minutes. He toweled off, shaved, combed his hair, got dressed, fixed himself a travelling mug of strong black coffee, and headed out the front door, muttering to himself all the while. He was almost to his pickup truck when he stopped, thought hard for a minute, trying to remember something, and limped back to the house. When he came back out, he was walking with his wooden cane, just for good measure, and had put on his old creased, black Stetson and his favorite well-worn bomber style brown leather jacket. In the front right pocket he had slipped his chrome plated Ruger .357 magnum revolver, also for good measure.

Trent climbed into his truck and started the engine and just sat there, carefully gathering his scattered thoughts, a routine he had learned he needed to follow. He took a long sip of coffee, letting the strong, hot liquid burn his lips and tongue, as if in penance. His head throbbed, but his mind was finally clearing, so he rubbed his face hard and took another long gulp. After a couple more minutes of this routine, he put the truck in gear and let it roll down the long driveway to the county road below. Soon, he was headed east on State Highway 72 toward Yankee Canyon. Ahead of him a harvest moon had just risen above the hulking mass of Johnson Mesa from a break in the clouds, as if fighting to escape the mists of rain scudding to the east. The haunting view reminded Trent that he may have cleaned up, dressed up, and somewhat sobered up, but he still felt very much enshrouded in a mess, both inside and out.

He also sensed that nothing but trouble was about to come from this business with Ms. Margot Van Ryan.

CHAPTER 2
TO THE LEAST OF THESE

Excerpt from the journal of Otto Eberhardt

"15.11.44 – Tomorrow is the day! I can't believe we are going through with this, after all the months of planning and preparations. My new uniform is terrible, though. That fool that calls himself a tailor here has gotten the arm lengths all wrong, and I'm not sure that the material is dyed the correct shade of green for an American uniform. But it's too late to change anything now. Tomorrow at dusk we go! I can't believe that we are going to try and just walk out of here. I wonder if we should wait. I hear rumors of a tunnel. I only wish I had learned to speak better English while I was here. Good thing Ernst is much more fluent than I am.

'My thoughts are rambling. I dare not write more in case I am searched! And if Ernst knew I was keeping a journal – well, I must make sure he never sees it."

#

The 1938 Chevy pickup nosed its way through the early winter evening. Dave Perkins was heading home to his small farm near Hoehne, northeast of Trinidad, Colorado. He rubbed his cold, weathered hands together as they draped over the top of the steering wheel. The snow was beginning to fall lazily, not enough yet to stick to anything, but the temperature had already dropped at least another ten degrees since he'd left the city limits a couple miles back. He was eager to get his load of groceries and supplies home, get the fire blazing in his old cook stove, and set a good stew boiling as soon as possible. His biweekly trip to town had to be carefully planned these days, what with gasoline and grocery rationing, plus, he was more than a little worried that the balding tires on the old truck were about finished, and his ration card not due to allow him new ones for another six months.

Dave blew warm breath on his fingers, flexed them, and winced as the arthritis in them grabbed hold. He searched once more between the seats for his worn mittens, found only one, and pulled it onto one hand before reaching up and swiping the inside of the windshield where his breath had fogged it. His eyes widened and he gasped as two dark figures suddenly loomed out of nowhere on the shoulder where he had allowed the truck to drift. He swore, stomped the brake pedal, and at the same time swerved back onto the road to hopefully avoid plowing into the two men. The engine died as the truck bounced to a stop at an angle across the centerline. Dave pushed his almost numb fingers – the ones without the mitten – underneath his old fedora and rubbed the left side of his head where it had banged against the side window.

"Dammit!" he swore again. He looked at his fingers, sure he would find a trace of blood, but there was none, only a tender spot and a slight welt under his sparse, graying hair. He then remembered the men he had surely run into. He quickly rolled down the window and thumbed the outer door handle as the inside one was broken and no longer worked the latch. He dragged himself out of the truck and hurried around to the back, fearing that he would find bodies lying there. Instead, two uniformed soldiers, American Army officers, were climbing out of the ditch at the side of the road where they had evidently made a nosedive when the truck had almost slid into them. One of them, wearing the uniform of a lieutenant, was short and stocky and scowled at Dave as he rubbed the dirt off his hands. The other officer, with captain's bars on his lapels, dusted off his trousers and chuckled as he straightened up and rearranged the cap on his head. He was tall and little thin, but appeared athletic and fit. He gave a brief wave, and then sauntered toward Dave, still smiling.

"Why, hello there, old timer!" the captain said, holding his hand out while taking a couple of springing steps toward him. "You gave us a pretty darn good scare there." His voice was clipped and precise and had a slight accent that Dave could not immediately place. The captain looked quickly up the road and then back the other way.

"Gosh! You fellas alright?" Dave asked, also looking down the road, following the soldier's gaze. No other cars were in sight anywhere. "I swear I didn't see you guys at all," he began to apologize, then pointed at his truck. "My windshield was freezin' up and I just barely caught sight of you.

I'm awful sorry about this!" The stocky lieutenant looked around nervously for something. Dave realized the man had lost his hat and ran over to help him look for it. He talked back over his shoulder. "I guess you guys are heading to town for the evening?" he asked and then rubbed his chin. "Seems a little late in the day to be starting a day pass. I thought everyone usually got away from the camp earlier than this." He shaded his eyes from the slight glare of the setting sun and then spied the hat lying a few yards away in the middle of the road. He retrieved it, knocked it against his knee, and then trotted back to where the soldiers stood at the back of his truck.

"Yes," replied the captain. "We got a late start today. There was a minor problem at the camp, and we didn't get away as soon as we had planned." He shifted his eyes quickly to the lieutenant and back again to Dave with a smile.

"Here ya go, Lootinit." Dave handed the hat back to the quiet officer who immediately snatched it from his hand and pulled it quickly back on. Dave noticed the man had scraped the back of his hand and that he frowned as he rubbed it. Dave couldn't help but notice something a little odd about his manner; he seemed a little nervous – more than what the situation dictated – for some reason.

"You sure you're all right there, sir?" he asked cautiously, but the lieutenant muttered something unintelligible under his breath and turned away. "I – I could give you boys a ride to town, if you'd like; maybe take you to the doctor or back to the camp? Maybe you got some important plans," Dave continued. "Maybe, you know, lady plans?" Dave chuckled and winked conspiratorially as he started to open the passenger door but abruptly stopped as he noticed the lieutenant was leaning over the side of the truck bed and checking under the old tarp that was covering the supplies in the back.

"Oh, no sir," Dave quickly reacted to the lieutenant. "That's just my groceries and such. Besides, you don't need to ride back there," Dave stammered as he reached over to pull the tarp back over his supplies. "I'll just clean off the front seat there. I think we'll all fit okay." Dave didn't have anything to hide, but he didn't appreciate the man snooping around in his truck.

"Yes – yes a ride would be much appreciated," replied the captain, stepping up to Dave, putting his hand on his shoulder in a friendly manner.

"But perhaps, since it's getting late, we could just ride to your place for the night. It is nearby, yes?" He tightened his grasp on the old man's shoulder and turned him to move him back toward the truck.

Dave detected that slight accent again in the captain's speech. East coast, maybe? He slowed his step, thinking, trying to place it, and hesitated. He glanced back again at the fit of their uniforms. Something seemed a little off. The captain noticed Dave's hesitancy and suddenly put his hand into his jacket pocket. Dave's heart missed a beat, his eyes following the captain's movement, but then he breathed a sigh of relief as the hand emerged with a packet of non-filtered cigarettes. He shook a cigarette loose, took it between his lips, and proffered the pack to Dave.

"Would you happen to have a light?"

Dave dismissed his wandering thoughts as quickly as they had arisen and fumbled in his pants pocket for the lighter he carried, although he himself had not been able to afford cigarettes for a couple of weeks. They lit up, and then finally, Dave moved back toward the truck.

"Well, let's get this truck turned around, so we can get you guys out of this weather!" Dave scooped up an armful of mail and newspapers and other trash from where it had all scattered across the seat and floor when he had slammed on the brakes. He muttered to himself and made excuses for the mess and tilted the seatback forward to drop it all behind the seat.

"Out of sight, out of mind," Dave chuckled nervously as he put the seat back into position.

The two men slid into the truck, the captain sliding to the middle of the seat where he straddled the stick shift in the middle of the floorboard with his long legs while the young lieutenant hopped in beside him. Dave slammed the passenger door, scurried around, and climbed into the driver's seat. He blew on his hands again, then cranked the engine a few times until it caught.

"What is your name, Old Timer?" the captain asked. His voice was soft, smooth, and he enunciated his words carefully.

"Name's Perkins. Dave Perkins," he answered, checking both ways and reaching over past the captain's leg to put the truck into gear. "What's yours?"

The captain suddenly grabbed Dave's wrist tightly with his left hand. His other hand darted into his inner jacket pocket. The next moment, Dave felt a small dagger stick him under his arm, jabbing his armpit. Dave gasped as he felt the extremely sharp point penetrate his denim jacket and flannel shirt and break the skin underneath. He hardly had a moment to wonder what was happening before the captain spoke again, his voice still soft and soothing.

"Well, Dave Perkins. You are going to do exactly as I say if you want to keep breathing." The other man, the lieutenant, had twisted his body in the seat and frowned, but was watching impassively.

"You live nearby, yes? Out in the country?" the captain continued. Dave was quiet, but sucked in air in short gasps. The knifepoint jabbed again.

"Y-yes! In the country! My farm – just down the road a bit! Not real far. Just right down there," Dave blurted a little too loudly, eager to please.

"This is good! So here is what will happen: you are going to drive us all to your home, very calmly, nothing out of order, yes?"

Suddenly, the other man nudged the captain.

"*Mein Herr*," he said urgently and nodded toward the road.

An old battered Buick had appeared over the rise in the highway just ahead of them and slowed to a gradual stop as it pulled even, the driver side window rolling down. The captain pressed the knife harder. Dave gasped again.

"Now, Mr. Perkins," the captain hissed. "Do not be foolish – you are going to wave them on, and not let on anything is wrong. We are all friends, yes?"

Dave nodded, quickly rolled down the fogged up side window, nodded again and grimaced a smile to the other driver, a middle-aged man wearing a fedora pushed back from his chubby face. He grinned back, a cigarette dangling from his lips with a long ash protruding precariously.

"Hey there, Dave! Having some trouble again with that old truck?" the man asked. He was overweight and wheezed when he spoke, either from the cold or from smoking too much or both.

"Nah, it's good. Everything's fine, Harvey – just fine!" Dave's mouth suddenly went dry and he coughed. The knife made its presence known again. "Just giving these two soldier boys here a lift." He jerked his head back to indicate the two soldiers. The smiling captain leaned forward a bit in the seat, let go of Dave's arm for a moment, and touched the brim of his cap with two fingers. "Howdy there, sir. Brisk evening isn't it?"

Harvey frowned for a second, then smiled broadly. "Yes, sir! Looks like that blizzard is finally moving in on us. You fellas must be from the POW camp." The captain and lieutenant exchanged quick glances before the man continued. "Cold night for a stroll, boys! You're lucky old Dave here stopped for you. He's normally too much of a bastard to pick up hitchhikers! Isn't that right, Dave!" He then laughed uproariously at his own joke as he rolled up the window and gunned the Buick away. Dave lowered his head, staring forlornly into the rear view mirror as the Buick faded from view.

The snow began to fall more thickly now. Dave began to shiver, not entirely from the cold.

"Well, Old Timer," the captain said. "You did very well. Time for us to get moving, wouldn't you say?" His knife hand held firm against Dave's side. "But not too fast, *ja*? We wouldn't want any accidents, would we?"

Dave swallowed, slowly eased the window back up, ground the truck into low gear, and moved back out onto the highway, moving cautiously.

With his free hand the captain took another cigarette from his shirt pocket and offered one to the lieutenant, who hesitated for a moment before plucking one and lighting it. He seemed grateful for the strong, soothing American tobacco smoke expanding in his lungs and watering his eyes. Dave noticed that this one still appeared uneasy – not quite as confident as his captain.

"*Komm jetzt, Herr Leutnant*," smiled the captain, patting the lieutenant's arm. "We are out of that damned prison camp and well on our way to better things." He turned to look at Dave again. "And now we are going to enjoy some of our new friend's hospitality, *ja*?"

The lieutenant said nothing, but quietly smoked as he stared through the windshield into the flickering stabs of snowflakes now coming hard at them like tiny silver bullets.

CHAPTER 3
INTO THE PROMISED LAND

Raindrops the sizes of quarters were smacking the windshield by the time Trent reached the bottom of the winding graveled road that ran a quarter mile from his house. He turned off onto the county road that carried him another mile or so before dumping him onto Highway 72. He then drove east into what was now a welcome shower. By the time the road had dropped into Yankee Canyon a few miles farther, the rain had become a steady downpour.

Abruptly, though, the rain had stopped by the time Trent pulled his truck off the highway and headed south down the dirt road that meandered and roughly paralleled a nicely running creek for a couple more miles. He topped a rise and dropped immediately into a valley filled with ancient cottonwood trees. The road from the highway had been well maintained, but was a little muddy after the shower so that his truck was now spattered with mud.

He slowed down upon reaching the massive log gateway that formed the entrance into the Van Ryan homestead. The logs were held in place by large welded straps of iron; carved into the log that formed the upper crossbeam was the name *Montaña del Sol*, with the ranch's distinctive *VR-* brand centered underneath. He drove through the impressive, but intimidating, gateway and entered the Van Ryan ranch.

The long driveway was lined with large cottonwood trees that formed a canopy overhead, and here the road was only slightly damp. The late afternoon light was golden green as it filtered through the leaves; Trent rolled down his window to enjoy the welcome scent of the passing rains.

The air was fresh and cool, mixed with the pungent aromas of tall grasses growing in nearby pastures and the musky odors of a working cattle ranch.

After another half mile, the road spilled out of the trees into a sprawling compound of ranch buildings. To the south, surrounded by a manicured lawn, sat a rambling, two-story main house that boasted a large covered porch stretching around the home on three sides. To the north and east were barns, stables, and various other outbuildings, all of which formed a large central plaza where a few ranch vehicles and implements were neatly parked. Scattered cottonwoods, live oak, and elms provided ample shade near the house where Trent pulled his truck up and parked. He eased stiffly out of the truck, reached for his cane, but changed his mind and left it on the seat. He limped up the flagstone walkway to the house and slowly climbed the wide steps to the porch. He reached out a hand to knock on the front door.

"Trent Carter! Well, there's a sight for sore eyes."

Trent froze for a moment, confused, for the voice sounded disembodied and distant.

"Over here, cowboy."

The voice came from somewhere behind him; he turned, squinted, and took a step back down the stairs before spying a figure waving at him from across the plaza. The person sat in a wicker chair that was tipped back to lean against the barn door. At this distance the person looked like a man in nondescript ranch clothes, but the voice had been unmistakably that of a woman. Trent limped cautiously down the steps, back down the sidewalk, and towards the barn. As he approached, he finally recognized the person as Margot Van Ryan. She wore an unbuttoned rain slicker over a red-checkered flannel shirt tucked into faded jeans and a man's brown fedora with a rain-dampened rolled brim. More disconcerting was the two-barrel shotgun she balanced on one knee by the stock, although the barrels pointed inoffensively upward.

Margot let the chair tip back down to the ground and stood up to greet him. She slung the shotgun over one shoulder and shifted her weight slightly to one hip. The pose suddenly struck Trent like that of a miniature John Wayne. The tip of her tongue poked out of the corner of her smile; she looked him up and down as he approached, as if appraising a prize bull in the auction ring.

"Well, your eyes have to be pretty sore then, Ms. Van Ryan," Trent finally said before stopping a few feet in front of her.

"Never too sore for you, Sheriff – even though you do look like you've been rode hard and put up wet!"

"Well now, Ms. Van Ryan," he answered. "You know I am not the sheriff. Hell, not even a deputy anymore. Didn't they tell you when you called that I had quit?" he asked, peering down at her.

"Yeah, What's-Her-Name down there at your office might've said something about it. But that doesn't mean much to me," she answered. She took the shotgun from her shoulder, broke open the breach with a clacking sound, and exposed the two loaded chambers. She crooked it safely over her forearm as she stepped toward him. "Must not mean much to you neither, evidently – seeing as you're here, "she responded, her voice trailing off coquettishly.

Trent shifted his feet and nodded at her shotgun. "You – uh –hunting rats with that popgun, Ms. Van Ryan? Out here in the rain?"

She stepped to within a foot of him, clearly into his comfort zone, pushed her hat up off her forehead, and tilted her face to look up at him.

"Might be," she answered mysteriously. She was a good ten inches shorter than he and was giving him that mischievous smile again. She was close enough that he could smell the lemon scent of the shampoo she had used today – and maybe just a hint of cologne.

"Maybe something bigger" she teased, gazing up into his eyes. "And it's Margot – but you can call me Maggie – if you want." She punctuated her words with her forefinger against his chest.

"It's Molly," he said, staggering back a step.

"No, 'Maggie.'"

"What? No, I meant," he stammered. "'What's-Her-Name,' the dispatcher." He cleared his throat nervously and repeated, "Her name's Molly."

She rolled her eyes, took a step back, letting the matter drop. Instead, she removed her hat and slapped it a couple of times against her rain slicker, scattering droplets of water onto both of them.

"I got caught in that shower earlier." She gazed out wistfully across her pastures that rolled gradually uphill to the southeast until they disappeared into distant tree line of mixed oak and pine. She remained quiet for a moment, as if communing with the creative force that had made this land. She breathed in deeply, then continued. "But I sure do enjoy a good rain, don't you?"

Margot Van Ryan had lived on this ranch all her life, born and raised here. Her grandfather, Werner Van Ryan, who had homesteaded the ranch after immigrating from Holland after World War I, and had been a tough and no nonsense old cattleman. But he had also gotten himself wrapped firmly around Maggie's little finger since the day she was born. He had died when she was five, the first loss like that she had ever experienced.

Her father Richard had then taken charge and had been the one responsible for incorporating the ranch and expanding its land and cattle holdings; in so doing, he had made them all a lot of money over the years while at the same time working himself into an early grave at the age of 45. Richard had had a sister, Evie, but after some rumored scandal, which had remained hushed up in the family, Aunt Evie had been married away to some rancher on the New Mexico/ Oklahoma border and had since also died tragically and mysteriously. Evie had had a couple of children, a boy and a girl a few years older than Maggie, but she had only seen her cousins a couple of times over the years.

As an only child herself, when her father died twenty-two year old Maggie had to leave her senior year at New Mexico State University where she had been pursuing an agricultural business degree to come home and help her widowed mother run the ranch. She had proven herself to be more than capable at the task and had taken the bull by the horns, literally and figuratively, working the cattle as well as – or better than – most men, and taking care of the business needs of a modern ranch as well. She had become known as a hard but fair boss lady, very much like her Grandpa Werner, particularly when it came to hiring and firing the seasonal ranch hands needed around the sprawling place. In her rulebook, if a body worked hard and didn't need to be bailed out of jail on their days off, they were pretty much guaranteed to keep their job.

Almost predictably, within a few years Maggie had finally fallen in love with one of those ranch hands and had married him. But his handsome movie star cowboy looks and sweet talk had belied an inner mean streak, and soon, clearly enough, he proved himself only to have been interested in the higher status of living afforded to him by the relationship and not the hard work that helped to earn it. He had begun drinking heavily and disappearing for days at a time to carouse with old friends – and with other women. When he was found tangled in his horse's stirrup and dragged to death up a canyon one day after riding off drunk the evening before, Maggie could muster no real sadness or grief, only a profound sense of relief.

Notably, she took back her maiden name shortly after.

She and her mother had continued to run the enterprise from then on, two strong cattlewomen who knew as much or more about the ranching business than a lot of other men, several of whom had lost many a cattle or land deal by underestimating their individual and collective business acumen.

However, Maggie had lost her mother to heart failure a couple of years ago. Now in her late fifties, and not wanting to be forced to rely on too much help from others, she had gradually downsized her operation to where she was running only a few yearlings of her own, a few cutting horses for fun, and leasing out the remainder of the grazing land to others. These decisions had allowed her to pretty much run the ranch by herself, except for the occasional need for day labor.

She had never re-married, though still a handsome woman, petite but nicely proportioned. Her auburn hair was pulled back into a French braid with hints of gray creeping in at the temples. Bangs hung right above her eyebrows that arched attractively above stormy gray, almond shaped eyes, which held tiny flecks of gold, if someone dared look closely enough.

Trent could not help but look closely right now.

He noticed that she wore very little makeup – didn't need to, in his opinion. The skin crinkled at the corners of her eyes into fine laugh lines to match the ones at the corners of her mouth as if she were perpetually smiling. Trent had been uncomfortable coming out here in the first place to talk to this strong-willed, independent woman, and was even more so now that he was reminded how attractive Maggie was.

He cleared his throat and shuffled a foot.

"Okay…Maggie. So, uh, just what is so urgent?"

"Out there," she answered. "Had a break in up at what I call the old homestead shack."

She nodded toward the southwest, beyond the compound. Trent

He tasted the stew again and added a bit more salt. The front door of the house suddenly flew open and cold air and snow howled in viciously as the shorter of his two guests – the quiet, troubled one – stamped his feet on the threshold, pulled the screen door shut, and pushed his way in quickly with an armload of freshly split firewood. A flurry of snow danced around his legs.

The other man – the tall unpleasant one with the perpetually strange smile – sat at a small end table in the corner. He was engrossed in the local Trinidad newspaper, one leg crossed over the other, stroking his cheek thoughtfully with one finger. He ignored the swirling blizzard forcing its way in through the open door. The other man had hurried over to drop his wood near the fireplace while Dave rushed to close the door behind him.

"I am so sorry about the door," the man muttered over his shoulder to Dave. He stacked the firewood efficiently and then tended to the fire.

The Germans had been here for over six weeks now, holding him as a prisoner in his own house, waiting out this storm that had dumped several inches of fresh snow over the past several days. They had burned the fake American Army officers' uniforms they had used to escape Camp Trinidad, had scrounged through the old man's closets and trunks, and then helped themselves to the less conspicuous pants and shirts of a typical Colorado farmer. The shorter one was more of Dave's height and build so had taken some of his old clothes. Dave's father had been built more like the taller German, and they had found some of those old clothes that fit fairly well.

By now Dave had learned their names, so he knew with certainty that the taller one, Ernst, was clearly in charge. He could see that the quieter man, Otto, treated Ernst with deference and referred to him as "Herr Oberst," which Dave assumed meant that Ernst held the higher rank. Dave had also remembered some of the German his mother had taught him, so he could understood a smattering of what they said to one another, but pretended not to.

He was afraid of Ernst, who often struck him at the slightest provocation. But he rather liked Otto, who spoke kindly to him and always offered to do a few chores like gathering wood and tending the fire while Ernst was more than satisfied to sit and expected to be waited on like royalty.

Ernst folded his newspaper, laid it carefully on the table, and looked up.

"Dinner is almost ready, I think—yes, Mr. Perkins?" he asked with mocking politeness, the corners of his mouth curling into a tight smile again.

Dave paused for only a moment, clenched his fists, then hurried back toward the kitchen, not looking at Ernst and not answering. Otto stood from his work at the fireplace and wiped his sooty hands on his pants.

"You should wash up, Otto. Our host does not like to be kept waiting."

Dave scooped up bowls and spoons, cups and saucers, and brought them quickly back to the table where he set them carefully and precisely. He had learned the hard way that Ernst expected the table to always be set exactly the same way – or else there would be hell to pay.

Dave fussed over the silverware on the table, aware that Ernst watched him, and flinched as the German waved him away impatiently. Dave headed back to the small kitchen and squeezed past Otto, who dried his hands at the kitchen sink.

Dave hated Ernst. He hated that he had ever picked these people up on the highway, and he hated himself most of all for not feeling brave or strong enough to do anything about it – and for fearing for his life.

Dave grabbed some sourdough bread, put it on a small serving plate, and picked up the coffee pot. Otto turned and reached out a hand, offering to take the bread.

"I am sorry for all--this," Otto apologized quietly in his broken English.

Dave stopped and frowned for a moment, but softened and nodded. He wasn't mad at Otto and handed him the plate of bread. They both went out to the dining area where Dave carefully poured coffee into Ernst's mug, holding a dishtowel around the spout, not daring to spill or splash any. He touched his split bottom lip with the back of one knuckle; it was still swollen and tender from yesterday's incident when he had inadvertently sloshed hot coffee onto Ernst's sleeve.

He poured some for Otto and then set the coffee pot at the side of the table. Otto placed the plate of bread in the middle, turned, and looked sympathetically at Dave, who had stepped over to pull his chair out for him. He sat down with a sigh.

"Trying to play the good host, Mr. Perkins," Ernst sneered, picking up his mug with both hands and sipping. Dave waited anxiously. "The coffee is adequate tonight, Mr. Perkins. You may serve the main course now."

Dave nodded and stepped quietly back to the kitchen. Soon, he returned holding the pot of stew between two towels and set it down near the bread. Next, he took the men's bowls and ladled stew into them generously, again careful not to slosh it over the edges. He gingerly set the bowls in front of them and stood quietly back by the kitchen door with his hands folded in front of him and stared off into the distance, looking at nothing, as he had been instructed to do.

Dave was embarrassed and ashamed. Not only was he a hostage in his own home, but he was also expected to stand at attention and wait on his German "guests" like a common servant, or else suffer more consequences. The whole setup was demeaning to him, but he felt powerless to do anything about it. He was at least grateful that his wife had not lived to witness his cowardice, or worse, to be victimized by it.

Ernst had made it very clear that Dave's life was hanging by a mere thread, and only at a whim. He was not allowed eat his own dinner until the Germans had quite finished theirs. And next, Dave had to go prepare the one bedroom – his old bedroom – for "Herr Oberst" to retire to. The bedclothes had to be turned down just so, the pillows properly fluffed, and fresh towels laid out. Only at that time was Dave allowed to go clean up the dinner dishes and to finally sit down for a bite to eat in the kitchen, while his guests finished the night by smoking and reading the newspapers around the fireplace, where he dared not disturb them further.

Later, Dave heard Ernst walk to the bedroom and close the door, and he breathed a sigh of relief. He sat at the kitchen table and picked at his food, but was not hungry. He heard someone clear their throat and looked up to see Otto standing in the doorway, a sympathetic look on his face and a chessboard under his arm. Dave allowed himself a smile.

They were both avid chess players and playing chess with Otto had turned out to be one of the only pleasant aspects of his forced imprisonment. They would often be up until all hours happily challenging one other's abilities – and talking quietly. Otto seemed to enjoy the opportunity to practice his English, and each night Dave learned a little more about his "guests."

Dave cleared the last of the dinner dishes from the table and watched Otto methodically set up his black chessmen on the board. Dave preferred the white chess pieces, a small concession Otto had made to him during their games.

Tonight's game was no different.

"You realize that white is the color of the 'good guys,' don't you, Otto? And black is the 'bad guys." Otto raised his eyes and glanced at Dave, then back to his work with the chess pieces.

"If you are trying to – how do you say – get the rise out of me, Mr. Perkins, you are not going to succeed." He finished setting up the chessmen, sat down, and smiled. "I am – um – 'cool like the cucumber!'"

They made their opening moves, both quickly taking turns moving pawns. Otto then moved his queen's black knight, sat back, lit a cigarette, folded his arms, and watched to see what Dave might move in response.

"Do you want to know one of the most interesting things I have learned since I was brought here to your country, Mr. Perkins?"

Dave grunted as he studied the board.

"It was that the famous Santa Fe Trail runs right through here, practically right outside your doorway. You see, I have heard of this Santa Fe Trail. When I was a boy in Germany, I read about your history here, your Wild West, and all the Indians and cowboys and gunfighters. We had all the storybooks – picture books – with stories."

"You mean comic books?" Dave asked.

"Coma? Coma books?" Otto repeated, trying to repeat the strange word.

"Comic. C-o-m-i-c. Comic book," Dave spelled out.

"Comic book. Yes, very good." Otto smoked his cigarette and peered off into the cloud he had exhaled, seeing something there. "And so I was very happy to find out that Wyatt Earp and his brothers and Doc Holliday – all of them – stopped in Colorado, in Trinidad, for several weeks, on their way to live in Tombstone." He pronounced the town *Treenee-dad,* with the accent on the last syllable. "Did you know this about your history, Mr. Perkins?"

"Hadn't heard about that one, nope." Dave fingered one of his own knights then thought better of it and left it alone.

"Yes. And so, after they had the – uh – shoot it out of the O.K. Corral – "

"'Shoot out.'"

"Yes, 'shoot it out.'"

"'Shoot-out. SHOOT out," Dave enunciated slowly.

"*Ja*, shoot out. And so, they 'shoot out' the O.K Corral, and then I think you did not know, then, that later Wyatt Earp came back to Trinidad on the train, and his friend Bat Masterson, the famous U.S. Marshal, asked his good friend Wyatt Earp to stay and be a marshal here, also. But Wyatt Earp said to him, 'No!'" Otto puffed on his cigarette and gave Dave a smug look.

"Bat Masterson." Dave looked at Otto in disbelief.

"Yes,"

"THE Bat Masterson."

"Yes, yes. Mr. Bat Masterson who was the famous marshal back in Kansas, but also was in Trinidad!" Otto smiled with satisfaction and gestured at Dave with his cigarette. "You are – surprised, *ja*? – that you do not know your own history, Mr. Perkins."

"Know what I need to, I guess." Dave finally moved his white bishop to take Otto's black knight.

"I think that is why you Americans will still lose this war – no sense of place in history."

"You mean lose, like when you was captured in Africa by us Americans? That kind of 'lose?'" Dave grinned and sat back and waited for Otto's move. Otto quietly leaned forward in his chair, mashed out his cigarette in an ashtray, and studied the board.

Otto had already shared with Dave, over previous matches, how Ernst and he had served in a Panzer tank regiment of the *Deutsches Afrikakorps*, like several of the other prisoners at Camp Trinidad, under General Field Marshall Erwin Rommel. In February of 1943, almost two years to this day, they had been sitting at night with their respective Tiger tanks in North Africa, near a place called Kasserine Pass, awaiting orders. The sand had permeated every orifice of their bodies. Even at night, they had been miserable, sleeping outside their tanks in the open air for even a little relief from the unbearable heat that topped 55 degrees centigrade during the day and dropped to only 35 at night. Their regiment had just won a strategic victory over the Americans, who had fought their first ground battle of the war at Kasserine against hardened German veterans.

Ernst had never imagined he would now be sitting out the war in the middle of the American heartland, enduring a freezing blowing blizzard rather than the sweltering heat and sand. Flushed with their victory, and awaiting redeployment, their Tiger tanks may have been superior to the

American tanks, but they had not been impervious to the American warplanes that suddenly strafed and bombed them that night. Many of their tanks had been destroyed, many of their comrades had been blown to pieces in front of their eyes, and many more had been routed in hasty retreat. The wounded and starving survivors, including Otto and Ernst, had been left behind by the German army to be hunted down and captured by the Americans.

"And I must tell you that I am now grateful for that," Otto had admitted to Dave. "Otherwise, I think I would now be dead in that damned desert." They had been marched to a holding facility outside of Tunis, fed well, and doctored. They had, in short, been quite amazed at their excellent treatment and had even been given real American cigarettes and allowed to write home to their families – although he suspected that their letters had been held up for a while, perhaps for security reasons. In any event, he had never received a reply from his wife.

After a few weeks of recuperation, they had been transported as prisoners of war to the United States, a miserable three-week cruise on a converted freighter where Otto said he had been seasick for much of the trip and in constant fear of being sunk by his own country's *Kriegsmarine* submarines – the highly effective and deadly *U-boats*. They had finally docked in Florida, and along with maybe fifty other German prisoners had been trundled aboard a fairly comfortable passenger train that had taken another four days to travel across the vast North American continent to this place called Camp Trinidad in Colorado. Along the way, they had stared out the train windows in awe at the comparatively thriving American cities, towns, and countryside, which rolled by totally unscathed by the devastations of war.

A rail spur had allowed their train to offload them right at the gates of the prison camp, which had been built on the high desert plains east of the Rocky Mountains. The camp was a large compound, built to house over 2,500 German prisoners, but by the time Ernst and Otto had escaped, the number had swelled to almost 3,500. Ten-foot high double barbed wire fences, with guard towers armed with .50 caliber machine guns, surrounded it. The prisoners had been further surprised to find that the POW camp boasted its own movie theater and canteen where the prisoners, using camp scrip earned from work details, could purchase various sundries and toiletries and watch what to them were decadent American romantic comedies.

Overall, Otto had told him they had been very well cared for, even if the American commander had had his office floor entirely painted blood red to psychologically intimidate his charges when they were first checked into the facility. The camp was where Brandt and Eberhardt had remained for the last twenty months in relative ease, getting close to the other prisoners who shared an increasing determination to escape.

"One thing I'm confused about," Dave began, waiting for Otto's next move, "if you guys were so well treated, why did you escape at all? I mean, where's the sense in it all? You're just gonna get caught again – maybe shot this time." Dave looked at Otto curiously.

Otto didn't answer right away. Dave couldn't tell whether Otto was thinking about his next move or of an answer to his question. The fireplace in the next room crackled and popped as a gust of wind moaned down the chimney. The familiar smell of wood smoke made both their eyes burn and tear up. Dave suddenly feared he had been too bold to ask such questions.

Otto pursed his lips, rubbed his eyes, and looked up from the game. "For me, I have not seen my wife and daughter now for three years. My baby girl was two months old when I left home." He stared down at the board, but didn't appear to be looking at it, and in an almost whisper, "I do not know if they are even alive still."

He shook his head, as if rousing himself, reached out, moved his Queen's bishop diagonally across the board, and took Dave's knight. Nothing now was standing between his bishop and Dave's king. "I wrote them from prison, but no reply – for two years now." He shrugged. "I so badly want to write them again – but it is now dangerous to do so, *ja*?" He turned Dave's knight over and over in his fingers and then carefully deposited it with the other captured pieces in front of him. "Besides, I am not even sure where they are now. So many families are displaced in Deutschland right now, I fear – at least from what I read in your American newspapers."

"And Ernst? Doesn't he miss his family, too?"

Otto shrugged.

"*Herr Oberst* has no family, at least that I know of."

"Now, I don't doubt that at all," Dave replied. "That ornery son of a bitch was probably hatched in a cave!" He almost immediately regretted his comment and glanced nervously toward the other room.

"Sorry," he muttered sheepishly. After all, as friendly as Otto was, he was still one his captors.

Otto paused, tapped the table with a forefinger, and then pointed at the board.

"Check," he said.

Dave stared back at the board, incredulous.

"And that is also 'checkmate,' *ja*?"

#

By the next day, the storm had subsided, leaving behind a clearing sky, ten more inches of fresh snow on top of the drifts already accumulated, and a temperature hovering around 15 degrees Fahrenheit. Dave and Otto busied themselves shoveling snow, cleaned the pigs' pens and sheds, spread clean straw, and then fed the animals that squealed in delight at the attention. The hard work pleased Otto. He felt good to get into the fresh air and move around; the work reminded him of home. Ernst, on the other hand, seemed bored and passed the day alternately smoking and muttering while he paced on the porch of the house or sat by the fire inside and reread the newspapers. At one point, he had shoved Dave hard when he passed too near him as he came in from caring for the pigs.

"You stink to heaven of those pigs!" he had shouted at Dave. "Make sure you wash yourself and change clothes before you touch my food tonight! "

The dinner routine that evening was much the same, with Dave especially walking on eggshells so as not to draw Ernst's attention, but seemingly of no use.

"And so, Mr. Perkins--what were dear Otto and you talking about out there earlier in the pigsty? Pray tell: he wasn't apologizing to you again for your horrid predicament?"

Ernst glared across the table at Otto as he spoke. Otto met his eyes, quickly looked back down, and continued to eat his stew hungrily. Ernst took his napkin, shook it out, and carefully laid it across his lap. He toyed with a piece of pork in his stew, picked it up on his spoon to eye level, and gazed at it curiously.

"I should wonder if Mr. Perkins knows how to prepare any delicacies other than pork stew," he mused. "Aren't you getting rather tired of it, Otto?"

Otto slurped and chewed, glanced up, and immediately down again.

"No, *Herr Oberst.*"

Ernst rolled his eyes, dumped the pork back in his bowl, and dipped a piece of hard bread into the soupy liquid.

"I suppose all of you dirt farmers do have the same unrefined appetites." He nibbled at the bread and wiped his mouth daintily with his napkin, smiling at Dave.

"Mr. Perkins, Otto likes to talk to you, *ja*? And so, he must have told you he, too, was raised on a farm back in the Fatherland, yes? Back in Germany – a potato farm, I believe it was, yes, Otto?" Otto glanced up again at Ernst, hesitating before finally answering.

"Ja wohl, Herr Oberst. Das ist rechtig."

"Auf Englisch, bitte, my dear Otto – practice, practice! You must stop slipping into German so easily. We are in America now." He sipped his coffee while looking over the rim at Dave.

"Mr. Perkins, I believe I asked you a simple question. Is it not polite to answer?"

Dave stood at his usual spot near the kitchen and glanced down at the back of Otto's head, expecting some sort of support, then quickly shifted his eyes back straight ahead, focusing on nothing.

"A – a question, sir?" he stammered.

"Yes. I asked you whether or not Otto had told you he had also been a filthy farmer – like you." He carefully set his coffee cup onto its saucer and turned back to Otto. "Potatoes – or turnips – wasn't it Otto? Some such thing you have to get down on your knees and grub out of the ground."

An uncomfortable silence settled over the men as Otto had stopped chewing and merely stared at his plate, his neck growing red.

"No, sir, I did not know that," Dave finally blurted.

"Well, it is the truth," Ernst replied softly as he played with another chunk of pork. He grimaced suddenly and dropped it unceremoniously back into his bowl before slamming his spoon down.

"Which is exactly why he is not nearly as disgusted as I am!" he said, raising his voice. He shoved away from the table and stood up; the chair clattered behind him as he stalked the floor.

"I am sick and tired of eating nothing but this drivel made from the meat of those stinking, nasty animals you have rooting around out in their stinking pens, so close to the house you can hear them and smell their shit all night and day!" He stomped over to Dave, grabbed him by double fistfuls of his shirt, and pulled his face to within inches of his.

"And I am sick to death of being cooped up for weeks in this filthy old shack, listening to the wind howl, listening to you two laughing late at night, playing your stupid chess games, and talking about who-knows-what!" He punctuated his last words with a backhanded swat to the old man's ear and threw him like a child to the floor where Dave lay trembling at Ernst's feet, covering his head with his arms.

"Herr Oberst!" Otto had stood up, shoved his chair back, and made a move as if to intervene, then froze as Ernst gave him a stern look, fists clinching and reopening. Ernst breathed heavily, in and out, but finally appeared to calm down.

"And so, here we all sit – waiting for something to happen – something meaningful to do," Ernst continued, turning finally and stepping aside, "waiting – waiting, to do anything – something that is worthy of the Fatherland – worthy of me!"

At that moment, the dishes on the table began to vibrate, slightly at first, the table trembled, and they could all feel a familiar rumbling through their boots.

"And—and then – this!" Ernst shouted again, his face reddening again as a freight train roared past the house, shaking it on its foundations, not fifty yards away. He ran to the door, jerking it open, allowing the crisp cold air to pour in along with the acrid smell of burning coal and the thunderous shudder of the train flying past. "Why must we put up with this incessant noise and aggravation all the day long?"

Dave slowly picked himself up from the floor, wondering with trepidation whether or not he was supposed come up with an answer. They all three stood watching the freight train roar by. Dave visualized its route, wishing he were on it. It was right on time and on its evening run, having just left the Hoehne depot, now picking up a little speed again before it stopped briefly at the Trinidad train yards and refilled its engines' water tanks. The train would continue to steam on through town, turning south, toward the mountains, where it would struggle its way up the gradually steepening grade until it reached the top of Raton Pass, and then through the tunnels that had been blasted through the mountain and across the state line there, where it would pick up speed again and drop off the Pass on the New Mexico side, past the roundhouse and train yards and finally roll to a stop at the depot at Raton.

Ernst suddenly stopped his ranting, looked at Otto and Dave each in turn. His face lit up as his unsettling smile creased his face even wider. He turned and gazed back out the door as the train whisked by. When the caboose passed by, he finally spoke, a look of joyful revelation on his face, and just loud enough to be heard over the diminishing clatter of train cars as they receded into the distance.

"That's it!" Ernst said, almost to himself. "Otto! I know precisely what we are meant to do!"

CHAPTER 5
IT IS WRITTEN

As Trent stepped through the shattered doorway of the adobe house, he caught the odor of stale wood smoke mixed with the musty smell of a long closed up space. He found himself in a one room cabin, dimly lit with the golden light of the setting sun filtering in through a green checkered curtain pulled across the only window on the west wall just above an old tub sink. An antique water pump was mounted on one side of the sink looking as if it might still be functional.

The plastered adobe walls sagged a bit, betraying their age, but were solid. They were painted an off white color, which grew darker toward the ceiling from the years of wood smoke that had leaked out of the old stove sitting in one corner. As Trent moved on into the room in the dimming light, he almost tripped over the snarling head of an old bearskin rug unceremoniously tossed in a pile off to the side. The rug had evidently covered a trap door that now stood open in the middle of the room. The rough-hewn wood floors creaked as Trent stepped over and squatted painfully. He pointed his light into the opening and peered into the dark crawlspace below.

"Nothing down there, much," Maggie said.

"What do you mean, 'much'?"

"I mean I already crawled in there and looked," she answered. "Only thing down there's an old trunk. Been there for years. Just a bunch of old clothes, a few old books and papers that somebody left a long time ago. Guess I never thought much about it, except when I was little I used to play down there," she cut her eyes at him and grinned, "that is, when my mama wasn't looking."

"What sort of books and papers?" he asked, ignoring the obvious flirt.

"Couldn't tell ya," she mused, trying to remember. "Just papers – couple of old letters, and stuff. They were in some sort of foreign language." She stood up from the trap door and wiped her hands together. "It wasn't Spanish – I know that much. Anyway, most of them are gone now."

"Gone?"

"Yeah, like I said, I looked earlier – trunk's dumped over down there – old clothes strewn all over. But most the papers are gone."

Trent straightened up slowly, stifled a groan, and played the flashlight beam around the room, studying things.

"Whoever did this was looking for something in particular," he commented, absently.

"Ya think?" Maggie answered sarcastically, but with a sly grin.

She walked over to where an old double bed and its sturdy iron frame had been turned over and tumbled against the south wall, its comforter thrown aside and the feather mattress ripped to shreds. Feathers were scattered about, a few now floating, disturbed by their footsteps. Maggie reached down and picked up a corner of the bedding, frowned, and shook her head.

"Bastards!" she seethed through clenched teeth. "Why do vandals always have to tear shit up?"

Trent shrugged. "Well, you just said it – maybe because they're vandals. Trying to live up to their name, I suppose."

A small wooden table lay turned on its side near the cook stove. Two wooden chairs – one of them smashed to bits – had also been tossed aside, their matching stitched seat cushions ripped apart. The stovepipe had been knocked away from the cook stove and left dangling from its mount on the ceiling. The burner covers had been thrown aside and the kindling door on the front flung open. Ashes were spilled all about, pulled out of the stove where someone had dug and sifted through them.

The remaining corner of the room had been arranged as a small sitting/reading area with a small rocker next to an end table where a broken lamp now lay shattered. A small wooden bookshelf had been shoved over against the table and its books now scattered indiscriminately around the room where they had been tossed, many with their pages torn out. Trent picked one up and thumbed its yellowing pages. He turned it over to find its faded title, *All Quiet on the Western Front,* by Erich Maria Remarque. It had been a favorite from his boyhood, and he smiled at the memory, but shook his head at the wanton desecration of the book.

"Anything else missing?" he asked.

"I don't think so – at least from what all I remember was here. But this right here is a little weird."

She stood looking down into the metal sink where the charred remains of what appeared to be random papers had been burned. Trent came over and pointed his flashlight into the sink.

"Looks like you just found those missing documents."

"Maybe," Maggie reflected. "Almost like they deliberately burned them, though – not just out of meanness. Wonder why that was?"

Trent reached in his pocket and produced a pair of latex gloves and a small plastic evidence bag. He put on the gloves, then gently scooped up the remnants of charred paper, sealed the bag, and replaced it in his pocket.

Maggie suddenly gasped and Trent looked up at her.

"I just thought of something else," she said, her eyes widening.

"What?" he asked.

"Not here – up at the house." She whirled and stomped to the door. "Let's go!"

#

"They're coming out again," observed Jimmy, careful not to speak too loudly. Voices carried across open ground in these high country valleys, especially on a still afternoon like this. He could already hear Trent's and Margot's muted murmurings as they came out of the cabin below, though he couldn't tell exactly what they were saying as he continued to watch them through the rifle sight.

Carl Neumann pulled his binoculars back up, refocused, and had a look. Neither Trent nor Margot appeared to have brought anything out of the hut.

"You see anything?" he asked. "They bring anything out with them?"

"Nope. Nothing I can see." Jimmy's finger began to itch, and his upper lip trembled into another sneer.

"I could sure take them both out right now, Carl. Hell, if I time it right, could even line them up and get them both with one shot!" The sneer turned into a wide smile as he continued to peer through the sight.

"Well, as much as I sure would like to see that," Neumann answered, then suddenly, thinking of something else, looked over at the gunman. "Jimmy – I'm sorry, but I'm still fretting just a bit. Please tell me once again exactly what it was that you found down there. I," he hesitated, "I just need a little reassurance, that's all." He paused again but then added, "And the old man's certainly going to want some reassurance, too – if you know what I mean."

Jimmy pulled his cheek away from the gunstock again, leaned over, and spit. "Like I told you," he answered, not bothering to hide the impatience in his voice, "couple of old letters, some old train tickets," he paused, thinking for a moment, "and some old maps – hand-drawn stuff – some of those little notebooks, the kind you slip in your pocket – bunch of lists, and stuff."

"And, you're very sure you burned it all – completely?"

"Yeah, I burnt it – like I said – in the sink."

"Nothing left, right? Nothing anyone could identify?

"I said it's burnt—it's burnt!" Jimmy didn't like to be grilled about his actions. He took great pride in his work. Still, he hesitated for a moment, thinking hard. "Nope," he continued, "I'm sure of it. Nothing left but ashes." He put his eye firmly back to the scope.

Carl looked back through his field glasses. He slowly raised an eyebrow and turned back to the gunman.

"Jimmy, you didn't happen to – read any of those notes or documents, did you?"

"Oh, hell no!" Jimmy exclaimed. "I did just like you said. I grabbed any old piece of paper that had any writing on it at all and burned it right away." He shuddered. "I sure don't need to get crossways with no one – particularly your dad!"

Carl nodded slowly in agreement. The old man had been quite specific regarding anything they might have found. Evidently some secrets were never intended to be divulged – ever – and Carl, too, understood fully that the old man was never to be questioned – or crossed.

They both turned back and watched now as Trent moved around the side of the building, carefully looking at the ground. Jimmy squinted through the riflescope once more, licking his lips.

"Yes sir, I could sure nail them both right now," he repeated. "It would be mighty clean and easy."

Carl gazed down at the scene through his binoculars, his eyes bright, and the tip of his tongue wetting his lower lip.

"I really would like that, Jimmy—that would really be something, too!" He lowered the binoculars and looked back over his shoulder, almost wistfully, at the pickup parked below them in the steadily darkening ravine and sighed. He had left his video camera back there. He glanced back up to the horizon where the sun was about to slip away. He knew by the time he got to the truck, retrieved the camera, got it back and set up by the time Jimmy could take the shot, that the resolution on the video at this distance and in the low light conditions would be terrible. He knew better than to take back a poorly made video, especially of such a momentous event. The old man would never forgive him.

In any case, Margot and Trent were now moving back toward their utility wagon: it was now or never. Carl made a decision.

"No, Jimmy, as much as I would surely like to see that, I think we need to wait." Carl let out a sigh of genuine disappointment. "Let's get on out of here," he continued. "Doesn't look like they found anything in there, anyway," he said. "We can't kill them yet, anyhow – not til we find out just what else they may know."

They watched as Margot and Trent drove away back toward the main house before both men stood up and brushed at the damp dirt on their pants. Jimmy folded the short bipod stand of his rifle before slinging it over his shoulder. The two men turned and picked their way back to their truck. Carl Neumann clapped the gunman on the shoulder.

"Soon, Jimmy – real soon."

#

Maggie slid to a stop in front of her ranch house with a final bounce of the 4x4, almost throwing Trent out. He cursed under his breath while she jumped down and chuckled. He eased himself out and stood unsteadily for a moment, then moved slowly to his truck. She headed up the sidewalk toward the house, stopped, and turned to him.

"You can't leave yet," she admonished. "You're going to want to come on in and see this," she said. She took the porch steps two at a time and went into the house, but not before turning once again at the screen door and giving him a wink. "Well, come on – I'm not gonna bite you!"

Trent watched her open the door and paused for a second or two, feeling his face flush. What the hell was he getting into with this woman?

He moved slowly up the sidewalk, leaving the gate wide open, as if leaving a quick escape route. His hip and knee were screaming and his head throbbed. He was finding it a real chore to keep his thoughts from rambling away inside his head. He wanted a drink more than anything right now. *No, that would only numb his mind some more,* he thought, and he knew he needed to think clearly right now, commit everything he had seen to memory. Not that he even planned to be involved in any ongoing investigations; in fact, he intended to report all of this back to the sheriff's office and wash his hands of it as soon as possible.

Yet something nagged him; something important he couldn't quite put his finger on yet.

What was it – something back there at the shack?

As they had walked out, his old police training had automatically kicked in and he had methodically checked the shattered doorframe, trying to determine the usual clues and perhaps come up with some corresponding answers: like, what sort of tool exactly had been used to gain entry, or were there any identifiable footprints or vehicle tracks around the premises that could be cast in plaster and examined more closely? Those details alone might not tell him much, but tools and tires could often be identified and traced to where they had been purchased, which, in turn, could turn into viable leads.

Just as he was thinking on these questions, he remembered that Margot's horses had been grazing around this meadow and had churned up the dirt and mud, effectively obliterating any tracks. He had found faint outlines where a vehicle had recently mashed the grass down with its tires, but, unfortunately, nothing that left an identifiable tread print. The driver had been cautious and had kept the wheels on the grass and rocky surfaces, and had managed to stay out of the mud and dirt.

Trent came back to his senses and found himself standing stock still on Maggie's porch steps, trying hard to file the various tidbits away into his mind. The evidence would need to be analyzed later; his mind had sure been playing a lot of tricks on itself lately, and he was finding it exhausting.

He took a deep breath and made his way methodically up the steps to the porch where Maggie still waited and held the screen door open for him.

He stopped in the doorway and turned to her, remembering suddenly what it was he had forgotten. He couldn't believe he had missed something so basically important.

"Maggie, I'm going to have someone from the department come back out tomorrow and process the place for additional clues, primarily fingerprints." *Not that they're going to find anything,* he thought. "So, if you wouldn't mind, don't go back over to the crime scene until they tell you it's okay."

Maggie smirked and gave him a quick salute and a smart, "Yes, Sir!"

He raised his eyebrows at her, shook his head slightly, turned, and went into the house. He removed his hat but received another sharp glance from Maggie as she breezed on past him.

"Boots," she ordered. Trent sighed, returned to the doormat, and dutifully wiped his feet before following back inside.

He took a quick look around. It had been a long, long time since he had been in the Van Ryan residence; the last time had been when Maggie's father Richard was still alive and Trent had been hired to come out and do some day work at branding time. He had been about 24 years old, home on leave, and had needed to make a little pocket money. He remembered Maggie back then as a cute, but irritating, little tomboy sitting on the corrals or jumping down to help hold a calf or telling him how he was doing it all wrong. In fact, in his recollections, she had been a little snot-nosed nuisance, flirting with him even back then. As he came on into the house, he reflected with an expression between a smile and a grimace how she really hadn't changed much in that regard.

"Boots!" Maggie barked again, once more pointing at his feet, her other hand perched imperiously on her hip, as Trent stepped obediently away from an ornamental throw rug of some sort. "I'll have you know that's an original, hundred-year-old antique Navajo rug you're tromping all over there." She turned abruptly and left him gawking after her.

"Geez," he muttered, and then looked around.

The entryway of the rambling old home was furnished with a wide hall tree on which were hung a few jackets, caps, and hats, and was fitted with a bench for just such a purpose. Trent sat and removed his dirty boots and glanced around. The long, rectangular and expensive looking throw rug was indeed woven in some sort of intricate Native American design and covered most of the hardwood floor and led on through the wide, open pocket doors into the large, brightly lit living room of the house.

The entire room was a hexagon, with not a square corner in it, which probably made it a little difficult to decorate—hence, the sparse, but large, furnishings. Three huge couches arranged in a U shape surrounded one end of a massive varnished coffee table, hewn and carved out of a large tree stump. The arrangement generally faced a huge fireplace on the wall constructed of large river rock. Its chimney disappeared up into the high ceiling, itself crossed with Vega style beams in the New Mexican tradition. A large elk head balanced its imposing rack of antlers above the mantle and was turned and looking downward and to the left, as if taken off guard when he had been shot and was now frozen in time. From this position the elk stared curiously straight at Trent as he entered the room. Three large double hung windows peered out to the west at what remained of the brilliant sunset that flickered back in through full-length Belgian lace curtains. The overall design and decoration of the room were that of a hunting lodge, a place for rugged men to kick their boots off, prop their feet up, and sip expensive Scotch whiskey as they embellished their tales of the day's outing.

Maggie had immediately disappeared up a staircase on the east side of the room, its beautifully carved banister winding upwards as it rounded a couple of landings. He could hear the distant banging of closet doors, desk drawers, and her footsteps bustling around up there.

"Take a load off for a couple of minutes," she yelled, her voice echoing through the upstairs hallways and back down the stairs.

Trent chose one of the massive leather chairs with the best view of the fiery sky gradually extinguishing itself in the west, and collapsed into it with a groan. The day had been long and the night promised to be even longer. He suddenly felt weary, maybe a little feverish, and just wanted to leave. Sophie would be home by now, would have some dinner ready for him soon, and had probably started to worry about him. He reached into his pocket, found his cell phone, and flipped it open. Yep. Sure enough, he had missed two messages from her in the past half hour. He began to redial when he suddenly jumped at the sound of Maggie's voice coming from the stairs behind him.

"Check it out!" She had blurted.

He stood as she bounced on down the stairs, carrying something in her hand. But what really caught his eye was that she no longer looked like the middle-aged ranch hand that had been throwing hay to the horses all afternoon. Gone were the work boots; in their place were casual pumps. Gone, too, was the fedora, as well as the French braid. Instead, her long, freshly brushed sandy hair was pulled back, clipped behind her ears, and tumbled freely across the shoulders of a cream colored dress that was printed with light yellow flowers, its half sleeves ending right above her dimpled elbows. The dress was belted with a thin leather belt at her slim waist and was buttoned almost to her throat, with the notable exception of the top two buttons that seemed to be strategically unfastened – not too much, but just enough.

In other words, Maggie knew when to dress for hard work, knew exactly how to dress to impress, and certainly seemed fully aware of the effect she was now having on Trent.

"Put your tongue back in your mouth, Cowboy," she smiled, striking a little pose on the bottom step, one hand on a slightly swelled hip. Trent quickly broke his stare, made a move to remove his hat from where it lay on the coffee table, then straightened up and stopped, as Maggie had now made her way into the room and was leaning with one hand propped on the back of the couch, effectively blocking his way to the door. He could now also see what she held: an old book of some sort, which she now wagged at him and smiled conspiratorially.

"I just got to thinking this might have been what those yahoos were after," she suggested as she held it out to him. "Go on: take a look at it."

Trent looked at the worn leather-bound book and back at Maggie. As he reached for it, she pulled it back a few inches, playfully forcing him to move closer to her. He grasped the book gingerly. She held onto it for a second longer than necessary before releasing it. He moved back a step, frowned at her, and turned to examine the book.

The leather cover was scuffed and worn, the pages thumbed and well used, and the spine creased and cracked along its edge. He opened it carefully. The inside front cover contained many hurried scribbles, mostly numbers, and scrawls like someone had used it to jot down information when they had nothing else to write on at the moment – random items, not in any particular order or format. He carefully turned the cover page. On the next page were some numbers separated by dashes, written in faded blue ink, probably from an old fountain pen, and judging from the broad, firm strokes, the penmanship was stylish, yet masculine. The numbers read simply *21-10-42*. Trent shrugged. They communicated nothing to him immediately. His gaze wandered to mid-page where the following inscription had been written – same faded blue ink, same handsome, broad pen strokes, centered on an otherwise blank page:

Zeitschrift von
Otto Franz Eberhardt
Stuttgart, Deutschland
(Persönlich und Vertaulich)

He furrowed his brow, more confused than ever, and just thumbed through several pages. The book seemed to be a journal of some kind – and was written entirely in German.

#

Trent had driven his pickup out of the gates of *Montaña del Sol* after dark, then back west through Yankee Canyon toward Raton. Lightning snaked along the horizon in front of him, illuminating a fast running, angry sky. He was exhausted, his head still throbbed, his sore joints screamed, and he was just glad to be heading home.

The wipers beat a slow rhythm against the drizzle of rain, which spattered again from the darkened sky. Their pattern began a slow waltz in his head, and eventually segued again into the tune his wife had been humming right before the accident on Cordova Pass.

"I am Far and Away from the one that I love..."

The song was one he had written specifically for her – indeed, the last one he had ever played for her on his guitar – and it had been one of her favorites, or so she had said.

"Far and Away from my home…"

The song continued to play subconsciously as he began to try and make sense of the events of the day. He had left Maggie Van Ryan standing on the porch with a perturbed pout, a stray strand of hair falling down over her eye, wiping her hands on a dishtowel as she watched him drive away. She had been puttering around in her kitchen, insisting that he should stay and let her cook him dinner, but he had begged off, using his daughter's impatience back home as an excuse. Maggie had been clearly disappointed, but finally relented and had walked him to the door. She had warned him she was going to be calling him in a day or two to see if he had any leads, and he had reminded her he was no longer in active law enforcement, was planning to turn it all over to the sheriff's office, and that maybe she should deal directly with them from now on.

As he drove, he glanced over at the book that he had tossed into the passenger seat. Before he had left, Maggie and he had spent a little time thumbing through the journal and picking out certain familiar words and phrases. The cryptic numbers continued to appear sporadically on certain pages and mystified them until Maggie pointed out that if this were a journal, they would probably be dates. Trent did recall, finally, that European serial dates were written numerically backwards from how Americans wrote them. Instead of a date in October 1942 being written *10-21-42*, a European would have written *21-10-42*.

Trent had just stared blankly at the verbiage scribbled out in the book. Truth was, there had been a time when he had been able to speak and read passable German—at least well enough to get the gist of anything he was reading. In fact, being fluent in German had been a requirement of his job as a military policeman while stationed in Germany and the U.S. Army had sent him to language school before he was posted there in the late 70s. Knowing the language had definitely come in handy at times to be able to adequately communicate with the local tavern owners and bouncers in the various beer halls and strip clubs he had regularly broken up fights in, usually between the local patrons and the uniformed ones.

Concentrate as he might, though, the words and sentences now merely spilled across the page of the journal like so much gibberish. The doctors had warned him after his head injury in the car accident that certain aspects of his life were going to seem different, that some normal activities he had once been able to do – even think or say – were going to become harder or maybe even impossible for him to do. Some differences, they had said, he would notice immediately – like this ongoing dizziness when he stood up too quickly. Other differences would only become obvious over time—gaps in certain memories or forgetting simple words. Now, those differences also seemed to include recalling languages he had once been somewhat fluent in.

Some of these abilities, they had told him, might gradually return to him, but for now, the words that appeared before him in this strange journal were just pretty much words, not anything meaningful.

Curious as to how far the journal went, they had thumbed on through to the last entry, a few pages from the end, dated October 23, 1972, as written in the journal *23-10-72*. This entry had been hastily scribbled, as if the author had been in a hurry to get it done, punctuated with numerous exclamation points and heavy underscores indicating that he had given it some importance, perhaps under some sort of desperation or duress. But as to what, exactly, only the author knew, for neither Trent nor Maggie had been able to decipher the entry or its importance.

Lightning struck closer now, up ahead on the left and outlined the dark, looming bulk of Johnson Mesa. The lyrics of Vicky's song floated on its mournful melody as it clawed its way deep into his heart.

How he wished it would stop.

Trent glanced again at the journal. Maggie had told him she had found it years ago when she had been a teenager, cleaning the old adobe house one spring with her mother. The book had been hidden in the small corner bookshelf behind all the other books and it had fallen out when she had removed them to give everything a good dusting. She had stood there, thumbing through the old journal, when her mother had walked back in after dumping a pail of mop water outside. Maggie had felt a sense of guilt for some reason and had tucked the journal under her jacket that she had draped on the chair. She had later smuggled it back home, hidden it in her bedroom, and over the next few evenings had tried to make heads or tails out of all the funny writing under the covers with a flashlight when she should have been sleeping. However, her mother had caught her reading one night, had taken it, and shown it to Maggie's father who had taken one look at the cover page, turned beet red, and demanded to know if she had read any of it. She told Trent she had never seen her father react so angrily, so quickly, and her wide eyes had filled with surprise and tears at his ire as she had shaken her head at him and told him *no,* that it was in a strange language she hadn't understood. The last time she had seen the journal, for a long time, was when her father had stormed out of her room with it.

She had assumed he had destroyed it, but many years later, when she had been going through his belongings following his funeral, she had found the journal in the bottom of his sock drawer, wrapped in an old t-shirt. She had taken it and put it on a bookshelf in her room, thinking she would have it translated one day, just out of curiosity. But she had never gotten around to it and had pretty much forgotten about it—until today – when they had found the burnt traces of the other documents in the sink.

She had reluctantly allowed Trent to take the journal with him when he left. He couldn't entirely explain to himself why he should be interested in it. Now, though, as he continued to drive in the gathering darkness, which was stabbed occasionally by lightning, he had too many questions bubbling up to the surface of his mind: like why had Maggie's father Richard been so upset at the journal? What information was in it that would be of concern to anyone today? Was it really evidence that related to the break-in? And just who wrote the damn thing, anyway?

And why should I really care?

All of these questions were getting so jumbled up in Trent's mind again, he couldn't think straight. He feared for his mental and emotional health more and more these days and his ongoing inability to concentrate too well on certain activities. All of the questions and their mystery only increased his desire to get back to the relative safety, seclusion, and quiet of his home; the solace of his daughter and his cat; the comfort of a large glass of bourbon whiskey. He drove a little faster.

In fact, to tell the truth, lately, he had often thought of just going off somewhere—escaping to wherever – run away to maybe find an answer in the unknown, a cure for his melancholy; drop everything he was doing, without even a moment's notice, jump into his truck – or better yet onto the back of his motorcycle, with nothing but the leather jacket on his back and his wallet full of credit cards, and just head for the horizon, destinations unknown; just anywhere different than the streets of his hometown. Even these familiar and beautiful, rocky vistas around him no longer offered solace or a promise of adventure, or even romance, regardless of Margot Van Ryan's undisguised advances.

What then was wrong with all of that – desiring a little adventure that might finally swab at this heart full of hurt, perhaps dab away the dull ache until it was eventually washed clean? And why did such notions always carry such a vague sense of guilt, like they were a betrayal to Vicky? Such thoughts were always followed by what seemed like her still, small voice that whispered, *this is no responsible way to feel – there's no escape for you – go on – carry that cross until your back bleeds.*

He felt a great, eternal fatigue, a weariness not only of his losses, and of all these disjointed thoughts, but also of the idea of having let others down so many times and of having lost precious things in the process.

No, he would stay around. Deep down inside, he knew that any attempt to escape was merely that: an escape for escape's sake, pure and simple. Because no matter how far he ran, and no matter how many exotic and new horizons came into view, there would be no reprieve. He feared that his spirit would always be left with all these unhealed internal wounds and that his very soul would continue to burn and gasp for the oxygen of forgetfulness.

"…far and away from my home,"

The verse continued to play out in his head, *'Where my heart yearns to go is to the one I love so…"*

"…and fore'er and a day I will roam," suddenly sang out a clear, unmistakably familiar voice that came now, inexplicably, from his back seat, directly behind him.

Trent slammed the brakes hard; the truck began to slide, veering finally to a stop half off the slick pavement onto the shoulder as he grabbed the rear view mirror with one hand and peered into it hard. For a moment, he could swear he saw a dark profile of a woman gazing peacefully out the side window and twirling a strand of long hair in her fingers, her voice still lilting and humming sweetly. Lightning flashed, and he suddenly saw her profile perfectly: the beautiful long line of her nose, the full pout of her lips. She languidly turned and met his eyes in the mirror with a sideways glance. Her eyes glowed like embers, and her scent was suddenly overwhelming – and unmistakable.

It was Vicky.

"I truly love that song, Trenny," she said, her voice slow and smoky.

Another flash careened across the sky, followed almost immediately by a crash of thunder. In the mirror, Vicky's face was lit up brilliantly and clearly, but only for a moment. "You shouldn't have been so rude to Maggie, you know – she has a lot of important answers for you."

Trent stopped breathing.

"Besides," the apparition continued, "she likes you a lot, you know!"

He whipped his head around and looked directly into the back seat.

No one was there.

At all.

Trent reached over and flipped the interior lights on, then raised abruptly half out of his seat, scanning the back floorboard, swiping the back seat with an outstretched hand.

The seat was warm.

His pulse throbbed in his head as he sat there for another full minute, then slowly turned back around and stared blankly out the windshield. His hands grasped the steering wheel tightly. His breath came in ragged bursts. Every bone in his body ached; his head was about to explode. Rain drummed steadily now on the roof, punctuated by distant rumbles of thunder that blended with the sound of blood pumping hard in his ears. He hyperventilated, and suddenly slapped his forehead several times with the heel of his hand in frustration before closing his eyes, and leaning his head on the wheel, he trembled and moaned.

The sudden blast of a car horn speeding past just inches away jolted him back to reality. He had lost track of time and wasn't quite sure how long he had been sitting there.

He felt exhausted and numb. He rubbed his face with his hands and turned his head to look cautiously into the backseat once more.

Nobody there, of course.

He checked for oncoming traffic and slowly pulled the truck back onto the highway. He picked up speed, nudged the gas pedal, and forced the road by sheer willpower to slip more quickly beneath his tires. The visibility ahead grew worse as the rain splattered in sheets across the windshield. One part of his mind kept telling him to slow down; another part told him to speed up – that maybe the thing to do would be to simply end it all with another well-timed accident.

He shook his head and tried to force his mind back onto the business at hand. He slammed the steering wheel again with the palm of his hand. He wished now he hadn't left his house, hadn't answered Molly's call, hadn't

stumbled, startled, and fell to the ground. He touched himself all over to see where the bullet had hit him, but then realized he hadn't been shot at all. His mouth opened and closed, gasping for air. He then sat very still, embarrassed when he realized he had just urinated on himself.

Otto rushed to his side and stooped to help him.

"That's right, *Herr Leutnant* – see if the old fool is alright," Ernst chuckled. Otto frowned at Ernst as he helped Dave to his feet.

"*Was tun Sie, Kapitän*?" Otto demanded in alarm through clenched teeth.

Ernst crooked the rifle in one arm, pulled a cigarette out of his shirt pocket and lit it, and inhaled deeply. "Dear, dear Otto – what shall we do with you?" he asked with the air of a man who already knew the answer. He exhaled the smoke slowly. "I am afraid all these months in America have already softened you." Ernst then stepped over and grabbed Dave by the arm and wrenched him out of Otto's grasp. "You seem to have forgotten, my friend, that we are still at war with these people," he growled as he walked, "it is our duty to the *Vaterland* to continue the fight – and there will continue to be many casualties before we are finished!"

Dave tripped and stumbled as Ernst pulled him roughly with an iron grip on his upper arm, pain seared deep into his muscles. Ernst pulled him further until he had dragged Dave roughly several yards into the field and dropped him hard on the ground. He then turned abruptly, marched back to the main road past the front the truck, and scrambled up and over the railroad embankment until he was just over the top, where he had a vantage point over the surrounding area. He silently and slowly turned around to look out over the frigid fields that lay beyond Dave. From below, Dave watched him fearfully, not believing what was happening. He knew that Ernst was confirming there were no other farms or houses anywhere near here, the closest one being a couple of miles away. Besides, gunshots around here were commonplace. He himself had gone off many a time, hunting a coyote or fox, or maybe rabbits for his stew pot. Kids growing up in this area would often ride their bicycles up and down this road, set up cans and bottles, and pop them with their .22 rifles. Even if gunshots were heard near his place today, Dave had known with a sinking heart that no one would give them a second thought.

He rubbed a sore ankle where he had twisted it, and looked at his captors, from one to the other. He watched as Ernst knelt down on one knee and raised Dave's Winchester up to his shoulder. Ernst turned slowly, squinting through the scope, and surveyed the 180 degrees of fields and landscape around them. Dave then turned to look at Otto, who hadn't moved and stood looking down at the ground until eventually, slowly, he looked up to sadly meet Dave's gaze. Dave felt an odd satisfaction that Otto had turned pale and he looked as if he would be sick – satisfaction that at least one more human being would feel some compassion for him before the end.

Dave slowly regained control of himself, gave Otto a rueful smile and a nod, and worked his way painfully to a standing position.

War, Ernst had said. *So be it,* thought Dave. He brushed himself off, determined to dredge up what little dignity he had left. He glared up at Ernst in utter hatred.

"You damned stinkin' *Kraut,*" Dave said to him evenly, then spit on the ground. Ernst merely looked at him with that infuriating, sickening smile, and chuckled. Dave shook his head, turned slowly, and began to shuffle away, one arm holding the other at the elbow. He looked around to orient himself. *The Johnson place is just across the creek, just over that rise,* he reminded himself. Barlow's farm is just over yonder. It was somehow important to him to identify as nearly as possible where on this earth he was about to meet his end.

He felt his back tighten up between the shoulder blades where he expected to feel a horrible impact.

Nothing.

He lifted his feet and picked up the pace. He dared not think that there might actually be the tiniest hope he would get away from them, and he dared not look back to check. Instead, he trotted, stumbled every few steps, but still made headway.

Maybe they're really going to let me go! He began to feel somewhat euphoric, and the pain where Ernst had squeezed his arm subsided as the adrenaline kicked in and gave him energy. He felt a surge of hope for the first time in weeks.

He ran maybe fifty yards when the first bullet hit him high in the left shoulder, tearing through muscle and shattering bone, and spinning him around. He lost his footing and began to fall, although at first he really hadn't comprehended what had just happened. The impact felt as if someone had hit him as hard as they could with a baseball or a rock or the baseball bat itself. But he strangely felt no pain at all, only a numbness, which permeated his entire arm and spread across his back. He gazed curiously as the high grass and the bare trees and the cobalt blue sky spun around in his field of vision in slow motion, around and around, but suddenly stopped spinning when he felt himself hit and bounce, and slid on his knees on the hardened road.

He sat there, dumbly, for what seemed like hours, his head bowed low over his lap, and wondered where he was and how he got there. *Oh yeah,* he remembered, *the war – something about the war.* He raised his head slowly as dullness began to throb somewhere – *shoulder,* he thought. He tried to twist his head to look at the wound, but couldn't. He suddenly knew with urgency there was something he desperately needed to do – something he needed to prove not only to himself but to his executioners – something that proved to them all that he was still free.

He placed his right hand on the ground to steady himself, found his feet, and then stood up shakily. He wobbled for a few seconds, feeling like he might fall again, be he refused to let his body dictate his actions. One foot finally lurched out, then the other. He began moving again; he was now unclear where he had been heading. He felt at peace, somehow, as though he were finally accomplishing whatever it was he was meant to do, and as if God in His heaven were also pleased.

What more could I ask for? he thought he heard himself mutter.

He then looked up at the blue sky and saw high scudding clouds floating along with him, like angels, he thought. He smiled at one of them and suddenly recognized the lovely face of his wife, smiling down at him. She was young once more and achingly beautiful. He felt his cheeks grow wet and lifted his hand to brush the tears – tears of joy – but joy that vanished into despair as he watched the shape of the cloud change slightly and his wife's smile turned to sadness.

He stretched his hand to the sky as she turned her angelic face away.

"No!" he cried out – or had he only thought it? He reached for her again, waving his good arm wildly. The cloud was morphing and his wife's face disappeared into a dark thunderhead. *"Don't leave me again!"*

That clear thought had been the last Dave Perkins ever comprehended.

Something massive exploded silently inside his head and a brilliant white light washed over him from the inside out. He was vaguely aware of seeing something – someone – but couldn't formulate enough of a thought pattern to decipher what – who – it was. Whoever they were gradually grew dim. Dave's eyes locked onto this other set of eyes – such wide and sad and somehow familiar eyes – and he thought he heard someone shouting something at him – a name, perhaps? Maybe his own name? *What is my name?*

Then, even those simple questions eluded him as he gratefully felt himself slipping away.

Into the darkness.

Into forever.

#

Otto continued to stand in the kitchen, and still felt Dave Perkins' vacant eyes fixed on his, just as they had been when he had run up the path, dropped to his knees, and held the dying man's bleeding head in his hands. He saw those eyes every night now, in his sleepless hours.

Otto knew that he would see them for the rest of his life.

He felt something odd in his hand and looked down at the old man's chess piece he was still fingering. He stared at it for a full minute, then slipped the white king into his pants pocket.

He jumped suddenly at a rifle shot, which rang out in the near distance, and another, and a third one in rapid succession. *What the hell, now?* His heart thumped as he spun around and raced to the screen door, flung it open, ran out onto the porch and froze. What he saw horrified him, as if he could feel more horror and disgust.

Twenty yards away, Ernst sat on the top of the three-rail fence that formed the pigpen, his feet hooked under the second rung of the fence. He was alternately cocking the lever of the Winchester rifle, bringing it up to his cheek, aiming carefully, pulling the trigger, and then repeating the actions – laughing.

Screaming in terror, the pigs raced around the pen, stampeding over one other, their eyes wide in sheer terror; one by one in loud, unearthly screeches they died as they tumbled like bloody rag dolls, legs scrambling, flying and splaying as the bullets tore wetly through their bodies. Ernst giggled maniacally as he fired and then cocked, fired and cocked, fired and cocked, again and again.

Then silence.

Otto's mouth hung open; he gasped for air as he backed slowly into the room, the screams still echoing in his head. His backside bumped hard into the table; his hands flailed behind him to find a purchase and keep himself from falling. He steadied himself, tried to catch his breath and slow down the swirl of thoughts in his brain. He brought his hands up to rub his face, but stopped suddenly when he saw they were dripping with Dave's blood. He squeezed his eyes shut and shook his head. *That is impossible,* he screamed in his head. He opened his eyes to see that his hands were, indeed, quite clean. He felt he would pass out and then slumped to a sitting position on the floor. He needed to concentrate – grab onto one of his spinning thoughts – any of them – any would do. He needed to center himself, quickly, before he went mad. He finally found the one he reluctantly knew he needed desperately to deal with, latched onto it with the tendrils of his pounding mind, and let it soak deeply into his consciousness.

Ernst Brandt was, indeed, a monster.

CHAPTER 7
CONDEMNATIONS

Vicky always looks serene, humming softly to herself like a little girl, "…far and away from my home," the song he had written for her. Although she never could sing very well at all, her unrefined vocal efforts are still precious to him – and he smiles. Spangled light dances colorfully over them both, while she pulls her sunglasses halfway down her nose to take in all the magic washing around and over them. He glances over at her as he drives and feels all the cares of the day drift away as they both totally immerse themselves into the palette of hot oranges, brilliant yellows, and soft greens that splash across the canvas of the mountains and valleys around them. Autumn has begun her magic, and the changing of the colors has worked its wizardry and drawn them out for an afternoon drive.

Vicky cocks her head and props it in the palm of her hand as she catches him sneaking looks at her. A smile coaxes one corner of her mouth, and she teases him by pushing her sunglasses back up to hide her pretty green eyes from him.

"You'd better just watch the road, mister."

"I could drive this thing blindfolded."

"Then you'll do it without me. Let me out!" She grabs the handle and pushes the door open a few inches as if she will jump out. The Jeep works its way up a pretty good grade, inching along slowly. At this speed, she could step out and be okay. Trent chuckles and pops the gas pedal just enough to make the Jeep lurch, which forces them both back into their seats and causes her door to slam shut. Squealing, she reaches over and playfully digs her fingers into his ribs, which she knows he hates. He negotiates the next sharp curve as the road flattens out, allowing him to gain a little more speed.

Trent suddenly feels the Jeep lurch violently. His first thought is that it must have hit a deep pothole in the road. The steering wheel wrenches hard in his hands, spinning as if it has come alive. He fights as the vehicle careens off the roadside, down a steep embankment where it flies off of a rise and becomes airborne, twisting slowly in the air. Trent and Vicky seem to float out of their seats in slow motion, only to slam back down again hard, pulled back by their seatbelts that cut into their bodies. The world twists and blurs, the engine roars unrestrained, and Trent suddenly smells gasoline. He feels completely helpless and begins to panic while at the same time he is also filled with a surrealistic wonder at what will happen next; wondering when they are going to hit, wondering how hard they will hit, wondering when the pain will materialize, wondering what part of their bodies are about to be damaged – and just how bad it will be – and mostly, wondering if this is it – if this is where they are about to die.

Abruptly, he wonders where those screams are coming from – distant at first, but growing in intensity – until he realizes the sounds are coming from Vicky, wailing like a wounded animal, clawing at his arms and at his head, grabbing for anything. He turns and sees her eyes searching his, desperately pleading with him to stop whatever it is that's happening to them. He stretches his hand toward her helplessly, unable to reach her, her face just there at the end of his fingertips, almost touching: she may as well be twenty feet away.

Finally, almost mercifully, all he knows is a blinding flash of light accompanied by a deafening absence of any noise whatsoever – except for her dying screams.

#

Trent jerked wide-awake, breathing raggedly, with sweat pouring from every pore. Vicky's screams still echoed in his ears. The bed sheets were knotted in his fists and drenched with his perspiration. His eyes were wide in terror but stared at nothing, at first, but slowly, slowly focused on the dim room around him. Until he realized where he was, his gaze wandered as he got control of his terror and willed his thumping heart back to normal. He looked over at the clock on his bedside table – 4:30 A.M. He sat up on the edge of his bed, closed his eyes, and ran a hand over his sweaty face.

"It wasn't really your fault you know, Darling." The silky smooth voice coming from behind him was strangely reassuring. He then felt cool fingertips trace the hot skin on his shoulder.

He twisted his head around and could just make out in the dim light the figure of a woman lying under the bed sheet. She lay on her side, her head propped on her hand and her elbow on the pillow. Her light brown hair was tousled and loosely spilled over her cheek as if she had just now awakened and had run her fingers through it to get it out of her eyes.

"Good mornin', Baby Boy," a familiar voice murmured close to his ear.

It was Vicky.

Here.

In his bed.

Right now.

He momentarily closed his eyes, soaking in her voice and touch.

She smiled and reached for him again.

This time, though, in shock but with his eyes wide open, Trent lurched away from her, cursed, and jumped out of bed. He slammed his toe against the table, lost his balance, and fell back against the nearby chest of drawers. He twisted back toward the bed and stared, then rubbed his eyes.

Vicky was nowhere there. Nowhere. Anywhere.

Instead, Jarhead raised himself up from the pillow, stretched his hind legs, yawned at Trent, and started his loud morning serenade, purring while kneading the pillow contentedly with his front paws.

Trent slowly slid to the floor and put his head in his hands. The dream had always started and ended the same way, always beginning with one of the most memorable times he had ever spent with his precious wife – the picnic drive two years ago to look at autumn colors in the Sangre de Cristo Mountains, but it always morphed into the most horrible experience he had ever had – the car crash that had ripped her from his life.

The nightmare had been recurring, over and over, ever since he had gotten home from the hospital. Small details changed subtly within the dream from time-to-time and were all fairly irrelevant but always disconcerting. But some overlapping meanings still eluded him – something that always seemed vitally important, which hovered just beyond the continual mists in his mind.

Now, something entirely new was manifesting itself.

Vicky was not only appearing in his dreams, but was also now visiting his waking hours.

#

Trent didn't know how long he had sat on the floor of his bedroom, staring into space, but at some point, Jarhead started rubbing his head and body insistently against his knee, then jumped into his lap, purring extra loudly. The cat wanted to be fed and meant to communicate its demands clearly. After all, feeding Jarhead was what he did every morning at this time. And right now, doing so was actually a welcome routine that Trent needed, something concrete to pull him back to a semblance of reality.

A half hour later, Sophie stumbled into the kitchen where Trent sat drinking coffee at the kitchen table, watching Jarhead clean himself beside his recently emptied breakfast dish. Trent was barefoot, dressed in jeans and a white t-shirt, eyes puffy. He looked up and watched his daughter make her way to the coffee maker and pour herself a cup. She wore one of his old New Mexico State Police t-shirts as a nightgown as she had loved wearing his shirts to sleep in ever since she had been a preteen. It hung on her like a bag and came down to mid-thigh. Her shoulder length hair, the same color as her mom's, was tousled from sleeping, and she scratched at the crown of her head absently and yawned loudly. She might have looked like her mother in many ways, but he knew she had inherited his own stubbornness and devil-may-care attitude – and it made him smile.

She turned and came toward him. Stopping behind him, she leaned around and sat her mug down on the table so she wouldn't spill it, then wrapped her arms lovingly around his neck.

"Good morning, Daddy. You're up early," she said softly, her voice still a little gruff from sleep. She put her face against his, turned, and kissed him lightly on the cheek.

"Ooh! You're scratchy! You need a shave!"

"What if I want to grow a beard?"

"Well, I do like how you look in a beard," she acquiesced. She moved around and sat across the corner of the table from him, sipping her hot coffee carefully. "But until it grows out a little more, you can get your morning kisses from Jarhead!"

The cat stopped licking himself, one back leg still hiked over his head, hearing his name, and seemed to know what was said. He shook his head and went back to his work.

Sophie took another sip of her coffee and looked at her father reproachfully. "You didn't rest well, did you?" she asked over the rim of her cup.

Trent sipped his lukewarm coffee and shrugged with his eyebrows.

"I heard you come in last night. It was very late," she said, sipping her coffee again. She hesitated when he didn't respond, looked at him more closely, and asked, "Where were you?"

He shifted in his chair uncomfortably, peering down into his cup. "I was just out on a call – got caught in the rain coming back in. Didn't want to wake you."

"Out on a call?" she continued to probe. "I thought you quit!"

Trent shrugged again. "Some unfinished business. I'm done with it, now."

Sophie looked around the kitchen. She saw no dishes in the sink or signs of a mess. She stopped looking, though, when she saw a yellow sticky note still on the refrigerator.

"And you didn't get anything to eat last night, either, did you?" She set her cup down hard. "Dad, I left you a note there, with dinner in the oven," she chastised, and then continued. "Didn't you see it?"

"Guess I wasn't hungry – just too tired to eat." He glanced at her, then away again. "Like I said – didn't want to make noise – wake you up."

She ducked her head, trying to get him to look at her. He wouldn't. She got up and walked over to the oven, opened it, and began busying herself dealing with the spoiled remains of last night's dinner.

"You're upset about something," she concluded. "And stop saying you were 'too tired' because you obviously didn't sleep!"

He avoided her eyes.

"It was that damn dream again, wasn't it?" she demanded to know.

Trent looked up at her briefly, then went back to fiddling with his cup.

"Yes, it was the damn dream again," he conceded.

Of course, his curt response was only half an answer. He wasn't about to tell Sophie about his visit with Margot Van Ryan. He wasn't at all sure if he understood himself what that visit was all about, much less be able to explain it to his daughter.

Trent had learned a long time ago, even when Vicky was alive, that to avoid the bigger problem it was best to confess to the lesser problem. In this case, the bigger problem was that he now saw her dead mother during the day. Sophie had insisted on temporarily interrupting her own life and dreams to come live with him and help him back to some semblance of health. She had been a saint about it all, but he doubted she would stand idly by while he began hallucinating, without forcing him to go seek counseling, or worse, go for an extended stay in a psychiatric ward somewhere.

Sophie sighed and put her hand on his forearm. "How long now since your last visit?" she asked determinedly.

"What?" he asked, a shocked look crossing his face.

"Dad! Your last visit with the doctor?" She frowned, and tapped the side of her head with her fingertip.

"Couple of weeks," he answered casually. But the truth was he really couldn't remember if it had been that recent or not. He suspected not, but quite honestly, his mind right now was trying to grapple more with Vicky's ghostly presence over the past two days rather than how often he'd been having dreams about her, much less how often he'd been seeing his shrink.

What the hell was going on? he asked himself.

Earlier, as he had sat drinking coffee alone, trying to still his mind from the shock of seeing is dead wife not once, but twice now in as many days, he had finally reduced the answer down to three possibilities: he was either seeing Vicky as a subconscious projection onto his reality because of exhaustion or stress, he was seeing a figment of her as a result of the injuries to his brain from the accident, or he was seeing her actual ghost.

Any of the three was equally disturbing.

#

They had talked a while longer – father and daughter – idly discussing their day and the rest of the week. He listened and smiled, like the proud father he was, while Sophie spoke of her new project at the newspaper, cataloguing and organizing the old news archives, getting information computerized and more easily retrievable. Trent had then talked about wanting to get more focused on his workouts down at the gym, wanting to get more committed to his physical therapy to get his body completely back to normal as soon as possible. And – slowly, quietly, assuredly – as they talked about these daily routines, his trepidations concerning Vicky's appearances finally subsided.

Trent got up from the table, opened the sliding door to let Jarhead out, then went to get himself a shower while Sophie busied herself cooking breakfast. He stood very still in the spray of water, which he had turned on as hot as he could stand, and allowed it to spill onto his head and chest to beat away his remaining anxieties. Afterwards, he shaved as the smell of bacon, scrambled eggs, and fresh coffee filled the house. As he stepped into the bedroom to finish dressing, he reflected that breakfast always smelled like what morning should smell like; the kind of smells that always made the day feel fresh and new.

He smiled again.

He was beginning to think that today just might mark a new chapter in his mental recovery process, too. Maybe that's all Vicky's "visits" had been about – to force him to get on with his life – and get back to normal, whatever that was.

They were still eating breakfast when Trent's cell phone buzzed in his shirt pocket. He gulped coffee to wash down a mouthful of eggs and looked at the phone. It was the sheriff's private number. Trent stared at the number for a few seconds. The phone vibrated again and he flipped it open.

"Yeah," he said.

"So, I guess you thought it was real funny to just break into the office in the middle of the night, waltz in here, and dump a bunch of crap on my desk without so much as a 'Kiss my butt!'" Sheriff Ben Ferguson was never one to mince words.

On his way into town from Maggie's the previous night, Trent had swung by the office, knowing no one would be on duty that late, unless there had been someone on lockup duty, which there wasn't. Even though Trent had unceremoniously resigned several days earlier, he had kept his office keys, had let himself in, sat down at his old desk, and typed out a full report of his trip out to the Van Ryan ranch. He included his direct observations of the break in, gave a few recommendations as to sending someone out to gather physical evidence, and had finished his report by saying he suspected it to be a simple case of vandalism by transients, with nothing much to suggest anything more specific or sinister. He had then printed up the report, signed it *Trent Carter – former Deputy,* emailed a copy to the desk clerk for the archives, wrapped the report around the old journal Maggie had given him, tossed it all on the sheriff's desk, and had gone home.

"And what's this musty old book you left here, anyway? Not even in English! What the hell am I supposed to do with all this stuff?"

Trent felt a slow burn coming on. "Well, I guess I thought it was all self-explanatory, Ben. It's all there in my report.

Ferguson cut him off. "Well, I'm not making heads or tails out of any of it at all," he barked. "Looks like that crazy Van Ryan woman is just trying to stir up the crap for some reason – and she picked you out as the stick to stir it all up with! You owe her some favors, or something?"

"Look, Sheriff –frankly, it's not my problem anymore. I told Molly the same thing when she dispatched me, and I told Ms. Van Ryan that – and now I guess I'm saying it to you. I quit, if you recall, and I just brought you what I know, as a concerned citizen!" He counted to ten, but it didn't work. "So yes," he continued, gritting his teeth, "you can just kiss my ass since you apparently didn't hear it before!"

In the span of silence that followed, Trent could hear the sheriff take a couple of deep breaths and could picture him tapping his fingers on his desk in exasperation.

"Well, the best chance of that happening is to get that ass of yours down here – right now! We have things to discuss." Ferguson hung up abruptly.

Trent sat for a moment, the phone still up to his ear as if he had forgotten what it was there for.

"What is it, Dad?"

Trent moved the phone away from his ear and closed it with a snap and a frown. He looked over at Sophie and shook his head.

The day no longer felt fresh and new.

CHAPTER 8
DARKNESS & LIGHT

Excerpt from the Journal of Otto Eberhardt

'07.05.45 – "What the hell are we thinking? This is terribly wrong! I no longer know what is the honorable course of action. I am so very weary -- weary of this war, of what it has done to me. I consider myself a good soldier, and I have never questioned my actions – until now. But I seriously doubt that what we are about to do will bring any glory to the Fatherland – or to us. This war is long lost. I think I have long known this in my soul, perhaps ever since we were captured after our tanks blew up around us in that godforsaken North African desert, only to be brought thousands of miles to die here in America. I feel like Moses – a stranger in a strange land.

"Germany is about to fall – Der Führer is a madman – at least, that is what all the American newspapers say. They also say that we murdered all the Jews – put them away in some sort of labor camps – starved them and gassed them, by the millions! I just cannot believe that. But if it is true, then God help us all. We will be regarded as the most despicable people on earth. It is only a matter of time now. Germany is a bombed out wasteland, they say. I have now written several letters home, but have yet to receive a reply. I fear that my precious wife and young daughter are dead in the ruins of Germany. I now wish I had died there, too. At least we would be together right now, in Heaven – if there even were such a place for me anymore. If my countrymen have done all those horrible things, then surely God has reserved Hell for only us Germans. I suppose I shall find out soon enough, for Ernst has decided we shall set out on our 'mission' any day now. We have spent the past couple of weeks gathering what we need, mainly by stealing – clothes, luggage, money. We even broke into a shack on a construction site and stole explosives. There is no dissuading Ernst from this insane plan. But what does it really

matter? We are killers – and we are about to kill again.

"I fear I shall surely not survive this."

#

Sergeant Alberto Armijo scrambled up the last few yards towards the top of the ridge, small rocks and dirt bouncing in his wake. He had to carefully climb the last six feet up a vertical outcropping of rock before he could finally stand and look over to the other side. He rose slowly, breathing hard, brushed his hands together, and put them on his hips. He then looked out and took in the magnificent vistas that flowed away before him – from the knee-high buffalo grass rolling around him in the breeze like ocean surf to the budding scrub oak crowding the hillside down below – eventually across the carpet of dark pines that spilled miles away to the northwest all the way to the snow-tipped Sangre de Cristo Mountains and the gathering gold of the setting sun. Up here, atop Raton Pass, was one of his absolute favorite places to be, especially at this time of day. He welcomed the cool evening breezes that dried the sweat on his face and body as it swept across the flat ridge, which spanned an area the size of a couple of football fields.

Alberto liked to measure his world in terms of football, having been the star quarterback at Raton High School. He had graduated three years ago and at any other time might have gone on to earn a scholarship to play college ball. But the country had been at war and his two older brothers were already overseas. One was somewhere in Germany fighting Nazis, the other in the South Pacific fighting the Nips. Even though he had been sorely needed at home to work and help make ends meet for his family, Alberto had still tried to join up, but he had been denied because of an undiagnosed heart murmur that had shown up in his army physical. He had finally been allowed to join the New Mexico National Guard a few months later when it seemed the Guard had been struggling to fill its ranks following the tragedies at Corregidor in the Philippines, soon after the attack on Pearl Harbor. The entire New Mexico battalion had been taken prisoner by the Japanese and had been forced on what would become known infamously as the Bataan Death March. The Guard's numbers back at home had then gotten so low that they had eased a few of the less critical enlistment requirements. Alberto was able to take quick advantage.

Finally in uniform, he had ironically found himself stationed no further than a few miles from his hometown where his platoon was assigned to guard the vital train tunnels on Raton Pass where the freight and passenger lines of the Santa Fe Railroad passed from Chicago to Los Angeles, often carrying important military cargo, vehicles, weapons, and troops to be shipped out to the Pacific Theater of war. After Pearl Harbor, and with rumors of West Coast sightings of Japanese submarines and the threat of possible homegrown saboteurs, the tunnels had been identified as a potential target. Such an attack on them, if successful, could cripple commerce and vital transportation of war materiel, and the Army was determined that another surprise attack would never again catch them with their pants down.

Somewhere far beneath his feet right now lay those tunnels. Sergeant Armijo often spent his down-time up here, straddling the state line between Colorado and New Mexico, daydreaming of jumping onto one of the trains as it crawled out of the tunnels and riding it all the way to California, just to see how much closer he could get to the war. Right now the Pacific Theater seemed like the only real conflict left, now that the papers were already reporting that Berlin had fallen to the Russians; the Americans and British had flooded over the Rhine River and on through the remainder of Germany; Benito Mussolini had been captured and executed in Italy by partisans. Adolf Hitler himself was nowhere to be found and was possibly lying dead in the rubble of the dying Third Reich. Already, reports were surfacing about large numbers of German soldiers surrendering by the thousands all over Europe. Unconditional surrender seemed imminent.

In the meantime, here stood Sergeant Alberto Armijo, on top of his peaceful world at 7,835 feet above sea level where he could almost forget for a while his disappointments at being sidelined in this war; forget the glowing college football career he might have had; and resign himself to the fact that, in his own eyes, he was already an aging old man, not only with no future post-war prospects but still working in his father's feed store in Raton to provide a living for his widowed mother, his young wife, and their two children.

His thoughts and melancholy were interrupted by the long wail of a far off train's whistle as it echoed up from the oak-filled valleys to the north and signaled its southbound approach to the tunnels. He had a few minutes yet – he knew by the tone of the whistle that the train was still several miles away and would be ascending the Pass slowly. He sighed, squatted on the flat hard table rock, lit a cigarette, inhaled deeply, and watched the tobacco smoke drift away to perhaps mingle somewhere below with the smoke of the approaching train. He pictured the smoke wafting further on into the sunset – along with the remaining – and best – years of his life.

#

Hauptmann Ernst Brandt and *Leutnant* Otto Eberhardt, late of Field Marshall Erwin Rommel's *Deutsches Afrikakorps*, sat silently in the rear seats of the last passenger coach as the train labored to ascend to the summit of Raton Pass, both dressed in the non-descript civilian clothes of common laborers. In case they were arrested, they had stitched into the linings of their jackets their old *Wehrmacht* identification papers along with their documentation and IDs that had been issued to them at Camp Trinidad, all of which identified them as officers in what had been, until recently, the most powerful fighting force in the world. Hopefully, their being recognized as enemy officers would prevent them from being shot as spies – but Otto really doubted it. In any case, they would probably be dead soon anyway, so no sense worrying about being accused of espionage.

He stared straight ahead at the backs of the heads of the other passengers, some idly chatting, others reading newspapers. A young mother seated across the aisle and one row up was trying to keep her two young sons in line as they fidgeted and fought with one another. They occasionally escaped to the aisle to chase one another, noisily playing war. She looked around, saw Otto, and gave him an embarrassed smile and a shrug as she pushed a lock of loose hair wearily back from her forehead. Otto tried to return her smile, but only managed a tight-lipped grimace. He looked away, embarrassed that she had caught him looking at her, and shuffled in his seat.

The heel of his foot struck the bag under his seat. The heavy bag did not move as he nervously jerked his foot back. He glanced at his watch – 6:25 p.m. He took a handkerchief out of his jacket pocket and wiped away the perspiration on his upper lip for the umpteenth time, but suddenly became aware of Ernst staring at him. They held each other's eyes for several seconds until Ernst raised a cautionary eyebrow, and looked slowly away.

They had boarded the train in Trinidad, Colorado, at 4:45 p.m., and had been careful to arrive at the ticket counter separately where they had purchased one-way tickets – Ernst's to Las Vegas, New Mexico, and Otto's to Albuquerque. Ernst had said not being seen together was a precaution in the event they were questioned or detained before they could complete their mission. They had made their ways separately to the last passenger coach where they had been fortunate to find the rear seats empty as the train was already about three-quarters full of passengers. The last two cars behind theirs were the observation car and the caboose.

The two young boys were now running back down the aisle, pointing their toy pistols at one another. "Blam, blam, blam," they yelled at each other, diving behind seats for cover. As they neared the two Germans' row, the older of the boys staggered, grasped his chest, croaked, "Ya got me!" and sprawled dramatically onto the floor in the aisle between them, playing dead. His hand flopped over heavily onto the bag under Otto's seat. The boy's eyes suddenly flew open, and he jerked his hand back and held it up to his mouth. "Ow!" he exclaimed and gave Otto a frown. The boys' mother stood up and grabbed them both by their collars.

"Now, that is quite enough!" she told them forcefully. "You're disturbing these folks!"

"But Mom, I hurt my hand on that man's bag," the boy whined, pointing back at Otto.

"I am so sorry," Otto mumbled, standing up quickly, removing his cap, and squeezing it between both hands. "I hope the boy is not hurt I should have put this out of the way." He pushed the bag further under the seat with his foot.

"No, they shouldn't be rough-housing," the young woman replied. "They are just excited. Lots of energy to burn off." The boys continued to squirm until she turned and deposited them back in their seats. She started to sit back down before turning back toward Otto.

"We are – all excited," she said, explaining further. "Their father – my husband –is returning from the Pacific, and we are going to meet him in Los Angeles. Haven't seen him in almost four years." She looked toward her boys. "Walter here, my oldest, was only eight when my husband enlisted. And Timmy was barely three." Her voice trailed off as she blushed and looked down.

Otto saw that she was a handsome woman, strongly built and stout, but not plump, with a pleasing figure and beautiful green eyes. She appeared to be more than able to handle two rambunctious boys and still project charm at the same time.

"Well, where are my manners?" She exclaimed, looking up at Otto again and extending her hand. "My name is Penelope Carter. But just call me Penny." Otto removed his cap and shyly shook her hand.

"Very pleased to meet you, Mrs. Carter. I am Otto – er – Bauer."

"Well, we've never been so far from home. It's just taking a lot longer than I thought it would." She smiled again apologetically. "Are you headed to LA, too?"

Otto had been shifting his feet while she spoke and had succeeded in pushing the bag even further out of sight under his seat while she spoke. He looked up nervously. "No – no, I am only going to Albuquerque," he said.

"Oh, I see – Do you have family there?"

Across the aisle, Ernst coughed loudly, like someone who had swallowed wrong. Otto glanced over at him, but Ernst was gazing out the window, seemingly ignoring the conversation. Otto looked back at Mrs. Carter.

"No. Just – just looking for some work," he stammered, before attempting a poor excuse for a smile. He wished that she would sit back down, but instead, she continued to stand there attempting to make conversation with him. He began to perspire again.

"You have such an interesting accent," she said eventually after looking at him for a moment. "Is that Italian?"

Otto could now feel Ernst's eyes boring into him. He didn't dare look over.

"Yes – yes, Italian," he said. "My mother was from there." He now made a move as if to sit.

"Well, there are certainly a lot of you folks that have moved in around here, what with the railroad, and the coalmines and such. Oh, not that I mind it, you understand! I'm as open minded as they come. Glad to have all you interesting people around." She blushed, and gave up trying to explain. "Oh, just listen to me, will you, chattering on and on. I am so sorry. I didn't mean to pry. Guess I'm just nervous, what with the trip and the excitement. I do apologize, Mr. Bauer, and I wish you good luck on your trip," she said, extending her hand, which he self-consciously took. "And I will try to keep these little hoodlums quiet from now on." She chuckled nervously, then wiped the seat before she finally sat down.

Otto hazarded a quick glance over at Ernst, who was now tightlipped, glaring, and shaking his head slowly at him.

The twin locomotives chugged in tandem and puffed their way up the steep inclines of the approaches to the Raton Tunnels. As the train gradually made its way around the switchbacks and bends, the black smoke from their stacks swirled and eddied about the cars. Some of the passengers began to close a few of the opened windows as the acrid smell of the coal smoke wafted through. Otto nervously checked his watch again. They had to be very near by now.

After noting the time, he looked across the aisle, ignoring Ernst, and out the windows toward the setting sun in the west. The sky burst with brilliant oranges and reds; on any other evening, Otto would have marveled and allowed the view to take his breath away. But right now, this minute, all it reminded him of was a devastating explosion in slow motion, full of foreboding and death.

Ernst cleared his throat softly again, getting Otto's attention. Ernst then nodded toward Otto's bag. He gave Otto that unnerving smile of his and touched his watch. At that moment, the train's whistle blew shrilly several times, signaling its impending approach to the tunnels.

It was almost time.

#

Sergeant Armijo finished his cigarette, watching the fiery clouds lit up by the sun as it began its descent behind the jagged peaks of the distant mountains. He stood up and dropped the butt on the ground, mashed it under his boot, and hitched up his pants and holster belt. He reached down out of habit and checked that his Remington Model 1911A1 .45 caliber semi-automatic pistol was securely snapped into its holster. He was proud to have it, as he had learned it was usually only issued to officers. Even so, he reflected once again that he had never fired this or any other weapon during this war except at the practice range. Sighing audibly, he figured, regretfully, that he never would, now that the war was drawing to a close.

The train blew its whistle again several times, noticeably closer now, and Armijo could now hear the faint chugging noises of the approaching engines. He could picture them as they dragged the train slowly up the Pass. He closed his eyes, took a deep breath through his nostrils, and caught the faint, familiar odor of coal smoke. It was time to get back down to check the tunnels.

#

Ernst frowned and nodded again. Otto looked away and let his gaze travel back over the heads of the passengers in the car. He sweated profusely now and wiped again at his lip and his face. He glanced at Ernst once more, then reached down until he felt the edge of the bag under his seat and slid it out carefully. His eyes wandered back over to Mrs. Carter and her young sons. He froze with the bag halfway out from under the seat, closed his eyes, and tried desperately to quell his thoughts – the horrifying mental images of exploding metal, wood, and flesh, screaming people, and of fire and blood everywhere.

He wasn't sure how much time had passed when he felt the car lurch into another curve. He felt around and gingerly unzipped the bag. He winced as it made a loud ripping noise, which seemed to fill the entire car. He stopped and looked nervously around, but no one paid any attention whatsoever. The boys, Walter and Timmy, were sitting on either side of their mother. Their heads had begun to loll against her arms. A golden aura from the setting sun surrounded Mrs. Carter's profile like a halo, and she looked strikingly peaceful and full of hope at the moment. Otto thought about how kindly she had spoken to him and, remembering his own lost family, his heart began to hurt inside his throat. He watched for a moment or two longer. Finally, after taking and exhaling a deep breath, he made a decision. He stood up, stepped over the bag and across the aisle, and removed his hat.

"Excuse me, Mrs. Carter," he said quietly. She looked up with a start. Her boys squirmed and frowned up at him, rubbing their sleepy eyes. It was now Otto's turn to blush and apologize. "I am very sorry to intrude," he stammered. He stopped, briefly at a loss for words, but suddenly had an idea. "Did you hear the conductor – just now?" he asked brightly, gesturing up the aisle.

She looked at him, apparently confused, but shook her head.

"Well," he continued, hopefully, "I suspected you might not have heard him. But he has announced that dinner is about to be served in the dining car." He paused, but only for a moment, then continued earnestly. "And perhaps this would be a good time to let your boys – how did you say – burn off some energy?"

The woman looked around, still looking confused, as if noticing that no one else was making a move toward the exit.

"Here – I can help you and the boys, if you wish," Otto continued the ruse. He offered his arm to her. "You will surely want to beat the crowd."

She looked first at his proffered arm, then back up at him. She smiled appreciatively. "Yes," she answered, hesitatingly at first, but then, "yes, thank you very much, Mr. Bauer. That's probably a very good idea!"

Otto took the youngest boy Timmy gently by the arm and led him into the aisle. Penny stood up and coaxed her other son up out of his seat.

"Come on, boys, let's go eat," she said brightly. Otto then led the little family up the aisle toward the exit to the adjoining passenger cars. On their way out, he glanced over his shoulder.

Ernst glowered furiously at him.

#

Sergeant Armijo made his way back down the loose rock, through the scrub oak and waist high buffalo grass to the small group of outbuildings that served as temporary quarters, office, and supply shack for the platoon. They were located near the entrance to the tunnels on the New Mexico side of the Pass. The twin north- and south-bound tracks of the Santa Fe Railroad lines entered into separate tunnels that had been blasted through the mountain here five decades ago, 500 feet underneath the summit of Raton Pass and the length of ten football fields from one side to the other, to serve as a much-needed shortcut through the mountains between Chicago and Los Angeles. As he trudged on toward the tunnels to check on his guards posted there, Armijo reflected briefly on their overall purpose here: to guard the tunnel against possible attack and sabotage. Earlier in the war, securing the tunnel had been seen as a real threat and guarding it an important job. But now, only a few years later, with the realization that his war was almost over, he had to wonder if there was any real threat left at all.

He walked up to the private on duty there who was looking off into the distance, smoking a cigarette, and hadn't noticed Sergeant Armijo's approach.

"Put out that smoke, private, "Armijo growled.

"Yes, sir!" The private quickly threw the butt down and ground it out. He was no more than eighteen, just recently assigned to Armijo's platoon, and extremely nervous.

"And it's 'Sergeant,' to you – not 'Sir.' I work for a living."

"Sorry, Sir – I mean – Sergeant – sorry!" The private snapped to attention, shouldering his rifle. Armijo shook his head. Even though none of this protocol seemed to matter at all anymore, he would still try to maintain some discipline, go through the motions, and do his duty.

He pointed to the flashlight clipped to the private's shoulder strap. "Let's take a quick look," he continued. "The 6:45's coming up."

"Yes, sir – er – Sergeant!"

The private unclipped his flashlight, turned, and started into the tunnel. Armijo went into step a few feet behind him. The light played up and around along the curved, thick concrete ceiling of the tunnel, casting weird, dancing shadows around them as they made their way along the crossties between the tracks and began their inspection. Their footfalls echoed loudly back at them. They were 500 yards in when a piercing whistle blew three long blasts, which echoed up from somewhere far ahead and bounced eerily through the tunnel around them. The black silhouette of the private moved quickly away from Armijo.

"Slow down there, private," he called out. "That train still has a few minutes." The private slowed his pace, but looked back over his shoulder at Armijo nervously.

Armijo gestured ahead of them. "It always sounds a lot closer than it is. We'll be okay. We'll get all the way through before it gets here."

#

Otto opened the adjoining doors between each of the other passenger cars and carefully led the small family out onto the moving iron plates that covered the spaces where the connecting cars bounced against each other. Here, the noise of the clacking tracks was not as insulated as it was in the cars and the wind made whooshing noises around them while unseen chains and connecting cables clanged and bounced somewhere beneath their feet.

"Step carefully," Otto said to them, calmly. The boys were hollering with delight, and jumping up and down. Penny gripped Otto's arm tighter.

"Oh, do be careful, boys," she said nervously, stepping cautiously herself.

Otto led them through the other two passenger cars, then finally pulled open the door of the dining car and ushered them through, closing it just as quickly behind them, and the noise subsided. The car was relatively quiet and almost empty, except for an older couple who was drinking coffee at a table about halfway down. A steward stepped out of the nearby galley, looked at them with an irritated frown, then glanced at his watch. He opened his mouth to say something, but Otto cut him off.

"I think they really need to be allowed in a little early," he said to the steward, and nodded knowingly toward the boys who were fidgeting. The steward glanced at the boys with a frown, then at their frazzled mother, and relented, perhaps thinking how much of a nuisance the boisterous boys could be later when the dining car was bustling with business.

"Yes, I think we can accommodate you," he reluctantly agreed, gesturing toward a nearby table.

"Oh!" Otto interrupted. "Can you perhaps seat them at the far end of the car – so the boys might not accidently disturb the other passengers?" The steward hesitated, then led the way to the far end. The boys trailed after him, with their mother bringing up the rear. Otto didn't follow, but stood quietly at the door for a moment. Mrs. Carter turned one final time as she was seating her boys, smiled, and mouthed a *thank you* to him.

Otto smiled and nodded, then turned and stepped back into the connecting passageway. There he let the door close before letting out a huge breath. He closed his eyes and leaned back against the door for a moment. *Perhaps they will now be far enough away and safe from the danger,* he thought.

Please, God? Let it be so!

CHAPTER 9
LAZARUS

Colfax County, at 3,768 square miles, is one of the largest counties, by area, in New Mexico with its 13,750 residents spread over terrain ranging from mesquite covered sand hills and high desert prairies, wild rivers cutting their way through rugged canyons, to pine forests covering high-mountain passes. Its population density is only 3.7 people per square mile. Add to this the thousands of vehicles per day travelling the 1,067 mile major corridor that is Interstate Highway 25 from its starting point just north of El Paso, near the U.S.-Mexico border, all the way up into Montana, and a good number of people pass within a few hundred yards of the Colfax County Courthouse. They are all either heading to or from Colorado across the Raton Pass, or spilling in from West Texas.

Either way, all of these facts equated to a whole bunch of variables that made the job difficult for nine deputies and a sheriff to adequately patrol, investigate crime, and enforce the law, even on a good day, which Trent had already decided it definitely was not – a good day – at all.

He purposely parked his truck in the visitors' area of the courthouse, turned the engine off, and sat there for a couple of minutes glaring up at the windows of the building. He took a deep breath, got out, and walked across the parking lot to the front doors and into the lobby. The offices of the sheriff's department were located on the first floor here since a large part of the duties of the department was to supply security for the court system.

"Mornin' Manuel," he said with a curt nod, walking steadily.

The security guard on duty there, a wizened, grey haired man who looked as old as Trent felt stopped him short at the metal detector, just inside the doors. Normally, Trent would have been waved around the machine, but this time the guard shrugged sheepishly and indicated that he would have to step through the detector.

"Sorry, Trent," Manuel apologized. "But rules is rules."

"Right," Trent said, remembering he was now just an ordinary citizen. He moved forward, but just as quickly hesitated, suddenly remembering something.

"Uh – I'll be right back," he finally said and turned and walked back out of the building to his truck where he removed his revolver from his jacket pocket and locked it in the glove-box. He then re-entered the building, smiled, and nodded to the guard, and was cleared right through without incident.

The granite floor and the high ceilings echoed with his footfalls as he walked through the lobby toward the heavy floor to ceiling glass partitions that marked the department's offices. He pushed open the heavy glass door, which made a sucking sound when it swung back shut, giving him the distinct impression he was entering a hermetically sealed chamber. The air conditioning was set way too cool in here and he immediately felt the temperature drop twenty-five degrees. He was glad he'd kept his leather jacket on.

He stopped for a moment at the counter to his right that was fitted with a bullet resistant glass barrier and equipped with a speaker system. Molly Evans, the dispatcher, sat on the other side, and Trent waited for her to look up from her computer screen – and waited. He was sure she was making a point of ignoring him. He reached up over and tapped the glass with his knuckle. She smirked but continued to ignore him. He muttered under his breath and looked around. In front of him was another locked glass door in yet another glass partition, beyond which was a bullpen filled with desks, all with stacks of in-baskets overflowing with paper. *So much for computers doing away with all the paper,* he observed absently. The room was staffed with a couple of clerks and a few other deputies, all of whom were either busy on the phones that were continually ringing, clicking away on computers, or interviewing people. Toward the rear of the room, a uniformed Hispanic deputy was busily writing and nodding, his chin cupped in one hand while a concerned looking older woman sat at the side of his desk. She talked excitedly and gestured animatedly with her hands. Within this heavy glass enclosure, Trent could not hear what they were saying.

"Well, well. To what do we owe this dubious pleasure?" Molly had finally looked up from her work, apparently satisfied that she had made Trent wait the obligatory amount of time needed to reinforce her role as official gatekeeper. She was an attractive middle-aged woman with dyed-blond, short hair, dressed tastefully in a dark blue pantsuit with a pale blue blouse showing under the jacket. She wore a modest amount of jewelry and makeup – although she was given to bright shades of lipstick. She leaned forward on her stool, took off her glasses, and smiled knowingly.

"Last time you and I talked, you weren't ever stepping foot in here again. And if memory serves, you were more than a little abrupt with me – *former*," she emphasized, "Deputy Carter."

Trent's immediate answer was to tap his fingertip restlessly on the counter.

"Hmm," he grunted, then with a grimace, "Sorry – *Ms.* Evans."

He tapped his finger for a few more seconds, determined not to prolong the discussion any further. He pointed through the glass toward the office door in the far corner.

"He wants to see me, I guess."

"So I've heard." She slid her glasses back on, punched a button on her keyboard, and glanced at something on the screen before looking back at Trent. "It seems someone's been sneaking in at all hours filing mysterious investigative reports – which has also made *my* life so much easier, thank you very much."

Trent looked down, shuffled his feet, and cleared his throat. "So, you going to call the sheriff and tell him I'm here, Molly – or just keep me standing here and kick my ass some more?"

"Don't need to – he left instructions to send you right in, minute you arrived." She reached under her desk, the door buzzed loudly, and he turned to push it open as she continued. "Seems some people have *carte blanche* around here. Oh – that's French, by the way, for, 'do whatever the hell you please, whenever the hell you want to do it!'"

Trent ignored her and stepped through the glass wall.

"Holler if you need me to bring you a bandage," she said, loudly enough for the rest of the room to now hear.

He stopped halfway through and turned. "For what, exactly?" he asked.

"For the real ass-kicking you're about to get, speaking of which." Her fake smile unnerved him and Trent rolled his eyes as the door whooshed shut behind him. He zigzagged among the desks and suddenly noticed everything had gotten very quiet, as if everyone in the room held their collective breaths. He could feel all eyes on him – although no one directly acknowledged him – at least not until he passed the desk of the Hispanic officer's desk.

"Good to see you, Deputy, uh, Mr. Carter!" The officer had looked up from his work and beamed at him.

Trent slowed down enough to give the deputy a perfunctory nod. "Uh – good to see you too, Hector," he stammered. Trent noticed that the elderly woman who had been chattering at Hector non-stop in Spanish now stopped talking altogether and frowned at Trent for the interruption. He tipped his hat towards her.

"Ma'am," he said and then walked on toward the sheriff's office.

Hector Armijo had always taken time out of his routine to speak to Trent, almost going out of his way to make sure Trent noticed him for some odd reason – even brought him coffee or doughnuts, or both, without being asked to, as if constantly trying to impress him. At times his efforts amused Trent and at other times merely irritated him. This instance was one of the irritating times, for Trent had his mind on the coming storm and had no time for Hector's supposed hero worship.

He stopped in front of the sheriff's closed door, raised his hand to knock, fist poised, but lowered it. He thought for a moment, shook his head, grabbed the doorknob, and barged on in. He slammed the door behind him, ready to do battle.

Ben Ferguson sat behind his large mahogany desk, writing quietly and steadily on a legal pad. He didn't flinch nor look up at all and never broke his concentration, but continued jotting thoughts on paper, evidently refusing to take the bait.

Ferguson was a 49-year-old retired detective who had moved from Denver a couple years ago for the dual purpose of getting away from a nagging ex-wife, not counting getting out of one of the fastest growing metro lexes in the country in favor of quiet, easy-going rural living. He loaded up whatever he could fit in his truck and a small trailer, headed south on I-25, figuring to stop at the first quaint and interesting place he drove through.

He had crossed the state line at the top of Raton Pass and the interstate had dumped him seven miles later into a quaint town called Raton, situated at the beginning of the high desert plains of New Mexico.

But a man like him, accustomed to a little more action, had quickly grown tired of long morning walks and the eventually boring evening trips to nearby Lake Maloya to fish off the bank with the other retirees and watch the beavers work on their dams. So, consequently, as often happened in small communities, as soon as anyone with any professional experience moves in, they soon find themselves pushed back into service – and truthfully, it hadn't taken much nudging for Ben Ferguson to agree to run for sheriff of Colfax County when the next election bid came up.

"Sit down, Deputy," he said quietly after several seconds, still without looking at Trent and continuing to write.

Trent stood, making fists, unsure where to channel the tension he had built up over the last few minutes in preparation for an intense shouting match. With two nicely upholstered leather chairs arrayed in front of the desk, Trent glanced from one to the other and then back over the desk at the sheriff who finally looked up, put his pen down, and leaned back in his overstuffed leather chair to stare passively at Trent. He held an even look on his face as he finally gestured to one of the chairs with a nod.

"I think that one right there should do nicely," he said dryly. .

Trent took off his hat, sat, and eyed his former boss cautiously.

Ferguson steepled his fingers at his chin and sat for a while, looking at Trent with an empty expression, his eyes squinting a little as if sizing him up. He suddenly slapped the desk, having made some decision, opened the top right drawer, took some objects out, and closed it again. He pushed the items in a stack across the desk toward Trent, who now could see it included his Glock .45 service pistol in its holster, the extra magazine for it, and his badge on top. Underneath them all was a book of some kind and a bulging 8x10 envelope.

"You and me, we've worked with a lot of people in our day, Trent," Ben began. "Ever wonder who was crazier – the people that are messing up the world out there," he gestured somewhere beyond the window, "or those of us who have to go mess with the mess?"

Trent looked from the sheriff to the stack in front of him and back again. "I suppose it depends on how bad the mess is – and how bad it needs cleaning up," he answered quietly, but hesitated before continuing. "Guess I'm not necessarily a good one to ask about the crazy part just yet."

"Well, hell – I've about decided we're all just half a bubble off the plumb. And if that's what the job takes these days, then so be it. Besides, I don't need a lawsuit under the 'Americans with Disillusions Act.'"

"I think you mean, 'Americans with Disabilities."

"Yeah, whatever," Ben dismissed, waving the error off. His gramar had never been top notch, but he didn't really care. He nodded down at Trent's badge and collection of items. "You know – the last time you walked out of here, you went off half-cocked and threw those things at me. So I am probably half out of my mind to say this –," he paused to look at Trent, his eyes squinted again and his mouth pursed, but continued, "but you had best pick those back up before I quickly think better of it."

Trent frowned at the items, then looked at Ben, and saw that he was quite serious. He didn't move for a full minute as he weighted the pros and cons at this unexpected turn of events. All of a sudden, he smelled wild strawberries and cloves and thought he heard a familiar voice singing softly in the near distance, but couldn't quite make out the words. The sensation passed.

Trent eyed the items lying before him. "You sure you want me back, either half-cocked or half-minded?" Trent tapped the side of his head slowly with the tip of his finger. "I most likely won't change, and this thing isn't as sharp as it once was, you know. Lots of details missing."

Ben leaned back in his chair and studied Trent for a while. "Well, half-brained – or even half-witted – or not, you're still the best damned investigator I've ever had around here – disabled *or* disillusioned." He grunted as an afterthought, shrugging his shoulders. "And besides, the same box-loads of crap piled up in that office of yours when you left are still right where you left them. I'll be damned – and I possibly will be – but I need you to get busy on it again – not to mention all this new crap you dumped in *here* last night." Ferguson tapped the large envelope before sliding it across the desk.

"Disabled and disillusioned. Yep, that's about right." He rubbed his eyes then scratched his head. "Guess that would describe the both of us pretty well, Ben – at least, if I'm fool enough to take you up on it again."

Trent sighed, followed by a grunt. "More fool, me, then."

He slowly reached over, picked up the badge and gun, and clipped them onto his belt.

"Good," Ben muttered, nodding his head slowly and ever so slightly in the affirmative. He breathed what seemed to be a sigh of relief, pushed himself out of his chair, dragged his coffee cup off the desk, and walked to the window. He was a couple inches shorter than Trent, a few pounds heavier, several years younger, and moved like a prizefighter. He appeared to still be mostly muscle, judging by how his barrel chest and thick biceps threatened to burst out his shirt He also moved like he carried the weight of the world on those broad shoulders. He lifted one edge of the window blind and squinted out, took a long sip of coffee, and grimaced. He turned to Trent and gestured at the window.

"Now, would you please get your deputy-ass outta here and go move that piece of shit truck of yours out of visitor parking before I have it towed?" he demanded, much louder than necessary. "Makes the place look like a used car lot!"

Trent raised an eyebrow because Ben had made his remarks with a crinkle around his eyes and a half smile. Ben now winked and spoke again in a quieter, more conspiratorial voice over the rim of his cup. "Gotta keep up the appearances. Everybody is probably gathered around the coffee pot out there, expecting me to really lower the boom on you."

Trent didn't react at all, just looked back down, and finally picked up the envelope and the book, which he hefted in his hand. It was the journal Maggie had given him. *Now what the hell am I supposed to do with this?* he wondered.

"Well, consider the boom lowered, then," he finally muttered as he turned and left the Ben's office, slamming the door behind him for additional effect.

#

Trent's old wooden desk had scratches on the edges where it looked as if someone had been in the habit of propping their feet on it. He stepped over and swiveled his high-backed, worn leather office chair and sighed as he eased himself into its comfortable familiarity. Everything in the office looked pretty much the way he had left it. A few framed citations commemorating his military and state police days sat on the credenza behind him – and one framed 5X7 photograph of Vicky sat off to one side of the computer. Even the trashcan beside the desk looked as if it had not been emptied in his absence. The only things new he had found were a few sticky notes on his dark computer screen and some pink message slips shoved under the edge of his telephone.

He took the large envelope Ben had given back to him, spilled the contents onto his desk, and shuffled through them. On the top was the five-page incident report he had written the night before, plus a few photos he had uploaded from his cell phone and printed off – pics he had taken out at Maggie's place yesterday, primarily of the damages in and around the adobe hut, including a couple of close-ups of what could've been boot prints and other tire tracks.

He stopped shuffling when he came to a photo of the damaged doorway. Maggie had been standing off to one side, in profile. A sunbeam had streaked down and created a faint rainbow aura around her head, and her hair glowed like a halo. She was standing with one hip cocked and her fingers were pushing away a strand of golden hair from her face. She was really quite lovely, and, for a second there, he thought she looked like Vicky. He glanced back over at the framed photo of his dead wife, exhaled slowly, and shuffled Maggie's photo back in with the other photographs.

Next, he picked up and opened the old journal. He squinted at the first page, thumbed a few more pages, and looked around the room. The room had gotten a lot darker, but he had not bothered to turn on the lights – hadn't needed to as the fluorescent wash spilling in from the squad room had been sufficient lighting at the time. As he stood now and walked over to the light switch, a sudden flash of light appeared out the window, followed shortly by a loud cracking boom. He pulled the shades open and saw that a pretty good rainstorm, complete with dark skies, plenty of erratic lightning, and percussive thunder, had started up at some point. In fact, it had already developed into quite a deluge with the drainage gutters in the street already running like small creeks.

He watched as another flash of lightning struck nearby, waited for the roll thunder which soon followed, and sat back down to wait out the storm. He picked up the old journal again and turned to what would have to be the title page:

Zeitschrift von Otto Eberhardt
(Persönlich und Vertaulich)

Zeitschrift? he wondered. He racked his brain for the lost German words he once knew.

Persönlich? "Person?" he muttered. That could've meant *personal,* he supposed.

Vertaulich? No clue, whatsoever. The only possibility that made any sense was that *Otto Eberhardt* was clearly someone's name. *The Journal of Otto Eberhardt,* perhaps? *Personal and* – something or other.

Private, maybe? *Confidential?*

Trent laid the book down, thought hard for a moment, and reached over and switched on the computer. He had never liked using the contraption much and wasn't too adept at it, except for getting into the department's data base files and report forms. What had Sophie called it? *Computer illiterate?* She had tried to get him into the 21st century with email, which he had refused to use, and by trying to teach him something called "Googling." She claimed there was not much in the world anymore that was secret and that anyone could find practically anything on something called Google. So maybe this magic Googly thingy could show him how to translate some of these words. The computer booted up, and, sure enough, on the opening screen was a selection of icons that included one sporting a large "G." He double clicked on it, and the screen replaced itself with a white field containing the stylized word "GOOGLE" across the middle and a big blank underneath. He typed in the word "German," and an entire list of topics containing the word spilled onto his screen, from food to films to Hitler. He frowned, not seeing what he needed. He scrolled back up to the top, added the word "translate," and was taken to a screen that seemed to be asking for either a word in German or in English. He stared at it for a few more seconds, unsure what to type next. The unexpected ring of his desk phone startled him. But before he could pick up the receiver, Molly's voice came over the intercom.

"Hey, Trent, Bobby Orsini called for you when you were in with the sheriff."

Trent drew a blank and searched his memory. "Bobby who?" he asked.

"Bobby! You know, down at the Shuler Theater? Anyway, he says you better get down there right away."

"Why? What's going on down there?"

"Wouldn't say. He sounded a bit excited. Said he found something you might be interested in, given the previous cases everyone knows you were investigating all over the place before your – well, before your, uh, you know, uh, sick leave."

"So, you heard the good news already?"

"Yep," she answered. "It do travel fast around here."

Molly hung up and Trent sat back in his chair, thinking. *Previous cases,* he thought. He opened a couple of his desk drawers and flipped through a few files, looking at the headings. Nothing jarred his memory. He then let his gaze roam the office. His eyes stopped to rest on a pile of file boxes shoved into one dark corner. The lid was off of one of them, and some of the old files were half pulled out. Some faded writing in magic marker was on the side of the box with what looked like a series of old dates. He could just make out the words *Cold Case Homicides* above them.

For some reason, his pulse quickened. Something about those boxes was of critical importance to him – but he couldn't quite remember why.

#

The torrential rainwater had cascaded down the alley steps behind the old theater and found its way under the basement stage door entrance to form a steady stream through the hallway that extended behind the theater's dressing rooms. Fortunately, the stream of water turned here, instead of flooding the dressing rooms, and continued to run down into an open utility door that led to yet another set of steps to the building's sub-basement. Here, it managed to divert itself from doing any real damage to the rest of the theater. The flow now had subsided to a slow trickle, but the water had had nowhere else to drain and now lay collected in a two-foot deep pool in the sub-basement. Boxes, old furniture, and other discarded items, which had previously been utilized as theatrical props and set pieces, now floated in the ruined room.

"Bobby?" Trent called out as he followed the flow of water.

"Down here," came the caretaker's disembodied voice from somewhere before him.

Trent stepped through the doorway and searched with his hand for a light switch. The air felt close and its odor ancient. The Shuler Theater had been built in 1914 and had housed the old city offices as well as an opera house style theater auditorium. It had originally been built to showcase touring stage stars from the east and west coasts travelling through on the train from the larger venues in Chicago and Los Angeles. Someone had had the brilliant idea that, with a built-in audience made up of the burgeoning surrounding population of coal miners and railroad workers and their families, building a quality theater would be an excellent way to improve the amenities in the growing Wild West town of Raton. The city fathers had already coined the town slogan – "Gateway to New Mexico." Having weathered the winds of time, almost being demolished in the late 50s, early 60s, the old theatre was rescued when enterprising citizens had saved it from the wrecking ball by dumping a ton of money into it and restoring her to her former glory so once again the theater had echoed, if not completely thrived, with musicals and semi-professional touring shows.

"No electricity down here anymore," reminded Bobby Orsini, the aging maintenance man who knew all the ins and outs of the old building. "Here, use this." He handed Trent an extra flashlight.

Trent watched skeptically as Bobby stepped down into the water that had filled the basement, his lower pants legs and boots already soaked from having previously waded through the room. He disappeared into the shadows as he sloshed around a corner. Trent stooped down, looking for him, and snapped on the flashlight and let the light play over the flooded basement before stepping cautiously forward. He stopped on the last three steps, not sure that going any farther was worth getting his boots wet for.

He cursed under his breath and splashed his way down the last steps only to become quickly aware that the dirt floor underneath was now slippery mud. The water immediately poured over the top of his boots and soaked his feet and his pants up to mid-thigh. He cursed, reached to steady himself on the grimy wall, and sloshed forward, carefully feeling his way by sliding one foot gingerly after another, slipping and catching himself now and then. *What in the hell am I doing down here*, he thought and wondered if he should've brought his cane. He was getting angry.

"Bobby! You sure there's something here I need to see?"

The light from his flashlight now danced over the water, creating fluid reflections and illusions on the ceiling and illuminated diaphanous networks of spider webs undulating spookily like in a bad horror movie. The basement was musty and dank and echoed wetly as Bobby called back from the shadows.

"Over this way," Bobby directed, the light from his flashlight bouncing like a pointer toward the outermost foundation wall.

In the dancing light, Trent could just dimly make out some disturbance over in the corner of the crumbling limestone foundation. Evidently, that the rainwater had also seeped through a weakness in the wall at this point as dirt and stone had crumbled onto the floor leaving a dark opening beyond. He waded several yards more toward the back wall, still not able to see much except for the disorienting effects as the light splayed along the water, and came up behind Bobby, who was leaning over and peering down into the dark space intently. Trent looked over Bobby's shoulder, but could really see nothing.

"Gotta stoop down here to see anything much," Bobby commanded. "But this here is what got my attention." Trent moved to the side and bent over. Something protruded from the opening in the old foundation that Bobby lifted up gingerly with his hand.

Trent squatted a little further, intent on not slipping, and then squinted at what appeared to be a small, shriveled branch, suspended in the remains of ancient spider webs, and with a filthy piece of moth-eaten cloth wrapped around it. He reached in to pull the cloth out of the way and suddenly inhaled sharply as he felt his heart thump and jerked his hand back.

The shriveled branch was not a branch at all: he now clearly recognized the skeletal remains of a human forearm, the fingers of a bony hand still attached and extending out of the rotten sleeve of an old coat of some type. The remainder of the grisly arm disappeared back into the darkness of the washed out opening in the wall.

Trent regained his composure, sucked in his breath, and trained his flashlight back into the hole.

CHAPTER 10
APOCALYPSE

Excerpt from the Journal of Otto Eberhardt

'08.05.45 – By all rights, I should be dead, blown to bits! It would have been justice and mercy – and I would have welcomed it. It is strange, however, that I have no clear recollection of the event itself – only of a sudden stoppage of time, like the earth had ceased spinning on its axis, and we all went floating out into space, as if I had died and passed through the diaphanous veil that separates life and death, straight into a peaceful oblivion, only to be jerked rudely back across the barrier and back into the sheer chaos and carnage of what my world has become."

#

The dancing light from their flashlights suddenly revealed up ahead a place where the tunnel curved slightly. Sergeant Armijo and the private quickened their pace and continued their inspection, walking around the curve until they could see the hole of light materialize at the other end. Even though it was late afternoon outside, the daylight appeared very bright to their unadjusted eyes, causing them to shade them for protection against the glare as they walked from the dark tunnel. Once his eyes were adjusted, Alberto strode steadily along, continuing to look left and right, up and down, methodically checking for damage or anything suspicious looking where something might've been disturbed. *A rather pointless task*, he thought, but it was his duty. So he did it.

The private, ahead of him a couple of yards now, finally exited the tunnel, turned off his flashlight, and breathed a sigh of relief as he stepped quickly to the northbound tracks. A second sentry already stood at his post, guarding the southbound tunnel entrance. Armijo nodded to him as he too stepped out, stopped between the rails, shaded his eyes with one hand, and squinted up the tracks to the north just as the tandem locomotives wheezed around the final curve and rolled fully into view, coming out of the tree line. Black smoke billowed from twin smokestacks with white clouds of steam puffing at intervals from underneath the massive, churning drive wheels. The huge engines straightened out, working their way onto the flatter grade as the train started its final approach less than a quarter mile away now. From here Armijo could already see the familiar face of the engineer, grinning broadly as he leaned out of his perch high up on the back of the first black locomotive to wave to him.

As bored as he was of his duties here at times, and as about as far from the real war as a guy could get, Sergeant Armijo never tired of watching these majestic, giant workhorses plowing along. As a small boy, he had loved riding his bicycle down to the big roundhouse at the Raton train yards where the massive engines would roll in and out to be repaired or refueled. He had loved how the earth shook, trembled as they passed through town. Even now he still enjoyed feeling their sheer power surge up through his legs and shudder in his belly.

He allowed the iron and steel monsters to pound their way nearer to him another few yards, then stepped calmly off the tracks to the side at the last minute – the only dangerous thrill he figured he was likely to experience today just like all of the other days.

#

The door adjoining the dining car to the passenger coach suddenly burst open and Ernst charged through. In one fluid motion, he leapt across the cramped passageway, grabbed Otto roughly by the lapels, lifted him half off the floor, and slammed him into the opposite door frame.

"You listen to me, you stupid *Schweinhund*!" he snarled in German, his face just inches from Otto's. "We have only a few more minutes and only one opportunity to do this. So you and I are going to get back there and finish what we have begun, or else I am going to take care of you right here and now!"

As he spoke, Ernst had reached into his jacket, pulled out a pistol, forced the barrel between Otto's lips, and cocked it. The cold metal tasted bitter and acidic and the forward gun-sight raked the inside of his mouth between his cheek and teeth. Otto felt it tear into the tender skin and tasted his own blood. He began to tremble as rage slowly took the place of shock. He reached up, grasped Ernst's hand in both of his, jammed his thumb in front of the pistol's hammer, and slowly but firmly wrenched the barrel out of his mouth.

"You would murder anyone, anywhere – no matter who, wouldn't you? Even me!" Otto shouted, wiping his mouth roughly with the back of his hand. The un-muffled pounding of steel wheels and the whistling wind drowned their voices out.

He rubbed his mouth gingerly, looked at his hand, and pulled out his handkerchief and spat blood into it. "You are insane," he burst out in fury. "Nothing noble or glorious comes from what we do today!"

Ernst stumbled back a step in stunned silence. He turned slowly and glanced toward the dining car and began to smile knowingly. He un-cocked the pistol and put it back into his coat as he began to chuckle.

"Oh, my," he said. "Have you now also grown a pacifist's heart, my old friend, in addition to your cowardice?"

Otto glared back. "Call it what you will," he snarled between clenched teeth, pushing his way quickly past Ernst and reaching for the door handle. "At least I still have a heart."

Ernst grabbed him by the upper arm, stopping him in his tracks, and whispered harshly into his ear. "Heart?" he sniggered. "You forget that I know who you are, my friend – who you really are and what you are really capable of! You remember El Alamein – those Americans at Kasserine Pass, on their knees, weeping, and trying to surrender? I saw you myself, Otto – swimming in the blood of Yankees – walking up behind them, one by one, and putting a bullet in the back of their heads! And now," Ernst scoffed, looking him up and down, "now, look at you!"

He paused for a moment, watching the pallor wash over Otto's face. Otto's eyes grew wider; his mouth moved awkwardly. Images of bleeding and dying American soldiers filled his mind, and he again saw himself back in that miserable desert, holding a smoking pistol in his outstretched hand, the stench of war filling his nostrils.

"No," Otto murmured, shaking his head slightly. "That was mainly you – and that was war – that was orders." He swallowed hard, his eyes still wide and searching the wall and floor beyond Ernst for answers that still weren't there. His hand came up to his mouth and he bit his knuckle in consternation. Had he really done such horrible things?

That was different! Was it not?

Ernst pulled himself even closer to growl into Otto's ear. "And this is still war – and I am still giving you orders – *Herr Leutnant!*" He pushed Otto away from him in disgust, then continued. "I do not know what has happened to you, *Leutnant* Eberhardt, and I do not really care. But I tell you this: if you screw up this mission I will shoot you dead, here, now."

"Mission!" Otto scoffed, jerking his head back to Ernst with a new resolve. "Is that what you still call it – *Herr Oberst?*" He spit out the honorific like it was poison. He jabbed his forefinger into Ernst's chest, hissing, "You know damned well that this war is all but over! You are not the only one who reads the newspapers. Germany is finished – Berlin is burning to the ground, and the Soviets have overrun it all, and Patton's tanks are almost to the outskirts." Otto paused for a second. "And for all we know, Hitler is probably dead!"

Ernst's slap on Otto's face was hard and cut him short. "How dare you speak of *Der Führer* in such a disrespectful manner!" He immediately backhanded Otto on the other cheek and pushed the pistol hard underneath his jaw. "I should shoot you where you stand – for treason!"

Otto's eyes flicked back up to Ernst's. "Go ahead, then," he snapped. "Shoot me – *please!* It would solve both our problems!"

Ernst moved back slowly and glanced back into the dining car.

"Yes," he answered, eyeing Otto again closely and nodding knowingly. "That would be so very easy for you, wouldn't it? It would solve all your problems." He gestured with the pistol toward the door. "But not before I let you watch as I march in there and put a bullet between the eyes of that pretty bitch and her two brats, who you seem to have grown so inexplicably protective of. Then, and only then, I should come back and shove the still hot barrel back into your throat."

Otto glared now at Ernst with pure hatred, but said nothing.

"You know I will do it," Ernst snarled under his breath, grabbing Otto's arm again, "And understand this: I *will* pull the trigger this time." Ernst's voice trailed off as a smirk gathered at the corners of his mouth. "But on the other hand, perhaps you don't get off so easy, for now – Dear. Old. Friend!"

Otto jerked his arm free, then backed away in disgust.

They both stood breathing heavily, glaring into each other's faces.

At that moment, the train's whistle blew three distinct blasts. Otto clenched his fists and with each blast of the whistle felt his rage start to slip away, resigned that there really was not much more he could do. After all, Mrs. Carter and her sons were safe now – hopefully – and he must now remember his place: the war was still officially on, he was still a soldier of the Third Reich, behind enemy lines and still under orders, as awful as they were.

He let his arms fall to his sides. He straightened his clothing, stood erect, but not quite fully at attention, and stared blankly into space. He would continue to do his duty – but he wouldn't like it – and he would never again apologize to Ernst Brandt – for anything. It was small consolation that, in a very short while, they would probably both be dead anyway.

"*Ja wohl, Herr Oberst,*" he said evenly, with no more emotion, and saluted smartly.

Ernst looked at him intensely, nodded with a degree of grudging satisfaction, and glanced at his watch.

"Then it is time, *Leutnant.*" He turned and pulled on the door handle to the next passenger car. In a measured, almost jovial tone, he continued, "Let us go finish this, once and for all, shall we?"

Otto followed him back through the passenger cars, trying very hard not to look into the faces of the other passengers as he had passed their seats. Several were soldiers coming home on leave – some obviously coming home from the war, judging by their hollow eyes, arms in slings, or heads bandaged. He tried not to think of the ironic horror that awaited some of them shortly: to die just when they thought they had escaped Death's clutches on the battlefronts of Europe and the Pacific.

Finally, back at their seats at the rear of the last coach, Otto sat down, dutifully reached under his seat, and slid the bag out where he could get at it. He reached cautiously inside to begin work on the bomb inside. He cursed the day he had learned to make bombs and cursed even more that he had become so expert at it, which he was convinced was the only reason Ernst had kept him alive up until now. He glanced up one more time at all the men and women in their seats in front of him.

If he survived these next few minutes, he prayed to God he would never see any of their faces – any of them – in his nightmares.

#

The huge locomotives picked up a perceptible amount of speed as they dragged their cars through the final curve and settled down onto the relatively flat meadow and straight rails. They were now only about 75 yards from the mouth of the tunnel, and the chugga-chugga of the steam escaping in rhythmic bursts from their huge boilers began to pick up in tempo. Dark coal-fired smoke billowed in inky clouds from the smokestacks and trailed away along the right side of the train, partially obscuring the cars. A couple more loud blasts on the steam whistle with a final wave and tip of the hat from the engineer, and the lead locomotive plowed into the dark entrance of the tunnel at about twenty miles an hour.

Sergeant Armijo and the other guards all took an involuntary step back as hot air belched out of the tunnel, displaced by the bulk of the locomotive as it inserted itself forcefully into its narrow confines. The second locomotive followed almost immediately. The guardsmen now watched as the various cars slid by, just a few feet from their upturned faces, with rhythmic clackety-clacks from wheels against the tracks – steel against steel: the baggage car, the mail car, two Pullman cars, the dining car, and finally, the first of three passenger coaches, all with the faces of laughing and waving passengers, some hanging out of the windows, some calling out to the soldiers. Sergeant Armijo smiled and waved back.

#

Twelve-year-old Walter Carter sat at a table on the left side of the dining car with his mother and little brother and stared out the window while absently gnawing on a fried chicken leg. His little brother Timmy sat next to him slurping vanilla ice cream from a large spoon.

"Oh, darn it!" Walter's mother exclaimed under her breath from across the table. She had been searching the seat next to her and glancing under the table. She now looked up and dropped her hands resignedly in her lap.

"What's wrong, Mom?" Walter asked, talking around a mouthful of chicken. His mother looked over at him and gave him a tired smile.

"I think I left my purse in the other car – under our seats." She reached over and picked up the dinner check the waiter had just left on the edge of the table. She sighed, dabbed her mouth with her napkin, and pushed at her hair. "Guess I'll just have to go get it. You boys wait right here." She began to stand up.

"Want me to go get it, Mama?" Walter asked. He was bored again and ready for a small adventure. His mother hesitated, glanced over at Timmy, and then down the aisle at the waiter.

"No," she replied cautiously. "No, I'll go, Sweetie. But thank you for offering." She reached over and patted his hand. "It'll only take me a minute. And besides, you're the man of the house while your daddy's away, remember? And I need you to stay here and keep a good eye on your little brother!"

She stood up, self-consciously smoothed her dress, and touched her hair once more. "I'll just have to explain to the waiter on my way out."

"I wanna go!" exclaimed Timmy. His spoon clattered noisily on the table as he jumped up from his seat. The waiter looked up the aisle in their direction with a frown.

"No, Honey – you just wait here with your big brother like I said. Besides, you haven't finished your ice cream. I'll be right back – I promise!"

"Ah, geez," moaned Timmy, slumping back into his seat, pouting and folding his arms dejectedly.

"Walter, you watch him close, now – okay?"

Walter and Timmy scowled at each other.

"Walter – I'm speaking to you, and I want an answer…"

"Okay," he muttered.

"That was, 'Yes – What?'"

Walter squirmed. "Yes, Ma'am," he muttered, finally.

His mother smiled at him again, blew him a kiss, turned, and walked away. Walter thought that his mother was the prettiest lady he'd ever seen, and when she smiled she was even prettier, if that was possible. She stopped at the end of the dining car and spoke briefly to the waiter. Walter watched her gesture toward the doorway, then back in their direction. The waiter nodded at her and opened the door for her. She paused for a moment, caught Walter's eye, waved goodbye, and disappeared out the door.

The dining car lurched suddenly, and Walter turned back to look out the window. From here, he could see that the train had entered a long curve. Up ahead, he could now actually see the two black locomotives angrily churning and belching smoke, struggling their way out of the trees onto a flat meadow. He excitedly tugged on his little brother's jacket.

"Look, Timmy! You can see the engines!"

Timmy got on his knees and scooted over the bench to crowd in next to his brother at the window.

"Wow!" he exclaimed.

Walter's eyes quickly grew wider with amazement as he saw the black hole of the tunnel in the near distance and the mass of rock and grass on the side of the mountain that loomed overhead. He realized excitedly that the train was crawling straight toward it. Men were milling about the tunnel entrance and along the tracks in front, and he suddenly realized they were in uniforms and carrying slung rifles.

"Oh look, Timmy! Soldiers! Just like Daddy!"

#

Otto took a couple of deep slow breaths and carefully felt around for the detonator cap that he had just pushed deeply into the explosive compounds. He gingerly located the timing ridges on the cap and counted them off. Next, he pushed a crimping tool onto the correct ridge, took another deep breath, and held it. The thought crossed his mind that he might accidently set the thing off now while he was arming it. Sweat poured from his forehead into his eyes; he stifled an involuntary shudder.

He closed his eyes tight and squeezed the pliers slowly until he felt the rod crimp. He inhaled sharply, waited a few seconds, and slowly opened his eyes.

He was still alive.

They had only minutes now. Otto carefully closed up the bag, eased it back under his seat, and stood up and straightened his cap and jacket. Ernst already had his hand on the exit door. They glanced around the coach one more time. No one seemed to be paying them any attention. Ernst nodded to Otto and opened the door, and they both went out to the noisy platform that connected their coach to the observation car. Here, they paused for just a moment to see if anyone else was coming their way from the next car. Determining they were alone, they each turned to the side exit doors opposite each other and slid them open. Two more sharp blasts sounded from the train whistles, and from out here, they were so loud that Otto's ears ached. The wind gusted through and he braced himself against the doorframe with his hands while looking down at the railroad ties flying past three feet below him. Beyond that, the rail bed fell away precipitously. He briefly wondered what he would do if he broke a leg. In any event, he decided broken bones – or anything, for that matter – would be better than being blown to pieces.

Or would it?

He counted to three, held his breath, and jumped.

#

The mail car had barely entered the tunnel when Sergeant Armijo saw something out of the corner of his eye. He looked toward the rear of the train and did a double take as he saw a tall man – dressed in dungarees, denim jacket, and a leather cap, shrouded by dissipating black smoke – rise up slowly like a wraith from out of the tall grass within feet of the moving train. Armijo was almost positive the man had just jumped from the train. At first he couldn't quite believe his eyes, but as the passenger coaches drew nearer, he could, for sure, see the door to the last one was swinging wide open. The two men stared at one another seconds before the strange man calmly pulled a pistol out of his jacket and started walking steadily toward Armijo. From here, Alberto thought incredulously that the man had an oddly troubling grin on his face.

"You there! Stop!" Armijo shouted as he fumbled with his own sidearm, trying to get the holster flap unsnapped. The man continued toward him and now raised his pistol as he came. Armijo also stepped forward as he finally got the flap undone. He had his pistol half out of the holster when he saw a puff of smoke spit soundlessly from out of the advancing stranger's weapon, followed a second or two later by a loud pop, halfway drowned out by the clattering of the train. Armijo could hardly believe it: the man was actually firing at him from over seventy yards away, an incredible and hardly accurate distance. He still felt adrenaline kick in and felt that he must be dreaming.

Armijo heard a soft sound -- a sort of thud – to his left, followed by what sounded like a sigh, and then another delayed pop of the man's handgun. He stumbled backwards now, incredulous, and turned to the guard on his left, and gasped in horror at what he saw: the private standing very still, one hand frozen on the stock of his still-slung rifle on his shoulder, staring straight ahead with a face filled with shock. A small dark hole had blossomed in the exact center of the soldier's throat out of which a steady stream of dark maroon blood began to pulse. The soldier gurgled, dropped his rifle, grabbed his throat with both hands, and began to slump.

Armijo found himself reaching a hand toward him, as if to help him, but the guard had crumpled to the ground in a lifeless heap.

Armijo immediately felt something buzz angrily within inches of his ear, heard another delayed *pop,* and then simultaneously heard the bullet splat and whack and ricochet behind him, off of the concrete wall of the tunnel. He turned his head and his gun arm simultaneously toward the stranger who had now advanced to within twenty yards of him. The attacker's gun arm was still outstretched and he was tightening his finger for another shot. Armijo's big semi-automatic .45 bucked in his hand has he fired twice in quick succession, but the shots were not well aimed and went wild. He found himself watching the entire scene unfold as if he was a non-participant, everything starting to move in slow motion. He stumbled backwards again, fired a third time, and watched incredulously as he saw his own bullet blow off the bottom of the attacker's ear. The man flinched, stopped walking, touched his ear, and just frowned down at the blood on his fingers. He slowly raised his eyes up to Armijo's – and again smiled.

A deep chill shuddered through Armijo: he suddenly felt that he was facing the devil himself. He instinctively dropped into a shooter's crouch and now concentrated hard on aiming the forward sight of his pistol against the center mass of the man's chest as he had trained for so many times on the practice range. Everything around him continued to move in extreme slow motion – as if minutes and not seconds had passed since the attack had begun.

The observation car entered the tunnel and the caboose was now moving past the sergeant. His feet were spread wide apart as he crouched lower and fired a fifth, sixth, and seventh time in quick succession. He thought he heard someone screaming long and hard – almost like a warrior's angry cry of rage intermingled with fear – and was immediately shocked to realize the person screaming was himself.

Alberto, as if in a trance, watched with a certain thrill as a puff of dust and blood leapt from the stranger's left shoulder as one of his bullets finally struck home. The man stumbled once, almost fell, but quickly straightened up and kept coming and firing back in rapid succession at Alberto – one, two, three more shots. Armijo fired twice more and gasped as he felt something slam into his chest like a sledgehammer. His eyes blurred; he lost his senses for a few moments. When he came back to himself, he found he was on the ground, his legs splayed out in front of him. His breath had been knocked completely out of him, but he still didn't understand what the hell had just happened. He felt a warmth and numbness spread through him – then, an inexplicable peace. He stared down at his gun arm, which was still outstretched and locked in firing position, but he found he was suddenly unsure what he was supposed to do with it. He looked down at his shirt and was surprised to see a stain blossom and grow there, the tan color of the uniform shirt slowly blooming into a beautiful, red flower. He felt himself laugh once because it struck him as rather ludicrous that he couldn't identify what had happened – but he knew something was terribly wrong.

Armijo felt a shadow pass over him and became aware of someone standing off to his left. He turned and saw a man silhouetted against the final light of the sunset and hovering over him. He could see that the man's left arm dangled helplessly and blood dripped from his fingertips onto Alberto's boot. The attacker's other hand held a pistol loosely at his side – and the man still smiled that devil's smile. Armijo stared with his mouth wide, tried to form some words, but was not exactly sure what he needed to say. He was suddenly very tired and his own pistol felt extremely heavy, so he let his own gun arm drop. Somewhere in his fog, he realized the other man was now speaking to him.

"What is your name, soldier?"

"Wha-what?" Alberto muttered, confused. The man spoke in a strange accent and Alberto tried very hard to focus on his assailant's face above him, but everything was an increasing blur.

"I suppose it doesn't matter," the gunman said, matter-of-factly as he slowly, deliberately, raised his pistol until all Alberto Armijo could see was the large black hole of the barrel pointed at his face.

All he knew to do now was to pray as he waited for the inevitable impact of the bullet that would end his life.

#

Walter continued to gaze in fascination as the train cars entered the tunnel, one after another. He had lowered the window so that they could hang out for a better view.

"Woo-hoo!" he crowed into the wind as it whipped through his hair.

The black maw of the tunnel grew larger as their car drew closer, and Timmy suddenly whimpered and jumped back down, then out of the seat.

"Timmy – come back here!"

"I want Mama!"

Walter scooted out of the booth and started after his little brother who had run to the rear of the dining car and was now shoving at the door, which wouldn't yield to his weak efforts. The doors suddenly opened wide, as if of their own accord, and an elderly couple came through from the passenger cars. Timmy darted between them and disappeared out the door.

"Oh, geez," muttered Walter. He had stopped in his pursuit halfway through the car when it had appeared that his brother would not get through the door. He now scowled at the slowly closing doors.

"Well, phooey on you then!" he groused after his brother and flopped back into the seat just as the dining car went entirely dark.

The dining car had finally entered the tunnel and it took a minute for the staff to find the light switches. Finally, enough yellow light spilled through the car, and everyone chuckled appreciatively before going back to their conversations and meals.

Walter sat and fumed for a few more seconds, then decided he had better go find his little brother. After all, his mother had put him in charge.

He stood up and started back down the aisle, reached out his hand, pushed open the door, and stepped out onto the clattering platform between the cars.

At that moment, something tremendous and inexplicable happened: Walter felt himself tumbling wildly, his arms and legs flailing about in thin air that was filled suddenly with a horrific flash of brilliant light, followed immediately by total darkness, along with an indescribable vacuum and sudden absence of sound as his eardrums shattered.

Then there was nothing.

#

Otto had hit the ground and rolled several times down the cinder embankment. He had skinned his hands and knees and had finally stopped in some high grass where he lay as still as he could, almost in a fetal position with his arms clasping his head, and waited. He listened as the train clattered on just above him and suddenly heard gunshots popping in the distance. He opened his eyes and raised his head a little. He next heard what sounded like footsteps running his way, getting louder and nearer. He desperately felt under his coat for the pistol he knew was there, but couldn't find it. He must've lost it in the jump.

He looked up again in a panic and could now see someone about ten feet away. One of the soldiers guarding the tunnel was trotting toward Otto's hiding place while slipping his rifle from his shoulder. *Had the guard seen me?* he wondered. *No – not yet! He was not even looking this way!* The guard had slowed his run and ducked down to peer underneath the passing train cars at the commotion on the other side. Otto dropped back down and thought quickly. The soldier had now crept to within three feet of his position, still searching underneath the moving train.

If he turned, he would see Otto immediately.

Otto's instincts kicked in. He needed to strike first. He took a deep breath, pulled himself into a crouch, then pounced onto the soldier's back.

He kicked him hard in the kidney with his knee, wrapped his strong forearms around his neck, and squeezed. The guard had had a precarious grip on his rifle that now flew out of his hands as he began to fall forward to the ground. Otto held on tightly, riding the guard's back all the way down. He felt the man's head hit the ground hard and saw his helmet flying off. Otto pushed the man's face into the rocks and dirt, his forearm digging hard into his throat. The soldier bucked and squirmed and screamed mutely into the dirt, his hands scrabbling like claws at Otto's arms. Otto clenched his teeth and pushed his other forearm harder against the back of the man's head and squeezed tighter and tighter, until slowly the guard ceased to struggle. Otto could feel the muscles in the man's throat constricting violently and his jaws and chin flexing against his arm. Somewhere in the distance, he heard shots, shouting, followed by the sound of a long, drawn out scream and even more shots being fired. But Otto didn't allow himself to be distracted and stayed focused on his grisly work.

In reality, less than sixty seconds had passed since Otto had jumped from the train, but that had seemed like an eternity. He was suddenly aware that the noise of the train was receding as its final cars entered the tunnel. He continued to squeeze the guard tightly while allowing himself to glance up to see the caboose disappear into the tunnel, about forty yards ahead. He then looked over to see a strange and terrible sight – Ernst was standing a few yards to the right of the tunnel. His face and left arm was dripping in blood, and he was grinning like a madman. He was pointing his pistol toward a soldier sitting there on the ground with his legs stretched out before him, his head bowed down, and the entire front of his shirt soaked with blood. Otto watched, mesmerized.

The soldier beneath Otto suddenly stirred, gave a huge grunt, and elbowed Otto hard in the ribs, breaking his grip. The soldier heaved up, twisted his body, and threw Otto onto the ground. Before Otto could react, the man rolled on top of him and then grabbed his throat with both hands and began to squeeze. Now, it was Otto's turn to kick and buck, and he stretched out his arms to try and find his enemy's neck. His fingers finally found purchase and he dug his thumbs hard into the American's throat. They struggled together, choking the very life out of one another as hard as they could, heaving and twisting, their hands like vices, their faces turning blue.

Otto's lungs began to burn, desperate for air. He slowly felt a darkness swim over his vision. He could not tell if it was the deepening dusk or if he was passing out, but either way he knew he would not be able to hold on much longer.

An instant later, it no longer mattered. The American disappeared completely. Otto felt a huge pressure wave suddenly wash around him; the earth itself moved; and the hand of God picked him up completely off the ground and tossed him upwards and sideways through the air, torn, and tumbled like a small stuffed doll as something horrific and inexplicable happened.

#

Alberto Armijo also felt something tremendous and inexplicable happen: all the sounds and understanding of his world instantly and totally ceased. A tremendous pressure filled his ears with a vacuum, the man pointing the gun was jerked impossibly backwards, away from Alberto, and he felt the earth he sat on suddenly rise up several feet. He felt himself become airborne, flipped end over end, and finally ripped apart within some sort of terrible finality; an inferno of heat and dust, concrete and metal, and fire and flesh.

The very last thought, in fact, Sergeant Alberto Armijo had before everything went soothingly dark was a very odd question: *Where was the gunman with the idiotic grin?*

His world went forever dark before he ever knew the answer.

CHAPTER 11
HONOR THY CHILDREN

A double blast of a locomotive's air horns echoed up from the train depot below in the distance, a couple of miles away from Trent's house, and bounced off of the mesas and canyons around him as he sat on his back deck.

He had closed his eyes and breathed in the clean, crisp, fall mountain air, and now opened them again. He took a long sip of bourbon and looked out across his property: ten acres of low sagebrush and cedar trees sloped away below. Further on, the old railroad and mining town of Raton nestled into the foothills of the Sangre de Cristo Mountains.

He usually loved this time of day with the distant noises of a relatively peaceful community drifting up to him and settling down for the evening – of dogs barking and children laughing and playing after school; car doors slamming as parents returned home after work; the muted hum of diesel engines and the rhythmic clanking of steel rails as the Amtrak arrived and departed from the old train station, still in operation after 140 years; and the distant whir of semis and cars as they made their way north, south, east, and west on the various highways that utilized the small town as a crossroads..

Living out here, far enough away from town where he had no close neighbors, he could usually unwind and watch as the emerging parade of brilliant cumulonimbus clouds marched daily across panoramic skies, the best entertainment on earth, so far as he was concerned. Lately, though, this colorful dance of the clouds had seemed to draw someone, or something, else out of the shadows – out of his subconscious, perhaps. Either way, he waited anxiously to see if the magic would conjure up something more ethereal again this evening.

And he waited.

He felt sure she would come. But then again, what if she didn't? He felt himself tensing up. What if he was too keyed up and anxious? After all, hadn't she only appeared to him when he was least expecting her?

He really needed for that magic to work – right now. Inside the house, he knew he had a drawer full of prescription pain meds, which he had foregone months ago for fear of becoming addicted to them.

Addicted, he snorted to himself over the rim of his glass. Seems he was now in jeopardy of trading one addiction for another, but right now the numbness of the alcohol had yet to kick in. Every part of his body seemed to hurt today – his hip, knees, and neck ached, his lower back had tightened up, arthritis flared in his fingers – and his head throbbed fiercely, right behind the scar high on his forehead. He didn't want to dwell tonight on these aching injuries, which, at his age, seemed to be taking an inordinate amount of time to heal up. His therapist, a pushy, no-nonsense, retired Marine sergeant who had served two tours in Afghanistan, had told Trent he could, at best, help him to get back about 75% use of his leg, and to expect his lower back to continue to seize up on him a good deal of the time, as well as to expect, perhaps, additional surgeries. A real sweetheart of an optimist he was.

His neurologist, on the other hand, sounded a little more encouraging. According to her, his recovery from his head injuries had been remarkable, but Trent wasn't sure he agreed. He still suffered from short-term memory loss and, at the most inopportune times, had trouble remembering certain simple words or phrases, which often got him in trouble. .

Getting back to work was helping him refocus on a routine – retraining his thought processes. But tonight he didn't want to think about work – not the skeletal remains unearthed beneath the theater nor the break-in at the Van Ryan place nor some old German's musty, yellowed journal nor the stacks of unsolved case files boxed in his office nor Brad Ferguson's constantly dour disposition.

And tonight, he didn't even want to think about Maggie's undisguised attempts to seduce him. The fact that he had found himself tempted by her flirtations only made him more determined than ever to stay clear of Margot Van Ryan. For the truth of the matter was that Trent was no longer sure he was in control of his own emotional, or even mental, stability, especially where matters of the heart were concerned.

No, tonight, all Trent could think about were these visits from his dead wife.

He pinched his eyes, drained the amber liquor in his glass, reached over to the redwood table beside him, and picked up the bottle he had just opened.

Trent had never remotely believed in ghosts, spirits, hovering angelic beings, little green men, Ouija boards, or things that go bump in the night; he had always looked askance at anyone who had ever claimed to see these apparitions. But now, and for whatever reason, he was experiencing just such visitations – *and not by just any old chain-rattler*, he murmured out loud to whomever might be listening, but by the shade of that most precious one who had always known him better than he had ever known himself; that one who had always loved him unconditionally and had unwaveringly, and often irritatingly, forced him to look into the shadows of his own soul and identify for himself the deficiencies lying there that needed attention and correction; the only one who could get away with such criticism; and what's more, the one whose haunting visits he now actually craved.

God help me, he moaned under his breath. *I'm falling in love with a damn ghost.*

He froze, suddenly catching a fragrance on the evening breeze – the smoky, sweet scent of wild roses and clove – Vicky's signature scent – and that seemed now to be the harbinger of her arrivals.

"So – are you going to sit out here all evening, guzzling that poison?"

Vicky – or that which looked a lot like Vicky – had come up behind him quietly, as usual, her voice slow, languid, husky – and had begun softly, tenderly twirling her finger around that stray lock of hair that grew untamed from his double crown. She had begun this endearing action early on in their relationship, but later the gesture had only irritated him.

"I grew tired of waiting," he muttered under his breath, twisting his head away from her like a restless child, "and so I started without you." He casually picked up his tumbler and took a long gulp.

She slid smoothly and silently around his chair, trailing the backs of her fingers along his upper arm, raising goose bumps in their path, floated over to lean on the deck railing with her forearms, and gazed out toward the fiery mesas.

"Still so breathtakingly beautiful," she murmured. The voice he was hearing was definitely Vicky's, but her manner of speaking was otherworldly – her words flowed in a peaceful, drawn-out drawl that washed over his very soul and soothed the jagged edges of his conflicted thoughts immediately, and yet a bit unnerving in her measured delivery.

"Y – Yes," he stuttered. "Yes, truly."

Trent slumped deeper into his chair, scarcely daring to move, watching her – remembering her – allowing his eyes at last to drift from her flowing hair to her neck, down along her slim back to the attractive curve of her backside, then on past the flair of the well worn, blue flowered dress he had always loved to see her in – the one she had been wearing when she died. The hem ended just above that cute crease behind her knee. She had lifted the shapely calf of one leg, which slimmed seductively toward her ankle, and had poised it so that her sandal dangled precariously off the ball of her foot. She was humming softly – the same familiar song again – *her* song. He knew that every gesture, every tone of voice, was all a practiced pose calculated to fill him with an aching desire.

"O, whatever became of the one that I love…" she sang softly, but then hesitated, looking back over her shoulder at him. "What made you write such a sad, sad song?"

He swallowed hard, unable to speak, but remained still. He was determined to remain calm and composed this time. Even so, he couldn't help but allow his gaze to roam again to her light brown, shoulder length hair wafting in the warm breeze in concert with the movements of the sagebrush in the field beyond.

"You missed me, even a little?" her voice purred, as if honey had coated her throat. Her back was still turned to him, but she had cocked her head and rested her chin against her shoulder and he could see that her downturned brown eyes were lidded, almost hidden in the waning light, as if she could not – or would not – meet his eyes.

"You know," he paused for air, "that I have," he said, the words coming out in an uneven, ragged stammer.

"You know what else, too, don't you?" she purred.

"No," he paused again, trying to catch his breath. "No, what else?"

"Of course, you do," she teased softly, now turning a bit more of her profile toward him. "You know there are things that remain to be said between us." He caught his breath suddenly at the innocent, coquettish beauty that he had so often missed about her face. Her mouth dimpled at the corners as she noticed his reaction. He was finding it extremely difficult to breathe, much less to answer her.

"Like – what things?"

"You see there? Just like that," she continued, turning completely around now, facing him. "Things that we both know you don't want to see. Things that you always refuse to acknowledge or maybe even comprehend." She spoke slowly, carefully enunciating her words, her eyes bold and serious now.

Trent visibly shook as he tore his eyes away and desperately sloshed more whisky into his glass.

"I think you'd like me to go away," she said assuredly, leaning back on the rail on her elbows, "wouldn't you?"

He felt that she was toying with him, but she wore a terribly sad expression on her face.

"Oh, Lord, no," he breathed, transfixed on her. The liquor spilled onto his pants leg as his hand shook.

"Sometimes, I think I am a nuisance to you."

"Infuriating, yes – a nuisance, no!" Trent drained the remainder of his glass in one gulp, no longer tasting the burning liquid that did little to bolster his bravado. "But you really enjoy seeing me uncomfortable; I've no doubt about that."

Her face became strangely shadowed, her eyes harder to see. Perhaps, the effect was only the quickening dusk, for he could still make out her dimpled smile. As she leaned in nearer, he caught her smoky fragrance, more intoxicating than any liquor. Trent's head began to swim as she moved even nearer and bent her face close to his. Her hair tickled his neck.

"No, Darling," Vicky breathed, her scent flooding his nostrils, "never that." He almost fainted as her cool lips brushed his cheek and stopped near his left ear, an ethereal chill crawling down his spine as she continued. He felt the panic rise and wanted to kick the chair over and run blindly away, but his body refused to obey the impulse.

"Victoria – I – I'm not myself anymore. So much is so wrong with me – confused…" His voice trailed off hoarsely.

"Shhh, Trenny, I know," she hushed into his ear. "But you must listen to me, my Love."

Trent suddenly felt weightless as if they both were now floating just above the deck. He dared not look down.

"Surely, you understand that I am trying to help you," she continued in her measured, alien speech pattern. "Help you with your battle."

"Battle?" Trent could barely breathe.

"You are embarking too quickly down a dangerous path, Dearest One, a path that could very well destroy you, but one that I also know I cannot dissuade you of." She paused, pulled her hair back, an endearing but somehow disturbing gesture that filled him with longing – and pain – but kept her shadowed face only inches away from his.

"So, if I cannot dissuade you," she continued, "I must try my best to convince you to use extreme caution." Her breath softly caressed the tender flesh under his lower eyelid. Trent was swooning.

"You know of what," she paused while leaning closer, "and of whom," she now whispered, "I speak."

Vicky's mouth barely touched his lower lip – so very light and gentle. It was the most sensuous kiss he had ever experienced. "My Love," he tasted the breath of her words now, "there are terrible dangers for you – both in your world," she paused for the briefest moment, "and in mine." Her lips now moved to his ear and he trembled uncontrollably.

"Above all else, my Darling One," she barely whispered on the breeze, "you must remember that *none of this is as it seems.*"

Trent's entire body twitched in his chair with a gasp and he was suddenly fully alert. His empty glass fell from his drooping hand and shattered on the deck, throwing shards everywhere. He leapt from his chair.

Vicky was gone.

"Wait," he pleaded suddenly. "Come back!" His heart thumped wildly; his lungs gasped for oxygen as he stared and searched around him.

The glass door of the kitchen slid open and Sophie, wiping her hands on a dishtowel, stuck her head out. The aroma of simmering meat sauce and onions escaped around her and quickly drove away the haunting scent of clove and roses.

"Say, what's all the racket out here? You okay?" Sophie looked back and forth along the deck. "Who were you talking to, Dad? Somebody here?"

At the sound of his daughter's voice, he shuddered; he shrugged and didn't answer.

"Well, supper's almost ready," she said, then went back inside after looking again in the yard and then back at him and shut the door.

Trent took a step, but stopped when he felt glass crunch under his boot. He looked anxiously around the deck and the yard below, all the way to the line of cedar trees.

Vicky was no longer there at all.

He knew that.

But still, he looked again.

#

The storms came again that night, which was good because the patter of rain on the roof and windows had helped Trent to finally fall asleep, but was also not so good because the nightmare tormented him worse than ever these nights:

A horn blares in the distance, urging him to do something. He tries to claw himself out of the white, swirling mist. He feels disembodied, but finds he can only move sluggishly. And there is something else, something that doesn't seem quite right; something that is terribly wrong. He feels he has missed it, something important that he needs to know. But whatever it is, he knows that he is still alive and has managed to survive – something – whatever it was he survived – and that his next concern is to find her again – find Vicky – because only she can tell him. But there is that damned noise again!

The beeping grows louder and even more insistent, taking on a life of its own, each blast reaching out like a fist and punching him on the side of head, rhythmically harder and harder, then seeming to come from within his head, right behind his eyes, until he can take no more. He tries to escape. Part of him wants to run far away, but another part wants to stay and find – who? What?

He can no longer remember. But it doesn't matter – he can't move at all. Instead, he screams, and then screams some more – again, and again – but no sound comes out of his mouth. And then the screams morph into the intrusive blaring of a nearby rhythmically bleating horn.

#

"You okay?"

Trent jerked awake, feeling a cool hand on his forehead. *Was it she?* A bright light was to his right and a loud incessant beeping coming from the same area. He could just make out a woman's head silhouetted within the light; her fingers reached over and pushed a button on top of the clock radio, and, blissfully, the beeping was silenced.

"Daddy, are you okay?"

Sophie leaned over and came into view, and gently stroked his forehead again.

"You were having another nightmare."

Trent sat up in the bed and looked around. He was back in his own room, his own bed. The light was coming from the bedside lamp that Sophie had switched on. He heard purring and looked to his left to see Jarhead stretching and yawning on the pillow next to him. He looked back around the room.

"Where is she?"

"Who, Daddy – where is who?"

Trent sat up and searched the room again. "Vicky." He pressed the heels of his hands to his eyes. "Your mother," he continued groggily. "Where'd she go?"

"You were dreaming about her again – is that why you called her name out?"

"She was just here," he mumbled, but looked around. Then he paused and rubbed his face again, realizing with sudden embarrassment what he was saying. He whipped the covers off, swiveled his legs around, and sat on the edge of the bed, steadying himself. "It was awful," he said finally, a little more awake. He looked away from his daughter in shame. "I'm really getting tired of all this."

"Daddy …" Sophie let her voice trail off. "Dad – Mom's not here. You know that, don't you?" She examined his face more closely, her brows furrowed.

He looked up at her blankly. "What are you doing here, anyway? Did I wake you?"

"Well – yeah," she paused. "I could hear you from my room. I always do. But this time you sounded really, you know, scared?"

His knee touched hers where she was sitting in the chair she had pulled up beside the bed. He glanced back over to the bedside table and spied an empty bottle next to the clock. A beat up old book was lying open there, face down. It looked familiar. Sophie must have been sitting there reading while he slept. He looked back at his daughter. He could see she had not slept well with dark circles clearly visible under her eyes, also red rimmed. He reached over and lifted her chin.

"You've been crying." he said softly.

She sniffed, wiped her nose on a tissue she had wadded in her hand, and looked up at him. "Yeah, well, maybe – a little."

"Why?"

She shrugged. "Not sure." She paused. "Maybe because I'm scared, too."

"Scared of what, Baby?" He reached up and traced her cheek with the back of his finger.

"I dunno – maybe just scared for you."

"Why, Sweet Pea?"

"You've been doing a lot of scary things lately, Daddy."

"Like what?"

Sophie shrugged again, tilted her head sideways until it gently trapped his hand between her cheek and her shoulder. Her misty eyes turned up to gaze at his. She was his little girl again.

"The drinking," she paused, "your nightmares," she continued. "Those other – you know – *things*."

Trent hesitated. "What other 'things?'"

"Well, like I said. I've overheard you – talking to Mom," she said, finally.

Trent looked away and was quiet. Sophie took a deep breath and continued.

"Dad – I mean, you act like she's really there – like she's telling you things, and asking you things. And, well – Daddy, you're answering her!" Sophie raised her head and wiped her eyes, waiting for her father to speak. "Aren't you going to say anything?"

Trent glanced at her face, smiled weakly, opened his mouth to speak, but then shrugged, so Sophie continued. "I mean, you go to work early, I don't see you till late in the evening, and then you go straight out there on that deck and sit there for hours with a bottle, mumbling and swearing, and – having conversations with – with my dead mother!"

"I – really don't know what to say," he finally stammered. His head was throbbing, and he suddenly needed coffee – or even a drink.

Sophie shook her head but continued insistently, "Well – at least saying *that* is saying *something*. I mean, you never talk to me about any of it." She paused. "And that really hurts me, Dad, because I really want to help you. I really, really do!"

"And I'm really, really trying here, Sofe," he said, using the nickname he had always called her since she was little. "But if I don't tell you anything, it's only because I'm not sure of anything right now! How do I talk to anybody about something when I don't even know the difference anymore myself?"

"The difference? Between what?"

Trent swallowed hard. He shook his head, then stood up shakily, rubbed his face, and stumbled toward the hallway.

"Dad, where are you going?"

"I need something to drink."

Sophie jumped up and followed him. "Dad, you don't need something to drink!" she pleaded with him and called out after him, "not at six o'clock in the damned morning!"

Trent wandered into the dining room and opened the hutch. No whiskey. He went on into the kitchen and opened a cupboard where he kept extra bottles. This shelf was also empty.

"Where is it?" he demanded.

"Dad, tell me the difference," she called from the other room.

"What? What difference?"

"The difference you were just talking about – you know …" She had followed him into the kitchen now, sat down at the table, and pulled her robe around her. Trent stalked around the kitchen, opening cabinets and drawers, the utility closet, looking under the sink, under dishtowels, in the dishwasher.

Sophie reached out and patted the chair next to hers. "Daddy, come sit down."

"Where is it?" he growled through clenched teeth.

She hesitated and squared her shoulders.

"Daddy, I – I dumped it out, okay?"

Trent stopped roaming the room and turned to stare at her in disbelief.

"You what?"

"It's all gone, Dad, so you can yell at me all you want. Guess that's what I'm here for, too – if it gets your attention!"

Trent stood motionless for a couple of minutes, licking his lips. He rubbed his face again, put one hand on his hip, and with the other, wagged his finger in his daughter's direction.

"You poured out three liters of Maker's Mark?" he asked, incredulous. Sophie shrugged.

"Guess that means it was the expensive stuff," she quipped, but when he didn't smile she looked up at him defiantly. "And it was four bottles, by the way. I found the one you had hidden in your bathroom, too."

Trent rubbed his forehead for a moment. "I forgot about that one," he mumbled to himself, then looked at her again. "But you didn't have any right to do that," he said, much quieter. He leaned on the counter, wiped his mouth with the back of his hand, and began to say something else, but then stopped suddenly.

Sophie was laughing.

"What's so damned funny?" he demanded.

"You should see yourself," she snorted and then put a hand over her mouth to stifle the laughter. "I mean, how am I supposed to take you seriously?" She pointed at him.

Trent looked down and surveyed himself: he realized he was standing, dressed only in his underwear, in the middle of the kitchen floor. He looked up again and glared at his daughter, who was now convulsed in laughter and could hardly contain herself.

"I mean seriously," she guffawed, "I'm being chewed out in the middle of the kitchen by an old man in his 'wife beater' undershirt and 'tighty whities!'"

Trent turned beet red. Jarhead had wandered into the kitchen, evidently to see what all the fuss was about, and was now rubbing himself back and forth against his master's bare legs, purring loudly. No matter the ruckus, to Jarhead it was time to be fed. Seeing that, Sophie lost all composure and dropped her head into her arms, slapping the table with one hand as laughter consumed her. "I feel like I'm in a movie," she gasped, "a really bad comedy!"

Trent spluttered for a second, pushed himself away from the counter, and stomped out of the kitchen, his bare feet making slapping noises as he disappeared down the hallway toward his bedroom where he slammed the door behind him.

A little later, the phone rang. From his bedroom, Trent heard Sophie answer it and could hear her speak indistinctly for a few minutes. Soon, she knocked lightly on his bedroom door.

"Come in," he said softly. Sophie opened the door and walked in carrying two steaming mugs of coffee.

Trent had dressed in jeans and a clean t-shirt and was sitting in the chair she had sat in earlier. He was trying to read the old book that had been lying on his table. Sophie walked slowly over and sat on the edge of the bed, their knees once again touching, but now their positions reversed. She handed him the coffee, which he took and sipped gratefully. He then looked at her over the rim of his cup and smiled, and she smiled back over her cup.

"It was really nice to laugh," she said with a slight giggle. "I haven't laughed like that in a long time." Trent nodded and grunted.

"Well, I'm so happy to oblige," he said. "Glad to know I'm at least good for something around here." He sipped more coffee. "By the way, who was that on the phone?"

"Oh yeah – Grampa Walter," she answered.

Trent let a brief grimace cross his face, then thought better of it. But it was too late – she had seen it.

"Now, Dad – don't be that way."

"What way?"

"You know what way – about Grampa."

"He's grumpy."

She chuckled. "And you're not?"

Trent snorted and blew at his coffee to cool the next sip. He had not been on the best terms with his father for a long while now.

"So what's Walter want, anyway?"

"*Grampa* Walter wants you to come out and talk to him. He said he's got something he thinks you'd be interested in hearing."

"Like what?"

"He wouldn't tell me. But he did say he might have something important to tell you – something that might have to do with a case you're working on?"

"Can't imagine what that could possibly be – or how he would even know about it."

"Well, just go see him, okay? When's the last time you saw him?"

"I called him on his birthday."

"That's not what I asked, Dad – when did you last go over to the nursing home and visit face to face?"

Trent really couldn't remember. He searched his memory. Had he been out there at all since the accident? *That would've made it almost two years,* he thought.

"Can't really recall," he answered, sheepishly. Sophie shook her head at him.

"Well, then I think it's way past time we went out for a visit, don't you?"

Trent grimaced again, then held up the book. "You were reading this old journal?" he asked.

"Don't try and change the subject," she said.

"You know it's in German, don't you?"

She rolled her eyes and answered. "Yes, don't you remember I minored in German in college?" She immediately regretted the question.

"No, I didn't remember that," he answered quietly. He thought about it for a moment. "Lots of things I'm not remembering these days." He paused but continued thumbing the pages of the book. "Does it say anything interesting?"

"Oh, it's pretty interesting, all right," she answered. "It was written by a German soldier who apparently escaped from that prison camp over near Trinidad, during the war. I mean, it's kind of slow going – I haven't used my German since school, the dialect isn't familiar to me, and the handwriting is difficult at times – like it was written in a hurry. So I haven't really gotten that far, yet."

Trent flipped the pages once more, closed the book, and offered it to her. "Here. How would you like a job?

"Doing what?" she asked, taking the dog-eared old book from him.

"I'd like you to try and translate it for me, if you have the time. I'll even pay you for it."

"Oh, you don't have to do that."

"Yes, I do. It could turn out to be something useful – you know, some kind of evidence or something – for the department, of course."

"Well, in that case, sure, if you insist." She thumbed the streaked cover of the book. "I'll get right on it."

"No, no rush – I mean, you've got your job and everything. Just keep track of your hours – the department would pay you a little something for your time and trouble."

Sophie scowled at him. "No more trouble than you've already been," she said and nudged him on the thigh with her knee.

Trent smiled and nudged her back. "You, too," he responded fondly.

He lowered his head, looked into the steaming cup of coffee, and then offered, "I owe you an apology, Sofe – about the whisky, I mean. I shouldn't have yelled at you, not when you're trying to help me."

She paused for a moment. "Well – guess I shouldn't have poured it out. It was just that when I came in here earlier to check on you and I saw that empty bottle by your bed, I got so mad – I lost it. So, I guess I should be sorry, too." She waited for a beat, and then looked at him. "But I'm not! And I still think you drink too much!"

"Probably," he said, "but the doctor did tell me some red wine in the evening was good for the heart."

"I'm not even going to try and make any sense out of that comment," she remarked with a frown.

He smiled at her and lifted his mug in a toast. "Great coffee, though – I'm guessing some more of this could do me a lot more good right now."

They both sat quietly for a minute, lost in their own thoughts, drinking their coffee. Trent could hear the comforting noise of the water dripping through the downspouts outside the windows.

Sophie leaned forward and put her hand on his knee.

"What difference, Dad?" she asked.

"Huh?"

"What you said earlier – when we were talking, you know, after the nightmare."

Trent shrugged, got up, and walked over to the window.

"I don't remember what I said."

"Well, I do – you said, 'I don't think I can tell the difference anymore,'" she reminded him. "So, just what does that mean? Tell the difference in what?"

Trent separated the blinds with two fingers and peeked out. The rain had slowed to a drizzle, but he could see that the rising sun peeking between the horizon and cloud layer was casting a brilliant, iridescent undercoating of red and purple on the clouds' bellies. He stayed quiet for some time, remembering part of the dream.

#

He finds himself in a beautiful mountain meadow, very relaxed at first, and lying on a soft bed of grass and fall leaves. There is far off, strange music, and the golden aspen leaves tinkle like wind chimes in the breeze. He is vaguely troubled and tries to move, but he can't. He catches the sudden fragrance of roses and cloves, feels a cool fingertip trace his eyebrow and push a lock of hair off of his forehead. The worries fade for a moment.

"Hey, Cowboy," a familiar, lovely voice says.

She leans over him, smiling, her hair shimmering like the sunlight through the canopy of aspen trees above them. He smiles, content to quietly gaze adoringly into the most beautiful face in the world. Her soft brown hair dangles down and tickles his face.

"You screwed yourself up pretty good this time, Sweetie," she coos. Her lips brush the corner of his mouth, and her breath tastes like honey. He swoons from vertigo – and something else – and closes his eyes.

"What do you mean?" he asks, his voice slurring.

"I mean that I'm going to need you to be real brave now, Trenny," she breathes near his ear, "because it's about to get really hard for you – dangerous." She begins to pull away from him. He opens his eyes. Clouds start to scurry across the lowering sun like outriders of a coming storm.

"Victoria …" his voice trails off.

"Shhh – you need to listen to me, Trenny, very carefully." She speaks in that low, measured, drawn out tone of voice that now defines her. "You are going to need to gather all of your wits about you – all of your strength, all of your love. There is danger all around you. And most of all, Dear One, you are going to need to find your faith again."

Trent's eyes close; he feels her stroke his cheek with the back of her fingers. He is frustrated now; sure that what she is saying is vitally important – that somewhere her words hold what he desperately needs. But something also feels wrong – very wrong. He feels weak and tired, groggy, dizzy. He is missing something. His forehead throbs at the hairline and he idly reaches his fingers up to touch his scar, but Vicky pushes his hand away.

"Don't touch that, Sweetie."

"What are you trying to tell me, Vic?"

"I am trying to tell you that you need to pay very close attention to everything that has happened – and everything that will happen; everything that has been said – and all that is yet to spoken. I am trying to tell you that once you have done all of that, you are going to have to force yourself to push it all away. Only then will you be able to really see anything – to remember anything important, at all.

"And I am trying to tell you that only then will you finally learn that none of this is at all what it seems!"

#

The rain finally stopped. Trent turned from the window and looked at his daughter.

"What I meant, Sofe, is that I can't tell the difference anymore – with your mom," he finally answered.

Sophie looked up at him sadly, her hands folded in her lap. She looked back down, brushed at her robe, then back up, her eyes misting.

"In what way?" she asked, peering at him more intently.

He stared into his mug, like it might have some answers there.

"Well, now, Sofe, you're going to think I'm really nuts, but when I see Vicky – when your mom comes to me – I can't tell if she's a nightmare, or a ghost, or else, plainly and simply, because I am going crazy." He drained his cup, set it down on the nearby dresser, and stepped over to look down at his daughter. He lifted her chin with his fingertips lovingly.

"But what I can honestly tell you, Sofe – and nothing that you or anyone else can say will convince me otherwise – is that when I'm talking to her, she really *is* there." Trent paused, put his hands in his pockets, and looked back out the window. "And I hope I keep seeing her – because I feel like I am right on the verge of remembering something really important – to all of us."

Sophie said nothing, but looked back down as a tear splashed on the cover of the old journal in her lap.

CHAPTER 12
THE WAGES OF SIN

Excerpt from the Journal of Otto Eberhardt:

"07-05-45 - 'An act of war,' Ernst calls it! An act of sadistic cruelty is what it was! Oh, yes, we fought the enemy – a handful of inexperienced civilian militia known as the National Guard – scared young men who have never come face to face with seasoned fighters – and most of whom, I presume, are now dead. But how could the murder of so many other innocent people – those passengers – be justified by any cause?' I am sick to my stomach at my actions and the people that have now died at my hand, and I want no more part of this! So what if Ernst calls me a traitor! I no longer care. Two years ago when we were captured in North Africa I surrendered my body and my freedom. But today, I hereby surrender this damned war!"

#

Twin spires of black smoke billowed up over the top of Raton Pass and could be seen from miles around as well as from the highway, north and south of the summit. From a distance, they looked like ancient smoke signals – apocalyptic warnings in the dying light of day.

Traffic approaching from both Colorado and New Mexico began to slow, then stop and stack up in a two-way traffic jam as drivers screeched to a halt and hurriedly jumped from their vehicles, some leaving engines running and doors ajar as they raced on foot to discover the cause of what they were witnessing. They climbed or crawled under fences and plowed through knee high grass and oak bushes to get over to the railroad tracks and steadily hiked, jogged, and tripped up the rail beds as they yelled back and forth, urging each other on to determine the scale of the tragedy that had certainly happened just out of sight a few hundred yards ahead.

What they discovered as they topped a rise and clambered around a short bend was a scene of chaos and utter confusion. Soldiers ran about disorganized with their rifles held at port arms, unsure what else to do, shouting at one another and the would-be rescuers. Some crewmembers from the train stumbled around the two locomotives that had gradually rolled to a stop and now protruded from just outside of the southbound tunnel. Steam still chuffed from beneath them, but the thick, black smoke poured ominously from elsewhere within the dark recesses of the tunnel. An evening breeze had whipped up and begun to flatten the acrid smoke out to spread greyly across the meadows and up the hillsides.

A scene straight from hell.

As the people from the highway made their way nearer, they began seeing passengers who had climbed or fallen or been blown off the train emerging like ghostly shapes through the smoke from somewhere back in the tunnel. In a daze, now, they stumbled about like lost wraiths searching for eternity. Most staggered, bloodied, their clothes torn and shredded, their faces smeared with soot, their eyes vacant in shock, their mouths hanging open wordlessly. Some wandered away downhill aimlessly, and a few of the rescuers ran to wrangle them like lost sheep back up to where they could get help. Others floated out of the swirling shrouds into fresh air, stopped, and looked around in confusion, but collapsed near the tracks in a daze. Some just lay down where they were and wept uncontrollably.

One scarecrow of a man, dressed in the tattered remnants of a conductor's uniform, the bill half-torn and dangling from his smoldering cap, stepped carefully as he searched the ground about him for something. He clutched his upper arm tightly with the opposite hand, just above the elbow, where a white stub of bone protruded nakedly and obscenely out of bloody, ragged flesh, right where his lower arm used to be. He finally collapsed on the ground where he sat and stared back in shock at the huge locomotives and the dark smoke clouds enveloping them. After a moment, he began to rock himself like a child and moaned.

A young boy, perhaps ten or twelve years old, wandered out of the smoky haze, coughing and rubbing his stinging eyes. He was covered with scrapes and cuts on his face and arms, but was otherwise apparently not injured seriously. His clothes were tattered, and one shoe was missing as he plodded steadily and purposefully down the track.

A burly truck driver was trotting up the track and had just rounded the bend, a dead stub of a cigar clamped in his teeth. He stopped suddenly, taking in the scene in disbelief and horror before he leaned over with his hands on his knees to catch his breath. Something just ahead caught his eye; he peered closer to see the tattered boy approaching him resolutely. The boy advanced to within five feet of the big man, but abruptly stopped, his arms straight down at his side. He looked defiantly up into the gruff face that towered over him.

"Where's my mama?" the boy demanded in a clear firm voice, a challenge in his eyes. He held the big man's gaze for several seconds, coughed again, looked back toward the tunnel, and dropped down cross-legged in the middle of the tracks. He picked absently at his bleeding, bare foot, and tried to brush dirt from his ruined clothes.

The truck driver had no immediate answer to the boy's question. Instead, the big man spat out his cigar, choked back an involuntary sob, and squatted down on his haunches to get to the boy's eye level. Thick smoke filled the air and stung his nose and eyes, for which he was grateful as it gave him an excuse to wipe away the tears that he felt already brimming.

"What's your name, boy?" he finally asked as he reached a huge hand over and began gingerly touching the boy on his extremities, prodding gently here and there, checking to see if there were any serious injuries. The boy flinched when the trucker carefully poked around his ribcage, then looked back up at the man's face stubbornly.

"What?" the boy asked, much too loudly. It became apparent that the boy was having trouble hearing.

"Your name, son – *your name!"* the trucker asked again, louder this time, but touching the boy gently on the shoulder.

"Walter James Carter!" he answered proudly. "What's yours, mister?"

#

About a mile to the north, over the top of the pass and down at the tunnel entrances on the opposite side, a slightly different scenario was playing out. Here, the carnage had been much worse with the brunt of the explosion having blasted its way out of the mountain like a huge shotgun blast, obliterating everything in its path – metal, concrete, wood, glass, and, of course, flesh and bone. The National Guardsmen who had been standing anywhere near the entrance had virtually disappeared in a spray of blood and matter, leaving only random body parts scattered about. Rescuers here picked their way over from the highway below and from the service road that wound around over the top of the tunnels. As they neared the disaster site, many of them stopped in horror, abruptly leaned over, and retched violently. A severed arm, still inside the shredded sleeve of a military uniform with sergeant's stripes, lay in the gravel just to the left of the rails near the tunnel entrance, its pale white fingers clutching a .45 caliber semiautomatic pistol, the forefinger still firmly on the trigger. The remainder of the body was nowhere to be seen.

Across the track and about fifty yards north of the tunnel entrance, Otto Eberhardt lay face down in the dirt. He tried opening his eyes. He had no sense of time or place, no idea where he was, no notion of what had just happened. He could hear nothing but a loud, incessant ringing in his ears; his head felt like a sponge soaked full of liquid and two times its normal size. His mouth was filled with dirt and blood, but he felt too weak to even spit. He tried to move, but couldn't. A huge weight pressed down on him. He lay still, listening carefully, trying to figure out where he was and to recall what had happened, but the ringing only grew louder, and his head started spinning with vertigo.

He was suddenly wracked with coughing and immediately noticed the coppery taste of fresh blood in his mouth. He raised his head and was finally able to spit, and watched dispassionately as his own blood spilled onto the ground. He lay still for another moment, then wrenched himself up hard and pushed to one side to break free of whatever had pinned him down. He rolled over onto his back. Every joint and muscle in his body cried out in tremendous pain, and he felt a shortness of breath and great pain in his ribs. He feared he might have punctured a lung. As he lay now on his back, gasping, he glanced to his right and froze, startled to see the dead eyes of a man staring back at him, only a couple of feet away, and realized this man was who had been on top of him. The dead body lay face down on the ground. Otto could see that the back of the man's skull was simply gone; all the way down his backside was a smoldering mass of ruined and bleeding flesh; the back half of his entire body had been torn completely away. Even so, Otto recognized the remnants of an American uniform, and his memory was suddenly jogged: he had been fighting with this soldier, whose body must have shielded Otto from the brunt of the explosion.

Explosion? Was it an explosion?

Otto lay back and squeezed his eyes shut, trying to remember anything at all. He lifted himself back up onto his elbows and looked around, first at the black smoke still spilling from the railroad tunnel in front of him, then catching sight of several people scrambling around, shouting and pointing – except that he could hear nothing at all – only the dull, steady ringing in his ears.

Now, a couple of the men who were shouting indistinctly pointed in his direction and headed his way. Otto felt a certain dread, but could not explain why. He looked back at the dead soldier and slowly began to process the associated memories – jumping off of a train, hearing gunshots, and fighting desperately for his life with the soldier.

Gradually, Otto's senses started to stabilize. He was remembering small details of what must have happened and began to piece things together – a little like waking from a dream and trying to remember all the specifics, but only getting small glimpses. Finally, he recalled the bomb – and his eyes opened wide in horror. He felt extremely exposed all of a sudden, filled with tremendous guilt and terror, followed immediately by a great wariness. One part of him needed desperately to get up, run away – far away – change his clothes, hole up somewhere until his wounds healed up, find a way out of this cursed place – this country fraught with danger at every turn, and somehow find his way back home – to Germany.

The other part of him just wanted to lie down right here, and die.

He stiffened as the two shouting men made their way closer, talking excitedly to one another. He could still make out nothing they were saying, but he could hear the echoing noises of the voices. Otto coughed again and tasted more blood, though not quite as much as before. He shrank back as the men neared and flinched as two pairs of arms reached down and grasped him under his arms. The men were speaking to him now, seeming to ask questions, but he could only make out that they were speaking in English. He was suddenly so exhausted that he couldn't translate it in his mind at this time. He was aware of trying to say something to the men, but they only looked at one another curiously, then back down at Otto. He closed his eyes and let himself be half carried, half dragged by the two men. He became aware of the distant wails of approaching sirens, and suddenly realized his ears were beginning to work again; a strange sense of peace descended on him as he idly wondered where they were taking him, feeling that he was floating away. He thought about this sensation for maybe ten more seconds before his eyes fluttered, and he succumbed gratefully back into the dark, soft womb of unconsciousness.

#

When he came to again, Otto didn't know how much time had passed, but felt that he was now somewhere totally different – and strange. He became aware of a gentle swaying motion and the hum of tires and the occasional grind of engine gears. He gradually awoke and found himself half sitting, half lying in the back seat of an automobile, crammed between two other individuals. He tried lifting his head, but it was pounding with excruciating pain and he was having trouble focusing clearly. His head lolled back down and he once again veered toward unconsciousness.

He roused himself again. What felt like hours had passed, but it could've only been minutes. He wasn't really sure, as he still had no sense of time. *Had he been arrested?* He attempted again to raise his head enough to get his bearings and to identify the people in the front seat.

Soldiers, perhaps? Police? He wasn't sure.

What he was sure of was that he was in tremendous pain. Not only did his head pound and his ribs ache terribly but also every joint and sinew felt as if they had been pulled and then snapped back into place, like rubber bands. Even his fingernails and hair follicles ached. He looked himself over in the dimming light. His clothing was literally so ripped to shreds that he could see through to his skin in several places. He was bleeding from a dozen small wounds, but which ones were caused from his jump from the moving train, from his fistfight with the soldier, or from the explosion, he couldn't determine.

He looked out and tried to get his bearings. The car seemed to be moving down a highway, perhaps south toward the town of Raton, bouncing along, weaving in and out of other traffic. He then looked back at the man seated to his left. The man's head was flopped to one side; his staring, bulging eyes were fixed on the floor. Otto nudged him, with no response. He did it again – still nothing. He cautiously grasped the man's wrist and squeezed slightly, searching for a pulse, but found none. The man was dead.

Well, Otto thought, *so much for being rescued.*

He next looked to the right to where the other man sat and gave a start. This man was barely conscious and in a very bad way, bleeding profusely from several places. Otto squinted at the man's features through the mask of blood and filth.

He gasped.

This bleeding mess was Ernst.

Otto quickly checked his pulse and found it weak, but steady.

So the Monster survived, he thought.

Otto lifted Ernst's shirt – or what was left of it – and discovered what appeared to be a bullet wound in the upper shoulder, oozing blood. He looked around the backseat area, checked his own pockets, and the pockets of the dead man next to him. All he could come up with were two handkerchiefs and a box of tissues that had been on the floor. He turned back to Ernst and pressed the handkerchiefs to the wounded shoulder to try and staunch the bleeding. He tore strips of cloth from Ernst's tattered shirt and tied the handkerchiefs as tightly as he could. He finally used the tissues to wipe some the blood and dirt off of Ernst's face.

Ernst stirred, half opened his eyes, and moaned, but let his head loll back against the car window, seemingly unconscious again. Otto decided not to disturb him anymore. *Let him sleep, if he can. And if he can't,* he thought, almost praying to himself, *then, maybe, he'll die too!* Otto sank back, let his head fall against the back seat, and shook off the previous thought as being less than charitable. If not for Ernst – psychopath that he was – neither one of them would probably be alive today.

His eyes turned to the front seat and focused onto the back of the heads of the two men there. Their attentions were fixed on the road, but pretty soon one of them caught Otto looking at him in the rear view mirror.

"Hold on there, buddy," the driver said, returning Otto's dull stare. "We're gonna have you guys to the hospital in about twenty or thirty minutes. I'll try not to bounce you around too bad." He and the other man exchanged strange looks, and then the driver glanced back at the mirror.

Otto held the man's eyes for a moment before he spoke in a soft monotone.

"There is a dead man back here," he said nonchalantly to the mirror. The man in the front passenger seat suddenly turned to look, and reached over the seatback to shake the dead man on Otto's left. As Otto expected, the dead man did nothing but fall further forward, his head now mashed against the front seat.

Otto watched, almost detached, as if he were moving through a dream. The man in the passenger seat glanced at Otto and frowned. He wore a spiffy looking fedora and appeared to Otto like a cartoon gangster from an old Hollywood movie.

"Damn it!" the man muttered. He nervously glanced over at Ernst and quickly reached over to check his pulse also. Fedora Man's face seemed to relax, but only a bit. He frowned at Otto once more then turned back to the driver. "One of them is dead," he confirmed.

"See?" Otto murmured, but the men didn't respond to him.

"What do we do now?" the driver asked. Otto watched as the two men exchanged quiet glances again. He felt his heart rate increase and his senses suddenly go on alert.

Something did not feel quite right.

"Let's get off the highway," Fedora Man ordered. He seemed to be the one clearly in charge and must have made a decision.

The car slowed down and entered a long curve as the driver searched the roadside for a suitable place to pull off the highway. Otto was fully alert now, but didn't move. He kept his eyes half closed and his demeanor calm, attempting to appear half conscious. He heard the blinker clicking, felt the car slow down to a crawl, bump as it lurched off the pavement, and onto a dirt road. The car bounced on down the rough road, which wound back and forth, and finally rumbled across a small wooden bridge over a shallow ravine about half a mile from the highway. The driver steered a few more yards around another bend until the road opened into a small, secluded meadow surrounded by trees. He finally slowed to a stop and turned off the engine.

All was abruptly very quiet and dark. The two men sat still for a moment before Fedora Man switched on an interior light. He then reached into his jacket pocket and pulled something out. He twisted to look into the back seat.

"So, you guys are German, huh?" His words were a statement, not a question. He then held up two familiar looking small booklets to the light. "Says so right here," he continued, a smile creeping onto his face. Otto could now see he was holding Ernst's and his identification papers. "Kraut army officers," Fedora Man continued. He chuckled and looked back at the driver and slapped him on the arm with the documents. "Bet there's some good reward money for three escaped POWs!"

Otto said nothing, but shuddered involuntarily. Fedora Man was no longer a cartoon, but now exuded real danger. Otto quickly regained his composure, and continued to hold the man's gaze. He breathed slowly and deeply, attempting to keep his face calm and devoid of all expression, while his thoughts raced into survival mode. He had often wondered what would happen if they were captured as escaped prisoners of war. He had assumed they would be arrested, turned over to the military authorities, and taken back to Camp Trinidad, if not to one of the other POW camps scattered across the Southwest. He had also expected to be subjected to intense interrogation, perhaps even beaten. He had even assumed that they would not get away with the bombing of the train. But all of these assumptions were based on the relatively good treatment they had received from the Americans, ever since they had been taken prisoner in North Africa. Otto expected justice to be meted out – maybe even execution – but only after due process of the laws Americans so proudly upheld.

Until now.

He would never have guessed that, instead, self-righteous gangsters would murder them on some isolated back road. More rotten luck.

Otto sat still and watched as both men chuckled, then simultaneously opened their doors and got out of the car. The door to Otto's left then opened; the driver grabbed the dead man by his lapels, dragged him out of the car, and dropped him unceremoniously in a heap on the ground. His partner, in the meantime, had opened Ernst's door. Ernst had been slouching against the door, half conscious, and would have fallen out if the man hadn't caught him by the shoulders. Ernst moaned as the man began to roughly pull him out of the vehicle. On the other side of the car, the driver had bent over the dead man and begun searching his pockets, rifling through a wallet, and laughing when he pulled out wads of cash.

"Yeah, bound to be a reward on you Krauts," the driver chortled. "Not only that – I'm bettin' you had something to do with blowing that train up, didn't ya!"

"Yeah, *big* reward, I'm thinking," said Fedora Man as he struggled with Ernst's dead weight. The man's coat fell open and Otto glimpsed the butt of a pistol shoved into the waistband of his pants. He looked back up to see Fedora Man smiling at him, and sucking on his teeth. "And with dangerous, escaped war criminals," the gangster continued, "nobody's going to think twice whether we bring you in alive," he paused and grunted as he adjusted his grip around Ernst, "or dead!"

Just then, Otto thought he had caught a familiar glimmer in Ernst's half opened eyes – almost a wink; had these thieves woefully underestimated their captives? Somehow, some force of nature – *perhaps God?* – had always managed to intervene at the most dire moments, although in their present, weakened conditions, Otto could not for the life of him think how they were going to extricate themselves from these gunman.

But then again, he knew that Ernst was still alive.

"C'mon, you!" the man grunted and tried to pull Ernst to his feet. "Or don't you *sprecka da English?*"

Otto watched, fascinated now as if it were all still a dream unfolding before him, as Ernst slowly reached behind to the small of his back to a hidden scabbard tucked into his belt there and pulled out a six-inch knife. He waited for just the right moment when suddenly, he pushed up off the balls of his feet, plunged the knife upwards into the soft flesh under the man's chin, and twisted it hard. Fedora Man's eyes went wide in total surprise and shock. He became rigid, trembling slightly as blood suddenly exploded over Ernst's hand, which still gripped the knife. The driver on the other side, still squatting over the dead man, looked up in dumb surprise.

Otto sat very still, transfixed, and marveled that he knew Ernst so well, what he was capable of doing, and that he had been able to anticipate every move that was unfolding in front of him like a macabre dance. He also anticipated what was about to happen next, so he pushed himself down even further into the upholstered seat back, trying to make himself smaller and part of the fabric.

The driver continued to crouch, but now reached inside his jacket and fumbled out his own pistol. Ernst flicked his eyes first at the driver, back to Otto – and smiled, again knowing exactly what was about to transpire. Without looking away and in a matter of only seconds, Ernst let go of the knife, which remained embedded in Fedora Man's neck, slid his hand down into his victim's waistband until it found the butt of the gun, pulled the weapon out, cocked it with one fluid motion before twisting the dying man's body around to act as a shield. At the same moment, the driver nervously fired a badly aimed shot that tore into the headliner just above Otto's head. Otto flinched, but only made himself smaller.

Ernst calmly raised the .32 caliber pistol up at arm's length and fired one precise shot.

In his dreamlike state, Otto actually saw the bullet exit through the spurt of flame at the muzzle of Ernst's pistol, watched it travel through the airspace of the back seat, passing within six or eight inches of his own nose, and saw it pick up some speed through the open doorway to his left where it punched a clean hole into the center of the driver's forehead. The man's eyes sprang wider, unbelieving; he was frozen in place as the small black hole began to leak a single dribble of dark red blood between his eyes and down the side of his nose. He stayed in this position for what seemed to Otto like minutes before he finally tottered and fell across the dead train victim. Otto swiveled his head and now watched out of the corner of his eye as Fedora Man also finally collapsed and slid straight down in a heap.

Suddenly, another shot rang out: Otto jerked back around to see that the driver's gun, still clutched in his dead right hand, had fired harmlessly into the other victim's stomach as the gunman's trigger finger had twitched involuntarily in a single death spasm.

Wads of stolen bills clutched in the dead gunman's other hand began to flutter away into the twilight breeze, along with his and Fedora Man's souls.

CHAPTER 13
FATHER, SON, AND SPIRIT

"There was a fire…"

Walter James Carter glanced over his shoulder as the woman shuffled behind his chair, moving listlessly, muttering to herself. She paid him no mind.

"There was a fire," her voice drifted off, only to pick up again, "and Papa got burned," she mumbled again.

Walter shifted restlessly in his chair and turned his attention back to the chessboard. He looked at his pieces, back up at the old priest across from him, and waited.

Father Michael pinched his lower lip thoughtfully, the thumb and forefinger of his other hand poised above his white bishop. *If he moves that bishop*, Walter thought, *he just may have figured out the end game.*

Walter tapped the heel of his left foot lightly and nervously against the tiled floor.

"There was a fire," the litany began again, "and Papa got burned."

The woman – he believed her name was Caroline – moved past the small table where their chessboard was laid out in the dayroom. She was modestly dressed in a jumper – he thought they were called – with light pink stripes, a narrow belt cinched around the waist, and an unbuttoned, tan sweater which slouched off her shoulders. Her graying, shoulder length light brown hair was brushed neatly back from her face and behind her ears. Caroline had a pleasant enough face and didn't look much beyond her mid 60s, though she was possibly a little older with the hints of silver beginning to show at her temples. In her hands she clutched an old, threadbare rag doll with one button eye, and straggly hair that looked as if it were as old as she. All Walter knew was that Caroline had been here at the rehab center when he had moved in here four years ago; he suspected she had even been here for a while.

Still younger than me, he thought to himself, *and I ain't near as crazy.*

She stopped right beside the two elderly men, although her clear blue eyes were focused on something else in the far distance, out beyond the walls somewhere. Walter glanced at her nervously as one of her sleeves brushed dangerously close to the table, almost knocking over their chess pieces. She suddenly raised her arm to point a trembling finger at something evidently only she could see. She hesitated, brought her hand slowly to her mouth, looked down as if remembering something, pinched her lower lip, and made a soft mewing noise behind her fingers. Her eyes finally drifted back to the chessboard that she now studied for several moments.

"King's bishop to queen's knight," she said softly through her fingers, not looking at either player. "Checkmate – two moves."

She raised her eyes, a hint of familiarity flashing in them, to Father Michael's face. The old priest's eyes twinkled back, and Caroline leaned over toward him. "Papa got burned," she repeated, nodding her head earnestly. Father Michael smiled at her and reached over to gently pat her arm.

"Yes, my dear one," Father Michael now said softly, a brief look of sincere sadness crossing the old man's face for just a moment. "Yes, we know – your papa got hurt." He paused and sighed. "But it's all okay now." He studied his pieces as he spoke. He always insisted playing the white pieces, and Walter had noticed that when the old priest was contemplating his moves, he always nervously toyed with his white king, even though he hardly ever resorted to moving it. .

"How are you this evening, Caroline?" Walter asked, smiling at the woman and trying to make conversation as she turned her blank face to his. The corner of her mouth twitched in what was almost a responsive smile, but stopped. Her brows furrowed abruptly.

"There was a fire," she insisted in an intense half-whisper, staring at him. Walter rolled his eyes. She pointed again, beyond him somewhere, tilted her head slightly, and said it louder. "There WAS a fire! And Papa got burnt! Real bad!" She held both her hands at her chest, wringing the worn rag doll between her hands as she stared, horrified, into the distance. "And Mama," she began, then hesitated, her lower lip quivering.

This woman is a one track record, Walter thought, shaking his head: always a fire, and "Papa" was always getting burned. Poor thing was fixated on some tragedy, lost in the recesses of her memories to some horrible nightmare. He shook his head again. Her shared visions were surely terrible, but also surely getting tiresome to listen to day in and day out.

A nurse's aide came around the corner and saw Caroline standing there, clenching and unclenching her fists, picking at the loose threads of her doll, while moving her lips, mouthing unspoken words.

"Come on, now, Miss Caroline; let's let these guys finish their game in peace."

Caroline was led away, mumbling and shuffling, to the other side of the dayroom. Father Michael's eyes followed her for a few moments, but eventually turned back to the chessboard. The old priest sure loved his chess. He was pretty good, too, but hardly spoke two words during their matches. He could sit for long minutes at a time, focusing on the board, contemplating several moves at once, extrapolating all the outcomes, gently tapping his king – all to Walter's ultimate irritation. He loved his chess, too, but was a less patient player and could only figure out a couple of good moves ahead at a time, which made his turns comparatively swift.

He looked at the clock on the wall, and back at the priest, willing him to make his move. But then, what was the use? The priest would finally move, Walter would waste no time making his own next move, and he would be right back to waiting on the priest to study the board and take his good, sweet time again. *Oh well,* he sighed to himself. *Got nothing else to do all afternoon.*

Speaking of which, Walter wondered what went through the old priest's mind during the rest of the day when he wasn't staring at a chessboard. He often seemed preoccupied with his thoughts. Chess seemed to be the only activity Father Michael would come out of his room for anymore.

What was definitely clear was that the old man had infinite patience with the woman Caroline, and seemed to be very close to her – a bit protective, paternal, actually. Oftentimes, he could be found walking with her in the gardens, sometimes with another rather stern, mysterious woman – a frequent visitor of Caroline's, perhaps a relative? At those times, Caroline seemed to be the most calm, and it also seemed to Walter that Father Michael seemed the most content, for some reason.

Most days, however, anyone could find the priest sitting in his chair, fingering a worn leather-covered Bible, and staring blankly out his window. At these times especially, he always wore the face of one who had witnessed more than his share of the consequences of human frailties and failures, or else just the plain evil that one person could perpetrate upon another in this world.

On one such day, when Walter had wandered into Father Michael's room to see about a chess match, he had found the old priest weeping silently and rocking himself on the side of his bed, hugging himself tightly and gazing out the window. Walter had overheard him muttering, "All the death – all those poor souls," over and over again. "Why? Oh, why?"

Walter had tip-toed away without disturbing him and his memories – his secrets.

Walter certainly had never considered himself any sort of saint; his litany of sins could probably fill an entire day in the confessional, yet he had hardly ever seen the need for confession. However, Father Michael had something, something – he was not sure what it was – that touched a chord in Walter. He felt that here was someone who had shouldered the burdens of so many people – had experienced vicariously more than one lifetime of suffering and mental anguish – that he, more than anyone else Walter could think of, could probably use a good friend – and be one.

The feeling was strange, but felt to Walter as if they had been friends for much longer than the four years he had been here.

In fact, their daily chess match had evolved into one of the few ways to be just that sort of a friend. If he had to admit it, he was actually enjoying the old priest's friendship, even if he wasn't much of a conversationalist – and partly because the old man had never tried to convert him to his faith.

Father Michael stopped pinching his lip, glanced up at Walter, and smiled, having made a decision. He grasped his bishop, swooped down on Walter's knight, and deftly claimed the kill with another twinkle in his eyes. Walter and the old priest looked at each other with satisfaction, before looking back at the board. The game was finally back in play.

"Well, I'll be damned," muttered Walter. The twinkle left the priest's eyes to be replaced by a look of reproach.

"Oh. Sorry, Father."

Father Michael's eyes now focused beyond Walter and the twinkle returned, along with a wide smile. Walter heard footsteps coming up softly and felt a pair of arms encircle his neck from behind. A soft cheek pressed against his.

"Hi, Grampa!"

Walter turned in surprise to see Sophie standing there with a huge smile on her face. She held out a plastic grocery bag to him.

"Well, now – what's this?" he asked, taking the bag. He opened it, peered inside, grinned, and pulled out a package of his favorite cream-filled finger cookies.

"I didn't have time to wrap them for you," said Sophie.

"Oh pooh, that's quite alright," he chuckled. "One less thing to tear open."

Sophie leaned over and kissed him on the cheek and gave him another hug. Walter subsequently pulled back so that he could gaze into his granddaughter's face for more than a few seconds. "You look every bit as beautiful as your sweet mother," he said wistfully. "More every day." He leaned and put his forehead against hers. "I sure do miss her," he whispered.

"I do, too Grampa – I do too."

Sophie finally pulled gently away and wiped her eyes. "You'd best not let them catch you with these," she whispered conspiratorially, pointing to the cookies, "or they might take them away!"

"Oh, I've got a hiding place or two where old 'Nurse Cratchett' will never find them.

"Who?"

"Nurse Cratchett – that's what I call her. You know, like the one in that old Jack Nicholson movie."

"I think you mean 'Nurse Ratchett,' Walter," growled Trent, who had just at that moment stepped around the corner into the room. He had been parking the truck while Sophie had gone on ahead.

Walter Carter's smile disintegrated into a frown.

"Now, I *will* be damned – never expected to see you again until the funeral."

Father Michael cleared his throat loudly and tapped his finger on the table. Walter glanced sheepishly at him. "Sorry again, Father," he said.

"Funeral? What funeral?" asked Trent.

"*My* funeral!" Walter thumbed his chest before turning back to his game.

Trent rolled his eyes.

"Nice to see you again, too, Dad."

Trent turned toward the old priest. Father Michael was smiling and had folded his arms and leaned back in his chair. He didn't seem to mind the interruption, obviously enjoying their banter. He seemed genuinely glad to see Trent, who stepped over to shake his hand.

"Don't let this old thief cheat you, Father Michael."

"Oh, he does not cheat, young Mr. Carter," the priest responded. His voice was high-pitched and a little wheezy, and his manner of speaking was very precise and proper. "At least, not that he gets away with."

"I see," said Trent. "Well, just don't press your luck, Father."

"I really hate to break up this sweet reunion," Walter interrupted, then glared at Trent. "But what in the name of doggone hell are you doing here, anyway? And don't say it's because you miss me!"

"Okay – 'Because I miss you.'"

"Liar."

Trent pointed to the cookies. "You know those things will hurt your teeth."

"Not if I dunk 'em in my coffee first."

Sophie turned and looked around the room. "That's a great idea! Looks like there's a fresh pot of coffee over there. Who wants a cup?" She glanced at each of them. "Grampa? Father Michael?"

The old priest pushed back from the table. He was in a wheelchair.

"Oh, no, thank you," he said. "I really should excuse myself. You folks need to visit."

"Nonsense," Sophie said, "you haven't finished your game yet."

"Well, then – let us just take care of that, shall we?" Father Michael wheeled back to the table, leaned over the board, and looked back up at Walter.

"Your move, Walter."

Walter looked at him with surprise, and down again at the pieces. He studied the bishop Father Michael had just moved, allowing a brief look of discovery to escape his face. He reached out, slid his queen over the board, and devoured the bishop. He crossed his arms, sat back, and lifted his eyes to the priest with a look of triumph on his face.

"Check!" he declared.

Father Michael frowned for only a moment, slowly smiled, reached back over the board to where his other remaining bishop had been resting unobtrusively, and sprung his trap by moving it with confidence to where Walter's queen was resting. He deftly picked her up with the little finger and ring finger of the same hand that held the bishop and smiled back at Walter's shocked face with a brief shrug.

"Check!" the old priest quipped, in turn, twitching a forefinger and knocking Walter's king over on its side. "And mate, I do believe!" he added with a flourish, backing his wheelchair up a couple of feet, then swiveling and rolling himself toward the hallway. "There! Game over!" he called out over his shoulder. "Now, you folks can enjoy your visit!"

Walter glared after him with chagrin.

"Bye, Father Michael," Sophie called after him. He raised one hand and waved without turning or slowing down and disappeared down the hall.

"Old bastard!" exclaimed Walter. "More words than he's said all week." He suddenly became thoughtful as he recalled how Caroline had earlier predicted the outcome of the match.

#

The three of them took their coffees and went out to the back patio. The two-story, U-shaped rehab center had been remodeled in recent years to a Santa Fe adobe style structure that surrounded a well-landscaped garden area. Numerous nooks and crannies set among skillful arrangements of flowerbeds, bushes, and trees provided several great places to have a private conversation in such a public place. The variety of flowers exuded a pleasurable potpourri of fragrances. Sophie and her grandfather chose their favorite spot to sit: wrought iron chairs that sat around a moderately sized fountain that spilled into large sculptured bowls that served as birdbaths. The bubbling water also added a sense of privacy.

"Thanks for the cookies, Munchkin," Walter mumbled around a mouthful. He had sat down and eagerly opened the package and immediately doused one of the finger cookies in his hot coffee to soften it. "You want one?"

He proffered the package to Sophie, who smiled but shook her head. Walter glanced over at Trent, who had just now wandered up and sat down with Sophie between them. "You don't get one," Walter said, snatching the bag of cookies away.

"Well, why doesn't that surprise me any, Walter?"

Sophie kicked her father's boot. Trent gave her a look and then turned back to Walter, who had gobbled down his first cookie and had already dunked a second one in his cup, and was now sucking on it.

"So, *Dad,*" Trent exaggerated, glancing briefly at his daughter, "what did you have to tell me that was so important?"

Walter chomped on his treat and wiped his mouth with the back of his hand.

"Not really sure what you're talking about."

Trent sighed heavily. This visit, as usual, was already turning into a big waste of time. He started to get up to leave, but Sophie touched his arm.

"Grampa, you don't remember talking to me on the phone this morning?"

Walter chewed his cookie, looked over at the fountain, scratched his head, and made a show of thinking hard for a moment.

"Did I? Oh yeah! Guess I did." He fished another cookie out of the package and went about the business of properly dunking it. "Believe it or not, there is an actual art to doing this," he smirked as he held the moistened cookie up to examine before devouring it. Trent frowned at him.

"Well?" he asked. "You going to tell us or not?"

Walter glared back at Trent and took a gulp of coffee to wash down the remnants of his cookie. "Tell you what, Smartass – I'll tell Sophie – and you can listen in if you want, I guess!"

He leaned forward to them and glanced around, checking to see if anyone else was listening. Trent looked around also. An elderly man in a big slouch hat sat in a wheelchair being pushed by a younger man on the other side of the garden. Other than that, they had the place to themselves.

"Couldn't talk to you about it inside," Walter continued furtively. "Not in front of the priest."

Trent just looked at him with skepticism on his face.

"Why not?" Sophie asked.

"Because I think it involves him!"

Trent and Sophie exchanged a glance.

"Involves who?

"Father Michael!"

"Oh, for crying out loud," Trent protested under his breath and started to rise.

Sophie elbowed her father softly. "How does it involve him, Grandpa?"

"Why, all those murders, of course."

Trent frowned again. "Which murders?" he asked cautiously.

"You know, all those killings you used to talk about – that you've been investigating forever now, you know – what did you call them? 'Cold Criminals,' or something?"

"'Cold Cases,'" Trent corrected.

"Yeah! That's it – all those cold cases you were looking into before the, uh – the, uh…" Walter's voice trailed off to silence, suddenly morose.

"Before the what, Walter? Say it."

"I think he means 'before the accident,' Dad," explained Sophie quietly when her grandfather remained quiet.

Walter looked down on the ground. Trent also looked away.

"I knew what he meant," growled Trent, exasperatedly.

"Yeah – before all that," Walter said finally, clearing his throat.

"So, I don't understand," Sophie interjected. "How does this all fit in with Father Michael, Grampa?"

Walter began to answer, but stopped suddenly. The wiry, younger man who had been pushing the wheelchair had come back into view now, his Denver Broncos cap seeming to float just above the bushes behind the nearby fountain. He chomped on gum and was hunched over with his face turned half away as he pushed the elderly man who could have been his grandfather. The old man wore a wide-brimmed straw hat pulled down over his brow and a scarf wrapped around his neck, effectively hiding the lower half of his face, with only the gleam of his eyes visible. They stopped for a minute on the opposite side of the fountain, supposedly to watch the birds frolic there. After a moment, the younger man leaned down and listened as the old man murmured something and gestured. Just as suddenly as they had stopped, they moved on.

Something disturbed Trent about the two of them as he watched them disappear around the side of a building. He couldn't quite put his finger on it.

Walter waited until they were out of earshot and continued in a hushed tone. "So, get this: Father Michael knows about all those murders!" He went on to tell how he had come upon the old priest more than once, crying and saying something over and over about some killings, and rubbing on his rosary beads the whole while.

Sophie pondered it for a bit. "So, why do you think Father's memories have anything at all to do with the same things Daddy's been investigating? Maybe, he's just rambling – another confused old man locked away in a nursing home."

She was immediately sorry for what she had said.

"I didn't mean it that way, Grampa," she said softly, reaching over and touching his hand.

Walter looked up and smiled. He patted his granddaughter's hand on top of his other one. "I know you meant nothing by it, Munchkin," he said. "At least, not the way *others* might have meant it." This last comment he directed at Trent who stared down sheepishly at his outstretched boots, one crossed over the other.

"So, Walter," Trent said, then looked up. "Just how the hell do you suppose Father Michael knows anything about any of my unsolved murders?" Trent asked.

"Well, how do you think?" Walter asked. "He's a priest!"

"You mean God told him," Trent said flippantly, after a pause.

"No, dummy! I mean the killer told him!"

"The confessional!" Sophie suddenly blurted in realization.

Walter sat back and grinned. Sophie smiled back; Trent nodded slowly.

"Well, that's wonderful! Isn't it, Daddy?" Sophie said, excited now, still smiling and looking from one to the other.

"Could be," Trent murmured.

"Just think what that means," she continued exuberantly. "You can go talk to Father Michael, find out what the killer said, and who it is – just think how many of those cold cases might get resolved, and how great this will look for you!"

Trent continued to nod, a knowing look on his face, but allowed his nod to turn to a shaking of his head.

"Yeah, just great. Except you're both forgetting an inconvenient detail."

"What's that?" Walter asked.

"A little thing called 'the Sanctity of the Confessional.'"

"The whatity of the what?" asked Walter.

Trent rolled his eyes. "Something a non-Catholic like you would obviously know nothing about, Walter."

"Well, you're not Catholic either, smart guy! So how do you know anything about it?"

"Just something I've run into a time or two in the past regarding the Church, that sometimes makes things difficult where the law's concerned."

"So," mused Sophie pushing a stray lock of her hair from her eyes in the quickening breeze, "does that mean what it sounds like, Daddy? Like, a priest can't tell you what he knows?"

"That's right. Under Church law, a priest cannot divulge what was confessed to him, so long as the person confessing made what's called '*a good act of contrition.*'"

"What the hell does that mean?" asked Walter.

"Well, Walter – since I am also not a Catholic, I'm not entirely sure what all that means – except that if a person is truly sorry for his sins and is willing to do something to make up for it, somehow, that in the eyes of the Church his confession is sealed."

"Sealed?"

"Private."

"Oh." Walter thought hard. "What about a warrant, then?"

"Doesn't work that way, either – not with the Church, at least not in this case."

"So – Trent," Walter began, then hesitated before continuing. "Just how do you – remember all this, uh – detail? I mean, about the Church and everything." He paused and looked at his feet as he scuffed them self-consciously on the ground, then blurted the rest of it out. "I mean, aren't you supposed to be suffering from all this 'memory loss' crap, and such?" Trent stared at him for a few moments, then looked away.

"Gee, I don't know, Walter," he murmured, finally, still looking off in the distance. "I guess some stuff I still retain well enough," he said, then looked over at his father with a scowl, "and others I would just as soon forget."

They all sat silently for a long time, listening to the softly flowing water and the happily chirping birds splashing in the fountain. Trent glanced around the patio garden. The two men with the wheelchair were back on the other side of the garden now, maybe thirty yards away, looking at some roses. Trent's eyes squinted as he watched them.

Something still nagged him. Something about that younger guy.

Something.

But as quickly as the feeling had come, it had gone from his mind.

Trent froze suddenly as he caught a strong fragrance of those roses – which was impossible at this distance – but mixed subtly with the scent of some other spice or perfume. He stood up and looked around anxiously over the tops of the bushes. He took a few tentative steps but stopped.

No one else was there. The scent began to fade.

"What is it, Daddy?" Sophie asked, noticing her father's discomfort.

Trent glanced around once more, sitting slowly back down.

"I don't know," he said, looking around again. He nodded toward the two men, the old man now being wheeled through the doors of the nursing home. "Something about one of those guys. Who are they, Walter?"

Walter had been staring off into space, but now looked over at the two men disappearing inside. "Him? Oh, you know him, don't ya? He's that's rich old rancher – you know, Neumann, I think it is. Used to be a big muckity-muck around here. Even ran for governor once. Story is he got badly burned up a long time ago. Comes here to visit every so often. He's not a resident – Ha! He's got more money than God, so he can afford *not* to be here.

"Anyway, he comes around occasionally to visit that girl of his, Caroline – at least I think she's his. You know – that crazy one that walks around talking about some fire all the time. I think he's her father. Least, he's the only one I know who fits her story – being burned up and all." Walter shook his head. "I don't know who that other guy is. Just works for him, I think." He fished in the bag for another cookie and stuffed it in his mouth. ""Poor thing. I sure would like to know her whole story. She does seem to listen to Father Michael, though," he mumbled around his mouthful. "And he's the one you still need to go talk to anyway," he said, with a fresh gleam in his eye. "Maybe you can get him to tell you *their* story, too – along with the other's he probably knows."

Trent shook his head. "I told you – it wouldn't do any good. Besides, a lot of those murders took place a long, long time ago. Probably not even related. Could be several different killers, over the years, for all I know."

Now, Sophie began to look thoughtful. "But maybe Grampa's got a point, Dad," she said.

"Oh, now don't you start, too."

"No, seriously. Think about it. You said a priest can't say anything if there was a confession of a crime. And then this person confessing to the crime had to perform this 'act of contrition,' right?"

"Yes – so?"

"So – what if the person never completed that *contrition* part of it?"

Trent thought hard about her question. He wasn't at all sure what the overall conditions were. He had only run into it a couple of times when he had tried to get information from the Church, but had been road-blocked. He had never thought about it that much beyond the confessional itself.

"Well, I think you still oughta go talk to him," Walter emphasized. "You never know."

"Yeah, it couldn't hurt, Dad," Sophie chimed in.

"Besides," Walter continued, "it's really eating him up, I can tell. I mean, all he does when he's not playing chess or coming out to eat is to sit in his room by the window and play with those beads – or thumbing through that old Bible that never leaves his sight."

"So come on, Boy," Walter continued. "Pull your head out and go talk to the good Father about the killers and that crazy woman and her strange daddy. Make yourself useful for a change!"

#

"Why do you call him *Walter?*" Sophie asked Trent later as they were heading home. "I mean, after all, he is your father. Why are you so mean and disrespectful to him? You didn't always talk so ugly to him, did you?"

They were in Trent's old pickup, driving back to Raton from Clayton, about an hour or so drive. The sun was dipping down and glaring into Trent's eyes right at that point where the sun visor didn't quite do the job. He fished for his shades in his jacket pocket, put them on, and took a deep breath.

"I don't know – I guess I've called him Walter for about as long as I can remember. Guess ever since I felt like he didn't really approve of me much anymore – never really cared for any of my choices, I think – high school sports, the military, nor my career. So, he ceased being a father to me and became just – a *Walter* – I guess."

He paused. "And *no*, I didn't always talk to him that way," he finally answered. "But he sort of started it."

"Oh, now *that* sounds awfully mature," Sophie scoffed. "How was he the one who started it?"

"Do we really need to get into this right now?" he asked, looking over at her and feeling exasperated.

"Oh, come on, Dad! Hasn't there been enough drama for one day? Besides – you promised this morning you'd start opening up to me more about," she hesitated, "things – that you'd start being honest with me!"

Trent blew his breath out slowly and thought about it. "Well, once again, it involves your mother," he began tentatively, glancing over at his daughter, "and your grandmother." Sophie just stared straight ahead now, anger still clouding her face.

"Walter – I mean, your grampa – was very fond of your mom. I mean, he really thought the world of her, and as far as he was concerned, she really hung the moon." He hesitated, and then continued. "Guess he thought marrying your mother was about the best decision I had ever made -- especially when your grandmother got sick and it was your mom who came and stayed with her and nursed her, day in and day out – I mean, tirelessly. I couldn't do it because I was still working as a state cop, down in Santa Fe. I mean, I came up to visit when I could, but your grampa thought I should've dropped everything I was doing to be up here with my mom; never mind that he himself wasn't up to it, either, physically or emotionally. Guess that's about when he and I stopped talking to each other much – as father and son, anyway."

Trent grew quiet for several moments.

"And then, when Vicky was killed, he – uh," Trent glanced back at Sophie who was now watching him sadly. Trent reached over and gently touched her cheek.

"What I am trying to tell you is that your mama meant the world to a lot of people, Sofe; most of all to you and me, right? And also to your grampa and grandma. And then – well," his voice trailed off as he briefly turned his misted eyes from her and stared back at the highway rolling toward them.

Sophie reached over and placed her soft, warm hand over his on the steering wheel.

"You don't have to go on, Daddy."

"Yes. Yes, I think I do, Sofe." Trent wiped his nose hard with the back of his other hand.

"When your mama died, your Grampa blamed me – said it was me who killed her." His voice broke with a soft croak. He turned and looked back at Sophie, his eyes wet. "And you know what, Kiddo? If your grampa was ever right about anything, he was sure right about that! And he's never let me forget it, either. Not for a single instant!"

Trent heard a loud horn blare and lights flashed behind him. He looked up into his rearview mirror, saw the outline of a huge semi truck trying to pass him, and, startled, realized that he had drifted a little over the centerline. He steered the pickup back over a few inches to let the big rig pass, and waved to the driver apologetically.

Trent was in no particular hurry, so he continued driving a bit below the speed limit as they rode on in silence. Sophie's hand rested gently on his knee, but he thought he could hear her crying softly, and tried to give her some privacy by not saying anything else for a while. Instead he turned his thoughts elsewhere.

The day had been excruciatingly long; now, he was feeling doubly frustrated – especially after his visit with the priest earlier.

#

After leaving Sophie and her grandfather to visit some more in the day room, Trent had found Father Michael's room and, just as Walter had said, he had been sitting and staring out the window and fingering his rosary beads in his lap. A well-read Bible sat on a nearby desk. Trent had knocked softly on the open doorframe and excused himself; Father Michael had smiled and welcomed him in. They had sat and talked for awhile, the priest calmly, politely, skillfully deflecting all of Trent's attempts to turn the conversation to the priest's history – or the unsolved murders – almost as if he had spent a lifetime doing so. But when Trent finally asked about Caroline, the woman who supposedly went about talking about some fire, the priest suddenly reacted.

"You have no idea how it torments me to see that poor girl suffering so," Father Michael had said intensely, his words clipped and precise, but his eyes welling up with tears. "If I thought there was something – anything

– I could do for her, do you not think I would do it?" He looked imploringly at Trent. "She and I once conversed about many things, but lately there is no talking to her. I fear she is too far gone, the poor soul. The tragedy of all that happened with her parents has been too much for her mind."

At this point, Father Michael had turned abruptly away. He stared back out the window, as if no longer aware Trent was there.

"So, what happened, exactly, with her parents, Father?" Trent finally asked softly.

"That night was the center of so much else," the old priest mused, almost to himself. He groaned, picking his beads up again from his lap. "The beginning of the end – for Caroline, I am sure of it. At least, for her, she has escaped into the safe recesses of the mind."

At this, Trent looked away, suddenly identifying uncomfortably with the old man's remarks.

"But for the others – her, um, family," Father Michael continued, suddenly guarded, "it was only the beginning of the worst part of it all." The priest had paused, sighed, and momentarily closed his eyes, then lowered his head, shaking it slowly. "Death brings no real release for some."

Father Michael had opened his eyes and seemed to become aware once again of Trent's presence. He swiveled his wheelchair back to him and peered closely into Trent's face.

"Are you a man of faith, young Mr. Carter?"

Trent had looked up sharply, startled at the abrupt, unexpected question. He had felt a sudden chill.

"What was that, Father?"

"I asked about your faith, Trent. Do you trust in God?"

Trent thought for a moment. "Well, yes, I guess so. I guess I believe in God."

"That is not what I asked you, my friend. Even the devil himself believes in God – and the devil is going to hell, eventually. No, what I asked you is do you trust in Him – have you ever trusted that Someone, besides that proud intellect of yours, has your life in His hands?"

Trent hadn't been able to answer right away.

"No," he finally admitted. "I guess I don't believe that there's a God like that – or much anyone else – who cares for me that much, Father. I mean, maybe God does care a little bit – but no, I can't say I've seen much evidence these days that I'm in His thoughts at all, much less His hands, as you would say." He had thought a little more about it and nervously chuckled. "Father, I haven't stepped inside a church since I was a kid. In fact, I'm pretty sure that your God's been letting the devil have quite a field day at my expense, lately!"

Father Michael looked down, nodded his head slightly, pursed his lips, and wagged a long, thin finger at Trent. "Going to church, young man, makes you a follower of the Lord about as much as stepping into your garage makes you a car." The priest thought for a moment, reached over to the desk, and picked up his worn Bible. He caressed the old leather cover and slowly held it up so Trent could see it clearly.

"Of course," he remarked pointing to the black book in his hand, "you know what this is."

Trent looked at the bound book, at Father Michael, and back at the book. He answered finally, more with annoyance than amusement.

"Of course. It's a Bible."

"Have you ever heard about the Bible, that it actually contains revelations?"

Trent glared at the old priest and managed to nod affirmatively. He was getting slightly perturbed at this game of 20 Questions.

"Yes. Of course," Trent answered, uncomfortably. "Isn't there even a chapter in there called Revelations?"

Father Michael chuckled and waved his hand dismissively. "Revelation – in the singular – a very common mistake. And it's a Book of the Bible, not just a Chapter."

He tilted his head a bit and smiled at Trent. "And please, Young Mr. Carter – no need to be so defensive. I am not trying to convert you, I assure you. After all, it was once just a book to me, also – nothing more, nothing less," he noted, rubbing the outer cover of the black leather book almost affectionately. He continued, "But then, over time, even until today, this book here has come to reveal more than I could ever have known alone."

His eyes twinkled when he looked at the lawman, who had by this time sat back in his chair with arms folded before him. The old man chuckled and slightly moved to the edge of his chair, his voice becoming more serious. "One day, if you let it, when the time comes, if you really look into it, it is going to reveal much to you, as well."

He sat back in his chair and put the worn Bible on the table beside him.

"Yes," he continued with his eyes closed and almost to himself, "that is what I have come to know for sure, for myself."

After almost a full minute, Trent had thought the priest had drifted off to sleep and that it was time for him to leave, but inexplicably he felt rooted in place. Suddenly Father Michael opened his eyes, looked at him with an intensity bordering on mania, leaned forward, gripped Trent's knee tightly, and whispered urgently, cryptically, "Pontius Pilate tried to wash Christ's blood off of his hands – he tried over and over, to no avail!"

Trent pulled back instinctively, slightly alarmed. The fever went out of Father Michael's eyes as quickly as it had arisen; he sat back, exhausted, and rubbed his forehead for a few moments.

"You would not believe how many others have had blood on their hands," the priest continued, his eyes frowning and focused somewhere else, "blood that they, too, are still trying to wash off."

He suddenly focused back on Trent, his voice back to a more conversational tone as if what he had been saying was of no consequence whatsoever.

"I may not be able to tell you much of what you would like to know, my young friend – but what I can tell you is this: you must begin to pay very close attention to all that has happened, to all that is happening right now, and to all that will happen; and to all that has been said to you, not only by me but also by others."

Trent sat back slowly, trying to digest the old priest's mysterious and provocative words.

"But most of all," Father Michael added, his eyes coming back into focus and locking onto Trent's, "you must find your faith, my son – at all costs – and you must wrap it around yourself very securely, for you are going to need it!"

The priest's next words had been delivered almost as a dismissal, but had caused the hair on the back of Trent's neck to stand up: *"You know of what I speak. None of this, Young Mr. Carter, is as it seems."*

Trent's eyes went wide. His dead wife had spoken very similar words to him.

CHAPTER 14
SANCTUARY

Excerpt from the Journal of Otto Eberhardt:

"9.05.45 - I am not at all sure where we are, and I care even less. I feel little sympathy with the thieves that Ernst was compelled to kill. Indeed, if he hadn't, I am positive we would now be lying dead in their places. I argued lamely to bury the bodies – at least to bury that other innocent, unfortunate, nameless passenger who had died next to me in the back seat, but Ernst refused to spend any time on graves. Instead, we took their car further up the old road until we were well hidden in the trees, dumped the bodies in a ditch there, and spent a cold night in the vehicle, fearful of making even a small fire. Before dawn, we drove the car back up to the highway, merged with the sparse traffic at that early hour, and drove on south into the sleepy little town called Raton, just past the New Mexico state line. There, we spied a milk carrier making his early deliveries and so were able to steal a couple of bottles of fresh milk from the porch of a residence there. We drove aimlessly through town, filling our empty bellies with the wonderful milk, but then became nervous after passing a local police car patrolling the area. We found the first road out of town and headed east into the early dawn lighting the sky over the mesas there. Still fearful of being caught in a stolen vehicle, we finally ditched the car up a canyon, just past a very small settlement of houses identified by a road sign as simply, and ironically, "Yankee." From there, we wandered off the highway on foot and up into the woods.

That was two days ago, and we are now lost, exhausted, injured, and starving; and now Ernst has gotten delirious and feverish from his wounds.

Perhaps God will, at last, be merciful and just, after all, and allow us to finally die out here in the wilderness, unknown and abandoned – as it probably should be."

#

Excerpt from the Diary of Evie Van Ryan:

"May 12, 1945 – Dear Diary: Yesterday was one of the most thrilling days of my life! I have never experienced anything like this before – and I am torn! Part of me feels like a traitor, and another part heroic, like Wonder Woman, from those comic books my brother hides under his mattress.

Oh, I know I should not toy with these matters, even at my age. It could be so dangerous! But both those men are injured – one of them so terribly! How could I have done otherwise?

Besides, the younger one is so very – well – handsome, in a rugged sort of way.

But how in the world am I going to keep this all from Papa? Should I tell him or not? And what if Richard finds out? He would shoot them for sure! Oh, Lord, help me to understand what I am supposed to do!"

#

The little four-year-old buckskin mare snorted and raised her head from the stream from which she had been drinking, water dripping from her mouth. She turned her head to the left with her ears perked forward and stood still, listening and watching, twitching her nostrils. The young, dark haired woman leaned forward on the beautifully tooled saddle and patted the mare's neck.

"What'd ya hear, girl?" she asked as she also looked upstream.

The early afternoon sun dappled through the cottonwood trees as they spread their massive canopies over the shallow spring-fed creek that wound its way down the twisting canyon. The sunlight danced and sparkled along the surface of the water, making it difficult to see anything more than a few yards away. The girl thought she saw movement and figured it must be some of the ranch yearlings that grazed up here this time of year. But it could also be a predator of some sort and her father would surely want to know.

She gathered up the mare's reigns, shaded her eyes, and let her horse step a few feet further upstream, allowing her to pick and choose her own way until she stopped to dip her nose into the cool rushing waters once more. Suddenly, though, the mare coughed, backed quickly away from the streambed, and shook her head vigorously.

"What's the matter, Miss Priss? What's wrong, girl?"

She leaned over again to stroke the horse's neck. Once the animal seemed calmer, she looked past her snout, down towards the water, and stiffened, sucked her breath in, and held it. A ribbon of pink threaded its way downstream like a long, threadbare silk scarf floating just under the surface. She looked back upstream where the water was actually redder and darker; she sat mesmerized as she watched the bloody strands float steadily toward her, then pulled the mare's head up to continue forward to find its source.

#

Evie Van Ryan loved riding through the beautiful, peaceful meadows and these rugged canyons that rose into the foothills behind her father's ranch. A few afternoons a week, she would saddle up Miss Priss, her little buckskin, and disappear into her own little world, not only to get away from the chores and the business – and the boredoms – of a working ranch in the summertime, but also from the eyes of her overprotective father and her prying, older brother Richard. Evie knew that she was attractive with her raven hair and green eyes that she had inherited from her Irish mother and her clear complexion with just a hint of ruddiness in her bright cheeks that she had gotten from her Austrian father.

She also knew the effect she had on most of the ranch-hands in the valley, especially the hot-blooded young wetbacks that did most of the real work around the place, driving her father's herd up into these hills in the early spring after the snows had melted, and driving them back down in the fall for sorting, branding, and shipping. In their leisure time, the young Mexican *vaqueros* showed off their skills at breaking the raw young horses that the ranch also raised. As Evie would drape herself flirtatiously over the top rails of the corral fences, her green eyes would flash, and she would smile at the handsome young cowboys trying to catch her eye and impress her with their makeshift rodeos.

However, she was getting tired of her father's apparent mistrust of her. She wasn't stupid. After all, she was sixteen years old, practically a grown woman, and her mother had been all of seventeen when her father had married her. Evie just didn't understand her Werner Van Ryan's unreasonably prudish attitudes these days. After all, it was the 1940s; almost the middle of the 20th century. Besides, her teasing was all in innocence, flirting idly with the ranch-hands, giving them a little wink and a toss of her long, curly black hair. She had fun seeing that she could make them stop whatever they were doing and stare by merely walking nonchalantly near the stables and corrals where they could be found early in the mornings. She never meant anything by it, being playful, but she would giggle at how they would shake their heads and suck on their teeth, muttering softly to each other in Spanish. Then, they would quickly get back to their work after glancing up at the big ranch house across the way to see her father standing on the veranda, drinking his morning coffee, and glaring down at them over the rim of his cup. If Evie enjoyed practicing her recently developed feminine powers, it was very clear, both to her and any potential suitor, that her father's power to intimidate was greater still – and not to be tested too far.

She had also suspected that her father had instructed her older brother Richard to keep a watchful eye out for her. Whether or not this conspiracy against her was true, Richard's watchfulness was reinforced in no uncertain terms when he had grabbed her by the arm one morning right after he had spied one of the handsome young Mexican cowboys returning her smile with a nod and wink of his own. Richard had pulled her none too gently around the corner of the barn and pushed her against the wall.

"You better watch out, you little troublemaker!" her brother had hissed at her. He had just turned eighteen, only a couple of years older than she, but had already filled out to a lean two hundred and ten pounds of pure muscle, and at six foot two he towered over Evie. She glared back at him defiantly as he leaned in close, continuing his warning: "You better be very careful, you little slut – or you're gonna wind up with a little wet-back in your belly!"

No one had ever spoken to her that way; such a thought was, frankly, shocking to her. Evie began to breathe hard and her blood boiled as she tried to come up with an angry retort. She continued to glare at Richard, but had felt her anger well up in her eyes until she choked up and couldn't speak. She wasn't about to let her brother see her cry, so she jerked her arm away from him and stomped away into the meadow behind the barn.

The next day, a little chagrined, she had walked a little less enticingly past the corrals, looking resolutely at the ground, trying not to do anything to catch the young men's eyes. Still, she couldn't help but notice that the handsome *vaquero* named Raul wouldn't be winking at her today, what with the huge black eye he sported that had swollen shut, a puffy dark cheek, and a bloodied split lip.

Later at the breakfast table, as Richard had passed her the peach jam, her favorite, she had put two and two together when she noticed his skinned and scabbed knuckles and had looked up to find him silently observing her reaction with a satisfied smirk on his face.

#

Now, Evie was once again looking at blood, this time flowing past her in the cool mountain stream. She stopped Miss Priss while her breath came shallowly as she gingerly dismounted and stepped carefully onto the rock-strewn shore of the stream. The sound of the rushing water hopefully covered any noise she might inadvertently be making by dislodging stones, and she held Miss Priss's halter close and stroked the mare's muzzle with her free hand to prevent the animal from snorting again. Evie's heart thumped loudly in her throat as she stepped further, her eyes darting from the rocks at her feet back up to the tree line ahead. She couldn't help but glance occasionally at the bloody water flowing to her right. She squinted as she tried to see around the bend up ahead that disappeared into a gathering of low foliage that enveloped the stream.

With the sound of another sudden cough, Evie froze as she realized this one had not emanated from Miss Priss, but rather from the other side of the oaks just ahead. She stood still for a moment, patted the mare again reassuringly, and moved quietly to the saddlebag strapped to the animal's side. She unlaced the leather flap and fumbled around inside. Her hand came out holding a small .32 caliber revolver that she then tucked into the waist of her canvas riding breeches. The handgun had been a gift from her father for protection against snakes and varmints. He had taught her to shoot when she was twelve and had been increasingly impressed with her marksmanship.

Having the pistol now gave her a welcome boost of courage, but her heart still thumped in her throat.

She quietly pulled Miss Priss around to a small patch of grass in the shade, just a few feet away from the stream. There, she tied the mare's reins loosely to a small scrub oak, allowing enough slack for Miss Priss to graze, hopefully contentedly and quietly, while not being able to wander off.

Evie pulled the handgun from her waist, checked quickly to see that it was loaded, took another deep breath, and advanced carefully toward the bushes. She worked her way up the embankment to a place that became relatively flat again and edged around the other side of the oak bushes, moving cautiously and closely around a large cottonwood trunk in case she would need it for cover.

She heard muted voices nearby and suddenly stopped. She hugged the tree with her body, shifted the pistol to her left hand, and aimed it, as her father had taught her to do with either hand, toward the direction of the voices. Evie deliberately, slowly, moved to the left, leaning until just her eye cleared the tree. She held her breath, brought the pistol up, and steadied it against the trunk.

Fifteen yards away, at the stream, were two of the most terrifying men Evie had ever laid eyes on. One knelt at the edge of the water, alternately wetting and squeezing out a strip of cloth torn from one of their shirts. The other man was lying on his back, barely conscious, his head and one arm fully extended into the water. Blood trickled and dripped from unseen wounds into the stream where it mingled with the water and flowed away. Occasionally, he moaned and turned his head painfully and deliriously from one side to the other.

Both men's clothes were so ragged they looked like weather-beaten scarecrows, or worse. Evie had seen hobos before, roaming the land and sometimes asking for work and food back at the house. But these men's shirts and trousers were not only worn, but were shredded and burned and hung in tatters from their limbs, as if they had come through some horrific ordeal. Evie could see through the rips and tears in the clothing that the skin underneath was also torn and filthy – and bloodied. Their faces, heads, arms, and hands were torn and crimson where dozens of small wounds had not only oozed blood, but also looked terribly burned in places. The man kneeling at the stream was barefoot, his feet swollen, red, and blistered. He busied himself gently cleaning the older man's wounds and rinsing the wet cloth between washings. Occasionally, he placed the rag on the injured man's swollen lips to let cool water dribble into his mouth. The injured man would cough and gag and then reach weakly with his good hand to press the cloth harder to his parched lips. He fell back again, the back of his bloodied head splashing into the stream. At that time the kneeling man turned back and scooped water from the stream into his battered, cupped hands, raised it to his own face, and slurped loudly. Evie stood transfixed as the man drank as if he had never tasted water before. He then repositioned himself to stretch out on his stomach and lie face down in the water, taking it by the handfuls over his filthy head, rubbing his face hard, and combing wet fingers back through his hair. After a couple minutes of this routine, he got back up on his knees, unbuttoned what was left of his shirt, and stripped it and a ragged, filthy undershirt off, revealing a scarred but muscular back and arms. His skin was laced with streaks of blood and abrasions, bruises and burns.

What on earth had happened to these men?

The scarecrow soaked his washcloth again and began giving himself a bath. He was just about to dip the cloth into the stream again when he suddenly froze, hand in midair, water dripping from the rag. He cocked his head slightly and slowly raised both arms above his head where the rag now dripped water onto the top of his head. Evie stood still, wondering what on earth he was doing.

"Whoever you are," he finally croaked, "I am not armed."

Evie suddenly came to her senses, only at that moment realizing that he was speaking to her, even though she still hid behind the tree. She hesitated for only a second more.

"Yeah? Well, I sure am!" she shouted, a little louder than necessary, and took a couple of long, quick strides away from the tree, careful to keep about thirty feet distance between herself and the strangers. She brought the .32 pistol up to a shooter's stance, aimed it at the scarecrow's head, and cocked it.

"Now just who the hell are you two?" she demanded, just a bit less loudly than before. Evie had never really cursed much, certainly not when other people were around. So *hell* was about the only foul language she would ever have dreamed of using on someone. If the truth be known, her bravado had already left her, and if the man hadn't become aware of her, she probably would've tried to sneak away by now to go find her dad and let him handle the situation.

"What the damn hell are you doing on our – *my* land? And what the hell – " Evie's voice began to soften as the shirtless man with his hands up began to slowly turn around where she could see him better. She noticed he had a handsome jaw line under that dirty face and tired, but somewhat kind, blue eyes. "Wha – What the hell happened to you guys?" she stammered.

She looked at him in shock and lowered her pistol slightly. The man started to lower his hands; Evie jerked the gun back up and he, likewise, raised them again.

"I said 'don't move!'" she shouted. The man smiled weakly.

"Um – no…you did not," he protested quietly.

"What?"

"You only pointed your gun at me."

"Yeah? So?"

"You did not tell me, 'don't move.'"

Evie looked at him, her eyes still wide, and began to shift nervously from one foot to the other.

"Okay, smarty pants. Then *don't move!*" She nodded once, with what she hoped was an authoritative look, and added, "Or I'll shoot ya! That plain enough for you?"

Neither of them said a word for several moments, after which the man shuffled a little to more fully face her, still uncomfortably on his knees. He allowed his arms to drop a few inches.

"And stop moving around!"

"I do not think you will shoot an unarmed man," he said. "At least I would hope not."

"I sure will," she yelled at him, waving her gun, "if I have to!"

Evie noticed the man had an accent that sounded somewhat similar to her father's – that was to say, European.

"Where you from, anyways?" she asked. "You sound like my daddy – the way you talk, I mean. What is it?"

The man turned to look at his friend lying very still in the water. The injured man moaned again and turned his head as if trying to shake it. His eyes were trying to open, but remained heavy and finally closed again. The other man glanced back at Evie but lowered his hands a few more inches, as if testing her.

"I must tend to my friend. He is badly injured – we both are, in fact – as you can surely see." He looked back up to her again with an eternal weariness in his eyes that Evie felt would break her heart if she looked at him much longer.

"Can you, perhaps, help us?" he asked, exhaustion gripping him.

"Why? I mean, what happened to you, Mister?"

The man's deep blue eyes gazed down at the water gurgling past them for a moment as if trying to decide what to say. He suddenly seemed to have made up his mind and turned back to her. She couldn't help noticing just how ruggedly handsome he looked, even beneath the dirt and bloody streaks. His blue eyes pierced hers and held them while he slowly lowered his hands tiredly into his lap. Evie did not stop him this time.

"Is your father, by any chance – German?" the shirtless man asked.

"German? Why, no. No, he's not." She stopped and looked at him curiously. "Our family is from Austria – well, Mama's Irish, so I guess that means Ireland and Austria – but why would you think we're from Germany?" Evie had lowered the gun down further. The man shrugged and smiled again.

"Because," he began, as if patiently instructing a child, "Austria is near Germany, and the people there speak similarly – and we are German." He gestured to indicate the other man as well as himself. He paused, lowered his face, and continued in an almost relieved tone. "We are actually German soldiers, from Germany, and we are wounded from a recent battle – an explosion…" His voice trailed off, and he lowered his head again. "I am so sick and tired of all the killing and the hate and the war," he muttered, almost to himself.

He looked up at Evie with the saddest eyes she had ever seen. "You did not hear about the train? The – accident? Two, three days ago, I think?"

"Train? No – no train." She felt confused. "But I do know that the war is over," she said, finally lowering her gun hand to her side, letting it dangle harmlessly. "I heard about it on the radio last week – Germany surrendered; and Hitler is dead, thank God!"

The man stared dumbly at her, nodded finally, lifted his hands again, and just as quickly let them drop back into his lap in resignation. He sighed and began to slowly and painfully stand.

Evie quickly lifted her gun again for just a moment, hesitantly, before lowering it, deciding the exhausted and injured men posed no immediate threat.

"So. It is true. Germany has surrendered," he said, taking the words in, standing in a tired slouch. "I suppose finally, so must we." He looked wearily at Evie and down at his companion lying unconscious and bleeding, and back up at her. "May I please know your name, *Fräulein*?" he grimaced as he painfully began pulling his ragged shirt back on.

Evie stared at him, at a loss for words.

"Um – my name? Why, it's Evie – Evie Van Ryan. I –uh – my daddy owns this ranch you're on."

The man nodded, smiled, and after a brief pause, continued with a slight, formal bow.

"And my name is *Leutnant* Otto Eberhardt – of the *Deutsches Afrikakorps, Dritte* – um, Third – *Panzer* Division."

The German officer tugged at the remaining hem of his destroyed shirt, trying pathetically and unsuccessfully to find a way to tuck it in. He made a show of smartly standing at attention and painfully pulled his arm up into a salute.

"And on behalf of my commanding officer here and myself – I, too, hereby surrender to you, and to your mercy, *Fräulein* Van Ryan!"

#

Otto awoke to the soft sounds of morning: the songs of birds calling nearby, adding their morning greetings to the squabbling chatter of a couple of squirrels; a soft rattling of leaves brushing against a window; and snoring coming from somewhere nearby. Wood smoke was in the air and his nose twitched as he swore he smelled bacon cooking.

He slowly opened his eyes, but something was pulled over his face. He squirmed until his head emerged from some sort of sleeping bag. Still unsure of where he was, he looked around at his surroundings. Although he felt a little confused, he also felt like he had just had the best night's sleep he'd had in a long, long time. He also felt something else he hadn't felt for awhile – totally safe and secure. He squirmed again until he was completely out of his bedding and could stand shakily. Every joint and inch of flesh seemed to cry out in pain as he slowly stretched and squinted to look around him, exploring his surroundings.

He seemed to be in a small, one room cabin of some sort with a single door in the middle of one wall and one window high above a metal sink with a long handled water pump attached to it. In one corner, a couple of comfortable looking chairs stood with a small table between them holding a kerosene lamp. This area appeared to be some sort of reading corner as there was a small bookcase filled with books here. The lamp was lit and a warm inviting glow emanated from it.

In the middle of the room sat a small wooden dining table set with plates, utensils, and blue metal coffee cups. Nearby sat a small black woodstove, its stovepipe angling up and disappearing into the ceiling. A coffee pot billowed steam and bubbled on top of the stove, along with a cast iron skillet that sizzled with the cooking bacon he had smelled.

Otto became aware of the snoring noises again and peered toward the other corner of the room where a low trundle bed of some kind sat in the shadows against the wall. The snoring came from within a jumble of bedclothes and blankets covering a shapeless form there.

Otto yawned and stretched again, but winced some more in pain. He slowly frowned as the peace he had felt took an ominous turn and the events of the previous days began flipping across his memory like an old grainy film. He recalled riding a train in the late afternoon, watching the changing colors of the clouds through the pines but not really comprehending anything except for the satchel of explosives under his seat; jumping from the train as it careened toward doom; a life and death struggle with some American soldier; and finally, time stopping entirely as his world lit up and turned inside out and upside down.

As the cold realities returned, so did the guilt and dread at what he had done. Now, in this same moment, parading before his mind's eye were all the haunted faces, all those innocent people who had probably died in the explosion. He had hoped and prayed that God would not let him remember them. Instead, though, here they all were again, each and every unique facial feature burned forever into his consciousness – the kindly Negro conductor; the civilian passengers as well as the homeward-bound soldiers who had been seated all around him, some still with bandaged wounds from their battlefield ordeals; the pretty young mother with her two boisterous boys – whom he had purposefully moved to the dining car hoping against hope that they might be safe from the explosion. He prayed now that they had, indeed, survived, but the woman's face haunted him the most and he feared that the worst had happened to them, too.

Otto felt a deep chill and shuddered as a powerful wave of guilt and shame washed over him. These people were all probably dead now – by his hand.

And all for what purpose: a wartime action when the war was, unbeknownst to him at the time, already over. This made all those deaths – *murder.*

He shuffled over to the stove, grabbed a cup from the table as he passed, and filled it to the brim with hot coffee. The pot was scalding, but he was grateful for the pain as it seared his shaking hand – anything to take his thoughts elsewhere. He sipped the aromatic, piping hot liquid, allowing it to blister his lips and tongue, almost happy at the punishment. Glancing down at the skillet, he picked up a large fork there and began flipping the bacon as it continued to cook. Only then did he begin to wonder how on earth the food and the coffee had gotten here – and who had started the cooking?

As if on cue, a slight footfall sounded on the porch and the door quietly opened with a soft squeak. He turned to see a young woman standing there in the doorway, her arms full of kindling, and a look of surprise on her face. Otto drew a blank for a moment before finally recognizing Evie Van Ryan, the girl he had "surrendered" to yesterday. He smiled as he remembered her and toasted her with his coffee cup.

"Good morning, *Fraülein* Van Ryan. What a pleasant surprise!" Evie nodded slowly, still wearing a curious look of shock on her face. Her eyes dipped, giving Otto the once-over, and turned red. He froze with the cup at his mouth and looked down at himself. He was shirtless and barefoot, and what was once a pair of long johns now hung off of his lower extremities in filthy tatters. Even from his angle, he could see that several of the tears and holes exposed more than he – or Evie, obviously – were comfortable with.

Otto also blushed furiously and dropped one hand down to casually cover himself. He then calmly took another sip of coffee as he turned away from the girl and nonchalantly walked over to the pile of bedding he had just crawled out of. There he began kicking at the pile and looking for his clothes. Evie finally came to her senses, walked on in, and shut the door with her foot; for the next few moments, they both tried to act as if all were normal.

"Well, I wondered if you boys were going to sleep the day away." She dropped the kindling in the wood box near the stove and busied herself at the skillet. She continued to talk non-stop. "But I am not in the least surprised. You fellas were both in pretty bad shape – still are, by the looks of it." She suddenly stopped herself and blushed again. "Well, I mean – you were both fairly well tuckered out." Here she glanced over and gestured at the bed with genuine concern on her face.

"So how's your friend this morning? He does seem to be sleeping soundly – guess that's one good sign."

Evie turned back to her work, scooting the bacon to one side of the pan and breaking a few eggs into the hot grease.

"I swear I thought he was going to just drift away in the middle of the night." She had quickly glanced back at Otto, who seemed to be having trouble finding his clothes. "Oh, here," she pointed. "You'll be wanting those," she continued and pointed to the chair by the door. "I took all your old things and burned them outside." Otto looked up at her perplexed for a moment. "Well!" she continued. "They were full of holes and fairly worthless!" She paused and nodded again at the folded stack of clothing in the chair. "So I brought you guys some stuff to wear – some of Daddy's and my brother's old clothes. Hope something there fits you." She turned back to her work.

"Um – thank you," Otto stammered and moved over to the chair, still modestly covering himself.

Evie blushed again. "I – uh – even brought you some – well, these," pointing to the underwear. "There. Probably underneath there – somewhere." She indicated vaguely in that direction with her spatula, but didn't dare look again.

Otto picked through the clothes and selected a flannel shirt and pair of dungarees and held them up to himself. In the meantime, Evie had grabbed plates, scooped eggs and bacon onto them, and placed them back on the table along with the coffee pot. She stood admiring her work for a moment, wiping her hands on a towel, pushing back a stray strand of black hair that played around her face, and turned and strode purposefully towards the door. She did this all without taking another look in Otto's direction.

"So, I reckon I'll just step outside here for awhile," she continued awkwardly, "give you a little privacy to – well – do what you need to do there." She stood and just stared at her hand on the doorknob for a moment or two longer than was really necessary.

Otto could see her neck was flushed red and he truly could think of nothing to say. For the first time, he suddenly realized just how beautiful the embarrassed young woman was.

Evie opened the door, stepped out, and shut it quickly, only to open it again almost immediately, but only a crack. Otto saw her fingers push something through the crack.

"And here – you're probably gonna want this stuff. I found them in your pockets." Otto took a step forward and reached a hand out tentatively to take two small pieces of pasteboard from her fingers – Ernst's and his POW identification cards – some folded currency, and a pocketknife. Her fingers disappeared and the door closed, only to open yet again.

"And – as you can surely see, I guess – your breakfast is ready." She paused.

"And I'll be back in a couple of minutes to check on your friend. I am sure those bandages need changing." Another pause, and when he didn't say anything, she pulled the door to with a loud thud. This time her footsteps faded quickly away until he could no longer hear them.

Otto stared at the door with his mouth open, the new clothes draped loosely over his arm, the I.D. cards in his hand, and hunger pangs – or something very like them – gnawing at his stomach.

CHAPTER 15
THROUGH A GLASS DARKLY

The next day Trent got up before sunrise, pulled on a pair of sweats and sneakers, put the coffee on, and fed Jarhead before letting him outside. Yawning, he made himself a thermos of coffee laced with honey and hot milk, grabbed a bottle of water, pulled on a stocking cap, and tiptoed out of the house into the pre-dawn silence. He stood for a moment and enjoyed the pine-scented moist air of the sleeping world. He could see his breath as he got into his truck. He pulled the door to, put the gear in neutral, and coasted silently down the driveway for several yards before starting the engine so as not to wake Sophie.

He drove down the dirt road off of Raton Mesa, then south all the way through the sleeping town, finally pulling into the empty parking lot of the physical therapy building. He climbed stiffly out of his truck and let himself into the back door with the key they had given him with his membership. He found the lights, turned on the music system, and cranked up the volume.

He pushed himself harder than usual today, first warming up on the recumbent bike before doing three sets on all the weight machines, concentrating mostly on the leg exercises. He groaned with the exertion, but was bound and determined to get his injured body back into some semblance of condition to match his equal determination to whip his troubled mind back into shape. He was tired of the weaknesses he could still feel in his legs, but even more tired of all these jumbled thoughts and disconnected memories that he kept tripping over. Time to get back on the horse, ride hard, and find the path forward he needed to be on. It was either now or never.

He finished his workout, trembling and dripping with sweat, then chugged and drained his water bottle. He toweled off his face and arms, wiped down the equipment he had used with disinfectant tissues, and pulled on his sweatshirt and stocking cap just as one of the therapists walked in to start her early shift. They nodded to each other at the door, part of a familiar routine. Trent was self-conscious and preferred to work out in private, so he was always pleased when he timed it so perfectly.

He sipped his coffee and thought about his day as he drove home. Today, he would dive back into those cold case files stacked in his office. Something about them had bothered him for a long time. *Could they all be linked?* Certainly, some patterns in each one seemed to be replicated in others. However, something else bothered him about one case in particular. He would start with that file today, even though he realized he would need some help to sift through it all – to find all the answers. Ben had told him to use anyone in the office he liked, but Trent wasn't sure he could think of anyone he liked well enough to work closely with.

Better strike that "like" part, he thought to himself.

He drove back through the wakening town and back uphill to his house perched on the side of the mesa where he parked and got out of his truck. He stood there and poured the last cup of coffee from his Thermos and sipped it, quietly waiting for the sun to blink and peek over the massive rim of Johnson Mesa three miles to the east.

He waited for something else – someone else – too, but didn't hold out any real expectations.

Jarhead jumped up on the warm hood, sauntered over to rub against Trent's shoulder, and purred loudly as he waited expectantly for a scratch behind the ears. Suddenly, the big orange cat growled and batted at Trent's hand before jumping down and quickly running away, clearly frightened.

"That cat never liked me too much," Vicky said as she appeared at her husband's shoulder. She gently slipped her arm through his and leaned against him. Trent didn't react at all, continued to wait for the sunrise, and sipped his lukewarm coffee calmly.

"That cat never liked anybody much," he answered quietly. He was getting used to his dead wife's appearances. They no longer surprised him, nor did they upset him. He had given up trying to explain her presence to himself – or to Sophie, who would not understand and only worry. Like it or not, real or not, Vicky was just there, and Trent had resigned himself to it, to her, or whatever she was.

Besides, she certainly seemed to know things. Then again, she was really making him work for what she knew, for some reason.

"*Things are not what they seem,*" he finally said, deciding to get right to the point. He gazed into the distant sunrise as it finally began to glimmer over the mesa. "You've said that to me on more than one occasion now."

"Yes – I have, My Love."

"Then, it's something important?"

"Yes – it is important. Very, very important, My Darling."

"So, what are you trying to tell me – what do you mean by it?" Trent continued to avoid looking at her.

Silence between them lingered for a long while. Trent felt Vicky snuggle tighter to him, but he felt no real warmth emanate from her. The feeling was fairly unsettling.

"It means that there is truth – and then there is – *Truth,*" she said finally. Her voice whispered and echoed simultaneously, which was also a bit disturbing.

Trent pondered her words. He was learning to carefully absorb information; let it settle into his mind a bit before responding; let it find the new synapses his brain was forming for itself in there; new ways of interpreting, thinking, finding meaning.

"So – you mean that there is more than one truth?" He turned his head and finally looked at her for the first time since she had appeared today.

"No. Only one *Truth.*"

"I don't understand."

"Yes, I think you do, Darling One – you understand, deep down. You just don't see."

"You mean that I don't hear, don't you?"

Vicky pulled around and faced him, placing her hands softly on his chest. She gazed lovingly up into his eyes; he felt his resolve begin to melt away.

"No, Trenny. You hear perfectly well. You're just not seeing what you hear. You look, but don't recognize what is right there, for what it really is. If you only had eyes to see – ears to hear – then you would also have the knowledge."

"Knowledge of what?"

"The Truth."

He rolled his eyes. "And so it comes, full circle again," he muttered, exasperated. "But I see you well enough, don't I?" Trent was suddenly finding it hard to breath. He reached out for her, but she moved away before he could touch her.

"Do you?" she asked.

"Vic?" he muttered, half way between a statement and a question.

She continued backing slowly away from him. Her voice became very low and echoed even more distantly now. "You see only what you wish to see. You hear only what you expect to hear."

"You mean what I see isn't the truth?" he demanded. "You're not real? Is that why you can't tell me what I want to know? Because you're only in my mind, which has none of the answers anyway, and I'm just trapped inside of a never-ending, vicious cycle in there?" His voice rose along with the desperation rising in him again. "Is that it?"

He took a couple of steps toward her, but she quickly eluded and outpaced him, drifting backwards from him across the driveway, and through the oak trees, ghostlike, her feet seeming to not touch the ground. The rising sun was now in Trent's eyes, as Vicky seemed to be fading into its brilliance. Her voice floated back to him – all around him, through him – on the morning breeze.

"No – your answers are already there in your mind, Darling – most of them, anyway. Look beyond your eyes – look behind them. Look beyond the light, and behind the shadows; think – and see." She stopped and turned back to him. Only a brilliant aura of light defined her now.

"Think about the end – where you last saw me in the light, once before – where all the beautiful colors live." Vicky's voice was a mixture of the wind and the sunlight now. Trent could no longer see her at all. "Go back to that place. Stop there awhile. Think beyond the truths you only thought were there. Then find the real Truth."

Trent heard the front door of the house open and turned to see Sophie letting Jarhead in. She was barefoot and again wearing one of his old flannel shirts as a housecoat that she wrapped tightly around her against the morning air. She squinted up and spied her father there.

"Well, good morning!" she said. "You got up and around early, I see. Already been to the gym?" Trent nodded numbly and turned back to stare at the spot where Vicky had just been.

Her figure, her aura, her scent, any trace of her presence had simply slipped away into the brilliance of the rising sun.

"Damned ghost," he muttered, finally, pouring out the remainder of his cold coffee, heading toward the house, and kicking at gravel in the driveway.

#

Trent had showered, shaved, and dressed while Sophie made their breakfast – eggs over easy, bacon, biscuits with gravy, and sliced tomatoes, just the way she knew he liked it. She enjoyed trying to please him, to try to help her father get his life back to normal – whatever that was. They ate together in the kitchen and talked about their respective upcoming days. Trent told Sophie he planned to spend a few days working on the cold case files to see if he could start piecing together the similarities that he suspected were there. He thought they might point to some sort of serial killer, but he needed to call some of the adjacent counties to see if they also had any similar cases going on.

"I began translating that old journal you gave me," Sophie mentioned finally. "It's intriguing. Might even be good enough to turn into a story for the newspaper – maybe even a novel."

Trent just nodded. "That's real good, Sweetie," he said, staring into his plate of food as he chewed absently. He seemed preoccupied again.

Sophie looked at him for a moment, then went on to say how this Otto Eberhardt fellow wrote with such emotion and detail and how he had, also, described another man, someone with whom he had escaped from the POW camp. But the way Otto had described the guy, someone named Ernst, had really sent shivers down her back. He seemed the epitome of evil. She chuckled to herself and said she was just as glad these two guys were long since dead and gone, for she would really have hated to run into them.

"Yeah, they sound like they could've caused a lot of trouble way back when," Trent said, wiping his mouth, rising from his chair. "Gotta run, Kiddo."

Sophie sighed again, feeling dismissed. She wished her dad would take more of an interest in the journal project. After all, he was the one who had asked her to do it. But she knew he was focused on more important matters these days and had probably just given it to her to keep her busy. Frankly, she was just glad that he was finally concentrating on his investigative work again, instead of ghosts.

She walked him to the door and called after him as he headed to his truck. "Oh, and I won't be cooking this evening. Going out – with – friends," she stammered. She started to say something else, but instead, bit her lip.

Trent waved at her as he climbed into his truck. "That's great, Honey. I'll just plan on working late then."

She watched his truck bounce its way down the dirt road and disappear into the juniper and oak bushes around the corner. She sighed again and went back inside the house where she dressed in jeans and a sweatshirt and sat down at her computer to do some work. She stared at the blank screen for several seconds, then turned to see the old journal lying there. She reached over and flipped it open to the page she'd last read – something about a train and the tunnel under the pass, right at the end of the war. She picked it up and read a little more before she began typing. The interpretation was still slow going, trying to capture the exact idiom and nuance of the German soldier's words.

Several minutes later, she dropped the journal and stared in amazement at what she had just translated into her computer. She read it again, thought for a moment, took a deep breath, picked up her cell phone, and speed dialed.

"Colfax County Sheriff's office," a voice answered.

"Hi, Molly –it's Sophie."

"Well, g'morning there, Sunshine," Molly said cheerfully. "Now, let me guess – your daddy's not here yet, so that can only leave one other person you could possibly want to speak to, I'm thinking."

"You guessed it as usual, Molly. I don't know why they don't have you out solving all these cases instead of fielding phone calls."

"Because they don't know what a good thing they have in me yet. Just a sec and I'll put you through."

Sophie bit her bottom lip until another voice came on.

"Detective Armijo," the voice announced. "How may I help you?"

"Well, Detective – you could help me in more ways than one, I'm sure," Sophie answered mischievously, awaiting the appreciative chuckle from the other end of the line. "But seriously, do you remember that old journal I told you about – the one Dad gave me to translate?"

"Sure do, ma'am," Hector answered, hesitantly, as if he was not entirely free to talk.

"Well, I've got some of it translated and – well – didn't you mention once that you had some uncle or somebody who had guarded the train tunnels during the war?"

"Yeah – my grandfather was up there. In fact, he got killed up there in some freak accident or something. An explosion, I think it was. But beyond that –" His voice trailed away in what she imagined was a shrug. "Why?"

"Well, you might find this pretty interesting," Sophie continued. "Something about that accident is in this journal." Sophie's tone of voice grew a little coy. "But I guess we'll just have to wait until tonight to discuss it further – that is, if we're still on for tonight."

#

Trent parked his truck right up front in its usual spot and went into the courthouse. He passed Molly's window and proceeded straight into the office area, Molly's voice following him in.

"Well, nice to see you too, Officer Carter – and good morning."

Trent kept walking and waved his hand in the air in some sort of acknowledgement. He spied Detective Armijo out of the corner of his eye, turned abruptly as he opened his office door, and stood watching and thinking for a minute. Hector was smiling and talking quietly on the phone, obviously not departmental business. Trent made up his mind and entered his office, leaving the door ajar.

"Get off that damn phone and come in here," he barked in Hector's general direction. Hector turned beet red, stammered something into the mouthpiece, and hung up as he jumped out of his chair and almost trotted to Trent's office.

"Yes, sir – right away, sir."

"Have a seat," Trent directed as Armijo rushed into the office.

Trent stood behind his desk, flipping idly through a legal sized, green pasteboard folder. Inside were several pages clipped to one side and a series of 5X7 photographs taped neatly on the other. Hector took a seat across from Trent and sat waiting quietly.

"You've worked on some of these old files, haven't you, Hector?"

"Yes, sir. I have. I helped put some of the newer ones together," Hector answered, trying to sound helpful and efficient. "I believe I could let you know where to find most anything you needed to – in the files, I mean – glad to do so, that is – Deputy Carter – " Hector's voice trailed away, embarrassed.

"At ease, Private."

"Uh – excuse me, Sir?"

"I mean calm down, Hector. You act like a fresh recruit, and you're making me feel like some grizzled old drill sergeant." Trent looked up at Hector and continued. "And if we're going to be working together, it's 'Trent,' if you don't mind."

Trent paused, looked over, and pointed to an unopened white cardboard box on the corner of his desk. "And Hector," he continued, "why do you insist on bringing me doughnuts?"

Hector was at a loss for words, blushed again, and shrugged.

"Well, please stop. It's irritating."

He turned the file around as he spoke and slid it across the desk to Hector, who nodded quickly and looked down at the file, then back up again. His eyes grew wide as he seemed to realize something.

"What was that – did you say, 'working together?'"

"Yes, that's what I said."

"As in, *working* working – or just working *today* – together – sort of thing?"

"As in 'working' working – together – sort of thing," Trent answered, sitting down finally. "That is, if you think you're up to the challenge." Trent tapped the file with his forefinger. Hector looked back at the file, up again, and broke into a grin.

"Oh, yes sir! Definitely up to it – definitely, sir – uh – Trent, that is."

Hector grinned again and shoved his hand out to offer Trent a handshake. Trent stared at Hector's hand incredulously for a second before slowly grasping it, frowned, and shook it once. Hector pulled his hand back, embarrassed.

"Sorry, sir – er – Trent, for the exuberance, that is," he blurted.

Trent continued tapping the file until Hector stopped talking, before continuing.

"I had asked Sheriff Ferguson for a little help. And I knew you'd done some work on these files in the past. So how about this one? Remember anything about it?"

Hector studied the file. The photograph Trent was tapping showed a close-up of a frightened and disheveled young Hispanic woman, seated in the back seat of a department cruiser. Her face was rather pretty from what he could see beneath a rash of scrapes and bruises, her lower lip bloody and swollen, her dark hair matted and wet. Hector looked at the other photos arrayed neatly and taped beneath hers. He cringed at the sight of a blood-soaked corpse of what appeared to be a man, his face half gone in a mass of blood and matter, his clothes drenched in blood. Several photos, taken at several angles, was the norm for a crime scene investigation, along with others of footprints, tire tracks, and establishing shots of the landscapes around the scene. Yellow crime scene tape had staked out a general area, and in a couple of shots, various law enforcement personnel were milling around.

In one shot, Hector even recognized Trent in the background, leaning against a department SUV and apparently talking on a cell phone. Sheriff Ferguson was standing near him.

"So, do you recognize this case?" Trent asked.

"Yeah, sure do," Hector answered, looking intently at the victims' photos again. "Couple of illegals. I remember putting this together myself." He glanced at the name on the file. "Segura, Rogelio and Mirielle – couple of years back, maybe?"

"Four and a half, to be exact. Notice anything in particular about this one?"

Hector squinted at the photos again. "Uh – no. Guy's face is blown away." Hector chuckled to cover his apparent horror, looked back up at Trent, and stopped laughing. He cleared his throat. "Should I be noticing something in particular, Sir?"

"Well, a couple of things stand out to me," Trent continued. "For one thing, we seem to have a photograph of Mrs. Segura – apparently alive, if not entirely well – obviously taken *after* the incident." Trent paused as Hector looked more closely. "And we also seem to have a statement on file from her here that makes for interesting reading," Trent noted further.

Hector still looked puzzled, so Trent spelled it out. "If a lot of these cases are tied together by one killer – which, by the way, we still have to prove – and in all of the other cases the victims are dead, then Mirielle Segura seems to be our only surviving witness to any of these attacks."

"Wow!" Hector exclaimed, before looking back up, a somewhat confused look on his face. "So, you're saying we have a lead?"

Trent leaned back in his chair and placed his hands on his thighs. "Well, one would hope for a lead or two. But her statement there is all over the place and filled with ambiguities and a couple of contradictions."

Sort of like me, Trent wanted to add, but didn't.

"So, maybe we need to go interview her again and see if we can learn anything new?" Hector offered, getting excited.

"I think you're absolutely right. Mirielle Segura could very well be the best clue we have in these cases." He paused for effect. "But Hector, there's one more important fact that jumps out of that file at me," Trent continued. Hector waited, studied the file again, then looked back at Trent, and shrugged. Trent caught Hector's clueless look, and chuckled. Hector looked chagrined.

"Oh, don't worry: you wouldn't have noticed it, Hector. Not in a hundred years. In fact, no one but me would've seen it."

Trent reached over and pointed at the photograph of himself talking on the phone. He sat back again, looking carefully at Hector as if sizing him up, and decided to continue with full disclosure.

"Detective, if we're going to be partners, there's one thing you need to understand up front, for your sake as well as mine. Because you and everyone else out there," Trent gestured toward the rest of the office, but he could have been indicating the world, "know that I have not been myself for quite awhile. In fact, some would think I'm downright crazy."

Hector began to mildly protest. "Oh, no sir – I have never thought anything like that, believe me."

Trent cut him off with a wave of the hand.

"Skip it, Hector. I understand. But I was in a bad accident that is still causing me major difficulties. Now I won't go into all the clinical details, but suffice it to say – " Trent paused, searching carefully for the words, "suffice it to say I am experiencing more than a few – uh – lapses." He leaned forward and nodded towards the photograph once more.

"For example – and this is going to sound very strange to you," Trent paused, pulling his words together carefully, " – as far as I'm concerned, I was never at that crime scene that day."

"Sir?" Hector looked from Trent to the photograph and back again. "Well, how could that be? Somebody doctor the photo?"

"No, nothing of the sort – and you're not listening, Hector. What I am saying to you is that I must've been there – there's the photo. But I have no distinct memory of being there. What's more than that, I have no recollection at all of working this case, or ever meeting Mrs. Murielle Segura." Trent's face took on a more serious demeanor as Hector simply looked shocked.

"You see what I mean, Hector?" he continued. "So, I'm afraid that if you're going to partner up with me, you'll possibly have a lot of babysitting to do with me," Trent paused, "at least for awhile." Trent paused once more. "You willing to put up with a lot of my crap?"

"Yes, of course, Mr. Carter – Trent – anything I can do to help at all. Anything."

"Well, I guess that makes us partners, then."

There was silence in the office for a few seconds.

"There is just one more thing, Hector." Trent leaned forward, motioned his new partner closer, then slid the white cardboard box across the desk to him.

"For the love of all that's holy – no more doughnuts.

CHAPTER 16
MY BROTHER'S KEEPER

Excerpt from the Journal of Otto Eberhardt:

"7.03.47 – I am such a conflicted man. God picked me up from a time and place of unbelievable brutality, horror, and blood, and dropped me into a piece of heaven itself – this beautiful ranch hidden away in the mountains of the fabled American West where we have been welcomed and been given honest work. In my wildest dreams as a boy, I would have never believed I would be living the life of a real cowboy in such a beautiful sanctuary of peace and safety. Herr Van Ryan could have so easily turned us in to the authorities. Instead, he took pity, perhaps because of our common European heritage, but more probably because we are all so sick of that war. The work is hard and I go to bed each night exhausted, but we are well treated and well fed, and even paid a modest wage in real American dollars – not that I would dare venture far to spend it. Instead, I send most of my money to my precious wife and daughter in Germany. And therein lies the quandary. I fear that all my letters home to them have gone astray. Several of them have been returned undeliverable. Ernst tells me they are dead or else that she assumes I am dead and has perhaps remarried – 'Probably to an American soldier,' he says, laughing at my dilemma, 'who is sleeping with her in your bed – eating food from your dinnerware – and bouncing your daughter on his knee.' He infuriates me! But I really have no way of knowing – it is not as if I can freely contact the German consulate. I would probably be immediately arrested. As an escaped prisoner I have no official status. Even so, I continue to send the letters and I resign myself a little more daily that I will never see them again.

And so, this has become our new home, for almost two years now. Montaña del Sol – Mountain of the Sun – such a perfect name for a place so near to Heaven that it even has its own beautiful angel – an ever present, ever caring, ever real and alive angel – one who stays on my heart and mind – and, therefore, keeps me consumed with guilt.

If only I knew that my wife really lives -- that I would see her again, I might be able to control myself. Otherwise, may she and God both forgive me for my sins."

#

Excerpt from the diary of Evie Van Ryan:

'May 10, 1947 – I have never been in love – is this what love feels like? A little bit of heaven and whole lot of foolishness? Because I certainly have the foolish part down! Oh, how is this ever going to work out? And if Papa ever finds out, he will surely kill us both!

But I don't really care.

#

Evie Van Ryan arose an hour and a half before dawn, dressed warmly, and crept quietly downstairs. Her father would be stirring soon enough, and she wished to be well on her way before he could question her. Hopefully, he would think she was merely on one of her early morning rides. She tiptoed to the kitchen, grabbed bread, cheese, a jar of homemade peach jam, a quart of milk, bacon, and half a dozen eggs. She carefully wrapped it all and stuffed the bundle in her rucksack before sneaking out the back door and hurrying to the stables.

Once there, she slipped inside, tiptoed quietly through the alleyway, roused Miss Priss from her comfortable stall, and saddled her quickly. She slung the rucksack over the saddle horn and led the mare out through the corrals, mounted, and turned the animal with a light rein and a firm but gentle heel to the ribs. Soon, they were trotting up the hillside path that meandered through the pasturelands toward the pearl-grey dawn outlining the eastern horizon over the mesa.

The air was still crisp and cold on these early spring mornings, and both she and her little buckskin mare blew foggy breath. The mare knew where they were going, so Evie let Miss Priss have her lead to get her blood flowing and ward off the chill. They rode a little over a mile, further up into the tree line of scrub oak, juniper, and pine until Evie could see an amber light glowing through a distant window with warmth that seemed both inviting and a little forbidding. A finger of smoke curled out of the old stone chimney of the small adobe shack, and the combined odors of burning pine and cedar and coffee greeted her with the further promise of welcoming heat on this chilly dawn.

She pulled the reins in on Miss Priss, who obediently halted beside a short rail fence. Evie quickly dismounted, opened a saddlebag, and removed a rolled up feedbag into which she had previously stuffed a few handfuls of grain. She unrolled it and slipped it over Miss Priss's mouth and ears. The buckskin snickered at her with satisfaction and began to quietly munch.

Evie turned toward the house, adjusted the bag of food on her shoulder, pushed her hair back from her eyes, and stepped forward. She stopped, wide-eyed, as the door of the house opened slowly, orange and yellow firelight dancing out in a growing stream across the yard. The dark silhouette of a man suddenly broke the light as he stepped lightly out the doorway onto the porch.

Evie caught her breath; her heart raced. She gripped her bag anxiously as the man stepped abruptly off the porch, crossed the yard, and quickly narrowed the gap between them. He reached large hands out toward her and grabbed her lightly by her shoulders. Evie looked up but could barely make out the rugged features of his face. Her eyes widened even further; her breath came in short gasps as he took her chin in one hand and leaned his face closer to hers.

"I have been awake for hours," he murmured huskily, the warmth of his breath tingling her ear as he whispered, "I thought you'd never get here!" His mouth closed hungrily on hers; Evie returned the kiss just as desperately. She felt her knees buckle as Otto pulled her impossibly closer while she wrapped her arms tightly around his neck, held on, her lips and moans meeting his again.

#

"Raul! *¿Dónde estás?*"

Werner Van Ryan leaned over the corral gate and spit. "Damn," he muttered under his breath. *Where is that boy?* He opened the gate and strode into the stables where he surprised a couple of his Mexican workers sweeping out stalls.

"*¡Oye! ¿Has visto a Raúl?*" The two ranch hands looked at each other worriedly, then back at Van Ryan and shook their heads in unison.

"*No, jefe! No lo hemos visto desde anoche.*" They noted their boss's annoyance, glanced at one another again, and quickly got back to their work.

Van Ryan cursed again, took off his hat, and wiped the sweat from the inside rim with a handkerchief. Nobody had seen Raul since last night, and he needed him. Raul was his top hand, had been on the ranch for five years, and it wasn't like him to just wander off, even after a day off on Sunday – which yesterday wasn't.

I do not have time for this bullshit!

He slapped his hat back on his head, stomped into the tack room inside the stables, and quickly counted the saddles.

Two were missing.

One, he knew, belonged to his daughter Evie. No surprise there, as she would still be out on her early morning ride. The second missing saddle was now the mystery. Van Ryan walked back through the stable, counting noses along the way. All the good riding horses were there. A couple of the old timers nickered at him as he passed by and stroked their muzzles. He reached the other end of the alleyway and opened the upper half of the door and leaned over it on his forearms, peering out into the horse pasture just beyond where several of the rougher stock was grazing in silhouette against the sun now rising behind the tree-lined hillside in the distance. He did a quick count, but couldn't be sure they were all there. Some could be just over the hillside, out of view. He spat again, cursed, and left the stables.

Van Ryan walked over to the maintenance garage where the ranch vehicles were kept. He quickly determined none of the trucks were missing before turning at approaching footsteps.

"Morning, Pop."

Van Ryan's son Richard had entered the back door of the garage. He was sweaty, his shirtsleeves were rolled up, and he was wiping his hands on a red work rag.

"You haven't seen Raul this morning, have you?"

Richard frowned, caught his dad's eye, and quickly looked down and continued to clean his hands. "No sir," he answered respectfully. "Not since yesterday, to be quite honest."

Van Ryan frowned at his son. "You sure about that? I mean, you didn't take him out back behind the barn and whip his ass for him again, did you?"

Richard looked up, peeved. "No! Why in the world would I do that?"

"Because it wouldn't be the first time, that's why. Seems you've taken a liking to beatin' up the hands lately – especially Raul."

Richard shuffled his boots on the hard dirt floor. "Well, sometimes those beaners need a bit of reminding, that's all."

"Reminding about what? And you know I don't like that word!" Van Ryan had never held a person's race and origin against them so long as they were willing to work hard and earn their keep. His own father had emigrated from Austria just a few decades ago; Werner had learned the hard way the value of a man's work ethic.

"Well, reminding them of their proper place, Pop. And I've told you before, I don't like the way that Raul looks at Evie – like he's undressing her with his eyes!"

"Oh, hell! He's not stupid! He isn't gonna try anything with her! He knows something like that would get him into a world of hurt." Van Ryan thought for a moment. "And I know Evie's not stupid, either. Besides – anybody needs to be taking care of your sister, it sure isn't you! And anybody needs a beating around here, it'll come from me." Van Ryan scowled at his son, who looked sheepishly away. He leaned against the fender of an old pickup and folded his arms. "And besides, Raul's my top hand. He knows I needed him to go out to the north section and work on that windmill today. Thing's not pumping right and those calves we're weaning this week are going out there – they gotta have water."

"Well, maybe he's up there already working on it."

"No, he isn't up there working on it," Van Ryan mimicked impatiently, "because I just came from there – he isn't there and hasn't been there, because nobody's touched it at all."

Well, I can go fix it..."

"No, you can't go fix it because I need you to go roust those Germans and have them ride out with you to start sorting off those calves."

Richard frowned again. "I don't like them Krauts much, Daddy. Don't know why you ever let them stay around here in the first place."

"I don't care who you like or don't like, Boy – and again with your damned language, please! They've turned into about the best cowhands I've got – like ducks to water." Van Ryan pushed away from the truck and began counting on his fingers. "They ride good, they got a second sense for when a cow's sick, or dry, they don't complain about the room or the board, they work almost as hard as I do, and they don't show up on

Mondays with a tequila hangover!"

Richard looked down, chagrined. "Well, I still don't trust them – especially that younger one – Otto. He's just a little too self –assured, you ask me. And that taller one, that Ernst fella, just sometimes gives me the willies – looks at you sorta crazy when you ask him to do something – like he'd just as soon slit your throat."

Van Ryan sighed, adjusted his hat, and turned to walk away. "Well, maybe it's all in the manner with which you speak to people, Richard. You have a lousy attitude with folks. Can't attract the bees with vinegar, you know."

He walked around to the other side of the truck, opened the door, and started to get in, but looked over the top of the cab. "I'm gonna drive back out to that windmill myself – see if Raul showed up – and maybe scout some other places, if he didn't. He may have fallen somewhere, or gotten thrown, and got himself hurt – dammit to hell!" He got into his truck, started it, and backed it out of the garage. He rolled the window down and called back through the doorway.

"And you've got work to do, too. Quit messing around here, get saddled up, go find Otto and Ernst, and get to it! I'll see you at dinner, and I will expect a good report on a good day's work!"

Richard stepped out the door and watched his father drive off in a cloud of dust. *A good report on a good day's work*, his father's daily mantra; Richard cringed when he heard it, like his father never trusted him to do what was right – still treated him like a child. Wasn't he also a *top hand?*

"Damn Krauts," he growled.

#

Raul's breath was ragged and burned down deep in his lungs with every gasp. His legs were shaking with fatigue, but he still picked his feet up and plowed uphill. He knew every inch of this ranch, and if he could just get to the top of this next hill, he knew that on the other side there was a rocky ravine he could drop into and hide to catch his breath and wits.

But where was that crazy pendejo he wondered to himself. He had never thought something like this would happen, not here on this ranch – five years earlier, maybe, when he had been crossing the border, trying to get out of *Méjico* into *Estados Unidos*. He had heard stories of bad things happening to people, especially in the badlands of Southwest *Téjas,* where a person could just disappear and never be found again; where someone would just shoot you for sport, like a jackrabbit, or a coyote.

But not here – not now!

Señor Van Ryan was a good man – *un buen jefé*! And Raul knew the boss respected him, too. He would be furious if he knew this was happening!

Raul slid and dropped down the side of the ravine, collapsed heavily, and sat leaning against the side. He had lost his hat awhile back, but took his handkerchief and wiped the sweat from his eyes, caught his breath, and held it, listening hard. He thought he had heard a noise in the distance, just beyond the ravine.

But not so much the *jefé's* son, Ricardo – Richard, he now reflected. He knew the boy hated him. Just because I whistle at the *señorita*, his sister. But the *jefé* knows I would never dare touch her!

He froze again, hearing a stone clatter in the distance. So what if it had been Ricardo who ordered this crazy hombre to do this? To hunt me like a jackal! Beating me is no longer enough – now he is going to have me killed!

Raul listened closely for several more minutes, but heard nothing else. He couldn't stay here for long. The crazy German was relentless. He had rousted Raul well before dawn, in the still cold darkness – had told him that *jefé* wanted them out to the windmill earlier than planned, and that they were both to go – now. Raul had never liked the tall German. He was arrogant and rude. Why couldn't it have been the pleasant one, he had wondered, the one called 'Otto?' He hadn't liked the idea of spending the entire day working alone with this *hombre loco*. And when they had met up behind the corral, his trepidations were confirmed when there had been only one horse – one of the recently broken ones – and the German was already mounted. "I think the walk will do you good," he had told Raul. So, he had walked, sometimes trailing the horse, sometimes leading. He didn't mind – really. The windmill was only a little over two miles away, and he could walk that in his sleep. He just didn't want to give in to this *Alemán's* sense of superiority.

Suddenly came the running, and the loco one pulling his rifle out of the saddle scabbard, and brandishing it at him, shouting at him, *corre por tu vida* – "Run for your life!" At first Raul thought he joked, but then out of nowhere, the *pendejo* had jumped down from his horse, moved toward him, shoved him, pointed the rifle right between Raul's eyes – and smiled that crazy smile. "Run," he had said again, this time almost in a whisper. "I will even give you a good head start." Raul knew then by Ernst's eyes that he was deadly serious – and that it had somehow given the *loco* one great pleasure.

So, he had run.

Now, three hours later, the sun was blazing down, and here he sat in this ravine, exhausted. He looked around. Nothing. Perhaps he had gotten away? He decided to take his chances. He stood up into a crouch, listened again, turned to run up the other side of the ravine – and froze in his tracks, staring up above him. Twenty yards up and at the lip of the ravine was the German, sitting with his legs crossed and a Winchester rifle propped on one thigh. A straw cowboy hat was pushed back from his brow and he had that frightening, loco smile on his face.

"Good morning there, *mein kleiner Kojote*," Ernst said, his voice smooth and friendly. He reached in his shirt pocket and pulled out a pack of cigarettes, shook one out, and lit it. He sucked the smoke into his lungs and slowly exhaled it. "You have given me quite a nice little outing today – a better chase than I have had in a long while!"

Raul's mouth went bone dry; he could barely breathe. He felt like he would pass out. He finally got a breath. "But why?" he croaked. "Why are you doing this, *Señor* Ernst? I thought we were *amigos* – friends…"

"Friends!" Ernst smirked. "Now, why would I want to call you my friend?" He uncrossed his legs and stood up with a slight groan, rebalancing the stock of the old Winchester rifle against his hip. He smiled down at Raul and tilted his head, like he was studying an interesting insect on the ground. "You really have no idea who I really am to you, do you? Who it is I represent?" He took another drag of his cigarette and looked at it like an artifact as he held it between two fingers.

"I represent a holy race that does not – indeed, dares not – call too many others 'friends' – particularly one of such a mongrel people as yours."

Raul twisted and took a step, halted, and stepped the other way, unsure which way to turn in the deep, dry arroyo. He stopped again when he realized there was nowhere to run.

"Oh, yes, please do, Raul – I do so enjoy the chase more when they run."

Raul looked up, gazed hopelessly down the rim of the arroyo to his left, then to his right, and finally rested his eyes back on Ernst. He took a deep breath and put his hands on his hips, and shrugged. "Then I do not wish to give you any further pleasure, *Pendejo*!" Raul summoned what little moisture he had left in his mouth and spit it defiantly toward Ernst.

"Ah, but you must run, my little coyote," said Ernst, a false look of disappointment crossing his face, "else there is no sport in it for me."

He lifted the Winchester and cocked the lever. Raul flinched but otherwise stood still, staring back up at his tormentor. He still could not believe this was really happening.

Ernst raised the rifle and gestured with it, up the ravine.

"Not even a little run – to pretend?"

Raul licked his dry lips, but chased all emotion from his face.

Ernst lowered the rifle and aimed from his hip. He fired once. Raul jumped as the bullet struck the ground a few inches from his left boot and ricocheted away with a whine.

"Is this because of the *señorita*? *Señor* Ricardo makes you do this?" Raul shouted, his hand now raised above his head in surrender.

Ernst scoffed, then chuckled. "The *señorita*? Oh, no, my little cockroach…this has nothing to do with her – although I have seen how you devour her with your eyes." Ernst looked down and thought for a moment. "Or, I suppose we could say that is also another good reason to kill you, then – to protect the young woman from becoming something impure – from bringing another possible mongrel into this dismal world." Ernst took another puff then flicked the cigarette to the ground and mashed it under his boot.

"But, you see, Raul – in the end, I just really don't need another reason, do I? I can just do this because," Ernst shrugged, "I can."

Raul watched in horror and fascination as the barrel of the Winchester lowered again until all he could see was the round, dark hole of the bore locked on him.

They say the last thing to go when someone dies is the hearing. Almost simultaneously, Raul saw flame and smoke spit from the small hole and felt something powerful tear through his chest. He felt himself floating slowly through air for what seemed like long, horrible minutes, felt the air knocked out of him as he slammed to the ground. He could not move a muscle – only lie there, staring up as the clear blue sky above grew gradually grey, then dim to darkness.

Only then Raul curiously heard the roar of the rifle echoing from the ravine walls, and wondered vacantly just what it was.

#

Otto lay on his side in bed, his head propped on one hand. He smiled as he watched Evie finish dressing across the room before she started to brush her dark hair out. She hummed a quiet song, one that Otto didn't recognize, but he could tell she was humming it out of tune and it made him chuckle. Her actions formed a routine he had grown to love watching. She stopped brushing and turned to him with a scowl.

"What are you laughing at?" She demanded.

"I am laughing at you, my little flower!"

Evie raised her arm and threw the brush at him. Otto yelped as it hit him on the chest and bounced to the floor. Evie rushed toward the bed while Otto tried to scramble out of from the covers to beat her to the fallen brush. She got to it first, grabbed it, and pretended like she would hit him with it again. Otto wrapped her in his arms and pulled her over on top of him. At this point, they were both laughing and she flailed at him playfully with the brush. Soon, they were quiet again, kissing deeply, and the brush dropped from Evie's hand. They held and caressed each other for a while longer, but Evie suddenly groaned and pulled away.

"I've got to go," she declared. "They're going to wonder where I am." She tried to get up, but Otto held her arm gently.

"Stay for just awhile longer," he begged.

"Won't Ernst be back soon?" she asked.

"Ernst never comes back until late," he answered, but the thought caused him to frown for a minute. Ernst had left well before dawn, without a word, and had taken the Winchester with him.

Otto let go of Evie's arm and sighed as he stood up.

"What are we doing?" he finally asked, as he watched her brushing her hair again.

"You know what we're doing, silly," she giggled.

Otto smiled, but he soon lost the smile. She suddenly looked very much like a schoolgirl while he felt every bit that much older than she.

"You know what I mean, Evie. This is a very dangerous thing we are doing."

Evie stopped brushing and looked down quietly, thinking.

"And there are just too many ways this will get us into trouble," Otto continued.

"What if I don't care," Evie murmured.

"You do not care if I am ruining your life?"

She turned to look at him. "How are you ruining my life," she asked. "It's my life – and I do with it as I wish."

Otto smiled again, and shook his head. "That is the stubborn Irish teenager talking now," he said.

"So?"

"Well, so – I happen to like the Irish part of you – very much!" Otto slipped out of bed, came up behind her, and lifted her long hair off of her back, combing it through his fingers. He then leaned over and held it up to his nose and breathed in her scent. "But I am afraid it is the Irish part of you – and the German part of me – that is going to bring us big problems, my flower."

"I still don't care," she pouted. "And I am a woman now, not a teenager – you made sure of that."

When they were both dressed, they sat at the little table and drank coffee. Evie looked at him over the rim of her cup, her eyes glistening.

"I think you are going to leave me soon," she said slowly.

"Why would you say that?"

"It's a feeling I have – a premonition, really."

"So, what if I tell you I do not believe in premonitions?"

Evie set her cup down and reached over to take his fingers in both hands, looking him in the eyes. "I am usually very good with premonitions," she whispered. She looked around the small adobe cabin, then back at Otto. "Anyway, I'm going to keep this place exactly as it is now – after you're gone. It will probably be the only thing I have to remember you by.

"But I do not plan to go anywhere, silly one," he chuckled

"I'm going to keep the same furniture, the same books," she continued, ignoring his comment. "And I am going to keep the same sheets and blankets and pillows – and not wash them.

"And why would you do such a thing?" he teased.

"So I can still smell you on them from now on – because I am going to sneak down here every day and take a nap – and hug the pillow as if it's you."

Otto gazed at her for a long while, then kicked his chair behind him, grabbed her around the waist, and half-dragged, half-carried her back to toward the bed, while both of them melted once more into searching embraces and languishing kisses.

Later, Evie quickly and silently made up the bed while Otto washed the dishes, relishing even in these moments together. When the tasks were completed, they both grabbed their hats and jackets and embraced once more by the door before stepping outside onto the porch together – and straight into trouble.

"Well, well – now, isn't this just about the coziest little bit of domestic bliss you ever did see?"

Otto and Evie froze and stared in shock as they looked up at her brother Richard, who sat on his sorrel gelding near the porch, one leg propped lazily over the saddle horn, and grinned down at them.

#

Werner Van Ryan's pickup bounced around a curve in the dirt road, topped a short rise, then slowed to a stop. He leaned over the steering wheel and peered through the windshield, down into the ravine below where a shallow stream ran across the road. On the other side of the stream sat a cowboy on one of Van Ryan's younger horses that was drinking from the stream. The rider raised his head, tipped his straw hat back from his brow, and waved at Werner.

It was one of the Germans – the one called Ernst.

"Hmm," Van Ryan grunted. He put the truck in park, opened the door, stepped halfway out, and leaned through the open window. *"Guten Morgan, Ernst,"* he called down to the cowboy, then switched to English. "You out for a morning constitutional there, or are you looking around for a little work to do today?"

"You know that I would never say 'no' to a good day's work, *Herr* Van Ryan," Ernst answered, still smiling. He obviously knew the drill.

"Where's your buddy Otto?"

Ernst had reined in his horse and shrugged as he rode across the stream toward his boss.

"I am afraid I am not my brother's keeper, *mein Herr.* But my guess would be that Otto – um – slept in this morning." He now stopped his horse just a few feet from the truck.

Van Ryan's nose twitched and he thought he had caught a whiff of burned gunpowder. He noted the butt of a rifle protruding from a scabbard on Ernst's saddle.

"Been doing a little hunting this morning?" Van Ryan gestured toward the rifle.

Ernst raised his eyebrows for a second. "Oh," he finally answered after delaying a moment or two longer than necessary. "I did shoot a rattler earlier." He poked his thumb back behind him. "Back near the calving pasture there. Pretty big one, too. Didn't want him around the calves, you know."

Ernst smiled slowly while Van Ryan glanced at the rifle once more.

"You haven't, by any chance, seen Raul this morning, have you?" Van Ryan asked, a hint of unease creeping into his voice.

Ernst paused, his eye glancing briefly at the pearl handled .45 revolver strapped to Van Ryan's belt. Right now, Werner was glad that he never went anywhere without it.

"Yes," Ernst answered after another moment's thought. "Yes, I have seen him. I saw him when I was in the corral earlier. He said he was headed out to work on a windmill somewhere. I did not ask him where, and he did not seem to want any help – not from me, at least." Ernst rubbed his cheek. "Is there something wrong, *Herr* Van Ryan?"

Van Ryan looked down and swore. "Damn Raul!" he said, mostly to himself, and slapped the door panel. "Damn fool probably hurt himself somewhere. Suppose we should go find him." He looked back at Ernst, thought for a moment longer, then made a decision. He got back into his truck and slammed the door. "Let's go find Otto first," he ordered, throwing the truck in reverse, then whipping the wheel to turn it around. "The more people we get looking for Raul, the better. I will meet you back at the bunkhouse," he shouted back as he disappeared in a plume of dust he churned up as he spun tires.

#

Otto hit the ground hard and the breath burst from his lungs. He tasted copper in his mouth and spit out blood. He shook his head to clear it and thought he heard Evie crying somewhere, and alternately screaming, "Stop it!"

"Get up, Kraut!"

Richard Van Ryan's voice growled from somewhere behind him. Otto tried to raise himself up, but felt two strong hands grab the back of his shirt and jerk him upright none too gently. The hands then whipped him around until he was staring into Richard's snarling face. Sheer hatred gleamed in those eyes and spittle ran from the corner of Richard's mouth as he wound up his fist and forcefully, deliberately, plunged it deep into Otto's belly, doubling him over. Otto retched and threw up what little breakfast he had left in his stomach to only fall face down into the mess he had just created.

Richard's heavy boot flew into Otto's ribs. Otto heard rather than felt the ribs crack; at this point in the beating, pain was now his constant companion, the only thing he had any real cognizance of – so much so that any absence of pain would have seemed unusual. Otto's consciousness wavered now between light and darkness; woven throughout the two extremes was a thread of a sound wave – a lilting, dancing, feminine voice that wailed one second, and faded to almost a melodic sigh the next. Somewhere deep in his mind, Otto associated the wailing voice with Evie, but he could no longer be certain of reality.

Otto sensed more than felt another heavy thud of a boot in his midsection and heard what strangely sounded like a racing engine growing louder before abruptly stopping. Next, he thought he heard shouting, but again, could not be sure of it because by this point his world went finally, peacefully dark.

#

"What in the name of holy hell is going on here?" Werner Van Ryan's truck had hardly slid to a stop when he had the door open and flew out of the vehicle. "Boy, I am talking to you!" he shouted at Richard, who had his leg back to kick the man on the ground.

Van Ryan reached Richard in just a few long strides and grabbed his son by the upper arm. Richard whipped around in rage, his fist raised as if to strike his father. Van Ryan didn't let go, but clenched his teeth and glared back at his son, raising his chin as if daring the boy to punch him. Richard was breathing heavily with murder in his eyes. His breathing began to slow and his expression softened when he realized who was intervening. He finally lowered his fist and pulled away from his father.

"I asked you a question," Van Ryan growled low in his throat, "what is going on here, Richard?" He stepped around his son as he spoke and went to look down at the man on the ground. "Is that Otto?" he asked. He knelt down and rolled the German over on his back and winced when he got a look at the bloodied face.

Richard stood to one side, looking back over his shoulder. "He dead?" he breathed.

Van Ryan looked up at his son and shook his head. "Just about, but not quite yet – although not for a lack of trying." He stood up slowly and just then noticed his daughter Evie on the porch, clutching her hat, and crying. She was stared at her father, then back down at Otto in utter horror, and suddenly ran over and threw herself across his chest, sobbing uncontrollably.

Van Ryan looked back over at his son, down at his daughter, nodded slowly, and continued. "And still – nobody yet has bothered to tell me what the hell is going on here – or just why it is that I am starting to get a bad feeling about all this?"

He was interrupted by the sound of horse hooves beating a rhythm in the near distance, followed by Ernst appearing around the corner at a gallop. He skidded the winded gelding to a quick stop, jumped down, and walked quickly over to where Otto and Evie were.

"Is he dead?" Ernst asked in an even and unemotional voice.

Werner Van Ryan suddenly laughed; they all turned to stare at him in shock.

"Well now," Van Ryan chortled, "that seems to be just one of many unanswered questions of the day around here, doesn't it?" He finally stopped laughing and his face turned dark.

"And someone had better start answering, right now."

CHAPTER 17
RESURRECTIONS

Trent turned off the computer and glanced at his watch. It was about noon. He thought for a second, then abruptly grabbed Mirielle Segura's file, turned off the lights, and left his office. On his way out, he refilled his travelling mug with hot, over-cooked coffee from the machine in the corner of the office. His stomach growled, and out of the corner of his eye, he spied the now half empty box of doughnuts that Hector must have left here. Trent looked around casually and, seeing no one paying attention, grabbed one and shoved it into his mouth.

He checked out a department cruiser, gassed it up, nosed it out of town onto I-25 South, and settled down for the long, fairly boring drive to Las Vegas, New Mexico, about 110 miles away. The late model Ford Explorer picked up speed as he nudged it a bit over the 75 mile per hour limit, which didn't mean much, but he liked to think it would shave off some time. The four-lane highway wound its way lazily around and through a few mesas and foothills before it flattened out across the high desert plains.

He sipped his coffee, grimaced at it, and glanced down into the passenger seat at the green pasteboard file of the one known survivor of these murder cases he had been investigating. He hadn't wanted to let on to Hector how badly he was bothered that he could not remember a single detail about Mirielle Segura's case, nor even the day at the crime scene itself, although plainly, by the photographs in the file, Trent had, by all accounts, been there. That particular memory sat smack dab in the middle of the vacant tract of his brain cells, the area raked clean by his accident and not yet fully functional again – if it ever would be.

He rubbed his temples with his fingers. His cell phone suddenly buzzed insistently in his shirt pocket followed a split second later by a loud tone that blared out of the vehicle's speakers as the Bluetooth program picked up the call. Trent jumped and fumbled clumsily at the volume. He hated digital technology.

"Carter!" he finally shouted into the air.

"Hey, good lookin'!" Margot's voice purred through the speakers. Trent sighed.

"What can I do for you, Margot?" It was an impatient statement, not a question.

"Well, you don't have to sound so damned excited for one thing!"

Trent sighed again and shook his head.

"And you can just stop that ridiculous sighing, too," she continued.

Trent was immediately embarrassed. He hadn't realized how well the car's sound system would pick up extraneous noises.

"Um – sorry, Margot, uh, Maggie," he stammered, "just preoccupied with something, that's all."

"Uh-huh." She paused. "Where are you, anyway? You driving?"

"Yeah, just headed out of town. Gotta go interview a witness down in Las Vegas. She might know something about an old murder."

"Aww – I was hoping you were in town. Thought I might talk you into taking me to dinner tonight." She sounded disappointed.

Trent could imagine Maggie's bottom lip pouting from her mouth as she chewed absently on the nail of her little finger, as she did. He was surprised that the image had popped into his mind – and even more surprised that it pleased him. A smile played at the corner of his mouth. He wasn't sure how to respond.

"Trent?" she asked, finally.

"Yes."

"Uh – 'yes,' you're still there? Or 'yes,' to dinner?"

"Yes to dinner," he answered, almost too quickly.

Now, it was Maggie's turn for a moment of silence.

"Wow!" she said, finally. "I was ready to hear a whole bunch of 'too busies,' and 'maybe-some-other-times!'"

"Well, I think I can wrap this up and get back by dinner time. Besides –

fellow's gotta eat, doesn't he?"

"Oh. Gee. Well, I wouldn't worry too much about sweeping a girl off her feet or anything, Cowboy. Your charm is fairly underwhelming."

Trent straightened up in his seat, cleared his throat, and started over.

"Maggie Van Ryan," Trent paused, "would you give me the distinct pleasure of dining with you this evening – say, around six o'clock – that is, if you're not too busy?"

He could feel her smiling through the phone.

"Six o'clock it is, Mr. Carter!"

Trent glanced at the clock on the dashboard and then at the thick file next to him.

"Better make it 7:00."

#

A short, stout Hispanic woman pulled the heavy wooden door open and peered up at Trent with severe eyes. Her silver hair was pulled back into a tight bun and she appeared to him to be in her late seventies. She blocked the door protectively with one arm, the other resting defiantly on her hip. Clearly, no one was getting past her without her permission.

"*Que deseas*?" she asked in a strong, clear voice. She looked Trent up and down, then glanced quickly behind him at the sheriff's department vehicle parked at the curb. Her eyes grew even flintier; she glared at him suspiciously now.

"Deputy Trent Carter, *Señora*," he answered, holding out his badge and identification at which the woman squinted through the screen door. "Colfax County Sheriff's Department," he continued officiously. "*Por favor, Señora* – I was wondering if there is a Mrs. Segura still living here, by any chance – um, *Señora* Mirielle Segura?"

The woman glanced from Trent's ID back up to his face, at the green pasteboard file tucked under his arm, then looked worriedly back into the cool darkness of the house. Another lilting female voice came from the interior. "Who is it, *Tia*?"

"*Polizia, hita*!" The older woman hissed over her shoulder, then lowered her voice and rattled off something else intensely in Spanish. She glared back at Trent and prepared to push the heavy door shut. At the same time, a prettier, younger version of the older woman walked into the sunlight that streamed in through the doorway. The aunt leaned close to her niece and whispered something else in Spanish. Trent recognized the words *Border Patrol.* The younger woman waved away her aunt's concerns.

"Oh, come now – I'm sure it's alright, *Tia.* Besides," she added as she moved to open the screen door and gestured Trent inside with a pleasant smile, "I think I know this man."

Trent stood confused for a moment, politely took off his hat, carefully wiped his boots on the doormat, and stepped inside.

"Ma'am," he said, nodding to the young woman. "*Muchas gracias, Señora,*" he offered politely to the woman's aunt. An aroma of baked goods and cooking oil greeted him warmly as he entered the living room, belying the continued frown of Mirielle's aunt, who, nonetheless, stepped aside to let him in.

"Please," Mirielle Segura motioned with a wide sweep of her hand. "Won't you have a seat?" She had walked over to the only comfortable looking chair in the room, an overstuffed lounger with crocheted doilies on the arms, and indicated that he was to sit there. She casually moved over to a worn couch nearby. A small coffee table arranged with photographs sat between the couch and the chair. "Would you like some iced tea, Deputy Carter?"

"Oh, please don't go to any trouble for me," Trent answered.

"No. No trouble at all, Officer Carter." She turned and touched her aunt's shoulder. The older woman was still standing, frowning at Trent with her arms folded. "*Tia – Algo fria, para nuestro huésped, por favor,*" she instructed politely.

The older woman took the hint, but sucked her teeth and muttered something under her breath as she turned and left the room briskly.

Trent couldn't help but notice that Mirielle Segura wore a simple one-piece cotton dress decorated with small red flowers on a light blue background with a modest collar and sleeves. The rather plain but pleasing dress was not too snug, but form fitting enough to accentuate her build and was hemmed modestly just below her knees. The brown calves of her legs looked strong as if they had known lots of exercise and sunshine. Trent studied her, not so much admiring her looks – although she was a striking woman – but trying to remember her from years ago.

He couldn't.

She moved toward the middle of the couch and sat down on the edge of the cushion, her posture erect. She wore her long, black hair pulled straight back behind her ears, but instead of a severe bun like her aunt's, she had gathered it in a silver clasp that allowed it to fall loosely down her back. Trent noticed that her eyes were dark brown, almond shaped, and carried a distinct seriousness way beyond her years. Her lips were full and the skin of her face dark but carried fine lines, especially at the corners of her eyes and her mouth, as if she was used to being outside in the wind and the sun. She wore little or no makeup – didn't need to, in his opinion – and wore only a faint shade of red lipstick. Mirielle Segura was, for sure, attractive, but life had aged her beyond her years. Trent recalled that her file had cited her age at twenty-six at the time of the shooting, which would make her just over thirty-two now.

Overall, she had the look of a proud young woman who knew what she wanted in life and was not afraid to go after it, a woman who knew that some goals carried a tremendous cost – a cost, Trent knew, that she had already paid dearly. That much was obvious. She had made her way over five hundred miles from Mexico, on foot, with her husband when they had been attacked. As if those hardships weren't enough to try anyone's spirit, her husband Rogelio had been killed, gunned down in front of her. But Mirielle Segura sat here now, not with the look of a victim about her, but with the determined eyes of a survivor.

Mirielle demurely pulled the hem of her dress down over her knees, folded her hands in her lap, and smiled politely over at Trent. He suddenly became aware he had been staring at her, and blushed.

"*Señora* Segura, please excuse my manners," he quickly apologized, "but it seems we must have met before, yes?"

The young woman looked at him curiously. "Yes, of course," she replied. "We have met before, *Señor* Carter."

Trent looked away quickly and scanned the room, looking at the meager furnishings and decorations, most of them old, possibly hand-made family treasures. His eyes stopped on the framed photographs on the small table between them. One showed a beautiful young woman – a much younger Mirielle – in a bridal grown, gazing adoringly up into the face of a ruggedly handsome, tall, and dark young man dressed in a suit that was perhaps a size too small for him. The young man's eyes glistened with pride as he gazed back lovingly at his bride.

Trent cleared his throat and gestured toward the picture.

"Is that your husband?"

She followed his eyes, and then smiled sadly.

"Yes – that was my Rogelio." She let her gaze linger.

"*Señora* – "

"Please," she interrupted, looking back at Trent. "Call me Mirielle, Señor Carter."

"Mrs. Segura," he repeated, shifting forward to the edge of his seat, trying to appear earnest. "First of all, I need to assure you that I am not here on behalf of the Border Patrol or INS or anything to do with your legal status here."

"Yes. I understand this." She looked at her hands in her lap and then glanced again at Rogelio's photograph. "I am thinking I know why you are here. And please – it *is* Mirielle – I insist." She grinned now, and nodded toward the kitchen, "'Mrs. Segura' is my husband's aunt."

"Well, I do need to ask you a few questions – Mirielle."

Trent paused, fingering the edge of the file in his lap, before opening it and extracting a single photo. He glanced at it uncertainly and handed it across to her. "Do you recognize this photograph?"

She took the photo from his hand and studied it, an expression of surprise growing on her face. The photograph depicted Trent and Sheriff Ferguson standing by the Sheriff's car.

"Why, of course. This is you, *Señor*."

"And you recognize where this photo was taken, do you?" She peered down at the photograph again, her eyebrows knitting.

"Yes, I do." Mirielle paused, frowning, then slowly raised her face. "It is the place where my husband Rogelio was murdered – and where I, too, was shot." Her voice grew quieter and a little wary as she handed the photo back to Trent.

"Now, Mirielle, this is going to sound very strange, I know – but, you see, I myself had a pretty bad accident right after this happened," Trent paused, "right after this tragic attack on you and your husband." He continued to struggle with how he was going to say what came next. "Well, truth is, I don't seem to have any recollection, no memory, of this day whatsoever – the day this photograph was taken – and I'm here to get some help from you regarding that."

Mirielle gave Trent a puzzled look that gradually turned to consternation.

"How can this be, *Señor*? You mean," she began with a puzzled expression, "you do not remember anything about this?" She pointed back to the photograph, thinking for a moment, and looked up at Trent again. "But I don't understand. You and I spoke – first at the hospital where they took me – then later, a couple of times." She now looked hurt. "You – you say you do not remember me, then?"

Trent looked at his hands and slowly shook his head.

"No, I don't, Mrs. Segura. And I'm so very sorry about that because I know that I should, particularly regarding such a terrible event in your life." Trent paused before he pointed back at the photo. "I mean I evidently was the investigator on the scene. And I have read through your file here a dozen times in the last couple of days, and I don't remember any of it – not the place, your husband – nor you."

They both grew quiet as Mirielle's aunt returned with a tray of glasses filled with iced tea and a small plate of cookies. They looked homemade and smelled like they had just come out of the oven, and the tea glasses had crushed mint leaves suspended in the amber liquid. She sat the tray on the coffee table, quietly scooted past Mirielle, took her seat straight across from Trent, and stared at him coldly as if to show him that he would have to go through her to get to her niece. Mirielle leaned over, patted her arm reassuringly, and spoke softly to her in Spanish. Trent heard her say, "*no INS,*" and watched the hardness finally leave the aunt's face. She finally smiled and nodded at Trent before pushing the plate of cookies toward him.

"My apologies, *Señor.* My sweet *Tia* is very protective, as you may understand. And," Mirielle quickly added, "she does not speak much English, so you may feel quite comfortable talking in front of her – about any of this." She gestured down at the file in Trent's lap.

"So – what else do you need to ask me, *Señor* Carter? I don't know that I can be of much further help to you besides what you must already have in your file there. You see, my own memory of that particular day also plays tricks with me. I was not – at my best, shall we say."

Trent hesitated, his throat suddenly dry, and gratefully took a gulp of iced tea. He wished it were something a lot stronger. He cleared his throat and rushed ahead with the next question.

"Can you to tell me anything you remember at all about the men who attacked you and your husband."

Mirielle paused, chewing her lip thoughtfully, and looked up at him and shrugged. "They were just men – two men who were always laughing – one was very skinny and also very scary looking. The other one – the one who drove the shiny black truck – he was even scarier, in a way. He spoke very kindly, at first, but he was always smiling at me – but not in the good way, if you understand what I mean."

"What did you say?" Trent sat back suddenly with a gasp. He felt like something had broken loose inside his head – a vague memory that was now floating free but had nowhere to land or to make any purchase inside the blank areas of his mind.

"I said he was smiling at me – you know," she blushed, "as some men do – staring at me in a vulgar way. And there were two of them, one skinny and ugly, the other better looking, but a little older. And at the end – after we were shot – they both just stood over us, laughing. And laughing and laughing."

Mirielle's voice trailed off and she shuddered, but Trent wasn't noticing anymore. He was remembering. *Shiny black truck. Laughing men. Why did those images mean something? What did they mean? And where?*

The memories suddenly flooded in on him in a deluge, coming from somewhere deep inside, as if a floodgate had burst open from some bruised and broken place; swirling quickly at first, then a little slower, dipping and falling, almost coming into view, before skittering just out of sight in his mind's peripheral vision; memories of a crime scene – except not this particular crime scene where Murielle and her husband had been attacked on a hot summer's day out on the high desert plains of New Mexico.

No, these memories evoked a crisp fall day in Colorado and a leisurely drive on Cordova Pass, just below the Spanish Peaks in the Sangre de Cristo Mountains – and his beautiful wife's smiling face beside him in their Jeep, laughing at his bad jokes – but from out of nowhere, another, more sinister laugh, from someone else, someone with a slightly disturbing smile. Next came a feeling of despair and panic, punctuated by crashing sounds and screams – and woven throughout was another vague memory: a shiny black pickup truck slowly disappearing around a bend and music blaring from its radio and the cold laughter of two men fading away in the distance.

As those particular memories could no longer be kept at bay and now swam fully into view, Trent slumped further down into his chair and stared into space as the file slipped out of his numb fingers and hit the floor, photos and documents scattering.

Suddenly, at that very moment, the room was filled with the familiar and overwhelming scent of wild roses and cloves, and everything swirling about him began to fade as he squeezed his eyes shut, one detailed memory after another coming finally into view and surging and skipping through the damaged areas of his mind like an long forgotten horror movie.

#

Light glitters brilliantly through aspen trees like shimmering handfuls of gold coins thrown into the air. Late afternoon sunlight splits through a prism and spectacular rays cut through the shadows – splashes of color dapple everything in their path. Even so, all has an air of mystery, as if filtered through gauze or a light misty fog. Trent drives and glances at Vicky, her light brown hair blowing like a gossamer banner in the breeze, her elbow resting casually on the windowsill of the Jeep as it bounces over the rough and winding dirt road. Even in this wonderland, she is the most beautiful sight he has ever laid eyes on.

Vicky looks serene, humming to herself like a little girl, then softly sings under her breath, "Will you say when you see him, the one that I love." It's the song he had recently written just for her, but when she sings it, it's the most enticing music he's ever heard.

"Tell him my heart is still true," she continues. She stops and pulls her sunglasses down her nose to take in all the magical color spinning around her. Just watching her, Trent feels all the cares of the day drift away as they immerse themselves into the palette of hot oranges, brilliant yellows, and soft greens painted across the canvas of mountain and valley and sky around and above and below them.

Suddenly, they are not alone.

In the rear view mirror, Trent spies a late model 4X4 pickup easing up close behind them. Not ready to move on yet, he obligingly slows down and pulls the Jeep as far to the side of the road as possible. The black pickup pauses for a moment too long and then slowly passes by. The windows are tinted and seem to vibrate as loud country music blares from within. The pickup slows, stops as it draws even with the Jeep. The passenger window whirs down to reveal the shadowy forms of two men. The passenger doesn't turn to look at Trent but continues to stare straight ahead. He is maybe in his late fifties with blond hair cut very short, a military cut. He is wearing yellow tinted sunglasses with narrow lenses, is clean-shaven, except for long sideburns ending at a point on his jaw-line, and sucks on a wooden kitchen match.

The driver leans forward slowly and Trent finally sees him, beyond the passenger. He appears to be in his late 60s, clean-shaven, and wears dark aviator shades and a well-worn baseball cap on his head with tufts of graying hair escaping out the sides. The man slowly reaches over, turns the volume down on the radio, and pulls the sunglasses off to reveal steely grey eyes.

Now, Trent recognizes him: Carl Neumann, a member of a well-known area ranching family located just northeast of Raton.

"Afternoon, Deputy," Carl calls out and then leers over at Vicky. "Ma'am," he adds, with a lazy tip of his hat with his forefinger.

"Afternoon," replies Trent. His sense of imminent danger increases dramatically, but he can't say why – something about the man that doesn't settle right with him – he should remember, but can't. He slips his right hand down beside his seat and touches the butt of the Ruger .357 magnum pistol hidden there. At the same time, he instinctively repositions himself in the seat as more of a protective shield to Vicky.

He forces himself to breathe deeply and slowly, forcing oxygen through his body – an exercise akin to slowing down the pace of footsteps and becoming more aware of surroundings as if a rattlesnake is nearby – and talking to Carl Neumann feels like handling a whole basket of snakes.

"Help you boys with something, Mr. Neumann?"

"Nah, we're just taking in the beauty of the changing of the colors – much like I imagine you and the pretty lady there are doing!" He nods again to Vicky, who simply stares back at him with a tight-lipped expression. She was raised around rough and rude cowboys and knows how to put them in their place with a mere look. She slips her hand over to rest lightly on the top of Trent's knee where she pats it a couple of times as if to remind him.

"Don't think I've been introduced to your friend here," Trent nods towards the skinny stranger.

"Oh, I do apologize," says Carl with feigned embarrassment. "Where are my manners?" He grasps the man in the passenger seat by the shoulder and squeezes it lightly. "This here's my old army buddy, Jimmy Streck – from Amarillo. Jimmy's come out to help me attend to a few – uh, shall we say, 'chores.'" A wide grin splits Carl's mouth.

The man called Jimmy turns his head and slowly removes the match from his mouth. He says nothing, but just stares at Trent, who can now see that the man has a jagged pink scar across the left side of his upper lip. Something unnerving and sinister resides in his manner.

"Chores, huh?"

"That's right," Carl grins again. "Clearing out some – vermin, you might say."

He puts the truck into gear and is already pulling slowly away as he calls out, "See ya around, Deputy – Ma'am. And please be real careful on this bad old road! Wouldn't want any accidents way up here," he chuckles. "You know, out here in the middle of nowhere."

As the black Chevy truck gains some speed and pulls away around the next bend, Trent hears their laughter on the breeze mixed with the thumping of their radio, then hears it all begin to fade and tumble and meld back into the wind chime tones of the aspen leaves.

#

"*Señor Carter!*"

The wind chimes faded as Trent's vision slowly cleared and the mountain aspens morphed into the dappled afternoon sunlight playing on the ceiling of Mirielle Segura's living room. He found himself still sprawled across the easy chair. He heard Mirielle's voice coming from somewhere to his left and raised his head slightly.

"Are you alright, Señor Carter?" Mirielle Segura's voice held concern, and she was on her knees beside his chair, picking up scattered photographs and documents from the floor, carefully placing them back into the file that lay open on the coffee table. Her aunt was standing on the other side of the table, a hand covering her mouth, staring at Trent with a troubled expression. She now picked up his glass of iced tea and offered it to him with a nod and a concerned smile. Trent shakily accepted the glass and took a couple of appreciative gulps.

"*Muchisimas gracias, Señora,*" he said softly, wiping his lip.

Mirielle finished her work, stood, and looked at Trent.

"How long was I out?" he asked.

"Out?" answered Mirielle, puzzled for a moment. "Oh, only for a few seconds." She hesitated. "I – er – thought you were having a seizure, like my *tia* sometimes." She pointed to her aunt. "If she doesn't take her medication, she also gets light-headed."

Trent downed the remainder of his tea.

"No," he answered. "Well – yes, I do take some medication; as I alluded to earlier, I do have a few – uh – *conditions.*" He stood up slowly, straightened his shirt, tucked it into his trousers, and ran his fingers through his hair.

"But nothing I can't," he hesitated to clear his throat, "handle," he lied, as much to himself as to the two women.

#

Later, as Trent's cruiser was headed back north on I-25, he continued to replay these newfound memories that now augmented the older ones; as he did so, it occurred to him that maybe his doctors had been right: evidently, as time went by, some re-connectivity was, for sure, occurring in his brain and sparking forgotten details of the accident two and a half years ago and its aftermath.

"I told you so," Vicky said softly as she leaned over from the backseat. He flinched away from her as she reached up to twirl the cowlick on the back of his head.

"*You told me so?* Just how, exactly?" he asked, focusing his eyes on the road ahead and not his dead wife's face in the rear-view mirror.

"I told you – that things were not as they seemed. Do you not you believe me when I tell you these things, Trenny?" she asked.

"Believe you about what, Vic?" he demanded as he glared at her now in the mirror. "Believe that I'm certifiably nuts? Or believe that you're just trying to drive me even crazier? I mean, sure – you tell me a lot of things, but it's not real information or answers! It's all mysterious clues and spiritual lingo and – and *crap!* How am I supposed to use any of *that* to solve anything, or – or," he balled his fist and tapped it against his forehead several times, "or to bring back what's trapped up *here?*"

Vicky pouted; her face in the mirror became shaded to him as she slowly leaned back in the seat. Only her eyes shone out of the darkness that had enveloped her.

"I mean," Trent continued, "do you know how ridiculous I felt back there with those women – after all that lady has been through? Surviving what she did? Losing her husband? I mean, she was the one trying to really help, here – and all I could manage to do was pass out and dream, after – after smelling that damn cologne of yours again."

"You don't believe I am trying to help you," she whispered. "You really can't see that, can you?"

Trent couldn't tell if it was disappointment he heard in her voice or hurt. He rubbed his face with his hand and took a deep breath.

"Victoria – I'm sorry. But if you'd only – " his voice trailed off. "I wish you'd just give me just one single solid clue, for once."

Trent squinted into the mirror as Vicky's face started to dissolve into thin air, the bright pinprick lights of her eyes the last things to fade.

"Oh, great," he muttered. "Now, you're just going to leave – and I can't believe I just apologized to a ghost."

He squeezed his eyes shut tight; at that instant, Vicky's disembodied voice shouted and echoed throughout his head.

"*Neumann!*"

The SUV suddenly shuddered and the right-hand tires whined as they ran over the zipper line on the shoulder; Trent jerked awake and whipped the vehicle back onto the highway. He glanced around sheepishly to verify no other vehicles were near him, leaned back in his seat, and blew his breath out sharply.

Soon, the Explorer topped a rise where Trent saw a distinctive rocky butte come into view before him. From this vantage point, the hill looked like the profile of an old Conestoga wagon being pulled by a team of oxen along the nearby Santa Fe Trail, hence, its name: Wagon Mound, which was also the name of the small town that now nestled around its base.

"Neumann," Trent muttered under his breath. "Carl Neumann."

He glanced at the clock again – a quarter to 4:00, and dinner was at 7:00. He might still make it.

He whipped the cruiser off the interstate at the next exit, glided through the Village of Wagon Mound, and barreled east on State Highway 120 toward the rugged canyons and badlands of Northeast New Mexico.

It was time to go make the acquaintance of a particular person of interest – right away.

CHAPTER 18
CANE AND ABEL

Excerpts from the Journal of Otto Eberhardt:

"01.06.47 – I suppose I should be grateful I am not dead. I am still not so sure how I survived. I awakened being bounced around jarringly and painfully in the back of some truck where I found myself lying on sacks of onions. The odor gagged me; I retched, and all I could finally manage to do was to roll over and watch the sky swim by nauseatingly above me. Ernst sat there, looking down at me blankly as we flounced along some dirt road, the dust boiling into the truck and choking us.

Ernst seems so nonchalant about us being on the run again. He says that Herr Van Ryan and he had arrived back at the cabin almost at the same instant and that it had taken them both to pull Richard off of me. I have no doubt he would have beaten me to death and then continued beating me long after. Ernst tells me Herr Van Ryan was extremely angry at the entire situation – rightfully so, I admit – and that he had ordered him to gather up our things and get off his ranch immediately before he changed his mind and let Richard finish me off. Ernst said that, for some reason, the old man was angry with him too – something about a missing vaquero – and seemed just as glad to see us both gone. He said after that Van Ryan had dragged Evie away to his truck, crying, and drove away.

I am miserable – and I have no earthly idea where we are headed or what we will do now. This time, it is Ernst taking care of me instead of the other way around."

#

"23.07.49 – I had so hoped that the violence and uncertainties of our lives were finally subsiding and that my sojourn in these quiet and beautiful valleys and mountains of New Mexico and Colorado would continue to heal not only the visible wounds, but also the hidden ones of my heart and soul. We have been working on various cattle ranches and

farms in Southern Colorado for the past couple of years, since being chased off of the Van Ryan place. Ernst and I now wander wherever there is work, not allowing ourselves to get tied down in one place for too long. My affair with Evie Van Ryan was a breath of fresh air – but I now know that it was terribly wrong of me. I hope and pray she has forgiven me, as I have her, and that she is finding some happiness in her life.

I will never forget her. I love her still – I always will.

The money from the work, though migratory, has also been good – I am trying to save some and send it back to Germany, to my wife and daughter there -- although I never hear back from them. Are they even alive? Does it matter? After Evie, I must ask myself how a man could still care about his family – his wife and daughter, from a previous lifetime – after falling in love with another woman? Is it possible to have the gift of love for two women, in one lifetime – and to continue to love them both equally? These are questions I will never fully know the answer to; this sort of love, for me, is clearly over, but remains buried in my heart like a curse.

Truth is, I am enjoying this type of work, I am seeing a lot of variety of the terrain here, from pine-forested mountains to oceans of grasslands, and these vistas would, at any other time, take my mind off of my troubles and disappointments, but not so.

The evil continues.

Ernst concerns me more and more. I fear he is addicted to the killing that he learned in the fields of war; he has grown to love it, and like a jealous lover, he will never give it up. He occasionally gets very surly and fidgety, wanders away with his rifle – the old Winchester he stole from Dave Perkins after he murdered him. God knows where he goes, but he returns a day or two later much calmer – but with that disturbing smile on his face. He claims he goes hunting but seldom brings back any game, and even so, too often has spatters of blood on his clothing and boots. Unfortunately, I suspect exactly what sort of 'hunting' he is doing, as he brags often of "doing away with the vermin."

Ernst has descended deeper into his personal hell that began with that damned war, and I fear he will soon drag me there, also."

#

"13.05.50
Mrs. Erika Eberhardt
#35 Frankfurtstrasse
Munich, Germany

My Darling Wife:

Once more I set my hand to pen in hopes that this letter will find you. I fear it is in vain, and that it will merely go the route of all the others I have written. I have now received several of them back undeliverable. I see that the last two were forwarded to a new address in München, so I will attempt to mail this one there, rather than to our old apartment in Stuttgart, which I understand is, like most of the German cities – and like our lives – a bombed out ruin.

No! I refuse to dwell on the horrid possibility that you might have perished there, although after so many years it seems increasingly hopeless that we will ever be reunited. Whether or not you live, my fervent prayer is that our beautiful little girl – my precious little rosebud – somehow survived the war and even now thrives. It will remain my lifelong dream that I will one day at least hear from her, if not actually see her face to face. I weep every time I realize I can no longer see your faces – no longer remember what you look like, for I unfortunately lost your photograph years ago in North Africa.

I am now working in what is known as the San Luis Valley of southern Colorado on a large potato farm. It is wonderful to get my hands back into the clean soil and let the good earth try and cleanse me. It is a beautiful area and the nearest town is called Alamosa. It is there I will check for any mail – which, alas, I fear will never be forthcoming.

I have nothing more to say that I have not said in all my previous letters, except that I remain:

Your devoted husband,
Otto.

P.S. I have enclosed a dried, pressed Columbine, a beautiful flower found in the region of Colorado I am in. I send it as a gift to our precious daughter, so she will have something to remind her that she has a father who loves her. Please tell her she dances for me in my dreams with this flower in her hair."

#

Excerpt from the journal of Otto Eberhardt

"20.08.51. I am at my wits end, roaming from farm to ranch, ranch to truck farms, always staying one step ahead of disaster. I fear we shall soon be forced to move on yet again.

Ernst has steadily gotten worse (if that's even possible) with his bloodlust – indiscriminate and careless now. The local newspapers recently reported the discovery of the body of a young murdered hitchhiker, who was eventually identified as a runaway student from Denver. He had been shot once in the back and once in the head by a high-powered rifle, and his body left to rot a quarter mile off the highway. It sounded ominously like Ernst's handiwork, but when I asked him about it, he just shrugged – but then that devil's grin crept onto his face, and I knew it was true.

I am sick to death of these murders. They don't seem to bother him in the least, but I am now feeling their dark stain on my own soul; just by knowing about them and not doing anything about them I am complicit.

I must do something before Ernst ruins what little is left of my life!

I have an idea that I have been contemplating – it is rather drastic, and if it fails…"

#

Otto sat perched on a stool nursing a beer, his third of the afternoon, at the dimly lit end of the smoky bar. He was positioned at a slight angle so he could watch the door. Even with the whirling of the ceiling fans in the old saloon, the late summer heat had not subsided: each time someone swung the door open to enter or exit a blast of dusty heat washed over the sticky, sweaty patrons.

It was payday, and the saloon was packed with farm workers and truckers who, like Otto, had spent all week laboring in the potato fields or in the overheated warehouses containing the harvested crop or shuffling and heaving seventy-five pound bags of potatoes onto the backs of trucks that would haul the produce to markets near and far.

Music blared from one of those machines that played records of several selections of popular songs for a mere dime – a *jukebox* he thought they were called. A lone couple slow danced near the machine, sweating and groping one another as if they were the only people in the room. Balls clacked loudly from the other side of the room as a group of men surrounded a pool table where two others brandished well-used cue sticks. The onlookers clutched wads of cash in dirty calloused hands, betting on the game, and shouting with each new smack of the balls.

Otto drank and watched the doorway. He was waiting for the right person to walk through. Although he had never met them before and wasn't exactly sure what they would look like, he was fairly certain he would know him when he saw him.

"Another beer?" The bartender had walked over to pick up Otto's empties. Otto shrugged.

"Sure, why not."

He didn't notice the bartender glance beyond him with a quick raise of his eyebrows. Nor did he notice that a short man wearing a clean white Stetson, a fresh blue checked shirt tucked into starched jeans, which themselves were tucked into tooled leather boots, had materialized from the dim corner of the room and sidled up and onto the barstool to Otto's left. The man had been holding a large tumbler of amber liquid and now sipped it, swallowed, and studied his glass appreciatively.

"So – you the German?" the strange little man asked with a drawn out Texas drawl, without looking up.

Otto set his beer down and swiveled his stool toward the man.

"Yes," he answered finally. "I am German."

"Not what I asked you – exactly. I said, 'are you *the* German – the one who's looking for, uh – certain services?'"

Otto squirmed on his stool to study the man more closely. The Texan continued to stare straight ahead as Otto sized him up. He appeared to be around one hundred fifteen or twenty pounds, short, wiry, and he toyed with his glass with hands that had a scrubbed, pink look like they had never seen hard work at all. Otto cleared his throat.

"Are you – him?" Otto asked, uncertainly.

The Texan sipped his drink again and stared down in the glass.

"I would sure 'preciate it if you would not stare quite so purposefully," he answered, "If you know what I mean."

Balls clattered and dropped again behind them, another chorus of shouts and groans rose from the crowd, and the wads of cash changed hands. Otto glanced in their direction, then turned back. He tried to match the Texan's unconcerned posture by also looking straight ahead, but stole an occasional glance out of his peripheral vision. The Texan drained his drink, caught the bartender's eye, and tapped the rim of his glass to signal another.

"You bring it?" he asked quietly, once the bartender had refilled the glass and walked away.

"Excuse me?" Otto asked, then realized what the question was. "Oh. You mean the money." He reached quickly inside his jacket. The Texan cleared his throat softly and slowly put his hand on Otto's nearest forearm.

"Just give me a quiet but firm 'yes,' or 'no.' That will be quite a sufficient answer for now."

Otto slowly removed his empty hand from his jacket. "Yes," he said quietly, with a slight nod.

The Texan caught Otto's eyes in the mirror. Otto thought his eyes looked like a shark's – dead and dark. He shuddered.

"You got the subject's name and a way for me to know him?"

Otto started to reach again for his pocket, but with an afterthought, stopped. "Uh, is it alright if I go to my pocket now?"

The Texan gave a slight nod. "Alright. Just do not make such a big fuss about it."

Otto pulled a slip of paper wrapped around a card from out of his shirt pocket and slid it slowly onto the bar. The Texan picked up his drink, took another sip, and at the same time, slid the paper over with his other hand. He opened the paper, which was folded over a dog-eared identification card of some sort, took a moment to read the name and commit the photo to memory, folded it, and slid it back over to Otto.

"You do not want to keep it?" Otto asked.

"Don't need to. Memorized it." The Texan paused, then continued. "So, where is he going to be at?"

Otto looked around the bar again, nervously, and turned back around to face the Texan. He looked the small man up and down again.

"Um – you know, I am no longer sure if this is going to be such a good idea. This guy is – "

"Listen, you son-of-a bitch!" the Texan interrupted with a snarl, just above a whisper. "I do not spend my time uselessly, nor do I allow myself to be made a mockery of." He shifted almost imperceptibly on his stool, adjusted the trim of his hat on his head, and took another slow sip to calm down. "Now – I don't think you were intending to do either. Were you?"

Otto looked at the man numbly. The Texan calmly set his tumbler of whisky on the bar, turned his head, and, for the first time, looked Otto directly in the eyes. He had been correct about the man's eyes – dead and flat. "Here is where you can say, 'yes' or 'no' again."

"No – sir," Otto stammered. "No disrespect at all – and I do not wish to waste your time."

"Okay, then." The Texan turned back to the bar and waited. "Well?" he finally asked the wall.

Otto hesitated for only a moment. "You will find him out at the Gardner Farms Warehouse, any time tomorrow. For the next couple days there are shipments that have to be loaded up. Early in the morning might be the best time to – uh – find him."

The Texan calmly drained his glass, placed a five-dollar bill underneath it, and stood up.

"I am going to leave now," he said quietly. "You, on the other hand, are going to stay here. You are not going to watch me leave, but you will order another beer and take your good sweet time about drinking it. When you have drunk half of it, the bartender is going to come over and ask if you are done. *Then*, and only then, will it be alright for you to quietly remove the envelope of cash from your jacket and slide it right under the bar towel he is going to have at the ready. He will then walk away from you and you may then walk away and leave this bar – but only then." The Texan glanced at Otto again in the mirror with those dead eyes and furrowed his brow.

"Is any of this making any sort of sense to you at all?" the Texan asked, paused, and sighed. "You know the drill by now – 'yes' or 'no.'"

Otto nodded once into the mirror.

"Good! Now, my German friend – I do trust we will never see one another again – and I do so hope that is your wish, also."

"How are going to do it? Otto interjected abruptly.

"Say again?" the man asked, after a beat.

"I mean, will he see you first? Or will you – um – you know, shoot him from a distance?" Otto caught the Texan exchanging an incredulous look with the bartender. "You must be very cautious with this man," he hurriedly added; "You have no idea what he is capable of."

The Texan didn't answer, but merely shook his head slowly and walked away. Not daring to breathe, Otto watched him through the mirror as he sauntered away toward the door of the saloon, adjusted his Stetson once more, and disappeared into the blast of heat and bright light as the door opened and slammed quickly behind him.

#

A few days later, Otto rode back to the bunkhouse in the back of the stake bed truck with three other exhausted men. They had all just spent the last few hours unloading potatoes from the truck into the sorting barn at the edge of the fields. A few more acres and they would be done with this season's harvest. Then, and only then, would be the time to move on to the foothills and seek some fall cattle work at the ranches up at the end of the valley. The ranchers would be wanting to move their herds out of the high country pastures and onto lower winter pastures, sorting off weaned calves and yearlings and taking some to the auction rings or feedlots.

Otto jumped down stiffly from the back of the truck and helped a couple of the older workers down. Most were migrant Mexicans, hard working all, and Otto got along fine with most of them. They lined up at the single water spigot outside their bunkhouse and took turns filling a bucket with cool water and dousing it over their sweaty, dusty heads in relief. Otto allowed most the other men to go first; when it was his turn, he rubbed his face and neck vigorously under the water, cupped his hands, and drank deeply and thankfully. He finally took his shirt off and rinsed it under the stream of water. He wiped his torso and under his arms with the wet shirt and put it back on to create a cool flow of air over his hot body as he tiredly ascended the steps to the bunkhouse.

He opened the door and crossed the room toward his bunk at the far end. Most of the other men were either already lying down gratefully on their bunks or changing clothes in anticipation of the dinner wagon that would be coming up the road shortly. Dinner usually consisted of beans, potatoes, and bread – sometimes a piece of chicken or even ground beef, but the food was always good and filling. If they were lucky, they would often have fresh apples or peaches for dessert.

Otto was still wiping the water from his eyes as he approached his bunk. He slowed down and after hesitating a bit, stopped, staring down uneasily at his bunk. Sitting squarely in the middle of the blanket spread over the thin mattress was a once-white Stetson cowboy hat. The hat was now filthy, the brim torn on one side, and blood and other matter caked along the inside brim near a single hole that looked to have been made by a bullet.

Otto's heart first skipped a beat and then thumped in his throat as he recognized the Texan's bloody hat and pondered what it meant.

But what it meant didn't take him long to understand; the meaning was stark and quite understandable – Ernst was still alive, he knew what Otto had done, and he had just sent him a very clear message.

Chapter 19
FRUIT OF THE SPIRIT

Trent stood on the deck overlooking the back yard behind the sprawling Neumann ranch house where he had been ushered by the stern-faced housekeeper, Mrs. Meeks. A large, beautifully manicured lawn lay before them like the first tee box of a well-tended country club. Beyond that a huge orchard of gnarled old peach trees spread into the distance, like a haunted wood. An elderly troll of a man was seated in a rattan chair on the edge of the lawn, underneath a huge peach tree, but the sun had evidently moved so that he was no longer completely shaded. The bodies of several half rotten peaches lay scattered about where they had fallen and were being patiently and methodically disposed of by a number of bees, flies, worms, and a few competitive sparrows.

Conrad Neumann was turned in slight profile to Trent, the old man's face, as if in a trance, upturned and gazing through the speckled sunlight filtering through the leaves. His eyes were concealed by a battered, broad brimmed planter's style straw hat pulled down around his ears, and he was dressed in a loose fitting flannel shirt buttoned to the neck and wrists and tucked into baggy brown trousers precariously held up by loose suspenders. He leaned out of his chair, perched birdlike over a large, gnarled cane, and with his upturned face, he gave the distinct impression of an inverted question mark—or a wizened, ancient troll.

"Wait here, please," Mrs. Meeks ordered as she brushed passed Trent and strode purposefully down the steps of the deck and across the freshly mown lawn. She leaned over and spoke quietly to the old man, then briefly touched his shoulder with her fingertips before returning to the deck. She gave Trent a cursory nod.

"Mr. Neumann will see you now," she said brusquely in her clipped German accent. "But please do not get him excited." She hesitated as she looked back at the old man and continued, "He is not entirely well, as you can easily see." She moved to the door, looking back once more. "And I will be right inside here – if needed." The statement was as much a warning as it was informational. Mrs. Meeks disappeared back into the house without another word.

Trent took his hat off, squinted up at the late afternoon sun, and let out his breath in a puff as if trying to put off something inevitable and unpleasant. He took control of himself, swallowed hard, put a tight-lipped smile on his face, and stepped off the porch.

The somewhat soothing drone of bees belied the scene before him. Neumann had lowered his face slowly and waved away a meandering bee; he gave a feeble cough, and now, turned his head around in acknowledgement of his visitor. The left side of his tanned face showed the natural, well-earned leathery wrinkles someone would have expected of any ninety-eight-year-old man who'd spent a lifetime working outdoors. Even so, Trent felt a sudden chill and shuddered involuntarily; now, the red puckered visage of Neumann's right profile was turning into full view, revealing a horrific map of shriveled scars that transformed his appearance into that of a ruined, two-faced Janus.

Trent's mind recoiled.

He stopped and took a sudden breath: this side of the old man's head wore a mockery of a face, the results of a terrible accident of some kind that had left him with this nightmare mask, like melted wax, the ear just a boiled nub and the hairline non-existent; naked eyebrow and eyelid fused together in a permanent flap that all but obscured a sightless, pale eyeball. The melted skin continued downward to where the lips on this side of the mouth drooped into a grimace from which the old man frequently dabbed a trickle of saliva with a grimy handkerchief gripped in his gloved left hand. He now waved the handkerchief feebly to gesture to Trent to come closer.

The odor of rotten peaches rose up to greet Trent's nostrils; he had to will his feet to move again toward this burned out shell of a man before him like someone methodically walking into a nightmare.

Conrad Neumann stared at Trent out of his one clear eye. Although he recognized the old man from the garden at the nursing home, Trent fought every impulse to turn his eyes away from the horror before him. He held the old man's gaze, fascinated, as if he were watching a plane crash.

Neumann gestured again with his handkerchief toward a bench across from him.

"Please – seat yourself, Officer Carter." The old man's breathy voice gurgled with phlegm, but he didn't bother to cough and clear it, only satisfied himself with wiping away spittle from the corner of his ruined mouth with his damp handkerchief. His gaze was unwavering and unapologetic. "I am pleased to see you. I receive so few visitors anymore."

Conrad Neumann's voice slurred a bit, but clearly bore a strong German accent, which was not unusual. Colfax County had experienced an influx of European immigrants over the past 120 years – Italians, Austrians, Swedes, Germans, Slavs, primarily, all hungering for the good steady work offered by the coalmines and by the railroads built to haul the coal. Hardworking and industrious, their descendants had fanned out, acquiring property, starting businesses and ranches, many becoming the burgeoning backbone of the local economies as well as scions of politics and community affairs.

Trent had never met Conrad Neumann – at least not that he could remember – but knew of his history and reputation as a brutally efficient rancher, businessman, and politician who had struggled greatly to overcome the tragedy of his younger years when he had been carving out a living by building his ranch. He supposedly had been horribly injured and disfigured in a devastating fire that destroyed half his ranch and had taken the life of his young wife. Their two children had been spared: the older son Carl had seemed fine, but the young daughter Caroline had ended up so traumatized, she had to be relegated to institutional care – or so the story was told. Overall, a tragic accident, although rumor had it that Neumann started the fire himself after catching his wife with a lover, that he had killed them both, then set the fire to cover the murders.

Either way, Neumann had become legendary, and later, when his son Carl had returned from Vietnam, together they rebuilt and grew the cattle ranch into a small empire. He had been a ruthless competitor in business over the years. Eventually his old injuries had drained him of ambition and energy, making him a virtual recluse under the watchful eye of his loyal housekeeper/caregiver, Mrs. Meeks, who had emigrated from Germany years ago. Tongues had occasionally wagged that they had become something more to one another than just servant and boss. Whatever the case, clearly she seemed to be very protective of her employer.

Trent glanced toward the house to see Mrs. Meeks even now standing and watching them out the window, sternly and unabashedly.

"So to what do I owe the pleasure, Officer Carter?"

Trent looked away from the house and cleared his throat. "Mr. Neumann, I apologize for the intrusion – "

"No, you do not, Mr. Carter," Neumann replied, abruptly cutting him off. His clear eye bore into Trent's like a probing searchlight. "You have come here to do your duty." He licked his lower lip with a pink tongue. "And duty is one thing that I understand – and something I happen to admire greatly in a man."

Trent stared as Neumann leaned toward him ever so slightly, the eye honing in on him like a laser.

"So. Your duty here today has something to do with my son Carl I am guessing, *ja*?" The old man attempted a smile, but what crawled onto his mouth was a mocking grimace, instead. He batted weakly with his handkerchief at a bee that veered too close to his ruined face. "Carl may be many things, Mr. Carter, including having been a dutiful son – a great help to me in running this place. But also, in his own way, he has been at times troublesome, indulging far too many of his – what shall I call them – baser obsessions, perhaps, *ja*?" Trent broke the old man's cold, piercing gaze and looked away, grateful to allow his eyes to follow the meanderings of the bees – anything but dwell on Neumann's horror of a face.

"As a matter of fact," agreed Trent, "I'm afraid that Carl is now a suspect in an investigation I am involved in, Mr. Neumann." He hesitated, but continued, "I'm sorry to say he is a person of interest in a series of murders, some that have stretched back for some time." He paused.

"No, you are not," the old man blurted out as he slowly raised his handkerchief, this time to dab at his ruined eye.

"Excuse me?"

"You are not in the least sorry about my son, Deputy Carter," he continued. "You are a hunter, and I happen to know hunters – very well. You have the scent of blood in your nostrils and you thrive on it." Neumann suddenly lowered the handkerchief to cover his mouth and began a soft hacking sound deep in his throat. The noise gurgled and rolled around, growing louder as the old man's frame shook. Trent began to get alarmed that Neumann may be choking and started to rise to help. Neumann shook his head and motioned him to stay put, and only then did Trent realize the old man was chuckling.

"And, of course, he is a suspect," Neumann finally chortled. "Carl is nothing if not cruel and sadistic. After all, he learned from the best." Here, he poked a gnarled thumb into his small bony chest hiding somewhere in the folds of his flannel shirt and chuckled some more. "We Neumanns have fought long and hard for what you see around you. We have not accomplished anything by being soft or accommodating. We can smell out weakness and indecisiveness, and we have taken full advantage over those who exhibit it – and with relish!"

Neumann took a deep, rattling breath, the air wheezing out of his ancient lungs, and sat back, momentarily exhausted.

"Do you know where I can find your son, Mr. Neumann?"

Conrad Neumann at last turned his good eye away from Trent and squinted out across the manicured lawn beyond the peach trees and their rotting fruit, over the distant pastures to the foothills of the Sangre de Cristo Mountains on the horizon, and up toward the Raton Pass. He weakly and shakily pointed his cane in the direction he was looking.

"I have driven cattle in blizzards out of those very mountains there to safety, and almost froze to death doing it. I have taken everything I ever wanted – never asked or begged for anything. And I dare to tell you that there were things I have done – things I was forced to do to survive, mind you – that, if you knew about them, you would have to do your duty and arrest me right here and now. Everything that you see between here and those mountains there I have taken, Mr. Carter – in my timing and for my own pleasure. And I have raised my son to do the same," he croaked. He lowered his cane and looked down at the rotten peaches on the ground.

"No, Deputy Carter – if Carl has done these things that you say he is suspected of doing, then you shall have to prove it – in a court of law. But first, you shall have to find him – and then you shall have to catch him. And you shall have to do all of that with no assistance from me, whatsoever. No sir. I will not sully my hands with such matters. He is my son – yes. But he, too, has made his own way, in his own time, and, for whatever reasons, he himself has done these deeds."

Neumann lowered his voice to a growl and leaned forward. "But be warned, Deputy Carter. Carl is not just another rich man's spoiled boy, incapable of fending for himself."

Trent wanted badly to look away as the old man's grisly death's head moved ever closer. He could smell the rotten breath in the space of air between the two of them.

"Tell, my, Mr. Carter: you are a fan of football, yes? You played when you were younger – you understand the strategies of the game?"

Trent raised his eyebrows, slightly surprised. "Yes," he answered. "Of course."

Neumann leaned forward, wiped his glistening lips with the handkerchief. "You do not want to let Carl make the 'end run' around you," he continued. "If he knows you are coming for him – and believe me, he probably knows already– he will be very dangerous…" The old man's moist growl conveyed both a warning and a gloat, "the most dangerous foe you have ever known."

Trent shook his head out of curiosity. "And just why are you telling me this, Mr. Neumann? It's almost as if you want me to catch your son."

Neumann looked up and made a gesture somewhere behind Trent. Trent heard the door open behind him abruptly and Mrs. Meeks's heavy tread on the porch. He turned to see her standing at the stop of the steps, her arms folded defiantly as she glared his way.

"Let us just say, Mr. Carter," Neumann lowered his voice as he looked down at his feet and swatted his cane at flies crawling on a rotten peach lying there, "that I love a good game. And at my age, there are not too many good games left to play. So may the best man win!" The sound that gurgled from Neumann's throat made Trent cringe as the old man looked back up at the deck and nodded at his housekeeper.

"Mr. Neumann is finished talking with you now," she informed Trent as she stepped down to the lawn. She deliberately unfolded her arms and turned to one side, indicating that Trent should make his exit with her into and through the house. "If you will, please come this way, sir."

Trent stood up slowly and swatted a bee away with his hat. He looked disgustedly down at the old man.

"You know, Mr. Neumann," Trent murmured as he leaned down and placed his hands on either side of the old man's chair, meeting the watering, glaring eye with his own, "I will track him down, and I will know the truth," he continued, "and I will do my duty." Trent leaned even closer to the grotesque face staring back at him. "And, Old Man, if I find that you have had anything at all to do with any of this, I will be back – and I will not hesitate to slap the handcuffs on you, too."

Trent stood up, glanced back at Mrs. Meeks, and smiled, then back at Conrad Neumann, "and as you alluded to, sometimes doing one's duty *is* the admirable thing to do."

He turned on his heel and followed the stern housekeeper across the deck and on through the house, waving away the flies and the rotten odors that now seemed to permeate every fiber of his clothes.

Trent vowed never to eat another peach so long as he l

CHAPTER 20
PRODIGAL

Excerpt from the Journal of Otto Eberhardt

"10.10.53 – My life has become one of perpetual movement. I cannot remember a time when I was not on the move, from place to place, job to job – and continuously looking over my shoulder or sleeping with one eye open or feeling the constant tingle in the back of my neck, waiting for the inevitable bullet to plow through my skull, explode me into nonexistence.

Ernst is still out there. I feel his eyes on me, even after all years – and I know he is only biding his time, awaiting the perfect moment, just the right place, to exact his revenge against me.

And so I will continue to wander – perhaps until I find that one special place where I can at least pretend that I am safe – someplace he would never dream I would be.

But I know that is all a lie to myself – that it is all just a matter of time. Ernst is good at this game. He is out there, hiding in plain sight.

I am a walking dead man."

#

The rugged terrain north of the town of Clayton encompasses an area that, within just a few miles east, forms the conjoined borders of five states: namely, New Mexico, Colorado, Kansas, and the Panhandles of Oklahoma and Texas. To the west, this land rolls across high desert plains, but abruptly and unexpectedly spills into hidden canyons and fertile valleys cut by ancient waterways. A couple of these hidden valleys still flow with live water, meandering through tree lined creek beds to further feed an ecosystem of surprisingly fertile land. In and around these virtual oases are tucked homesteads, cultivated fields, and small ranches whose tenacious existences depend solely on that water to continue to nurture them and their owners.

The water has always depended on two dynamics – the cycle of good rainy seasons and snowpack on the mountains, year-in and year–out, and the landowners' abilities to hold onto their valuable and sometimes tenuous claims of enough water shares to keep their meager agricultural endeavors viable. The former required the Almighty Himself pouring out His wet blessings at the proper times while the latter often required the almighty gun wielded by a trustworthy hand or two as well as a judge who was friendly to a claim, or at least susceptible to a good bribe.

Conrad Neumann was neither very wealthy nor very knowledgeable concerning manipulation of water law – but he did know an opportunity when he saw one, and he was good with a gun – even better with his fists. Through the years, he watched as one neighbor after another wore out their stamina struggling hand-to-mouth; however, he had prided himself on timing events just right: being in the right place at the right time to make just the right offer to ease his neighbors' of their burdens and acquire their water, and often their land. By adding their parcels to the homestead he had inherited from his father, he now possessed one of the more desirable small ranches that spread out along the entire width of valley, itself bisected by one of the few steadily flowing streams in the area that rarely ran dry. This possession and control afforded him both a healthy herd of cattle and allowed him to cultivate and grow his own hay crop to feed them with as well as often producing a surplus that he could sell to his remaining and now less fortunate neighbors.

Neumann's father had moved the family from the Alsace-Lorraine border area of Germany and France right after the Great War when the Treaty of Versailles had taken the coveted and disputed land away from the defeated Germans and had given it back to the French. The German citizens who had owned farms there for generations were often suddenly displaced. Those farmers who weren't had two choices – stay and suffer additional war reparations imposed in the form of crippling taxes along with the ignominy of living with the stigma of being a defeated people or they could leave. Conrad's father chose to sell out at a huge loss and emigrate to the United States where he had heard that the limitless resources of North America offered tremendous opportunity and jobs, particularly out in the proverbial Wild West where they were digging coal and silver, building railroads to ship it with, and building cities and towns to ship it to. After several years of living in coal camps and digging King Coal under dangerous conditions, Conrad's father had finally scraped together enough to purchase a small plot of arable land in the canyons along what was known as the Dry Cimarron, roughly forty miles north of Clayton and hugging the Colorado state line.

With farming in their blood, the family was finally back to a lifestyle they knew, albeit a struggling one. But they were happy eking out a living from the dirt they understood and gradually built up their farm. Conrad grew tall and lean; when he turned twenty, he took a wife in a marriage arranged by his father and a neighbor, and the farm continued to grow by yet another several hundred acres in the negotiations. But a scarlet fever epidemic swept through the homesteads in the late 30s, killing dozens of people who had somehow survived the Great Depression only to succumb now to illness; these victims included Conrad's parents, his sister, his wife, and two-year old son. Conrad had been devastated with the toll of these losses, had begun to drink heavily, and had almost lost his farm to neglect.

Then came the next world war, and although Conrad was too old to be drafted and he hadn't yet sobered up completely, he did see clearly enough yet another opportunity and straightened up enough to put the small ranch back in shape just in time to start supplying the insatiable demands of a nation on a war footing for agricultural products.

By the end of the war, Neumann was comfortable, out of debt, and successful. He also found that he was also quite lonely. At the age of 45, then, he began looking for another marriage opportunity. He had overheard at the feed yard outside of Clayton about a fellow rancher over in neighboring Colfax County who had a marriageable daughter. Neumann wasted no time in writing a letter, followed by making a more formal introduction to the girl's father. He knew from experience and tradition how these marriage arrangements worked, so he was surprised and delighted just how quickly the girl's family agreed to the proposal, especially since, at age 23, she was about half his age. He was doubly surprised and delighted when he finally laid eyes on her that she was one of the most beautiful young women he had ever seen with her raven dark hair and unblemished, creamy skin. Her perpetually sad eyes, to him, only enhanced her desirability; besides, he had hoped he would be able to put some happiness back into them, given time.

July 1947, then, was when Conrad Neumann became the proud husband to Miss Evie Van Ryan, who a little over eight months later presented him with a strong son, whom he readily named Carl after his late father.

#

Excerpt from the Diary of Evie Neumann

"June 7, 1954 – Conrad has been gone for most of two days again. It frightens me when he does this. Not that I am afraid of being home alone, even if it is just me and the kids here, along with a couple of ranch hands. I'm not worried about any of that – I can more than fend for myself – have done so on more than one occasion.

It's just that the longer he is gone, the worse it will be when he finally returns – I know he's spending all this extra time with his drinking and carousing – even with other women. I'm not stupid. He hardly touches me anymore, not since Caroline was born. Not that that bothers me in the least, all his drunken pawing and grabbing – and worse. And I don't even mind when he hits me now and then – I am a little mouthy at times. I just don't want him ever to start in on the children. He's already taken his belt off to my son a time or two. Little Carl tries so hard to get attention – a little too hard at times, I know. But he's just a typical boy who needs his father's approval. And Conrad has never been one to show real affection – I surely know that. Even when Carl was born and he was so very excited, at first, to have another son. And, of course, there was so much I was relieved about, also.

But then Caroline came along, and after a while it was clear something was different about her, maybe not quite right. I know Conrad blames me for that. Oh, she's as pretty as a picture and as precious as any four-year-old girl could be – but she is just not always there, staring off into space, singing her little songs to herself, not answering right away when she's spoken to. I know it makes Conrad furious, and thank God I have never seen him raise a finger to her – and I know that deep down Caroline loves her daddy, and needs him. She just doesn't know how to show it. But I fear that this has also driven him further away.

I just wish he would come home and stay. Because when he's been to town, drinking and whoring – well, I've already said it all. He was supposed to go to town this time to hire us some good seasonal help. Always a few experienced migrants that wander in over at the feed yards. Calves will be weaned soon, and it'll be branding time. Also first cutting of grass hay coming up in a few weeks. Sure need some help to stay on top of things.

And I think I just might get some peaches this year from the little peach orchard I planted out back a couple years ago. It has taken off so nicely, and oh, how I am so looking forward to fresh peaches!

#

Conrad Neumann had gone straight to the feed store when he pulled into Clayton. There he had found a few men sitting or milling around in front, hoping for some day work. The trick was to find two or three who actually had some experience and could be counted on to put in a full day's work. Conrad prided himself on being able to size up such men, learned through years of experience. He quickly looked these over, shook his head at a few, asked others some informational questions, and after only a few minutes, ended up hiring three of them. One of these, a scruffy looking bearded fellow, looked capable enough: late 30s, clear-eyed, stood up straight, and had sturdy legs and arms and strong, calloused hands. He answered Conrad's questions quietly but firmly and directly and seemed to understand cattle work. The man also surprisingly spoke with a slight German accent, which didn't bother Conrad in the least, since he himself still retained a similar accent.

Conrad promptly put his new hires to work loading his truck with the feed and supplies he had just purchased. He then paid the men a little money, against their coming wages, of course, and as it was late in the day ordered them to go buy themselves something to eat and come back and stay with the truck overnight. They were to make themselves comfortable in the back, amongst the sacks of feed, and be ready to go in the morning. Instructions being given, he walked on down the street and around the corner to the Elkhorn Saloon where he drank half the night away and spent the other half upstairs in the bed of his favorite whore.

He awoke promptly at 9:00 a.m., soaked in the woman's bathtub for an hour, got dressed, paid his debt, and went downstairs and ate a medium rare sirloin steak with three eggs, all smothered in onions. After he ate, he purchased a pint of whisky, slipped it into his coat pocket, and walked back down the street and around the corner to where his truck was parked in front of the feed store. The three men he had just hired were seated on the curb in front of the truck smoking cigarettes. Conrad walked up to them, pulled the pint of whisky from his pocket, broke the seal, and took a big gulp. He grimaced and momentarily offered the pint to the three men. Two of them smiled up at him and both of them took an equally large drink from the proffered bottle; but the other one – the bearded quiet one – shook his head and looked away, up the street. Conrad took the pint back, looking back and forth at the faces of the men in front of him.

"You're fired," he said, finally.

The two men who had shared his booze looked at one another in shock, but stood up slowly and made their way up the sidewalk, cursing under their breaths. The third man – the bearded man – continued to look up the street into the shimmering heat glaze, said nothing, tossed his cigarette butt in the gutter, and stood up. He made a show of tucking his shirt neatly into his pants, straightened his hat, and turned to walk away in the opposite direction of the first two men.

"Not you," Conrad murmured, looking the man over. "You still work for me – your decision." The bearded man stopped, his back still turned to Conrad, grunted once, then slowly turned around and stood there, looking at Conrad with his arms folded in front of him. He waited.

"Can't abide having a drunk on my place," Conrad continued, looking at this man directly in the eye. "Sign of poor character, if you ask me." He took another deliberate sip of whisky, screwed the cap back on, and slipped the bottle back into his pocket, his eyes never leaving the bearded man's as if inviting a comment.

The man said nothing, but stood waiting patiently.

"You are certainly not one to waste words, are you?" Conrad turned on his heels suddenly and slapped the fender of the truck with a loud bang. "You drive?" he asked.

The bearded man nodded slowly. "I do," he answered.

"Well, look at that – you do have a tongue."

Conrad threw him the keys across the hood of the truck, then opened the passenger door. "So, let's get going then!" Conrad barked as he slid into the passenger seat, leaned back, and gestured toward the windshield. "About thirty miles, straight north out of town on 370 until you can't go any further – then turn left into the Dry Cimarron." He pulled his hat down over his eyes. "Then just keep driving west til you see the gate says 'Neumann Ranch.' Can't miss it."

He was snoring by the time the bearded man had the truck turned around and had passed the city limits heading north.

#

Evie was almost done hanging the day's wash on the wire clothesline strung in the yard. The early afternoon sun was nice and warm, but a gathering of cumulonimbus clouds crawling up over the southeast horizon caught her eye and made her pause as she stretched her back. Static electricity was in the air, a sure harbinger of a pending thunderstorm; knowing the signs, she quickly and expertly tossed the remaining damp bed linens up on the line. They needed time to get dry, along with her husband's favorite shirts, well before any storm arrived or there would be hell to pay and she knew who would pay it – that is, if he even made it back home today.

Carl was running around the house playing cowboys and Indians with the homemade gun one of the hands had carved for him out of a piece of scrap wood. It was shaped like a rifle and had a clothes pin tacked to the top, which, in turn, held a piece of rubber cut from an old inner tube of a tire. Carl could pull the big rubber band back until he clasped it in the pin, then "shoot" it at his chosen targets: usually ants, flies, or sometimes, his little sister, a favorite target he seemed to enjoy tormenting.

Caroline was sitting cross-legged by her mother's laundry basket rocking back and forth and crooning softly to her favorite doll, which was missing one of its button eyes and had half its blond woolly hair pulled out.

Carl stopped running suddenly and looked off into the distance where a dirt plume was rising.

"Is that Daddy?" he called out.

Evie stopped her work and stepped out from behind a hanging bed sheet to take an anxious look up the road. She cupped a hand over her brow to shade it and squinted.

"Yes – yes, I do believe it is." Her voice was hesitant and just a little disappointed.

The plume drifted off behind a moving dot that grew larger by the minute until it materialized into Conrad's familiar old Chevy truck, bouncing and weaving along. Evie bit her bottom lip, sighed, and stepped back until she was half obscured behind the safety of the hanging wash. She squeezed her eyes shut for a moment and whispered a quick prayer. *Oh God, please don't let him be too mean today.* She opened her eyes and saw Caroline looking up at her steadily.

"God says He likes it when you talk to him, Mama," Caroline crooned and quietly busied herself with her doll once more.

Evie continued on with her work, only listening now instead of watching as the truck drew nearer, its engine overworking in the heat, and its gears beginning to grind down. She hazarded one more sideways look around the corner of the linens and spied the silhouettes of two people in the cab of the truck.

So only one she thought to herself. *Gonna have to be one heck of a worker to get things done around here that need doing.*

She shook her head and returned to her washing. She listened for the familiar creaking noise of the truck doors opening, slamming, and then waited for her husband's inevitable shout.

"Where's your mama, boy?" he called out to Carl with only silence as a response. Evie could picture Carl pointing around to her side of the house.

She waited a beat, took a deep breath, and stepped out from behind the sheets – but suddenly froze.

"There you are, woman," Conrad said, his voice slurring and way too loud. "Get on over here. Found me a guy in town – think he may be all right. We'll see. But it's been a long day and he's probably hungry, so see what you can rustle up for him to eat before I show him around."

Evie's eyes had widened as her husband spoke, but she wasn't looking at him; she was staring at the man who had been driving. He was of average build, wore old but clean clothes, scuffed up boots, and a broad brimmed straw hat that shaded deep blue eyes. His tanned and weathered face was half covered with a full reddish brown beard. The man took a hesitant step forward as he pulled his hat off slowly but politely to reveal unkempt, shaggy hair of a sandy blond color, and his eyes had also widened in stunned surprise as he stared back at Evie.

As she recognized this man standing before her, she gasped and put the back of her hand quickly to her mouth. Even with the beard and rough demeanor, Evie Neumann would know this man's eyes anywhere.

The eyes that belonged to the love of her life: Otto Eberhardt.

CHAPTER 21
REVELATIONS

"What the hell are you doing here?"

The other diners in the main dining room of The Santa Fe Trail Supper Club grew noticeably quieter. Trent and Maggie had just walked in and stopped in the doorway between the bar and the dining room so he could help her off with her suede jacket, an expensive looking beige garment with a few glittering sequins across the back. Underneath the jacket, she wore a turquoise blouse with colorful Indian patterns, a long strand of round turquoise beads, beige slacks, and light gray boots. Her hair was pulled up behind her ears, clipped in the back, and hung straight down past her shoulders. Trent idly wondered for a brief second or two, as she gently smoothed her slacks, if she somehow knew that was the same way Vicky used to wear her hair when they went out.

He liked it.

Trent had just made it home in time to take one of the fastest showers he had ever taken, shave quickly – hence, the small scab near his chin – and change into fresh jeans, a black shirt and gray tie, and his favorite light blue tweed sports jacket.

But now, he froze with Maggie's coat halfway off her shoulders as he glared at a couple seated at a table across the room.

It was Sophie and Hector.

"What the –, " he started to say.

Maggie shrugged her wrap the remainder of the way off and, in a manner he was becoming accustomed to, took charge.

"Oh, hush up now and come on, Honey Bunch." She smiled and

shrugged apologetically at the diners seated nearby as she left him behind and made her way over to Sophie and Hector, seated cozily across the corner of their table, but now looking nervously their way. Trent still stood in the doorway, holding her jacket uselessly, and watching her walk away with an exasperated look on his face.

Maggie stood expectantly beside one of the empty chairs, made a face at him, and with a smile, gestured with her head for him to come. He scowled, looked down at her coat in his hands, audibly sighed, and strode over to the table. He stood beside her and scowled from Sophie to Hector and back again.

"Hey, Sweet Pea," Maggie said, poking him in the arm. "Can't a lady get a chair pulled out for her?"

Trent frowned, seated her, and carefully placed her jacket on the back of her chair. He thought he saw Maggie and Sophie exchange knowing looks as he glanced from his daughter to his date first with surprise, then comprehension.

"I'll be damned," he growled in measured words. "You two cooked up this little get together, didn't you?" He glared across the table at Hector, who was seated straight across from him. "What the hell is this, Hector?"

Hector blushed deeply, looked quickly away, and took a long drink of his beer. To break the awkward silence, finally, Sophie spoke.

"Daddy, please sit down," she began, just above a whisper. Trent paused for a moment, his hand on the back of the chair, frowning at them all suspiciously before he finally sat.

Sophie continued: "Hector and I have been seeing each other, and – "

"Hector and you have been doing *what?*" Trent almost came right out of his chair before he had even settled.

"We've been seeing one another – and we didn't know how to – "

"Since when?" Trent demanded, loudly. He glared back at Hector. "How long have you been sneaking behind my back with my daughter, Hector?" People nearby grew quiet again and looked over at their table.

"Oh, do shut up, Trent," interrupted Maggie sweetly," and order me a drink like a good boy."

#

Sophie spent the next ten or fifteen minutes patiently explaining to her father why it was not such a terrible idea that Hector and she had been dating for several weeks now while Hector spent the next ten or fifteen minutes studiously avoiding Trent's glare by nursing first one beer, then another, and Maggie spent the next ten to fifteen minutes kicking Trent under the table each time he opened his mouth to argue.

Trent himself spent the next ten to fifteen minutes alternately frowning around the table, trying to say something, and reaching under the table to rub his sore shins.

Sophie had concluded her well-rehearsed justifications; a space of silence settled around the table while around them the low murmurings of other conversations and the tinkling of cutlery from the surrounding diners ebbed and flowed.

Trent looked impatiently at Maggie.

"May I speak now?" he asked defensively while moving his nearest leg away from her reach.

"Long as you keep a civil tongue in your head," she murmured around a mouthful of Caesar salad that had arrived at their places.

"And that's another thing," Trent began, irritated. "How in the world did it happen that you're the designated matchmaker around here?" Maggie chewed her food meticulously and then washed it down with a gulp of her margarita.

"Oh, that's the easy one to answer." She held up her glass and wiggled it at the waiter. "I was coming to town the other day and invited Sophie to lunch."

"And just why would you invite my daughter to lunch?"

"Because I have called a couple of times now over the past few weeks to try and take *you* to lunch, but you're never in the office – off gallivanting around somewhere, I suppose – so I suddenly hit upon the brilliant idea of taking Sophie instead. You know – girl-to-girl sort of thing."

"Again I ask 'why?' I mean, Sophie's half your age, and – "

"Watch it, Mister!"

"*And,*" he picked up where he'd left off, "I doubt that you two have anything in the least in common."

Another awkward silence rose around the table as Trent took a large drink of his double Scotch before catching Maggie and Sophie and Hector all exchanging glances. The two women both stifled giggles.

"What was that?" he asked, setting his glass down slowly. "That thing –

right there." He pointed his finger accusingly at each of them in turn. "I saw those looks, there." His glare finally rested back on Hector, who had tried to crawl into his beer bottle. "Hector? What the hell is this?"

Hector shrugged dumbly and quickly renewed his attack on his salad.

Trent looked around at each of them again and finally stopped at Maggie. "What did you mean, Margot Van Ryan, when you said, 'that's the easy one to answer?'"

At this point, everybody but Trent was hungrily eating their starters as if there would be no entrees to follow.

"Well, I will be damned," he finally muttered, watching them all, and finally nodded knowingly. "I've been ambushed here, haven't I, Maggie?" His fingers drummed a tattoo on the edge of the table as he squinted his eyes at his dinner date. "I don't know whether to be more upset over finding out that my only daughter is sneaking around behind my back with my new partner, or by learning that all three of you have been conspiring to get you and me together, somehow!"

Trent grabbed his napkin off his lap and threw it on top of his untouched salad. He quickly drained the remainder of his Scotch, slammed the tumbler on the table, pushed his chair out, and got up. The nearby tables grew uncomfortably silent and the diners glanced in their direction.

"Daddy, now stop it," Sophie said in a tight half-whisper through gritted teeth. "You're embarrassing us – and yourself!"

"Good!" he declared, after looking around the room at the now silent diners who stared at him. He spread his arms to include them all. "Embarrassment is something I happen to excel in – and I am sure that all these fine folks here have seen it often enough before – the crazy, burned out cop who talks to himself -- and to ghosts, no less!'"

"*Stop now, Baby Boy.*"

The voice was merely a faint echo in his mind, matching the faint, familiar scent that wafted past his nose and made him choke on his words. He stopped and glanced around nervously, breathing heavily, sweat breaking on his brow. *Please, not now,* he thought to himself. *Not here!* He pressed his eyes with his fingers.

Vicky's presence passed on.

"You done, Cowboy?" Maggie asked tenderly after a moment. She had leaned on one elbow and was sipping her refilled margarita thoughtfully while watching his tirade. "Trent?" she asked again more directly, raised eyebrows peering over the salted rim of her glass at him as she finally caught his eye. She reached over, patted him lovingly but firmly on the back of his hand as it clenched his chair-back, smiled sweetly, and continued in a softer tone. "Then just sit your sweet ass back down right now because these kids have a lot more to tell you. And I think you are going to want to hear what they have to say," she continued in a lilting drawl, "that is, if you'll stop your asinine blustering long enough to listen – Sweet Pea," she added demurely.

Trent stood transfixed, staring at her with a mixture of fascination, admiration, and trepidation. He would never cease to be amazed by this woman. She continuously pulled the rug out from under him, but seemed to always soften the fall, somehow. And, having nothing left to say, nor any inkling of how to respond at all, Trent sat down obediently.

"Dad," Sophie began again, trying to get his attention. She reached down in her lap, fumbled in her purse, and pulled out a familiar-looking worn book. "This is that old journal you gave me to translate, remember? From that German soldier?"

Trent gave his daughter a tired, resigned look. "What about it?"

"Well, that's what I've been trying to tell you – and all of this is part of it, really." She indicated Hector and Maggie. "All of us, actually."

She thumbed excitedly through the book and Trent could see she had marked several pages with yellow tabs. "I'm only about halfway through it, but I've found some things – things I realized you really need to know about!"

Sophie proceeded to tell Trent that she had struggled, at first, in translating the language. She had pulled out some of her old college German textbooks, and when those references hadn't helped much, she had gotten onto some internet translation sites and started making better progress.

At first the story had peaked her interest merely as a fascinating historical account and human-interest story of World War II era German soldiers who had managed to escape from a POW camp in Colorado. But as she continued to read, it had begun to turn dark, with some really disturbing events being documented, including kidnappings and even murders. One of the men seemed to be quite sadistic – and according to the author, evil incarnate. Reading about this guy – Ernst was his name – was slightly akin to watching an auto accident – horrifying, but hard to look away. She had even begun having thoughts that if the project were handled correctly, the story could be turned into a great book – or maybe even a movie script. But by that time, she had worked her way through to an account of sabotage the two escapees had perpetrated at the train tunnels on Raton Pass in the closing days of the war, and her attention had become even more focused than on a mere human-interest level.

By now Trent had ordered another Scotch and was nursing it, but at this point of her story, he grew very still and set his glass down, waiting to hear more. Part of him was still annoyed at the entire evening, but another part was intrigued, and very impressed, that his daughter had taken such a keen interest in the project he had given her – and there was something else, too, about what she was now sharing.

The effects of the alcohol were suddenly wearing off of him. She had his full attention now.

"Go on," he said in a measured voice.

"Well, for one thing, that's how I actually met Hector." Sophie stopped, her mouth open in exasperation as her father pinched his eyes between a thumb and forefinger. "Dad! This is important!"

"Well, forgive me if I am not seeing the relevance that Deputy Armijo brings to the table," Trent said, feeling a slow burn rise in him again. "Can we just eat our meals and get the hell out of here?"

"Shut up, Trent, and listen!" Maggie said softly through a tight smile, like wielding a hammer wrapped in a velvet glove. Trent squirmed, crossed his legs, and sat back.

Sophie continued to explain how she had come down to his office one day to show him just how far she had gotten on the project. Instead, Hector, who had told her that Trent was out of the office, met her, and politely offered her coffee and donuts – here, Trent rolled his eyes again – and one thing led to another. Pretty soon they were discussing the contents of the journal, and Hector had suddenly perked up and gotten intensely interested.

"Dad, Hector said his grandfather was killed in that same tunnel attack – he was with the National Guard, assigned to guard the tunnel against possible sabotage."

"Yes. His name was Alberto – Alberto Armijo," Hector interjected excitedly, speaking up for the first time that evening. "My grandmother has told me the story many times. He is a family hero."

Trent looked over at Hector as if he were some inanimate object that had suddenly come to life. Hector, for once, did not look away but met Trent's eyes with a sobering look, then pointed over at the journal. "It *is* in the book – Mr. Carter."

"And Dad," Sophie continued in a quieter tone, "you've never said anything about your grandmother – my *great* grandmother – also being on that train, along with Grandpa Walter, and his little brother." Trent stared into his glass, saying nothing.

"Dad," Sophie continued intensely, "this Otto Eberhardt guy met her! He wrote about talking to a Penelope Carter, and her boys. They're all mentioned here by name – *Walter Carter.* That can't just be a coincidence." She tapped a highlighted page with her fingernail. "Dad, these men – they were responsible – the same man who wrote this journal – he and that Ernst fellow blew up that train!"

Trent said nothing, but studied the ice in his whisky. He suddenly felt a numb and a little sick.

"Innocent people died that day," Sophie continued softly. "Daddy, just what happened to Great Grandma Penelope – and Grandpa Walter's brother? I mean I never even knew he had a brother. You've never spoken about it."

Trent was silent for another moment, set his glass down on the table, and held out his hand for the journal. He thumbed through the dog-eared pages for several seconds before looking up at Sophie and shrugging.

"That's because I never knew them – my grandma and my Uncle Timmy. Walter talked about them some," he murmured, and then handed the book back to her.

"They were both killed in some railroad accident during the war," he blurted, finally. "And that's about all anyone ever knew – until now."

#

They finished a tense, quiet dinner, each of them seemingly lost in their own thoughts, but everyone eyeing Trent cautiously. The steaks were excellent but he had tasted none of his meal. It tasted to him like cardboard.

Sophie's revelations shared from the old journal, concerning the destruction and death on Raton Pass, had left him exhausted and a bit confused, and he had fueled his sour mood with a couple more drinks before announcing to Maggie that it was time to call it a night. He paid the ticket, stood up, and helped Maggie with her jacket, but hesitated before turning back to Sophie and Hector. He was about to caution Sophie not to stay out too late, but was interrupted by Maggie's firm hand on his bicep as she abruptly led him to the door.

"Say goodnight, Cowboy."

Trent turned his head back to his daughter while he was being marched away. Sophie's sad face prompted him to, at last, give her a little smile and quick wave, followed by a determined scowl for Hector's benefit.

In the parking lot, he fumbled in his pocket for his keys, found them, but only to look up to see Maggie standing by the driver's door of his truck with her hand outstretched.

"Keys," she ordered. He started to protest, but caught sight of her arching eyebrow and tightened lip, and thought better of it. He dropped the keys in her hand and shuffled around to the other side, fumbled open the passenger door, then dropped into the seat with a groaning sigh.

Maggie was thankfully silent as they drove through the quiet streets, until she steered the truck out of town and turned onto the road to Bartlett Mesa.

"Well, that went rather well, I thought," she finally offered, breaking the silence.

Trent had been leaning his head against the door, his elbow propped on the armrest and his chin in his hand. "Maggie – please. Not right now," he mumbled.

They rode on in silence for a couple of minutes. The truck entered a curve in the dirt road, and as it straightened again, the headlights suddenly illuminated a woman standing in the middle of the road about thirty yards in front of them. She was dressed in the familiar blue print dress that came to her knees and she was barefoot. But the dress was torn and ruined, her legs and arms were scraped and bleeding, and her head bowed so that her long light brown hair billowed around her shoulders and hid her face. Trent grabbed the dashboard with both hands and grimaced as he sucked in his breath loudly.

"Watch out!" he cried.

Maggie gritted her teeth and stomped on the brakes. The truck went into a slide, straight toward the woman who, at the last moment, raised her head. Trent winced as he saw blood pouring from some sort of horrible head wound at the woman's temple and down her face, washing her features in shimmering red. She slowly raised her bloody head, opened her eyes, and grinned ghoulishly at Trent. His breath began coming in gasps, the air flooded with the overpowering smell of roses and cloves.

Vicky!

Trent began to shiver and he felt as if he would pass out. The temperature seemed to have suddenly dropped twenty degrees inside the cab of the truck and his breath became visible and fogged the windshield. His fingernails dug into the dashboard until they hurt. He then unexpectedly reached for the door handle even as the vehicle was still moving.

"Where are you going?" Maggie shrieked, panic in her voice and face.

"We've got to help her! Can't you see? She's hurt!"

"Help who?"

Trent had the door open and one leg out.

"Hey! Knock it off! Stop it! Now, you're really scaring me!"

The truck finally skidded to a stop. Maggie threw the gearshift into park and breathing heavily, simply looked ahead for a second and over at Trent. After scanning the road, she leaned over and grabbed Trent by the arm, her nails digging in hard. He glanced at her hand on his arm, then grimaced back at her and jerked away angrily.

"Let go of me! What's the matter with you? It's Vicky!" He stepped out of the vehicle and stumbled away.

Suddenly, a flash of fur and horns appeared before them as a young buck jumped and bounded away from where it had been grazing at the shoulder of the road, caught in the headlights in front of the truck. It clattered away to the other side of the road and disappeared into the darkness, apparently unharmed. Trent stood at the side of the bumper, completely confused and breathing hard. He leaned heavily against the fender and raised a hand to his eyes, searching the road up ahead. Vicky's perfume had faded just as quickly as it had manifested, replaced now by a mixture of smells: the sweet scent of sage, the musky odor of the deer, and the dirt that had been kicked up by the truck tires and still floated in a haze in the headlights.

"But she was bleeding," Trent stammered and pointed out into the darkness helplessly. "Didn't you see her?"

Maggie said nothing, but sat still and stared at him through the windshield with deep concern, her lips tight. "Get in, Trent," she finally said quietly. "Let's get you home."

Trent turned and looked at her uncomprehendingly. He ran his tongue over dry lips, wiped them with the back of his hand, and got back into the truck. He pulled the door slowly shut, leaned back in the seat and closed his eyes. He remained that way as Maggie put the truck back in gear and headed on up the road to the house.

She had left her own truck parked at Trent's earlier and now pulled up behind it in the driveway. She killed the engine and lights. They both sat for a while in silence.

"Sophie told me you were doing this," Maggie said finally.

"Doing what?" Trent muttered.

Maggie turned in the seat and just stared at him, her lips parted slightly and her eyes wide. "Talking to your dead wife!" she said louder, the words enunciated distinctly.

Trent said nothing, but opened his eyes slowly and looked at her in defeat.

"It was a freakin' deer, Trent! I don't know what you thought you saw on the road down there, but it wasn't Vicky!"

Trent just looked away. Maggie shook her head in disbelief, turned, and opened the door. She stopped halfway out and looked back over her shoulder.

"You know, Trent – I know you've been through the wringer. You've got a lot of crap going on in there." She tapped the side of her own head with her fingertip. "But you know what? There are a lot of people pulling for you, trying to help you through all this."

She paused and took a deep breath.

"People who actually love you. And besides, you're not the only person who's ever lost someone. The world is filled with loss. And heartache. And brokenness! There are actually a lot of us that have had to deal with it!

She paused when her own voice broke a little and continued. "So maybe it's about time you quit acting like you're the only one in this whole damned world who's trying to get through a crisis – and maybe start to recognize a little nurturing, when it's right there in front of you!"

She got out of his truck, slammed the door hard, and started to walk away. She then stopped, came back, and opened the truck door again.

"And, by the way," she added. "All of that stuff I just mentioned? It's called 'living.' But you wouldn't know anything about that, would you, Trent Carter? All you seem to care about is sitting up here in this old haunted house, crawling around inside a bottle, and talking to ghosts day in and day out!"

Maggie slammed the door again and walked away. "Oh, who the hell cares," she muttered as she stomped away.

Trent squeezed his eyes shut as he felt the rebuke settle over him like cold ashes. She walked up the driveway to her own vehicle, her boots crunching angrily on the gravel. Trent sighed, rubbed his face, and got out of the truck. He felt a warm breeze begin to pick up and weave its way around him.

"Maggie – wait!" he called as the breeze swirled after her. She reached her pickup and fumbled in her pocketbook for her keys, ignoring him.

"Maggie, I'm sorry."

She stopped fumbling, stared away up the drive for a moment, then turned around to face him.

"Wait for what, Trent?" She stood with her arms crossed defiantly, her cheeks glistening. For the first time since Vicky, Trent wanted to go put his arms around another woman. Maggie had never looked lovelier. He took a step toward her but then stopped uncertainly when she turned her face away. Trent thought she was maybe embarrassed for him to see her upset.

"What you said just now," he admitted, "about not being the only one who's lost someone – just how am I supposed to do that – stop acting that way, I mean?"

Maggie looked back up, wiped her eyes, and took a couple of steps slowly toward him. "Well, I don't know if anyone really knows the answer to that," she reflected with no expression on her face, but moving nearer to him. "All I can tell you is you just decide to do the next thing that comes up. Then, you do the very next thing. And then the thing after that and again and again after that." She stopped briefly to look into his face," until you're functioning again."

Trent stepped toward her, meeting her halfway. "And then what?"

She stopped in her tracks, about a foot from him now, and turned her face up at him. "Well, then – when you think you just can't push it any further, you give it one – more – big – shove." She placed her fingertips on his chest and pretended to push him. Trent didn't move, but was at a loss for words.

"Then, you know what'll happen?" she continued softly, gazing up him expectantly.

Trent said nothing, nor did he move.

Maggie waited several moments, before she shook her head sadly, turned away, and wiped at her cheeks. "Yep. Just like that. Probably nothing – except you will eventually feel something break. And then you're gonna need to decide what it is that's broken, exactly – because it's either you or it's that ridiculous wall you've built around yourself that will finally fall down, broken beyond fixing – and you'd better hope it's the latter.

"But you know what?" She started to move away. "Either way, it's not going to matter much because certain people will no longer be around."

Trent reached out and gently touched her wet cheek with the back of his finger and wiped a tear away; the invisible force of the tear being taken away seemed to pull her back around to him. Trent's hand then dropped, his arm circled around her waist, and he pulled her close. Her body melted against his just as his lips crushed into hers.

Time simply stopped.

Trent felt the warmth of her from her mouth all the way down to her knees, and his mind emptied itself of all else, along with the lightly nagging guilt that had played around the fringes of his thoughts all evening – guilt over the first time he had been out with another woman since he had awakened from the coma. Now, guilt over a kiss that was like nothing he had experienced, ever since – *since* –

Trent found he could not complete that thought. In fact, he didn't want to go there at all. He just wanted to swim and drown in this moment, whatever this moment was.

Whatever it was – the moment, the kiss – it felt right.

When he came to his senses, time had begun again. Maggie was tilting her head back a few inches, smiling up at him with her eyes swimming over his face. His hand cradled the back of her head. She reached up and pushed his hair away from the scar on his forehead.

"Are you real?" she whispered, at last.

He tried to smile back but felt like he surely had the look of an idiot on his face. He had heard the question somewhere before.

Maggie patted him on the chest and tiptoed to peck him lightly on the corner of his mouth.

"Not exactly how I had planned it," she continued, finally, "but not bad for a first kiss."

She turned and walked over to her pickup door. Her words echoed in his head as his eyes were transfixed on her slender back, the shoulder muscles moving subtly underneath her sequined jacket as she walked. His mouth opened and closed, desperately searching for something profound to say, but no words formed.

She opened the door of her truck, put one foot on the running board, turned, and looked at him as he stared dumbly back at her. She smiled once more, shook her head slightly, and placed her finger on her lips.

"Shush," she murmured. "Let's just leave things right there for now, okay? It'll keep."

She got in and shut the door, and in a moment, her truck roared to life. She expertly backed it up and pulled even with him. Her window rolled down and she leaned out on her forearm. Her face looked angelic.

"Things aren't always what they seem, you know? But it's all going to be okay," she smiled. "I know there are just a lot of things you don't yet understand or comprehend. But no more pressure here – okay?"

She put the truck in gear and it started rolling away. She called back to him over the noise of the engine. "But I'm going to be here all the way, Baby Boy, to help you through it all." She finally disappeared down the dark drive, the engine fading away like a dream.

Trent froze in astonishment as he digested her last – disturbingly familiar – words.

#

Vicky again.

Her face floating in and out of focus – and now it's Maggie coming into focus – and now it's a grainy old black and white movie of Trent's mother, except it's not Trent's mother – it's his grandmother, whom he never knew because she was killed before he was even born.

And now it's Trent in his out of control old jeep, careening around the corners of the old road on Cuchara Pass which now morphs into Raton Pass – and he's no longer in his jeep, he's on an out of control locomotive plowing into the maw of a dark tunnel – and then there's nothing but darkness – and train whistles – and screams – and a brilliant, deafening explosion. And as the darkness fades to gray and the swirling mists grow brighter, he sees Vicky once more – and once more she is beautiful, lustrous, and radiant, exuding the light of angels – and whole, with no signs of blood or injury whatsoever, smiling down at him as she floats just inches above him, waiting to be kissed, and gently touching the scar on his head.

"No more worries, Baby Boy," she breathes into his ear with a silky-smooth voice. "You're getting much closer. Almost there – just listen and follow the Truth!"

#

Once again Trent awakened in a sweat-soaked bed, heart pounding, clawing between the dream and reality – and unable to distinguish for a very long while the difference between the two.

CHAPTER 22
FIRE BY NIGHT

Excerpt from the Diary of Evie Neumann:

"May 13, 1956 – I cannot imagine a more impossible situation to be caught in: smack dab in between the wondrous and the torturous – the "best of times and the worst of times," as I read once in some classic book. My nights are spent embracing my pillow in dangerous dreams, and my waking hours are filled with as much work as I can possibly find to do just to keep my attentions focused and from enticing me toward just those actions which would fulfill those destructive dreams – and damn my soul to hell.

I am torn straight down the middle. At best, I want to remain the dutiful and faithful wife to my family that I know I must; at worst, I want to throw that all out the window and give full rein to the betrayals I have so readily committed in my nightly dreams.

Oh, why has God allowed me to suffer this trial of fire?

Why, oh why, is Otto still here to further these temptations?

And why do I feel such a premonition of doom?"

#

Excerpt from the Journal of Otto Eberhardt:

"19.09.56 – I am the most wretched of men – oh, what have I done?"

#

Otto was in his living quarters in the barn, located just across from the house. A couple of unused horse stalls in the corner had been knocked apart and rebuilt into a bunkhouse of sorts that accommodated three men with a bunk bed in one corner and a single bed in the other. After almost two years at the Neumann Ranch, Otto's seniority among the other hands had earned him the single bed, which just so happened to be located beneath the only window in the room, that was great in the summer evenings when he could open the window and have a cool breeze wash over him after a long day's work with the cattle or in the hayfields. In winter months, though, it wasn't quite so nice since the poorly insulated window provided little protection, even when closed, against the frigid air and moisture that seeped into the room.

But Otto had learned long ago not to expect much in the way of luxuries in his life and was just glad to have the small comforts of this corner of his world to call his own. He now sat on the edge of his bed enjoying the early evening breeze drifting through the window. A change of season was in the air and the earlier setting sun these days was forcing a drop in temperatures.

Two letters lay on the bed beside him. One was contained in an unopened envelope bearing the last known address of his wife Erica and had fallen out of another cover envelope that had been addressed to Otto and postmarked three weeks earlier from Stuttgart, Germany, in care of General Delivery, Clayton, New Mexico, USA. Enough light remained spilling in the window for Otto to again make out the handwriting, in German, on the two pages of the cover letter in his hand:

'My dear Herr Eberhardt:

'I don't know that you will even receive this letter (and I hope that, if you do, you will remember me after all these years), but I was your old headmaster at the gymnasium here in Stuttgart. I am now approaching 70 years of age and, as was the case with most of us, the war was not kind to me at all. A man of my age should by now be enjoying grandchildren and great grandchildren. Alas, I am the only one of my family now left alive.

'The Wehrmacht began drafting the older of us as the war dragged on and I found myself in the final, futile fight to defend the Fatherland, up to the gates of Berlin itself, where I finally laid down my rifle and surrendered – I thank God it was to the British and not the Soviets, who took few live prisoners. After a few months, I was released to make my own way back home to the pile of rubble that once was Stuttgart.

'But our American occupiers, with their seemingly endless supply of rations and building materials, soon began making our lives tolerable again and very soon there was work for our hands and even a little money to begin to rebuild our lives. I am now the local postmaster for the reconstructed postal system – a perfect job for a man my age, and I am grateful for it.

"Which leads me to your letter which I have enclosed, unopened, and which I had found in what the Americans call the 'dead letter' files – thousands of undeliverable letters to people no longer here, many of whom, I fear, have perished in the bombings. Imagine my surprise to have found your letter and recognize the names of you and your dear wife Erica. It was the least I could do to return it to you, for it pains me to tell you that I have had no luck in locating her and I do fear the worst.

"My dear Otto, I wish I had better news for you. Again, I hope my letter finds you. If you know of any other names of relatives that I might approach, please write back to me and I will be very happy to pursue this further.

"In the meantime I will pray daily for the souls of Erika and your daughter, and for yours also, my young friend. May God bless and keep you, and bring you some peace.

"I remain your faithful servant,

Maximillian Bruell."

#

Otto let the letter drop into his lap as the words soaked into him.

So Ernst was right after all, he thought to himself. Erica is most probably dead. He picked up the dog-eared and undelivered envelope from beside him on the bed and weighed it in his hand, like something of questionable value.

"But what, then, of my little Rosebud?" he asked himself out loud.

'Rosebud?" echoed a small voice from the doorway. "Who is she?"

Otto shoved the letters behind him instinctively, looked up, but smiled. Six-year-old Caroline Neumann stood quietly on the threshold of the door cradling her ragged one-eyed doll protectively. "Well, if you come give me a big hug, then I will tell you," he answered, motioning her over to him with his head.

Caroline stood, swaying back and forth, gazing down at her doll thoughtfully before holding it up to her ear for a moment. Looking at the doll, she finally nodded in agreement and slowly looked up at Otto. "Irena says she thinks she loves you, Mr. Otto," she uttered softly.

Otto stood up, walked over to the little girl, and squatted down until he was eye-level with her. He touched two fingers to his lips, reached over, and gently patted the kiss onto the doll's head with his fingertips.

"Well, Irena – I think I love you, too," he replied to the doll.

Caroline smiled, but continued to sway gently and gazed back down at her doll. After a few seconds of looking lovingly at Irena, she raised her eyes to look at Otto. "I think that I love you, too, Mr. Otto," she whispered shyly, and leaned into his arms for a quick hug. Otto felt an ache form in his throat. He gently cupped the back of her head with one hand as it rested against his upper arm. Her long, dark hair was tied with a light blue ribbon and smelled of the same fresh soap that her mother used. Caroline silently, quickly slipped away and was halfway out the door when she suddenly remembered something and turned around.

"So, who is Rosebud?" She asked again. "You didn't tell me."

Otto remained squatting at her level. "Why, don't you know? It's a very special name that I have for only special little girls."

"Like Irena?"

"Like Irena."

"And – like me?"

"And especially you!"

Caroline grinned, whispered something to Irena, and brought the doll to her ear to again listen. "Irena says if anything ever happens to me, she would like to come live with you, Mr. Otto."

"Well, you tell Irena that I think I would like that very much. But also tell her that I don't think anything will happen to you at all – because I won't let it." Otto gently pinched Caroline's plump cheek between his thumb and forefinger.

"Ever!" he continued.

She took a couple of steps before she stopped again. "But, Mr. Otto – she says you will have to promise to keep her secret."

"Her secret?" Otto stood up and leaned on the doorframe. At that moment, Evie's voice rang out from outside the barn somewhere.

"Caroline – it's time for dinner…"

Caroline gasped, started to leave, but stopped, looking intently at Otto. "Mr. Otto, I was going to tell you Irena's secret, but she says she cannot tell you right now." She turned and began skipping away through the barn toward the big door. "But maybe soon – maybe soon." The words trailed away in a singsong voice as she slipped out through the barn door, which stood slightly ajar, and away into the evening. Otto smiled after her.

"Goodnight, little Rosebud," he whispered – to more than one little girl.

#

Sunrise found Otto already awake, dressed, and out in the corral behind the barn feeding the two mares who were kept there, one suffering some congestion and the other about to foal any day now. He cooed soothingly to the latter one as she fed and he ran his hands expertly down her sides, checking her gently.

"Any day now, my pretty one," he whispered. "Any day, *meine kleine Mutter*." She turned her head and nickered back at him trustingly.

"You surely do have a way with the girls," a voice came from behind him. Otto turned to see Evie with her arms propped over the top rail of the corral gate. She wore a beautiful smile on her face that belied certain sadness in her eyes that always seemed to be there lately.

"She is going to foal, um, soon," he stuttered, as if that response fully answered her statement.

"Did you work with animals before?" she paused and looked away briefly. "I mean, I know you worked them at my father's ranch before. But I meant before the war – back home, you know, in Germany?"

Otto shrugged. "A little, I guess. I was mainly in the city – in Stuttgart – factory work – labor, mainly. But I did have an uncle who had a farm nearby and I spent some summers there, growing up." He was gently leading the mare around the paddock, exercising her, letting her work out some of the stiffness of the cool night. He glanced back at Evie now and again. The melancholy in her eyes was disconcerting.

"Caroline really likes you," she observed finally, looking away briefly – sadly. Otto didn't reply, so she continued, "Like I said, you have a way with women – of all ages." She turned to look at him again and Otto tried to ignore her eyes and focus his attention on the mare's needs. "You've never told me about your family, you know – back home."

"No – I have not," he answered. He led the mare back to her stall and began brushing her down. Evie waited for him to say something further.

"Well?" she asked after a minute.

"Well, what?"

"Well, I think I deserve to know – don't you?"

Otto wiped his hands on his jeans, sighed, crossed his arms, and looked directly at her.

"Deserve to know what, Mrs. Neumann? And why do you deserve it? Because we were together once? Because we had something wonderful, once, and then it was all over – and now, all this?" Otto indicated the ranch buildings around them before he looked down at his boots and scuffed one in the dirt. He removed his hat, slapped it lightly a couple of times on his knee, and continued to speak to the ground.

"So what do you want to know, exactly, Evie? That I was married before? Yes – of course I was – to a wonderful woman named Erica." He shook his head with an exasperated look on his face.

"And that I have children? Yes – a beautiful little girl named Angela, who was not even two years old when I last saw her, and whose face I would not even know if I saw her today!"

He took a couple of steps toward her, his voice softening the closer he came to her.

"And that I still try to write to them, wondering if it is even worthwhile to do so any longer because they are probably both dead? And that I have an entire packet of letters in my room there, all returned undelivered and unopened?" He gestured toward the barn with his hat. "Is that what you want to know? Is it?" he demanded.

He had begun to walk toward her more quickly as he spoke and now stood face-to-face with her over the gate and looked her up and down hungrily. "Or that I look at you, Evie, every single day, and at your life here with that – man, who does not appreciate you in the least; I look at that boy of yours who is in danger of turning into a recluse – or something worse – because he doesn't think his father even knows he's there; I see that beautiful little girl of yours who is so starved for affection; and I…" Otto choked on his words, his eyes filling with tears, and stared down at his hands gripping the top of the gate until the knuckles were white, "and I see all of this," he continued, looking up and nodding at the cattle in the distance pastures, "as something that we might have had together, Evie, and would have been so much better at it – but that we now will never, ever have."

Otto suddenly pushed open the gate, forcing Evie to step quickly backwards, out of the way, and he walked through. He then turned abruptly and backed her up against the fence, his face just inches from hers. He could smell the soap on her skin and the hint of mint on her breath: his eyes glistened and burned into hers fiercely.

"Is that what you wanted to hear from me – *Mrs. Neumann*? Or that every time I see you it is all I can do to not get this close to you, or even closer – is that what you wanted to know – wanted to feel again?"

He reached an arm around her, his head brushing the hair near her shoulder; she sucked her breath in and closed her eyes in some sort of anticipation. Otto took his hand, latched the gate behind her, turned, and abruptly walked away from her toward the front of the barn.

"Otto – " she began. He stopped a few feet away, but didn't turn back around.

"How could you marry him?" he whispered hoarsely. "I mean – so soon after – us?"

"Otto, you don't understand. What if I told you that – that –" her voice trailed off.

"Told – me – what, Evie?" he asked, finally, over his shoulder, pronouncing one word at a time.

A deafening, hot silence grew between them until it filled the space for half a minute; they both became very hesitant to say anything else for fear of what might come next. Otto finally shook his head slowly, moved off, and disappeared around the corner without another word.

With her face in her hands, Evie wept.

#

At least 250 yards away from atop the canyon ridge overlooking the ranch headquarters, a lone gunman knelt behind a large rock and peered through the scope mounted on his Winchester rifle, the crosshairs following Otto as he went around the barn and disappeared. The gunman's finger caressed the trigger lightly, lovingly for a moment, and audibly sighed. He moved the rifle imperceptibly, still gazing through the scope, his view now swinging to the left until the crosshairs stopped on Evie, her face still in her hands and her shoulders shaking.

The man licked his lips as a thrill of anticipation thumped through his chest and he began to subconsciously will his finger to tighten on the trigger. Instead, the thumping subsided and he finally slipped his finger away and rested it momentarily on the trigger guard in case he felt further compelled to act.

Not just yet – not yet, he breathed to himself. He pulled his eye away from the telescopic sight, lowered the rifle, sat back on his lean haunches, and squinted into the brilliant dawn that was just now bursting over the horizon to his left.

Ernst Brandt finally stood up, stretched, groaned, and slung his rifle over his shoulder. He allowed a cock-eyed smile to play across his face along with the new sunlight that signaled the beginning of a momentous day. Now that he had finally found his quarry, he knew he had all the time in the world for his plan to unfold.

#

That afternoon Otto made up his mind. He walked around the barn to take one more look at the pregnant young mare. She was lazily munching hay and turned her head to look at him. She stopped chewing for a second and neighed to him softly as if she knew something was up. He unlatched the gate, walked over, and stroked her muzzle, clucking to her softly. When he walked back out, he left the gate to her stall open so she could wander around the paddock at her leisure.

He went back into the barn, gathered his extra clothes, the packet of returned letters, his journal, and a few additional personal items, and stuffed them all into his well-worn canvas tote bag. He pulled on his old denim jacket and shoved his straw cowboy hat onto his head, slung the bag over his shoulder and then took one more look around the bunkhouse before walking across the barn floor toward the big swinging doors.

In anticipation of the bright sunlight he could see filtering under the doors, Otto reached into his jacket pocket and pulled out his sunglasses. He had just slid them on, was adjusting them onto the bridge of his nose, and had a hand on the door when heard a soft noise behind him and turned just in time to see a shadowy figure swinging a pick axe handle toward his head.

Light burst across his eyesight as he felt the sunglasses explode into his face; he staggered and fell into the dusty, rough-hewn wooden floor.

"Guess you didn't see that one coming," snarled a familiar voice that floated somewhere above Otto as he lolled in a daze and tried to focus.

He shook his head and tried to clear it and pushed himself up to his knees. His hand wandered to his face where he felt pieces of jagged glass imbedded in his cheek below his right eye. He fumbled to remove the shattered frame of his glasses and pulled his hand back to look dumbly at blood dripping from his fingers. He braced himself with his other hand against the wall. "What the hell – " he sputtered.

"Guess I never saw you coming, neither," slurred the familiar, drunken voice again, which Otto now identified foggily as belonging to Conrad Neumann, just in time to have Conrad lean over and slam a big, hammy fist into his stomach. Otto doubled over and fell face forward into the dirt. He tried to get a breath, but couldn't.

"Came home to Evie crying in the kitchen," Neumann continued. "Hadn't even bothered to make me any lunch!" He punctuated these words with a boot-heel hard into the small of Otto's back. Otto almost passed out and clawed the ground in a desperate attempt to pull himself away, gasping to get air back into his lungs.

"She was blubbering so hard, I couldn't get a coherent word out of her," Neumann shrugged. "Nothing left for it but to slap her around a little!"

Conrad Neumann was drunk. Otto watched as he began to circle him, like a cowardly coyote circling his prey. Otto coughed and tried to crawl away. Neumann staggered back a step and began to pull back his leg to deliver another kick.

"Didn't take too many good slaps before she finally told me it was you made her cry – that it was you she's loved for a long while now – has since before she married me!" Neumann stood precariously now as he lifted one foot off the ground. "I should've known!"

Receiving a beating himself was something Otto was used to, but as the idea of Evie having been struck by this same man – husband or not – sank in, he felt a surge of anger invigorate him; he whipped his leg around and drove his boot hard into Conrad's other leg just below the knee. Neumann cried out and suddenly, off balance now, toppled over onto Otto, who had twisted onto his back as he had lashed out. They both flailed their arms, trying to disengage themselves. Otto took this opportunity to pull his knee up hard a second time, landing it with a hard crunch into Neumann's cheek and temple. He drove his left fist three times straight into Neumann's face, then fell back exhausted. Neumann let loose a muffled, high pitched scream and pushed himself away in a sudden, snarling rage.

Otto tried to catch his breath and roll away, but Neumann had already scrambled back up, this time straddling Otto, his knees squeezing Otto's chest. Otto's broken ribs screamed in pain as they ground together. Neumann bent over suddenly, spittle and bits of blood flying out of his lips and into Otto's face as Conrad grasped his neck with both hands and began to slowly, powerfully, squeeze.

"I'm going to kill you now, you son of a bitch!" he growled between clenched teeth.

Grunting loudly, Neumann bent over even further, giving more leverage to his arms as he strangled Otto, who clawed at his assailant's fingers that buried themselves in the soft flesh of his throat but otherwise felt entirely helpless to fight back.

Otto's efforts slowed, he gasped unsuccessfully for breath, and he finally closed his eyes and resigned himself to the worst.

He was unaware how much time had passed when he started to regain some consciousness; he was alive, and still on the dirt floor of the barn, but was now vaguely aware of other voices shouting, noises of scuffling and grunting and what sounded like heavy blows nearby, followed by a long silence – and the unmistakable odor of gasoline.

He coughed, still struggling to breathe and his head swimming, when he suddenly felt himself being dragged by his ankles; the sudden sensation of the cool evening air wafted over him blissfully and he finally sucked it deep into his lungs in long, gasping breaths. After being dragged a bit further, his feet hit the ground with a bone-jarring thud and he lay there perfectly still, gaining his breath, listening, and trying to focus. He sensed someone near him.

"Safe for now, dear Otto," he heard a familiar voice mutter – but immediately knew it was not Conrad's, but inexplicably another – a voice from his past – and Otto felt an ominous thud in his heart.

No, it cannot be!" he murmured to himself, tasting blood in his mouth and spluttering. He rolled his head, struggled to open his eyes, and finally got one slightly open.

Ernst Brandt stood over him, a look of false concern on his face, and a gasoline can in his hand.

"Hello, *meiner altes Freund!"* Ernst smirked. He noticed Otto staring at the gas can. "Oh, no, not to worry, my dear Otto – this is not how you are to die. I have some – how to say it – more elaborate plans for you."

Ernst looked around him, shook the gasoline in the can until it sloshed, and smiled again. "This is a little present for this sweet family here – and, of course, for your entertainment."

Otto watched, horrified, as Ernst turned and disappeared back into the nearby barn. He suddenly felt very cold and tired, a feeling of ennui descending on him; he lay his head down and turned away, only vaguely aware now of the odor and sound of gasoline splashing about somewhere inside the barn.

Ernst had finally, unbelievably, tracked him down. But if Otto were to be honest with himself, he had always known that he would. But now, they were all about to pay the terrible, exacting price of Ernst's vengeance – and he no longer had the energy to do anything about it.

Ernst's vengeance was the punishment God had evidently chosen, and Otto closed his eyes, hoping to finally sleep, forever.

#

"Otto! Wake up!"

Otto could hear someone – a woman, screaming his name. He also heard some other noises – something he thought he should know – something ominous, but that he could not yet identify.

"Otto! Please wake up! You have to get him out of there!"

He felt someone shaking him, and he began to rouse himself. His eyesight was swimming, light was flashing, and he could hear distant crackling noises. One eye wouldn't open, so he reached up with his fingers to find it was caked shut with dried blood. But his good eye finally focused on the lovely but terrified face of Evie just above his, her face glowing alternately yellow and white. Otto was suddenly aware of the smell of smoke and the nearby roaring of fire and raised his head from where it had been on Evie's soft lap. They were on the ground in the middle of the driveway between the house and the barn, which now flared in the night with fingers of flame escaping openings in the doors and walls. He was beginning to feel the heat from the flames.

But how did I get out here? Otto sat up in a panic, then fell back in horrified fascination.

Flames suddenly burst through, licked their way up the side of the barn, and crackled loudly from inside the structure, whipping out through the door. Huge gouts of sparks were flying above him and in all directions, shifting with the wind that had sprung up and had been responsible for the fire spreading over the dry, parched wood so quickly.

Evie stood up suddenly, pulling Otto with her and pushing at his back, and he gasped again as broken ribs scraped against each other. "You have to get him out of there! Please!" Evie shouted again, jumping up to her feet.

"Get who out?" Otto asked, confused and groggy, and rising finally on unsteady feet.

"Conrad! He is trapped in there! Please, you must get him out," she pleaded again, pushing him now toward the barn. "Hurry!" Otto turned to her and stared, wide-eyed. Evie saw the confused look on his face, then clenched her teeth and shoved him once more, hard. "He doesn't deserve to die like that!" she yelled. "No one does!"

Suddenly, she screamed; Otto turned. Evie was looking back towards the house, terrified. Otto followed her gaze, stopped, and stared up at the house's roof. Sparks swirling around had caught the wood shingles there on fire that was now spreading quickly up to the peak of the roof and on down the other side, almost as quickly as it had taken them to turn and see. Evie turned to Otto, her face white as a ghost, clearly in shock, unable to move.

"The children – Evie – " Otto began. She just continued to stare at him with a vacant look of shock. Otto grabbed her by the shoulders and shook. "Evie! Where are the children?" he shouted. Evie broke out of the trance.

"Oh my God, no," she whimpered. A faint keening sound came from back of her throat, and then began to rise in volume. She quickly turned on her heels and ran to the house, crying out incoherently.

"Evie! Come back!" Otto started after her, then stopped as she turned around and glared at him, reflections of fire flashing in her eyes. She gestured wildly back toward the barn, suddenly alert and purposeful again.

"You get him out of that barn!" she screamed back at him, taking charge. "I must go find the children!"

Without another word, she bounded up the stairs to the porch, wrenched back the screen door, and disappeared into the billowing smoke that now poured out of the house.

Strangely, Otto kept hearing other screams, this time coming from somewhere behind the barn. And then he suddenly knew.

The horses!

He stumbled, then fell into a loping run around the smoldering barn toward the attached corral at the back. From here, he could see the two mares running back and forth, careening in wide-eyed madness and terror, the flames from the back wall of the barn licking out at them, foam flecking their mouths and screams tearing from their throats. They both saw Otto simultaneously and galloped toward him in terror, and would have crashed headlong into the gate had he not fumbled it open and at the very last moment thrown it wide. The horses practically bowled him over as they whipped past him and disappeared into the smoke billowing across a nearby pasture.

Suddenly, a crash exploded somewhere behind him. He whipped around in time see the far corner of the barn collapse in an explosion of sparks and flame. He wiped his eyes and mouth, and trotted painfully back to the front of the barn where he could see that the outer edges of the entire roof of the structure now howled in flame, but the big barn doors appeared to still be accessible – for the moment. Otto stood awhile, his hands on his knees and his breath coming in ragged heaves while he wondered what use he was going to be to anyone left inside – if they, in fact, were even still alive in there.

Had he really heard two men in there earlier? And had one of them really been Ernst! His heart thudded dully. *That's impossible! It couldn't have been.* Otto briefly entertained the idea to just walk away, allow the barn to burn to the ground, and destroy anyone who was inside once and for all – both of his enemies at the same time – probably the easiest solution.

But he immediately shook off the notion, knowing he couldn't allow that kind of fate to happen to anyone. Besides, he now convinced himself Ernst had been a hallucination, that only one man – Conrad Neumann – could be in there, and even though he had just tried to kill Otto, Evie was right – no man deserved such a death – and he was, after all, Evie's husband. Otto forced his feet to move forward, one step after another toward the barn, lurching painfully. He finally found himself just inside the doorway.

The threshold of Hell itself.

The interior of the barn was an inferno with all three walls ahead of him sheeting with fire and the roof high above him crawling with burning, living, writhing devils. Fear, as well as smoke, snaked down his throat. He glanced around and spied a water bucket near the gate of a stall, just a few feet away. He crouched, ran to the bucket, and was relieved to see a few inches of water in the bottom. He whipped his shirt off, pressed it into the water, and wrapped it around his head and over his nose and mouth so that all but his eyes were covered. He remained squatted down and squinted ahead.

Through a break in the blinding smoke, he finally saw them – and this time what was before him was no hallucination.

The bodies of two men, not one, lay near one another in the center of the alleyway; one was draped across a smoldering bale of hay, and the other a couple of yards away on the floor. Adrenaline kicked in and Otto scurried across the floor like a crab, swatting away sparks and smoke, choking and coughing until he reached them. Both men were of similar build, lying within a few feet of each other; both were face down and completely unrecognizable. The body on the hay bale was the most badly burned, still blazing like a torch with a human shape. Otto would not, could not reach him or do anything at all to help him without causing himself grievous injuries. The man was long gone.

He turned to the other man and took in quickly the nightmare before him. The fire had already swept over this poor soul: his clothing still smoldered with smoke along one side; a blistered area of pink skin was over a large patch of the head where hair used to be; the shirt and pants were half burnt away, with any visible flesh burned black and emitting the gagging odor of charred meat.

But was this Conrad? Or was it Ernst? From what he could identify, Otto had no way to tell, and for all he knew, this man could also be dead.

But Otto's questions were interrupted: the man on the floor suddenly groaned and rolled over to reveal his horrid head and face to Otto. *He was still alive!*

Otto heard an otherworldly sound from above him, and glanced up to see the center beam of the barn completely engulfed in fire and starting to pop and split, move and sway. He knew it would collapse any moment, and the remainder of the barn with it, so he lunged, grabbing the smoldering man by his belt, and heaved. Otto jerked and dragged the injured man steadily toward the door. He looked up again as the center beam began to wobble and then explode as it split in the middle in a burst of sparks and crashed down toward them, bringing a third of the roof with it. Otto lunged once more with the body tightly in grip and flew through the door of the barn just as the beam smashed into the spot where he had been standing. Both he and the body collapsed and rolled over and over on the ground in a heap.

Otto was now lying just outside the collapsing barn and was on the verge of passing out again, gagging and retching as the odor of burnt flesh crawled deep into his nostrils. He sensed a heavy weight upon him and gradually became aware that the injured man was lying on top of him now, almost cheek-to-cheek. Otto's eyes stared in horror into the puckered, blistered burned visage just inches away from his, almost tasting the putrid, cooked flesh in his mouth. He grimaced and frantically squirmed and gibbered like an idiot until he had rolled the smoldering, cooked body off of him and onto its back. Otto finally sat up, pulled his feet under him, hugged his knees tightly, and began to sway like a horrified child as he tried to regain his composure, the roaring and crashing sounds of the fire behind him ironically soothing now as he gradually calmed down and finally forced himself to look back down at the ruined face in front of him. Only at that moment, and curiously, Otto frowned at it as if displeased.

He could not, for the life of him, recognize any of the poor wretch's features that would identify who he was.

Ernst or Conrad?

After a few minutes, Otto only shook his head slowly and turned away.

Suddenly, he spied Carl walking slowly up the road like a ghost out of the smoke into the firelight that flickered wildly over his features. He dragged a wooden toy rifle behind him.

Carl was staring up at the barn with an incredulous look of fascination as it continued to be consumed.

"Carl?" Otto spoke to the boy softly.

Carl's eyes flickered over to Otto briefly, then over to the injured man on the ground.

"You do this?" Carl inquired off-handedly.

Otto opened his mouth a couple of times, but couldn't think of what to say, amazed that the boy thought that he could've done something like this. Before long the boy shrugged, then slowly turned and walked back up the road in a daze, disappearing into the smoke. Otto stood up to go after him, when suddenly, he heard glass shattering from the direction of the house and turned to dumbly stare as Evie burst out of the doorway, as if in a nightmare, her long hair trailing smoke and the hem and sleeves of her dress smoldering. She was coughing and dragging Caroline by one arm. The girl was dressed for bed in her nightdress and clutching Irena, and also coughed heavily and was crying, wailing at the top of her lungs. Evie caught Otto's eye as he moved on into the front yard of the house, and she shoved little Caroline down the steps and into his waiting arms, shouting something at him.

"You watch her!" he thought she commanded, wagging her hand at him.

"Don't let her out of your sight, whatever you do! I'm going back in for Carl!"

The entire house was a conflagration. Flames leapt from the broken upstairs dormer windows, just above the porch roof, also now running with fire. Smoke poured from all the downstairs windows.

"Evie!" Otto yelled, but his voice only croaked, about to tell her Carl was already outside. He wobbled and staggered up a couple of porch steps, pulled the screen door open, but he was too late to stop her and the unbearable heat drove him back.

Inside the house, Evie had disappeared back into a wall of fire.

Caroline had fallen on the grass near the bottom steps of the house and was crying softly. Otto stumbled down the steps to her and painfully picked her up. She buried her head on his shoulder and sobbed. "Irena's scared," Caroline moaned into his shirt.

"I know, honey – I know." He stumbled back toward the driveway to a spot further away from the smoke billowing up from both the house and the barn now, the black plumes roiling away into the gathering darkness. He looked back over at the burned man lying nearby. He hadn't moved again, but he swore he could see the chest rising slightly as the man possibly breathed.

Otto heard a cough and turned around to see Carl stumble once more into sight, this time from the other side of the house. His eyes were red and dazed and wisps of smoke arose from the shock of blonde hair, which stood on end – he looked like a young demon.

Otto saw now that the boy was barefoot as he stumbled towards them and was clearly in shock. Otto set Caroline down on the ground and told her to stay there. He moved toward the boy and met him halfway into the yard just as a great spout of white-hot flame burst out of the front door. Otto snatched Carl up and held him to his chest as he backed quickly away from the house, staring up at it in horror.

Evie, he breathed to himself numbly and realized that no one else would be coming out of that inferno.

"Papa?"

Otto heard Caroline's small voice behind him and turned, still holding an almost catatonic Carl limply in his arms. Otto stumbled over to where little Caroline knelt beside the horribly disfigured man on the ground. She was singing softly to the man, but stopped as Otto walked up with Carl.

"Papa's hurt," she announced, looking up at Otto with a deep sorrow in her eyes.

"Papa?" Otto asked softly. "You're sure that's, uh," he hesitated, himself looking and nodding down at the horribly burned body, "Papa, Caroline?"

The little girl looked back down sadly, shrugged, and suggested, "Why, yes – but he's hurt. See? He got burnt – he's hurt – real bad – Papa's hurt!"

Otto slumped slowly to the ground, cradling Carl in his lap, and watched the fires on either side of them roar on into the darkening twilight. The barn began to collapse in on itself, folding its fiery arms over the monster Ernst Brandt inside and spraying the dark sky above them with showers of orange embers from his funeral pyre.

Otto's exhausted gaze wandered over to the children, sitting and guarding over the burned husk that had once been their father. He knew that all of their lives had just drastically and irrevocably changed.

Caroline's singsong voice lilted surreally over the hellish scene, like a childish dirge. She leaned over and kissed the burnt man's hand tenderly, only afterwards to sit back and hug Irena very close, listening to the doll's secrets, rocking and singing again.

Otto looked back over to the house and a great sob clutched his throat. It was now completely engulfed; what was left of Evie was trapped in there too, somewhere, never to come out. He continued to stare in a trance at the roaring inferno that had been this family's home, devastated, yet at the same time part of him strangely calm – an emptiness over the sudden loss of Evie, but also an odd peace that he was at last free of Ernst.

But at what cost?

CHAPTER 23
KEYS TO THE KINGDOM

Trent spent most of the morning at his office throwing paper around, working files, digging out old leads, and following up with phone calls that went nowhere. He pored over case notes, mostly in his own handwriting no less, which seemed as unfamiliar to him as if a stranger had written them and made them doubly frustrating to him.

He pursed his lips and rubbed the scar on his forehead. How could a brain just suddenly forget such a myriad of details?

He gulped a mouthful of cold coffee, grimaced, and remembered something else. He picked up his mobile phone and fumbled through the contact list. He punched the button to dial the medical examiner's office in Santa Fe. A gruff, familiar voice answered.

"Emerson," the voice said.

"Bill, this is Trent."

"Well, Trent Carter, a voice from the past. *'I thought you was dead,'*" the ME responded with a clear smirk in tone. Trent was surprised that he had at least remembered the reference from an old John Wayne movie.

"*'That'll be the day,'*" he answered, picking up on the shtick they used to kid one another with. The banter put a brief smile on Trent's face.

"What can I do you for today, Carter?"

"Wondering where you've gotten with my John Doe, Bill."

"You mean your mystery man from the nether world of the theater? Oh, he's been a piece of work, that one. Thirty or forty years of moldering in that damp basement should've pretty much dissolved him away. But I was surprised at how well he had maintained himself since he died. Must be something in all that coal dust that layers everything up in your neck of the woods. Sort of acted like a preservative, I suppose. Of course, you would know all that if you had bothered to read my report."

"Report? What report?"

"Carter, you must be as disorganized as ever you were. I finished the autopsy and mailed everything to you last week – as promised. You said to put a rush on it – and I do remember how awful surly you can get when you don't get your way, not that I really give a damn."

Trent leaned forward and shoved papers and files around on his desk until he spied the corner of a large official looking envelope peeking out from under a pile of magazines and other unopened mail in his overflowing in-basket. He pulled it out of the stack, scattering envelopes and paper, and laid it in front of him.

"Yeah, I see it right here, Bill," he admitted apologetically. "Sorry to bother you – I'll let you get back to it. I probably made you late for your tee time – or interrupted you chasing your assistant around the lab."

"Oh, she's much too young and fast and smart for this ugly old man. Besides, did you know that a guy could actually get sued for that crap these days? What is the world coming to, says I?"

"Well, I happen to know your wife would shoot you before it even got to court. Anyway, thanks again, Bill. And keep those sharks at bay down there in the Land of Mañana."

"Bye-bye, Trent. Oh, and Trent?" There was an awkward pause in Bill's voice, "I never got to tell you how sorry I was about Vicky."

Trent held the phone to his ear in silence for a moment and looked off into the distance.

"Thanks, Bill," he finally responded and disconnected the call.

Trent put the phone back slowly into his pocket and continued to stare at a blank spot on the wall for a few seconds before he looked down at the large envelope. He wondered how long it had been buried in his mail. He took his pocketknife out, slit the envelope open, and dumped the contents consisting of a sheaf of papers and photos clipped together. He removed the clip and skimmed over the report, detailing the medical examiner's autopsy results for one "John Doe – Colfax County, NM."

After gleaning the details of the three-page report, Trent set it aside, then spread out the dozen or so photos beside it. The grisly skeletal remains, according to the report, were of a male Caucasian and approximately 45-50 years of age at time of death. His estimated height and weight were five-foot-ten inches and 145 pounds. How such facts could be even remotely determined from a deteriorated skeleton was beyond Trent's understanding. The cause of death was assumed to have been a gunshot from a .32 caliber bullet fired at relatively close range. This fact itself was determined from a fragment of bullet found embedded in the dead man's backbone. From this evidence, the ME had posed an assumed trajectory of the bullet entering the upper chest and presumably travelling straight through the man's heart. If true, death would have been instantaneous. Other slight wounds may have been present, based on marks on the skull, but decomposition made it practically impossible to determine if those particular wounds were from the time of death or from earlier injuries. The ME's general observations noted that the man appeared to have been very active throughout his life, based on relative bone density, condition of the joints, and evidence of a couple of older broken bones that had healed well. Given his relative age, he might have also seen military action at some point in his life, but the ME was quick to point out this was mere speculation.

Trent shuffled through the autopsy photos. The cadaver had been still clothed with the remains of what appeared to be a moth-eaten, long sleeve flannel shirt, Levis jeans (Trent could tell by the tattered leather label still attached), a leather jacket, and a pair of Wellington-styled boots. He continued to flip the photos a few times but kept coming back to one in particular that zoomed in on the deceased man's face. Trent stared long and thoughtfully at the face – or what was left of it. Mummified dark and leathery skin still covered sunken cheeks and was pulled tight over the facial bones. Dried lips were pulled back from the teeth in a rictus grin. Wadded leathery nubs were on the sides of the head where ears would have been. Tufts of light colored hair still sprouted from the rotten scalp. The longer Trent absorbed the horror of the spectacle in the photo, the more he was certain he could detect a distinct look of sadness on the man's ruined face.

He set the photos aside and finished reading the summary page of the report:

'DNA analysis revealed no match in the law enforcement databases – therefore, subject remains unidentified. However, the key found lodged in the pocket of the subject's jacket

may provide additional evidence pertaining to subject's identity, although no discernible prints were found on it."

Trent stopped and looked off into the distance for a moment, thinking.

Key? What key?

In the jacket?

Trent picked up the large envelope, turned it upside down, and shook it. A small sealed plastic evidence bag dropped out heavily on his desk. He picked it up and held it close to examine it.

Huh! He grunted to himself. *How'd we miss that?*

The key inside was flat metal, flatter than what normally fits a vehicle or house lock, and had a patina of rust and tarnish. He squinted closer at what appeared to be faint lettering stamped on the headstock. Trent rummaged through his desk drawer and produced a small magnifying glass, held the key up to his desk lamp, and peered through the glass. He could barely make out an *F*, then a rubbed-out space, and finally *nk*.

Trent squinted for another minute, turning the key at various angles in the light. He slowly looked up as he heard familiar quick footsteps passing his half-opened door.

"Hey, Molly," he called out. Molly stuck her head through the doorway. "Come tell me if you can read this thing any better than I can."

Molly walked over to his desk, picked up the key, turned it over a couple of times, and then handed it back.

"Safe deposit box," she identified, matter-of-factly.

"Like, to a bank?"

Molly nodded. "Yep. Just like that."

Trent peered at the key once more. "Well – okay. Then how can we tell which bank? All I can make out is *F – something – something – nk."*

Molly shrugged, impatiently. "I don't know." She looked down and thought for a moment, then continued, "Only bank around here starts with an *F* is the Federal Savings Bank.

Trent thought out loud again. "But this key's got to be over forty years old."

"So?"

"So, Federal Savings isn't that old – twenty, twenty-five years, maybe."

"Forty years old? You sure?" Molly picked the key up again, turning it over to examine.

"Well, the body they found it on was buried for over forty years."

"You don't mean that old body you guys found under the theater?" Molly asked the question but already knew the answer. She made a face and stuck the tip of her tongue out. "Oh, yuck!" She dropped the key on Trent's desk and wiped her hands on her hips. "Why the hell didn't you say something?"

Molly turned abruptly on her heels and stomped out, muttering as she went and shaking her hands in front of her like they were wet with bacteria. Trent picked up the key again, sat back, and twisted it slowly in his fingers.

Bank … Bank … F, something, Bank.

He suddenly sat up straight and dialed a number on his phone. The phone call lasted for only a few seconds. He politely thanked the person and hung up, shoved the old key into his shirt pocket, grabbed his coat, and left the office.

#

The Sangre de Cristo Educational Foundation sat on the busiest corner of downtown Raton, which wasn't really saying much other than this particular corner boasted one of the few traffic lights in town and occupied a post modern, single story building with a façade of glass, metal, and faux stonework, and sandwiched in between 120-year-old buildings..

Trent parked his truck, walked in through thick, double glass doorways and into a spacious, well-appointed reception area. The receptionist recognized him, smiled, and told him to go on in. The next glass doorway led into a larger room filled with cubicles where numerous clerks and representatives were busy at their computers or making phone calls. Beyond the cubicles and along a long wall at the back were several glassed-in offices. From one of these offices emerged a tall, lanky man in a crew shirt and chinos. He quickly donned a broad smile and held out his hand as he approached Trent.

"Trent Carter, as I live and breathe! How the hell are you, my friend?" Trent took the proffered hand.

"Good, Scotty, good," he lied. "And good to see you, too. Glad you had time for me." He looked around at the similarly dressed employees. "Casual Friday, I see. I feel overdressed."

Scott Wellborn was the administrator of an organization whose function Trent was not entirely sure of, other than that it worked with all the public schools in the northeast region of the state, providing continuing education and other services to teachers. He knew they employed a lot of people and somehow brought in some money, always great for their little town's struggling economy.

But what Trent had suddenly remembered back in his office was that the Foundation had moved into the building previously occupied by the old First National Bank of Colfax County, itself founded in 1918, making it one of the oldest banking institutions in the state of New Mexico. The bank had built this newer facility in the 1970s, vacated the building in the 1990s, but back when it was founded, the entire area was bursting at the seams with immigrants flooding in to dig the coal from deep underground and build the railroads with which to haul the coal to the big city markets. They had arrived in droves from diverse countries, such as Italy Germany, Austria, and the Baltic States, and even China. Today, someone could open up a current phone book and find a colorful variety of surnames still carried by the descendants of all those hard working people who had followed a dream. Colfax County in New Mexico, along with its neighboring Las Animas County in Colorado, was a true melting pot of European cultures.

Wellborn ushered Trent to his office. He was about ten years younger than Trent, but they still went way back to their childhoods. Wellborn's older brother Jonathon had been Trent's best friend, so much so that they had even enlisted together in the Marines during the last couple of years of the Vietnam conflict. They were getting ready to ship back to the states when Jonathon had been killed by sniper fire, only fourteen days before the fall of Saigon.

Scott looked across the desk at Trent, a look of concern and sadness on his face. Trent was suddenly reminded of the earlier look he had imagined in the photo of the John Doe's sunken skeletal face.

"Trent – really," Scott finally spoke. "How have you been doing? Jeannie and I have been concerned."

Jeannie Wellborn, Scott's wife, had been Vicky's best friend – or so it had seemed. Trent and Jeannie had never really liked one another, though. And like many of Trent's so-called friends, neither Jeannie nor Scott had ever called or come by to visit him after Vicky's death. Oh, he figured they had probably gone to the funeral, but he wouldn't have known since he had still been lying in a coma at the time.

"Oh, I'm getting along, Scott – I guess."

Scott nodded, still with that look of deep concern. Trent not only wondered how much of the concern he saw was real, but also how many of the rumors Scott had heard – rumors of how Trent was out of it, couldn't remember crap, and talked to his dead wife. Trent shook it off, gave Wellborn a terse smile, and pulled the key from his pocket.

Trent coughed. "But what I'm really here for is to ask a favor." He pushed the key across the desk. Scott picked it up and turned it over. "You recognize that?"

Scott looked at it closely and then shook his head. "Should I?"

"Well, this used to be the old bank, right?"

"Yeah, that's right. First National. From way back."

"Well, I'm thinking that's an old safe deposit box key."

"Yeah? Where'd you find it?

"Well, not really at liberty to say right now. But it could possibly produce some evidence in a murder case I'm investigating."

Wellborn gave a low, appreciative whistle, and raised his eyebrows. "So, what's the favor, exactly?"

"Well, since this is the old bank premises, I was figuring it might still have the old vault, right? I mean those things are usually built to withstand a bomb. Would've cost a fortune to blast it out of here."

Wellborn nodded. "Yeah, the old vault's still here – just right around the corner." He jerked his thumb back towards his shoulder. "But there isn't much in it. We just use it for supplies and records and such."

Trent hesitated, pursed his lips, and asked, "Any chance I can get a look inside?"

Wellborn stroked his lower lip thoughtfully, not answering.

"Scott, you know I could get a warrant – "

Wellborn looked back at Trent, a hurt look crossing his face, and shook his head. "Aw, you know that's not necessary – of course, you can take a look. If I hesitated, it was only because I couldn't think of anything at all in there that old key would fit."

"You mean – no safe deposit boxes?"

"Oh, gosh, no – no safe deposit boxes," Scott thought for a moment, rubbing his chin, "or anything remotely similar, to my recollection."

Trent felt a wave of resignation. He sighed and returned the key to his shirt pocket. Wellborn saw his disappointment.

"I would still be glad to show you the vault. Who knows? Something might be helpful to you."

Trent thought for a moment and shrugged. "Well, wouldn't be much of a cop if I didn't take advantage – at least cover all the bases."

They left Wellborn's office. Trent followed him around the corner and down a short hallway. They made one more corner and came face-to-face with a large, very thick, polished steel vault door standing wide open on massive hinges. A gate consisting of thick steel bars sat closed across the doorway to the vault. Wellborn reached up to the top of the doorframe and retrieved a small ring of keys from a hook there. He selected one, slipped it into the gate lock, and opened it.

"Bet they never left the keys hanging there in the old days," Trent smirked.

"No, I bet they didn't. But as I said, we keep nothing real important in here nowadays."

Wellborn switched on the lights that revealed a large, silent room filled almost floor to ceiling with several rows of metal shelving, each one containing neatly arranged and labeled file boxes. He led Trent down one aisle between the shelves to the back wall and stopped. He turned to Trent and with his long, index finger, pointed up at the wall. Trent looked up to see a faint difference in the hues of paint, noticeable along a straight line all along the wall, about twelve inches from the ceiling.

"As I recall," Wellborn began, "all the old safe deposit boxes were along this wall here, and on around the corner, in both directions – and they were all quarter-inch-thick steel." He shook his head appreciatively. "I mean, they must have had to use a forklift to get them out of here."

Trent walked toward the dimly lit corner of the room and peered back that way, his heart sinking.

"Any idea at all where they would've taken all those boxes, Scotty?"

Wellborn shrugged. "I wouldn't know, right off hand. It's only a wild guess, but I figure they'd try and sell them to another bank. Or maybe they just sold them for scrap metal."

"Yeah, probably right." Trent stood in silent thought. "I wonder what they did with stuff that wasn't claimed out of those boxes, though? Might be important if we could find out." He had taken the key out of his pocket again and was examining it once more.

Wellborn thought for a moment. "You know, I might have somebody that might know – one of the retired vice presidents that used to work at the bank here. Let me go check my office for his number."

They left the vault, Wellborn turning off the lights and replacing the keys back on the hook by the outer door. They walked briskly down the hallway, turned a corner, and almost collided with a smartly dressed woman.

"Oh! There you are, Mr. Wellborn. There's a gentleman here to see you – says he had an appointment with you?"

Wellborn looked puzzled for a moment. The young woman consulted a message slip, and then continued. "A – Mr. Collins?"

A look of recognition came to Wellborn's face. "Oh, yeah – the contractor. Thank you, Sheila." He resumed his walk with Trent at his heels. "We're having some much needed renovations done in the old basement. Hasn't been hardly touched in decades. In fact, it sits under where the old original bank building sat, before they built this newer annex back in the 70s. That basement is practically the only thing left of the original bank at all and – "

Wellborn's voice trailed off, and as he slowed to a stop, a look of realization came on his face. He turned suddenly and faced Trent.

"I just remembered something!" He looked up at Trent, his eyebrows raised. "There's the remnant of an old vault of some sort down there, Trent! I never even thought of it until now. I mean, if I told you this newer vault up here is now just storage, then that ancient one in the basement is less than that – only used as a janitor's closet now."

Wellborn turned in his tracks and led Trent back the way they had come, except instead of turning toward the newer vault, he continued on down a longer hallway until he came to another door. He pulled it open to reveal a set of concrete stairs with an old fashioned steel handrail bolted into the concrete wall. A dank and damp odor rose from below. Wellborn fumbled along the wall until he found the light switch; the stairway and beyond blossomed into light. They started to descend into the cold air rising to greet them.

"Any reason to think it's going to have anything I'd be interested in?" Trent asked.

Wellborn nodded knowingly, but suddenly stopped halfway down the steps and turned to Trent.

"Oh, yeah," he replied with a smug smile. "There's a whole wall of really old safe deposit boxes down there." He tapped his finger against Trent's shirt pocket. "I'm guessing at least as old as that key of yours."

#

The sun had dipped low toward the Sangre de Cristo Mountains when Trent pulled his truck back into the customer parking lot of the sheriff's department. He loved to park here because he knew it still irritated Ben Ferguson. Life did continue to have its small pleasures.

He grabbed a large paper bag from the passenger seat. Its top had been neatly folded and taped shut. He walked into the building and passed Molly in the lobby on her way out. He looked at his watch.

"Where you going so early?"

"Girl's gotta go get herself dolled up every once in awhile," she replied, giving him a wink and continuing to walk past him, exaggerating the swing of her hips for his benefit. Trent wished he hadn't even opened his mouth.

He went to his office, hung up his coat and hat, and placed the paper bag in the middle of his desk right beside the medical examiner's envelope. He was standing there tapping the desk with his fingers, deep in thought, and then sat down and pulled the bag toward him. He took out his pocketknife, slit the top of the bag, and peered inside.

A few moments later the door opened. Hector stuck his head in.

"Had a message you tried to call me?" Hector asked hesitantly.

Trent looked up at him with a frown. "Not going to ask where you've been for the last hour and a half," he huffed. Hector blushed in response, while Trent, noticing Hector's response, quipped, "But I suppose I can guess – and I also suppose you would probably insist that the only thing you and my daughter were working on together was that old journal."

Hector spluttered in protest, but Trent held up a hand to cut him off.

"And I also suppose, if you've been working on the journal together, that hopefully you can give me a little more information to go on here."

Trent had leaned back in his chair while he spoke and now pointed at the mysterious bag on his desk. "You remember the name on that old journal, by any chance – the name of the guy who wrote it?" Hector moved over now and sat down on the opposite side of the desk.

"Yeah – Otto something or other," he answered. "Otto Ever – uh –

Ebert?"

"Otto Eberhardt," Trent finished for him as he reached over, opened the bag, and upended its contents onto the desk. "Seems as if somebody kept a safe deposit box at the old First National Bank – and judging by most of this stuff, it just could've been your friend Otto."

Documents of various kinds had spilled out of the bag: a large packet of old letters tied together with twine, some small booklets of some kind, other loose papers – and a curious, single white chess piece. Trent reached into the pile and picked up the two small booklets with worn gray covers bearing a faded stamped insignia of an American eagle, superimposed with the title 'Camp Trinidad, Colorado.' He sat down and opened one of the books.

"*'Lieutenant Otto Franz Eberhardt,*" he read, "Serial number 429375AK – late of the *Deutsche Wehrmacht Afrika Korps* – issued June14, 1943." He opened the second booklet. "*Hauptmann Ernst Josef Brandt* – serial number 428946AK, *Deutsche Wehrmacht Afrika Korps,* etcetera, etcetera."

Trent tossed the ID books over to Hector and leaned back in his chair. "Looks like we've found us a couple of German soldiers – escaped POWs from back in the day." He watched Hector's face change expressions multiple times as he looked at the IDs. "You probably oughta call your girlfriend and tell her we may have just found a big piece of the puzzle – the author of her journal – especially if the handwriting on these old letters matches the writing in the journal."

Trent pulled the autopsy photographs out of the envelope in front of him and once more studied the close-up of the skeletal face thoughtfully. He then tossed the photo across to Hector.

"Trouble is – we've got to figure out which one of these guys is our John Doe here."

#

That evening Trent paced slowly back and forth along the length of his deck. He had earlier poured himself a large tumbler of bourbon that he normally would have drained by now, but he had barely taken a sip. He finally stopped at the far end of the deck and leaned against the railing. He gazed blankly out at the refracted color blossoming in the clouds over Johnson Mesa, but was unmoved by its burgeoning beauty.

What the hell am I missing? he thought to himself repeatedly, wracking his brain. John Doe's safe deposit box had held several intriguing items, including the probable identity of John Doe himself – the key to the box was found in John Doe's jacket; it stood to reason that he had to have been one of the two Germans whose identification cards were found in that box. But a couple of IDs and a few old letters to Germany didn't really offer hard, conclusive evidence.

And just why had he been killed? And why had his body been meticulously hidden in the masonry of the foundation?

Trent continued to stare off into the distance, frustrated as usual that he wasn't able to think the problem through any further. He massaged his eyes with his fingers and tenderly touched the scar that itched and burned under his hairline. His head swam; he felt he was right on the verge of something being revealed through the fog in his brain.

Jarhead suddenly jumped up onto the railing, startling him, and began purring loudly and rubbing against Trent's arm. Trent scratched behind the cat's ears and frowned to himself as the animal rolled over onto its back to allow its stomach to be rubbed briefly.

"What do you think I'm missing here, mangy cat?" he muttered. He found himself wishing his life were also that simple – eat, sleep, then wander off into the evening to look for a little excitement. "Not a care in the world, huh cat?"

Just at that moment, Jarhead rolled back to a sitting position and fixed his eyes on something down below them in the distance, towards the tree line of juniper and piñon. The cat's fur bristled on his neck and tail, and he growled deeply in his throat. Trent squinted into the gathering dusk and tried to follow the cat's line of sight.

Then, he saw her.

Standing just within the tree line in the fading light was Vicky, half-hidden among the shadows as she moved from one tree to another. Trent could hear her song echoing from the somewhere otherworldly. "*I am far and away from the one that I love.*" Her voice lilted up and swirled around Trent like surreal surround sound, echoing and carried with such clarity that it seemed she was standing right behind him instead of thirty yards away.

Vicky finally drifted from out of the tree line into plain sight; she stopped, still at a distance, and lifted her head slowly and silently up at Trent. Jarhead hissed and let out a final yelping growl, almost falling all over himself as he leapt back down onto the deck. He raced around the opposite corner of the house and disappeared.

Trent straightened up, but not before taking a quick gulp of the whisky.

"Victoria?" he called down softly to the ghostly figure of his dead wife.

Something was not quite the same about her tonight. She wore the familiar light blue summer dress – the same one she had been wearing on the day of the accident. Her luscious brown hair was tousled and hung down around her face and shoulders in an unkempt, windblown – but quite sexy – look. But Trent couldn't quite put his finger on what was disturbing him about her tonight.

"Vicky," Trent called out again, but she didn't answer. Instead, she took a couple of languid steps toward him, but stopped again, several yards away in the tall grass, and lifted her head to stare up at him. Her eyes glowed faintly in the waning light of day. Something was really beginning to trouble Trent.

"Far and away from my home…"

Vicky began moving again, and he then saw what disturbed him as she came into sharper focus: a thin line of blood at her left temple was streaming – pulsing – from her hairline and down her left cheek. He sucked in his breath and gripped the deck rail.

"Vicky!" he exclaimed.

She took another step toward him, and another, and another, and he could hear her softly humming her song again. Trent's eyes begin to burn; he swiped the back of his hand at them. When he opened them again, Vicky was now almost below home, several feet below the railing, still looking up at him with a haunting, languid smile on her pale lips, and with even more blood streaking her face.

Trent took a step back from the rail and drained the remainder of his drink in one gulp. When he lowered the glass and looked again, she was no longer down in the yard. He leaned way over the railing to look below, but saw nothing. He stood upright and jerked his head left and right – and suddenly, there she was, up on the deck to his right now and moving slowly toward him, reaching out for him, her face and arms dripping blood. Her mouth smiled at him, and even though her eyes gazed at him lovingly, the entire left side her face was streaming with blood emanating from a hideous, terrible head wound at her temple.

"My love." Her words exhaled in a low tone and in exaggerated slow motion.

"Vicky," Trent breathed, hardly speaking at all. He felt as if he were in a horror movie. He tried to back away but his feet felt nailed in place.

"You still don't see it, do you, Sweet Boy," she continued. She was inches away from him now and stared up at his face as she lifted one wraith-like hand toward his hair. He caught his breath. The scent of cloves and roses was simply overpowering; he almost gagged.

"See what," he gasped. He trembled now and closed his eyes as her finger moved a lock of his hair from his forehead, moved towards the scar, and then softly stroked it. The burning sensation quickly faded away with the coolness of her touch.

The next sound Trent heard was his own scream, but it could've been only within his mind.

Vicky had suddenly pushed hard at his scar, so hard that he had felt her fingers tear open the old wound and dig deep into his head. Blood had begun to gush out of the hole she had created there and spill down into his eyes. She began to twist her forefinger around and back and forth as if searching for something within the wound. Trent had fallen backward onto the railing and was jerking his head back and forth, flailing his hands at Vicky, trying to get her fingers to dislodge from where they were probing his forehead with a certain macabre precision. Blood was flecking everywhere; he screamed her name, imploring her to stop. Her face remained serene and peaceful with no evidence of concern at his violent reaction.

"Almost there, Baby," she cooed. "Almost – just hold still."

He felt, and then heard, her forefinger and thumb pop back out of his head. He staggered a couple more steps away from her and pressed the palm of his hand against his forehead. She now had something between her thumb and forefinger and held it up to get a better look at whatever it was. She smiled back at Trent.

"There," she declared and reached over and dropped it with a loud ring into his empty glass on the railing. "That's going to be so much better for you, now!"

Trent dared not to move and leaned back on his elbows, trembling against the railing. He finally got up enough nerve, reached a shaky hand up to his forehead and again touched the hole she had put there – except there was no longer a hole, just a scar again. He rubbed hard before he pulled his fingers away and dared to look at them.

No blood, whatsoever.

He twisted back around, picked up the whisky tumbler, and peered into it. He could just make out in the gathering gloom that something was, in fact, at the bottom. He rattled it around and held the glass up. His eyes widened. There, rolling around the bottom of the glass lay a bent piece of lead – a spent bullet, still covered in his blood.

"What the –," he began and looked around.

Vicky was no longer there. Her fragrance was also quickly fading before he caught her singsong voice trailing away, and he looked back down to the juniper and piñon down below. Vicky was sashaying across the yard below the deck and soon disappeared into the darkening trees and bushes, but not before stopping and turning to look at him from afar. She left him with one more cryptic comment, called out to float ethereally on the breeze as she faded from sight.

"*A bullet for your thoughts, Baby Boy.*"

CHAPTER 24
OFFERINGS TO IDOLS

Excerpt from the Journal of Otto Eberhardt:
"14.09.61

'Five years ago today, we lost our precious Evie. Two people died in that fire, but it has consumed us all, one way or another. If it weren't for this obsession that I must now protect Evie's children, I would have disappeared from this place long ago. We all carry the scars now. I fear that it took what was left of little Caroline's sanity, robbed Carl of his childhood, and I know it consumed my own heart's capacity for love.

As to Conrad Neumann, I now also have a guilty obsession with protecting him as though he had some sort of invisible claim on my life, and I on his. He survived the inferno at a physical cost of not only third degree burns over half of his body, but also the psychological toll of never being the same man again – for, indeed, he is not the same.

Although it has taken all these years of treatment and therapy to get him back home and functioning in any sort of normal capacity, his character seems to have changed subtly. He has become as different as night and day, no longer drinking nor given to fits of anger, and exhibiting a calm, almost calculating air that he never had before. On the other hand, he wants little to do with his children and often refuses to allow them near him, even though 11 year old Caroline sits in the hallway outside his bedroom door, singing to him and talking to her doll, and Carl sneaks in when his father is asleep and stares in fascination at his hideous face, yet never saying a word.

Of course, I now take care of everything – caring for the children, the household, and overseeing the ranch, though I do hire occasional day laborers in the busy seasons. And I am the one who usually tends to Neumann's physical needs. At those times, I am acutely aware that he watches me, almost preternaturally, and a nagging, recurring thought has started to resurface in the back of my mind, causing me to once more begin looking over my shoulder as I did years ago.

Yes, two people died in that fire – one was the love of my life, and the other was a killer who had been hunting me down, a man with whom I had served through the entire war, risked my life for, escaped from prison with, and who then forced me to help him perform or cover up some of the most disturbing deeds that haunt me to this day – and who finally died horribly; it was his charred, barely recognizable remains I single-handedly pulled out of the ashes, dug a grave for, and buried – and God please forgive me, but I give thanks daily for Ernst Brandt's death!

Now, this ranch has become a valley of silence and of secrets – and still something crawls in the shadows here – a disturbing presence, almost like Ernst's spirit still roams, just out of sight.

#

Otto hammered the last of the shingles onto the roof, straightened up, and balanced himself on the peak of the roof. He took his hat off, wiped the sweat from his forehead with the back of his hand, and glanced at the afternoon sun about to disappear into a bank of clouds that could harbor some rain. He took a look at his watch. It was a little after 5:00 p.m. and they were at a good stopping point. He looked over and signaled the other two hands on the other end of the shingle run.

"Let's call it a day," he called to them. "Tomorrow we will start on the back porch. Who knows? Might even be done with the whole thing before the first snow flies."

Otto descended the ladder, went over to the nearby pickup, filled a ladle full of water from the cooler mounted on the side, and drank deeply. He took another one and doused it over his hair. The other ranch hands came over and helped themselves to water, methodically gathered their tools and ladders, put them into the truck, and drove off down the road to their quarters inside the new metal barn that had been built in place of the old one. Even though the house was being rebuilt on the site of the one that burned down, Otto had felt a degree of superstition in rebuilding the barn as close to the house as it had been before, so it now sat fifty yards further away.

It had been a long time coming, but they had finished rebuilding the majority of the house, Otto felt like something major had been accomplished. He had rebuilt it as a true ranch style house, single story this time, and completely modernized it with four bedrooms, two bathrooms, a huge living area, and a separate dining area with a large, serviceable kitchen. The house looked nothing like the previous one – the way Otto wanted it. He wanted nothing about the place to remind him of the one Evie died in – and after all, he was the only one around to really have a say in it this time.

As the noise of the truck engine faded away, Otto heard a bell ringing insistently in the near distance and turned toward the peach orchard that spread away several yards to the west of the house. He rubbed his eyes, slicked his wet air back, and sighed. Evie's grave was down there, at the edge of the grove of trees she had personally planted a few years ago. Caroline sat cross-legged a few yards away, leaning against her mother's headstone, singing to her doll Irena. And there, too, was Conrad Neumann, sitting in his wheelchair, turned toward the sunset, repeatedly slinging the old-fashioned school bell he gripped in one hand, which was the only way he had to signal to whomever that he was in need of something.

Conrad Neumann had not said a single word since the fire.

Otto blew out his breath and walked down that way. He wasn't sure where Carl was. The boy had jumped off the school bus earlier, scowling; ignoring everyone, he had tossed his books in the house only to emerge with his .22 rifle. He had wandered off to the tree-lined creek about a quarter mile below the house, presumably to shoot small game.

Evie hadn't lived long enough to see her trees bear fruit, but now, at the end of the season, the branches were heavily burdened with peaches – so many that the sparrows had gotten to many of them and others littered the ground where gnats and flies buzzed over them lazily.

None of it seemed to bother Mr. Neumann, who sat slumped to one side, waving the old wood handled bell back and forth, its clanging growing more jarring as Otto neared the back of the chair. The man had an old straw cowboy hat shoved down to his ears. Otto circled to the front of the wheelchair and stopped, crossed his arms, and frowned down at its occupant.

Conrad looked up at Otto and locked his one good eye on him, but continued clanging the brass school bell almost belligerently. The puckered pink and red flesh looked like badly butchered meat over the entire ruined left side of Neumann's head, down to his neck, and disappeared into the collar of his shirt. Massive scars covered most of his nose and half of his mouth; the shiny flesh was grossly swollen and made his head appear unnaturally lopsided. Otto knew that under the hat there was no hair, to speak of, except for stray long strands that Neumann had refused to allow to be trimmed and that stuck out at random from beneath his hat to complete the perpetual scarecrow effect that he exhibited. Drool had gathered at the corner of his ruined lip and dribbled down onto his shirt in a steady stream.

Otto stared down at the man and allowed the bell to continue ringing for several more seconds, almost a game between them; calmly, he finally reached down and grasped it in midair, stifling its noise. Neumann's pale blue eye glared at him while they played tug of war over the bell for a few more moments.

"So, we are going to play games again, are we?" Otto gritted, before jerking the bell away, finally, and setting it firmly on the small table next to the wheelchair.

Neumann gurgled something in an attempted but unintelligible answer. Otto had not heard him speak a word in nearly five years now, communicating only by pointing and grunting. Otto reached back down to the table and took a folded, dry hand towel there. He quietly dabbed at the corner of Neumann's mouth, sopping up the spittle before neatly folding the towel back and replacing it on the table next to the bell.

"I cannot understand how you can manage to ring that damned bell so much, but it is downright impossible for you to grab your own towel to clean yourself up."

Neumann looked up at him, still glaring, but suddenly dropped his head. Otto turned, and saw Evie's headstone a few feet away. He stepped over to it and squatted down. He picked up a half rotten peach from the grave, tossed it aside, and brushed at the engraving on the stone.

Loving Wife, Mother, & Friend.

Otto touched the last word, closed his eyes, and let his fingers linger there. Through his insistence the word *Friend* had been included, the sentiment being as close as he had dared come to saying what he had really wanted to say. Choosing the inscription had not been, after all, his place. Still, he couldn't shake the guilt that Evie's death had all been his fault. Had he but left the ranch sooner than planned, all of this might not have happened. Hell, if he had only followed his original instincts and never accepted Neumann's job offer.

If, but, should have …

He looked deeper into the shadows of the orchard in the direction he had tossed the rotten peach. Ernst Brandt's unmarked grave was down there somewhere, hopefully never to be found or acknowledged. The monster was gone – perhaps the only good thing that had come of all this.

Otto felt a small hand gently cup the top of his on the headstone. He smiled and opened his eyes to see Caroline gazing at the letters engraved on the stone, sounding out the words slowly and methodically. When she had finished repeating her mother's name, she looked up at Otto and smiled.

"Mr. Otto, Irena says I should show you her secret tonight." Otto cocked his head, curiosity in his face and then he remembered. They hadn't spoken of it in over five years.

"Oh, yes. I remember – the secret."

"Well, would you like to know what it is?"

"Oh, yes. Very much, Irena," he answered, patting the doll with his fingertips. "Very much!"

Otto suddenly felt Neumann's eye on him. He pulled his hand away sheepishly, then stood and turned, expecting to see Caroline's father frowning. But, instead, Neumann's good eyebrow was arched above his eye creating a bemused look, and the right half of his mouth was cocked into a strange, grimacing smile. The look was more than a little unsettling.

A distant roll of thunder broke the spell and Otto turned to Caroline. "Time to head to the house, little Rosebud," he softly directed to her as he stepped behind her father's wheelchair. He reached down and unlatched the locks on the big wheels, swiveled the chair around, and pushed it across the yard to the back steps. Otto parked the wheelchair, relocked the wheels, and bent over to scoop Neumann out of the chair and carry him up the steps and into the house. Although the man had lost weight and was rather easy to carry, Otto was looking forward to finishing the deck here as he planned to incorporate much-needed ramps for the wheelchair.

He carried Neumann on down the hallway to a bedroom at the back corner of the house and sat him on the edge of the bed. Neumann had given him no help whatsoever and had felt like stone in Otto's arms, as if to make it as difficult for him as possible. But once on the bed, he now sat upright and straight with his feet firmly on the floor. He defiantly watched Otto move around the room with that same bemused look on the normal side of his face. Otto refused to look back.

Otto went to the closet and came back with a button up cardigan sweater and house slippers that he helped Neumann change into. He gently pulled him into a standing position and guided him across to an overstuffed rocker that sat nearby and deposited him there. Otto went over to a chest of drawers and found a clean handkerchief that he took to Neumann and placed in his good right hand. He finally reached across Neumann and flicked on the radio that sat on the bedside table. Patsy Cline's low, melodic voice was soon crooning something about "falling to pieces."

Quite appropriate, Otto thought, then turned back to Neumann.

"Now – you are all set, Conrad," Otto murmured, somewhat out of breath. "Just sit here patiently while I go fix us some dinner." Otto moved to the door but turned again. "And Conrad – please lay off the damned bell – alright?" Neumann made no sound but just stared vacantly back at Otto with his pale blue eye. Otto shuddered, turned, and gladly left the room.

He went back out to the porch, folded up the wheelchair, and was bringing it up the steps when he heard a *crack-crack* in the distance from somewhere downstream. It had to be Carl, shooting at a rabbit or one of the many porcupines that infested the trees and caused painful problems to cows grazing the area.

"Carl?" Otto called out from the top step of the porch, cupping his hand to his mouth. Out of the corner of his eye, he saw lightning flash inside the dark clouds that had rolled in from the west. A breeze had picked up and made a shimmering noise as it moved through the limbs of the peach orchard. He could smell rain in the air.

"Carl," Otto called out loudly one more time, his voice hopefully carrying on the breeze. "Time to get home – storm's coming, and dinner is going to be ready soon!"

Otto squinted into the darkening light down among the big cottonwoods lining the creek about a hundred yards away and thought he saw movement, but wasn't sure. He suddenly felt very exposed out on the open porch and wasn't sure why he felt uncomfortable – until he remembered that lately he had the distinct impression Carl didn't like him at all, and the boy was now wandering around in the twilight out there with a loaded rifle. That old feeling of being hunted ran up his back: Otto trembled before forcing himself to turn and walk back into the house. *This is ridiculous,* he thought. *Frightened of shadows – and of a fourteen year old boy at that!*

#

Carl prodded the dying porcupine at his feet with the muzzle of his .22 rifle, blood oozing from a small wound in the animal's side right behind its front leg that still trembled and pawed weakly at thin air, as if it would jump up momentarily and scurry away. Carl pushed the barrel behind the ear of the suffering varmint, cocked the bolt of the single action weapon, loading another shell into the breech. His finger tightened on the trigger with the intent of putting a bullet into the porcupine's skull and thus putting it out of its misery.

But Carl hesitated, lifted the barrel away, and slung the rifle across the back of his shoulders. He knelt down, leaned close, and peered with great interest into the animal's beady black eye that was fixed upon him in terror; Carl watched, fascinated, as the light in the porcupine's eye gradually faded and the forelegs ceased their twitching.

Carl hated these ugly creatures. Good for nothing and only caused problems for the livestock. Not that he cared that much about the other animals, either; he was old enough and smart enough now to know that the cattle were a large part of their income, and that some day sooner than later he would be called upon to step up and run this place. He might as well at least start trying to care about it now. At least, that's what that stupid Otto always told him.

He hated Otto.

He hated ranch work.

He hated his retarded sister.

He even, at times, hated his mother for dying and leaving him in such a useless, impossible situation, with such useless, good-for-nothing people.

The only person that he didn't really hate, that he felt even halfway understood or cared for him, was his father. Even though his dad was maimed and spent most of his days in silence, he occasionally shared secrets with Carl – secrets that he knew were just between the two of them. This secrecy was a precious thing for Carl, who knew something that the others did not: his father, Conrad Neumann, could actually speak after all, but only to him. His father had been quick to warn Carl not to let Otto or Caroline know. Carl had wondered why the stealth, at first, but realized over time, through their secret conversations, that his father had no real patience for his mentally challenged sister and that he actually despised Otto Eberhardt – an emotion they both shared.

Beyond all that, Carl's father had promised that as he continued to get better, he would help Carl to grow up and be the man he needed to be – to take his rightful place at the head of the family business.

Carl must bide his time – for now.

He heard the distant rumble of thunder and turned his face to the quickening breeze. He closed his eyes and lifted his chin as he smelled the clean rain on the air and smiled – and suddenly stiffened.

"Carl?" Otto's voice echoed to him from the house in the distance.

How he especially hated Otto, that worthless German ranch hand who, according to comments that his father had occasionally said, was the real reason for the fire that had handicapped his father and killed his mother.

Carl took the .22 rifle from his shoulders, shifted from a squat to his knees, lifted his head until he could just see the house through the underbrush, about a hundred yards up from the bank of the stream, and spied Otto on the porch.

He carefully aimed the rifle, squinting his left eye and sighting down the barrel with his right as he lined up the forward bead on Otto's chest. Otto had his hand shading his eyes and was looking away off to the west, toward the gathering thunderheads on the horizon. Carl dropped his forefinger to the trigger and slowly squeezed.

"Crack!" Carl blurted at the last minute, without really firing, eased off the trigger, and lowered the rifle as he watched Otto turn and disappear back into the house.

He smiled slowly.

Damn, it would be so very easy. But for this, too, he would bide his time.

#

Caroline was sitting at the kitchen counter swiveling back and forth on one of the barstools and singing quietly under her breath. Irena sat in front of her on the counter. The worn out doll had mere strands of hair, only one button remaining for an eye, and half of her sewn lips had been pulled out so that she only had half a smile. For the first time, Otto realized how much the old doll reminded him of Conrad Neumann, damaged and grotesque. He forced his eyes away and busied himself pulling out some pots and pans and taking food from the refrigerator.

"Tonight, what do you think about Mr. Otto's Famous Meatloaf, Rosebud?" he asked Caroline. She raised her eyebrows and formed an *Oh* with her lips and nodded excitedly.

"Irena and I would like that very much, Mr. Otto! Very much!"

"Then, would you like to help me cook?" Usually, Caroline would have already jumped down and scooted up next to him to help break the eggs, or mix the cracker crumbs. But tonight, she sat very still and said nothing. Otto looked over his shoulder at her from across the kitchen. "Well?" he asked.

"When is Daddy going to get better?"

Otto had his hands and fingers in a mixing bowl, kneading the ingredients into the ground beef. He paused for a moment.

"Well, your Daddy is trying very hard to get a little better every day, Honey."

Caroline paused for a minute to think about his answer and then asked, "And why is Carl so angry all the time?"

Otto thought hard for a few moments before answering.

"Well, you know how sad you got when your mama went away?"

"You mean," the girl corrected, "when she burned up in the house fire?"

Otto stopped his preparations at the counter, startled by the bluntness of her comment. Turning from the counter, he picked up a dishtowel and continued, "Yes, I guess that is what I meant. But I think it is nicer if we just say she went away to live with the angels."

Caroline nodded her head affirmatively but then frowned. "I tried to tell Carl that once – but he just pushed me down and told me 'No – she got burnt to a crisp in the house!'" She looked thoughtful for a moment. "He said that there was nothing left of her to find. That's not true, is it, Mr. Otto? Because otherwise, why do we have a grave for Mama down in the orchard?"

Otto stopped his work feeling suddenly awkward. He did not want this conversation right now – but it was happening, so he felt as if he should try to comfort Caroline somehow.

"Caroline, like I was trying to say – when you got sad at your mama's – uh – passing, Carl got angry – for pretty much the same reasons."

"But, why?" she pressed. "Why can't he just be sad, too, instead of mad?"

"Well, Honey, different people handle things differently. Some of us – like you and me – get sad when people we love die. People like Carl get angry."

He thought again and, after a few moments of silence, continued. "I guess he is more like his daddy in that way, huh?"

Caroline became quiet for a couple more minutes. Otto finished preparing his meatloaf, molded it into a baking dish, and put it in the oven, which had been preheating. He washed his hands, walked back to Caroline, and sat on the stool next to hers.

Caroline fidgeted with the edge of her dress but then looked up at him with a serious look on her face as if she had made a decision of some kind.

"Irena says she really wants to show you her secret. She thinks it's time now."

Otto smiled indulgently, propped his chin in his hands, and looked the doll straight in the face.

"Well, now, Irena. I guess I am ready to hear about this famous secret of yours." He glanced at Caroline and winked. "If you think I can handle it, that is."

Caroline looked at him once more, seemed to make up her mind once and for all, then abruptly grasped Irena by the legs and turned the doll upside down. She stuck the tip of her tongue out, concentrating hard as she pulled its skirt up over its head, revealing a series of snaps sewn into the broad cloth back. She then began unsnapping them, gripped the exposed opening, and pulled it gently apart. Otto eyes widened; he raised his head from his hands and continued to watch in stunned silence as Caroline dug her thumb and forefingers into the opening, gripped something inside, and methodically began wriggling it out. Finally, with an audible grunt, she freed what turned out to be a small, well-worn, leather bound book.

She slowly raised the book to her lips and kissed it tenderly. She lowered it and gazed at it lovingly for a while before laying it on the counter and sliding it slowly toward Otto and whispered. "Mama always told me to never ever let anyone see this – nobody – ever!"

Caroline got very quiet, lowered her head before continuing, "But Irena says that she thinks you and Mama were special friends, and that Mama would be happy for you to have it now." Irena paused for a moment. "Were you special friends, Mr. Otto?"

Otto slowly reached over and touched the cover of the book. He traced a finger around its edge.

"Yes, Caroline," he answered softly. "We were very special friends."

He pulled the book over in front of him and opened it carefully. Inside the cover was a neatly handwritten, feminine scrawl, which read *Personal Diary of Evie Van Ryan – Private!* The first entry was dated August 1, 1944. Otto thought for a minute before concluding that she would have been fourteen years old – her son, Carl's, age – at the time. He began to tremble, slowly closing the diary and turning to Caroline.

He felt as if he were a vile intruder on the thoughts of someone he loved dearly.

"Caroline," Otto asked, "why do you think your mama would want me to have this? I mean – it does say 'Private' and 'Personal,' right? You do know what those words mean, don't you?"

"Yes, Mr. Otto. They mean 'None of Your Business,' which is what Carl is always yelling at me." Caroline picked Irena up and put the doll's dress back in place. "Just a minute – Irena wants to say something else." She held the doll up to her ear and listened intently for a moment. She laid Irena back on the counter. "Mr. Otto, Irena says to remind you that she and I can both read real good – and that – well, Mr. Otto? Do you think a lot of people have your name?"

"*My* name?" Otto asked, confused.

"Yes – your name – 'Mr. Otto," I mean, without the 'mister' part."

"You mean, 'Otto?' Well, I guess there are a few others. But probably back in the land I came from – you remember me telling you about Germany, the country where I am from? Well, there are probably more *'Ottos'* there than here in America." He hesitated, looking intently at Caroline, and continued. "Why do you think my name is so important, little Rosebud?"

"Well, because it's all in Mama's book – where she wrote stuff about you and her." Caroline blushed and looked down again. "I think Mama liked you a whole bunch, Mr. Otto," she smiled softly. "And that's why Irena and I like you so much, too – because Mama did." And with that, it now was Otto's turn to blush.

He picked up the book and thumbed through it, caressing the cover, trying to imagine Evie's hands lovingly turning the same pages, touching them gently with her fingers. He searched the pages, searching until he found a particular range of dates, and began to read.

Caroline suddenly jumped down from the stool and skipped across the kitchen. "Irena says 'thank you,' Mr. Otto, for taking the book. It was getting really heavy for her to carry around." She skipped out of the kitchen, but suddenly reappeared in the doorway. "And Mr. Otto," she started in a conspiratorial whisper, "Irena says to remind you to not tell anybody else about the secret – okay? You swear?"

Otto sat very still, staring at a particular entry he had just stumbled upon in the diary, dumbfounded. He had read it once, and read it again, and now read it for a third time before looking up at Caroline, realizing he hadn't really heard a word she had just said.

"What was that?" he asked, barely above a whisper.

"I said, 'Do you swear not to tell?'"

"Yes," he nodded absently to her. "Yes, of course – I swear."

"Swear what!" Caroline stood with her hands on her hips.

"I swear – I swear not to tell," he stammered, still distracted.

Caroline giggled and then ran down the hall.

Otto watched her leave, then turned back to the diary. He couldn't yet absorb what he had just read, yet here were Evie's own private thoughts and words in her own handwriting, so what he was reading here must be the truth.

He glanced back at the entry once more, confirming what he had just read. He slowly closed the diary and rubbed his eyes in disbelief.

He agreed completely with Caroline and Irena. No one must see this diary – ever – certainly not Conrad and definitely, absolutely not Carl.

Only the dead should know this Secret; no one alive ever could, or would, if he had anything to say about it.

#

Thinking of nowhere else to keep it, Otto had tucked Evie's diary into the waistband of his pants, then tucked his shirt over it. He must never let this book out of his sight.

Ever.

He quickly and numbly got back to the work of making dinner, adding a mixed salad and fresh green beans to the meal. He had just set the table when the screen door slammed. He recognized the clomping of Carl's boots on the wood floor as the boy passed through the living room, stomped up the stairs, and into his bedroom, where he slammed the door. Otto would have normally called out a greeting; but this time he feared that his voice would shake or that he would not be able to get the words out, so he let it go. He knew Carl would come out for dinner after he cleaned up. The boy was sullen, but he never managed to miss a meal.

Otto prepared a tray of food, took it into Neumann's room, and set it on the table beside his chair. Conrad was snoozing with his head propped in his good hand, his elbow on the arm of the chair. Otto took the handkerchief and wiped the man's wet face and chin, which awakened him with a start. He glared when he recognized Otto, but brightened a little at the sight of supper. Without a word, Otto positioned the tray where Conrad could reach the fork, put a towel in his lap, and left the room. Eating was one of the activities Conrad could do for himself.

The two kids were already seated and eating when Otto returned to the dining room and sat down. No one said a word. Otto picked at his food, deep in thought while Carl and Caroline wolfed theirs down. His mind kept wandering away, only for him to jerk it back to the issue that swam in circles around everything else in his head.

Why? He kept asking himself.

Why?

But like so many of the other *whys* in his life now, he had no good answers. And even if he had, he wouldn't have been able to know what he was supposed to do now.

The clanging of Neumann's bell jarred him back to his senses. He looked around and realized the children were gone, having finished eating and leaving behind dirty plates. Normally, Otto would've yelled upstairs for them to come back and take care of the dishes, but he was still not thinking clearly – only responding to outside stimuli, like that damned bell.

He threw his napkin on top of his uneaten food, scooted the chair back, and stomped into Conrad's room. Without a word, he snatched the bell out of the man's hand, moved the tray away, and wiped Neumann's face, now stained with the evidence of his meal.

He took the tray back to the kitchen, but came back and methodically prepared Neumann for bed. He helped the man go to the bathroom, brush his teeth, change into pajamas, laid him onto his bed, and finally began to pull the bedclothes up over him. The night's routine was nearly complete.

"So," came a raspy voice unexpectedly from somewhere deep within Neumann's throat, breaking the normal silence between them during the nightly ritual and startling Otto. "Since it seems as if we are both getting sick and tired of that damned bell," Neumann croaked, "why don't we just agree to get rid of it altogether – and communicate like civilized people?"

Otto froze in horror, not quite believing his ears. *Carl Neumann was speaking!*

"*Komm jetzt, mein ältester Freund*," the voice continued, now in very familiar German. The half-cocked smile appeared on the ruined lips, and the single, clear blue eye twinkled knowingly at Otto. "Oh, please tell me you haven't forgotten me after all these years, my dear *Leutnant*?" he chuckled. "That would disappoint me no end."

Otto stood numbly with the edge of the bedspread still in his hands and stared down at this horror in the bed before him – this physical and mental and emotional nightmare. For he might well have mistaken the strained voice, but there was no mistaking that the words, the tone, and the familiar *sobriquet* he used belonged to his ghostly nemesis from his past.

As ragged and scarred as it was, this voice was not that of Conrad Neumann at all.

No, this was the familiar voice of another man who was supposed to be dead – the man who still haunted his nightmares; the man Otto thought he had successfully buried and forgotten years ago in Evie's orchard: the monster, *Ernst Brandt.*

CHAPTER 25
GREATER LOVE HATH NO ONE

The next morning Trent got up at 4:00 a.m., showered, and put the coffee on to brew while he shaved and dressed in a uniform shirt and jeans. Not wanting to wake Sophie, he carried his boots and tiptoed back to the kitchen where he poured a travelling mug full of hot black coffee before sitting down at the table to put them on. On his way out, he grabbed three oatmeal cookies – his favorites – for breakfast, slipped them into the pocket of his leather jacket, and quietly pulled the door to.

He had slept fitfully the night before, afraid that if he fell fully asleep he would only descend into his tiresome world of nightmares. His encounters with Vicky had grown increasingly disturbing; last evening's shocking visitation, in particular, when she had mysteriously pulled a bullet out of his forehead, had left him drained physically and emotionally.

After she had disappeared, he had stood there on the deck in shock, gripping the glass tightly and staring off into the darkness. He had stayed that way for a long while, losing track of time, when he had heard the sliding door open and the deck lights had suddenly bathed him in their white blaze.

"Dad? You out here?" Sophie had stuck her head out from the kitchen and after she spied him, continued with an additional note of alarm: "Dad! What the hell happened?"

Trent had turned to her absently and noticed her staring at this hand. He looked down to see that his bloodied fingers clutched only shards of the glass. He hadn't even noticed the broken tumbler until then, nor had any idea how long he had been holding it, but it had obviously been long enough for blood to drip down and form a small pool around and over the toe of his boot.

He had opened his fingers to allow the remnants of the glass to fall where they tinkled and scattered on the deck. Sophie had hurried to him and picked carefully at the smaller slivers still imbedded in his palm and fingers. She had tenderly wrapped his hand with the kitchen towel she had been holding and ordered him to sit down in the deck chair.

"Stay right there," she had told him. "I'll be right back."

Trent quietly did as he was told, but when Sophie had reappeared with the first aid kit, she found him on all fours searching among the pieces of glass and blood on the deck.

"Dad!" she had shouted in alarm, rushing over to him.

"Do you see it?" he had asked urgently, his eyes frantic, scanning the deck and frowning.

"See what? What the hell are you doing?"

"It was right there," he stopped searching long enough to point, "in the glass."

"What was right there, Dad?" Sophie had asked as she looked from the ground to him before continuing, "What in the hell are you looking for?"

Finally, after searching through the shards a few minutes more, Trent had sat back on his heels and looked up at her, despair on his face. "You don't see it, do you?"

Sophie had knelt beside him. She touched his shoulder softly, as she would a child's, and tenderly lifted his wounded hand into her lap and opened up the first aid kit.

"Daddy, you're scaring me again," she had reasoned softly. "What is it I'm supposed to see there?"

Trent had looked forlornly back down at the blood-streaked deck, glittering with broken glass.

"The bullet," he finally admitted, "the bullet your mother gave to me – the one she pulled out of my head."

He had gingerly touched the scar on his forehead with his uninjured hand. Sophie looked up at him with deep concern and then bent back to her work. She uncapped a small bottle of disinfectant.

"This is going to sting like hell," she had cautioned and poured some on his cuts.

Trent had not acknowledged the pain at all, only stared blankly back into the darkness, toward the trees – toward where Vicky had disappeared.

#

By 4:45 in the morning, his hand was throbbing. Sophie had tried to convince him to go to the emergency room last night, but he had refused and, instead, had her dress the wound as best she could by cleaning and wrapping it in gauze and tape. Now, blood was seeping again through the bandages; Trent was finding it awfully difficult and painful to maneuver the stick shift in his old pickup truck as he bounced down the road off of the hillside and on into town.

He finally pulled into the parking lot of the sheriff's department, let himself into the darkened offices, and went to work. By the time the custodian had arrived at 6:30, Trent had the contents of several case file boxes strewn all over his office. The material covered every possible space, including his desk and chairs, even the floor. He had been looking for a particular file and now, having found it, stood quietly, hovering over it as it lay open in the middle of his desk.

He was breathing heavily and sweating as he stared down at several photographs from the file. Some were too gruesome to look at for long, even for a seasoned investigator and former combat soldier like himself, used to the horror of violent death and its aftermath. The difference with this particular file was that it was labeled with the name of Victoria Anne Carter, and the photos depicted the sadly mangled and torn body of his beloved wife as she had been found four years ago at a crash scene on Cordova Pass before the paramedics finally took her lifeless body away.

Despite the violence to her body shown in the photos, Trent was surprised at the small details he himself now focused upon: she had been wearing her favorite summer dress – the light blue one. She was wearing one brown slipper, which dangled off of a bloodied foot, but the other was missing and her delicate bare foot looked unharmed and girlishly innocent, her toenails painted a bright red. Her beautiful brown hair was splayed out on the ground as if she had simply laid down to rest for a moment in a meadow of wildflowers.

Those details were the ones Trent chose to dwell on now rather than the ones the other photographs revealed: her body and limbs twisted into unnatural positions impossible for a body to be in – and the close-up shots of her brutalized head. He stifled a sob and quickly turned those particular grotesque pictures over and slipped them under the others, out of sight.

Instead, he turned his attention to the investigative report and came upon the medical examiner's summary page: "*Cause of death – severe blunt force trauma to the head, due to multiple injuries incurred in a single car rollover accident.*"

Trent flipped the reports back over and he looked again through the photos. Something bothered him. Something was missing, something Vicky had been trying to communicate to him last night. What was that 'something,' and why couldn't he see it?

He pored through the file once more, scanning the reports, searching for details. He turned to the section of the file that should've contained an autopsy report, flipping through the file, until he stopped suddenly in realization and gazed into the distance – there would have been no autopsy ordered, as there had been no suspicions of foul play. This was an auto accident, pure and simple.

Wasn't it?

He thought a moment, then flipped hurriedly back through until he found a particular photo, a close-up detail of the crushed and bent Jeep. He grabbed the photograph and held it close, squinting at it, again looking at details. He twisted his desk lamp around until the photo was bathed in artificial light and peered closely at the photo again. He sighed impatiently, angrily jerked open his desk drawer, and rummaged quickly until he located his magnifying glass that he now focused on one particular area of the photo. He moved the glass slowly – and froze. His hand began to tremble; he sat down heavily in his chair. He looked up and stared again into the distance vacantly.

After a few moments, he flipped back through the report pages, scanning for certain information. He finally stopped, closed the file, and sat back, incredulous. Was that it? Was that what Vicky had been trying to show him? The report contained no mention of the details he thought he had seen in the photo, but no other explanation could be plausible. His fingertips wandered unconsciously to the scar on his forehead. Still, nothing registered at all in his memory. He closed his eyes, clenched his fists, and knocked them against his head in frustration.

He suddenly opened his eyes. He knew where he needed to go.

Trent jumped up, grabbed the file and his jacket, and moved quickly across the office. He jerked open the door and almost ran straight into Sheriff Ferguson who had his hand poised to knock.

"Whoa, there! Uh, morning, Trent."

"Ben."

Both men stood looking at one another, neither of them making a move. The sheriff craned his neck to look at the disheveled office behind Trent.

"Something you're working on here?" Ben asked. "Maybe something I can help with?"

Trent sighed and rubbed his neck, exasperated at the interruption. "What are you doing here so early, Ben?"

"Kind of thought that was supposed to be my line," answered the sheriff. "Besides, your daughter called me a few minutes ago, worried as hell about you." He glanced down at the bloody bandage on Trent's hand, then over to Vicky's file under his other arm. "Said you'd cut yourself up pretty good – and were talking crazy-like – some bullshit about bullets in the head and stuff." Ben folded his arms and leaned on the doorframe. "Now, I'm no shrink or anything," he continued, "but I don't suppose there's anything of that nature you'd like to talk to me about, would you?"

Trent rolled his eyes impatiently, looked down at his feet, sighed, and pushed himself firmly past the Sheriff.

"No, Ben – nothing worth talking about – yet." He weaved his way through the other desks scattered throughout the department and made his way to the exit. "But I promise," he called over his shoulder, "you will be the next to last to know anything."

He made it halfway out the double glass doors before abruptly turning around and coming back in. He stepped around the dispatcher's desk and went to the wall to rummage through various sets of keys hanging from a pegboard there. He selected one and looked over at the sheriff sheepishly.

"Checking out a cruiser," he mumbled apologetically as he disappeared back out the door.

Ben sighed and called after Trent before the door swung shut completely. "Say, if you should get yourself killed or anything, at least do me the courtesy of a call, will you?"

#

Twenty minutes later, Trent's white Ford Explorer, emblazoned with the blue markings and logo of the Colfax County Sheriff's Department, sat parked in the gravel driveway of Curly's Salvage Yard, located a mile or so east of the Raton city limits. Curly Johnson pulled up to the old frame house, which served as his office, opened his truck door, and eased his 300 some-odd pounds out of the truck. He glanced over to where Trent sat leaning against the wall of the house on two legs of an old metal chair that had once graced someone's dinette set. Trent had sunglasses on and had the brim of his Stetson pulled down over his brow against the rising sun that was just now slipping above Johnson Mesa, five miles to the east. He raised his head and pulled his sunshades down his nose to peer at Curly over the rims.

"Morning, Sheriff," Curly said as he limped stiffly in the chilly morning air and fumbled with a large ring of keys to unlock the front door of the office.

"Curly," Trent answered, letting this chair drop to the ground. "And it's 'Deputy Sheriff' to you." He stood and stretched before following Curly inside.

The office smelled of stale cigarettes and grease and was stacked everywhere anyone looked with old newspapers and well-worn car magazines, along with years of dust. Heavy wooden shelves that lined the walls were overloaded with various used parts, starters, pulleys, belts, mirrors, and jars of about every size and type of hardware a body could possibly need. An old metal desk sat in the middle of the floor. It, too, was covered with a disarray of papers that looked like bills and invoices. Curly had moved his bulk around to the only chair in the room and plopped himself down with an audible sigh. The chair groaned and creaked as if in pain.

"We're getting too old to be getting up and around this time of day," he wheezed. He then pulled an inhaler out of the breast pocket of his greasy coveralls, put it to his mouth, and sucked on it noisily. He replaced it in his pocket, took a couple more deep breaths, and looked up at Trent with red-rimmed eyes.

"So – something I can do you for Sheriff – uh – I mean, Deputy?" Curly glanced out the screen door. "Don't believe I got any parts for that new Explorer you're driving out there." He dug into another pocket while he talked, produced a well-used red handkerchief, and blew his nose loudly.

"S'cuse me," he mumbled, wiping his nose back and forth. "Must be allergies. Or a storm comin'. Always starts to hit me when there's a storm in the air."

Trent grunted, pulled a photograph from inside his leather jacket, and slid it across the cluttered desk.

"Gray, '82 Jeep Scrambler, with a T-top. Involved in an accident – four years ago, Cordova Pass. I believe it was towed here to your place."

Curly glanced at the photo of the wrecked vehicle and back up at Trent with red eyes, nose running, and a general look on his face that pleaded silently that he not be asked to stand back up again. Trent glared back with no sympathy.

Curly sighed. "'82 Jeep, huh?" He pushed himself slowly away from the desk, and then with another loud groan forced his considerable bulk back up to his feet. He limped over to a shelf of ledgers, ran his fingers along their spines, grunted in satisfaction, and pulled a thick binder down. He manhandled it back to his desk where he let it drop loudly, sat back down, caught his breath for a minute, and opened it.

"'82 Jeep – '82 Jeep," he mumbled as he idly flipped pages. "What time of year did you say?"

"I didn't say," answered Trent. "But it would've been September – maybe early October before they got it towed in here. Anyway, fall of the year." His voice trailed away slightly as he caught a mental vision of shimmering gold aspen leaves and Vicky's crystal clear laughter echoing in his mind.

"Don't get too many Jeeps in here," Curly continued, licking a pudgy finger to more easily turn pages. "Hopefully, we didn't crush it and scrap it out. That would be the norm – wait a sec, here's something."

Curly's finger traced a page for details while his lips moved, reading to himself. Trent sighed impatiently.

"Care to read it out loud?" he chided.

Curly frowned up at him and read, "'82 Jeep Scrambler – totaled – September 29." He paused, stabbing the page. "Now, this is interesting. Says here, 'Do not scrap, per order of Colfax County Sheriff's Department – ongoing investigation.'" He stopped reading and squinted back up at Trent curiously. "Well, then, I suppose that's what you're doing here, isn't it – *investigating in an ongoing manner?*" Curly chuckled at his own joke. Trent did not.

"You reckon you still got it here – or not?" he asked gruffly. Curly stopped laughing and consulted the page once more, mumbling under his breath and tracing once more with a stained, pudgy finger.

"Yeah, it's here – southwest corner, Lot 3." Curly jerked his thumb over his shoulder vaguely. "Back that way." He glared up at Trent's unsympathetic eyes, sighed, and groaned as he got up again. "Guess I'll have to unlock the gate for you – but you're gonna have to go on back there and find it for yourself – these old knees of mine aren't up to a lot of walkin' around these days."

Trent followed as Curly shuffled out the door, around the opposite side of the house, and several yards down the driveway where a large, steel-framed gate covered in sheet metal was chained and padlocked. Curly fumbled once again with his keys, unsnapped the big padlock, and removed the chain, letting it fall to the ground heavily. He managed to pull one of the gates open just wide enough to let Trent through.

"Go on in, *Señor*," he said in a sudden friendly manner, gesturing with a flourish, his grin revealing a mouthful of crooked, nicotine-stained teeth.

Trent slipped sideways through the gate, took a couple of steps, but suddenly turned in a panic and shoved his way back out the gate just as two mangy looking pit bulls, who had appeared from amongst the nearby ruined hulks of vehicles, charged toward him, snarling and snapping, saliva slinging from their jaws. Curly slammed the gate loudly just as Trent made it through. The dogs jumped up and clawed on the opposite side, yelping and growling, slamming their bodies noisily against the sheet metal. Trent stood pushing both hands heavily against the gate, only to turn to look at Curly incredulously.

"What the hell, Curly?"

Curly doubled over with laughter, slapped his knee, and banged on the gate with his fist a couple of times. The dogs whimpered and got quiet.

"Guess I plumb forgot about the burglar alarm system," Curly chortled. Trent just looked at him and shook his head. "But you should see the look on your face!"

Curly moved to open the gate again, but Trent pushed back against it. "Oh, they're alright now," Curly said. "Zeus! Thunder!" he hollered as he motioned Trent away and opened the gate. The dogs nosed their way out excitedly, tails now wagging, and tongues slobbering as Curly petted them and roughed up their heads a bit. "Here – put your hand down here so they can smell you."

Trent held his hands up in mock surrender and took another step back. "No, I'm good – I'm just fine." The dogs came over to him anyway and milled around his legs, smelling his boots, sniffing his bandaged hand, and glancing up at him, lapping their mouths with wet tongues. He thought they still looked at him like he was breakfast. Curly whistled once and began shuffling back toward the office. The dogs promptly forgot Trent and loped eagerly after their owner. He stopped and opened the screen door and the dogs went inside. Curly looked back over at Trent.

"Now, don't you get lost in there. But not to worry – if I don't hear back from you in a couple hours, I'll just send the boys here back in to find you!" Curly chuckled again and disappeared inside.

#

Trent took another forty minutes of picking his way cautiously through the salvage yard before he found his wrecked Jeep that sat forlornly amongst an overgrowth of weeds and grass, sandwiched in between a rusted Buick sedan and a wrecked Ford Aerostar van. Trent had actually passed it once without recognizing it before doubling back when the row hit a dead-end.

When he finally identified it, he had to stop and take a breath.

It was one thing to see the aftermath of an accident in photographs; it was quite another to see it up close, in twisted steel.

The Jeep was bent almost double at mid-body from having rolled over and over down a mountainside. It was creased across the middle where the bed met the roll bar, which was probably the only part that had kept Trent and Vicky from being crushed beyond all recognition. The hood was torn half off its hinges and hung to one side, and the passenger side door was opened slightly and folded over. He caught his breath and cringed as he realized that was where Vicky had been seated. He stepped timidly over an axle, which was loose and lay separately now with one wheel and tire still attached. Trent stopped just short of the passenger door, then reached over and touched the handle with two fingers of his bandaged hand. He pulled slightly and the door creaked and fell open. He stepped closer and peered into the seat area. The leather seats had been weathered and torn by time as well as animals and birds, and the seat frame itself had been twisted and laid skewed across the dashboard and crammed underneath the steering column, which itself had doubled back until the steering wheel lay mashed flat against the other door frame.

Trent didn't know what he had expected to see – maybe blood – and he was relieved that there was none to be seen – or maybe even Vicky's missing shoe. He cautiously reached across and, after a couple of attempts, wrenched the glove box open, but found nothing there either, its contents having probably been emptied during the initial investigation.

Trent stepped back and took a deep breath and after a few seconds remembered the photo in his pocket. He slipped it out again and began studying it. He squinted closely, then after putting the picture back in his pocket, moved toward the right front wheel well of the Jeep. This part of the wreck was wrenched upwards and away from the ground so that the wheel actually lay horizontal and almost at the level of Trent's waist. He recalled from the investigative report that this was the tire that had presumably blown out. He leaned over and peered across the ruined tire back into the exposed wheel well itself and ran his fingers along the wall of the rotten tire and the various fibers from the composite rubberized materials that poked from several torn areas. The damage was so severe, and so much time had passed that the cause of blowout would now be nearly impossible to determine. Trent removed his hat and leaned over the tire until he could almost put his head into the wheel well and peered underneath. He reached in and ran his hand slowly along the interior metal wall, careful about any protruding sharp areas. He suddenly felt something odd, moved his fingers back and forth over a small area, and cautiously stepped back. He took a small flashlight from his pocket, flicked it on, and bent forward once more, playing the light over the same area he had found with his fingers.

He reached back inside along the metal wheel well, felt for a moment, searching the area, and suddenly pushed a fingertip straight into a good-sized hole. He couldn't quite tell for sure what he had felt, but whatever it was didn't feel normal. He twisted his finger gently in the smooth sided hole, his mind considering the possibilities, and stood up to more closely examine the tire again, around the area of the blowout.

Trent stepped back, rubbed his chin, and pulled the photograph out of his pocket and peered down at it. He once again looked back and forth from the photo to the vehicle and stepped in closer to look at the crumpled passenger door. He leaned down and stretched out his hand until it touched the large creases that ran from corner to corner where it had crumpled in the rollover. He ran his forefinger along the seam of each one, but suddenly stopped. He knelt down on one knee and brought his light to bear at the spot where his finger had stopped.

There it was – what he had been looking for – what he felt certain had drawn his attention back in his office earlier, what he now felt certain Vicky had been trying to tell him. His finger probed an almost identical hole, exactly the same size and shape that he had found in the wheel well; these holes, due to their close similarity, couldn't have occurred during a typical rollover.

The holes could only have been from one other particular source: bullets.

Bullet holes – and judging from their shape, size, and similar trajectory, fired from a high-velocity rifle.

A bullet – *a bullet hole*, not a pothole – had blown out that tire.

Trent suddenly felt lightheaded; he staggered back, turned, and sat down heavily on the ground. The accident hadn't been an accident after all.

He hadn't killed his wife – the accident had not been his fault.

Beginning to feel numb, as if the world was spinning about him, he put his head between his knees and began to shiver and hyperventilate. He felt like he was about to throw up. He took deep breaths, and suddenly froze as he caught *her* scent – and felt her unmistakable presence once again. He looked up, tried to focus, but everything continued to slowly spin: he felt himself losing control. He leaned his head back against the damaged door panel, squeezed his eyes shut, and began rocking back and forth.

When he opened them again, he was still seated beside the wrecked Jeep, but now, he was back on Cordova Pass, down the side of a steep embankment, in the middle of a peaceful meadow where the wreck had finally come to a rest.

Trent shook his head slowly and moaned as the waking nightmare began again and lost memories began flooding in.

#

A field of wildflowers stretches away from him as far as he can see, dancing in the afternoon breeze, and the golden aspen trees shimmer overhead. The Jeep lies on its left side, its right wheel spinning just above him with the inertia of the rollover; dust billows around them; he isn't alone, but sits stunned while cradling and rocking Vicky, her bloody and ruined head in his arms and lap, her beautiful hair shrouding the worst of her wounds; her beautiful, but vacant eyes staring ahead, sightlessly. Trent himself is badly hurt, but he is oblivious to exactly what those injuries are or whether all of this blood he is trying to wipe away from Vicky's face and hair is hers, his, or a mixture of both. All he knows is they are both terribly injured, and somehow, he has gotten them both out of the wreckage; but they have collapsed here beside the mangled Jeep.

He moans and calls to her frantically, repeating, "No, no, no," tears dropping onto her waxen face and mingling with the blood. He puts his cheek next to hers and whispers her name over and over into her bloody ear.

Then, he remembers small details: coming to after the Jeep had stopped its fateful roll, finding himself draped over the steering wheel, his torso hanging half out of the shattered windscreen; his seatbelt had torn loose at some point in the rollover and his chest and sides burn with broken ribs. He recalls trying to move, feeling disembodied, in shock, and somewhere down deep his mind telling him to stay still, that it suspects he has other critical injuries. But then he had opened his eyes to see Vicky slumped and hanging over him, still strapped into her seatbelt and her head dripping blood all over his shirt; in an adrenaline rush, he ignored what his mind and the pain were telling him and he had somehow pulled himself up to a crouching position, straddling what was left of the steering column. He had struggled to get her seatbelt unlatched, and when he finally did their combined weight had caused them both to spill out of the wreckage onto the grass. He remembers the blinding pain exploding through his body, but he had somehow, after an excruciating amount of time, been able to push and pull himself to this sitting position, with his wife's broken body draped across his lap.

"Please, baby girl, please – please – come back – please!"

He rocks and moans and rocks some more and cries and plants numerous kisses on her blood-matted hair, willing her to come back to him. He looks around frantically, desperate for help – from anywhere – but he knows they are miles from anywhere and that it is getting late in the day, and the chances are slim of any more sightseers coming up this old road today. Suddenly, he hears someone screaming hysterically, uncontrollably, like a wounded animal – before realizing they are his screams.

In that horrible moment, and for the first time within this dream within a dream, Trent remembers everything.

Instant clarity floods his mind and he knows exactly what happened. And he sees himself continuing to wipe Vicky's head with her own hair, vainly attempting to staunch the blood flowing from what he now knows is the gaping, grotesque exit wound that a high-powered bullet has blown out the side of her crushed head. And he kisses her dead lips and his tears splash into her blood on her cheeks and he moans and sobs as her blank, unseeing eyes stare back him, her pupils fixed and dilated.

He then hears another noise – a distant but unmistakable sound of an engine – and looks up to see a black pickup has pulled to a stop on the road, maybe 75 yards above him. At first he feels elation as he spies two men standing beside the vehicle and tries to raise his arm to wave, but a rush of pain reminds him that the arm, too, is broken and useless. All he can do is grimace at them and shout and wonder after a few moments why they just stand there, watching – just watching, and smiling.

His excitement at being rescued soon turns to dread, then to horror as he watches one of the men, the heavier blond-headed one of the two, raise what looks to be a rifle, and the sun flashes a reflection on what must be a scope. He thinks he recognizes them as the two men who had stopped to chat on the road earlier.

He watches, incredulously, as one of them pulls back the bolt of the rifle and slams another shell back home into the chamber.

He screams and screams again – but this time in a carnal anger that wells up inside him. He hugs Vicky's shattered head to his breast and screams so long and hard that he feels the blood vessels actually bursting in his throat, and feels his eyes bulging, and his mind becoming unhinged, and his thoughts swelling like straining balloons until they, too, burst in confusion. All he can now do is to channel all that screaming anger like venomous arrows straight at the two men who have obviously caused all this – who have torn his precious Vicky from him – and who are about to...

But suddenly, there is another awful flash as Trent feels something viciously slam the front of his head, causing it to jerk back hard and crash into the hood of the wrecked Jeep; then as the darkness quickly pulls him in close, he feels Vicky's head slip helplessly out of his arms and watches with his last bit of blurred vision as her body flops limply onto the ground.

As he also begins to slump over on top of her, the last sensation he is aware of in this nightmare world is the sharp, delayed crack of the distant rifle shot.

#

A familiar, angry buzzing grew more insistent as the darkness finally faded. Trent became aware of a vague hissing noise behind the buzzing; as he forced open his eyes, he found himself still seated on the ground beside the rusted wreck of his Jeep in the salvage yard, rocking slowly back and forth with his back against the ruined passenger door and cradling his knees in his arms. His cheek rested on his forearm as he stared off into the distance.

Suddenly, a crash of thunder awakened him from his stupor; he raised his head with a start and realized that he was wet. For a moment, he thought he was still covered in blood, but a quick inspection showed him there was no blood; there was only rain. There was no meadow, no aspens – no Vicky – only the cleansing rain and his fresh revelations of bullets, murder – and death.

Trent never wanted to see or remember her that way ever again, but he knew the images were forever seared on his mind – that part of his brain that had closed itself off to him, mercifully, for the last few years – and that those memories were now back, with a vengeance.

The insistent buzzing reinserted itself irritatingly into his consciousness, and with it came the realization of one final mystery he had finally remembered. He touched the burning scar at his hairline again, the one that he now knew had been caused by a bullet that had creased his forehead – a bullet that had been meant to kill him and had been fired at him by the same gun and by the same men who had shot and killed Vicky and had left them both for dead – Carl Neumann and that friend of his, Jimmy Streck.

The memories were, at last, back, but the only real satisfaction Trent now felt at all was the knowledge that he hadn't caused his wife's death after all, at least not directly.

Indirectly, though, he knew that he had – because of his investigations into all those cold murder cases. He had obviously been getting too close to the truth, like a jigsaw puzzle that was slowly coming together one frustrating piece at a time.

And his beautiful, innocent Vicky had paid the price.

The buzzing now clawed at him; Trent reached into his shirt pocket and pulled out his cell phone. He flipped it open and raised it to his ear without speaking.

"Daddy?"

Trent sobbed once involuntarily, then wiped the rain from his face, trying to compose himself.

"Daddy, are you there?" Sophie sounded frantic. "Can you hear me? What's wrong?"

"Yeah, Baby – I'm here," Trent answered finally, his voice barely above a whisper.

"I can hardly hear you, Dad – where are you? Are you alright?"

Trent took the phone from his ear and looked around. His Stetson lay soaking on the ground. He painfully unfolded his limbs and slowly stood. He bent over, grabbed the hat, and shoved it on his head. The rain made a comforting pattering noise on the brim of his hat. He started walking, then stopped and returned to the wrecked Jeep. He put the phone back to his ear. "I'm okay, Sophie. Just a second, okay?"

He switched the phone to camera mode and focused it at the smashed passenger door panel. He zoomed in on the bullet hole and clicked the shutter a few times. He put the phone back to his ear and started walking again.

"I'm okay, Baby. Just a little damp." He paused for a minute, and then continued. "And just a little shook up, I guess."

"Why? What happened?"

"Nothing that won't wait." He hesitated, looked around to find his bearings, made a guess, and began walking again until he saw the gate. "I'll tell you – soon as I get back."

The rain continued to increase and thunder rumbled in the distance. Trent was now soaked to the skin, but he didn't care.

"Dad?" she continued, uncertainly.

"I'm remembering some more things, Soph. A lot of things," he hesitated. "And they're pretty important. They explain a lot. I'll tell you all about it when I get there. I promise."

"Well, it's ironic you say that," she answered. "Because I've got something you need to know, too. I got more of that Otto Eberhardt's journal translated, and – well, you're just not going to believe this." She paused. "Are you out in the rain? It sounds like you're outside!"

Trent rubbed his face against his jacket sleeve. "Yeah," he croaked, glancing up at the sky. "I'm afraid I'm getting good and soaked. You better put the coffee on. And call that partner of ours – Hector." He paused and could imagine her eyes rolling. "Get him over to the house. We've all got a lot of work to do." He had reached the gate, pushed his way through, and began to walk toward his cruiser.

"Uh – Hector's here already, Dad."

"Now, why does that not surprise me in the least?" Trent muttered.

"Dad, you need to listen to me. You remember that old German rancher you went to talk to – the one over near Clayton?"

"Yeah – old man Neumann – the guy who was burned real bad years back. Sits around that dying peach orchard all day. Real piece of work that guy – real sweetheart." Trent was finally back in the car, had started it up, and turned the heater on high.

"Yes, he's the one – only, turns out he's not the one, after all," she continued, cryptically.

"What are you talking about?"

"Well, I think you were right about who your John Doe might be – from under the theater?" She paused and then went on in the silence. "Dad, I think it must be Otto Eberhardt, himself – the one who wrote this journal!"

"Why do you think that?" he asked. "Couldn't it easily be the other guy, too – that old Nazi he escaped with?" He sat back and sighed, suddenly exhausted. "Shoot, could be anybody, for all we know."

"Well, it's pretty obvious, to me at least, after what I just read in his journal. Dad, where I now am in the translation, Eberhardt has identified old man Neumann as the one behind all of this – all the years of unsolved murders, and everything – maybe even behind whatever it is you have to tell me." She paused again.

Trent remained silent for a long time. He had just turned back through town, and was heading toward the turnoff that would take him up the side of the mesa to his house.

"Dad, you still there?"

"Go on," he finally uttered.

"Well, Otto wrote that he was getting afraid for his life – that he might even be killed for what he knows. And then there was this awful fire, and his sweetheart Evie gets killed, and also the old Nazi got killed – and Neumann lived – but then Otto goes on to say that it wasn't Neumann after all!"

"Sophie, you're not making a bit of sense," he interjected. His forehead was burning again.

Sophie hesitated, took a deep breath, and continued excitedly. "Otto wrote that years later he discovered Neumann wasn't who he said he was. He was actually that other German, the escaped Nazi, who escaped with him." She paused again.

"Dad, it's really Ernst Brandt! Ernst was injured in the fire, but he lived. And he's been posing for the last fifty years as Conrad Neumann." Sophie stopped, but continued when Trent remained quiet. "Dad, he," she stammered, then continued. "Brandt's still alive! He's old man Neumann – after all these years, an escaped Nazi, hiding out on that ranch, right under everyone's noses!"

Trent pulled the truck to a stop in the middle of the road and just sat there, numb, his mind reeling now at all of the information – old and new – that it was trying to absorb. *If the old Nazi is still alive*, he thought to himself, *then what does this all add up to?*

Suddenly, he had a vision of all those boxes of cold cases lining themselves up neatly on his office floor, crying out to him.

"Dad?"

Trent stared dumbly down the roadway and up the side of the mesa ahead. He could just glimpse the back deck of his house about a quarter mile away through the rain.

"Dad, are you still there?"

Trent looked down at the phone in his hand, barely comprehending the tinny voice emanating from its small speaker. He raised it slowly to his ear.

"I'm here, Sofe," he mumbled.

"Dad? You okay? You sound strange."

"Sophie," he started to say, then stopped.

"Yes, Daddy?"

"Sofe," he hesitated, wondering how to continue.

"Sophie, your Mom was murdered."

CHAPTER 26
MAN OF CONSTANT SORROWS

Excerpt from the Journal of Otto Eberhardt

"23.10.72 – I am at my wit's end, on the run again, and this time not only from the devil himself, but from the devil's spawn! I fear this will be the last entry I make in this journal, for I must do something to keep it out of Ernst's hands! I must hide it where he will never suspect – perhaps right here. It will surely be the last place on earth where he would think to look."

#

Otto lay very still in the darkness, not daring to breathe for fear that not only the fog from his breath, but the noise of the very blood pumping loudly through his heart and veins would betray him and that the judgment from the past twenty-five years would descend upon him in a fury.

He was lying in the crawl space underneath the cabin on Evie's old ranch, Montaña del Sol, a place that should have held such tender, if bittersweet, memories for Otto – memories of where he and Evie had really last been happy, if only for a few weeks. Evie's father was now long since dead, and her brother Richard now ran the place – Richard, who even more so than Ernst or Carl held more terror for Otto this night; Richard, who, after all, had beaten Otto to within an inch of his life when he had caught him with his Evie. Had it not been for the intervention of Werner Van Ryan – and Ernst – Otto felt certain he would have died that day. Right now, he wondered if that wouldn't have been more merciful.

He lay still now, his mind amplifying every sound of the night – each creaking of a tree limb bending with the wind, every distant call of the night owl, the cough of a bobcat or fox – even the scuffling of small creatures scurrying outside along the cabin walls, or even the mice scratching in the corners of this crawlspace. Listening from within this cramped, dusty space to what should have been the soothing sounds of the night now shouted impending doom to him.

He was fairly certain he had eluded Carl, whom he knew Ernst had sent to hunt him down after he had fled the Neumann Ranch two days ago, with only his journal, Evie's diary, the clothes on his back, and whatever other small personal items he could stuff in a knapsack – including Caroline's beloved doll, Irina. The doll was, after all, what had precipitated the confrontation that had eventually led to Otto running for his life.

#

Along with Evie, then, Conrad Neumann, not Ernst, had died in the flames fifteen years ago. Otto now wondered to what extent Ernst had been willing to go to perpetrate such a long and brutal psychological war against him.

This is not how you die! I have "special plans" for you.

The words haunted him now – the cryptic threat Ernst had given him at the barn that night, right after he had dragged Otto out of harm's way, and then gone back inside and doused everything with gasoline, and in the process inadvertently – supposedly – caught himself on fire. Ironically, Otto was the one who had braved the flames to go back in to drag Ernst out – even though he had thought he had actually saved Evie's husband, Conrad. Had Ernst known he would do that? Had that rescue turned out to have been the beginnings of Ernst's elaborate scheme of torment and revenge against Otto? If so, Otto was amazed at the patience and resilience – and the willingness to sacrifice his own body to the flames – of his former commanding officer.

He should have left immediately after discovering Ernst's true identity, but against his better judgment Otto had stayed out of a continued sense of responsibility toward Evie's children, Carl and Caroline. He had made sure they had never learned of their father's fate, nor of the true identity of the man now posing as their so-called father – this brutal stranger – this serial killer.

Caroline had subsequently continued to grow closer to Otto over time, but conversely, Ernst had managed to turn Carl against Otto, often talking to the boy until late at night, murmuring quietly together in Ernst's room, often until late at night, gaining the trust that Carl had never developed with his real father, regaling him with wild stories of mystery and war and murder, with veiled Nazi philosophies, and sowing seeds of distrust regarding Otto's own motives and background.

Ernst/"Neumann" had continued to heal to the point where he could get out and do some activities on his own again; at that time, he began taking Carl hunting with him – sometimes for days, leaving Otto in charge of running the work of the ranch, as usual. They would return, often with traces of blood on their clothing and vehicles, but very rarely with any game they had supposedly killed. Otto's trepidations grew when he had overheard Carl threatening his sister one evening as she sat down in the orchard, watering the flowers on her mother's grave. He had pulled a .22 pistol from his belt, waved it around, and pointed it at her, telling her he could shoot her "just as easy as one of those wetbacks!"

Otto had immediately intervened, taken the pistol away from Carl, and reprimanded him with such an air of righteous authority Carl was taken aback for a moment, but then Carl had sneered at him. "You can't tell me what to do, you damned Kraut! You aren't my father!" He had clinched his fists and put his defiant face inches from Otto's, and for a minute, Otto thought the six-foot tall, muscular teenager was going to hit him. In a few seconds, he had backed off, looked Otto up and down, and laughed in derision.

"Don't you ever talk to me that way again! You work for the Neumanns, which means me! Now give me my gun back, asshole!"

Otto had just shaken his head slowly, opened the cylinder of the pistol, emptied the bullets onto the ground at Carl's feet, and deliberately shoved it into his own belt, all the while never taking his eyes away from Carl's. He coolly motioned for Caroline to come with him, and turned and walked quietly away hand-in-hand with her to the house, leaving Carl fuming and sputtering in the orchard.

#

Still, Otto had stayed.

Two years later in 1967, on his eighteenth birthday, Carl had enlisted in the Marines and spent the next four years completing back-to-back tours of Vietnam. He wrote letters back home to Ernst, whom he still fully believed was his father, Conrad Neumann, and occasionally, Otto sneaked a look at a letter. They were filled with lurid details of his missions into the jungles of Southeast Asia, describing the horror and blood with a relish only someone in the mold of Ernst Brandt would appreciate.

Otto knew that he had now lost any influence at all on the boy and that this alienation, too, was part of Ernst's elaborate "special plan" of retribution he had for him.

The building tension had all come to a head six months after Carl's return from Vietnam. He came home a fully formed fighting machine whose eyes now held the constant, cold dullness of a seasoned killer, deferring to no one but his "father," who took delight now in allowing his so-called "son" to take full rein in the business affairs of the ranch – yet another slap in the face to Otto, who had actually built the success of the Neumann Ranch over the past fifteen years, not Ernst, and certainly not Carl. With Carl's ascendancy, Otto felt relegated once again to the role of that tired, persecuted, directionless ranch hand that Conrad Neumann had hired off the streets of Clayton, New Mexico, all those years ago.

The ultimate blow came with Carl's decision to suddenly have his now twenty-two year old sister committed to the state mental hospital at Las Vegas, New Mexico, within just a few weeks of his return. Although she had continued to be the same quiet, soft-spoken girl she had always been growing up, Caroline was now an adult living in her own world, and an embarrassment to both Carl and Ernst/"Neumann," who, of course, had never had patience for her at all.

Only a few fabricated stories to the proper authorities, a couple of signatures, and Caroline's fate was sealed.

The day the car had arrived from the hospital, Caroline had clung to Otto on the porch, scared to death, sobbing and begging not to go. Otto had hugged her for the longest time, but as the men in white coats had finally walked up to get her, Otto had reluctantly let go of her, struggling with himself as they dragged her screaming to the car. After all, he had no legal rights to stop this. Halfway down the steps, she had dropped Irina and had screamed and kicked even harder. Otto stepped quickly to retrieve the doll, but by the time he had picked it up, the door had slammed and the car pulled away with a roar of an accelerating engine and a cloud of dust. When the dust had cleared, Caroline's weeping face had been framed in the rear window with her splayed hands against the glass. Otto had kept his eyes on her until the car was a mere speck on the horizon.

#

Barely a week later now, Otto rolled onto his side in this cramped crawl space under the cabin, trying to get comfortable and get some sleep. He had pried the lid off of an old abandoned trunk nearby with his knife, pulled out some moth-eaten clothes, rolled them into a makeshift pillow, and spread a few of the others over him to serve as a blanket. Of course, he could have utilized the bed above him in the cabin, but he dared not be caught up there, nor disturb anything there in case someone was to enter and find objects tampered with and hamper his ultimate getaway.

Otto got as comfortable as he could, the night noises that had troubled him earlier finally fading to the background of his consciousness. He allowed his mind to drift again, back to the final events a couple of days ago that had led to this predicament.

#

He had been working some cattle out on the rim of the canyon and had finished his work late and come home exhausted. Wanting to clean up, have some dinner, and go to bed, he had headed down the hall only to find the door to his room ajar and Carl inside ransacking the place.

"What the hell do you think you're doing?" Otto had demanded. He had stood in the doorway in shock. His bed was upturned, the bedclothes strewn about, along with his clothes that had been yanked out of dresser drawers that had been upturned on the floor. Carl stood halfway inside the closet, ignoring him, pulling more clothes off of hangers, feeling through them, and then tossing them aside. When he was done, he began searching the shelves. He finally turned and looked at Otto as if he had simply been caught in the cookie jar.

He shrugged.

"The old man wants to know where Mom's diary is," he uttered as a matter of fact. He had turned around now and faced Otto. "So where is it?" he insisted with cold malevolence.

"What diary?" Otto lied. Even as he uttered it, he felt the blood drain from his face. *How on earth did they find out about Evie's diary?*

Carl allowed a quick smile to flit across his face and took a couple of menacing steps toward Otto. He looked down at the floor, pushed some clothes around with his foot, bent over, and picked up Caroline's doll that had been in one of the drawers. He turned it over and pulled at the seam along its back to expose an empty cavity within the doll's body.

"The same diary that my sister once kept inside this stupid doll of hers – you know – the diary she gave to you?" He paused, seeing Otto's blank reactions, then continued condescendingly. "Oh please! Just who do you think you're talking to? Don't you think I remember seeing my mother writing in her precious book, especially when my father wasn't around?"

Carl had taken another step and now was only a couple of feet from Otto. He tossed the doll lightly from one hand to another.

"After she died, I always wondered what had happened to it. Oh, I searched for it, everywhere. And it wasn't til the other day, when I overheard my stupid sister talking to her stupid doll, telling it she was so glad she didn't have to hide mother's diary anymore that I put two and two together."

Carl advanced even closer to Otto, now holding the doll up into his face and grimacing at him as he continued. "And it was only when I slapped the little bitch around some that she confessed. Imagine my surprise when she told me who she gave the diary to?"

Otto clinched his fists and lifted himself onto the balls of his feet, anger welling up inside at the thought of Carl laying a hand on his helpless sister.

"I would not know what you are talking about," Otto muttered finally, and turned away from Carl before he did anything stupid.

"Don't walk away from me, asshole – it's not polite," Carl snarled. "And you very well know that diary is rightfully mine! So, where is it?"

Otto had stopped suddenly just outside the door. Ernst had been blocking the middle of the hallway, standing there balanced on his cane, watching and listening with a smirk on his ruined, burned face. "Why, what on earth is going on here?" he had croaked, feigning innocence. He limped closer, squeezed passed Otto's shoulder, and peered around the doorframe. He had clucked his tongue in disapproval. "Oh, looks like you have quite a mess in here – maybe quite a few messes, you think?"

He had turned to look at Otto with his one clear eye, his hideous face only inches away, and lowered his voice so only Otto could hear. "I am sure that, after all these years, we are all entitled to know what juicy secrets the lovely Miss Evie chose to keep from everyone, wouldn't you say, Otto?" He had smiled at Otto as if they shared an unspoken secret, which, of course, they did. He scratched at the pink, obscenely bubbled nub where his ear used to be.

Otto leaned close to Ernst's good ear and whispered harshly: "You can go straight to hell – *Herr Oberst!*" Carl had still been out of earshot, but had made a move to intervene. Ernst waved him away.

"That's alright, Carl. Let's leave Otto to clean up his own messes here. Perhaps he will discover something he would like to share later – or, perhaps he will not." Ernst moved away, his voice echoing down the hall. "And then we shall, perhaps, have to let Carl make some – other decisions, yes?"

Ernst and Carl left him alone after exchanging sinister smiles, Carl bumping Otto with his shoulder as he passed, but not before shoving the rag doll hard into his chest. "Here's something to help you sleep tonight, you son-a-bitch," he growled as he pushed on past him.

Later that night, when the house was dark and everyone else was sleeping, Otto had gathered a few clothes and the doll, opened the window of his room, and climbed out. He silently crept down to Evie's peach orchard and knelt at her grave. After a moment of silence, he looked around cautiously before reaching down and carefully pulling up some of the roses planted there, ignoring the thorns that tore into his palms. A few inches underneath, he dug up a parcel wrapped tightly in plastic that had been buried there. He had brushed the dirt off and pulled the plastic open to check on the contents. Inside, he had found what he knew would be there – his old journal and Evie's diary, along with his packet of old letters and some other documents. He shoved them into his knapsack, quickly replanted the flowers, and tamped them down. His mission accomplished, he had stood up, wiped his hands on his jeans, and kissed his fingertips before touching them to Evie's engraved name.

"Farewell, my precious One," he had whispered, the emotion welling up inside his throat. Looking around once more and quietly listening, he had finally crept away through the orchard and across a pasture meadow until he had reached the stream that he followed west.

By sunrise he had gotten eight miles away, along what was called the Dry Cimarron, keeping to the rocky ravines and creek beds to minimize his tracks, before finally thumbing a ride at a spot where the stream crossed underneath the highway. They had driven ever westward, through the sleepy village of Folsom – named after prehistoric remains discovered there a hundred years ago – and over the top of Johnson Mesa's windswept, sprawling grasslands to where it eventually dropped back down into Yankee Canyon.

Here, Otto had the driver drop him off. Watching until the car disappeared around a curve, he had left the highway and hiked the final few miles cross-country, keeping to the shadows of the tree lines until he crossed a fence onto what he knew was Montaña del Sol ranchland. Here, he knew he would find a temporary hiding place for himself if he was very careful – and hopefully, a more permanent one for his sensitive documents.

#

Now here he lay in the dusty, cramped crawlspace underneath the old adobe line shack, which held nothing for him but memories of his beloved Evie. He dozed fitfully for a couple of hours; just before dawn he tried to stretch the stiffness from his bones before cautiously opening the trap door an inch or two, listening hard, and squinting out into the dim light of the one room cabin. After assuring himself he was quite alone, he slowly emerged, like from a tomb, and stood still in the middle of the room, gripping his journal in both hands and thinking for awhile. He felt completely at odds with himself; part of him didn't want to let the journal out of his sight, yet another side of him felt desperately compelled to hide it someplace safe.

But where?

He stepped over to the small bookcase in the corner, started to slip it in with the other volumes on the shelves, but thought better. He looked around again before making up his mind. He let himself quickly back down the trap door, wrapped the journal up in the old clothes he had used for a bed, and placed them carefully in the bottom of the old trunk before shutting it firmly. Not the best hiding place, but maybe not the first place someone would think to look.

Ten minutes later, Otto Eberhardt stepped lightly onto the porch, gently closed the front door behind him, adjusted his backpack, and stepped quickly back into the nearby trees that were just now beginning to cast faint shadows as the sun broke over the horizon. He squatted down and became very still, just another shadow. Here, he quietly watched the familiar ranch come slowly awake a third of a mile away down the valley below him: the back screen door of the big house slamming as an overweight Mexican cook came out to toss breakfast scraps to a couple of cats who crowded around her legs, and ranch hands stepping out of their bunkhouse sipping from coffee mugs, stretching and lighting cigarettes before shuffling over to the stable area.

Suddenly, Otto caught his breath and almost stood up in shock.

Out of the big double doors of the stables briskly stepped a beautiful young woman pulling a buckskin mare by the reins. From this distance, she appeared to be quite young, given the spring to her step and the way her dungarees and jean jacket clung to her girlish figure. She stopped the mare to adjust the saddle cinch, removed her wide brimmed straw hat, and ran her fingers through familiar shoulder length black hair while turning her light complexioned face to the sunrise, closing her eyes, and smiling.

For a long minute – maybe two – Otto sat with his eyes wide and his mouth open, barely breathing; if he didn't know it was already impossible, he could swear that he had gone back in time and was basking once again in the stunning presence of the young Evie Van Ryan, preparing for her morning ride.

"Margot," a man's voice echoed faintly from beyond her. The girl turned back toward the main house. At first Otto couldn't see where the disembodied voice had come from, but subsequently recognized the tall, fit figure of a middle-aged man step from the shadows of the front porch, sipping steaming coffee.

The man was Richard Van Ryan, the one who had almost beaten Otto to death years ago. He was much older now, with graying hair at his temples. But if the girl was someone named 'Margot,' and not Evie, just who was she?

"You don't be gone too long this morning, you hear?" Richard continued. "Gonna need you to go to town later with your mama – help with the shopping."

"Alright, Papa," the girl replied with the reluctant tone of a teenager, then raised and placed her left boot in the stirrup and pulled herself into the saddle. She clucked to the horse, which briskly cantered away from the stable, across the pastures and to this side of the little valley – *right toward where Otto was hidden!* As the girl on her horse trotted nearer, he held his breath again, watching her face become clearer and more detailed, and began to feel panicked.

She looked briefly over toward the little cabin and the line of trees nestled around it – seemingly directly into Otto's face. He froze, sure that she had seen him, and waited for her surprised shout that would certainly alert the entire ranch below. Instead, she turned her lovely face and directed the mare to continue loping on past, turning her smiling eyes back toward the sunrise as she and the horse began to grow smaller again.

She hadn't seen him.

Otto let out his breath slowly and stood up shakily. He adjusted the knapsack on his shoulder and turned to watch the young girl called Margot – his precious Evie's look-alike – disappear over the next hilltop. He hitched his pants up, glanced back down at the ranch buildings, and cautiously stepped back to fade away into the woods.

#

Father Michael Shannon sat back in his desk chair and stretched his sore joints. He had been hard at work on his homily for Sunday and now needed a break. He turned and gazed out the window, affording him a beautiful view of the tree-lined rose garden situated between the parish offices and the church. The garden was shaded by blue spruce along the edges with a large cottonwood in the middle and bursting with color from the variety of roses and irises planted in a design that, if viewed from the third story where his office was located, depicted a huge sundial, bisected by a large, rugged cross formed by pink flagstones with a crown of rose bushes at the head of the cross.

Father Michael watched as a middle-aged gardener diligently raked and weeded under the bushes, scooping up the results of his work with a spade and depositing them into a small wheelbarrow. Father Michael smiled. He vicariously enjoyed watching the man's hard work. He had only recently hired the handyman, as much an act of charity as of need, but he had so far been very impressed with the man's work ethic.

The man had given his name as Frank Smith, which Father had known was an obvious falsehood as the man spoke with a trace of a European accent of some kind and carried the worried look of a man who didn't want to be recognized. His hair was clean and neat, but he wore it fashionably long; he sported a full but evenly trimmed beard that was beginning to show some gray, and usually wore a Dallas Cowboys cap pulled down low on his forehead, hiding his eyes.

Father Michael had met him over the winter when the man had become a regular, though quiet and unassuming, at mass, and at the weekly soup kitchen. Father knew that Frank had probably only been escaping the cold and the hard times, but unlike several others who were down on their luck and haunted the church, Father Michael had never noticed him inebriated, panhandling, or hanging around in the seedier areas of town. In fact, Frank had always managed to scrounge up enough odd jobs to make his meager ends meet. However, when he inquired of the man as to where he lived, Frank had told him reluctantly that he slept wherever he could; alley doorways, sheds, or occasionally on a good citizen's sofa in exchange for some work.

Eventually, Father Michael took pity and helped Frank rent a small two room house within walking distance of the church by putting up a damage deposit from his own pocket and promising the landlord that if anything at all went wrong with the arrangement, the church would step up and make it right. Of course, nothing of the sort happened, and after getting to know him for a few weeks, Father had offered Frank the job as groundskeeper.

The getting-to-know-him part had been difficult and intriguing, though. Today, as the priest stepped out into the fresh air and flowery scents of the garden and walked over to where Frank was hard at work, he carried two ice-cold soft drinks in bottles. The priest stood there for a moment not wanting to startle him, then cleared his throat.

"Think it's time for a break, don't you, Frank?" The gardener straightened up, turned, and grinned at the priest.

"I would not mind that at all, Father," he answered in a measured, precise voice as he smiled. Father Michael wondered once again about the man's accent – he still couldn't quite place it. Frank removed his cap and wiped the sweat from his eyes and brow with the sleeve of his work shirt. The priest moved a step closer, smiled and pointed at Frank's cap.

"Bet you get more than a little razzing about that cap," he chuckled.

"Razzing?" Frank asked, uncertainly.

"*Cowboys,*" Father Michael explained. "Most folks around here are die-hard Denver Broncos fans." He produced a bottle opener and popped the caps from the bottles with a frosty hiss.

"What good is a priest without a church key," he quipped and chuckled at his own joke. He sat down on a flagstone ledge under the shade of the cottonwood tree and gestured for Frank to do the same. They toasted one another with a clink of their cola bottles and both guzzled them with long, satisfying gulps. Father Michael was the first to belch.

"Pardon me – not very respectable for a Man of God, I guess," he laughed. "But sometimes you have to do what you have to do."

Frank looked at him curiously, smiled, and covered his mouth with a sleeve to burp in turn.

"Thank you," he acknowledged with a smile, took another grateful sip of the cold carbonated soda, glancing back over at Father Michael, taking his measure. "You are not like most priests I have known," he offered.

"Oh? And just how many priests would you say you've known?"

Frank looked down at the ground and scratched his beard. "Well, matter of fact, other than a couple I ran into in the army, you are about the only one, I guess."

"The army? What unit?"

Frank suddenly let that vacant look slip back over his face and turned away. "I do not really like to dwell on that part of my life," he answered after a brief silence, taking another long pull on his drink.

The priest didn't pursue the question, and they both sat there drinking and staring off into the distance. The drowsy drone of nearby bees floated on the warm air. Presently, Frank sat his bottle down on the flagstone wall they were sitting on, folded his arms, and took a breath.

"Father – may I ask you a question?"

"Of course!"

"A few Sundays ago you taught that a man's faith is only as strong as his trust in the Lord."

"Yes – that's right."

"And that faith in the Lord, and His forgiveness, is free to us all, correct?"

"Well, yes – to a point."

"But then you said last week that if we fail to forgive others, we are blocking the full blessing that God means for us to have? That it is, therefore, dependent on my willingness to forgive others?"

Father Michael chuckled again. "I'm very pleased to see you've been listening so closely to my sermons, Frank. I wish all my parishioners paid attention like that. I'm afraid many of them are only there for the free soup!" He looked up at Frank who said nothing, but sat looking at him with a serious look, waiting for a serious answer.

"I'm sorry, Frank. I apologize. I can see you're being sincere, and here I am making light of things. It's a fault of mine." The priest set the bottle down, shifted his weight, and turned to face Frank. "Yes. I believe that's exactly what I said last week – forgiveness is the primary action of Our Father, expressed through His Son. And we are to follow the same principal in our lives, offering forgiveness to those who have trespassed against us."

"Then why, Father, would God allow such hurt and evil to continue in a world where so much needs to be forgiven? Is there so much unforgiveness out there that it is beyond the Lord's ability? I mean, the God I read about in the Bible was just as unforgiving at times. He wiped out entire nations, including women and children and animals. Is this forgiveness?" Frank paused, thought another moment, and continued, "And if God can exact such vengeance, am I not also allowed to, if we are to strive to be like Him? Must we forgive evil and destruction that comes into our lives, with no satisfaction or justice?"

Father Michael felt compelled to offer an answer to this amazing set of questions coming from such an unassuming and scruffy man; but he also sensed that Frank was not finished, so the priest kept silent. Frank shifted his weight and straightened his cap, awkwardly, before he looked down at his feet and cleared his throat.

"And what of those that I, too, have caused irreparable harm and injury to, Father? What sort of God would ever be able to forgive me of those things, without demanding full justice?"

Father Michael sat with his mouth open. This conversation was more than Frank had ever opened up with before, not only on theological matters, but also touching on matters of such obvious concern to the man. He searched Frank's face, trying to discern the truth behind those troubled, gray eyes. What he finally saw there behind the intractable expression was a soul in desperation. Father Michael chewed his lower lip, before he spoke.

"Frank – would you like to continue this discussion inside – maybe in the confessional?"

Frank looked toward the sanctuary, then shrugged. "Might as well," he said, and stood up. "I have never tried that before."

Frank Smith picked up their empty bottles and his rake and followed Father Michael inside.

#

Father Michael sat alone now in the confessional.

No one else was around.

He felt absolutely numb.

He had listened for the past hour as the groundskeeper who called himself Frank had confessed not only his real name to him, but also the horrifying events from the last 27 years of his life, including war crimes, sabotage, kidnappings, murders, and cover-ups. What he had heard had made the priest's blood run cold; he felt like he was about to vomit.

After a few more minutes, the priest composed himself, exited the confessional booth, made his way to the altar where he made the sign of the cross, prostrated himself, and began to pray harder than he had done in a long, long time.

He began by pleading, "Almighty God, have mercy on me, a sinner," and several long minutes later he ended the prayer with, "and please, please have mercy on the soul of my friend, Otto Franz Eberhardt!"

#

Several weeks later on a clear Saturday morning, Otto stepped out of his front door, locked it, and looked around. He casually walked the mile or so downtown to the public library. The little house he rented was located across from the old cemetery near the church. The entire neighborhood sat atop what was known as Kearny Hill that overlooked the town of Raton, spreading out to the southwest. He loved visiting the library when he could and had recently discovered in a book of local history there that the hill had been named for Brigadier General Stephen Watts Kearny, who in 1846 at the outset of the Mexican-American War, had brought a military force of some 2,500 men south into New Mexico, ousted the Mexican government from Santa Fe, and took the territory for the United States without firing a shot. Kearny's army had entered New Mexico via the Old Raton Pass in what become known as the "Kearny Entrada" and encamped at the base of the Pass on this same hill before there was even a town there. Now, whenever he laid his head on his pillow each night, Otto liked to imagine that General Kearny had also laid his head down in his tent at that very spot.

It was now 1975 as Otto sat and read the newspapers at the library, as he did once a week: he marveled at such current events as the death of General Francisco Franco of Spain, who had been allied with Nazi Germany since 1939, but had somehow remained out of the forefront of the war and survived it politically intact; Britain's election of their first woman leader, Prime Minister Margaret Thatcher; and the end of the American war in Vietnam with the surrender of South Vietnam to the communist North. As he left the library and stood on the steps buttoning his jacket, he also marveled that three years had now passed since he had fled the Neumann Ranch and gone into hiding as "Frank Smith." For the first time in almost 35 years – since he had kissed his wife and his baby daughter goodbye back in Germany and marched off to take the world for the Fatherland – he almost felt as if he had found a home, a reprieve, and a safe harbor from the consequences of his life.

Almost.

He walked down the sidewalk, glancing up at the five-story bank building across the street from the library as he often did; he looked for the decorative brickwork lining the top of the building – the bricks that were carved with stylized swastikas. The sight of these hated symbols had shocked him to see them there years ago, but Father Michael had filled him in on their history. Otto had already known that the swastika had been an old Native American symbol, a sign of "peace from the four winds," generations before Adolf Hitler had appropriated it for his hated propaganda. However, what Otto hadn't known was that, prior to Hitler's domination of the world stage, the small town of Raton had had several businesses that used the name – Swastika Coal Company, Swastika Mine – and this building, which was originally the largest hotel north of Santa Fe, called the Swastika Hotel. Of course, with what was felt the misuse of the symbol by Hitler, the names around town were quickly changed, the hotel had become the Yucca Hotel, and the swastika had all but disappeared from the town – all, except, for the mysterious symbols indelibly carved onto the top of the building.

Today, as Otto walked beneath them as quickly as he could, they seemed to symbolize for him the fact that, as comfortable as he had gotten lately in his new life, he could never let his vigil down. He knew that for the rest of his days, while either Ernst or Carl were still alive, he would remain a hunted man, still under the shadow of his old life in Nazi Germany.

As a result, Otto was still very much a loner, and even while as he walked along, nodding and smiling to a few of his familiar neighbors who were already out early today trimming their lawns and walking pets, he remained distant and unattached to any real relationships – except for Father Michael, of course, whom he could say was his true friend now in this world. Indeed, the priest was the only one who held all of Otto's secrets, seemingly without judgment, and genuinely seemed to enjoy Otto's company.

Father Michael was an exact polar opposite of Ernst – light *vs.* darkness, good *vs.* evil, and life *vs.* death. Otto had found it such a liberating experience in making confession, and his gratitude and fondness toward the priest had grown profound.

His thoughts had now taken him about halfway back home when Otto turned and entered the little corner grocery store just a few blocks away. He gathered his few grocery items: a small loaf of bread, some cheese, a quart of milk, eggs, bacon, tomatoes, and of course fresh peaches, then returned the smile of the plump, middle aged woman who owned the store, paid her, and stepped out the screen door into the warm mid-morning July sunshine. He pulled his cap down over his eyes, peeked into his sack of groceries, and pulled out a peach. He put it up to his nose, closed his eyes, and breathed deeply. The fresh scent always reminded him of Evie and her final resting place amongst her peach trees.

He smiled again, took a big bite, stepped off the curb, and was wiping his lips and beard with the back of his hand when a blast from a horn made him jump back. He dropped the peach in the gutter and almost his grocery bag. His heart raced as he stepped back to get out of the path of a dark gray pickup as it pulled even. The young driver glared over at Otto, gesturing at him angrily with his middle finger. The driver then gunned it and tires squealed and smoked pungently as the truck sped away.

Otto stood rooted in the street, very still, not moving an inch – indeed, barely breathing – as he watched the truck recede into the distance.

He had just stared into the angry eyes of Carl Neumann, who had evidently not even recognized him.

#

Otto did not go to church Sunday. Nor did he go to work on Monday. Instead, he waited until 9:00 a.m. when most businesses would be open. He could've walked the mile or so downtown, but after his close call with Carl, he didn't want to risk being seen. Instead, he politely asked a neighbor for a ride. He had himself dropped outside First National Bank, then walked quickly to the door with his head down and his cap pulled low. He carried a small duffel bag under his arm.

Several minutes later, he was sitting alone in a small room, the bag opened on a table in front of him alongside a long shiny metal safe deposit box that he had just rented. He reached into the bag and began transferring items to the box. He first opened his journal to the back inside cover where there he had taped two dog-eared, wallet sized pasteboard folders, each stamped on the front with an eagle insignia of the United States Army and the black printed words "Camp Trinidad – Prisoner of War." He pulled the two ID cards loose from the journal, then opened them up to look at the photos inside of two much younger versions of Ernst Brandt and himself. He had kept them all these years, having had an intuition that he may need them someday as protection – against Ernst.

He hadn't been wrong, but he also realized that to be caught with these documents would be disastrous.

He slipped the cards into the metal box, then pulled out a packet of letters that were rubber banded together. They were all addressed to *Mrs. Erica Eberhardt & Angela,* his long lost wife and daughter in Germany. Otto had long ago presumed they were both dead and had stopped writing to them as all these letters here had been returned undeliverable. He closed his eyes and brought the packet up to his face, inhaled the musty odor of old paper, and kissed it before placing it carefully in the safe deposit box.

He next reached into his jeans pocket and pulled out a white chess piece – a king – and held it for a while. The piece had belonged to Dave Perkins, the old pig farmer who had innocently picked them up after their prison escape, and whom Otto had stood by and watched as Ernst murdered him so callously. He turned the piece in his fingers. The finer details of the carved king had all been rubbed off from the years of being in Otto's pocket where he would touch it and rub it frequently. It had become his good luck charm – but perhaps his luck was running out. He smiled, rubbed his thumb over the white king one more time, and placed it, too, in the box.

The final item he pulled out of the duffel bag was Evie's well-worn diary. Otto thumbed through it absently, lovingly tracing Evie's handwriting here and there with his finger, then turned to the pages near the back where he had been adding his own thoughts, now that he had hidden his original journal away under the old cabin. He pulled a pen out of his pocket, thought awhile, leaned over, and began jotting lines in the diary. Since he had been in America for over thirty years now, he was thinking less and less in German anymore, so that everything he had written recently was in English. He finished writing, read through what he had written, smiled, put the pen away, and closed the book. He placed it gently in the box, which he then securely shut and took over to replace in its cubbyhole in the vault.

He slid the small box back into its place and was just about to latch it when something stopped him. He closed his eyes and struggled with himself for a moment. He pulled the box back out, just far enough to get the top lid open again. He peered down into it, reached in slowly, and took the diary back out. He held it and weighed it in one hand. He could not bring himself to part with this last reminder of Evie, no matter what fear he had that Carl and Ernst were once again on his trail. But he also could not take the chance that they might catch him with it on his person, along with its remaining secrets that no one must ever know.

No one.

Ever.

He wavered for a minute, then decided on a course of action.

He slipped the diary into his jacket pocket, locked the safe deposit box, and bounced the key in the palm of his hand, thinking. He found himself with the other hand absently fingering the flap of his jacket pocket. The inner lining had become worn and unraveled on one edge.

With no additional thought, he dropped the safe deposit key into the torn opening of the loose pocket lining and covered it with the pocket flap, and made a mental note to sew up the tear later.

#

Father Michael had just dismissed his last penitent from the confessional and waited for a few minutes to see if there would be anyone else this afternoon. As he finally moved to leave, he heard quick footsteps outside, the opposite confessional door open and shut quickly, and the footsteps recede just as quickly. The surprised priest waited a moment, opened the door, and peered out just in time to glimpse someone turning the corner to the vestibule. He could not make them out in the shadows, which was probably just as well.

He shrugged, stepped out of the booth, and began to walk to the front of the church, then stopped. Something nagged him. *Why had the person just opened the door and shut it? Had they gotten cold feet?* He turned back to the booth and opened the door, then raised his eyebrows; there before him on the bench lay a small square package wrapped in brown paper and tied with twine. A handwritten note was scribbled on the wrapping in a firm, clear hand:

Father Michael – When you read this, you will know why I entrust it to no one but you. I give it to you in this manner so that you will know and understand it to be part of my holy confession, and therefore inviolable. I know you will find the best way to hide and protect it.

For protect it, you must!

The signature read simply "Frank / O.E."

CHAPTER 27
HE WHO HAS EARS

That night Trent, Sophie, and Hector stayed up way past midnight reading back through Sophie's transcription of Otto Eberhardt's journal. Working on a hunch, Trent had found large foldout maps of Colfax, Union, Mora, Harding, and Taos Counties in New Mexico as well as the contiguous counties in Southern Colorado and tacked them to all four walls of the dining room. Given his admitted lack of computer skills, he had left it to Hector to log onto the department's internal database and pull up the unsolved cold case files of Northeast New Mexico / Southeast Colorado so that they could crosscheck and tag the dates of all the murders onto the maps. Then, armed with highlighters and colored pins, the three of them had gone to work graphically and chronologically tracing the dates, locations, and details revealed in the journal onto the maps.

Sophie had also blown up the photos from Ernst Brandt's and Otto Eberhardt's prison camp IDs and taped them on a wall chart, alongside photos of Carl Neumann, Jimmy Streck – and a shadowy, unfocused photo of Conrad Neumann she had taken from newspaper files that had a piece of colored yard stretched between it and Ernst's prison photo. Another chart contained photos of the few identified victims, such as Rogelio and Mirielle Segura and another one right at the top center where Trent's attention was continuously drawn, depicting the smiling face of Victoria Carter.

By the time the third pot of coffee ran out, as well as their collective exhaustion levels, the clock read 2:00 a.m. and the walls had blossomed into a rainbow of pins, lines, colored yarn stretched to the photographs, circles, and yellow sticky notes covering the majority of the maps, all reflecting 83 murders spanning almost seventy years that had been committed somewhere in the vicinity where the suspects had supposedly all lived at various times.

This calculation averaged more than one murder per year that, given the time span and large area, was not a huge number. Certainly, not every one of them could yet be positively related to their suspects. But if the majority were related and if factored in with the stark possibility that the same one or two people might have committed the murders, then the data became staggering to behold.

If true, this research represented one of the worst serial killing sprees in American history.

Hours later Hector lay snoring on a couch while Sophie was draped over a pile of papers strewn on the dining table and sound asleep. Trent sat on the floor, back against the wall, his forearms propped on his knees, chewing thoughtfully on the stub end of a yellow highlighter. He stared around the room from one map to another, trying to make sense of it all.

How could one man pull off such an incredible crime spree, right under everyone's noses?

Moreover, how was he ever going to tie all this circumstantial evidence to Conrad Neumann, a prominent rancher who, according to Otto's journal, had been living a lie all these years? Not only that fact, but also who was ever going to believe all this sporadic data? Without a verifiable, dependable eyewitness, or a confession from the killer – or killers – none of these suspicions or information would ever lead to an indictment. The only known eyewitness, the author of the journal, had probably been murdered for what he had known and buried under the theater and his writings merely hearsay evidence, at best.

The primary suspect – the old man, Neumann – was now well into his 90s, and if he, in fact, were really Ernst Brandt, at his age, he had seen it all and knew every trick, enough, that is, to not be cornered into any confession of guilt. Even if he were to confess, he didn't seem to fear anything, including death.

The other suspects, Neumann's son Carl and his cohort Jimmy, could possibly be brought up on murder charges on the strength of Trent's own testimony, now that his memories of the events on Cordova Pass had returned. Of course, a good defense attorney could argue that his testimony might very well be tainted by his documented head injuries and general lapse of mental capacity, coupled with his not-so-secret visitations with his dead wife. In addition, the other eyewitness, Mirielle Segura, had yet to be able to positively identify photos of either Carl or Jimmy, although her statement describing the events of the attack on her husband and her certainly smacked of those two.

The physical evidence gathered at the break-in of Maggie's cabin had turned out to be, at best, inconclusive, with none of the identifiable fingerprints belonging to any of the suspects.

Trent had even talked Ben Ferguson into issuing a "bolo" on Carl Neumann and Jimmy Streck as persons of interest, but so far, they had both dropped off the radar.

In other words, tying any of this information to the known suspects and getting this case to go forward at all was going to be a terrific challenge, if not downright impossible, and one that Trent could not keep his sleep deprived mind focused on for another minute.

He would attempt to tackle it all again tomorrow.

Trent pulled himself up painfully with the aid of a dining chair, groaned, and moved stiffly toward his bedroom. Along the way, he touched Sophie on the shoulder and squeezed it. She opened an eye, then slowly raised her head.

"What time is it?" she moaned.

"Don't know – don't care," answered her father from the hallway. "Going to bed, and you should, too." He wandered into his bedroom and shut the door, but opened it again immediately.

"And turn out the lights when you do," he called out and then shut the door again, then opened it once more. "And wake up your boyfriend there and send him home."

"But," his daughter interrupted.

"Home!" he reiterated and slammed the door for the final time.

#

Five hours later, the doorbell rang. Trent stumbled out of his room, scratching his head and yawning while he tried to focus on his watch. He got halfway to the door, looked down, and noticed he had no clothes on. He turned around, went to his room, and came back a minute later, having pulled on a pair of dark blue lounging pants. The doorbell had continued to ring several more times before he finally got the door open.

"Yeah, yeah," he croaked as he pulled the door wide.

"Charming," mocked Maggie, standing on the porch looking fresh as a dream and looking Trent up and down while she chewed her lip. She affectionately patted him on his bare chest as she pushed past him and on into the house, leaving him standing there with the door open. "You can close that door, Swee'Pea, along with your mouth," she called over her shoulder, threading her way through the detritus of the dining room on her way to the kitchen.

Trent did as he was told, still half asleep, and followed in Maggie's wake like a lost pup. As he passed the couch, he heard soft snoring coming from underneath a quilt that had been tossed there. He raised one corner to discover Hector still sound asleep and now grasping unconsciously for his covers. "Thought I chased you out of here," Trent mumbled as he dropped the blanket back over Hector's head and then stumbled on into the kitchen where Maggie was starting a fresh pot of coffee, rinsing out dirty dishes, and pulling open drawers and cabinets. Trent ambled over to the sliding glass doors and squinted out into the sunrise. Out of the corner of his eye, down near his feet, he spied Jarhead patiently sitting by the door waiting for it to open, but Trent did nothing. Maggie glanced over, shook her head, and pointed in various directions as she spoke to him.

"Cat – shower – clothes – breakfast – in that order," she instructed firmly.

"Wha?" Trent answered, turning toward her.

"Let. The. Cat. In – Go. Shower," she enunciated, as to a child, then handed him a hot cup of black coffee. "Then come back in here, kiss me, and take me to breakfast."

Trent leaned over and absently tried to kiss her, but she pushed him away with distasteful wave of her hand.

"I said shower first!"

Trent turned and shuffled away.

"And brush your teeth," Maggie called after him, "before you try that kiss again!"

#

They had gone to eat breakfast at a 24-hour diner near the interstate, usually full of more tourists than locals, which was good because Trent was not in the mood this morning to smile and nod at people he knew. Maggie assumed it was for another reason.

"Still embarrassed about being seen with me in public?" she said, peering at him over her cup as she sipped coffee.

"What? Oh, of course not – don't be ridiculous," he answered between mouthfuls of eggs and bacon.

"Then why'd you have me park around back? Didn't want anyone to see us walking in from the street?" She reached over and put her hand on his, and he slid it away. She sat back and gave him a *told-you-so* look.

Trent had pulled his hand away to reach into his pocket and take out his mobile phone, which had started to buzz. He looked at Maggie and shrugged defensively.

"Carter," he spoke into the phone. "Yeah? Really?" A worried look crossed his face. "When? *Now?*" He looked at his watch: 8:55 a.m. "Yeah, okay. Be there soon as I can."

He snapped the phone shut and put it away. He picked up his coffee cup and drained it, stood up, and took a wad of cash from of his wallet, counted some bills out, and stuck them under the plate.

"Gotta run," he said, reaching down and grabbing his hat. Maggie sat looking up at him coyly, not saying a word. Trent fumbled with the brim of his hat, not quite knowing what to do or say. "So, uh," he stammered, "can I drop you somewhere?"

Maggie rolled her eyes, wiped her mouth on her napkin, and scooted out of the booth to stand next to him.

"We came in my car, remember?" she reminded him.

"Oh, yeah – right." Trent looked at his watch again, exasperated, then back at Maggie. "Well, damn," he muttered finally.

"Damn?" she asked, puzzlement on her face.

"Yeah, well – can't spare the time to go back for my truck." Trent was thinking out loud, now. "Could have you drop me at the station, check out a cruiser – naw, dammit, that won't work. This is personal business." They had started walking already and were now out on the sidewalk.

"What is?"

"This – thing I gotta do." He finally turned to her. "That was my father on the phone."

"Your father? Walter?" She got concerned and touched his arm. "Oh,

Sweetie, is he alright?"

Trent looked at her funny before he realized what she was saying. "Walter? Oh, yeah, he's fine. Never better." They had reached Maggie's car, a beige Lincoln Navigator. "It's just a friend of his – of ours, really – an old priest that lives there, too. Funny old guy. Plays chess with Walter – uh, Dad. Anyway, he's worried about him. Says the old fellow insists on talking with me. Says it's pretty urgent." Trent chuckled.

"What's so funny?" Maggie asked.

"Oh, just that Father Michael's always trying to get me saved or something, that's all." He stopped for a moment. "But there's just something about him I really like."

"You make him sound more like a Southern Baptist than a Catholic priest," Maggie mused. "But it does seem to me you could use a little saving." She tossed him the keys. "Here. I might as well go with you – and you're driving this time."

Trent caught the keys and started to retort, but gave up.

#

When they walked into the lobby of the Clayton Nursing Home, Trent's father was pacing the floor, waiting for them.

"Took you long enough – and who's this?" Walter asked, looking Maggie up and down.

"Good morning to you, too, Dad," Trent grumbled, then provided the cursory introductions. "Margot Van Ryan, this is Walter – Walter Carter, meet Margot."

"Van Ryan? Sounds familiar somehow." Walter rubbed his chin. Maggie smiled, stepped up and took Walter's hand, then leaned over and kissed his cheek.

"Hello, Mr. Carter. I am so glad to meet you. Trent has told me so much about you!"

"He has? / I have?" the two men said simultaneously. Walter grinned up at her like a schoolboy as Trent rolled his eyes. They began walking down the hall. Maggie took Walter by the arm as they walked ahead, leaving Trent to trail behind.

"Say – I do know that name," Walter began, scratching his head. "Your family run that spread out Yankee Canyon way, right? Montana something-or-other?"

"*Montaña del Sol*, Mr. Carter. And yes – one and the same."

"Well, Trent sure never mentioned anything about a pretty young lady," Walter flirted. "About time he stopped moping around, and find somebody to settle him back down, you ask me."

"Nobody asked," muttered Trent under his breath. Maggie turned and winked at him over her shoulder.

Walter led them around the corner and up another hall, about three doors down. He tapped softly on the door, only to skip ahead and push it open.

"Hey, Buddy – you awake?" he called softly into the dim room. The drapes had been pulled with only a bit of light creeping in from the bathroom door, itself pushed almost closed.

"Come on in," came a high, thin voice from the direction of the bed, crackling with age and fatigue. As their eyes adjusted to the dimness, Trent recognized the old priest, lying in bed, his long wispy white hair askew and fanned out on the pillow and his face unnaturally sallow. Trent also became aware that they weren't the only visitors. A chair had been pulled up close alongside the bed where an older woman sat. She had graying hair pulled into pigtails, like a little girl's, and was holding what looked to be an antique, threadbare ragdoll under one arm while her other hand held Father Michael's bony hand, gently stroking it. She glanced back over her shoulder with a worried expression, bent, and whispered something to the doll, then listened carefully.

"Irina says she doesn't like strangers," she whispered hoarsely to Father Michael, leaning over towards him.

The old priest patted the woman's hand and smiled at her. "Then let's not have any strangers here, okay?" he said. "Let's only have new friends, shall we?" Father Michael then introduced them to Caroline Neumann. "And Caroline, you know Walter – now don't pretend that you don't." Caroline had grinned sheepishly at Walter and ducked her head.

"Hi, Mr. Walter," she said bashfully.

"And this other man is Walter's boy, Trent. Say 'hi' to him, Caroline," he continued patiently.

"Hi, Mr. Trent." She looked down in her arms and mumbled to the doll, "He looks way too old to be a boy, doesn't he, Irina?" She listened for a quick moment, and then held up the barely recognizable ragdoll. "Would you like to say hello to Irina, Mr. Trent?"

"I sure would," Trent answered with a smile as he stepped over, knelt down by Caroline's chair, and touched the two or three threads of yarn that were all that remained of the doll's hair. "Hi, there, Ms. Irina. You and Ms. Caroline are sure looking lovely today," he complimented, gazing into the woman's eyes that twinkled as she smiled back at him. Suddenly, though, he felt a strange emotion well up inside as he suddenly put two and two together and realized this woman before him had to be the same girl that Otto Eberhardt had written about so lovingly in his journal. But how had she come to be here, in this exact place and time?

He eventually stood up and leaned over to take the old man's hand. "How are you doing, Father?" he asked. "Walter said you needed to see me."

"Raise me up a little, so I can see everyone better." The priest motioned to an electronic control wand hanging over the bed rail and indicated that Trent should activate it, which he did. As the priest's head rose to a more comfortable position, he squinted his eyes and asked for his glasses. Trent found them on the bedside table on top of a small worn Bible and handed them to him. Father Michael put them on and finally noticed Maggie standing off to one side, a little behind Walter even though the room was still dim.

"Open those shades a little – let's brighten up this place some so we can see each other," the priest instructed. "Besides, I haven't met this young lady, have I? That's not Sophie, is it? Is that your granddaughter, Walter?"

"No," Trent answered instead. "She couldn't come today, Father." He stepped over to the window and adjusted the shades to let in a little more daylight, just enough to chase away the shadows. "Father Michael, this is Margot Van Ryan, my – " he hesitated, "good friend."

Maggie let a trace of a frown cross her face, for Trent's benefit, stepped over to the bed, smiled, and took Father Michael's hand. "So wonderful to meet you, Father," she greeted him softly.

Father Michael's eyes suddenly grew wide and his mouth opened silently. He slowly took Maggie's hand and stared at her face. He tried to speak but abruptly began coughing, but with an effort, he composed himself and smiled.

"It is entirely my pleasure, dear lady," he said, measuring his words carefully, holding her hand warmly between both of his, and continuing to peer into her eyes.

"My," she said with a chuckle, "nice … to see I still have an effect on some men!" She looked over at Trent with that comment and gave him a quick smirk.

"I – apologize, Miss – Van Ryan, is it?" Father Michael continued. "It is just that – you are a remarkably beautiful young woman." He interrupted himself with another bout of coughing and dabbed at his mouth with a handkerchief. "For a moment, I thought we might have met before."

Maggie smiled again, turned to speak to Caroline, but froze with a look of concern. Caroline was still seated, holding Irina tightly to her chest, her lip trembling, and also staring up at Maggie with wide eyes. Tears sprang up; she gripped the doll tighter and tighter, kneading it like bread dough while whispering something unintelligible. Maggie cocked her head, a little confused, smiled again, and offered her hand.

"Hello there, Ms. Neumann. If you're who I think you are, believe it or not, I think that we might be cousins. I'm – "

Caroline suddenly careened forward in her chair, flung her arms wide, grabbed Maggie around her torso, and buried her sobbing face into Maggie's skirt. Maggie staggered back a step in surprise, stopped, and quickly glanced around at everyone else. The only sound in the room was Caroline's heart wrenching muffled sobs of what sounded like *Mama – Mama,* breathed into the folds of Maggie's skirt.

Trent and Walter stared in shock while Father Michael struggled to a sitting position in the bed. He leaned over and called to Caroline gently.

"Hey there, little Rosebud," he comforted. "Caroline – come here."

Caroline raised her head and looked at him. She disengaged herself from Maggie's dress and looked back up at her sheepishly as she wiped her nose on her sleeve. She quietly walked over and sat on the edge of Father Michael's bed and laid her head on his lap, sniffling softly.

"Yes – that's alright," he continued to speak softly, stroking her hair. "It's okay, Caroline." Father Michael glanced up at Maggie apologetically, then back at Trent and Walter. "She's just a little confused, you understand. Lost her mama years ago – in a fire. She does this occasionally." He continued to stroke her graying hair and speak softly to Caroline, but as he did so he stole a look at Maggie once or twice more. "I wonder – perhaps you remind her of her mother?"

"Yes," Maggie answered with a quick nod. "My Aunt Evie, my father's sister. She –" Maggie hesitated, glancing at Caroline, before she continued softly. "Aunt Evie – uh – passed before I was born. But I've seen photos of her." She looked down, self consciously, then back up. "I have been told there is a bit of a family resemblance."

Father Michael had been gazing at Maggie steadily, and now a small smile touched the corners of his mouth. "Yes," he offered, deep in thought, then seemed to catch himself. "Yes, I – I often hear of such a thing."

Caroline's sniffing finally subsided as she calmed down and pulled her doll up to hide her face in embarrassment. "You going to be okay, now?" Father Michael asked her, touching her arm.

Caroline nodded, looked up and smiled at the priest, and nodded again. "I'm sorry, Papa Michael," she mumbled. "We'll be good, now, won't we, Irina. We'll be good."

Maggie knelt down in front of her childlike, gray haired cousin, who was probably only a few years older than she. "That's alright, Caroline. I'm happy you gave me such a nice hug!" Caroline looked down, embarrassed, spoke to the doll, and put it up to her ear for a moment.

"We're sorry, Miss Margot. We didn't mean to get your clothes all wet."

"Oh, Sweetie, that's okay," Maggie said, reaching out and touching Caroline's hand, before leaning toward the doll. "Say, Irina – what say we all go out to the garden and play some games," she suggested conspiratorially.

Caroline looked up at her with wide eyes and put her doll up to her ear again.

"Irina says she would really, really love to play hide and seek!" she responded excitedly.

"Well, Irina – do you think Caroline would like to come, too?"

"Oh, yes, ma'am, please! Irina says we can both come. We love the garden, but they don't ever let us go out there by ourselves." Caroline jumped up, took Maggie's hand, and began to lead her from the room. She stopped and turned back to Father Michael. "Is that okay, Papa? If Irina and I go to play in the garden with Miss – I mean, Cousin Margot?

Father Michael smiled and touched Caroline's cheek. "Yes, of course, Angel. You go now, and Papa will talk with these nice men."

The door closed behind them, but Trent could still hear Caroline's excited chattering as her voice faded away down the hallway.

Walter made a move toward the door, too, but Father Michael stopped him. "No need for you to leave, Walter. Nothing you cannot listen to. Here – come sit down, before you fall down." He indicated the chair that Caroline had been seated in and then looked up at Trent. "Sorry – nice, strong guy like you will just have to stand, I guess." He gave Trent a wink, coughed again, but suddenly dropped back onto his pillow, motioning Trent to step closer. The priest looked exhausted, physically, and now, somehow, mentally.

"Gentlemen, I am an old, old man, and," he spoke while looking at them in turn, "I am dying."

"Oh, shut up with that damned fool talk, for god's sake," Walter scoffed and then saw the priest knit his brows sternly at him over the top of his glasses. "Sorry, Father," he muttered. "For gosh sake."

"The truth is, once you have lived beyond ninety," Father continued, "what is there left of any value for one to contribute to this world?" He stopped and coughed a few more times into his handkerchief. He motioned to Walter to hand him a glass of water that sat beside the Bible. He took a few sips, a few deep breaths, and handed it back. After taking a few deep breaths, he looked up at Trent with piercing blue eyes.

"And I am well beyond that particular benchmark, young Mr. Carter."

"Could'a fooled me, Father. You don't look a day over eighty-five."9 Trent guessed, shifting from one foot to the other, avoiding the priest's piercing gaze. He felt as if the old man was scrutinizing his very soul. Father Michael remained thoughtful for moment and spoke again.

"But before I drift away completely, I suppose there are one or two things left for me to do – things I know I must pass on, perhaps, to someone else – to someone I trust. Do you remember our last conversation, Trent – and have you thought about any of those things we talked about?" Trent shuffled again, uncomfortably.

"Uh – well, not offhand, Father. It's been awhile, you know." He felt put on the spot, like a delinquent schoolboy, suddenly caught without his homework.

"And he hasn't been entirely right in the head for a while, either," Walter interjected. Father Michael ignored the interruption.

"I had asked you about your relationship to our Lord, if you recall," the old priest began, before adding, "you know, it's my job."

Here we go, thought Trent, a bit perturbed that this topic was coming up right now.

"And I asked you about those issues that were snowballing in your life – the bad things that you continue to try and control, but that wind up manipulating you instead until you are completely bowled over and crushed by them." The priest paused for a long while. Trent grew uncomfortable in the sudden quiet.

"Uh – yes, I seem to recall some of that," he finally said, more to fill up the awkward silence.

Father Michael had closed his eyes and had lain back on the pillow, and a couple more minutes of silence passed. Trent leaned forward, a little alarmed, to see if the priest was still breathing, but straightened up quickly when the old man spoke once more, his eyes still closed.

"All of that – stuff – all of that snowball – ultimately represents all the things in your life that were never really as they seemed – and are not being dealt with properly."

Trent was suddenly alert, listening. *There was that phrase again, the same one the priest had said the last time, – the same one Vicky had used, over and over.* Trent stepped back and leaned against the windowsill for support.

"I'm listening," he finally said softly.

"Are you?" Father Michael's eyes shot open. "'He who has ears to hear let him hear.' Those were words actually spoken by Jesus, you know."

"Sounds familiar."

"Well, I should hope so. But do you know what he really meant? He was speaking about hearing things in two completely different ways – first, with our ears and then the right way. You, my friend, are still learning to not listen the wrong way – but you're doing a mighty poor job of it." The priest's eyes peered at him again thoughtfully. He nodded knowingly and spoke slower this time. "Others have told you this, I think, yes?"

Trent said nothing, but gripped the windowsill and swallowed hard. He knew from recent experience that every time he had heard certain words – phrases – they usually presaged something profound.

Father Michael continued to study him, curiously. "Tell me something, Deputy Sheriff," he said, suddenly changing the subject. "Have you discovered, yet, the identity of that dead person you found underneath the theater in Raton?"

Trent opened his mouth to answer, but was clearly shocked at the question.

"I do still read the newspapers, you know," the priest said, raising his eyebrows. "It has been all over the news. And Walter here says something about the body, perhaps, belonging to an old German soldier, or the like – oh, I do think that is so very fascinating, that part of your work."

Trent turned and scowled at his father who merely shrugged. "I was just making conversation," Walter answered in defense.

Trent sighed, thought for a moment, but went on to tell the priest that they did have a few clues, but weren't really sure about anything yet pertaining to the identity; that the only clues they really had were from a bullet found in the autopsy and some stuff from an old safe deposit box found in the old bank. He stopped when he noticed the old man's eyes squinting.

"Really?" commented Father Michael thoughtfully, then continued slowly, "What sort of items from the bank?"

"Oh, not much really – some old identifications, a bundle of old letters, personal papers – oh, and this was in there, too, for some inexplicable reason." Trent suddenly pulled something out of his pocket, reached over, and handed it to the priest. "Thought you might get a kick out of it, since you enjoy chess so much."

The old man slowly reached over and gingerly took a worn chess piece, a white king, from Trent's fingers.

"Looks like real ivory to me," Trent offered.

"Oh, my – " Father Michael gasped, his voice trailing off for a moment. " I cannot believe this!" He seemed to catch himself, then continued after a moment. "This is truly exquisite! Quite old, I think – like me, yes?" His voice expressed awe as he looked up at Trent and smiled broadly. "Thank you – a most unexpected gift! I shall treasure it for the rest of my life." He immediately began to chuckle at his joke.

Trent motioned to Walter. "Well," he began softly, "I guess we should really be going, Father. I'm sure you need your rest, and we …"

"Please, do not go yet," the old man interrupted. "Speaking of treasures, I, too, have a gift for you." He reached over to his bedside table, set down the chess piece, and picked up his old Bible.

"Oh, no, Father, I couldn't accept that – I mean, it's your Bible. You don't want to be without that."

Father Michael smiled, looked down lovingly at the leather bound book, and flipped through the old pages gently.

"Yes, I insist. There is a wealth of life in this book." He looked up at Trent intently. "A real treasure, in fact – at least, to me." He slowly extended the Bible to him. "There are...truths in here that will answer so many of your questions – truths that will help you in ways you may never have expected. But you must dig for this treasure, young Mr. Carter, as I also dug for it – labored for it – defended it, and kept it – until just the right person came along." He paused, watching Trent's face closely, then added, "You, Trent, are that person. Here, please take it."

Trent hesitated before he took the Bible. He touched its worn, fine leather cover, and ran his finger around the edges of the well-worn pages that seemed to exude an air of devotion and love. Father Michael leaned up off of the pillow suddenly, a strange light in his eyes. "Do promise me you will read it soon, Trent. Some things cannot wait. You must promise me!"

The old man's sudden urgency struck Trent with its hoarse insistence.

"Yes. Yes, I will. I promise," he answered. Trent suddenly knew that, this time, he really meant it.

He stepped over and took Father Michael's hand and squeezed it gently. "Thank you," he said to the old priest, sincerely. "It's really been an honor to speak with you. And I hope to see you again very soon."

"Not soon," the priest answered, his voice now barely above a whisper. "At least, not in this lifetime, I think. But we shall meet again one day – I am assured of that." He lay back on the pillow and closed his eyes, a peaceful look on his face.

Trent helped his father from the chair; they walked to the door and opened it to leave.

"And young Mr. Carter," Father Michael called feebly from across the room. Trent turned around. "Do not let that Ms. Van Ryan get away from you. She is a most lovely woman, in many ways – and another treasure. And she does, indeed," the old priest paused and looked away for a moment with a dreamy look in his eyes before continuing, "remind me of someone I once knew, many years ago."

Trent nodded and smiled, started to reply, but was again interrupted by the priest.

"And Mr. Carter," the old gentleman added urgently, raising his head from the bed and pointing a finger his way. "You must do everything you can to protect her — and my precious Caroline — from the Neumanns!"

CHAPTER 28
SINS OF THE FATHER

Excerpt from the Journal of Otto Franz Eberhardt

"22.05.77 – I fear that I will soon be a dead man. How foolish to think I could hide in plain sight for so long. Ernst has no forgiveness in him, and Carl, no mercy. I have no better plan than to stay right where I am – continue to live in plain sight. But I have a feeling of dread, that my days are numbered.

"If they find me, may God have mercy on my soul."

#

Brilliant explosions of color lit the late evening skies, followed a few seconds later by the delayed sound waves of earsplitting booms that cracked off of the surrounding mesas like distant artillery. At least such was the immediate impression Otto had as he trembled with mixed reactions of terror and delight.

The day was July 4th, 1977, a Monday, and like most everyone in town, he had the day off to wander and enjoy the festivities, including booths, food, and games in the park, and later, a huge parade. But now commenced the wondrous fireworks display that the town managed to put on magnificently year after year.

Otto separated himself from the crowd somewhat and, stepping back into the shadows of a storefront entryway, watched the revelers ooh and ahh with excitement over each new starburst of brilliance over their heads. After all these years living in America, these celebrations of his adopted country's independence still fascinated him with the outpouring of patriotism, frivolity, and the innocent homage to the sounds and fury of war. He had always wondered how many, if any, of these folks associated this annual spectacle with the same horrific memories that he possessed; with each explosion of light and sound and each whiff of gunpowder, Otto cringed and was transported briefly back to the interior of a cramped, sweltering Tiger tank in North Africa – the Battle of Kasserine Pass, fighting for the Fatherland in Rommel's *Afrika Korps*. He could close his eyes; the year was 1944, and he could once again feel his hands and feet on the gun controls of the unparalleled war machine. The sweat would pour down into his eyes and his heart would pound in his throat, anticipating death — either the enemy's or his own — as the turret began to swing and the gun sights zeroed in on yet another Sherman tank filled with an American crew about to feel the wrath of Otto's incendiary rounds fired almost point blank from his mighty 88mm cannon. He could again hear the burning, screaming – and dying — as he had slammed round after round home, hitting one target after another; a mixed thrill of the horror of battle and the exhilaration of survival had surged through him that he would never be able to fully explain to another person who had never experienced war. These were emotions he did not choose to dwell on, unless reminded of them.

Like right now.

Another firework burst over his head and he opened his eyes, back on the street with the celebrating crowd. He scanned the faces and marveled that here he was, thirty-three years later, walking unobserved and unhindered in the homeland of his former enemies, amongst their descendants; he wondered if he ever rubbed elbows with anyone whose father lay in a North African war cemetery, possibly even put there by his own hand. That man – that trained killer soldier he had once been – seemed a total stranger to Otto now.

The fiery artistry blasting overhead again made him cringe, so incongruous to him to hear the simulated noise of battle and then see it light up the laughing, happy faces around him — mothers bounced fussing babies; fathers held youngsters up on strong shoulders to get a better view as they pointed up to the blossoming, brilliant displays. Otto gazed at them, the normal citizens of this normal, American town he now also called home, and reflected on the simple, contented life he had begun to build here, with God's help.

"Quite wondrous, isn't it?" As if on cue, Father Michael materialized from out of the crowd. He stepped over to where Otto was half concealed in the doorway and stood beside him, hands in his pockets, looking very much at ease as he puffed on a cigar that was probably the priest's only guilty pleasure. He wore a black suede fedora that he had pushed up off of his forehead so he could see the fireworks better. Bursts of colored light reflected off of his wire rimmed glasses and clerical vestments.

The two men stood in silence for a while, each reacting in his own way to the festive atmosphere. Father Michael sighed and shook his head.

"I know far too many of these people," he chuckled. "I know their names, most of their parents and grandparents – christened most of these kids running around." He paused, put out his cigar in a nearby ashcan, and cleaned his glasses on his handkerchief. Otto watched him curiously. The priest's eyes glistened.

"This is going to be hard for you, isn't it?" he said quietly to Father Michael.

In just a few short years, the two men had become fast friends. The priest had been the first person in Raton to show Otto any kindness – any real trust, even. He had arranged his job for him, a home, and given him other help. But most of all, he had introduced Otto to a real faith in God and had guided his growth in that faith to a depth and importance that Otto had never before imagined, not to mention that the priest had shared all of Otto's deepest secrets – all of them.

"You all set then, Father?" Otto continued.

The priest smiled and patted his jacket pockets as he described the contents of each. "Got my ticket, my letters of introduction, my Bible – and my suitcase is packed and waiting back at the rectory. All set to just step out the door and catch that 5:00 a.m. train to Albuquerque."

Otto chuckled.

"What's so darn funny?"

"Just looks like you were genuflecting – patting yourself down like that," Otto answered.

A week earlier, Father Michael had invited Otto to lunch at their favorite coffee shop where they had made small talk as they ate hot roast beef sandwiches with slabs of melting Monterey Jack cheese and large strips of fresh New Mexican green chile, all on homemade sourdough bread and washed down by ice cold Italian sodas. When they had finished eating, the priest had abruptly informed Otto that he had formally stepped down from the parish and was leaving for a long needed sabbatical. He planned to travel for a while, maybe a year or more, wherever the urge and God took him, perhaps do some writing; and after he had gotten himself recharged, he would eventually land wherever God wanted him to be, doing whatever He had for him to do next in this journey of life.

At first the unexpected news had hit Otto like a ton of bricks; he had reacted selfishly, insisting that Father Michael had not thought this through at all. But there had been no convincing him to change his mind, so for a couple of days, Otto had sulked and did not speak to his friend. But one morning, after his usual early morning walk around the park near his home, he had realized just how childish he was being. That day he had gone to the priest, apologized to him, and thanked him for all he had done for him, wishing him Godspeed.

Now, the two friends stood together and stared at the fiery skies, which lit up hundreds of pairs of smiling eyes in the crowds with the continuous blasts and flurries of color. Not much more was left to say to one another. Otto's friend – perhaps the first real friend in his life and one of the few who had touched him so deeply – was leaving, and Otto was standing once again at a crossroads. Looking back on all other such moments, he realized that most of life's changes had been thrust upon him, unannounced, and without regard for his needs or desires: being drafted into the *Wehrmacht*, leaving a young wife and child and going off to war, being taken prisoner by the Americans and brought to this place, being with Evie and then being viciously torn away from her, only to unexpectedly reunite with her in time to watch her die horribly.

Tonight, though, Otto felt completely at peace with this particular crossroads. This time it all felt right; he still had no idea what the future may bring, but something deep in his spirit gave him an odd assurance that somehow things would be fine. He had nothing more he needed to say to the priest and merely reached over and clapped his hand on his friend's shoulder in the simplest yet most heartfelt gesture he could think of. He dropped his eyes from the skies and contentedly gazed around the crowd once more.

Otto froze as his eyes locked onto those of Carl Neumann.

Carl stood directly across the street no more than 100 feet away, his back turned to the crowds and the fireworks, staring right back at Otto – grinning like a death's head.

Carl was dressed in jeans and boots; his hands were thrust into the pockets of a windbreaker. He was bareheaded and his shock of blond hair changed color with each flash of light in the skies. He stood still as a statue, his gaze never wavering. Otto stared back as long as he could stand it, dropped his head, took his hand away from Father Michael's shoulder, and pulled his cap back down over his brow – as if that would do anything to help now.

"Father – I," he stammered.

Father Michael turned to give Otto a curious look, but his smile faded as he saw the consternation on Otto's face.

"Otto? What is it?"

Otto glanced quickly back across the way; Carl had not moved a muscle, but continued to stand and grin. Father Michael followed Otto's gaze.

"Is that him?" he asked suspiciously. "Is that your – is that Carl?" Otto didn't answer right away, staring back across the street at his nemesis, but looked back at his friend and nodded slowly.

"Father," he paused, "Michael, I have to go now," he said, finally. He could think of nothing more to say to this man who had given him his life back – had shown him the very path to redemption. But now he had to get away from his friend as quickly as possible, so that he would not also step into the path of the danger that hovered so near.

"Let me help!" the priest insisted.

"No!" exclaimed Otto and took a hesitant step away. He then softened his voice. "No, you have done enough, my friend. Please – just go enjoy your new life. You have earned it." Otto took another couple of steps to move away, glancing across the street again, and back. "Please, please listen to me, Father!" he continued to plead. "You must not follow me. That man over there is dangerous – almost the most dangerous man I know, except for the one who sent him!" Otto pushed his way into the crowd, then spoke loudly back over his shoulder, and over the crowd's noise. "Be well, my friend. I will be fine —I promise. Write to me soon. And go with God – and I will try and do the same!"

Otto speedily vanished into the crowd, pushing his way through a sea of faces as they flashed red, green, blue, and yellow. He could hear gasps and bursts of laughter as the skies continued to shriek and boom, but he was no longer looking at what they were seeing. The holiday spectacle was now merely serving as his vital cover and only means and hope of escape, for behind him he could feel that the hounds of hell themselves had smelled him out. He began praying earnestly that God would intervene miraculously, just once more, just as He had seemed to do so many times before, Otto realized in hindsight.

He also feared that God's mercies were probably now running out.

The crowds parted amicably for him, oblivious to the potential evil that stalked somewhere close behind. Otto had gone several yards when he stopped, still hemmed in by the milling crowd surging around him. He crouched down a bit and chanced a quick look behind him. He studied the sea of brightly lit faces for any sign of Carl, but could see no unusual movements, other than the waving and pointing of hands towards the sky. Yet his sixth sense told him that danger lurked right there in that sea somewhere, watching him, closing in on him slowly, prowling, stalking his prey as he knew Carl had learned to do so many times over the last few years under Ernst's sick guidance.

Otto felt the hair on the back of his neck stand on end with the sudden realization that this feeling of terror, of being hunted, must be exactly what Ernst's victims had all felt, each and every one of them. The ruthless predators had become masters of giving their quarry a false sense of hope, a sliver of an idea that escape was, perhaps, possible. In the end, though, their hopes would always dissolve in a rush of fear and the certainty of death right before their eyes. Otto knew without a doubt now the ultimate fate of all prey: to gain hope only to have it dashed at the last moment when the numbing mercy of the bullet struck home.

Otto was beginning to know that his hours – perhaps minutes – were now numbered.

He shook away such debilitating thoughts from his mind, uttered another quick prayer under his breath, decisively turned, and pushed on through the crowd. He finally emerged from the press of bodies and found himself at the corner of 1st Street and Park Avenue where the street lights had been temporarily, and thankfully, extinguished by the local power crews to accommodate the fireworks show. The resulting shadows offered a degree of comfort as Otto slipped around the corner, away from the crowd, and pressed in close to the buildings as he made his way west up the avenue. He finally came to an alley and ducked around the corner, stopped, leaned tightly against the darkened building, tried to regain his breath – and waited.

His heart raced, the breathing he had tried to calm was still ragged; he cringed as the fireworks continued to crack and the light of their explosions reflected off the opposite buildings, bathing him in occasional pale light before fading quickly back to darkness. He listened for any sound of pursuit, and after a few minutes got his breathing under control, squeezed his eyes shut, removed his cap, and wiped the sweat from his face with his sleeve.

"It's been a long time, hasn't it Otto," a low voice floated from somewhere out of the darkness. Otto jumped, turned, went into a defensive crouch and suddenly saw Carl silhouetted by the flashes in the sky. He had obviously circled the block, come down the alley from Otto's right, quiet as a cat, and now pointed a pistol at Otto's head, just out of arm's reach.

Otto suddenly heard laughter as a happy family walked up the sidewalk beside him and began to cross the street quickly. He resisted the urge to call out to them or to just fall into step behind them, but wasn't sure what Carl was capable of doing and didn't want to risk anyone else getting hurt. When the frivolity faded into the distance, Carl motioned with the gun and took a couple of steps back deeper into shadows, indicating that Otto should come with him.

"No, my friend," Carl warned, as if reading his mind. "Please don't be stupid."

Otto hesitated for just an instant, reluctant to abandon the semblance of safety afforded by the crowd, glanced back briefly to see if there was any possibility of escape, and resigned himself. He gritted his teeth and slowly followed Carl deeper into the alley with his hands raised in surrender.

Carl waved the pistol again to indicate that Otto should move in front of him. Otto passed around him and continued to walk slowly between the dark buildings, his path occasionally lit up by more fireworks and thinking feverishly.

"Why are you doing this, Carl?"

"Shut up and keep moving!" Carl seemed to know exactly where he was going, which did not settle well with Otto. This hadn't been a random encounter; Carl actually had a plan.

"Up there – to the left," Carl ordered. Otto squinted and could just see the large bulk of the four-story Shuler Theater loom up ahead of them. "Go on over there, between those buildings – and keep those hands up where I can see them!"

They moved on past the rear loading dock, past the darkened stage door entrance steps, and around the right rear corner of the theater. Here was a passageway formed by the recessed area between the buildings. Otto staggered on the uneven ground and stopped suddenly. He had almost toppled headlong into what seemed to be a large hole in the ground. Another flash from the festive skies revealed that the hole was a purposely dug pit, about five feet wide by eight long and maybe five feet deep.

My lord! he thought. *He's actually dug a grave!*

In sporadic bursts of light Otto could now see this was some sort of workman's ditch recently excavated for some purpose. Tools, buckets, and pieces of loose stone lay in the bottom and a small stepladder was in place to allow the laborers an easy way in and out of the ditch. The entire area smelled of dust, wet dirt, and cement and it soon became evident that repairs were being made to the old limestone foundation that had deteriorated at the corner of the building. Part of the foundation lay open in places. Work still obviously had to be completed.

"That's far enough," Carl snarled. Otto stood precariously on the very edge of the ditch and peered down into the hole. He still felt as if he was staring down into his own grave – as he very well probably was. Otto had a sudden premonition that it seemed right and just to be standing here at this very place that seemed to have been prepared for this very moment.

So, this is how it ends, he thought. *So much for prayers for a long and peaceful life.*

Otto glanced around, looking for any last vestige of hope – any means of escape.

"Don't you move an inch," Carl snarled. Otto felt the gun press into the small of his back while Carl's free hand roughly searched him from behind. He felt his wallet being pulled out of his pants pocket, along with his keys and money.

"Carl – please," Otto started, but then Carl leaned his face close to Otto's ear, the pistol still digging hard into his back.

"So, now you're going to beg for you life?" he growled. "Go on then –

beg! I love it when they beg!"

Otto pressed his mouth shut and didn't continue.

"Turn around!" Carl ordered.

"Carl – Son, you have to listen to me – "

"Don't call me *Son,*" Carl snapped. "You've got nothing to say that I could possibly be interested in – unless it's to tell me where to find them!"

"Find what, Carl?" Otto asked, turning slowly around.

"Don't play games with me, old man," he snarled. "You know what I mean! The diary – and that stupid journal you've been keeping." He had now jammed the gun into Otto's stomach and with the other hand searched through Otto's jacket pockets. He snatched the cap off Otto's head and felt around the brim and lining before slapping him hard across the face with it.

"Where are they?" Carl shouted. Otto slowly rubbed his stinging cheek, then turned his back to Carl, trying to quench the anger he felt rising inside.

"Is this for him? Or for you?" Otto asked evenly after a few moments.

"What?"

"Him? Or you? It is a very simple question, Carl, requiring a very simple answer. I mean, I cannot honestly see why you would be personally interested in my old written ravings. It is all ancient history to someone like you," Otto paused, his mind working up an idea, then turning back around and dropping his hands to his side, facing Carl now, he continued, "in which case, I am guessing you can no longer think for yourself – I know the military trains that out of a man – you know, I was in the army once, too. Well, not quite as elite as the U.S. Marine Corps, mind you – but *Der Korps,* nonetheless."

Otto was purposely rambling now, trying to rile Carl up, maybe get him to make a serious mistake. Otto was actually enjoying the game, deadly as it was, but watched Carl carefully.

"Shut up!" Carl barked. "You don't know a damned thing about it!"

"Oh. Right. I forgot. I do not know your 'father' any better than you do – even though we both know it is he who wants these – *histories* of mine." Otto paused again as Carl took a step back. Otto knew he now had him thinking. *And if I can get him to listen just a bit longer,* he thought.

"What the hell are you talking about?" Carl demanded.

"I am talking about something that has been kept from you, Carl, for years now, not only by your own – well, by Conrad Neumann. But also by me, and by your mother, even, and –"

Carl cut him off by swinging the pistol across Otto's face where it cracked against his upper lip and split it.

"Don't you dare speak of my mother again, you piece of shit!" He stepped forward and grabbed Otto by the lapels of his jacket and shook him like he would a child. He was a couple inches taller than Otto and outweighed him by probably thirty pounds of pure muscle. Their faces were only a few inches from each other and Carl's breath was hot against Otto's cheek. He breathed heavily and stared into Otto's eyes, daring him to speak again.

Carl's fury abated just as quickly as it had erupted; he let go of Otto and stepped back again, turning half away now, a troubled look on his face, as if trying to absorb some truth that hovered just outside the perimeter of his mind. Otto waited a few moments, barely breathing; the only sounds that could be heard were the continued occasional pops and shrieks of joy from the celebration on the next street.

Otto felt no more fear – no more worries regarding his life. A comforting peace had indeed descended upon him like angels' wings; he felt warmth emerging from his heart, spreading throughout his being, and then passing on through the pores of his skin to radiate outside of himself. He felt that if he could only direct it, like a stream of warm energy, toward this angry young man in front of him, then anything miraculous was possible. Otto had no more words to describe what he was feeling. The word love seemed entirely inadequate. What he felt, instead, was more a deep yearning to have this all end: all of this hate and pain and loss that had permeated his life, and for this pitiful, hateful young man to have an opportunity to deny the dark impulses that governed his being and to embrace the power of God's light.

Otto was also ready for all the secrets to end.

"Son – I do not really care anymore what you think –"

"I said don't call me *Son,*" Carl whispered huskily over his shoulder, the pistol hanging limply at his side now.

"Yes – I think I will. For it pleases me to call you 'Son,' right now." Carl's lips tightened and he glared back at Otto.

"Conrad wants that diary – but we both know that it is your mother's diary, not his – and as you've mentioned before, it rightfully belongs to you, not him." Carl shifted his feet and looked back at Otto for a second. "Carl," Otto proceeded to ask, "did Conrad warn you not to read the diary – or the journal?"

Carl rubbed his face with his free hand, then slowly looked away again. "So what if he did?" he asked.

"Because," Otto continued, "Conrad wants the diary so that he can prevent you from learning what it is your mother wanted you to know someday." Otto took a deep breath, then continued. "And since I'm the only one who does know, Conrad also needs me dead – among other reasons." He managed a weak smile.

"Carl," Otto continued, "Don't you see? *You* are that twisted man's perfect revenge against me." He paused and slowly reached out his hand and placed it on Carl's shoulder. "That's why I think that the day has now come – for you to know, also – so that we may both put an end to the charade and lies."

"You're the one who's lying," Carl growled in a low, deadly voice. He squirmed away from Otto's hand, took a step back, and slowly raised the pistol again until it was aimed at Otto's chest. "You're lying – and you're stalling and you're trying to distract me and get me all worked up so that I won't kill you." Carl smirked and went on, "But there's something you haven't figured out, my lying friend – and that is that my father actually loves me, in ways you could never know or understand — and he has shown me that the weak and sniveling scum of the earth – like you – have ruined this world and don't deserve a place in it, and need to be crushed under the boot like a cockroach! And that some of us – the very select few – have been anointed by Heaven to carry out a cleansing, a purge –"

Otto's smile began to fade during Carl's tirade. He took a step toward Carl, ignoring the gun pointed at him.

"Carl, there is no anointing of God for such an evil work as that. What you are spouting is not from your own heart. It is pure National Socialism – I should know – at one time I also bought into it entirely, until I knew better. This all comes from a man who has deluded you as he has allowed himself to continue to be deluded and misled."

Otto stopped to think some more, not wanting to lose this chance, choosing his words carefully. He looked back at Carl and continued. "Do you know what I have only recently learned myself? That all are created equal; all are deceived, originally, and fallen; and that all were then redeemed by a God who actually walked this earth, experienced the hardships, temptations – and even joys – that we do, and in the process, called us all to be better than we are?"

"Shut up with that crazy talk!"

"Carl," Otto continued, undeterred, "this heartless demon who calls himself your 'father' has deceived you, as he once did me, like the great devil that he is." He took another cautious step toward Carl's gun.

"He is not who he appears to be, Son!"

"Don't you move – not another step closer! And stop calling me that!" Carl's pistol shook in his hand.

Otto stretched out his arm slowly toward Carl's gun hand, the tips of his fingers almost touching the weapon. Whatever happened now, Otto was resigned to his fate: He was content with it.

He decided to get to the point.

"Carl, there is something I have needed to tell you for a great while now," Otto continued. The words were already swelling within him in power and truth; he was about to finally divulge Evie's long-hidden secret to her son.

Carl's fingers visibly tightened on the pistol grip; his forefinger curved toward the trigger. Otto opened his mouth to speak.

"Hey!"

The disembodied voice shouted out from behind them, and a quick and sudden flurry of confusion burst out of nowhere as a figure ran out of the shadows and threw itself between the two men. A panicked struggle ensued, with a flailing of arms, punctuated by grunts and more shouts as the three men fought and pushed one another. Otto heaved forward, stretching and clawing with his fingers, trying to find the pistol before it could go off. The three bodies surged as one grotesque, multi-limbed beast, stumbling about, arms flailing, deep and guttural sounds being emitted.

Fireworks burst and suddenly lit the area again; the colored skies illuminated the faces in front him. Otto gasped as he recognized the third man: Father Michael, who must have followed them into the alley, against Otto's specific urging, and had waited to intervene now upon seeing the danger escalate between the two men.

Another series of delayed explosions went off around them and in the air above them, but this time something suddenly felt strange and wrong to Otto, and all three of them froze seemingly in equal surprise. Otto stared into the other two faces as an odor of acrid gunpowder arose in their midst. None of them had heard Carl's pistol go off during the last explosion of fireworks.

It had.

The brilliant flashes of color began to fade on their faces, just inches from one another, but not before Otto noticed a trickle of blood dribble from the corner of Father Michael's mouth and he saw the light begin to go out in his eyes, just behind his glasses.

"No – no!" Otto whispered to the priest. He tried to hold him up as Father Michael's body slumped heavily between Carl and Otto. Otto tried to catch him, but suddenly, his own arms felt very heavy and would not work properly, his legs rubbery and numb. Otto stumbled backward, confused, and not knowing for sure exactly what had happened or why the unexplained dizziness he now felt in his head. A sharp stab of pain shot from his side. He looked down, pulled the corner of his leather jacket back, and discovered a slowly spreading stain of blood on his shirt over his abdomen. He shook his head, trying to clear it. His mind began going blank.

He felt the unmistakable sensation of falling.

The last coherent thought Otto had as all three of them fell into the tomb-like ditch was how quickly his previous sense of peace and righteous purpose had fled as he sensed the beating wings of demons all now flying far away.

All about him faded to dark and total silence.

#

Carl Neumann stirred, touched his head, and slowly rolled over to raise himself to a sitting position. He opened his eyes, surveyed his surroundings, and realized quickly where he was. He suddenly panicked, jumped up, and looked around. He checked himself out for wounds, running his hands all over his body, and found nothing serious save for some bruises and scrapes. He turned and saw the two bodies he had been lying on at the bottom of the ditch. He stooped and rolled the first body over.

He swore.

The blood-soaked body belonged to the man Carl had seen with Otto earlier, standing in the storefront on 1st Street, watching the fireworks. Carl caught his breath; the man was a priest. Carl had seen more than his share of dead men, but he had never seen a dead priest before; the fact that he had now killed one sent a strange and unfamiliar chill through his stomach.

He then looked over at Otto Eberhardt's pale, unconscious face, and dismissed the priest completely. Carl stood up and rubbed his head, thinking carefully. His father was not going to be pleased – not pleased at all. The mission was to have been so simple: isolate Otto, retrieve the two books his father had described, then take Otto someplace quiet and finish him off.

He had botched it all so badly. His father was not going to be pleased at all. Carl felt a fury begin to boil deep inside, along with an overwhelming need to express that anger.

"You son-of-a-bitch!" he shouted and then kicked Otto's body two or three times in the side and the ribs. Otto didn't flinch or move at all, which, of course, Carl never expected him to. He calmed his temper and glanced around quickly to ascertain if anyone was nearby, then knelt back down and searched Otto's body once more – every pocket, every fold of clothing. Perhaps he had missed something in the heat of the moment.

Nothing.

He stood back up, exasperated. In the sudden light of another flash in the sky, he saw something glint out of the corner of his eye and recognized his pistol lying there in the bottom of the ditch. He quickly picked it up, blew the dirt out of it, and with hatred in his eyes, looked back down at Otto's inert form. He gritted his teeth as he again felt uncontrollable anger well up; aimed the gun at Otto's peaceful face. *Death's too good for you,* he muttered. He started to squeeze the trigger.

"Hey!" he suddenly heard. "You, there!"

A large middle-aged man had come running up the alley, brandishing a flashlight that bathed the scene completely in a pool of bright white light as he walked forward. "What's going on over there?" The stranger was puffing hard, out of shape and out of breath, and wiped the sweat from his brow with the back of his free hand as he moved nearer.

Carl quickly hid the gun behind his back and turned to face the man, trusting that he could not see beyond him into the ditch.

"Nothing to worry about, sir. Nothing at all." Carl answered brightly, smiling as he put a foot on the ladder to begin to climb out. "Just lost my hat down there in that ditch. It's all good now, though."

The man was coming closer, beaming the light all over the area and then back into Carl's eyes.

"Just hold up a second there, friend," the man retorted, pulling back his jacket to reveal a security badge in his shirt. He had also placed his other hand onto the butt of a service revolver holstered at his side.

"If you went down there to get your hat, how come you're not wearing it? Where is it?"

The security guard had just made the ultimate mistake of taking a few more steps than was frugal and now paid the price for it when Carl brought the pistol up quickly from behind his back and fired once, instinctively, putting a .32 caliber round right in the center of the man's forehead. The guard opened his eyes and mouth wide in surprised silent protest, stood still for a moment, and crumpled slowly into a heap in the alley.

Carl stood quietly at the top of the ladder for several moments, his gun still drawn and ready, looking and waiting and listening for anything and everything. *What the hell else can go wrong tonight?* he thought. Hopefully, anyone who might have heard the gunshots would think the noises were part of the show. After a moment, he stepped out of the ditch, slipped the pistol into his waistband, walked over to the dead guard, and began to drag him over the ground with the intent of rolling him into the hole on top of the other two bodies.

Sprinkles of rain began to patter around and on him, and the sound of the raindrops suddenly merged with the muted sound of applause on the next block as the fireworks display was ending and the crowd began to quickly disperse. Carl heard their voices now passing on the avenues on either end of the alley. Soon, he feared, some might possibly decide to take a shortcut right through here. He needed to think, needed to know what to do next, needed some guidance, and to get somewhere safe.

He needed to get out of here.

For the first time in years, Carl Neumann felt at risk and exposed, unsure of what to do next. Abruptly, he dropped the dead guard's legs and feet, left the three bodies where they lay, and ran away panicked under the cover of the noisy, rainy night.

CHAPTER 29
THE WORD MADE FLESH

Trent and Maggie left the Clayton Senior Center in Maggie's Lincoln Navigator. Trent was once again driving and, once again, was losing an argument with Maggie, this time about taking her home before going out to Conrad Neumann's ranch to confront him.

"That would take you miles out of your way. What on earth would you do that for?" she had asked. "I'll just go with you."

"Well, for one thing, according to that journal, this guy's a serial killer," Trent answered.

"So?"

"So, he's been killing folks for decades, now – not to mention he's an ex-Nazi!"

"So?"

"So – he seems to have developed a knack for making people disappear!"

"So?"

"So, will you quit saying 'so'?" Trent was exasperated. This discussion was going nowhere. "It could be dangerous, that's what's *so*!'"

"He's ninety-something years old and in a wheelchair," Maggie continued. "What's he gonna do – throw his teeth at us?"

Trent stopped at a stop sign, looked over at her, only to shake his head.

"Margot Van Ryan, you are the most stubborn woman I have ever met in my life! I am a law enforcement officer and you're a civilian." He paused and glanced at her. "And one I happen to care about. What in the hell makes any sense about this? If you think I'm about to take you into a situation that could turn ugly in a heartbeat, you've got another think coming."

Maggie turned to him and held up her fingers one at a time as she spoke. "Count 'em! My car, my property they broke into, my family," she paused only to take a breath, "and don't forget that he is living on my Aunt Evie's property and that Carl is my first cousin – which doesn't exactly give me warm fuzzy feelings – and that most of all," she continued on, still counting on her fingers, "you wouldn't even have any of this information had it not been for me finding that old journal in the first place! So, don't you give me any of that 'dangerous' business, Mr. Sheriff-Man," she added. "You ain't seen 'dangerous,' yet!"

Trent fumed and glared at her for several moments, totally lost for words. "That's Deputy Sheriff-Man," he finally muttered, turned away abruptly, and rubbed his face in exasperation.

Maggie's eyes flashed, but just as quickly she smiled, sat back against her door, and put an exaggerated Southern drawl in her voice. "Trent Carter," her voice dripped, "Ah swear, Ah am flattered that you all are worried 'bout lil' 'ole me." She couldn't help but grin; then, back to her own voice, she shrugged her shoulders and noted, "But to my recollection, that *is* the first time I have ever heard you say that you care." She suddenly gasped in mock surprise, held up her hand again, and wiggled her fingers. "And you know what? That makes five, doesn't it! I believe that's called a 'Full House' in cards?"

A blast of a horn behind them made Trent jump suddenly as he noticed a car in the rear view mirror impatiently waiting for them to drive on. He blushed, looked quickly both ways, whipped the wheel, and gunned the big SUV out onto the highway northwest toward the Dry Cimarron and the Neumann Ranch. Maggie had won yet another argument; he frowned and muttered something else under his breath.

"What was that, Honey?" Maggie asked sweetly, reaching over with her finger to curl a lock of his hair at his collar. He shrugged her hand away.

"I said, 'Something happens, it'll just serve you right!'"

"Well, if it does, Darlin', you can put that on my gravestone." Maggie settled back in her seat with a satisfied look on her face.

Forty-five minutes later, they turned off of the highway and drove through the weathered wooden gates where Trent could just barely make out the faded name "Neumann Ranch." They continued on the dirt road running through stands of gigantic elm trees that had not been properly trimmed in years, some of which had shed large limbs scattered about here and there making a potential fire hazard. The road wound down and around until it reached the river, following it along a ravine for another half mile or so before it spilled out into broad meadows and overgrown pastures that appeared not to have been grazed or farmed in a long time. On either side of them, maybe a mile or so apart at this point, red sandstone walls of the canyon rose up over 300 feet or more in some places, marking the passage of geologic time and history. Anyone eyeing these vistas could imagine the spirits of Comanche warriors lurking and stalking from the rims of the canyon. The big vehicle bounced along the pitted and rutted road in great need of maintenance, as was the rambling single story ranch house that soon loomed up in front of them. Obviously, the years had not been kind to the Neumann enterprises. Trent wondered how the place even kept afloat.

Trent breathed a sigh of relief as he pulled up to the front of the house. No other vehicles were in the drive, which meant Carl was hopefully occupied elsewhere and would not pose an immediate threat to them. But they still had Ernst Brandt to deal with. Even if he were elderly, Trent knew they shouldn't take any chances with this man, especially if he were the killer and mastermind Trent suspected he was. He switched off the engine and turned once more to Maggie.

"I suppose it's useless to ask you to stay in the car," he said, resigned.

Maggie smiled at him coyly, removed her seat belt, and got out without a word.

Trent rolled his eyes, got out, too, but in a huff, and slammed the door. He reached under his jacket and adjusted the Glock .45 concealed in his belt at the small of his back. They stepped up onto the covered porch where Trent rang the doorbell, which echoed deep inside somewhere. Out of the corner of his eye, he saw a heavy drape being pulled aside in a nearby window, and just as quickly dropped. Trent heard the sound of brisk footsteps approaching, and suddenly, the big door was pulled open wide.

Neumann's stern housekeeper stood looking at them stoically through the screen door. She said nothing at first and kept one hand firmly on the door. Trent cleared his throat.

"Afternoon, Mrs. Meeks," he offered politely with a quick, professional smile. He pulled his badge from his jacket and held it open for her.

"Good afternoon, Deputy Carter. How may I help you?" She hadn't even bothered to look at his badge.

"I need to see Mr. Neumann, if he is available."

"May I tell him what this is about?"

"Oh, I think he'll know what it's about when you announce me," Trent remarked.

"Tell him it's about his damn son," Maggie mumbled. Trent casually slid the toe of his boot over and tapped the edge of Maggie's shoe to shush her.

Mrs. Meeks looked over at Maggie as if she were just now noticing her. The housekeeper raised an eyebrow, looked her up and down once, and nonchalantly ignored her again as she looked back at Trent and unlatched the screen. "Won't you come in and wait in the parlor?" she asked evenly in a clipped accent. Her words were an instruction, not an invitation.

Trent held the door open for Maggie. They both walked past Mrs. Meeks, who then shut the heavy wooden door behind them. They followed her out of the entryway and into the living room where she offered them a seat. Trent shook his head.

"We'll just stand here and wait," he insisted. Mrs. Meeks looked at him blankly for a moment, but briskly turned and left the room. After she was gone, Maggie began to snicker. Trent looked at her and frowned.

"*Wait in zee parlor,*" Maggie chuckled. "She sounds like a character from one of those old black and white movie mysteries, especially with that European accent. Where do you suppose they found her?"

Trent didn't answer, but looked around the large sitting room. Heavy drapes hung over all the windows, effectively blocking the daylight. The house felt blanketed in darkness with only an occasional lamp to throw any light about the room, which was decorated with massive pieces of antique furniture, some of which looked quite old and expensive. The walls were covered with large oil paintings, lit with muted studio lighting mounted on the high ceilings, depicting various classic hunting scenes of men on horseback and hunting dogs surrounding deer, foxes, and even a lion. Trent was no art critic, but the paintings looked quite well done and expensive in massive, gilt-edged frames, if somebody liked that sort of thing, and might have been found hanging in some nobleman's hunting lodge in Europe.

He could hear low voices coming from the interior of the house, then silence, then the housekeeper's echoing footsteps returning.

"Mr. Neumann will see you now," she instructed again, emerging from the shadows of the hallway to stand in the archway at the far end of the large living room. She extended her arm to show them the way and raised an eyebrow. "He says he has been expecting you."

"I'll just bet he has," whispered Maggie as they followed Mrs. Meeks once more. Trent took Maggie's upper arm in his hand and squeezed harder than necessary. "Ow!" she protested under her breath.

The hallway was plunged even deeper into darkness as Trent had the distinct feeling he was entering an inner sanctum, or perhaps a tomb. The housekeeper led them on a meandering route as they passed several closed doors before she finally took them through another archway that opened into an even larger room – a den – that looked as if it spread the entire width of the house. The walls here were lined with heavy bookcases interspersed with several trophy heads of animals. In one corner stood a large oaken gun case with a glass door and several rifles illuminated from the interior. In the opposite corner sat a massive stone fireplace with a mantle of oak five inches thick, two feet wide, and ran the twelve-foot width of the fireplace. Atop this mantle was mounted a large mountain lion, so life-like it appeared to have just now jumped up onto the mantle to snarl down at them.

Trent began to wander around the large room, taking in the various mementos on the shelves and photos on the walls. Some were older pictures of a much younger Conrad Neumann, posing in hunting attire along with his son Carl. Trent found it interesting there were no photos of anyone else that he could see, particularly not even of Neumann's late wife Evie or his daughter Caroline. Trent straightened up and let his gaze wander the remainder of the dark room and its memorabilia.

The place seemed more a mausoleum than a museum.

"My son's trophies," growled a low, disembodied, but familiar voice from somewhere in the dim recesses of the den. Trent looked around, surprised, then noticed a slight movement and detected the faint whir of an electric motor as Conrad Neumann's wheelchair rolled from out of the dark recesses and around the end of a large leather sofa in the middle of the room. Trent was a little disconcerted; it was impossible to determine whether Conrad had just entered the room or had been lurking there all the while.

Trent had prepared himself for what they were about to see, but heard a sharp intake of breath from Maggie as the ancient Neumann's ruined visage rolled gradually into view and stopped a few feet away from her. "I stopped hunting years ago," the old man continued, his voice emerging from a face that looked as if pink wax had melted down over one side of his head and then hardened again, leaving half of a functional nose and mouth and one clear eye.

"That will be all for now, Angela," Neumann rasped. The housekeeper hesitated, then turned, and clopped away down the hall.

"Thanks for seeing us. I trust we're not interrupting you from anything," Trent said.

"Not at all, Mr. Carter. Please make yourselves comfortable. I was just working on my memoirs." He started to chuckle, which turned into a wet and lingering cough. "Isn't that what old men are supposed to say? That's what they do with all their time, 'memoirs?'"

"No, thanks – we'll stand," replied Trent. "This shouldn't take too long." Trent wandered over to a large mahogany desk situated along one side of the room and began openly snooping at various papers and items there. "And funny you should mention 'memoirs,' Mr. Neumann – that is, if that's really the name I should be using." The old man cocked his head, curiously.

"What on earth are you talking about?" the old man chortled.

"Well, since you brought up Carl, when's the last time you saw your son, Mr. Neumann? Or that Jimmy Streck fella who works for you?"

"Oh, I see," Neumann answered. "You're still on that witch hunt of yours, aren't you – still trying to pin those half-assed charges against Carl? And I know nothing about any Streck person. He's a friend of Carl's, I suppose." Neumann's wheelchair whirred again and came back toward the desk. "We've had this same discussion before, Mr. Carter, if you'll recall – Oh yes, that's right – I don't think you can recall much of anything, can you? Well, what *I* seem to recall is that you've had some difficulty with your head, haven't you? Something about some memory loss, or a serious injury of some sort – some such tragic situation?"

Neumann glanced back over in Maggie's direction. "You really must be cautious with whom you choose to associate, my dear niece," he offered, gratuitously. "Oh yes, I recognize you now – young Margot Van Ryan, isn't it?" He continued, not awaiting an answer from her. "Anyway, you must be careful, Margot. You never know about some people or the danger they may pose for you." He lowered his voice conspiratorially, still speaking to Maggie but peering at Trent. "They say he was responsible for the brutal death of his wife!"

Maggie shuffled in discomfort and looked away from this horror of a man before her. Neumann wheeled even closer to her. He seemed to enjoy the look of sheer disgust on her face and licked his lips as he neared her. "You know, it's remarkable how you have grown to look so much like your Aunt Evie! Same raven hair, same piercing green eyes, and such a ravishing figure!" His good eye leered at her.

Maggie's face turned ashen as if she were about to be sick.

"Too bad she didn't survive the fire, isn't it?" he continued in a lower voice, leaning toward her. He absently scratched the nub of an ear with his forefinger. "Can you imagine it? We would've made quite a pair to look at, don't you think? Two mangled, hideous people, with nothing left to enjoy in life – just hiding out from the world."

"I – I never knew my Aunt Evie, Mr. Neumann," Maggie stammered, trying not to back away from him. "I wasn't born when she – when the accident happened." She looked away. "I'm so very sorry."

"*Sorry*?" the old scarecrow blurted. Maggie was taken aback, but he continued. "Why should you be sorry, you and your wealthy family? That father of yours – Richard – too arrogant and hateful to ever check up on his family here – or even come to his own sister's funeral! Never even called or asked after his own flesh and blood – his niece and nephew – or me. And you all only lived in the next county – not as if you were hundreds of miles away. Why, even now you can't even bring yourself to call me 'Uncle.'" He rolled a few more inches nearer to Maggie and studied her with animosity on the undamaged part of his face. "So, please give me no more of the Van Ryan self-righteous pity, My. Dear. Niece!" The last three words were measured out slowly and venomously.

"Alright, you quite done now, scaring the poor defenseless lady?" Trent interrupted from across the room. He had taken the opportunity to move around to the other side of the desk and now flipped open the laptop that had been closed there. The screen flickered to life and displayed a video that had been paused. "And what do we have here? Part of those memoirs you were talking about?" Trent continued while punching keys at random. "Never could get the hang of these computers. Never had much use for them, myself."

"Don't touch that!" Neumann spluttered, spun his chair around, and hurriedly rolled back toward the desk.

"Well, would you look at that!" Trent exclaimed as the video began to flicker and play on the screen. "Seems I got something working here, after all. Home movies?"

Muffled sounds emanated from the tinny speakers along with occasional voices. The scene jerked and moved with the camera movement and soon settled and focused on the figure of a person running across open ground in the distance. The camera next swiveled and revealed a man standing near the cameraman. A rifle was raised to the man's cheek, obscuring his features as he took careful aim. A voice came clearly out of the speakers.

"*Ya got him?*" the off-screen voice asked.

"*Yep,*" answered the gunman as the scene shifted off of him and back onto the running person in the distance, perhaps a hundred yards away. The camera zoomed in: the running man now looked only a few feet away, but the jerkiness of the zoom effect made it impossible to see who it was. Whoever it was clearly struggled in their exhaustion to keep running. Suddenly came the loud crack of the rifle and the camera jerked in reaction before settling down again, only now no running man was visible, just an unrecognizable heap on the ground that slowly moved and crawled, one hand reaching up shakily, then freezing for a moment, and then falling back to the ground. Nothing else moved. A shout of *Woohoo* burst from the speakers as the view swung again to the shooter who now lowered the gun and grinned for the camera.

The gunman was none other than Carl Neumann.

At that exact moment, the old man's hand flew over and slammed the lid of the computer shut.

"Well, now, that was a real interesting movie, there, my friend. Quite interesting, indeed. And if you ask me, not only interesting and entertaining, but also fairly incriminating."

"You don't have a warrant to be looking at that," Neumann blurted, trying to grapple the laptop from the desk with his one good hand. He abruptly began a coughing fit, dropped the computer in his lap, and grabbed a well-used handkerchief.

Trent stepped back, sat down in the high-backed leather desk chair, and steepled his fingers. "And it's comments like that one right there – regarding a warrant – that makes it sound to me like you've got something to hide, Mr. Neumann – Sir," Trent continued. "Oh, wait just a minute." He paused and pulled out a small notebook from his jacket, flipped a few pages, and referred to some notes there.

"Or should I call you, *Herr Kapitan Ernst Brandt*?"

Complete silence descended like a dark blanket on the room for what seemed like an eternity. Trent glanced over at Maggie, who stood rooted beside the couch. Her eyes were wide and watching the old German closely. Ernst continued to stare down at the computer in his lap and slowly raised his head. His one good eye bore into Trent malevolently.

"Where did you hear that name?" he demanded in a quiet, gravelly voice.

"Well, let's just say I have a rather unusual source," Trent answered, flipping a couple more pages in his notebook.

"Who told you that name?" Ernst demanded, slapping the edge of the desk with his good hand.

"Well, now, wherever I heard it – *Ernst* – it's clear that I finally have your full attention." Trent rose from the desk chair, glanced once more at his notes, then looked up again and smiled at the old man. "Surely, you remember a guy by the name of Otto Eberhardt, don't you? Excuse me – *Leutnant Otto Franz Eberhardt.* Good friend of yours from way back in your war days as I understand it."

The old man slumped back slowly in his wheelchair, his face going flat and expressionless. He gazed unflinchingly at Trent, who suddenly felt a chill slip up his spine as if he were only inches away from a coiled rattlesnake.

"It's the journal, isn't it," Ernst whispered.

"What was that?"

"You have Otto's damned journal, don't you? That's the only explanation. But how?" He leaned forward again. "Where did you find it?" Ernst turned his piercing blue eye toward Maggie. "Was it you? Yes, I think it must be." Ernst pointed a shaking finger and pierced her with his venomous gaze. The corner of his mouth twitched as Maggie visibly shuddered. "We searched your ranch," Ernst continued, almost to himself, then looked up with sudden revelation. "But, of course, you had already found it by then, hadn't you? I wouldn't be surprised if you have that damned diary, too," he snapped.

"Diary?" Maggie blurted. "What diary?" She exchanged a quick look with Trent.

Ernst caught the puzzlement that passed between them, but searched Maggie's face closely as a wretched smile crawled over what was left of his mouth. He looked back to Trent, who also had a quizzical look on his face.

"You haven't found her diary, then?" Ernst continued, incredulously, raising his good eyebrow in surprise, another welcome revelation crossing his face. "You don't know anything about it!"

Maggie took a couple of steps toward the old man, her courage returning. "You killed all those people," she exclaimed. "It's all in there – in Otto's journal. And there's even an eyewitness – a survivor. Tell him, Trent! And who cares about some dumb diary. It's all in the journal – we've all read it – what?"

This last was to Trent, who had, too late, held his hand up to Maggie to stop her from saying anything more.

"All?" asked Ernst slyly. "Who is *'All'*?"

Trent sighed, then stood up, and took his cell phone out of his pocket.

"Look, *Herr Brandt,*" he began. "I have enough already to call in for a warrant. I've got the evidence in that journal – it may be hearsay from a dead man, but everything still points back to you and Carl. And I'll bet if I turn this house upside down that I'll find even more," Trent's eyes drifted over to the rifle case and wondered to himself what all a set of ballistics tests would turn up on all those rifles. "But it would sure be a lot easier and better for everyone concerned if you'll just admit to all this: admit who you really are, tell us where we can find Carl and Streck, and we can be done with all of this, once and for all.

"I mean, aren't you tired of it all, Ernst? Living this lie, pretending to be Carl and Caroline's father?" Ernst kept his malevolent glare fixed on Trent's face, but said nothing.

"And just what about your old friend, Otto?" he continued. "I mean, you must have murdered him, too, I'm guessing. And living with the guilt of everything that's happened, for years now? Living with all those dead people on your conscience? Don't you want to die with even a little bit of dignity, some peace? I mean – don't you have even a little remorse for killing your best friend – for Otto? Or for what you've done to this family?"

Ernst Brandt had dropped his head into his chest, breathing steadily and deeply, gripping the arm of the wheelchair with his one good hand, the other one shriveled in his lap. He was trembling. Trent suddenly thought he might be having a heart attack. Brandt slowly raised his head again.

He was smiling and chuckling – it looked like a grimace.

"*My best friend.*" he growled, then continued. "I did not kill Otto – Otto killed himself if you must know. It would have been better had he died a long time ago when we were captured in Tunisia. At least, then, he was still a soldier, dedicated to our cause. But then he became weak and lost the heart of a warrior – never saw the greater need, to keep serving the Fatherland. Anything Otto suffered he brought upon himself." Ernst made a slicing motion with his good hand. "But I never laid a finger on him."

"So just how do you suppose he did die, then?" Trent asked, rising from the chair. "I mean, we figure that has to be his body we pulled out of the old theater basement."

Brandt put a blank look back on his face and stared at Trent for a long time before turning his head away. "I have no idea what you're talking about."

Maggie couldn't stand it any longer. "But you just confessed to it all – and – and there's that video there – and that other woman, who survived – and the murder of Trent's wife." Here Maggie took a step toward Trent. "Tell him, Trent – how you remember now about Carl and that other guy, shooting you and Vickie!"

Trent made a gesture for Maggie to keep quiet.

"Confessed?" Ernst blurted, whipping back around to face her. "You stupid bitch! I confess nothing. You have no proof of anything. That video there could have been made by anyone. And that so-called journal you say you have is no more than the written ravings of a lunatic who has been dead for years – and good riddance, if you ask me!"

"Maybe not by your own hand," Maggie taunted, "but surely by your order!" She turned back to Trent. "Tell him — tell him how Father Michael begged you to protect Caroline from him and Carl, just today, at the nursing home!"

Silence filled the room, as Brandt's squinted his one good eye and peered closely at Maggie. His wheelchair whirred as he then turned it again toward Trent.

"I fear your lady-friend has started to become hysterical. Perhaps it is time for you both to leave."

"Hysterical!" Maggie blurted. She started to say something else.

"Maggie! Please," Trent entreated her, and she became quiet.

And you, Deputy Carter," Brandt spat. "Go ahead and get your damned warrants for all the good they will do you! Your feeble-minded personal testimony regarding any so-called *shootings* will be in shreds in the hands of a good defense attorney, especially after they subpoena your psychiatric records, yes?"

At this last comment, Trent felt the blood rush into his face. Before he could muster up an adequate response, the old man straightened up suddenly and spun around to the doorway.

"Angela!" he called out, and only a moment passed before the housekeeper materialized at the door.

"Yes sir!" she answered quietly, not looking straight at him.

"Our guests are leaving now. Please show them out."

"That's quite alright; we'll find our own way out." Trent stepped over and took Maggie by the arm. They walked over to the doorway before Trent turned around.

"But I will be back with that warrant – *Mr. Neumann,*" he said, with a glance at the housekeeper, then back at Ernst. "You might want to save yourself some embarrassment, after you've had a chance to think about all this."

Trent turned and they stepped through the archway as he continued over his shoulder, "Give me a call – real soon."

#

Their footsteps faded off through the hallway; eventually, Ernst heard the front door slam shut. He waited a few minutes before he wheeled over to a bookcase, selected one of the many scrapbooks there, turned, and dropped it onto his desk. He opened it and methodically turned the pages of old photographs and newspaper clippings until he found the entry he wanted.

His gnarled finger traced a faded newspaper photograph depicting a young woman seated in the back seat of a sheriff's department cruiser along with a familiar deputy who stood near the open door. Ernst leaned back and opened a desk drawer. He pulled out a mobile phone and pressed a quick-dial digit.

"Yes, Sir?" Carl's voice quietly answered on the other end.

"It is time to tie up all of our loose ends," Ernst said. There was silence for moment.

"I understand. And it's about damned time, too, if you ask me."

"Well, I didn't ask you, did I?" He paused. "Just where are you?"

"Over in Raton. Shall I begin here?"

Ernst thought for a second. "No," he answered, finally. "Better not to be too hasty or careless this time – not like before, with Otto." Carl had rushed things then, and subsequently they had never found the journal – or that diary. "That's exactly why we are in this predicament now," he continued, "because of your past screw ups!"

Ernst knew that Carl's inept actions had only lit a fire under Trent Carter after his wife had been killed. Ernst wanted to make sure everything was tidy this time before they finished off this troublesome deputy – and whoever else had had the ill fortune of getting involved.

"No, just send a clear warning for now," Ernst finally continued. "Nothing too specific, but that will make them give some pause to their actions, perhaps. In the meantime, we have a couple more serious concerns to deal with." Ernst looked again at the grainy newspaper photo of the young woman in the deputy's cruiser.

"Call your unpleasant friend, that Mr. Streck. I want him to deal with one of them."

"What concern is that?"

"A survivor that you missed, a few years back. Her name is," he quickly consulted the newspaper article again, "Mirielle Segura. Streck can track her down. There seems to have been an aunt living in Las Vegas. And you will explain to him exactly what to do when he finds her – remember, I said *no loose ends."*

Ernst heard silence on the other end for a moment and then, "I understand."

And what about the old priest, Brandt thought to himself, *the one Maggie had inadvertently mentioned just now? Seems he somehow knows things, perhaps? Just what was his real interest in the Neumann family? Just a coincidence?* Ernst thought hard for few moments. He was not a believer in coincidence — at all.

"And once you've dispatched Mr. Streck, get back over here and pick me up. You and I need to go back to the nursing home to personally take care of another issue. I think I might finally know where that diary is, and it's been right under our noses all this time."

"Oh, yeah?" responded Carl.

"Yes," Ernst answered, then paused. "Carl — just what do you remember about that priest friend of Otto's? You know — the one you told me befriended him in Raton, years ago? The one who so conveniently disappeared, around the time Otto died?"

There was a pause.

"What about him?" Carl finally asked.

"Well nothing, really, Carl," Brandt answered. He then lowered his voice to an exasperated growl, "except that it appears he is alive and well, and perhaps in possession of a good many secrets."

Another uncomfortable silence descended on the other end of the phone. For a moment, Ernst thought they had been disconnected.

"You still there?"

"I'll be there in a couple hours," Carl finally responded.

"And Carl, bring along that special pistol of yours, won't you, you know, the one with the silencer? I rather like that gun — I like how it feels in my hand, when it fires…and this is one loose end I'd like to take care of personally – for old time's sake.

CHAPTER 30
ACTS OF CONTRITION

Excerpt from the Journal of Otto Eberhardt

"August 18, 1977 – I will never be the same person again. My life has completely changed, and I can honestly say I have peace. Otto Franz Eberhardt is dead, yet lives. Michael Francis Shannon is alive, and yet rests in peace. May God be praised, for these can both be very good things!"

#

Otto blinked his eyes several times as the rain that had awakened him beat steadily on his face. He didn't immediately understand where he was, what had happened, why he was lying out in the rain. He tried to raise himself up, felt his head spin, and dropped back heavily in a muddy pool of water. Thunder rolled but he lay still for a minute, trying to get his bearings. He suddenly caught his breath, thinking he was back on the battlefield, perhaps lying gravely wounded as the noise of artillery crashed around him. He blinked several more times before vaguely remembering some sort of festive atmosphere – fireworks – and suddenly recalled a very different feeling of dread, not from a battle, not of festivities, but something altogether different. He turned his head to find his eyes focused on a man's shoe, just inches away from his face. He rose up again on his elbows and peered curiously at it.

He rolled over. This time he was able to make his way up to his hands and knees where he remained for another minute or two trying to get his throbbing head to stop spinning and the nausea to pass. His ribs and stomach ached fiercely as if a mule had kicked him.

He tried to determine his surroundings but instantly froze in horror. He seemed to be lying in the bottom of an open grave, but he realized he was not alone down here. A dead man lay immediately in front of him – the one connected to the shoe – and what's more, he thought he recognized the corpse. Otto pushed himself up further until he painfully sat back against the dirt wall of the grave. He wiped his eyes hard and ran his fingers through his soaked hair, trying hard to clear the last strands of cobwebs from his memory: He found himself staring down into the face of Father Michael as rain bounced off of his friend's unflinching, dead eyes. In a moment of clarity, everything came flooding back to him: the fireworks, the struggle with Carl, the priest stepping between them – then the gunshots, followed by that seemingly never-ending fall into darkness.

Otto caught his breath, looked away from his dead friend's waxen face, before realizing he was not at the bottom of a grave at all, but in some sort of construction area. He suddenly panicked and pressed himself even further into the wall.

So just where was Carl? He dared not move until he knew for sure.

After a few more minutes, he realized that the fireworks had ceased and the streetlights were back on and provided just enough reflected light to see and distinguish shapes in the shadows. Even though still nighttime, he was unsure of exactly how much time had passed.

He forced himself to wait for several more minutes although the urge was overwhelming to jump out of this hole and run for his life. Instead, he tried to listen and determine and assess every little noise. *Was Carl still lurking nearby? Waiting for him to show himself and blow his head off?*

With each breath, a severe pain grabbed his side. He reached down and touched the source of the pain, flinched, and pulled back his hand. He held up his fingers in the light of the nearby street lamp; they were covered in blood. He pulled his shirt up and away from the seeping wound at his side and squinted as he let the rain wash the blood away from a single, small bullet hole he saw there. He cringed as he gingerly felt around to his back and discovered a similar hole – the exit wound. He felt a surge of relief – at least the bullet had passed straight through. He took a couple of deep breaths, held the last one, and continued to prod with his fingers in a circumference around the wounds. He was no doctor, but had treated his share of battlefield wounds. The bleeding also seemed to have stopped for the moment, so he felt hopeful that the bullet had only damaged fatty tissues and had avoided any major organs or arteries, breaking into fragments, or other serious damage.

Father Michael, though, had not been so lucky.

Otto looked back over at his dead friend. Blood covered the front of his shirt, indicating a bad wound somewhere on the priest's chest. Otto prayed that his friend's death had been mercifully quick, with no suffering.

He sat back heavily and waited a couple more minutes, ignoring the rain that washed over and through him while he listened carefully and thought hard. The rain began to lighten up; he suddenly knew he could waste no more time. Someone might be along at any moment, and he would not be able to explain this scene coherently. Worse, Carl might be back to double-check his handiwork or to dispose of the bodies. Otto needed to be long gone by then.

He slowly forced himself up to a crouch, bent over with his hands on his knees until the pin-prick of circulation returned to his lower legs, and carefully, slowly stood up just enough to peek over the edge of the hole. He stopped and let his eyes scan from side to side, paying close attention to the shadows, identifying objects, waiting to catch any possible movements of anyone before they saw him. Satisfied that nothing moved out there, he turned his head to the right and froze in place, his eyes wide.

There, just a few feet away, was yet another body.

Was it Carl? He chanced a closer look and climbed a couple of steps up the ladder. From this angle, he could now see that the body definitely was not Carl's – the man was larger than Carl, and what was more, Otto didn't recognize him at all. But he could also clearly see, even from here, and judging from the trickle of blood that ran away from a small bullet wound in the center of the man's forehead was that the man was dead.

Otto looked back and forth and seeing no one around dropped back down into the hole and sat against the wall again with great relief. Carl was nowhere to be seen, but he needed to think now, to formulate a plan. He guessed the time to be somewhere around midnight, but he could not waste time. He had to get out of here quickly. With two dead bodies and Carl Neumann still wandering around out there somewhere, he needed to think his options through carefully. If he simply ran and some unseen witness identified him, he could be wrongly accused of a double murder. If he did manage to get away without being seen, Carl and Ernst were probably just waiting for him to make such a break for it – waiting to finish him off.

Think – think!

He looked around the ditch and surveyed all he could see: the step ladder, Father Michael's body, a couple of five gallon buckets, some pieces of scrap lumber, a large tarp covering other materials, and a few neatly stacked limestone bricks apparently ready to be put in place to complete the repairs to the foundation of the building. Otto rubbed the rain out of his eyes, thought awhile longer, then let his gaze wander back over to his dead friend's body. He felt a twinge of guilt just leaving him there exposed to the elements. To do so seemed somehow indecent, especially for such a good man, and he also knew it would only be a matter of time until the body would be found and its identity determined – and probably tied back to him since a number of witnesses had more than likely seen them together at the fireworks show. Otto glanced back down at the open foundation that awaited its few remaining pieces of stonework.

Suddenly, he knew exactly what he needed to do.

But would this really work? he wondered to himself. *Who was it going to really fool? And what about the workmen who were going to come back to their supposedly unfinished job tomorrow?*

His idea troubled him at first, but after considering his options, he realized what Father Michael would have told him to do. Otto sat back, dropped his head, and prayed. *How could he do such a thing? Wouldn't this be some sort of sin? Oh, please, dear God, what to do?*

At that exact moment, Otto felt a wave of peace and warmth pass over him. All his panic, confusion, doubt had ceased; he knew all would be right. But time was now of the essence. He went into action and stripped off his leather jacket, followed by his flannel shirt. He then crawled over in the mud and reached under Father Michael's shoulders.

"Forgive me, my dear friend," he said quietly as he raised the body into a sitting position. He quickly removed the priest's jacket, collar, vestments, and black shirt, then draped them all carefully on the tarp, not only to keep them out of the mud, but also to allow the rain to wash away any of the blood that might have permeated them. He struggled to redress his friend's body in his own clothes, pausing only when he noticed that the priest had, indeed, been shot squarely in the chest, and probably straight through the heart. Father Michael looked somehow much smaller with his pale upper torso bare to the cleansing rain. Otto made the sign of the cross and methodically continued with his work. When he finished dressing him, he gently laid his friend back down in the mud and stood up again, careful to look around to ensure he was still alone. He checked the ditch to see if he had missed anything and with one part of his plan accomplished began to implement the next part of his plan.

He moved toward the building, careful not to step on his friend's body, and squatted down to peer inside the gap in the foundation. Here, the exposed work was level with the bottom of the ditch and the space for the remaining stones appeared to be roughly four feet wide, a couple of feet high, and extended back to a depth of maybe three feet between the outer limestone and interior brick walls. Otto looked back again at the new stones, the buckets that were now about half full of rainwater, and the tarp. He flipped back the tarp to reveal exactly what he had expected to find: several unopened bags of Portland cement, most of which appeared to be dry. Otto felt like his prayers had been answered.

He carefully rolled Father Michael over and slid him feet first into the gap of the foundation, grunting as he pulled and lifted and pushed the body further into the dark recess until it finally fit snugly. He tenderly folded the priest's hands over his stomach, quickly located a trowel amongst the tools, tore open a bag of the cement, and mixed half of it with the water in one of the buckets, stirring until it seemed the right consistency. He next used the trowel to begin to spread it evenly, forming a bed on the existing foundation. Finally, he carefully slid the new limestone bricks into place one-by-one, tamped them in, and re-pointed the mortar as professionally as possible.

He worked methodically for a little over twenty minutes, taking little notice that the rain had gradually let up and finally stopped. Even though the rain had cooled off the summer night, he sweated profusely and his side ached with each fresh exertion. He paused occasionally to check on the bleeding and to glance around to assure no one was nearby.

When he was all but done, he quickly dressed himself in the priest's clothes, including the white collar. He quickly looked around, found the priest's black fedora, and donned it. Finally, before sliding the final stone the last few inches and covering Father Michael's face forever, he reached in to gently remove the glasses from the priest's pale face and tenderly placed his fingers on his friend's cold forehead.

"Well done, good and faithful servant," he prayed quietly, and then added, "*Vaya con Dios.*"

#

Carl Neumann sat in an all-night truck stop diner on the Clayton Highway at the east end of Raton. He stared into his coffee cup for the longest time and listened to the rain beating against the plate glass windows. A slice of lemon meringue pie sat in front of him, missing only one bite. He had almost gagged on it, not because the pie was not tasty, but because of his disgust and shame.

Killing had never bothered him. His murdering of the priest and Otto had not affected Carl in the least. For some inexplicable reason, though, the death of the policeman haunted him. Why, he could not say, except that it had been unexpected, unplanned, and completely unnecessary – and now, completely inexcusable because he had let it interfere with the larger task at hand.

He sat, cold cup of coffee and uneaten pie in front of him, trying to drum up the courage to call his father and give him the news of the entire botched affair. Otto was dead, along with two bystanders, and nothing at all to show for it: the proof the old man would want of Otto's death, as well as the lost journal and diary; not to mention the bodies that still needed to be dealt with – that is, if they had not yet been discovered.

He waved away the waitress's attempt to refill his coffee, took a deep breath, stood up, and walked to the pay phone like a condemned man. He slipped a dime into the slot, took another deep breath, and dialed the number.

#

As he walked, Otto held the handkerchief he had found in Father Michael's jacket tightly to his wounds to staunch further bleeding. He had kept to the shadows and alleyways as he made his way unsteadily back home. He had no idea if anyone would be watching his house, but he knew if Carl ever returned to the murder scene, this place would likely be his next stop. Otto also knew to attempt to go back home was sheer folly and that he should just go with the plan and hide out until time to catch the train out of here, hopefully to freedom.

But here he was, instead, quietly sneaking through his back alley gate to break into his own house, unseen, through a basement window, for the sole purpose of retrieving the one priceless item he could not bring himself to leave town without.

Thirty minutes later, after obtaining the item and getting away from his home – hopefully undetected – Otto sat in the relative safety of Father Michael's rectory on the edge of the bathtub and grimaced. Sweat poured from his brow as he squinted into the hand mirror he had propped up on the toilet, trying to focus on stitching the holes in his side. He had poured a generous amount of hydrogen peroxide on the bullet's entrance and exit wounds and was now methodically and painfully pinching each of them closed and suturing them up with a regular sewing needle and some dental floss he had found in the priest's belongings. He wasn't sure, but had surmised the floss would be slightly more hygienic than regular thread.

When the task was done, he gratefully stood under a hot shower for several long minutes, letting the weariness wash away along with the remaining blood and dried mud on his body. Afterwards, he found a pair of scissors and a straight razor and shaved off his dark beard. He then used the remainder of the peroxide to lighten his hair color to approximate that of Father Michael's. He brushed out the priest's clothes, put them back on, and went into the kitchen. Even though he had no real appetite, he forced himself to eat to replenish his strength from some fruit, bread, and cheese he found in the refrigerator, poured a large glass of tap water, and sat down at the small dining table to eat and to collect his thoughts. When he was finished, he gathered all the trash he could find around the apartment, including beard trimmings, soap, the needle and scissors, and all other evidence of his being there, into a plastic bag that he would toss later into a random dumpster on his way to the train station. Looking carefully around one more time, he finally sat down in a chair near the front door, next to Father Michael's suitcase, to quietly await the dawn.

He looked at Father Michael's watch, now on his wrist, checked the time on his ticket, and slipped it back into his jacket pocket. As he did so, his fingers brushed against something firm inside an inner pocket. He reached inside and fished out a small Bible with Father Michael's full birth name inscribed in faded gold letters on the worn leather cover: *Michael Francis Shannon.* Otto opened it and began thumbing through the pages, but grew very still and gazed blankly into the distance for several seconds. He eventually looked back at the Bible, turned it over and over, examining it carefully, dropped his hands back to his lap, and smiled to himself.

His good friend had been better than his word.

Father Michael had removed the leather cover from one of his old Bibles and had carefully glued it onto Evie's diary to conceal it – right in plain sight. If anyone were to be searching for it, chances are they would pass right over a priest's worn-out Bible without a second thought. Otto smiled at his friend's simple ingenuity, opened the diary again, and flipped to a page where Evie's beautiful handwriting abruptly ended. Finally, he took out a pen and began to write on the first of the many blank pages that followed.

He had much to catch up on.

#

After Carl had begged forgiveness on the phone, his father had outlined in precise detail what he was to do, as Carl knew that he would. He was to load the three bodies in his truck – without being seen, of course – drive them several miles south past Kiowa Mesa to the desolate area where ancient lava flows formed what was known as *malpais* – a Spanish word for "badlands" – and dump them down a deep lava tube where they would never be found.

Easy enough.

By the time Carl arrived back downtown to finish the night's work, the rain had stopped completely. He pulled his truck into the alley, just off of the street, and turned off the motor, letting the headlights illuminate the alley in front of him. The place was empty and quiet. He checked his watch – only a couple of hours until sunrise. He rolled the window down, closed his eyes for a moment, and breathed in the fresh, cool dampness of the pre-dawn.

After a few minutes, he opened his eyes and looked carefully around as far as the cone of illumination from his headlights would reveal. From here, he could just see the dark rim of the workmen's ditch and the northern wall of the old theater that rose above it.

But something seemed out of place; it took him a couple of minutes to notice exactly what it was: the night watchman's body had disappeared from where he had left it.

Carl hurriedly put the truck in gear and drove further into the alley, slowing to a stop near the edge of the ditch. He cautiously opened the door, glanced around, and pulled his pistol out of his jacket before stepping over to the hole where there was just enough reflected light to see the ladder, the workmen's tools, and some materials that were covered by a tarp. But more importantly for Carl, he spied a body sprawled across the tarp. His pulse quickened as he scampered down the ladder for a better look. He then gritted his teeth, cursed, and kicked the body, which he could now clearly see belonged to the dead watchman.

The bodies of Otto and the priest were nowhere to be found.

#

At 10:30 that morning, the Southwest Chief pulled slowly to a stop at the Amtrak station in Las Vegas, New Mexico. No one paid much attention to the solitary priest who stepped quietly down from the train onto the platform. He wore a dark fedora and a dark jacket over his black shirt and priest's collar and carried a small suitcase and a raincoat draped over his other arm. He looked around, adjusted his wire-rimmed glasses, and quietly walked off to the ticket office where he politely asked for directions to the state hospital.

Twenty minutes later, still no one noticed as a taxi pulled up to the hospital and a priest stepped out, opened his wallet, selected a couple of bills from the substantial amount of cash there, and paid the driver. He stood for a moment in the driveway as the cab drove away and stared up at the windows of the facility. He took a deep breath and knelt down, opened his suitcase, removed something, closed it, stood back up.

No one gave the middle-aged priest a second look as he straightened his hat and glasses and walked confidently into the lobby of the hospital, his suitcase and raincoat in one hand while in the other, he held the priceless item for which he had risked his life the night before: an old threadbare rag doll.

CHAPTER 31
VENGEANCE IS MINE

Late in the day, Hector picked Trent up at Maggie's ranch in a department cruiser and they headed back to Raton. Trent was exhausted, having spent most of the previous night poring over maps and journals; most of the day with an old priest who kept dropping cryptic messages; and most of the afternoon with an ancient Nazi serial killer who had been posing for years as a prominent local rancher. Trent felt like the entire case — along with his head — was about to burst wide open like an overripe melon.

Something else now troubled him, though, something about some old diary, yet another loose thread that Conrad Neumann – or rather, Ernst Brandt – had unwittingly revealed in this increasingly complicated jigsaw puzzle that had begun with Trent's own devastating accident on Cordova Pass years ago. The pieces and threads by now seemed to be reaching backward and forward throughout time, all the way back to World War II and up again to today. Who knew how many more seemingly unrelated bits were going to need to fall into place before the many labyrinths of this investigation were all done with, or if he could even keep track of them all in his already over-worked and under-functioning mind?

Trent sighed, too exhausted to think clearly. He slid back into the corner of the passenger seat, dropped his Stetson over his eyes, and had dozed off by the time Hector turned the vehicle back onto the highway and headed west.

Ten miles away from town, the sudden blare of the cruiser's siren jarred Trent from his sound sleep.

"What the hell!" he exclaimed. Hector glanced over, then back at the road. The vehicle had accelerated to just under 100 miles per hour.

"Sorry," he apologized. "But Sophie just buzzed me on my cell. Some kind of trouble. She sounded upset."

"She hurt?" Trent asked, anxiously rubbing the sleep from his face. "What happened?"

"Don't think so," Hector answered. "Not real sure yet."

Trent cringed at the ululating wail of the siren and held his head. "Do we really need all this fanfare?" he asked, still blinking his eyes awake.

"*Lights and sirens* – standard procedure in response to an unknown risk. Section III dash 2."

Trent glared at Hector incredulously. "So now you're quoting the damn manual to me? Really?"

He leaned over, flipped the siren off, and sat back. A few minutes later, Hector slowed down and swerved onto the I-25 frontage road near town.

"So just where are we going?"

"Animal hospital."

"What the hell?"

"Sophie said to meet her there. Said she'd explain."

The SUV skidded to a stop on the gravel driveway of the Raton Animal Hospital. Hector left the lights flashing as they jumped out and rushed inside, almost bowling over an elderly lady coming out the doors with a Chihuahua in her arms. The tiny dog yapped and snarled at them in protest.

"Excuse us, ma'am," Hector offered, turning at the door and tipping his hat. Trent ignored her completely, pushed on past Hector, and charged up to the receptionist who had evidently been expecting them as she showed them on through two double doors into the examination area. There, Trent saw Sophie standing with her back to them next to a young woman in a white lab coat bent over an examination table, working on something.

"Sophie?" Trent gasped, slightly out of breath.

"Oh, Daddy," she answered with a catch in her voice. She turned and came toward them with her arms outstretched. He opened his arms to greet her, but was left standing empty handed as she went past him into Hector's waiting arms instead.

"What the hell?" Trent asked for the third time in almost as many minutes.

"I'm so sorry," she continued, looking up at Trent as she rested her cheek against Hector's chest.

"Well, I should think so," answered Trent, a hurt tone in his voice.

"No, I meant I'm sorry about your cat."

Trent looked back at the examination table.

"Jarhead?" he asked softly, just now realizing why they were probably there.

"It was just awful," Sophie continued. "He was screaming, in such pain."

Trent took a couple of steps toward the table and craned his head to look over the veterinarian's shoulder. A big orange tomcat lay very still there on the table, a long tube shoved down his throat, his tongue lolling out the side of his mouth. "Will he – I mean, is he dead?"

The vet turned and glanced at Trent. "No, he's a tough old kitty cat. Lost a little blood. Would've bled out, though, if your daughter hadn't responded so quickly and wrapped it up good till she got him here." She pointed over to a stainless steel tray at the edge of the table. Trent looked over and grimaced as he caught sight of what looked like a rabbit's foot, only bigger, the orange fur matted with dried blood.

"Had to go ahead and take that left front paw and leg off, though," the vet continued, turning back to her work. Trent stepped closer and looked down at his old tomcat. Jarhead was unconscious but breathing deeply, mercifully unaware of the entire procedure. He reached over and gently rubbed the old cat's neck as the veterinarian continued. "He's going to be one sore tomcat for a while – then he's going to have a bit of a time getting used to limping around on three legs, but I'm guessing he's going to be okay in the long run, I think."

"You guess? You think? What the hell does that mean?" Trent demanded. He had turned pale and was feeling sick to his stomach. *How the hell did this happen?*

"Daddy," Sophie had slipped up beside him and now took him by the upper arm and pulled him away, "leave the woman alone and let her do her job. You're being your usual 'not helpful' self." She led him back down the hall to a small employee lounge and poured coffees all around.

"So just what the hell happened, Sofe?" Trent grimaced after sipping some of the lukewarm coffee. "What happened to my cat?"

Sophie told them how she had just gotten home from work and was about to go get a shower when she thought she heard a commotion outside. Initially thinking it had been some of the neighbor kids trespassing, she had gone to the front door and walked down the driveway to chase them away. She had seen something thrashing on the ground beneath the branches of one of the piñon trees near the house. Then, thinking it was maybe a bird in distress, she had stepped closer and stooped down only to discover the creature was Jarhead, rolling around, hissing, and wailing. When she reached down to check him, she found he had been caught in a small game trap that had crushed one of his front legs in its steel jaws.

Trent's face went from pale to bright red, his eyebrows knitted dangerously.

"Did you see anything else? Anybody hanging around?"

"No," Sophie answered, and then looked up. "Well, maybe – I didn't see anybody, but come to think of it, when I had gotten Jarhead out of the trap and was carrying him to the house, I did hear a truck start up. Sounded like it was just down the driveway, around the bend, just out of sight, and then it spun gravel and took off. Could've been anybody, I guess. I didn't think anything of it at the time – I was so upset about Jarhead," choking back a sob.

Trent stared off into space while he slowly crushed the Styrofoam cup in his hand, causing the remaining coffee to spill out through his clenched fingers. He didn't seem to notice and sat quietly for a minute.

"Daddy," she continued when he didn't say anything. "That couldn't have really been an accident, could it? Why would anyone do such a cruel thing to a defenseless animal?"

"Because I think it was a warning," Trent finally growled under his breath. "Someone purposely set that trap, and I think they baited it just for Jarhead – but they were sending me a message."

Trent, like an animal himself, glanced back and forth between Hector and Sophie, his eyes wide. "And I've got a pretty good idea who."

He stood up, threw his crushed cup toward a nearby trashcan, and found a paper towel to wipe the spilled coffee off his hands. He suddenly stopped and looked up, his frown deeper.

"Damn it!" he exclaimed, reaching into his pocket for his cell phone.

"What is it?" Hector asked, standing up slowly. "What's wrong?"

"*A warning*," Trent muttered as he flipped open the phone, scrolled through his directory, found the number he was looking for, then dialed it. "Damn it!" he exclaimed again. "How could I have been so stupid?"

The phone continued to ring unanswered on the other end.

"*Answer the damn phone*!"

#

Just after dark in West Las Vegas, New Mexico, a nondescript dark blue sedan with no hubcaps and no other distinguishing marks pulled up with its headlights off and parked at a small playground. The driver killed the engine and sat quietly, watching a particular small frame house a half block away. He sat this way for almost an hour, glancing at his watch every few minutes, waiting.

Jimmy Streck's wait was soon rewarded as he saw the living room lights go out in the house, the less intense glow of another light coming on somewhere at the rear of the house. He opened the glove box, took out a small .22 caliber revolver loaded with hollow point magnum loads, and slipped it into the right hand pocket of his jacket. He rummaged around and found a pair of thin black leather gloves from the other pocket, put them on, and got out of the car. He gently pushed the car door shut and stood for a moment looking around. Seeing no one else, he turned and walked nonchalantly up the sidewalk toward the house. To the casual observer, he was merely someone out for a stroll after dinner.

He walked past the gate in the chain link fence that surrounded the front yard, then made his way quietly to the alley. Here, he doubled his pace, keeping close to the fences lining the alley, counted the number of houses, and stopped at the back gate of the particular one he was interested in. Again, he stood still for a full minute, watching and listening. After he judged it was safe, he reached over, gently unlatched the gate, opened it with only the slightest creak of the hinges, and slipped unobserved into the back yard of the house. He stopped just inside the gate and listened. The last problem he needed was to run into a watchdog that would then have to be silenced. He hated when he had to kill an animal, not that that had ever stopped him before, but animals rarely deserved to be killed, in his opinion, whereas Jimmy could almost always find a good reason to take the life of a human being. Besides, having a good reason always helped to ease his conscience.

He gratefully determined no animal was around to deal with and took out a small pocket flashlight. Cupping his fingers over the head of the flashlight, he turned it on so that only a tiny sliver of light illuminated his path straight ahead.

He made his way to the back porch and listened again. After a minute and more stillness passed, he pulled firmly but quietly on the back screen door, only to find it had been latched. Jimmy took out his pocketknife and silently and expertly slit through the screening material, then used the butt of the knife to pop the latch. The screen door squeaked once as he slowly pulled it open. He paused and listened, then reached in and gently tried the doorknob.

Incredibly, the door was unlocked.

Jimmy shook his head as he twisted the knob very slowly. He was constantly amazed at how many people carelessly left their doors unlocked, particularly in these smaller towns. Doing so, though, sure made his work a whole lot easier.

He pushed the door slowly open, gritting his teeth against a possible screeching of worn hinges. They seemed to be well oiled, so he leaned in, quickly glanced around the kitchen using his finger of light, stepped quickly inside, and stopped to listen. He could just make out distant voices coming from a television set somewhere in the interior of the house and the creaking of upstairs floorboards as someone walked around above him.

Jimmy stepped quietly and slowly across the kitchen on crepe soled shoes, carefully noting with his small light any obstacles to walk around or over. He made his way stealthily into the next room, which turned out to be the living room; it, too, was dark, with the only illumination reflecting through the drapes from a nearby streetlamp. He let his light play around the room and bounce off of a couch and a couple of chairs, a large crucifix on the opposite wall beside the front door, and brightly reflect from the glass picture frames scattered around. One picture in particular caught his eye; he moved close to peer at a photo of a young couple dressed in their wedding finery. He recognized them immediately, smiled, and let a gloved finger caress the face of the woman in the photo.

This face was, for sure, the one who had gotten away.

Muffled noises from the television came from a closed door at the end of a short hallway that led just off of the living room. The television's light flickered and danced from underneath the doorway. He moved the flashlight to his left hand, reached back beneath his jacket to the small of his back, and removed the .22 pistol from his waistband. He took a cautious step into the hallway, but immediately froze. He suddenly heard footsteps upstairs and waited until they stopped. A woman's voice called down from a landing just above Jimmy's head.

"Tia, I'm going to get in the shower now, okay?"

Jimmy waited, expecting the bedroom door to fly open at any moment and expose him, gun in hand. Seconds went by, but the door remained closed, the TV blaring from inside.

"Auntie?" called out the young woman's voice again, a little more urgently. Another few seconds went by while Jimmy held his breath. Finally, the young woman sighed heavily, muttered something in Spanish under her breath, and briskly walked away, back down the upstairs hallway. Jimmy heard another door shut before the sound of water being turned on in a bathtub, and finally, the sweet, lilting voice of singing in Spanish from the bathroom.

Jimmy Streck smiled again, listening for a moment to the woman's song, idly wondering what the Spanish were saying before he cautiously and slowly ascended the stairs, his gun leading the way as he climbed to the landing, tiptoed down the hallway where he put a gloved hand to the handle of the bathroom door, and prepared to step in to put a bullet into Mirielle Segura's head.

#

Father Michael sat in his chair near the dark window, a small lamp on the nearby desk providing the only light in the room. He was dressed in pajamas and a maroon terry cloth bathrobe cinched tightly around his thin frame. He peered out into the darkness beyond the window, lost in thought.

"Come in, gentlemen. I have been expecting you," he declared in a soft, measured voice, "for quite a long time now." He continued to sit with his back to them and stare out of the window. "You are just in time to watch the harvest moon rise with me – momentarily, I do believe."

The priest stood up, finally, and turned to look at the two men who had quietly entered the room. He squinted, patted his pockets, and suddenly chuckled as he reached up to find his glasses perched on top of his head. "There now," he remarked casually as he put them on and scrutinized the two men again, "that is much better."

The younger, middle-aged man stood just behind the wheel chair where an ancient fossil of a man was seated. They had stopped just inside the door, which the younger man had quickly closed behind them.

"Go ahead and wheel him closer, if you would – Carl," the old priest instructed matter-of-factly, motioning them nearer.

The younger man began to push the wheelchair, then stopped in sudden realization.

"How do you know –," Carl's voice trailed away.

'How do I know your name?" Father Michael finished the question for him, watching him closely. "Why, you might be surprised at what all I do know, young Mister Neumann." Carl glanced down at the man in the wheelchair, who had begun to chuckle.

"Well, then, this could be a fruitful endeavor after all, Carl," croaked the old man, watching Father Michael closely. "Seems the good Father here just might have the answers we're looking for." He motioned for Carl to roll him nearer. Father Michael watched as the ruined visage came closer into view, but the priest did not register alarm or disgust at all, almost as if he was accustomed to the grotesque in life.

"Mr. Neumann – Conrad," Father Michael began cordially, "welcome to my humble home." Neumann's smile wavered for an instant. Carl glanced from his father back to the old priest again, questioningly. "Oh, do not look so surprised, gentlemen. It is really no mystery. I have seen you around here before, many times. You have been here visiting my young friend, Caroline – Caroline Neumann. So I, of course, assumed you are her relatives, yes? The same loving relatives who probably had her committed in the first place – how do they say it? *Out of sight, out of mind.*"

Neumann glared at the old priest, then glanced at Carl and nodded at him. Carl acknowledged the signal and moved away to slowly but methodically examine the room, occasionally touching or picking objects up, opening drawers, the closet, and checking under the furniture, all without permission.

"Ah," noted Father Michael, "so, not only do I get to play twenty questions, but I also get to have my room searched by strangers. How delightful! Oh, I do so love games!"

"It would make our purpose here a lot simpler – and quicker – if you would just tell us what we need to know."

"Oh, I fully intend to do so, Mr. Neumann – only, you need to do a couple of things for me first," Father Michael said, leaning over toward Neumann with a conspiratorial tone of voice.

"And just what would that be – *Padre?*" answered Neumann cautiously, a crooked smile creeping onto one corner of his ruined mouth.

"First of all, I do not recall that you have yet asked a real question."

The crooked smile left Neumann's face. "You said there were a couple of things," he muttered after a moment.

The priest sat back on the edge of the desk, crossed his hands on his lap, then nodded toward Carl. "Tell him – uh, your son – to leave us for a few minutes."

Carl put down the book he had been flipping through, looked over, and smirked.

"Why on earth should he?" Neumann asked, irritated.

"Indulge me," the priest insisted. "Besides, it is the only way you are ever going to get what you need." He turned the object over through his fingers again. Neumann looked but could still not determine what it was exactly. "Carl does not get to listen to what we have to say to each other."

Carl frowned, slapped the book shut, and dropped it loudly on the table. The two older men ignored him.

"What if he does leave?" Conrad asked. "What's to prevent me from telling him things afterward?"

"Why, nothing prevents you, of course."

"So, what's the difference?"

"The difference is that I get to choose to whom I divulge this information. Whomever you choose to tell afterward is of little importance to me."

"And just why is that?"

"Because, my dear Conrad; by then, I will most probably be dead, yes?"

Father Michael sat back, folded his arms, and chuckled. Neumann pursed his lips and glared at the priest. "You are being most difficult, is what it seems to me!" he finally responded.

Carl suddenly stepped over, pulled a small caliber pistol fitted with a silencer out of his coat pocket, and pointed it just inches from the priest's head. "We can make that happen right now if you'd like!" he snarled. Father

Michael looked up at him, then closed his eyes slowly and took a deep breath. He looked quite serene and content.

"Ah, yes. The young hothead emerges, as usual, and right on time," he smiled softly. He opened his eyes, ignoring the pistol now, and looked back at Neumann. "You have, indeed, raised him well, Conrad –*a chip off the old block,* I believe?" Father Michael smiled again at Neumann.

"You idiot," Neumann snapped at Carl. "Put that gun away! Now is not the time."

"Yes, Carl," murmured the priest. "Let us not be too hasty – there will be plenty of time for that soon." He stood again slowly, groaning as he straightened stiff joints, and took a couple of steps toward the wheelchair as he continued. "Everyone gets what they want tonight – at long last."

Neumann's smile had now become a frown, and with suspicion mixed with impatience, he spoke. "Get out, Carl!" he barked. "I will handle this old fool myself."

Father Michael was pleased to see a slight tremor in Neumann's shoulders.

"But I haven't finished searching everything –" Carl began to protest.

"He's playing us for fools, Carl – you won't find it anywhere. You really think he's got it here? He's not saying anything until he's good and ready – or at least until we beat it out of him!"

"And there it is," the priest said, a pleased look on his face as he clapped his hands together. "The old Neumann charm and persuasion; I was hoping to see some of that tonight!"

Neumann sat back and put his good hand up to his cheek and scratched at it, a perplexed look on his face. Carl continued to stand there.

"Carl – do as I told you. *Get out!*"

"And just where do you want me to go?" Carl sounded like the wounded child that he really was.

"Just go into the hall and wait! Don't let anybody else in – and don't come back in yourself, unless you hear something."

"Like what?"

"You'll know it if you hear it – now go!"

"Yes, Carl – run along," cajoled Father Michael. "Your services will be required soon, I am sure of it. In fact, I very much look forward to it!" He looked up at Carl and smiled broadly, then gave him a wave of dismissal.

Carl shoved the pistol back into the inner pocket of his jacket, wiped his lip with the back of his leather gloved hand, turned abruptly, and walked out.

Total silence enveloped the room.

"You are insane," Neumann finally pronounced.

"Perhaps," shrugged Father Michael, as he made his way haltingly to the edge of the bed. "But I rather suspect insanity comes in many forms and flavors – and in many people."

"What are you playing at here – *Priest?*" He spat the word out, hatefully. "What game do you have up your sleeve?"

"Game? Oh, I guess you could call it that." Father Michael sat down on the edge of the bed with a sigh. "Actually, yes – probably the best game ever – one where all that has not been as it seems finally gets revealed." He leaned over conspiratorially. "And everyone goes home a winner tonight – and if you are really lucky, Mr. Neumann, you get a bonus. You get a shot at making everything that is wrong very right for a change."

He paused for the briefest moment before he continued.

"Oh, and by the way, I do not have either the journal *or* the diary that you are looking for – but I can tell whatever it is you would like to know about them."

Neumann jerked his face around and glared at Father Michael.

"How the hell did you know about the journal *and* the diary?"

"Hmm. Well, let me answer that by first asking you another question – why would you think I ever had them? And if I did, why are you just now coming around to ask me for them, after all these years? Oh, sorry – that was two questions, was it not?"

"Because your friends talk too much!" Neumann answered angrily, grabbing the large wheels of the chair and propelling it slowly forward toward the old priest. "I was here a couple months ago, visiting my daughter, and I overheard a conversation in the garden between that idiot deputy and his old man, that smartass you like to play chess with." He waited for a reaction from the priest, but got none.

"Do you know who they were discussing?" he continued. "You!"

"Ah, yes – my dear friend Walter. He does so love chess, but is less patient than I." Father Michael slipped a bony hand into the pocket of his robe, took something out, and slowly turned it in his hand. He fixed

Neumann with a piercing gaze. "You remember young Walter, do you not? Oh, but forgive me – I get ahead of myself!" Father Michael looked down at the object he was toying with in his hand with a practiced movement that gave him some comfort. "Suffice it to say that Walter Carter's game is to go for the short kill. I am more interested in the long strategy – the long game produces so many more satisfying rewards, don't you think, Conrad?" Father Michael rose slowly from the edge of the bed, winced from the effort, and moved toward Neumann. "But that doesn't tell me why you thought that I had this diary, or – what was it? A journal of some sort?"

The priest leaned forward now and peered into Neumann's face intently as if studying a road map. Neumann squirmed and looked away for a moment before looking back up. Something was disarmingly familiar about the old priest that made him want to explain – to be understood.

"There was this – *employee*, let's call him, who worked on my ranch years ago. He took off suddenly – just quit, in the middle of the night. And he stole some important documents, including my late wife's diary, and an old journal that had – well – certain important information – information that could ruin me."

"You don't say," said Father Michael, straightening back up to listen.

"And when I found out where this man had gotten off to, I also discovered he had been befriended by a priest – a priest that I have come now to believe was you, as a matter of fact, *Father!*"

The old priest paused, watched Neumann carefully, then responded.

"And just what do you suppose, Mr. Neumann, happened to this – this supposed friend of mine?

Neumann shifted uncomfortably. "He – passed away," he finally answered abruptly. "Years ago." He then leaned toward the priest. "But I think you know this – *Priest;* in fact, before he died, I think he gave those documents to you. Now, where have you hidden them?" Neumann slapped the arm of his wheelchair for emphasis. "They're my rightful property!"

Neumann suddenly became distracted by the white object the priest kept fingering; his eyes widened with a growing familiarity.

"Oh, I do not have those – documents, as you call them," answered Father Michael. "Not anymore, that is. But what I do have is just one more very important question for you, Mr. – *Neumann.*" The priest cleared his throat, reached over slowly, and placed the mysterious object on the desk right in front of Conrad Neumann, and then continued.

"Do you recall the name of this friend of mine, the one I was supposed to have been so close to?"

"No!" Neumann whispered hoarsely. "That cannot be!" He reached with his shaking hand and touched the old ivory chess piece, a white king, with the tip of a trembling finger. "Where did you get this?"

"Oh, I have had that for a long, long time now. It is, in fact, one of my prized possessions. You see, it has really been my good luck charm, ever since – oh, but surely you remember the incident, Conrad, where I obtained it originally – oh, let me see – there was a pig farmer in Hoehne, Colorado – Dave Perkins, I believe his name was? Oh, come now –," the priest teased, and suddenly moved inches away from his adversary's face; his voice changed in tone, "Please tell me that you do remember dear Mr. Perkins – *Ernst*?"

The priest slowly reached back over, retrieved the old chess piece, leaned forward to press it into Ernst's hand, and whispered hoarsely, "I know I shall never forget him – nor you, *Mein Kapitan*."

Ernst Brandt's mouth dropped open as he stared up at this ancient man who, up until this moment, he had truly believed to be Father Michael. He began to tremble uncontrollably, spittle dribbled from the corner of his mouth, and he began shaking his head in disbelief.

"*Otto*?" he whimpered finally and collapsed back into his wheelchair.

#

Jimmy Streck stood just outside the bathroom door, the .22 pistol raised in his right hand, and listened. He could hear the shower hissing inside and Mirielle humming a familiar tune as she bathed. She sounded content, peaceful, and completely unaware of her pending fate, just as Jimmy had planned. Just to be sure, he mentally ticked off one final time the steps he would quickly take: shoot the woman, tiptoe downstairs and shoot the old aunt, then retrace his steps through the back alley and around to his car, and drive away. No muss, no fuss. No one would probably find the bodies for days. He would then make a call to Carl on the way back to the ranch to confirm that one more loose end was neatly tied up. He just hoped he would be back in time to help them tie up the other loose ends as well.

Jimmy started to push open the door, then stopped. He suddenly had a better idea. He decided on one slight change of plans since a long time had passed since he had killed someone with his bare hands. He smiled at the thought, remembering how gripping someone by their tender throat would be, staring into their horrified eyes as they felt the life being slowly squeezed out of them. This one – yes, this one – was very special and personal, indeed – *the one who got away*. Jimmy felt an excitement and anticipation he hadn't felt in a long time.

He carefully put his pistol away, flexed his fingers inside the smooth, calfskin gloves, and gently pushed the door wide. A cloud of steam billowed out at him; he could just make out the woman's shadow on the cheap plastic shower curtain a few feet away. The room smelled of the freshness that comes from warm water, dampness, soap, and shampoo. Jimmy smiled as he felt himself somehow being ceremoniously cleansed while he stepped quietly but steadily toward the shower curtain, his pulse quickening in excitement, a ritualistic feeling of completion and redemption building inside.

He reached out and gripped the edge of the curtain, took a deep breath, and ripped it loose noisily as the rings that had held the curtain to the rod clattered around the room. The steam cloud was still heavy, but he could just make out the outline of the woman under the shower as he reached eagerly toward her – and then things went wrong.

Mirielle Segura had stepped toward him, meeting him halfway as if she had been ready for him. Despite her damp face and streaming wet hair, she was fully clothed in a t-shirt and jeans, and he fleetingly noted a fixed determination on her face; in his surprise and shock, Jimmy could not begin to guess what was really happening now: he felt the wind go out of him and a heaviness seep into his stomach.

Jimmy Streck felt stupefied. Something was terribly wrong.

His gloved hands trembled and were still outstretched toward her beautifully angular neck, but for some reason, he could not reach her. He continued to stare into Mirielle Segura's beautiful olive eyes, filled now with the unmistakable look of triumph as she backed a quick step away from him and Jimmy felt compelled to look down. He watched incredulously as his trembling hands slowly reached down to grasp the hilt of a large butcher knife now protruding from the middle of his abdomen. His eyes grew ever wider; his breath came in short gasps as he turned slowly to try and escape this nightmare. He pulled on the knife, blood began to spill over his clenched hands, and he doubled over in pain as he began to stumble towards the bathroom door. He stopped abruptly, still doubled over, when he spied someone else blocking his path to the door: it was the old woman, standing there as if she had been waiting for him.

"*Pendejo!*" shouted Mirielle's elderly aunt defiantly, right before swinging a small cast iron skillet as hard as she could at his head.

The last sound on earth Jimmy Streck heard was the curious crunching sound the skillet made as it smashed into his left temple.

#

Ernst Brandt had grown pale with shock, staring as the aged face of Otto Eberhardt slowly emerged from the façade that had been "Father Michael." Otto slowly dragged the desk chair as close as he could get it, and sat down so that the two old comrades were now face-to-face, just inches apart. Otto patted Ernst on the knee and smiled before he began to speak to him in hushed tones that could not be overheard beyond where they sat.

"Just look at us, old friend. Is this not absolutely ironic? Two ancient brothers in arms, both pretending to be people we are not."

"This is impossible," Ernst whispered shakily. "*You're dead*!"

"Oh, on the contrary, my dear Ernst; this is entirely possible. You see, you are the one who has made it very possible – by all of your choices." Otto leaned forward until he could have almost kissed Ernst. "You have chosen to ruin everything you touch, my old friend, *ja?*" Otto began. "Every time you saw beauty, you chose to crush it under your boot. Every time you saw happiness, you chose to destroy it. Every time you set your disgusting Nazi superiority above everyone else, you chose to simply murder them – first in the war and later just for sport. I cannot judge you for that, though. It is in your nature, *mein Freund*. Like the complete monster that we both know you are. But," Otto sighed, and looking more intently at the other man, continued, "you were never able to murder the memories – and it is those that have sustained me, along with my faith."

Otto paused and looked away for a moment, his thoughts travelling back in time, then shook his head slowly.

"Memories," he whispered, almost inaudibly. He looked back up at Ernst. "When you emerged from that fire, burning brightly like a human torch, you had finally balanced the external man with the charred soul you had already become inside, had you not?"

Otto paused again, reached into the other pocket of his bathrobe, and pulled out a dog-eared, yellowed black and white photograph and placed it beside the chess piece. He tapped it with his fingernail until Ernst turned in stunned silence to look at a photograph of Evie Van Ryan taken when she was still an innocent teenager.

"Every time you saw love, you chose to rip it apart in hatred, to make sure no one else could have it." Otto reached over and with two fingers gently pulled Ernst's face back toward him. He then pointed at the door. "And I will tell you this now, Ernst – you may have raised that boy out there, and turned him into a monstrous shadow of yourself – but that boy was never your son," Otto whispered fiercely, "no matter what name you go by!"

Ernst looked up slowly with a gradual look of understanding crossing his face.

"And *that*," Otto Eberhardt continued triumphantly, "is the real secret of Evie's diary."

Otto suddenly began to cough in deep, long wracking spasms. When he finally stopped, he continued in a softer voice.

"And so, it is now decision time." He dabbed his mouth with his handkerchief, which he looked at briefly. He was not so surprised to see flecks of blood on the white linen. "*Der Führer ist tot, Herr Käpitan,*" he continued. "He died decades ago for his crimes against humanity." Otto held out the blood-spotted handkerchief for Ernst to see. "The blood of the innocents cried out from the ground for his blood – and now, this same blood cries out for yours – and mine, also, it would seem."

Ernst glared at Otto defiantly. He lifted his chin slightly, almost as if daring him to strike him down. Otto began slowly shaking his head. "No, I shall not kill you – and the Lord God knows how long I have wanted to see you dead – but I shall not do it." He leaned forward again and pointed a finger at Ernst's chest. "For as much as I want you to suffer as you made so many others suffer – as especially you made her suffer – God does not want that for you. He has already put an alternative plan in place."

Otto leaned back heavily in his chair and caught his breath. The exertion was beginning to take a great toll on him.

"I have since learned," he continued finally, turning to gaze out the window into the darkness, "and have come to understood, while being on this earth for nine decades, any things about life, about love —the true nature of love —love that is expressed through death. And as much death that you have caused, Ernst, I have realized that there was yet one more Man's blood already shed for the likes of you," Otto paused and smiled, "and even the likes of me, that makes all the difference. And whether I agree with Him or not about forgiveness, that one Man would still want a monster like you come to Him for redemption."

Otto looked back at Ernst, then shrugged. "So, believe it or not, my friend, that is why God has really brought us together, here at the end. You see, God has a strange sense of humor. He thinks it is funny that I should be the one to tell you about His desire to make you His, for you to confess your sins through me, a supposed priest, and then for you to give your answer, here," Otto gestured with a sweep of his hand, "in my presence." He paused once more and softly chuckled. "Quite hilarious, you think, Ernst?"

Ernst was moving his mouth, trying to say something.

"So. What will it be? What is your answer, *Herr Kapitan*? Speak up – God and I are a little hard of hearing these days."

"I shall kill you," Ernst whispered finally, his voice raspy, his face vacant now of emotion.

"You shall what? Kill me!" Otto began to openly laugh and then stopped abruptly as he saw Ernst slowly pull a small revolver from an inside pocket of the wheelchair with his good hand.

"Well, go on then," Otto said, with barely a whisper, after staring at the gun for a moment. His eyes went glassy; he licked his lips with a certain anticipation and he leaned forward slowly until only a foot away. "Here, I shall make it easy for you."

Otto reached out, took Ernst's hand, and firmly placed the barrel of the pistol against his own forehead.

Ernst's hand was trembling; he clenched and unclenched his teeth in a death's head grimace. Both of their hands were now on the pistol pointed at Otto's head. Spittle began to leak again from the ruined corner of Ernst's mouth, the lips still moving wordlessly. Otto had closed his eyes and put his thoughts on God, his face reflecting a beatific peace.

Nothing happened.

Otto opened his eyes once more, looked at this misshapen man in front of him, with the misshapen soul, and then almost chided, "Out of all of the villainous acts you have done, both in war and in peace, you cannot do it, Ernst – can you?" he whispered. "You cannot do this one final act of evil." The spittle ran more voluminously down Ernst's chin. Otto continued. "You can end all of your hatred for me in one quick jerk of the trigger, but you cannot kill me, Ernst. Do you know why?"

Otto suddenly felt Ernst's fingers twitch beneath own hand as he abruptly pulled the trigger, not once, but three times.

Otto squeezed his eyes shut, then slowly opened them again to stare at Ernst.

The pistol had misfired.

The gun barrel was still pressed to Otto's forehead, but Ernst stared blankly at him with almost dead eyes, appearing almost catatonic. Otto slowly reached up and easily removed the gun from Ernst's fingers and set it on the desk beside the chess piece and Evie's photograph. He then reached up and gently placed the palms of his hands on each side of Ernst's face and began to speak to him as to a child.

"And so, God has spoken. It is impossible for you to take my life, old friend. You know why, do you not? You see, I *really am* a follower of a Lord I can truly do battle for – for all these years now – no longer pretend. For the first time in my life," I know Someone I can really follow – Who deserves my faith and love entirely." Otto moved inches away and gazed straight into Ernst's malevolent eyes.

"I give my own life, Ernst. No mere man can take it from me – ever again. And certainly not a demon like you!"

Ernst breathed heavily and glared hatefully at Otto: "Damn you and your god!"

Otto sat back heavily in his chair, took a couple of deep breaths, and shook his head sadly. He was growing fainter; he knew he needed to finish quickly.

"So, that is how it is to be, then," Otto resigned, but added, "I am sad for you, *mein Herr,* but it is exactly what I expected. You have chosen to remain the monster, and therefore, you alone must answer for all the innocent blood you have spilled in your lifetime."

Otto reached into his other pocket and took out a small prescription bottle. "*The wages of sin is death*, my friend."

Otto set the little bottle on the desk and continued. "And I, too, shall soon go to be with God – but on my terms, not yours. You see these pills? These are supposed to keep me alive, at least awhile longer."

"But a while ago, I made a decision, and I set in motion some actions that I knew would get you here, sooner or later, one of which was that I met with Officer Carter and gave him some information that concerned you, knowing he would be after you, and that, in turn, you would come after me, and so on and so forth." Otto shrugged and smiled. "And now here we are." He coughed blood again into his handkerchief.

"So two weeks ago, I stopped taking my medication. The doctor says without it, for even a few days, my poor heart will gradually slow down and then –*poof!* And do you want to know why I did this? Because I knew you were going to come and try to kill me – well, you thought you would be killing Father Michael, who, by the way, was probably the best man I have ever known – the exact polar opposite of you, the worst person and soul I have ever known. What a blessing in disguise, *ja*? Or should I say, 'a disguise within the blessing?'" He chuckled at his own little joke before he continued. "Either way, I think it is amazing that I have known both the best and the worst of human nature, together in one small lifetime!"

Ernst stared at Otto with undisguised hatred in his eyes. Otto leaned in close again. "You see, I knew you would say 'No' to God, Ernst; God forgive me, for I actually counted on it. I also knew you would then want to kill me. But you see, God will not let you take away from me that which I now give away myself – I have chosen my death. With me dies your long-planned revenge, thus, my own perfect revenge, *ja wohl?*"

Otto stood up slowly and painfully, took the medicine bottle, opened it, and shook the remaining pills into his hand, and looked at them. He leaned over to the trashcan by the desk and dumped them all in, then walked slowly back over to Ernst, looked down at him sadly, and leaned over and kissed him on his ruined, scarred head.

"I know you will not believe a word of this, but I truly forgive you, *mein Kapitan.*" Otto picked up the pistol from the desk, dropped it into Ernst's lap, walked around the wheelchair, slowly wheeled Ernst to the door, and knocked on it. Carl, who was standing just outside the door, opened it immediately, and looked at the two old men questioningly. Otto looked at Carl sadly for a moment and then pushed Ernst on out into the hallway.

"Take your – *Father* – home. He has his answers – and so do I."

Carl frowned at the priest and questioningly eyed Ernst, who simply stared down at his hands. Carl glared back at the priest. "What did you do to him?" he snarled. Not waiting for an answer, he put his hand inside his jacket, his fingers closing on the butt of his pistol, but hesitated, confused and, seemingly, suddenly powerless to draw his weapon, as if an unseen, powerful hand restrained his. Otto smiled knowingly at Carl and made the sign of the cross over him, turned, and went back into his room and closed his door quietly behind him, leaving his enemies alone in the hallway stupefied with their own thoughts. He stopped just inside the doorway, turned to place the palm of his hand on the door, raised his face, and closed his eyes.

"Go with God – my dear, dear son," he whispered through the door in benediction.

He turned and shuffled back to the window where he pulled his chair back around, looked around his room, momentarily stopped, and looked down at the desk beside him. He smiled, reached over, and picked up the objects that had caught his attention there: the yellowed, creased photograph of his beloved Evie, and Dave Perkins's worn ivory chess piece. He sat down slowly in his chair, kissed Evie's photograph one more time, and leaned back with a deep sigh, fingering the white king absently in his hand and gazing out of the window as the huge yellow curve of the top of the harvest moon finally broke from behind the Texas horizon just to the east.

The magnificence of the event always gave Otto both the thrill of anticipation and a long remembered dread: Otto's breath grew shallow; he stared through the window at the huge moon; his eyelids drooped until his vision blurred.

#

The four walls of his small room fade, and he is now standing in the middle of an ancient, windblown desert, staring up at another harvest moon from decades ago rising over the detritus of battle – burned out tanks and bodies — so many bodies — some charred and smoldering, for as far as he can see in the moonlit, drifting sands. He looks down and sees blood dripping from his fingertips; even more bodies lie in a rough semi-circle around him; dead soldiers wearing American uniforms. He hears a single gunshot in the near distance, followed soon by another, and yet another, evenly spaced, progressively louder. He looks toward the approaching sound; a long line of American soldiers extends away to Otto's right until they disappear over a sand dune. But before him now, the prisoners are on their knees and weeping with their hands clasped on top of their heads; a shadowy figure dressed all in black, its face hooded, walks slowly and methodically, pointing at the backs of the soldiers in turn; after a loud 'bang' they each fall over face first in the sand. The hooded figure stops and sees Otto, then points at him. Otto closes his eyes and waits for the inevitable gunshot.

It never comes.

He opens his eyes; he is walking slowly through a train car, filled with passengers. As he approaches each row of seats, they look up at him and smile. He recognizes each and every one of their faces but is filled with dread. As he reaches the end of the car, he turns and looks back up the aisle, where the hooded shadowy figure has now entered at the other end and is walking slowly towards Otto, turning and pointing at each passenger. as he points at them, a gunshot blast is again heard, and they each slump over, dead. Otto opens his mouth to scream, "NO," but only a groan comes out of his throat. Halfway down the aisle, the Shadow Man stops, looks up, and points at Otto.

Flame erupts around and through the train car; pieces of metal, wood, fire and bodies are flying everywhere; the world is devoid of sound.

Otto again closes his eyes.

He awakens to find himself rocking on the porch of an old cabin. Birds are singing in the trees, and the air is filled with the pungent mixture of odors: an aromatic cocktail of wildflowers, grasses, and barnyard smells right after a nice, long rain. Something intrudes on his senses; the idyllic scene is interrupted by distant screams, punctuated by gunfire. The horrific screams sound like animals being slaughtered. As he often attempted in a dream, he tries to force his eyes open, not wanting to look in the direction of the cacophony, but he cannot help himself. He turns his head and sees a sort of low corral nearby where a turmoil of activity churns inside. the Shadow Man is sitting on the top fence rail, pointing down into the corral, the source of the screams. Shadow Man is laughing, and the gunfire is getting louder. Abruptly, the corral rails burst apart and hundreds of people come running out, across the yard, straight towards the cabin – straight at Otto; they surround him, screaming and pawing at him, as if he can stop whatever torture they are suffering. Otto tries to leave, but sits helplessly paralyzed as the cabin disappears and he finds himself sitting cross-legged out in the middle of a beautiful meadow on a late afternoon, and the only sound he now hears is a single voice, weeping in despair.

He closes his eyes once more.

When he again opens them, he is sitting in the front pew of a large church, weeping, and staring up at a crucified form above the altar. Everything in the church, including the walls, ceilings, floors, and pews, is colored stark, blinding white – except that he himself is dressed totally in black. He hears a distant sobbing, realizes he isn't the only one weeping, then notices tears of blood flowing from eyes of the crucified man.

"Otto," he hears as someone speaks his name. He turns and sees Father Michael, dressed in full, white vestments, holding open a side door to the church, smiling, gesturing that Otto is to come with him.

He follows.

He walks through the door; the white brilliance grows until it blinds him. When it gradually fades away and his sight returns, he is back in the garden area where he once worked for Father Michael. A solitary figure of a man, wearing work clothes and an old baseball cap, with his back to Otto is raking in the middle of the garden, near the area where the flagstone forms a cross. Otto knows this because he is now above the man, looking down as if floating over the garden. He descends to the ground right in front of the Gardener, who raises his head slowly, removes his Dallas Cowboys baseball cap obscuring his face, and shakes his full, white hair loose.

His eyes are brilliant, inviting pools of flaming blue, and his full lips are like smoldering coals. His smile is more gracious and genuine than Otto has ever seen and the Gardener's clothes are now also completely white.

Suddenly, this peace is broken by yet another gunshot. Otto whips around to see Shadow Man walking purposefully through the garden towards them. Flowers on either side of him are withering and falling to the ground as he passes; darkness follows close behind. Shadow Man's eyes are glowing red inside his hood as he raises a bony finger to point directly at Otto, as if claiming him for his own. Otto takes a step back and stares down again at his own arms and hands that are once again dripping with the blood of the innocents.

At this moment, he is aware that the Gardener now stands between Shadow Man and him. He is holding a large, golden book sealed with what looks like dried blood. The Gardener breaks the seal, opens the book, holds it up to Shadow Man, and points to a particular name. Otto cranes his head but can't quite see the name. Bewildered, Shadow Man stops in his tracks, stares at the name, looks up at the Gardener, turns, and glares at Otto before disappearing in a flash of smoke and lightning.

At last and forever, peace beyond his understanding descends upon him as The Gardener turns, smiling still, reaches out, and beckons to Otto Franz Eberhardt.

#

Walter Carter couldn't sleep. Something was bothering him. After tossing and turning for what seemed hours, he finally got up, slipped on pants and slippers, and took a walk. Up and down the dim halls of the nursing home he strolled, pausing in the commons area to gaze out the large windows at the brilliant moon rising over the Texas panhandle to spill its brilliance over the New Mexican plains. Still troubled, but not understanding what it could be, a few minutes later Walter walked back down the hall, and slowed down when he saw light seeping from beneath Father Michael's door. He tapped lightly, and, getting no response, slowly pushed the door open and stepped inside.

The small desk lamp was on, casting its slight illumination across the small room. The bed was still made up as if it had not been slept in. Instead, the old priest sat beside the desk, staring out the window.

"Father?" Walter called out quietly. When he heard no answer, he moved across the room to the back of the priest's chair. He reached out and placed a hand on Father Michael's shoulder. Still with no response, he stepped around the chair.

From here, he could see the priest was holding two objects in his hands, which rested limply in his lap: a faded old photograph and a worn chess piece. Walter was surprised to find a faint smile frozen on Father Michael's face, but clear, unwavering eyes gazing vacantly out the window into the brilliantly moonlit sky.

"Father?" he repeated once more, softly, then gently placed two fingers on the priest's wrist.

Walter's friend, the old man of God, was gone.

CHAPTER 32
TRUTH WILL SET YOU FREE

Excerpt from the Journal of Otto Eberhardt

"August 9, 2015 – My 90th birthday today – a time to certainly reflect on many things – so much heartache, pain and loss on the one hand, then on the other so much joy and blessing in these final years. I can no longer remember the faces of my dear wife Erika or my precious little daughter, both dead in the war, so long ago. Or the faces of my comrades on the battlefield, so many young men – no, not men – boys, really, who marched away excitedly from their homes, off to some grand adventure and many of whom later died in my arms crying out in agony for their mothers. And the faces of all those poor innocents who died when we blew up that train; old Dave Perkins, that pig farmer who helped me with my English and with my chess game; and dear Father Michael, who gave his life for me, who haunts me still. Because of me he lay unprotected for decades in an unconsecrated grave. At least now they have found him, though I don't think they have a clue yet who he really is.

Perhaps I should let someone know the truth – perhaps I can arrange to get my "Bible" to that intense, troubled young Deputy Carter, the son of my friend Walter.

Oh, Walter. How serendipitous that I would discover him in this place after all those years – in many ways with that same rambunctious boyish spirit I first met playing cowboys and Indians in the aisle of that train – and whose pretty mother and little brother did not survive the explosion. It was one of God's small blessings – my penance, really, and perhaps a sign of God's forgiveness – for me to find him here, of all places, when Caroline was transferred here to make room at the State Hospital. Of course, I was not going to remain behind there. Caroline was the entire reason I was there in the first place, to keep a watchful eye out for her, under the pretext of being the hospital chaplain. But when I started to have health issues of my own, I arranged to transfer myself to the Clayton facility, also to stay near her. But I do pray Walter will never learn the truth – that I was one of the ones responsible for the death of his mother and brother.

Deputy Carter already has my original journal, which details the tragedy, among most other events, and the truth will soon be out anyway. My prayer is that, for a while longer and at least in their eyes, I remain "Father Michael" until the end. Yes, I think perhaps no one better than Deputy Carter should have the "Bible" – my precious Evie's thoughts, as well as my final truths.

But none of that shall matter soon. My old body is finally shutting down. And if all goes as planned, my old enemy will be confronting me again soon, one final time. It shall all play out according to God's plan.

Then shall I finally be at rest, and reunited with those precious ones who have gone on before me – Erika and Evie (is it possible to have had more than one 'soul mate' in this world?), and my darling little "Rosebud,' the daughter I never really got to know."

#

Trent sat in his office the next morning when the phone rang. After he had called Mirielle Segura and warned her that their lives were in possible danger, he had called the local police to check on her periodically. He had been expecting a callback from either the police, or if even luckier, Mirielle herself.

But this call was from neither. It was the nursing home administrator in Clayton who began by expressing her condolences. Trent held his breath, certain that the call concerned Walter, his father. Instead, he was told that he was on the list to be informed that Father Michael had died peacefully early that morning. Trent hung up the phone and slumped quietly in his chair for a couple of minutes, before suddenly remembering something.

"Be sure you read this" had been among Father Michael's last words to him. Trent felt in his jacket pocket, pulled out the Bible, and ran a thumb over the faded gold letters of the name embossed on the lower right hand of the cover: *Michael Francis Shannon.* He casually flipped open the cover and thumbed through a few pages, thinking that the old gentleman might have marked some of his favorite Biblical passages.

Presently, Trent stopped flipping and froze, his finger slowly opening a page.

Instead of helpful Bible verses, he had just found exactly the treasure the priest had intended for him to find.

#

Trent had lost track of time when he finally closed the priest's Bible, which proved not to be a Bible at all, but rather the diary of Evie Van Ryan Neumann – and not only that, but also in the back pages, the additional journal entries of Otto Franz Eberhardt, one of the escaped POWs from Camp Trinidad. Taken together with the German soldier's original journal, they documented Eberhardt's life from World War II, right up to almost the day that he died — and not in the dark alley behind an old theater.

Trent placed the "Bible" beside Otto's original journal on his desk and sat in stunned silence, digesting everything he had just read and feeling more pieces of the puzzle fall into place: Otto Franz Eberhardt, an escaped German prisoner of war, had been living right under their noses for all these years, posing as the Catholic Priest Father Michael; it was Father Michael's remains that had been found under the theater. Unlike Eberhardt's first journal that ended in the 1970s and was written in German, these newer passages were entirely in English, a reflection, perhaps, of the changes the former soldier had gone through in his life. As it turned out in the end, he had lived far longer in the United States than in Germany. Several times throughout his journals, Eberhardt had mentioned his diligent work in learning the English language, progressing from knowing very little when he was captured in 1945 to speaking fluent English with only a slight trace of an accent by the time Trent had gotten to know him.

The entire saga of Otto Eberhardt was now documented here for over sixty-five years, comprising one of the most astonishing tales of war, intrigue, sabotage, murder, love, betrayal, assumed identities, brokenness, and finally, redemption, that Trent had ever read in either fiction or non-fiction, or ever even seen in a movie.

But the revelation that had Trent really sitting now in deep reflection over was the explosive secret that had been revealed in Evie's part of the diary – a revelation that finally explained so much — and a part of the story that now, with both Evie and Otto dead, supposedly no one but Trent knew.

Carl Neumann was not Conrad Neumann's son.

Carl Neumann was certainly not Ernst Brandt's son.

Carl Neumann, in truth, was the son of Otto Eberhardt – a secret that had evidently been kept from even Carl himself.

Trent sat drumming his fingers lightly on the edge of his desk, mulling over all of this startling information. He then pulled his attention back to the present, slid the "John Doe" file across the desk, and opened it. He thumbed idly through the autopsy photos of the skeleton from the theater for several minutes, closed the file, found a black marker, and changed the name on the file label to "Michael Francis Shannon." He peered at the name for a long while, realizing that he really knew nothing about this man, the real Father Michael, that is. He picked up the telephone and punched Molly's intercom.

"Yes," she answered,

"Molly, I need you to get on that "googly" thing of yours and find out everything you can on a 'Father Michael Francis Shannon,' who just passed away this morning at the nursing home in Clayton. Evidently used to be the parish priest here in Raton years ago."

"Sure thing. Oh! And your daughter just called. Said she's been trying your mobile, but you don't pick up."

"Okay, thanks," he replied. "Oh yeah, and is Ben back from lunch?"

"Think so – want me to buzz him? Oh, wait. He's on another line."

"That's okay, I'll just grab him."

"And don't forget Sophie — she sounded a little upset."

Trent hung up and found the cell phone in his jacket hanging on the back of his chair. He flipped it open and saw that he had, in fact, missed a couple of calls from Sophie. He called her back; the call went straight to voice mail.

Trent put the phone in his shirt pocket and turned back to the priest's file. After a few more minutes studying the file, he glanced at his watch, picked up the file, the journals, and the letters, and took them down the hall to Ben Ferguson's office.

Ben was still on the phone when Trent opened the door, stepped on in, and sat down in front of Ben's desk.

"Yes – yes – I see – yes – thank you. We'll send someone right away." Ben hung up and looked across the desk at Trent blankly. "That's okay, Carter. Come on in and have a seat, why don't you," he said evenly. "That closed door there is obviously just meant for everyone else."

The sarcasm seemed lost on Trent as he slid the file and other materials across the desk and then tapped his finger on the file label.

"Got a positive ID on that body," he announced quietly. Ben took a quick look at the name on the file and then slid it back.

"'Michael Shannon?' Supposed to mean anything to me?"

"Well, I thought I knew him," Trent answered, excitedly. "But turns out I didn't, really. Turns out he wasn't who he said he was and has been hiding out all these years, but he's really the key to most of these killings we've been looking at, and now that he's dead and has left me more evidence, even though it's probably still circumstantial, I think we need to get a search warrant and get back out to Neumann's Ranch before that old Nazi destroys any more real evidence."

Ben fixed Trent with a tired but steady stare.

"I'm going to just sit quietly here for a moment while you and I both pretend that I know exactly what you're talking about," Ben retorted matter-of-factly. Trent sat back, took a deep breath, and tried again more calmly.

He cleared his throat but looked steadily ahead. "Case of mistaken identity," he explained carefully. "You recall this old journal here that I've been scratching my head over?" Trent picked up the journal for a second, then dropped it back onto the file.

Ben nodded slowly.

"Well," continued Trent, "seems the guy who wrote it has been passing himself off as this old priest, over there in the Clayton nursing home. And he and another guy were originally two escaped German POWs from over at that old WWII camp northeast of Trinidad – and the other old German's the one who's been responsible for a majority of those cold case murders we've got stacked around here.

Ben stifled a yawn and glanced at the clock on the wall behind Trent. "We know all this, how?" he asked.

"From the bogus Father Michael's journals — right here." Trent tapped the books. "He's documented the whole thing for us – over the last five or six decades!"

Ben looked skeptical. "And this other old German is...?"

"A real piece of work, that's what he is," Trent interjected. "And he's been passing himself off as Conrad Neumann – for decades. "

"Neumann?" Ben suddenly interrupted, sitting up in his chair a little straighter. "You mean that old rancher, out on the Dry Cimarron? That Neumann?"

"One and the same."

"And you know this for sure?"

"Well, he all but confessed it to us when we went there to investigate him the other day."

"Us? Who's us?"

Trent cleared his throat and looked down at his hands, realizing he had just said too much. "Well – I may have had Maggie Van Ryan with me – just circumstances worked out that way – didn't plan it."

Ben tapped his finger on the desk and stared with an eyebrow cocked high at Trent, then continued with a lowered voice. "Hold on here a minute: You're telling me you took a civilian into an active investigation scene – with the primary suspect right there?" It was a statement, not a question.

Trent felt himself turning red and didn't have an immediate answer. Ben shook his head slowly, sinking back into his worn leather chair.

"So, besides that one infraction, and being totally out of your jurisdiction for a second one, how many other regulations do you think you managed to break this week?"

Trent began to say something in response but Ben held up his hand. He picked up the journal and thumbed through it absently, scratched his cheek and hit the intercom button on his desk phone.

"Molly, get me that sheriff over there in Union County – what's-his-name? Bradley or something."

"First or last?"

"First or last what, Molly?"

"Bradley – that his first name or last name?"

"The hell should I know? He's the sheriff. They only have one, whatever his name is, and I need him on the damn phone!" Ben disconnected, rubbed his eyes slowly, and sighed. "Doesn't she retire soon?" he asked no one in particular.

"I think we all need to retire soon," answered Trent, also to no one in particular. "Anyway, when that warrant's served, I want to be there to help turn that place upside down."

"Ain't gonna happen," pronounced Ben, shuffling some papers on his desk until he produced a pink phone message with scribbling all over it. "Just got off the phone with West Las Vegas P.D. when you barged in here. Seems there's a body lying in some old lady's bathroom down there. They came up with a couple of names related to one of your other cold cases there…"

"Mirielle Segura," Trent interrupted quietly, nodded knowingly at the floor, then cursed himself. "I was afraid of this. So, she's dead?"

"Nope. But some lowlife goes by the name Jimmy Streck sure is. Got his head stove in by some old lady," he referred to his notes again, "Ms. Segura's aunt, I think?" Trent's eyes went momentarily wide in surprise, but Ben continued. "Anyway, since you were the one opened up that particular can of worms, I'm thinking you're the one gets to go down there and help them sort out the good guys from the bad."

"But what about Ernst Brandt?"

Ben shook his head in confusion. "Now, just who the hell is that?" he asked.

"Posing as Neumann – the old Nazi, the one I've been trying to tell you about, Ben," Trent's voice gradually rose in volume, increasingly exasperated. "The guy actually behind all this, Ben! Haven't you been listening to me at all?" Trent reared back into his chair, frustrated now. "We need to get that warrant issued, Ben, and now! Who do you have any better than me to send out there to help them serve it?"

"Me, that's who. I'll do it myself," answered Ben. "Tired of riding this desk while you hotheads get to go have all the fun." The sheriff looked at his watch. "Soon as I get a call back from Bradley who's-it. Neumann's place is in his jurisdiction – and I, for one, plan to pursue the correct procedures." He stood up slowly and leaned on the desk, eye-to-eye with Trent, who was still fuming. "But what I need you to do right now, Deputy, is settle yourself down, get out of here, get yourself some fresh air, and get down to Vegas, where there is an actual, bonafide crime scene for you to investigate – before you go off half-cocked and throw another set of bizarre mistaken identities my way!"

As if on cue, the phone on Ben's desk suddenly rang. He pushed the speaker button.

"Yeah?"

"Sheriff Bradley Marshall on line 1," said Molly.

"Sheriff Marshall," Ben smirked again at Trent and held a hand over the phone. "Bet that's good for a few laughs around the office coffee pot each morning!"

Trent said nothing, ignoring Ben's lame joke, stood up, and headed for the door.

"Ferguson," he heard Ben say into the phone. "Hey, hold on a sec, Brad." He put the Union County Sheriff on hold and looked up at Trent. "Take Armijo with you; between the both of you, you just might keep each other out of trouble and from muddying up the crime scene down there!"

Trent started through the door when Ben called him back again. "And don't forget to take all this crap with you!" He shoved the case file and journals back across the desk. "Might need to refer to something important."

#

"So what do you really know about this Streck fellow, anyway?" asked Hector. They were about twenty miles out of town, headed south on I-25 towards Las Vegas, New Mexico. Trent was driving and had set the cruise control on 85 miles per hour. He wanted to get down there, get done with this Streck business, and hopefully cut around and take a shortcut on one of the back highways and get in on the search of the Neumann Ranch. He felt he was being sidetracked on this investigation and just knew Ben was liable to overlook something critical, like the old man's computer and all those scrapbooks.

"From Amarillo," Trent answered finally. "Beyond that, all I know about Streck is that he's an old Marine buddy of Carl Neumann's from Vietnam days. Guess they taught each other how to go shoot up the jungles and rice paddies over there and learned to take no prisoners – skills they evidently, unfortunately, have now put to use back here."

"Wow! All that and then killed by a frying pan," mused Hector, rubbing his chin. "And wielded by a little old Mexican lady, you say? Dang! How does a guy not see that coming?" He chuckled.

"Don't forget that he presumably was a little distracted by a butcher knife sticking out of his belly, courtesy of Mirielle Segura herself. How's that for a little payback?"

"Still," Hector continued, "best not mess around with a ticked off *mamasita*!"

Trent suddenly remembered the missed calls from his daughter. He glanced over at Hector.

"You talk to Sophie this afternoon?" he asked.

"Yeah, earlier. Well, we went to lunch is all. Why?"

"She say anything about needing to talk to me?" Trent was already taking his mobile phone out of his shirt pocket.

Hector thought for a second. "Uh – no, not that I recall. Said she was going back home to finish cleaning the mess we made in the dining room the other night. And to check on Jarhead."

Trent had flipped the phone open and punched Sophie's speed dial. It rang three times before it was answered.

"Hey, Punkin'. Sorry I missed your call. How's my cat doing?" There was silence on the other end of the line, but Trent could hear steady breathing. "Sofe, you there?"

"Daddy," Sophie answered, but her voice was quivering. "I – I'm sorry, Daddy —" Her voice trailed off with a sudden rustling on the phone. Then, a different voice came on.

"Well, hello, Deputy Carter – so good of you to call. I was afraid we weren't going to hear from you today — and that would have been so tragic."

The voice belonged, with no doubt, to Carl Neumann.

#

Trent slammed on the brakes, putting the Ford Explorer into a long, fishtailing skid of squealing, smoking tires in the middle of the southbound lanes of I-25. The cellphone flew from his hand and down onto the floorboard somewhere. Files, papers, photos, and other items flew off the front and back seats. Horns blasted on either side as vehicles careened and swerved around them to the right and left.

"Mr. Carter – Trent!" yelled Hector as he grabbed the dashboard with both hands. "Get off the road!"

Trent was pale and grimaced as he gripped the wheel with both hands. He jumped as a semi roared by blaring its horns, bringing him back to his senses. He quickly glanced into the rearview mirror, jerked the wheel to the right, and gunned the cruiser until it ran totally off the shoulder and onto the grass. He slammed the gearshift into park, ripped off his seatbelt, and frantically groped around his feet until he found the phone. He sat back and shoved it to his ear.

"What have you done with my daughter, you asshole?" Trent growled into the phone.

"Oh, such language, Deputy Carter," Carl Neumann answered with mock astonishment. "I am shocked at your manners," he smirked, "but frankly, that would explain why this pretty young lady here is such a handful – and she's such a lovely handful, by the way."

"You touch one hair on her and you're dead the moment you see me," Trent murmured through clenched teeth.

"Who is it?" demanded Hector. "Is that about Sophie? Put it on speaker!" He grabbed for the phone, but Trent jerked it out of reach, scowling at him, then held up his hand to caution him. He searched for a few seconds before he finally pushed the button to activate the phone speaker.

"Are you still there, Mr. Carter?"

"I'm here."

"I certainly hope so, for your sake. And did I just hear another voice? Who is it there with you, if I may be so bold to ask?"

Hector lurched over toward the phone, his face livid. "This is Deputy Hector Armijo, you son-of-a-buck! And like the man just said, you hurt her and you'll have more than one of us to deal with – you – you piece of slime, you!"

"Deputy Armijo! So pleased you can join our little game. And speaking of 'game,' I think you really need to 'up yours' in regard to proper swearing. Perhaps you could take better note of your mentor's technique."

Hector looked confused for a moment, then glanced up at Trent. "Did he just say, 'up yours?'" Hector frowned and leaned to the phone again to respond, but Trent pulled it away and waved him off.

"Carl," Trent hissed, "why don't you just cut out the bullshit and tell us what you want?"

"And that's exactly what's wrong with the world these days," Carl mockingly offered. "No appreciation for a good conversationalist. Ah well – *c'est la vie*," he audibly sighed before lowering his voice to a menacing tone. "No more bullshit, then. Here's what you're going to do, my old friend. You are going to bring everything you've got on the Neumanns –

every piece of writing, whether it's a journal, or a diary, or whatever, along with any investigative files and photos you may have, and you're going to bring it out to your precious girlfriend's place in – oh, let's say an hour?"

A frightening pause ensued before Carl continued, mockingly. "And, say, Dep-u-ty, that reminds me: I totally forgot to let you know that sweet Sophie and I have some company with us this evening! Say hello, dear cousin!"

Another shuffling sound came over the speaker, and, with a shock, a very familiar voice.

"Get your frickin' hands off me, you piece of shit!"

"Maggie?" yelled Trent. "You alright, Maggie?"

"Hey there, Cowboy," she answered, her voice ragged and sounding a little scared. "Yeah, we're both fine – for now. Nothing this little pervert's done so far that we've gotta worry about. I think he only gets off on scaring women – and you know that we two gals don't scare too easy – Hey!" she suddenly shouted. "I said knock it off!" Maggie's voice was cut short with the sound of a hard slap, followed by more shouting, a quick scream, and finally, eerie silence.

"These women," came Carl's disarmingly soft voice momentarily. "You can't live without 'em, can't kill 'em," with a dramatic pause. "Hey, wait a second! I guess I can, can't I?"

"You son-of-a-bitch," Trent spat. "I'm gonna need more than an hour!"

"Hmmm – don't think so," Carl continued, undeterred. "Looks like you're just going to have to put the pedal to the metal! Well, and will you look at that. We are now down to 56 minutes, what with all these pleasantries we've been exchanging! Clock's ticking, Deputy. So, please have the aforementioned incriminating items delivered here to my dear sweet Cousin Margot's place – all of it, mind you – in my impatient little hands by then or else you can kiss these precious little ladies bye-bye. Hey, though, here's another thought: maybe I'll just kiss them goodbye for you!"

Hector gritted his teeth and slapped the dashboard with his fist.

"Oh, and good friend," Carl's voice lowered in pitch as he added, "no calls for backup, please. I would so hate for this evening's activities to escalate out of control, wouldn't you?"

There was silence again as Trent's mind raced.

"Deputy Carter," Carl growled, his voice now low and ominous. "I am getting the distinct impression that you aren't taking any of this seriously at all. So, just to get our little game off with the proper motivation and, shall we say, incentive," he paused, and Trent could hear Carl's breathing quicken over the speaker, "I am now going to shoot one of these sweet treasures of yours – just to show you that the stakes are, indeed, quite high – and serious."

"Carl, use your head!" Trent broke the silence finally, and shouted into the phone. "Don't be stupid! We're going to bring you everything you asked for. You haven't done anything irreversible yet!"

Carl grew quiet for a moment, then continued.

"Oh, now we both know that isn't true at all, don't we, Trent? Have you forgotten so soon? Tell me, have you not taken my beautiful cousin here up to see the aspens on Cordova Pass yet? So breathtaking this time of year, as I recall – particularly in the company of a beautiful woman, wouldn't you say – Trent?"

Trent said nothing, but gripped the phone so tightly he thought it might break.

"So don't you be telling lies regarding what is reversible and what isn't. Even if a judge and jury were to let me off, I don't stand a snowball's chance in hell with you, now do I? Which is why the bonus round of tonight's game has to end with only one clear winner, don't you agree? A bullet in the head for one of us – oh, but let's see – you've already experienced that, haven't you?"

"Carl," Trent struggled to control the emotion in his voice, "please —"

"Oh, come now! Begging does not become you at all, Trent Carter," Carl replied, raising his voice impatiently. He then sighed and continued. "Alrighty then. Now, here we are at only 52 minutes left. My, my!

"Carl!" shouted Hector, grabbing again for the cell phone.

"Tick, tock – hickory dock – who will live – and who will not – eeny, meeny, miny … moe!"

The next noise the men heard was the sudden, loud pop of what sounded like a gunshot over the speaker, followed immediately by screams; just as abruptly, the phone signal went dead.

"Carl? *Carl!*"

Trent stared at the phone in stunned silence for several seconds. He began to tremble, collected himself enough to punch Sophie's speed dial button again, but the call went immediately to her voice mail. He opened the car door, jumped out, and screamed at the universe at the top of his lungs. In a sudden fit of rage, he reared back and threw the mobile phone as hard as he could. It sailed over three lanes of traffic into the northbound lanes of the interstate where it exploded on the asphalt right before an oncoming 18-wheeler crushed the remaining pieces into oblivion under its wheels. Trent stood there staring at nothing, his chest heaving with deep sobs, wondering which of the two people he cared most about in the world had just been shot.

Hector had also been in a daze, but when Trent threw the phone, he shook himself out of it and got out of the passenger side of the vehicle. He watched Trent for a moment, then stepped purposefully to the back of the cruiser, opened the tailgate, and pulled out a large molded equipment box. He poked his head around the side of the car and looked at Trent, who continued to stand at the side of the highway staring into space and motionless.

"Now, that was real mature and helpful," Hector called out. He went back to work and pulled out a military style assault rifle, a short-barreled shotgun, and boxes of ammo for both. He also put on a black Kevlar vest with "SHERIFF" stenciled in yellow letters on the front and back. Trent finally walked back and joined him.

"What was that?" Trent asked.

"Nothing," Hector answered sullenly. "Except I think a much better response right now would be to gear up and get our rear ends over there instead of staring out at the remains of your trashed phone."

Trent frowned at him. "You know he's right about one thing," he said, as he pushed past Hector, reached into the weapons' box and grabbed a few magazines of .45 ACP ammo that he shoved into his jacket pockets.

"What's that?" asked Hector.

"You really need to work on some better swear words."

"I swear just fine." Hector glanced at his watch. "And it's now 44 minutes and counting. Time to go put an end to this bull hockey. You driving? Hector asked, barely hesitating, "or am I?"

"Get in the damn car," Trent ordered curtly.

Hector slammed the tailgate and hurried back around to get in, by which time Trent had already turned the key in the ignition. The engine roared to life just as Hector opened his door and looked in.

"You don't want a vest?" he asked.

"Screw the vest," snapped Trent as he gunned the engine. The SUV lurched and sprayed gravel while Hector made a dive to throw himself in.

"Crap!" he exclaimed as he finally hauled himself in and slammed the door behind him.

#

The cruiser barreled north on I-25 at just under 100 miles an hour before reaching the outskirts of Raton. Hector had switched on the lights and sirens.

Trent looked over and scowled.

"At least until we get close," Hector pointed out, trying to be helpful. "Then we can shut it down and go on in quietly if you'd like."

"Because you figure he doesn't know we're coming?"

"Well – no. Not that. It's just I know you hate the noise, so thought we'd turn it off later, that's all."

"I don't care about the frickin' noise, I don't care about the damn lights, and I really don't care whether that asshole hears us coming, or not!"

Hector nodded. He picked up the radio microphone and clicked it on.

"Unit 4 to base, come in," he said, his voice modulating with a professional tone. "Unit 4 – come in, base." He was abruptly cut off as Trent reached over, grabbed the microphone, and ripped the cord from the radio unit. He quickly threw it over his shoulder where it bounced into the back of the vehicle somewhere.

"Are you crazy? What the heck did you do that for?" Hector demanded. He fumed for a minute. "You got a vendetta against electronics, too, today? We're going to need backup when we get out there!"

"No," Trent answered deliberately, "we will not."

He gripped the wheel and swerved off of the interstate onto the Sugarite Canyon exit, barely keeping all four wheels on the ground as he took the turn. He had no intention of calling in for help. His mind had been whirling over the past few days and weeks with all the bits of information that had fallen into his lap – all the pieces of the puzzle, not only of the random killings over the decades, but of his own life. The swirling images of desolate crime scenes, unidentified maimed bodies, pages of journals, maps, skeletal remains buried under a building, assumed identities, escaped

POWs, crashing vehicles, exploding trains, gunshots, pain, blood, and screams had all coalesced now into a somewhat recognizable chain of events, all spiraling down into this exact moment in time and all bathed in golden spangles of aspen leaves. One striking image remained in the center of it all: the now indelible memory of holding his dying wife's bleeding head in his arms and peering uphill into the flash and reflection of the afternoon sun glaring from a rifle scope being steadily aimed at his own head – a rifle being held by Carl Neumann himself.

Like his Native American ancestors before him, Trent had now stepped out onto the Warrior's Way and was not going to be deterred by any restraints of negotiations, fairness, or the law. Carl had been right about another thing: this all would end once and for all tonight, and Trent knew he would again have his peace – one way or another – and hopefully, his sanity back.

He whipped the Explorer through the bends and dips as the tight, two-lane highway climbed steadily eastward up the twisting canyons toward Johnson Mesa, tapping the brakes occasionally to avoid careening into a ravine. He glanced at Hector, who was bracing himself in the passenger side of the vehicle with a grim look on his face.

"How much time left?" Trent asked.

"Thirteen minutes," Hector answered. Trent glanced at him again and then softened.

"Listen. Hector, I see how much she means to you, too, and I do know how much you mean to her, actually. I'm not blind or insensitive about that. You two are probably really good for each other."

Hector turned his head away and stared out the window at the slopes of the huge mesa slipping by them. The afternoon sun was reflecting brilliant color from its massive rock formations towering above them.

"But you've got to understand what the Neumanns have really done," Trent continued. "In addition to everything else, Carl and that Nazi stepfather of his have done everything they can to destroy my family – killed my grandmother and an uncle of mine, before I was even born, in that train sabotage on the Pass during the war – blew my wife's head off – left me for dead trying to do the same thing to me – even tried to kill my stupid cat! And now, Carl intends to try to kill me again, and you, too, if he can." Trent tried to continue, "And he's probably already –"

Trent's voice caught and choked up. He swiped his nose roughly with the back of his hand, then gripped the wheel again as they whipped around the curve and headed east into Yankee Canyon that ran between Johnson and Raton Mesas. He looked over at Hector again and continued, his voice thick with emotion.

"If he hasn't already, he intends to kill our girls, Hector – Maggie and Sophie – my only daughter —"

Hector looked back at Trent with some compassion. He licked his lips and cleared his throat.

"Whatever it takes, Mr. Carter – I've got your back."

Trent nodded and wiped his mouth. "I knew that you would, Hector. And that's exactly why this is how it's got to go down." He stole a quick look at the clock. Nine minutes left. He reached over and turned off the lights and siren, but nudged the accelerator a bit in the straightaway. "When we leave the highway and start on down to the ranch, I'm going to roll up to within a hundred yards or so of the house, jump out, and run into the trees there. Then I'm going to need you to grab the wheel, turn around, and head back up to the highway. You should be in radio range there and you can make your call for backup because by the time anyone gets out here, it's going to all be over."

Hector smiled and pointed to the damaged radio.

"Oh – yeah, I guess not, huh," said Trent.

"I have a better idea," said Hector finally. "How about we act like real partners and both jump out, go into the trees, and come up on opposite sides of the house, because you know I'm not about to let you go in there all by yourself without any cover!"

Trent frowned, looked at his partner, and shook his head.

"This is going to get awful ugly, my friend – more ways than one. And when it does go down, you need to know that I will throw the rulebook out the window, if I have to, and do whatever needs to be done. Badge or no badge, Carl Neumann does not walk out of here tonight – especially if he has hurt either of our ladies." He paused for a moment, but continued. " So, Hector, there's an even chance this night may end with you having to put the handcuffs on me, instead – depending on how this all goes down."

Trent paused again and looked at the young officer. "So, are you prepared for all that -- *partner*? Because I am."

Hector looked at Trent grimly and reached down, grabbed a box of shotgun shells, and silently began loading the riot gun in his lap. He finished and clipped the gun back into its mount on the dash. He reached into another box, pulled out a handful of rifle clips, and shoved them into his vest pockets.

"Guess that answers my questions," acknowledged Trent. "But Hector, when we get in there, first chance we have to get to Sophie and Maggie, while I keep Carl occupied it's going to be your job to get them out of there and safely back to the vehicle, no matter what else is happening, *capiche*?"

"*Capiche,*" Hector answered, and turned and looked back out the window without another word.

The sun had dipped closer to the Sangre de Cristos behind them by the time Trent took his foot off the gas and turned through the gates of Montaño del Sol Ranch. Looking up at the massive log work as he passed under the gate sign, he briefly reflected on how much of the history of this case down through the decades had played itself out at this place – and now appeared to be drawing itself to an equally violent close right here. He pulled up a few more feet then slowed to a stop, holding his foot on the brake. He reached inside his jacket and removed his Glock .45 semiautomatic pistol, popped out the 12-shot magazine, checked it, shoved it back home, and replaced the pistol in his shoulder holster.

"You taking anything else?" Hector asked. "A rifle, maybe?" Trent shook his head and smiled.

"Nope. I need to see his eyes, close up – want him to see it coming."

Hector blew his breath out nervously, then looked up at Trent again.

"I'm not going to get in your way, Boss, but I just have to ask the question: you going to give him any chance at all to surrender?"

Trent thought hard for a moment. "I'm not going to gun him down in cold blood, if that's what you're asking. But quite honestly, I don't think that sociopath has any intention of surrendering," Trent almost smiled, "which makes my part of it that much easier."

"You're thinking 'suicide-by-cop,' then?"

Trent thought for a second. "More like *No* Lives Matter," he answered. "And take as many others with him as he can."

He put the SUV in gear, glanced at the clock once more, then back at Hector.

"Four minutes to go – you ready?"

Hector unbuckled his seatbelt, checked that his sidearm was in place before pulling the assault rifle up to the ready. He took another deep breath and nodded.

"Let's go!" he confirmed, just a little too loudly, betraying his nerves.

Trent tapped the gas. The cruiser picked up speed as they headed into the canopy of cottonwoods that lined the road majestically. Trent was trying to recall the exact layout of the outbuildings and the house. He figured the house was where Carl would have taken them, but he couldn't be absolutely positive.

Trent could just now see the outlines of the barns about 100 yards ahead and Maggie's two-story Victorian ranch house looming up ahead on the right. They rounded the bend that opened up into the final stretch of road to the house. Trent gripped the wheel even tighter, preparing to whip it over to the tree line to make their jump, when he suddenly smelled wild roses and cloves and his mind panicked and went numb.

"Oh, Lord! No, not now!" he murmured and his eyes widened as Vicky materialized out of nowhere directly in the path of their vehicle, her cornflower blue dress and long, sandy hair flowing in slow motion behind her. She was frowning at Trent and held her arms and hands up urgently as if to block the SUV – or divert it, for some reason. Trent swerved to miss her, just as the windshield erupted with a staccato of star blossoms as bullets stitched across it, shattering glass and thudding into the interior of the cruiser.

Trent felt hot ice slam into his right shoulder. In that instant, the car plowed into the trunk of a cottonwood tree. The airbags deployed, leaves showered down on the car, and his world went black.

CHAPTER 33
VALLEY OF THE SHADOW OF DEATH

Trent woke up; that is, he tried to wake up. His head was swimming and it was dark outside. He realized that his eyes were closed, but he was having trouble forcing them open.

He kept hearing a beautifully lilting and familiar voice cooing, *"Wake up, Baby Boy."* The singsong words drifted on Vicky's wondrous, unmistakable scent.

He tried to remember exactly what had happened – or even where he was. *Back in the dream – on Cordova Pass?*

He decided to continue concentrating on what he could sense: the sound of the ticking and hissing of a stalled engine, the faint odor of gasoline, the hard smooth coldness of window glass against his cheek, the sound of someone moaning.

He realized it was his own moaning. His right arm felt as if it were encased in cement.

The tangy taste of copper was in his mouth and he choked on his own blood. He coughed, sending a spasm of pain through his shoulder, and the sensation helped him to finally open his heavy eyelids, only to find himself looking curiously at a deflated airbag on his lap. He moved and gasped as another stab of pain shot through his upper arm. He twisted his head around and looked down at a hole there in his leather jacket. He reached inside, winced, and then pulled back his hand to find it covered with his own blood.

He knew this was no dream; he knew they were in grave danger; he knew they needed to get moving.

"Hector," he mumbled. "We've gotta get out of here."

He looked over at his partner in the passenger seat – except it wasn't his partner. Vicky was sitting there, her head down and her beautiful sandy golden hair obscuring her eyes.

"Victoria?" he asked quietly. "Are you really here?"

He waited quietly for her to respond. She didn't move. By now Trent had learned that each time his dead wife had appeared to him – whether as a ghost, a figment of his own psyche, or scar tissue on the brain – her manifestation had always been for a very good reason, ultimately for his own good.

Vicky finally raised her head, turned to him, and smiled lazily. "You must save her, Trenny," she murmured languidly, her voice like honey. The wild roses and cloves permeated the air thickly, making him swoon; its intensity seemed to be in direct correlation to the sense of urgency he felt, despite Vicky's lazy attitude.

"Which one, Vic? Which one do I save? Sophie? Maggie?" he asked desperately. He suddenly remembered the sound of a gunshot over the phone. "What if we're too late, Vic? What if we've already lost our baby girl?" Trent choked on the last word, an unwelcome image of his daughter welling up in his mind's eye.

She gazed at him lovingly, slid over to him, reached up, and stroked the wayward hair away from the scar on his forehead, but this time the scar didn't ache like before. Her cool fingers felt good on his hot skin. "And what if we haven't lost her? What then? You may have to ask yourself to make a sacrifice, to save one at the cost of the other – can you do that?"

"Sacrifice?" he swooned, not comprehending.

"You never listen – what I've been trying to tell you all along," she continued, letting her fingers lightly trace his cheek. "There must always be a Sacrifice for there to be a Salvation."

Trent pursed his lips and tried to lift his hand to touch her, but instead, it fell heavily like a lead weight into his lap. He suddenly felt exhausted and older than the sum of his years.

"I'm listening, Vic. I really am. It's just – I just don't understand. Just tell me – and no more riddles, please – what do I do?"

Vicky continued to stroke his cheek, as she leaned back into the corner of the seat and smiled at him.

"When the time comes, you will know exactly what to do – and you will do exactly what you know to do, at exactly the right time. Listen to your heart – to the Spirit speaking softly inside you."

Suddenly, the smile changed to a deep frown and her eyes flickered and smoldered as if she sensed some great urgency. She clinched her teeth in a grimace; her eyes opened wide as she lunged to him, grabbed the lapel of his jacket, and pulled him hard toward her.

"Run!" she shouted into his face. "Run now!"

Trent came fully alert as Vicky immediately disappeared. In her place once again was Hector, who had collapsed against the door, his eyes closed and blood streaming from a wound somewhere on his head. His face was white and he didn't appear to be breathing.

Trent sucked in his breath in horror, pushed back against his own door, his hand scrambling behind him to find the handle. He fumbled it open and half fell out of the vehicle. He was still strapped into his seatbelt and dangled out of the doorway like a marionette. He finally unlatched the buckle, stumbled out onto the ground, grabbed the door for balance, and stood there wobbling for a moment, blinking his eyes, and looking around. Ravens high in the branches over his head cawed at the intrusion, then stopped for a second before suddenly flapping noisily away.

He watched the big birds wing into the distance; he suddenly realized that they were reacting to something else that he, too, should have been paying attention to. Too late, out of the corner of his eye, he caught movement and turned just in time to see the raised butt of a rifle coming toward his face, then nothing.

#

Trent awoke and squinted painfully into a flood of brilliant light. His head and shoulder throbbed dully. He tried to reach up to rub his head, but this time both of his arms felt paralyzed. His head swam; he couldn't determine which way was up. He lurched forward and felt his face scrape across something hard. He finally forced one eye halfway open, and his vision gradually focused until he recognized a hardwood floor just inches from his face. He struggled to push himself up with his hands but discovered they were tied in front of him, which explained his paralysis. He tried moving his legs, but they, too, seemed to be restricted at the ankles, probably also tied.

He suddenly grew still as he heard other movements besides his own – nearby sounds that indicated he was not alone: someone chewing, pages turning, and an occasional chuckle.

Trent opened his eyes and allowed them to adjust to the light. He slowly maneuvered until he could roll his head to the other side and glanced around a room that looked huge from this angle: high vaulted ceilings with log beams, massive pieces of leather furniture, and high windows along one wall to catch the magnificent explosion of color as the late afternoon sun prepared to set in the west – but quite familiar.

He realized he was lying on the floor of the large living room of Maggie's house.

He twisted his head around and saw the legs of someone seated, just a few feet away, in one of the oversized leather chairs in the middle of the room, one leg swung over the arm. The man held a half-eaten apple and chewed noisily on a mouthful of the fruit. In the other hand, Otto Eberhardt's journal obscured his face as he flipped its pages idly, shaking his head, and continuing to chuckle occasionally.

Trent knew that laugh: Carl Neumann.

At that moment, Carl looked up over the edge of the journal and spied Trent.

"Ah, our guest has decided to join us," he chortled, dropping the journal against his chest and watching Trent. "And here I had about decided you were going to sleep the afternoon away and miss all the fun!"

Trent tried to answer, but only managed a cough. His throat felt drier than dust, his head still spun.

"But, of course, where are my manners?" Carl asked sarcastically. He swung his leg off the arm of the chair, leaned over and set the apple and journal on the huge metal and glass coffee table, then stood up. Trent could also see the case files, photographs, and Otto's letters that had all been taken from Trent's vehicle and strewn on the table where they had been unceremoniously tossed. A long barreled .22 pistol was tucked into the belt of Carl's khaki pants as he sauntered over, his hands in his pockets. Carl's boots looked expensive and well made, probably from some exotic animal's hide. The boots stopped inches from Trent's face. "Well, let's get a better look at you, shall we, Deputy Carter? It's been a while"

Trent felt one of Carl's strong hands grip his jacket collar and the other his belt as he was lifted off the floor as easily as if he had been a child until he was in a sitting position. He rested his bound hands on his knees, which were now pulled up to his chest, and could now see that his ankles had been tied in a similar fashion. He was leaning against the flagstone hearth of the huge fireplace angled into one corner of the big room that poked and scraped the middle of his back. But of greater urgency, Trent now saw that Maggie and Sophie were seated three or four feet away from him, also bound and leaning against the hearth. They both looked generally disheveled, with a few visible scrapes and bruises, but more importantly, neither appeared seriously harmed – certainly not shot. They watched Trent with worried but grateful looks in their eyes as he felt a wave of relief wash over him.

"He made me think he had shot one of you," he whispered hoarsely, smiling wearily at them both. He wanted so badly at this moment to scoop them both up in his arms.

"Shot them?" Carl interjected, a shocked tone in his voice. "Oh, please give me more credit, Trent. I told you this was merely a game we are playing. I just needed to do something to make you hurry up and get here. And it certainly worked, didn't it?" He pointed down between Maggie and Sophie. Trent looked where Carl was pointing and saw a bullet-gouged hole in the hardwood floor. The whole incident had all been for effect, but with this lunatic, no one, least of all Trent, could ever be sure.

Carl straightened Trent's lapels and patted them in mocking concern. "Comfy, my old friend?" He then stopped abruptly and patted the front of Trent's jacket again,

"What's this?" he asked. He slipped his hand into Trent's inside jacket pocket and pulled out a small Bible. Trent felt the blood drain from his face but dared not react.

Carl turned the Bible over in his hand, examining the worn leather cover. "*Michael Frances Shannon,*" he read. He fingered the fading gilded lettering and glanced up at Trent. Trent tried to keep his face unresponsive as Carl's thumb slid along the edge of the pages.

Carl chuckled. "I would think that it's probably a sin to steal a dead man's Bible," he smirked. "Particularly a priest's!" He finally shrugged and slipped the small book back into Trent's pocket without examining it further. "Small comfort it's going to give you now."

Trent closed his eyes slowly and felt a wave of relief. Now was not the time for Carl to learn the truth. Trent planned to pull *that* particularly weapon at just the right time.

Carl stood up, picked up the remains of his apple and the journal, and strolled around to the other side of the table.

"Too bad about that poor Officer Armijo, though." Carl shook his head, took another bite of the apple, and sighed. "And he seemed like such a nice guy, too." He paused and put a finger to his mouth to pick a piece of the fruit from his teeth. "No one else needed to die today."

"For the time being, anyway, you mean," growled Trent. He glanced at Sophie. Her eyes had begun to glisten as she had lowered her chin slowly to her chest, staring blankly at the bullet hole in the floor. Trent realized this was the first time she had heard of Hector's fate, and his heart broke for her.

"I'm sorry, Punkin'," he said to her softly.

Carl smiled at Trent and wagged his forefinger at him as he walked slowly over to him. "No, no, Deputy Carter – you haven't been called on to speak." Trent flinched as Carl kicked the bottom of his boot. "But you're absolutely right when you say 'for the time being.' That time will come soon enough, but for now, you just listen, yes? And learn."

Carl had opened the journal again and now strolled around the room as he slowly turned pages. He looked over at his captive audience. "Perhaps you all can help me – I don't really see what my father wants with this book. Seems to me to be rather useless. For one thing, it's written completely in German – such a tedious, ugly, and unexpressive language, don't you think?" He flipped a few more pages, pointed at a section, and stopped behind the large sofa. "For example," he began, reading with some difficulty, "*I find the boy, Carl, to be troubled and unable to express real emotion, except for when he torments defenseless animals or his unsuspecting and innocent little sister, Caroline.*"

They all jumped as Carl suddenly exploded, slammed the journal shut, and threw it angrily onto the sofa in front of him. "What drivel! Troubled? Unemotional?"

He took another angry bite and spoke with his mouth full, punctuating his comments with the apple core, bits of the fruit spilling from his mouth. "*My innocent little sister*," he mocked, then looked at the three of them in turn as he paced the floor. "I tell you the truth, I personally knew this Otto Eberhardt fellow, years ago, when he worked for my family; he was as worthless as they come. He wanted little to do with me, but fawned over my pathetic sister as if she hung the moon."

Carl paused here and looked away, and for just a moment, Trent thought he saw a break in the sociopath's armor. "You know, I seem to remember he did the same thing with my mother, before –" his voice trailed off reflectively.

The moment passed. Carl turned and abruptly threw the apple core between the ladies' heads and straight into the fireplace, raising a sudden plume of cold ashes. They both ducked; he looked over at his hostages, shrugged, and chuckled. "What's wrong? If I had wanted it to hit you, it would have."

"What happened to him?" Trent asked, wishing to divert Carl's attention back to him. "What happened to Eberhardt?" A brief flicker of Carl's eyes, a quick look of doubt, followed by a malevolent squint, rewarded him.

"I killed him, of course," Carl shrugged matter-of-factly, the corners of his mouth playing with a smile. Trent said nothing, knowing it was a practiced lie, and waited for Carl to continue.

"I believed him to be a pervert – and I think my father did, too. And who knows what the man was capable of doing? I think that was a major reason my father had Caroline committed – to get her away from Otto. He shook his head in mock concern.

"You shut your filthy mouth," Trent blurted, surprising even himself that he would jump so quickly to the defense of Otto, a stranger he had only really known, until his death, as Father Michael, but a man whose heart he now strangely felt a kinship with.

Carl looked at Trent with genuine surprise. He stepped slowly over to him and stood looking down at him for a few quiet seconds, before bending down suddenly and backhanding him hard across the mouth, knocking Trent violently back into the flagstone hearth.

"I thought I was clear when I instructed you to speak only when called upon, Mr. Carter?" Trent felt blood trickle from the corner of his mouth where his lip had split. He looked up at Carl and began to respond, but Carl cautioned him, "No – that was a rhetorical question – not an invitation to speak. Do not test me further, my friend."

Trent glanced over to where Maggie and Sophie were watching with concern. Maggie frowned and opened her mouth to say something, but he shook his head slightly at her.

"Now, where were we?" Carl pondered as he walked back, picked up the journal, and resumed his seat in the large, plush chair, putting his feet up on the table. "Ah, yes. Well, I had always wondered just what importance this stupid little book had for my father. I mean, apart from several untruths, and an unsavory bit about Otto's perverted obsession with my mother and sister, there is nothing incriminating in here to my family at all that I see. It merely details the saga of two escaped Nazis and how they came to work for our respective families, my dear cousin." Here, Carl gestured to include Maggie, who simply glared back at him.

"As for poor Otto – well, I think we both know what happened to him, don't we, Mr. Carter? I mean, you were actually the one who found those rotting bones underneath that building, weren't you?"

Trent thought hard, trying to come up with any sort of plan in his mind. If they were to get out of this predicament, he needed to start playing the game, too – stay one step ahead of their abductor, and look for the right opportunity to throw him off guard. To do that, he needed to keep a clear head and not say anything else out of the ordinary that would inadvertently give Carl more information than he already had – or make him angrier. After all, Carl had only seen Otto's original journal, not Evie's diary, where Otto had revealed himself as Father Michael. To Trent's knowledge, he was still the only person who knew the entire story. He needed to use that to his advantage – as a weapon – and decided to take a chance.

"So you're finally confessing to a murder, Carl? Is that it?"

Carl said nothing at first. A smile slowly crept onto his face and he raised another cautionary forefinger and wagged it.

"And, so, what if I am, Deputy Carter? As I said earlier, very soon it will make very little difference what you may or may not know."

Trent continued, "Oh, hell – it doesn't matter, Carl. You can pistol whip me all you want. We all know you've got the upper hand here. And we all know how it ends tonight, right? I mean you've got us all tied up nice and neat – no way to fight back. Just the way you like it, right?

Carl's smile began to fade. Trent knew he had touched a nerve of some sort. Carl stood up and straightened his jacket, slowly reached down, and fingered the butt of the pistol in his belt. "Must I warn you again?" he said ominously.

Trent ignored him. "Two defenseless women and a worn out, beat up cop. Big deal! In a minute or two, whenever you get tired of listening to yourself whine, you're just going to walk over here and pop me in the head with that pistol. No muss, no fuss, right? I mean, a .22 caliber bullet's so small it'll just rattle around inside my head, scrambling my brains even more than they already are – no messy exit wound to deal with – and certainly a painless and quick end for me. What sort of challenge are we to a seasoned hunter like you? I mean, you like the thrill of the chase, don't you? The skill of the hunt? Why don't you give us a running chance – like you did for most of your other victims?"

The corner of Carl's mouth twitched as he took a step in Trent's direction, his hand tightening on the pistol grip. He caught himself and stopped, his hand relaxing. "Oh, you sure like to make things happen, don't you, old friend?"

He had taken the bait. Trent smiled and decided to press harder.

"And how about your father, Carl? I mean, how's he going to take it when he finds out you've still been lying to him all these years – Old. Friend?"

Carl stopped, knitted his eyebrows, and cocked his head. Trent thought he saw the chink in the armor again. "Lying?" Carl murmured slowly. "I've never lied to my father – about anything."

"Really? Then I'm curious, Carl. What did you actually tell him about Otto – about how you supposedly got rid of his body that night all those years ago?"

"You know yourself, Deputy – as you said, you found Otto's bones buried there."

"Yeah, I found some bones, but I don't think you were the one who put them there – and besides – I never said they were Otto's."

Carl grew very quiet, stepped slowly over to Trent, squatted down in front of him, and glared with malice into his eyes.

"What if those bones aren't Otto's, Carl?" Trent asked softly. "You ever think about that?"

Carl rubbed his jaw for moment, and studied Trent's face carefully. Trent forced himself to remain passive.

"So pray tell me, then, Deputy Carter," Carl continued quietly, measuring his words. "Just whose bones do you think you found?"

Silence pervaded the room for several seconds. Trent didn't say another word, hoping he had not overplayed his hand, but suspected that he had when Carl suddenly reached into his pants pocket, pulled out a skinning knife, flicked it open, and held it in from of Trent's face. The late afternoon sunlight streaming in through the west windows glinted off of the blade as it twisted menacingly near Trent's eye.

"No! Please don't!" yelled Sophie.

Carl looked over at her and licked his lips. "Oh, not to worry, my little darling," he sneered. "Dear Daddy doesn't get out of this quite so easily." He leered at her and continued. "In fact, he gets to enjoy watching what I have in store for his two precious ladies. And by then, he will be telling me everything he knows – and begging for me to kill him."

Carl suddenly reached down and in one swipe of the knife cut the cords that tied Trent's ankles together. He grabbed Trent by his jacket lapels and jerked him painfully to his feet before he stepped quickly to each of the women, similarly freed their ankles, and gestured to all of them with the knife.

"Time for us all to go for a little stroll," he ordered.

#

The blood had only begun to re-circulate through Trent's tingling lower legs as he stumbled out to the front porch of Maggie's house. The idea had briefly occurred to him to make a run for it, but he quickly realized that would not be immediately possible with the pinpricks of pain exploding through his feet and ankles; that, plus the fact that the short barreled shotgun Carl had taken from Trent's cruiser was now pointed at the base of Sophie's skull. Carl's other hand was entangled in her long hair, and she winced as he guided and pushed her along painfully in front of him. Trent looked down and noticed for the first time that her feet were bare and bloodied. The four of them made it down the front steps in a tight group, with Maggie and Trent in front and Carl and Sophie bringing up the rear. Trent knew neither Maggie nor he would try to run because to do so assured Sophie's immediate death.

Carl was well armed. Not only did he have the shotgun, pistol, and a knife, he had also slung an old Winchester rifle over his shoulder. Trent thought he recognized the old rifle from the collection that had been on display in Old Man Neumann's den.

Carl steered them across the yard and then continued over the large plaza between the house and outbuildings. They marched slowly but surely through the waning late afternoon sunlight that filtered through the autumn leaves and cast a surreal glow on everything. Trent felt a wave of nausea as the fall hues triggered something ominous and deadly in his memory: a similar cascade of seasonal orange and gold, once beautiful to him, but now tinged with red and black – the colors of blood and death.

Trent glanced around, hoping against hope that one of Maggie's ranch hands might still be around, but he knew they were not usually needed at this time of year and had probably been laid off. He knew also that had they been there, Carl would have already taken them into account and dealt with them in no uncertain terms. Trent prayed that no one else had died today because of him.

Trent slowed his walk as they neared the big barn, even though he already suspected what Carl was up to.

"Keep going," Carl barked and confirmed Trent's suspicions by indicating they were to continue around the barn, toward the gate to the large pastures beyond. Here, he had Trent and Maggie stop while he pushed Sophie forward to the gate that he maneuvered with one hand while continuing to hold the shotgun on her with the other. Trent caught Sophie's wide and white-with-fear eyes and tried to manage what he hoped was a reassuring smile.

"It's going to be alright, Baby," he murmured.

Carl looked back at Trent and snickered with genuine amusement. He pushed the gate and allowed it to swing open wide and motioned them all to go ahead of him. They stepped out onto the faint track of road that had been worn into the field over the decades, the same path Trent and Maggie had driven weeks before when he had come out to investigate the vandalism of the little adobe line shack that he knew sat just out of sight over the ridge ahead, maybe a quarter mile away just outside the line of pines – the same cabin in which Otto and Evie had consummated their love affair, resulting nine months later with Carl's birth; where Otto had later hidden away his journal; and from where, just inside that same tree-line, Otto had watched incredulously as a much younger Margot Van Ryan had ridden her mare breathlessly up the dawn-streaked hillside, evoking an unexpected memory of her aunt, his beloved, doomed Evie.

In a way, Trent reflected, they had all now come full circle.

What a fitting place to end it all. He just hoped that if none of them survived this, Ben Ferguson's search warrant would produce enough evidence to put Ernst and Carl away in a deep hole forever.

"That's far enough," Carl snarled when they had gone about fifty yards up the trail. He shoved Sophie over to Trent, who did his best to catch her and steady her even though both their wrists were still bound tightly. All the color had left Sophie's face; she was gasping for breath, almost hyperventilating. Trent looked down at his daughter and tried to pull her close protectively, almost as much for his own reassurance as for hers.

"I'm so sorry, Daddy," she whispered, her voice coming in shaky gasps. "There was a knock and I just assumed it was Hector. I just opened the door without even checking – I was so stupid! Especially after what had happened to Jarhead. He just grabbed me before I knew what was happening – " Her voice trailed away.

"It's going to be alright, Sophie," he reassured, "I promise," he added, but realized he didn't even sound convincing to himself. He kissed the top of her head. Her hair smelled like shampoo and her skin like lilacs. He surmised that she had probably just bathed right before Carl showed up. She had never even had time to put on her shoes.

Carl stepped slowly around in front of them, looked at each of them in turn, and smirked. He held the shotgun at waist level, but Trent knew it was still just as deadly in that position. He was just waiting for Carl to make one mistake. Carl turned and faced Trent.

"Our little game is drawing to a close, my dear my friend. So, I think it's now time for you to stop worrying about others and to answer for your own sins, yes?"

Trent stared straight ahead, focusing beyond Carl at the top of the hill maybe 150 yards in the distance.

"Got no idea what you're talking about. What sins would those be, Carl?"

Carl stepped closer to Trent and sneered. "Oh, we all have many sins, wouldn't you agree –*Trent?* Some souls are darker than others and colored by the burden of the many secrets they are carrying. So, why don't you unburden yourself to me, like you would to a priest in confession – much as you did with that old priest in the nursing home, hmm?"

Trent turned his eyes toward Carl and stared him in the eye.

"Oh, now there's a real irony," Trent muttered.

Carl cocked his head and looked puzzled for moment. He chewed his lip, pulled up the shotgun, and tapped Trent on the chest with the barrel.

"Before this day is through, old friend, you will tell me all that I want to know. In fact, you will beg me to listen," he growled menacingly.

"What things, asshole?"

Carl turned away, looked across the long, undulating fields, turned back, suddenly pushed the shotgun barrel hard under Trent's chin, and spoke softly and grimly.

"All the things I want to hear and many more that I won't even have to ask for – like whose body was that under the theater, if not Otto's? And since I have no time right now to properly translate it, what else does that damned journal say about me and my family?" Carl now leaned in very close until his lips almost kissed Trent's earlobe. "And where, pray tell, is my mother's diary?" he hissed.

Trent turned and stared at Carl with as much arrogance as he could muster, their faces just inches away, and whispered back harshly, "What the hell difference does it all make, Carl? I mean you think I'm stupid enough to think you're actually going to let us all go if I tell you – just like that?"

"Of course, I will! You all get to go free – just like that." Carl punctuated the last three words by jabbing the shotgun into the soft flesh of Trent's throat, where it broke the skin and blood trickled down his neck. Trent dared not move even an inch. He managed to shift his eyes to glance at the women and saw them both watching in horror. Carl turned and pointed back at the field with the shotgun. "I'll let you go – if you can each make it to the top of that hill there – as fast as you can run!"

Maggie moved closer to Sophie, who was still white-faced and now appeared to be having trouble standing, and was leaning against her.

"How about this, Carl," Trent said through clenched teeth. "I will tell you everything you want to know, and you can do anything you want to me, but you have to let the women both go first. Your quarrel isn't with them – it's with me. It always has been – even before Cordova Pass," Trent almost choked on the words, but continued. "After all, I'm the one that can put you in jail."

Carl leaned just inches from Trent's face. Trent detected a musky smell to the man, like a hunter excited about the impending kill.

"An excellent idea, Deputy Carter. I agree to your terms – wholeheartedly." He then stepped quickly towards the women. "And to honor your new terms, I shall now 'release' one of your precious ladies. Care to choose?" He looked from one to the other, as if appraising them, an ecstatic look on his face before he reached into his pocket and removed his knife, which he opened with a flourish. "Oh, come on, Trent – which one would you like to set free first? Your call!"

"Carl!" Trent yelled and took a step toward him. "You know that's not at all what I meant!"

Carl swung the shotgun back in Trent's direction and shook his head while making a *tsk-tsk* sound with his tongue. "Alright – then I'll choose for you."

Trent froze and in horror watched as Carl reached over to Maggie; the knife flashed with a snicking noise. Suddenly, her wrists had been cut loose from the binding cords. He then did the same for Sophie before folding the knife and slipping it back into his front pants pocket, while the women rubbed their raw wrists. He quickly grabbed Maggie by the upper arm, pulled her around to him, and shoved her, causing her to stumble a few steps out onto the uneven ground of the pasture where she stopped and turned around to glare at her tormentor defiantly. Carl nodded at her and pointed out beyond her into the field with the shotgun.

"There lies your freedom, my dear cousin," he gestured magnanimously.

"You can kiss my ass, then go straight to hell – *Cousin*!" she retorted.

Carl's smile faded slowly. He shook his head, bent down, and laid the shotgun at his feet. "Oh, such language! And why all the anger?" he admonished, straightening back up and unslinging the Winchester rifle from his shoulder. "I'm, after all, giving you a chance – a very slight one, for sure – but you should make the most of it – and do so as quickly as you can, I might add." He reached into his jacket pocket, pulled out a handful of shells, and began methodically loading them into the rifle.

Maggie stifled a nervous laugh, which turned quickly to a sob. "Anyone ever tell you that you are full of shit and talk way too much?" she croaked at him. "A bad case of diarrhea of the mouth, you ask me!"

"Carl," Trent called out, desperately trying to turn the events to their advantage, "you know I didn't mean this way!"

"Well, you're the one who set the terms, my friend." He paused from his task and spread his hand out in a questioning gesture. "How on earth was I supposed to interpret that?"

"I told you I'd tell you everything!"

"Yes," Carl answered smoothly. "I know you will."

Trent took a quick step toward Maggie, who stood rubbing her chafed wrists. Carl opened his mouth and took a step to intervene, then relented and stepped aside.

"Maggie – Honey," Trent said to her, trying to keep the panic out of his voice. She whipped her eyes to his. He could see the whites around her shocked eyes.

For the first time since he'd met her, Trent could see she was frightened. He reached out and took her hands with his bound ones.

"Maggie, it's really the only way," he continued in a softer voice, trying to get her full attention. He gulped, concerned that he wasn't getting through to her. He looked down, but then remembered something.

It just might work, he thought for a second, and looked up at Maggie again. "You run, Sweetie – run like the wind," he continued urgently. "Run like you've never run before." He paused, searching her eyes to see if she comprehended what he was saying. She still appeared to be in shock. He thought hard and looked at her intensely, willing her now to listen to him closely.

"Maggie – sweetheart – listen to me." She finally held his gaze, trying to concentrate on what he was saying. "You run this ground like only you can – do you understand me?" Trent paused and glanced quickly at Carl, who continued to load and didn't seem to be listening. "You know this ground like no else does," Trent continued, "except for your Grandpa Werner – remember?"

Maggie squinted her eyes questioningly for a just a moment longer, seeming to have shaken off the shock. "So you run it like no one else can. Okay? Now run, Maggie! *Run!*"

Carl cleared his throat. "Alright, alright. You've said your goodbyes. Let's get going!"

Maggie stopped trembling and looked intensely into Trent's face.

Suddenly, her eyes widened with a clear understanding and she gave him the slightest of nods. Without another moment's hesitation, she turned, crouched low, took a deep breath, and leaped forward, sprinting away like a rabbit; she darted first one way, then the other – leaping over a small bush here, dipping down a shallow depression there. Trent glanced warily over at Carl, who seemed exasperated at first at how Maggie had taken him off guard. He pulled the rifle stock to his cheek, fiddled with the telescopic sight, and smiled as his exasperation seemed to turn to appreciation.

"Ha!" he exclaimed. "Look at her run, will you? Now *that's* what I'm talking about!"

"Carl," Trent whispered one more time. "You still don't have to do this!"

Carl glanced over at Trent and giggled somewhat maniacally, cocked the lever to chamber a round into the breech, and raised the rifle scope up to his right eye. Trent could see the rifle barrel tracking Maggie, almost lazily matching her every move like it was somehow connected to her by an invisible thread; she was now about fifty yards away, dipping, darting and swaying with the terrain, seemingly in anticipation of each feature of the land. Trent glanced down at the shotgun at Carl's feet and for a moment thought about his bound hands. He made a tentative move toward the gun.

"Don't you even think about it, Carter," Carl responded evenly. Without taking his attention from his target, he slid a boot over and placed it firmly on the shotgun. "You make a move like that again –" he started, then swiveled the rifle and lined it up, almost point blank, on Sophie's forehead.

"No – please," gasped Trent, stumbling back involuntarily.

Carl continued to aim at Sophie's head, paused for a moment, then shrugged and smiled. Trent thought he saw Carl's finger increase pressure on the trigger and moaned.

"*Bang!*" Carl exclaimed, making Sophie and Trent both jump. Sophie lost her footing and collapsed on the ground, sobbing silently. Trent stepped quickly over to her. Carl laughed uproariously, propped the stock of the rifle on his hip, and pointed a finger at Trent. "You should see the look on your faces!" He guffawed for a few more seconds.

At this moment Trent realized just how disturbed Carl Neumann had really become – as deranged as the man he called his father, Conrad Neumann – as deranged as Otto Eberhardt had alluded to in his journals.

"Now – where was I?" Carl continued. "You've made me lose my train of thought. What was I doing? Oh, yes, now I remember. I was easing someone of their burdens, wasn't I?"

Trent turned quickly and squinted back out into the darkening field where Maggie leapt and darted to and fro. She was now almost a hundred yards away, but instead of heading straight uphill, she had woven her way to the right side, bouncing briefly out of sight, then back up again.

"What the hell's she doing?" Carl murmured, squinting in the same direction, then grinned. "Oh, this is going to be fun!"

Run little rabbit – run! Trent muttered under his breath, not daring to lose sight of her, when out of the corner of his eye he saw Carl move in almost one fluid motion: he swiveled around, trained his eye through the scope one last time, took a deep breath – and fired.

CHAPTER 34
TO LIVE AND DIE BY THE SWORD

Time stood still.

Trent stared in sheer horror. He thought he could actually see the bullet leave the rifle muzzle, traverse the hundred yards or so, and slow in its trajectory as he squinted ahead of it to try and find Maggie, who was now almost camouflaged in the underbrush at this distance. If anyone could outrun a bullet, it was Maggie – but with Carl Neumann as the shooter, Trent knew full well the hopelessness of such a thought.

All was still in slow motion for him; he held his breath for what seemed minutes as she darted once to the left, again to the right, jumped straight up, flailing her arms – and suddenly spun around like a dervish, like she had been hit by something hard and fast.

Maggie collapsed and fell completely out of sight.

The rifle shot echoed forever before being replaced by a sudden silence, except for the sound of the late afternoon breeze that wafted through the grass like waves, the flutter of birds somewhere in the aftermath of the echoing gunshot, and the sound of Trent's own heartbeat in his throat. Sophie had stifled a scream and clasped her hands over her mouth. All three of them stared expectantly across the field, collectively holding their breaths for what seemed to Trent an eternity.

Carl searched for a moment through the scope, but finally lowered the rifle and turned back to Trent with a bemused smile.

"Free at last," he said quietly.

Trent stared at him, but, suddenly nauseous, bent over at the waist, and propped himself up on one knee with his bound hands. His head pounded and he gasped for air. Some part of his mind had shut down defensively as it desperately tried to comprehend what had just happened.

"Well. That. Was. Fun," Carl chortled. "Now, shall we see who we have behind door number two?"

Trent's heart stopped as Carl stepped toward Sophie. He squeezed his eyes shut to try and stop the pounding in his head – to try to do something – anything.

"Wait," he croaked. "I'll tell you." He stared at the ground between his feet, focused his mind. "I will tell you – everything."

"Ah, the prodigal father sees the light." Carl cradled the Winchester carelessly in his arms, stepped arrogantly over to Trent, sucked in a deep breath, and smiled.

"So, Deputy Carter – tell me things – preferably things that I don't already know."

Trent remained bent over, breathing deeply, desperately thinking. "Something that you don't know," he muttered, as much to himself as to Carl. He straightened up slowly and glared at him.

"Well, Carl," Trent began slowly but determinedly, "speaking of prodigal fathers, how about this for starters: Conrad Neumann is *not* the real name of the man you've been living with all these years," Trent blurted.

Carl froze in mid-step, quiet for a few seconds.

"What did you say?" he muttered, his voice barely above a whisper.

"You heard me."

Carl stepped over to Trent, pointed the rifle barrel toward the ground, and stopped. "Then tell me again – plainly," he snorted derisively.

From out of nowhere, Trent felt a small thrill of hope and allowed a trace of a smile to creep onto his face. He had found the chink in the armor once more. *Now, time to pull out the final weapon, slip the knife in, and maybe twist it a little* – anything to throw Carl off guard.

"Guess you didn't get to that part of Otto's journal, Carl. If you had, you'd have found out who really walked out of that burning barn years ago."

Trent studied Carl's face, watching the muscles work across his jaw line and a frown dance across his brow as if the thoughts and memories worked their way across Carl's mind.

"No," he whispered. "That's not possible. My father told me that damned old Nazi died in that fire. Hell, I even remember seeing it myself."

"Well, that 'damned old Nazi' murdered Conrad Neumann," Trent continued quickly, pushing the envelope, "and left him to burn to a crisp in that barn. That 'damned old Nazi' assumed his identity and evidently convinced you and everyone else for all these years that he was your father, Conrad Neumann." Trent stepped to within inches of Carl; they were now face to face.

Carl squeezed his eyes shut and rubbed them tightly with his fingers. He then lifted a bloodthirsty gaze back at Trent. "You're a damned liar," he breathed through clenched teeth, "just trying to buy some time." He took a step backward and swung the rifle up again. Trent glanced down at the rifle barrel pointed toward his belly and back up to meet Carl's furious gaze.

The bait had been taken; the knife had been slipped in. Now, time to twist the blade a little.

"Well, Carl – if you think that was a whopper, you're going to love this one: Why do you think Otto really hung around all those years, putting up with all of 'Conrad's' and your bullshit? You think it was only his love for your dead mother, or to protect your sister? It ever occur to you that there was another really good reason he agreed to stick around you two misanthropic throwbacks for all those years?"

Carl's eyes opened wider, his head cocked a little to one side in genuine puzzlement.

"What the hell are you trying to say?" Carl demanded softly, menacingly. He abruptly dropped the old rifle barrel first to the muddy ground, jerked the .22 pistol out of his belt, and pointed it at Trent's head. He pushed the mouth of the barrel hard into Trent's head, an inch above his right ear. Trent felt the skin tear under his hairline.

"Oh, are my words too big for you now?"

"I said, *what the hell are you saying*?" Carl screamed.

There it was – the knife blade shoved home, and the curtain was ready to rise on the finale. Trent took a deep breath.

"I'm saying that of all your sins, Carl, that night in the alley behind the theater you committed a couple of really unforgivable ones. I mean – I can't think, offhand, Carl, of too many warped individuals who were hell-bent on murdering not only their own father, but also a cop and a priest at the same time – can you? I mean, there must be a very special section of Hell reserved for someone like that!"

Carl stepped back, his eyes and mouth wide open in utter shock, his face white. "How the hell do you know all that?" he mumbled, "about the alley?" He shook his head in slow confusion and glanced back down toward Maggie's house. "None of that was in Otto's journal. And just what do you mean by 'my own father?'"

"That man you tried to kill – the man that worked and lived on your ranch for years; the one you were raised to hate with a passion – Otto Frances Eberhardt? Well, get hold of yourself, Carl," Trent paused long enough to take a certain perverse delight in the suspense in Carl's eyes.

"That man was your real father."

Trent saw the barrel of the pistol waiver. Carl said nothing, but his face reflected the dozens of thoughts racing through his mind.

Trent continued. "Oh, you managed to shoot him that night, all right – but you didn't kill him. Instead, you shot and killed another very good man, a good friend of your father's – of Otto's – the priest named Father Michael Shannon. Actually, it was his bones we found buried under the building."

"No – impossible – that priest," Carl blurted out incredulously. "that priest is alive – why, my father," he paused momentarily, and then resumed, "My father and I just went the other day to see that old priest, at the nursing home."

"So, just what did you tell old man Neumann – I mean, *Ernst* Brandt – about that night, Carl – when he asked you about Otto's body? You tell him you buried him under the foundation of that building?" Trent watched in fascination as Carl's face transformed slowly from puzzlement to understanding and, suddenly, to horror. "And just what happened to that policeman and the priest?

"Otto?" Carl whispered, staring blankly, almost in a trance. He slowly lowered the pistol and shook his head. "Still alive? But how – who?" He then raised his eyes and glowered at Trent. "Just how do you know all of this, you son-of-a-bitch?" he mumbled hatefully.

Trent shrugged. "I just know things – like, that Otto and your mother loved each other." He directed his eyes up the hill, golden now in the last rays of the setting sun shining from over their shoulders. "They spent a lot of time together, over in that little adobe shack, just over that hill there." Trent paused, watching Carl, who now stared up the hill, his gaze distant and years away.

"So that's why he wanted us to search the cabin…" Carl said, as much to himself. "No!" Carl breathed deeply, looking down, fury building in his face again.

Trent decided to take a big gamble and turned toward the big house. "It's all in the journal, Carl, back there at the house, you know, where you left it. What say we all go back there and – "

Trent suddenly gasped as Carl swung the barrel of the pistol hard against the side of his head. Trent saw lights burst and felt blood pour down into his ear and down his neck as he collapsed on the ground.

"You shut your filthy, lying mouth!" Carl shouted, kicking Trent hard in the ribs with every word. "She would never have betrayed my father that way!"

The world spun and Trent fell over to his side and curled up with his bound hands over his head in futile protection from the blows. A wave of pain engulfed him; he thought he would pass out.

"Not betrayal, Carl!" he yelled, rolling this way and that in defense. "When she married Conrad she was already pregnant."

"*No!*" Carl wailed, like a wounded animal.

#

Later, Trent would not be able to reconstruct the exact sequence of events, or exactly how much time had elapsed. They would all remain a jumble in his dysfunctional memory for the rest of his life.

The kicks suddenly ceased; Sophie began to scream and cried out, "*No,*" several times; at some point, Carl shouted *Run, you little bitch – Run*; and somewhere, mixed up with all the chaos, floating in and out of his hazy, malfunctioning memory banks, Trent felt himself veer off suddenly into a separate reality altogether and the cool touch of soft fingers on his hot forehead.

When he finally reopened his eyes, he was looking up into Vicky's impossibly beautiful face – a face no longer streaked with blood and horror, but the way she had looked skipping through the meadows on Cordova Pass, right before her death. As he now lay in her soft lap, her brown hair tickling his nose as it swayed gently in the soft breeze, she smiled down at him, turned his head gently to the side, and pointed out into the field.

"Look," she motioned. Trent looked to where she pointed, to where time had slowed

down, to where their daughter Sophie bounced and danced her way barefoot through the grass and flowers, only a few yards away – only now she was once again their precious little six year old girl, long blond hair floating behind her, looking over her shoulder at them now, smiling and giggling. "Look," Vicky repeated.

"Look at what?" he asked, confusion threading through the fog of his mind.

"At our sweet miracle," Vicky answered, watching her daughter lovingly. "Isn't she the most wonderful thing we've ever accomplished?"

"Sophie," Trent moaned and stretched out his hand toward their daughter, choking back tears. The love swelling in his soul had become unbearable, rivaling the pain rolling through his body.

"It's time," Vicky pronounced solemnly.

"Time?" He turned back to her, questioning.

"Time to go now."

"No, Vic," he moaned. "No, I don't want to go back."

"Then do something about it," she commanded, more firmly now. "Only you can, you know – and it's time," she insisted again.

"Time for what, exactly?" he persisted, rocking and moaning on the ground.

"Time for you to save our little miracle, my Darling."

"Victoria – please," Trent protested.

Vicky's voice suddenly roared in his ear. "Stop him – now!"

#

Trent's eyes flew open: Vicky was nowhere to be seen, Trent was back to reality, and shock engulfed him.

A few yards away, Sophie was crying, sobbing, struggling through the knee-deep grass, brush, and muddy, rocky ground, her legs and bare feet scraped and bleeding, no longer his six year old toddler, but a terrified young woman, looking back over her shoulder, her mouth open in a silent scream as she ran for her very life from the bullet that Trent knew was only moments away from being fired into her head.

Trent looked to see Carl standing a few paces away, bringing the rifle up to his cheek to aim.

Death himself was stalking Trent's daughter; something snapped within him.

He felt a sudden inner surge as all the love, memories, failures, tragedies, and regrets of life welled up in his stomach and mixed with equal portions of pure rage and vengeance. Forgotten were his aching cracked ribs and the festering, throbbing gunshot wound in his shoulder. Without another moment's hesitation, in one fluid motion, Trent rose up into a coiled crouch and launched his body full force through the brief space separating Carl from him. Trent's bound arms were stretched out in from of him like a battering ram and his clasped fists connected with Carl's solar plexus. Carl's breath exploded out of his mouth as he was propelled off the ground, the rifle flying free from his hands that scrambled now to break his fall as he landed hard on his back. Trent followed closely and landed full force on top of Carl, his bound, clenched fists pummeling wherever they could land, pounding into his chest, neck, and face, whipping back and forth, splitting flesh and breaking teeth, blood and spittle flying from the blows. One small part of Trent was shocked as the rage and violence of the attack took full control of him, but a greater part of him blocked out all other thoughts and emotions as he surrendered himself completely, and gratefully, to the explosive release of his vengeful anger.

He flailed and screamed for what seemed an eternity.

He had no idea how much time had passed before he came to his senses and the realization that Carl had stopped moving.

"Daddy?" Sophie's shocked voice came softly from behind him.

She stood very still, eyes wide, her hand over her mouth, not looking at her father but at Carl lying very still on the ground. Trent looked back down at his enemy, whom he now straddled with both knees tightly squeezing his chest. Carl was unconscious, barely breathing, and his face a mask of streaming blood. Trent felt his hands shaking, but only now noticed the .22 pistol in his hands, the barrel shoved hard against Carl's forehead, his trembling finger beginning to squeeze the trigger.

Trent had no idea how the pistol had materialized in his hands.

"Daddy – please, don't," Sophie whispered. She had stumbled closer and reached out a hand toward her father. "Not like this."

Trent tried to ignore her pleadings – ignore all the years of his training and instincts for upholding the law in all circumstances, believing wholeheartedly in the concept of righteousness and justice.

No!

He wanted to continue feeding this wellspring of rage; to say *to hell with it all* and force his mind to remember all the pain and suffering this man's murdering family had caused him; to remember Vicky's bloodied, shattered head cradled in his lap; to remember Mirielle Segura holding her dead husband in the desert; to remember all those other souls lying murdered across two states and six decades.

And now Hector – and Maggie.

Just where was all their justice?

He felt a low growl build up from deep within his chest and his finger squeezed the trigger a little tighter.

Justice was a mere ounce of pressure away.

Suddenly, Trent remembered Hector's body, slumped in the cruiser just down the road, cut down by a hail of bullets – but more importantly, his partner's last admonition to him.

You going to give him a chance at all to surrender?

"Daddy?" Sophie's hand gently touched Trent's trembling arm. He swallowed hard, the rage gradually draining away, finally. He eased his finger from the trigger and lifted the gun away from Carl's head.

"Okay, Punkin," he whispered, his voice a mere rasp, "okay." He fought to regain his composure. Only when his eyes finally focused back on Sophie and he realized she was safe did he blow out his breath, allowing the anger to subside; exhaustion suddenly flowed through him in the wake of the adrenaline rush, and his wounded shoulder throbbed worse than ever.

The breeze had picked up slightly, soothing his hot brow, and the sun had finally dipped past the tree line behind Maggie's house in the distance.

Maggie!

He quickly slid off of Carl's body, shoved the pistol into his belt, then hurriedly patted him down and fumbled through the pockets until he found Carl's pocketknife. He gave it to Sophie to awkwardly cut the plastic restraints from his wrists. They were numb and swollen and burned as he rubbed them to return circulation to them.

He glanced back down at Carl's inert form at his feet. *Is he dead?* he thought to himself. He no longer appeared to be breathing, but Trent neither knew nor cared. He kicked the Winchester away from Carl anyway as a precaution. He located Maggie's old short barrel shotgun nearby, picked it up, broke open the breech to confirm it was still loaded, and handed it to his daughter, who took it uncertainly at first.

"Here," he said. "I assume you still know how to use one of these." Sophie examined the shotgun skillfully and nodded back up at her father.

"Good," he said, and nudged Carl once more with his foot. He didn't move. "Stay here and watch him," Trent continued, "and if he moves, at all, shoot him." He jerked his chin to gesture up the hill, toward where they had seen Maggie fall. He took a shaky breath.

"I'll go check on Maggie."

"I am not staying here," Sophie blurted, falling in step behind him. "Not letting you out of my sight for an instant." Trent started to argue with her, then saw her fiercely determined, face, and shrugged. He glanced once more at the inert figure of Carl, turned, and started up the hill.

"Suit yourself," he responded.

He took his time, given that Sophie was still picking her way carefully with her bare, injured feet, and followed the half-remembered path Maggie had taken through the sage and Grama grass.

With each yard they advanced, he sucked in his breath slowly, expecting at any moment to stumble across Maggie's body. He drew up short and stopped at the edge of an old drainage ditch – one that he had expected to find. The trench was half hidden by tall grasses and choked with dead brush. The ground nearby was disturbed as if someone's boots had shuffled and gouged the dirt.

But that was not all.

By the time Sophie made her way up to her father, he had knelt down, gingerly touching the ground at the edge of the ditch. He brought up his thumb and forefinger, rubbing the recently bloodied dirt between them.

Maggie was nowhere to be found.

Trent stood up and breathed a ragged sigh of relief. There might still be a chance after all. Just as he had hinted to Maggie earlier, she had obviously used her grandfather's old irrigation trenches and had, hopefully, escaped. *But to where?*

"Carter!"

The snarling scream from somewhere behind him made Trent turn around and he instantly froze in place.

Seventy yards downhill stood Carl Neumann, leaning heavily and shakily on the Winchester rifle, the stock under his arm like a crutch.

"This isn't over, *Deputy*!" Carl spat through bloodied lips.

Trent slowly pulled the .22 revolver from his belt and held it loosely at his side. At this range, and with his injured right arm, he knew he had little chance of doing any real harm with the small caliber weapon. But it was all he had, and it felt good in his hand.

"Get behind me, Sofe," he said quietly and firmly to his daughter. "When he shoots, you drop into that ditch there," he indicated by nodding in that direction, "and then no matter what else happens, you run like hell." He glared back downhill at Carl.

"Yeah, I'm afraid it is all over, Carl," he shouted back down. "Give it up. Throw down your weapon and I'll see you get treated fairly."

Carl raised his eyebrows, but only shook his head, spit, and laughed.

"Dad, I'm not going to leave you," Sophie protested, but Trent cut her off with a growl.

"You are going to do exactly what I said, Sophie!"

Trent immediately regretted his tone, and turned to her. "Look, Honey – I know I haven't been making a lot of good decisions these past several months. But this is probably going to be your only real chance to survive this, Sophie. And somebody's got to get out of here and go for some help – find Ben Ferguson – let him know exactly what happened here." He nodded down into the ditch, and took a breath. "Besides, if Maggie is still alive, you've got to go and find her – okay?" He hesitated, and looked away. "If she's wounded…shot, she'll need attention."

"And if she's dead? Then what?"

Trent scowled back down toward Carl, who was still softly chuckling as he slowly raised his rifle. "Then you make that son-of-a-bitch come to you. You find just the right place to hunker down, then wait 'til he gets close," he paused and glanced down at the shotgun in her hands, "and then you give him both those barrels, point blank."

"Trent!" Carl yelled, staggering a little, off balance, still, from the furious beating Trent had given him. He finally steadied himself enough to raise the rifle up to his cheek and aim through the telescopic sight. "Good," he continued. "There you are, right up close and personal." He leaned away briefly to spit out a mouthful of blood at his feet.

"Nice and steady, now. I want you to see this one coming," he continued, focusing through the sight again. "Oh – and after I put this bullet through your head, I just want you to know I'm going to take my good sweet time with your pretty little girl there," he snarled.

Trent glared back and clinched his teeth hard. "Not if you're dead first,

Carl," he called back, then glanced back over his shoulder to Sophie.

"Get ready, Punkin," he said. He reached over to find her forearm and gave it a little reassuring squeeze before turning back around, raising the pistol in his less dominant left hand, extending it straight out at the end of his arm. He judged the windage and elevation and, with the calm of an expert, raised the gun just a hair more.

"Besides, like the lady told you before, Neumann: you talk way too much!"

Trent dropped into a crouch, immediately squeezed the trigger five times in rapid succession, and watched hopefully as the bullets plowed up spouts of dirt in a straight line that ended right between Carl's feet, just missing him. At the same moment, Carl also fired – just once.

What happened next was completely unpredictable and unbelievable: the old Winchester rifle simply exploded. Sophie screamed, followed by complete and total silence as the gunfire echoed around the valley and died away.

#

For a moment, Trent wasn't at all sure what had happened. He had dropped into a defensive crouch as soon as he had fired, and when Carl fired, Trent's body had jerked back involuntarily in anticipation of the slam of a bullet that never came – and Carl couldn't have missed.

Instead, Carl stood very still, the Winchester rifle stock still up against his cheek, one eye continuing to peer into the telescopic sight. The other eye as well as the entire left side of his face was simply gone – a mass of bleeding, smoking pulp had torn away from the side of his head when the breech of the old rifle had blown up as he had pulled the trigger. The bullet had nowhere else to go because of the mud and dirt that had plugged up the barrel when he had leaned on it earlier, pushing the muzzle deep into the moist ground. The metal fatigue and crystallization of the breech of the almost 100–year-old Winchester that Ernst had stolen years ago after murdering the pig farmer could not withstand the explosive force. Carl's face and neck had taken the brunt of the shrapnel and burning powder as metal shards of rifle and bullet had viciously sheered away with an explosive force.

Carl's legs began to wobble. The rifle dropped from his trembling arms and he collapsed in a heap on the ground, convulsing. Sophie and Trent stood in shock for several moments before Trent realized what had happened. He began moving forward, then trotting back down the hill. Sophie soon followed.

By the time she had caught up with her father, he was kneeling down over Carl, who lay on his back, clawing the ground in agony with his fingernails, gasping and gurgling as blood pulsed from several wounds around his face, neck and chest. Clearly, he was losing a lot of blood quickly and wouldn't last. His frightened eyes locked on Trent's as he reached a hand up shakily and motioned him nearer. Trent hesitantly leaned closer, the pistol still firmly in his hand. There was one more bullet left in the chamber, but Carl Neumann was clearly no longer a threat. Instead, he shivered violently, and was trying to mouth something, barely audible above a whisper.

"…journal," he wheezed through clinched teeth.

"What?" Trent asked.

"Not in – journal," Carl gasped. "… proof?" Blood bubbled from his lips and he began coughing, half of his words unintelligible.

"What about the journal, Carl?"

Carl's words now came in breathless spurts, like the blood pumping from his wounds. One entire side of his face looked like a horror mask. The "son" now resembled the "father," in every way.

"You said the journal – the part about – Otto – *my father*?" he gurgled. "How – how do – you know?" he wheezed, barely able to choke out the words now.

Trent paused and smiled, not unkindly.

"Your mother told me."

Carl looked puzzled and shook his head in grotesque jerks, not comprehending, no longer able to speak, blood dribbling heavily from the corner of his mouth. Trent reached into the inner pocket of his jacket and pulled out the small, worn leather bound Bible.

"You really should've learned to search people a little better, Carl. When you found my Glock, you forgot to check this." He thumbed the Bible open, then held it out so Carl could see the diary that was hidden there, and his mother's name *Evie Van Ryan Neumann* written in her own handwriting in the front. Trent then turned pages and began to read aloud to Carl in his mother's own words.

As he listened quietly, Carl's eyes grew wider in surprise.

"March 9, 1948 – God has at last smiled on me. Seven days ago I gave birth to the most beautiful baby boy that I have ever laid eyes on – not that I have seen many babies, other than dogs, kittens, calves, or foals. He has his father's eyes and dimpled chin and I have named him 'Carl' after my grandfather. I would have preferred, of course, to name him after his own father. But that is, of course, impossible.

Conrad must never find out the child is not his. There is no real love between us, but he is a proud man and a good provider. I would never hurt him intentionally with this.

Otto is long gone – where, I do not know. And I doubt that I will ever see him again, or that he will ever even know he has a son. But I pray for him daily – the love of my life! And I promise to raise his boy to be true and strong, in every way!"

Trent slowly closed the diary.

"There's your proof, Carl. Otto never hated you – he was trying to protect you – his own son. But you made that impossible."

Carl Neumann's breath came shallower now, and shortly ceased altogether as he became still. His eyes, still locked on Trent's, filled with astonishment and finally glazed over. Trent slowly reached over and pressed two fingers to his neck, but found no pulse. He stood up, slipped the diary back into the inner pocket of his jacket, put his hands in his pockets, and peered down at the ruined face of his nemesis.

Trent could not fully define the calm that was enveloping his spirit; he certainly wouldn't call it a feeling of justice, but he supposed it was as close as he was ever going to get.

Suddenly, Sophie cried out. She had a hand over her mouth and was looking into the distance. Without a word, she sprinted off toward Maggie's house where Trent now saw what appeared to be the ghosts of Hector and Maggie coming from around the far side of the house and stumbling toward them. Hector held his assault rifle at port arms, his head wrapped in some sort of makeshift bandage, using Maggie for support with one arm around her shoulders, and smiling and waving in their direction. By now Sophie had reached them and practically tackled Hector and smothered him with kisses.

So much for him being a ghost, Trent thought, as he stood up wearily and shakily.

As they stumbled near, Hector trained his assault rifle on Carl's prone figure. Trent shook his head, and motioned the rifle away.

"About time you got here," Trent muttered to Hector. "What the hell happened to 'I've got your back?'"

He turned to look at Maggie, and grinned. She smiled at him for a few seconds only to fall suddenly into his arms. Trent pressed his face into her hair and breathed deep.

"Ouch," she protested lightly, reaching up and removing his hand from one blood stained shoulder. He leaned back and frowned at her, his eyes suddenly filled with concern. Another makeshift bandage, torn from the bottom of her shirt, was tied tightly around the meaty part of her upper arm. "It's nothing," she said, looking up appreciatively at his concerned eyes. "At least, according to Hector. Says the bullet just grazed me about half an inch – more blood than any real damage."

Trent looked back and forth at Maggie and Hector. "Well, since I know for a fact I saw both of you shot – you two ghosts mind telling me just how the hell you learned to dodge bullets so well?"

#

As they all limped back to the house, Maggie told them that earlier when she had run for her life across that field, she had been certain she was going to be shot and killed; but that she had taken to heart what Trent had whispered to her right before – to use her knowledge of the terrain that rose up before her as only she could. She described how she had felt Carl's crosshairs on her back the entire time, so she had swerved and jumped about with almost every step, hoping to throw off his aim and either dodge the inevitable bullet or at least suffer a less serious wound.

She had known exactly where she needed to head: the shallow system of old irrigation trenches that had been dug decades earlier by her grandfather and had long since been abandoned. They were now overgrown with vegetation, and all but invisible to the naked eye.

"I just can't understand how Carl missed you," Trent told Maggie, incredulously, "as good a shot as he was."

"I knew one of two things would happen," she answered. "I'd either reach the ditch and jump in, or he would shoot first. Either way, I needed to just keep bouncing around, making myself a difficult target, while trying to get to that ditch. I had thought I would hear the shot, but forgot how slow sound travels. As it happened, when the bullet actually hit me, I couldn't believe how I never even heard it! It hurt like holy hell, but something inside told me to react really big, right then, before I could even think about it much, so I spun around to make it look like it was worse than it really was."

"Yeah? Well, you were way too convincing," Trent grimaced.

She went on to tell him that afterwards, she laid very still for several minutes, hoping that Carl would think she was dead, not bother to come over to check on her, and hopefully not notice when she finally made her way, stooping and crawling along the old canal until it disappeared into the tree line out of their line of sight. She had then climbed out, circled wide behind all the outbuildings, and headed toward the back of her house. That's when she had run straight into Hector, who had made his way through the trees along the road. His bleeding head had only been creased by one of Carl's bullets, and his Kevlar vest had stopped two other rounds, albeit painfully. She had torn strips off their shirts to quickly bandage their respective wounds. They had gone on around the house, sneaked close enough to find a location where Hector could get a good shot, and were just getting into position when they witnessed Trent and Carl's final standoff.

"That's when Carl's rifle exploded." Maggie grew silent as she glanced back at Carl Neumann's body and shuddered. "Always heard rumors a gun might do that – first time I've seen it, though.

Trent stayed quiet for a few minutes as the four of them limped and winced their way slowly up the steps to the porch. There, he stopped and pulled both Maggie and his daughter close and tight. "I just knew I had lost you both," he whispered into their hair. He raised his eyes over the tops of their heads, looked at Hector, winked at him, and mouthed, *Thank you.*

#

The lights of emergency vehicles threw haunting and alternating blue and red flashes over the house, outbuildings, and grounds of the ranch headquarters. Trent sat on the edge of a gurney while an EMT worked on his shoulder. Hector had already been looked at and loaded into the nearby ambulance. Sophie sat inside with him, holding his hand to her cheek. Maggie stood hovering beside Trent, her arms folded as she closely watched the EMT carefully bandage his wounds. The bullet had passed all the way through his shoulder, barely missing bone, his head contusions had already been cleaned and sutured, and he was now having his shirt cut away so his bruised ribcage could be wrapped.

He would live.

Trent watched Maggie with a bemused look on his face. She had already chewed out the young female EMT for being too rough and was now keeping watch like a mother hen.

Trent turned his head and looked over to where Carl Neumann's body had already been zippered into a nondescript black body bag and now lay isolated and alone off to the side, awaiting transport to the medical examiner's office. Trent trembled involuntarily, thinking how only a couple hours ago he had been fairly certain that this day was to have been his last one on earth – and not only his own, but maybe two or three other body bags would've been lying there now if events had turned out differently.

"Well, you're not too hard a guy to find these days," came Ben Ferguson's droll voice as he emerged from the shadows. "Just have to follow the trail of dead folks and wrecked vehicles. I can't wait to hear your explanation for all of this," he smirked.

Trent looked at the sheriff with a deadpan expression. "They shouldn't have hurt my cat," he replied without missing a beat.

Ben stopped, smiled, and hooked his thumbs in his thick service belt. "Now, that's a good one," he chortled. "Glad to see you have found your terrible sense of humor once more."

The sheriff turned and nodded to Maggie. "Hiya, Maggie. How's the patient doing?"

"Ornery and difficult as hell, as you can see," she answered.

Ben continued to look at her closely. "And how you holding up?"

Maggie started to answer, but her voice broke. She averted her face from the two men while she wiped quickly at her eyes.

"Damn it," she snapped, proudly. "I've done more crying and blubbering this week than I have in the last ten years!" She turned back to Trent and stabbed a finger into his chest. "And it's all *your* fault, Trent Carter! I wasn't this way before you breezed in here and swept me off my feet!" She turned abruptly and walked away, leaving Trent and Ben with their mouths hanging open.

Ben scratched his head and leaned closer to Trent.

"I do believe you are cornered with no way out, my friend," he murmured.

Trent looked at him dumbfounded.

"Huh?"

"Ahh. I see that you don't seem to know it yet, do you? But mark my words, you are going to end up spending a whole lot of time with that woman, so you'd best just put your mind firmly around the idea right now." Ben turned to the EMT. "Could you give us a minute or two, here?" The EMT quickly checked Trent's bandage, nodded, and walked off.

"Thought you'd like to know that Sheriff Marshall, or Marshall Sheriff – whatever the hell his name is – found old man Neumann – 'Ernst Brandt,' that is – lying across his desk with a bullet parked in his brainpan – close range. Says it was self-inflicted. Nice little .22 target pistol with a silencer on it was in his hand – just like the pros use."

Trent nodded knowingly and looked back over at Carl's outline inside the body bag.

"Housekeeper – a Mrs. Meeks – found him," Ben continued. "She evidently didn't get too upset about it. Guess he treated her about as fondly as he treated everyone else."

Trent thought for a moment and looked up at his boss. "I'm guessing he probably got rid of any evidence that was around, before he shot himself? I mean, there was a computer there and what looked like a shelf full of old scrapbooks, videos, guns and the like."

"Well, now that's the odd thing, isn't it? All of that stuff was actually still there – a gold mine of evidence, really. I guess that old Nazi was really proud of his accomplishments – a tribute to *Das Vaterland,* maybe? Hell, I don't know. But I think we're going to at least see a lot of old mysteries cleared up around here soon."

Ben clapped Trent on the back, making him wince, and walked away toward his cruiser, still talking as he went. "Now, see what you've done? I have to go back and get Molly to order a whole crap-load of *Case Closed* stickers so you'll have something to do when you get out of the hospital."

"See you, Sheriff."

Ben kept walking and simply raised his hand and waved over his shoulder as he stepped into the car, started it up, and drove off.

Trent smiled but then froze. He closed his eyes and breathed deeply.

It was Vicky.

He suddenly felt her cool fingers on the back of his neck and opened his eyes to see her seated next to him on the gurney. Emergency responders were milling back and forth, in front of and behind them, and, as usual, no one seemed the wiser that she was there.

She didn't speak at first, but just smiled and gazed into his eyes. She was the most beautiful he had ever seen her before, in life or in death. Trent felt that his heart was about to burst. He sighed deeply.

"So what do we do now, Victoria?" he asked.

Vicky reached up and found his errant lock of hair, pulled it free from where it had gotten trapped by the bandage, and let it dangle loosely over his brow. She nodded with satisfaction.

"You got it all done, Baby Boy – mostly, anyway."

"Mostly?"

"Well, you got the bad guys for sure," she admitted slowly.

"Yeah – got them for sure."

"And you saved our little girl."

Trent looked back at the ambulance where Sophie had her head resting on Hector's chest and was smiling peacefully.

"Yep. Looks like in more ways than one."

Vicky sighed and turned to look over toward the house to where Maggie was leaning with her back against the stone retaining wall, her hand covering her eyes.

"You've got some more work to do, my Love – this time for yourself." She looked into Trent's eyes and then nodded back toward Maggie. "You've got to let her into your life, and you've got to keep her there."

Trent looked surprised and glanced over at the house. Maggie's arms were folded as she wiped her nose, pouted, and gazed into the distance – she also had never looked more beautiful to him.

"You mean Maggie?" he asked. His eyebrows knit and he pursed his lips, pondering. "I mean – what about you and me? Now that you're here – " His voice trailed off as realization sank in. Vicky smiled and shook her head slowly.

"You can't be alone, Baby Boy – we both know that. You would never survive it."

"So you stay with me," he murmured, sensing the answer before she spoke.

"You know that I can't," she answered. "I told you, there always needs to be a sacrifice."

Trent looked conflicted. Vicky shrugged sweetly, stood up, put both her arms around his neck, and leaned over and kissed him full and deeply on the mouth. He closed his eyes and returned the kiss that would have to last for an eternity.

When he finally opened his eyes, she was gone.

He heard footsteps approaching and saw Maggie stride up to him purposefully, the young female EMT trailing in her wake, trying to finish dressing her shoulder wound.

"Time to get you all saddled up and out of here, Honey Bunch," Maggie said. She stopped, paused, looked at him intently, and with a coquettish grin, reached up to flick the stray hair on his forehead with a finger. Trent started to pull back, hesitated, and let her continue to play with his hair.

"Guess I could use a haircut," he said cautiously.

"Maybe – but don't you dare cut that forelock, Mister," she responded. "I've taken quite a liking to it, for some reason." She suddenly pulled back from him, sniffing the air suspiciously. "Nurse Cratchet there must be wearing some kind of strong cologne tonight."

Maggie gestured over her shoulder with her thumb. "Anyway, she says there's not enough room for Sophie or me ride in the ambulance with you boys to the hospital, so I guess since you two are the worst for wear, we're following in my car!"

"Uh – I don't think she's a nurse," Trent muttered, suddenly sensing déjà vu. "And I think that the name in that movie was 'Nurse Ratchet.'"

Maggie wrapped her arms around his neck, pulled him to her, and planted a long, warm kiss on his lips. She looked deeply into his eyes and smiled.

"Who cares?" she said.

CHAPTER 35
ABBA, FATHER

Three months later, Trent was in his office taping shut the last of the cold case boxes and labeling most of them with the new, bright yellow "Case Closed" stickers that Molly had purchased. He called maintenance to come get the boxes and have them filed away downstairs. As he hung up the phone, he heard a tap at his door and Hector stuck his head in.

"Got a minute?" he asked.

Trent cocked his head at him. "I thought you was dead," he said, his face deadpan.

Hector rolled his eyes and stepped on in without laughing. He was getting used to Trent's dry sense of humor, and this particular reference to the old John Wayne movie was already getting stale.

Hector sat down across the desk, fidgeted, and looked around sheepishly.

"Spit it out, Deputy," Trent ordered.

Hector hemmed and hawed for a few seconds more while turning several shades of red.

"Wait a minute," Trent commanded abruptly, leaning back in his chair and holding up his hand to stop Hector, who looked suddenly perplexed. "Let me guess: I'll bet you want to tell me what an upright person you are," Trent continued. "Responsible, gainfully employed, honest, and so on and so on, ad nauseam, am I right?"

"Well – um – I," Hector spluttered. Trent cut him off again with an upraised hand.

"And after making me listen to that litany of accomplishments, you were going to work your way around your bundle of nerves to tell me just how much my daughter means to you and just how much you love and cherish one another, right?"

"Yes! But I wasn't – "

"Well, Deputy Armijo – I do not have the time, nor the inclination, to sit here all afternoon and listen to you talk such foolishness when you and I both know there are much bigger fish for us to fry today." He paused just long enough to allow Hector to stew in his own juices, then continued. "So, am I correct to assume, Deputy, that the gist of this conversation is for me to give you permission to marry my only precious daughter and agree to allow the two of you to plunge into the most demanding, frustrating, impossible, and wonderfully miraculous enterprise that two people could ever attempt together?"

"Well, as a matter fact, Mr. Carter, I – what was that again?" Hector's brows furrowed.

"That is, if you've even gotten up the guts to ask her yet. Lord knows what Sophie even sees in you at all." Trent rocked back and forth in his chair, enjoying every bit of the consternation that now crisscrossed Hector's bright red face.

"Um – Yes, sir. That's exactly correct – what you just said there, Sir – I think."

Trent reached down and began scribbling nonsense on a notepad. Hector cleared his throat. Trent looked up again.

"Was that meant to be in the form of some sort of question, Deputy?"

"No, sir. I mean, yes. I mean," Hector suddenly stood up in exasperation, almost at attention. "Mr. Carter, Sir – will you do me the honor of granting your daughter's hand in marriage?"

"You mean, my daughter Sophie?"

"Yes, Sir," Hector stammered, "you – have another daughter?"

Trent tossed the pen aside, stood up, then smiled broadly as he offered Hector a handshake.

"I thought you'd never ask, Son."

Hector's mouth dropped open in genuine surprise. He took Trent's hand and shook it vigorously for quite a long time.

"Hector," Trent continued as they still shook hands, "I only have one requirement – I mean, beyond the usual *honor and cherish her and keep her in the manner she's accustomed,* blah – blah – blah." He was trying to extricate his hand from Hector's.

"And Hector, it's a real deal breaker."

"What's that, Sir?" He finally let go of Trent's hand and sat back down hesitantly. Trent continued to stand before putting his hands squarely on the desk and leaning way over.

"Don't you ever call me 'Dad' or 'Daddy' or 'Father,' or anything remotely endearing like that. Because if you do, Hector…" He had lowered his voice to a measured whisper as Hector listened intently, "I will kill you."

#

Later, Trent stood gazing out the window as several more of his case file boxes were wheeled out his office door on a dolly. He was still amazed at how much progress they had been able to make on tying these cases to what they were now calling the Brandt-Neumann serial killings. The district attorney's office was now performing some due diligence on the cases, but Ben Ferguson didn't expect any differing conclusions.

The door closed quietly and Trent was left in welcomed silence. He watched the cumulonimbus clouds boiling up over the Sangre de Cristo Mountains to the west like mounds of vanilla ice cream, and began seeing shapes in them: a cartoon character here, a wild animal there, galloping horses, and finally, a woman leaning her head back, laughing, and letting her long hair billow behind her through the sky.

Trent sighed, turned, and looked around his office as if searching for some lost meaning. He felt as if an important era had not only closed on his life, but had passed by entirely unnoticed by everyone else but him. *Who knows?* he thought. Perhaps this was how normal people usually felt. Could it be he was getting "normal" once more?

Whatever that is, he grunted.

His gaze drifted to a set of three framed photographs on the corner of his desk. He stepped over, sat down at the desk, and pulled one of the photos over to him.

Victoria's beautiful face smiled out at him. He smiled back.

His finger traced the curve of her hair, the tiny wrinkles at her eyes, her mouth – but his touch only registered the smooth coldness of glass. His smile faded.

What was he supposed to make of all this now? He had convinced himself that the visitations from his dead wife had all served a definite purpose. But all along he had suspected them to have been due to his clinical condition, a figment of his overwrought imagination, or a piece of overheated scar tissue in his brain firing off random synapses to his nervous system and affecting his thought patterns, his vision, and his sense of reality.

Hell – he was no psychiatrist. Even his own doctors had not been able to help him define it. According to them, Vicky's visits had been just that – visions. And now she had not appeared for over three months, since that night at Maggie's when she had said goodbye to him seated on the edge of an ambulance gurney. Trent was gradually, after all this time, coming to grips with her absence – packing her away into the attic of his mind, along with all the other perplexing or missing memories – and he was okay now with doing so.

Perhaps it was time – time to let his life begin morphing into different shapes, like those clouds lumbering by on the horizon.

He didn't know how long he had sat there staring at Vicky's face before his thoughts returned him to the present. He returned her photo back to its place between the other two that were prominently displayed on his desk: one of Sophie and the other of Maggie. He kissed a finger, touched to his daughter's image, then looked at Maggie's photo and lingered there.

You've got to let that girl into your life – and keep her there. Vicky's words still echoed in his head.

Trent glanced back at Vicky's photo, let out a sigh, and picked it up. He opened his desk drawer to place it gently inside, and then hesitated; he finally slid the drawer shut and put Vicky's picture back in its place on the desk.

Baby steps he thought. *And just who's to say a person can't have two "true loves" in one lifetime?*

At that moment, his intercom rang. He grabbed it reflexively on the second ring.

"Carter," he answered. It was Molly.

"Trent. Someone here to see you."

He glanced at his watch – 4 P.M. – he certainly was in no mood for any more visits this late in the day.

"Molly – can't they see someone else?"

"It's an Angela Meeks and she asked specifically, and very pointedly, to see you." Molly paused while she muffled the phone and spoke to someone else for a second. "She says you have met her before and that it's extremely important that she speak with you – *now*."

Trent rubbed his eyes and was silent.

"Trent?" Molly persisted.

"Yes, okay. It's all right. I do know her. Send her on in."

He took a moment to compose himself and straighten his jacket before he heard a firm knock on the door.

"Come in," he called out and stood to greet Mrs. Meeks as she entered the office. He shook her hand and offered her a seat. She nodded tersely, and Trent raised his eyebrows as he turned and went back around his desk. Her manner was certainly all business-as-usual, but he noticed her graying hair was no longer pulled into a severe bun, but hung stylishly loose and pulled attractively behind her ears where it then fell between her shoulders. She looked to be in her late 60s, but had applied only a modest amount of makeup, and instead of the dark clothes of a housekeeper, she had chosen a light, airy red blouse over which she wore a smart, tan jacket and knee length brown skirt. Her shoes were practical and showed off attractive ankles and calves. In short, Angela Meeks exuded warmth, charm, beauty, and confidence – although upon closer inspection Trent could see by the consternation in her eyes that the confidence may have been somewhat forced. She clutched a small handbag in her lap like a defensive shield.

"And to what do I owe the pleasure, Mrs. Meeks?" he asked, having taken his seat and pulling a notepad in front of him.

"Please – you may call me 'Angela,'" she answered perfunctorily.

"Well then, please call me 'Trent,'" he replied.

"No, I believe it will be better to refer to you as Mr. Carter, especially after you hear what I have come to tell you."

"As you wish," Trent responded. He was now intrigued. What was Ernst Brandt's former housekeeper doing in his office? Angela Meeks lost no time in telling him.

"Mr. Carter, Ernst Brandt – or 'Conrad Neumann,' as I had come to know him – did not kill himself." Mrs. Meeks hesitated, then continued, "I killed him."

Trent froze with his half smile in check.

"You – *You*," he repeated, dropping back into his chair, momentarily stunned by what he had just heard, "shot Ernst Brandt?" he asked in shock. "*You* killed him?"

Angela looked up and nodded grimly. "And, of course, you will want to know why I would do such a thing," she said softly but matter-of-factly.

She looked down in her lap, unclasped her handbag, and put her hand inside. Trent pushed back from his desk and suddenly raised his hand at her. His other hand went instinctively to the Glock holstered at his waist.

"Mrs. Meeks!" he suddenly warned her sternly. "Angela! I must ask you not to make sudden moves like that – not in a police office – for both our sakes!"

Angela froze in place, her hand still inside the bag and a look of surprise on her face. Again, she looked back at her bag and realized how her actions must have appeared. She shook her head and smiled apologetically.

"I am so very sorry, Mr. Carter. It is not what it must look like, believe me," she reassured, and added, "May I?" She slowly opened the bag wide and tipped it so that Trent could see inside. "See? No gun. I hate guns – always have." She once again reached in and cautiously removed a dog-eared, creased envelope.

"Ever since I moved here – from Germany," she continued, "and went to work for Mr. Neumann – um, Ernst Brandt, as it turned out – I was really looking for someone else."

She then looked back up at Trent and slowly slid the envelope over to him so that he could clearly see the information written on it. The handwriting seemed somehow familiar to Trent. The envelope had been postmarked March 12, 1973, but had been forwarded and re-stamped many times in its postal journeys until the various colored inks had almost covered all the blank places. The return address was from someone named Frank Smith, General Delivery, Raton, New Mexico, USA, and the addressee was a Frau Erika Eberhardt, Stuttgart, Deutschland.

Eberhardt! Trent caught his breath and looked up as the name jumped off of the paper. Mrs. Meeks, who had been watching him closely, now smiled at his reaction and picked up the envelope. She carefully removed the letter from inside and gently unfolded it. The letter was also worn and stained, possibly even with dried tears. She carefully smoothed it out on the desk, and Trent could see that it was all in German, though again in a very familiar hand. Angela then turned to the closing page, turned it so he could see, and pointed a manicured finger at the signature.

The letter had been signed by Otto Eberhardt. Trent stared at it for a long moment and looked back up at Angela Meeks.

"Where did you get this?" he asked, his voice barely a croak.

She took the letter, refolded it carefully, replaced it into its envelope, cleared her throat, and looked Trent evenly in the eyes, as if her confession of murder had only been the tip of the iceberg.

"Mr. Carter, this letter was mailed from Raton to Germany in 1973. It was finally delivered to my last home in Berlin in 1986. My maiden name is Angela Michele Eberhardt. I am the daughter of Otto and Erika Eberhardt, and after receiving this letter, I decided to come to the United States to find my long-missing father."

#

Angela Eberhardt had, obviously, survived the war, but her mother Erika had not, having been killed in a carpet-bombing raid by American B-17s over Stuttgart in late 1944. At the time of her mother's death, Angela had been eighteen months old but had been evacuated to live with an elderly aunt and uncle in the countryside in Bavaria. The defeat of Germany had brought mixed blessings and horror to the German people: Allied money and rebuilding projects quickly pumped up the devastated German economy, while roving bands of displaced persons had turned to thievery, and worse, before order could eventually be brought to bear and the police and legal systems properly restructured. Angela had struggled, along with most everyone else, and had been passed from one distant relative to another, having been told her father had also died in the war.

She had applied herself and eventually performed well in *gymnasium,* the equivalent of American high school, and won admission to university in Munich where she studied business and economics. There, she had met and married Hans Meeks, who went on to do well in the grocery business in West Berlin until he had died at age thirty of a brain hemorrhage. Angela continued to manage the small chain of stores until one day the wrinkled and well-travelled letter arrived from the U.S. from someone claiming to be the husband of her mother, a man who shared the incredible story of having fought in the war, survived as a prisoner, and had disappeared into the proverbial American Wild West.

The year was 1986, one of political unrest, with a pronounced movement toward tearing down the hated Berlin wall, which eventually did happen and led to reunification of the German states. By that time, though, Angela had made what for her was a huge decision: she cashed in all of her savings and investments, sold the stores, and embarked on the biggest adventure of her life by coming to America to find Otto Eberhardt, her father, using clues he had alluded to in the letter as to where he had been all those years.

One such clue was that he had evidently worked on a few of ranches and farms in New Mexico and Colorado. Having finally arrived in Raton by train in mid-1989 and poking around unsuccessfully for a few weeks, she found herself literally going ranch to ranch, door to door, throughout the entire area, trying to cover all the territory her father had mentioned in his letter.

She had finally exhausted most of her financial resources and, to extend her visa, had reluctantly had to find work until she either found him or could save up enough money to go home to Germany.

She had then found herself on the doorstep of Conrad Neumann, who, along with his strange and surly son Carl and an incompetent daughter named Caroline, who had been relegated to a nearby nursing home, seemed like people with great need for a good house manager. Of course, she quizzed the old man closely as to any knowledge of the whereabouts of her father, Otto Eberhardt. Conrad Neumann had just sat there, looked her straight in the face, and told her he had never heard of the man.

#

Angela paused in her story, looking down, and shaking her head. She trembled slightly and continued in a low, angry voice. "And that son-of-a-bitch of course lied to me about everything – about my father and about his own false identity – everything! And he knew all along that I was Otto Eberhardt's daughter! He knew all of Otto's secrets – and that my father had lived under the same roof for years!" Her voice trailed off to a whisper. "And – and how he had died…"

Angela broke into sobs. Trent reached into his desk and produced a box of tissues and slid them over to her. She composed herself and went on. "But for some reason, he kept all of that from me. I suppose it gave him some perverted pleasure."

She looked back up at Trent, dabbed at her running mascara, and tried to smile.

"I am sorry to come in this way, so unexpected. But I have been consumed with the guilt and the shame, and from the first time I met you, you seemed like such a forthright person."

Trent smiled faintly, thinking how ironic it was that, until now, Mrs. Meeks had always made him feel just the opposite.

"Please continue, Angela."

"When you and your lady friend arrived at the house a few days before – well, before Mr. Neumann and Carl died – I really had no idea what sort of monster I worked for. Oh, I always suspected that Carl was often up to no good, but I thought that had more to do with his unpleasant friend Mr. Streck, who was always hanging around. But any time I entered the room they would all grow suddenly quiet until I finished whatever it was I was doing and left the room again. I am just as glad I didn't know what they were discussing."

She softly blew her nose before continuing. "That day, at the house, when you confronted Mr. Neumann with his crimes – and you actually identified him as this 'Ernst Brandt' person, and then mentioned my father Otto's name in connection with him – well, I am ashamed to admit that I was eavesdropping from around the corner and I almost fainted! Then, after you both left and I overheard him on the phone with Carl, I knew he was not yet finished with his horrid crimes, and that even more people were about to become his victims!"

She stopped for a moment and wiped her nose. "And so, I decided then and there something must be done because he was much too crafty and smart to be cornered by anyone else – oh, no offense to your skills of course, Deputy Carter."

"None taken, Mrs. Meeks. But please tell me about the day Conrad – um, Mr. Brandt – died – the day you shot him. Tell me, please, how it all happened."

Angela went on to describe how the very next day after Trent's and Maggie's visit, Ernst had Carl drive him to the nursing home, which wasn't entirely unusual, since Caroline lives there, and her father – that is, Ernst – sometimes went for an occasional visit, if only to keep up appearances.

"You see, it had become obvious to me that he had no real fondness for his daughter, which had always made me a little sad, given that I would have loved a relationship with my own father. Of course, now I know why there was no love there for Caroline – she was never really his!"

She paused as if to catch her breath or perhaps remember.

"Often, it was me that he ordered to go into town and visit Caroline whenever there was business to do on her behalf, perhaps, or to take her some clothes or – uh – personal necessities, you understand." Mrs. Meeks blushed slightly. "But I must tell you that Caroline and I developed a real bond, a fondness for one another, almost like sisters, and it got to where I looked forward to our visits. It gave me something different and pleasurable to do – with someone who seemed to actually appreciate my efforts."

Angela paused thoughtfully and chuckled. "There was even this older, kindly priest there that Caroline had really seemed to have developed a genuine fondness for – and he for her – almost a father figure, actually. When I was there, sometimes we would watch him play chess – Caroline was actually very good at predicting the moves – or walked with him in the gardens, just talking about nothing really – but then again about everything – about life, and about faith. He seemed to be so full of life and of a love for God – and for Caroline. I was grateful for that, for her sake – and," she paused again, lowering her head, "regretted it a little, for mine."

"Regretted?" Trent asked.

"For my own father, you see – I had missed all of that."

Trent watched her closely as she continued with her story.

Her countenance turned dark once again. "On that last day, Carl and Ernst returned home very late following their visit to Clayton. I was very anxious and really did not want to know what had transpired. But I met them and could tell something had happened because they both were very agitated, as if something had gone wrong. I helped Mr. Neumann – I am sorry, I can't seem to stop calling him by that name – as he was getting from the car into his wheelchair and I prepared to take him back into the house. It was then that he slapped my hand away, then turned back and yelled at Carl that he wanted it all to end: *Get back there and take care of that damned deputy*, he told him, *and anyone else connected to any of this.*" She hesitated and looked into Trent's eyes. "I knew they were referring to you, and that you, and perhaps others, were in grave danger."

She paused and took a deep breath and took another tissue from the box. While she had been talking, Trent had buzzed Molly and asked her to bring Mrs. Meeks some water, which she now brought in and handed to her. Angela took a long sip, thanked her, and started to continue until Trent touched her on the arm, a signal to wait until Molly had left them alone again. When she was gone, Angela shrugged and continued.

"So I knew then and there that I had to kill him. I knew Carl was probably going to kill you and anyone else who might know about them, and I was suddenly terrified – for you, for that nice lady friend of yours, for Caroline, and for some reason deep down, for that dear priest. I was certain that if no one did anything to stop them, Ernst and Carl were going to get away with it all, and if there were to be any sort of justice, I had convinced myself that it now fell to me to find it." She took another deep breath, her face turned ashen.

"Just take your time," Trent said softly.

"The next morning, I took Mr. Neumann – Ernst Brandt – his breakfast to his study, where he always wanted it. As usual, he was watching his damned videos on his computer – oh yes, I was aware he watched these murder things, but I just thought they were movies or TV shows. I had no idea at the time they were videos of actual murders the three of them – Ernst, Carl, and that Streck fellow – had actually committed over the years!

"It was then," she continued, "that I saw the pistol lying on the edge of his desk where I think he had been cleaning it. I went away for a few minutes while he finished his breakfast until he called me back for the tray, and in that amount of time, I had decided what I was going to do. So I went in, picked up the tray, and in the same movement, dropped the napkin over the pistol, and took it all away."

She paused, but continued with a thickness in her throat. "I stood in the kitchen for the longest time, examining the gun, opening and shutting the thing that held the bullets, counting them, rehearsing in my head how I should do it, what I should say to him, and how many times I would need to shoot him." She sighed and gazed out the window thoughtfully. "I am still surprised at how methodically I thought about all this, and how much at peace I was at that moment." She shrugged and turned back to Trent.

"In the end, I simply walked back in, went straight up to him, and when he looked up with his horrible face and asked so hatefully what I was doing there, I just calmly pointed the pistol at his head and fired once."

Angela was silent for a few moments, staring off into space.

"I was surprised, you know," she noted almost nonchalantly, "at how very little blood there was. I don't know what I expected. I stood there for the longest time just looking at him, amazed at how peaceful he finally looked, in death anyway. Then I did what I had seen in the movies – I wiped the gun off completely with my apron, placed it in his hand, and pressed his fingers to it, for the fingerprints, you understand, and laid the gun in his lap.

She paused and took another long sip of water, and lightly wiped her lips with the tips of her fingers. "Then I went back to the kitchen, made myself a pot of tea, sat down, and called the police."

Angela Eberhardt Meeks grew very quiet, her story finally finished. She smoothed her skirt for a moment, sat up straighter in her chair, and looked Trent directly in the eyes.

"So, now I am a murderer, Deputy Carter. And I suppose now that you will need to take me to jail or something, yes? I have seen to it that all of my affairs are in order, and I am ready for you to," she touched her hair and pulled her sleeve down at her wrist, "do whatever it is you do at these times."

Trent had leaned back in his chair and was chewing on the eraser end of the pencil he had been using to jot notes with. He put the pencil down, thought hard for another moment, tore the page from the notepad, crumpled it up in a tight wad, and slipped it into his pocket.

"Mrs. Meeks – Angela," he began officiously, looking intently at her, "our investigation into the death of Ernst Brandt clearly proved beyond a doubt our suspicion that he committed suicide. I see no reason to go against the official record at this time. Ernst Brandt died of a self-inflicted gunshot to the head." He paused, stuck out his jaw a bit, and concluded, "And I, for one, would say that justice has been served."

Angela's eyes opened wide and her mouth formed a small *O*.

"So, you – you don't intend to arrest me?" she stammered in complete surprise.

"Nope. I don't see that anything much has changed the facts of this case. It's a closed case and will remain so as far as I'm concerned."

Angela looked down and nodded, dabbed her nose once more, opened her purse to put Otto's letter away, and paused to peer at it for a moment.

"You know, I had thought that justice would somehow feel different," she remarked. "Justice did get rid of a monster, and justice has made the nightmare go away – but justice never brought back my father to me, did it, Mr. Carter?" She looked up again and gave Trent a half smile. "That is my one remaining regret – that other than this one sad letter, and after all this time, I shall never really know who my father was."

Trent leaned back in his chair, folded his hands on his lap, and met her smile with his own.

"You know something, Mrs. Meeks? Once in a very great while, I get to do something in this lousy job that makes all the other lousy days worth it. And I believe that today," he added, "is going to be one of those days."

With that observation, Trent opened the bottom drawer of his desk and removed an old weather-beaten journal, a large bundle of letters, and what appeared to be an old Bible, all of which had been neatly banded together. He weighed the bundle in his hand for a second, paused, set the parcel in the middle of his desk, and gently pushed it over to her.

Angela looked at him, uncomprehendingly at first. Then she reached out and gingerly touched the leather corner of the old journal and ran a trembling finger over the edges of the unopened letters. She looked up suddenly in astonishment as she recognized the names on one of the envelopes, similar to the one in her purse.

"Are these…?" she started to ask, but then choked up. "I really don't know what to say," she finally whispered.

"Well, I don't guess you need to say anything," Trent answered and gestured at the documents in front of her. "But Angela Eberhardt Meeks, allow me to introduce you to a very fine man: your father, Otto Franz Eberhardt."

Angela looked at him, then down at the items at her fingertips, tears welling up in her eyes; choking back a sob, she pulled the stack to her, clutched it to her bosom, and bowed her head over the bundle. Trent suddenly felt as if he were intruding on something very private and looked down at his hands on the desk. He felt himself getting misty-eyed, swore under his breath, grabbed a tissue, and swiped quickly and embarrassingly at his nose. He then took a deep breath and looked back up at her.

"And Angela, there is one more very important thing I should really tell you regarding that kindly old priest that you said you met."

ACT OF CONTRITION

EPILOGUE – *A TIME TO HEAL*

Love produces many wounds. If anyone lives in this world long enough, love's accumulated wounds may eventually break them.

On the other hand, brokenness can also be the first step to healing, but only the first of many steps, followed by anger, acceptance, and a whole lot more gobbledygook Trent's psychiatrist had tried repeatedly to teach him.

But what had been finally revealed to him, after all this time, was that a certain level of "broken" also exists that remains untouchable, untreatable, un-healable even; a brokenness that eludes every finesse of the physician's scalpel or each of the counselor's probing words – a brokenness born out of awakening one day to find that any sense of well-being and wholeness has been brutally ripped right out of the soul. Such violence leaves such a devastation in its wake at all levels – physically, spiritually, and psychologically – that there can never be a complete healing – scar tissue, at best, but usually an open, seeping wound down deep, seldom to be staunched, that reminds constantly of the treasures of this life that have become so precious that when they are lost, as they might be, so will someone's humanity be lost, in the absence of another firm anchor to hold onto.

Trent had finally discovered that anchor and in so doing had also discovered that his deep brokenness was okay – perhaps even necessary to get him to the next truth. This great discovery, though, came not from doctors or psychiatrists – but from an elderly "priest," a former German soldier with his own secrets and blood on his own hands.

Nothing is as it seems.

This was the lesson that Otto – as benefactor of the wisdom of Father Michael – had been trying to get through to Trent in all their conversations and that had been reflected earlier throughout Otto's journals: that if someone would only put that brokenness to death and then surrender it as a virtual offering, as Otto had done, first to his friend the real Father Michael, and finally to a truer Father – a true act of contrition – then He, in turn, puts something in its place in the wounded heart: a helper, and advocate, that manifests His life force within in the form of healing touches that move someone gradually from the mundane to the majestic in everything they do, every single day, for the remainder of their life.

Without such a healing touch, Trent knew he would never be able to overcome and deal with those broken pieces, never be able to function in some semblance of normalcy, never again be capable to cultivate newfound feelings for the new experiences – the new people, the new transformations – in his life.

#

A couple of months had gone by and a lot of red tape had been cut for Trent and Maggie to finally convince the proper authorities that the remains of the man buried in the Clayton Community Cemetery as Father Michael were really those of another man, Otto Eberhardt, and that they should, therefore, honor his daughter Angela's formal request to exhume the remains so that he could be properly buried where she wished. In this case, Angela's desire was that her father be buried next to his beloved Evie in the old peach orchard that she had planted all those years ago just east of the house at the Neumann Ranch on the Dry Cimarron. Maggie, as Caroline's only remaining living relative, as well as her legal guardian and the conservator of her assets, had bolstered Angela's request by subsequently taking Caroline out of the retirement center and bringing her back to her proper home on the ranch. Legally, the ranch belonged now to Caroline as the only surviving direct heir of Conrad and Evie Neumann, but her competency would never be sufficient for her to be able to manage the place. With Caroline's strong attachment now to Angela, and at Trent's urging, consequently, Maggie had offered to Angela Eberhardt Meeks a lifelong position to stay and help manage the Neumann household and ranch, and most importantly, to look after Caroline.

The real Father Michael's remains had been released from the medical examiner's office to the Archdiocese of Santa Fe. After forty years of resting unknown and undisturbed beneath the walls of the old theater in Raton, Father Michael Francis Shannon would finally come to his proper rest in consecrated soil.

The charred remains of the real Conrad Neumann had been unceremoniously buried in an unmarked grave somewhere in the middle of the peach orchard, decades ago, by Otto, thinking he was actually burying Ernst, immediately following the tragic fire in the 1950s.

No one knew exactly where.

The escaped Nazi and serial killer *Hauptmann* Ernst Josef Brandt, late of Field Marshal Erwin Rommel's *Afrika Korps*, who had passed himself off for decades as Conrad Neumann, now lay buried in a pauper's grave in the Clayton Cemetery. Trent, Angela, and a hired local pastor had been the only ones in attendance at the graveside service.

No one had wept.

#

Otto Franz Eberhardt was now with his remaining family, resting on one side of Evie with their son Carl buried at her other side, near the edge of the peach orchard where his daughter Angela would be able to keep watch over their final resting places. Trent bent down and placed a single long stemmed red rose, with a flowering sprig of fresh cloves tied to it by a cornflower blue ribbon, on top of the soil on Otto's grave. There, it joined the other perfect roses that had already been placed, in turn, by Angela, Caroline, Walter, Sophie, Hector, and Maggie, who had all also gathered around to pay their respects. In addition to roses, a couple of other special mementos had been placed on the grave: Walter Carter had pulled a worn ivory chess piece out of his pocket and placed it carefully on top of Otto's headstone, right next to a very shabby, threadbare ragdoll that Caroline had already put there.

Angela and Caroline held each other and wept.

Trent winced as he stood up stiffly from the grave. Maggie stepped over, slid her arm through his, and leaned her head against his shoulder. For the first time in a very long while, he felt a peace wash over him, albeit one that he didn't yet fully understand.

Other pains remained, however, and were going to take a while longer to heal, if ever – such as the recently revisited pain of the loss of his wife.

Vicky's remains had been exhumed and autopsied following Trent's strong suggestions that her death had been the result of murder rather than a car accident. The autopsy findings clearly corroborated Trent's recent suspicion that her grievous head injuries had, in fact, hidden the evidence of a rifle bullet that had passed through her skull, and that his own injuries had also most likely included being grazed by a similar bullet that had contributed to his mental lapses.

Victoria Anne Carter, finally, rested in total peace, and Trent had come to terms with the fact that the hurt of her loss – and the ongoing healing of it – were part and parcel of his journey forward. He had not received any other visits from her since the shootout at Maggie's, nor had his sleep been haunted by recurring nightmares of Cordova Pass.

More specifically, Trent knew he was no longer alone.

Looking around him now, he knew that all of these here with him today – his real family, each and every one of them – were also part of that journey that had brought him to this place and would continue to take him – take them all – forward. He felt an unmistakable kinship with them here, the dead as well as the living. They all were an inseparable part of one another's ongoing legacies, still being written and played out, with frayed threads and stained patterns in the fabric created by their intertwining memories and lives.

THE END

ABOUT THE AUTHOR

Richard C. Trice was born in Abilene, Texas, sixty – some years ago. During that time he has worked as an actor, astronomer, banker, butcher, consultant, custodian, editor, freelance writer, journalist, musician, novelist, nurse's aide, photographer, playwright, poet, preacher, ranch hand, recording engineer, singer, songwriter, strategic planner, summer camp counselor, teacher, theatrical producer, and wildfire fighter, but not necessarily in that order. He's an incurable traveler of the world, and has been blessed by God with a love and appreciation of family, musical instruments, motorcycles, the outdoors, history, other people's pets, other people's points of view, other people's wine, good books, good art, good movies, good coffee, vanilla ice cream, any food with green chile, an occasional good cigar, and run-on sentences. He and his wonderful wife Linda have three wonderfully grown children, lots of wonderful grandchildren, a handful of wonderful friends, and live in a wonderfully rambling 135-year-old Victorian house in Northern New Mexico. Although a lifelong writer, ACT OF CONTRITION is his first published novel.

Made in the USA
Lexington, KY
11 August 2018